BEGINNING OPERATIONS

BOOKS BY JAMES WHITE

The Secret Visitor (1957)
Second Ending (1962)
Deadly Litter (1964)
Escape Orbit (1965)
The Watch Below (1966)
All Judgement Fled (1968)
The Aliens Among Us (1969)
Tomorrow Is Too Far (1971)
Dark Inferno (1972)
The Dream Millennium (1974)
Monsters and Medics (1977)
Underkill (1979)
Future Past (1982)
Federation World (1988)
The Silent Stars Go By (1991)
The White Papers (1996)
Gene Roddenberry's Earth:
    Final Conflict—The First Protector (Tor, 2000)

THE SECTOR GENERAL SERIES

Hospital Station (1962)
Star Surgeon (1963)
Major Operation (1971)
Ambulance Ship (1979)
Sector General (1983)
Star Healer (1985)
Code Blue—Emergency (1987)
The Genocidal Healer (1992)
The Galactic Gourmet (Tor, 1996)
Final Diagnosis (Tor, 1997)
Mind Changer (Tor, 1998)
Double Contact (Tor, 1999)

BEGINNING OPERATIONS

JAMES WHITE

ORB

A TOM DOHERTY ASSOCIATES BOOK
NEW YORK

BEGINNING OPERATIONS

Copyright © 2001 by the Estate of James White. This book is an omnibus edition comprising the novels *Hospital Station*, copyright © 1962 by James White, *Star Surgeon*, copyright © 1963 by James White, and *Major Operation*, copyright © 1971 by James White.

Introduction copyright © 2001 by Brian Stableford.

Edited by Teresa Nielsen Hayden

An Orb Edition
Published by Tom Doherty Associates, LLC
175 Fifth Avenue
New York, NY 10010

ISBN 0-312-87544-4

Printed in the United States of America

CONTENTS

INTRODUCTION
TO THE FIRST SECTOR GENERAL OMNIBUS

BY
BRIAN
STABLEFORD

This omnibus contains the first three volumes in the Sector General series. Because they were written at a time when magazines were gradually being displaced by paperback books as the core of the science fiction field, all three are "mosaic novels" made up of items that had previously been published as magazine stories. The five stories making up *Hospital Station* were published in *New Worlds* between 1957 and 1960, the novelette and novella making up *Star Surgeon* appeared in the same magazine in 1961–62, and the five novelettes making up *Major Operation* were published in the anthology series *New Writings in S-F* between 1966 and 1971. The series continued to grow thereafter until its author died in 1999, eventually spanning the greater part of half a century—a half-century which, as is nowadays a matter of routine, saw far greater political and technological changes than any of its predecessors.

Nothing dates as quickly as the future, but remote images tend to date better than nearer ones and a galactic culture spanning thousands of worlds is as distant a prospect today as it was in 1957. All fiction that deals with hypothetical futures is anchored in the present, so the Sector General series has had to evolve as time has passed, but the central themes of the series are as pertinent today as they were in 1957, and the argument developed in the series has lost none of its force. James White matured as a literary artist in the course of his career—and a considerable measure of that maturation is displayed within the pages of this book—but he was always a careful and clever writer, and his passion and sense of wonder did not diminish as the business of writing became familiar, so this almost-lifelong series maintained an evenness of tone, vivacity and moral concern unmatched by any of its rivals. It is a remarkable achievement, and a fitting monument to the life of a man whose unfailing modesty always tended to conceal the true extent of his intellect and the real strength of his character.

*   *   *

The first time that the author was invited to comment publicly on the Sector General series was in the June 1960 issue of *New Worlds,* which featured the last of the novelettes combined in *Hospital Station.* "The background idea for the Sector General series," White explained, "is one that developed gradually over the years. I have always had a fondness for stories with a medical slant—my ambition is to write one as good as Lester del Rey's 'Nerves'—and as it is always easier to do what one likes rather than otherwise, many of my leading characters have been doctors. To one with pacifist inclinations—feelings shared on both sides of the typewriter among the SF fellowship, I think—a doctor character is important in that all sorts of violent, dramatic and emotionally loaded incidents happen to him as a matter of course. So an author who doesn't relish killing off a lot of people or things can inject some legitimate bloodshed into his stories by substituting an accident or natural catastrophe for War."

Contemporary readers will readily appreciate that White's judgment as to the extent that his pacifist sympathies were shared within the SF community was a trifle optimistic, but that only served to make his efforts all the more necessary and all the more admirable. Alongside the Sector General series White produced other works of a similar ideological stripe, most of them—"Tableau" and "The Ideal Captain" (both 1958) are good examples—being satires whose manner and method recall the work of the other leading British SF writer of sarcastic anti-war stories, Eric Frank Russell.

White's was not the first extraterrestrial medical series to appear in science fiction—it had been preceded by L. Ron Hubbard's tales of "Ole Doc Methuselah" and Murray Leinster's Med Ship series—but neither of these authors had shown the same scrupulous commitment to the extension of the Hippocratic oath to cover all intelligent life-forms that became the moral foundation-stone of the Sector General series. The work of the medically-qualified Alan E. Nourse was much closer in spirit to White's, but Nourse's juvenile novel *Star Surgeon*—whose title was unnecessarily and confusingly hijacked for the second of White's mosaic novels—did not appear until 1959, two years after the first Sector General story.

In a later essay reprinted as a preface to *Ambulance Ship* (1979), "The Secret History of Sector General," White modestly confessed that the series got off to a shaky start because the magazine version of "Sector General" (1957) was slightly confused in its aims and execution, but once the basic location was established White knew that he had found the perfect format to develop his plotting skills within an appropriate framework. He eventually supplied a "prequel" to that first story which filled in the background more carefully—it appears here as the first part of *Hospital Station*—and reinforced the template which confronted concerned physicians with intellectually-challenging puzzles. The second major feature of the series has always been its brilliant ingenuity; there is no other which can match its prolific production of intriguingly bizarre aliens, or the care and cleverness with which alien biology is extrapolated into psychology and culture.

At first, the editor to whom White sold all the early Sector General stories, John Carnell, saw it as a light-hearted and comedic enterprise, and Carnell persuaded White to rewrite what was originally intended to be the third story in the series because it was "too serious." The ever-obliging White did so, but continued nevertheless, in a typically patient and subtle fashion, to import a necessary gravity into the series. By the time he produced "Resident Physician" and "Field Hospital"—the items combined as *Star Surgeon*—all the issues raised in the sidelined story that had become "Occupation: Warrior" (1959) had been re-raised and scrupulously addressed. Although Carnell may have been wrong to cast that story out of the series, his intervention ensured that White would make every possible effort to maintain a balance between the playful element of his stories and their earnest undercurrent—a balance whose delicacy always worked to their advantage.

*　　*　　*

The particular character of James White's SF, and the Sector General series in particular, is partly the legacy of his upbringing as an Ulster Scot, and an adult life spent in a province whose festering political sores are conventionally referred to, with telling understatement, as "the troubles." He was born in 1928 in Belfast, where he lived and worked until failing health hastened his retirement from formal employment in 1984. Having left school without any significant qualifications at the age of fifteen, he worked as a retailer in the gentlemen's clothing trade for more than twenty years before his writing skills enabled him to embark on a belated second career as a clerk and publicity officer for Shorts Aircraft. In the meantime, he obtained spiritual sustenance and solace from science fiction fandom; one of his closest friends was fellow SF writer Bob Shaw.

Although he rarely referred to them directly, "the troubles" are ever-present in the background behind the scenarios of White's stories and in every explanation that he ever gave of their content. The brief comment accompanying his entry in *The St. James Guide to Science Fiction Writers* observes that: "The attempt to understand the behavior and thought processes of . . . aliens frequently illuminate the human condition as well, and the problem of learning to adapt to a totally alien viewpoint places in proper perspective the very minor differences of skin pigmentation and politics which bedevil our own culture." White always saw the future in terms of a highly problematic but desperately necessary quest for lasting peace, whose establishment would require a respectful tolerance for all differences of form and faith.

As a professional writer, White's fortunes were very mixed. He sold the first story he ever wrote to John Carnell in 1953, and when *New Worlds* reached its hundredth issue in 1960 only one author, Francis G. Rayer, had contributed more stories to the magazine. White overtook Rayer soon afterward but his own tally was swiftly overtaken in the mid-1960s by J. G. Ballard (whose first *New Worlds* story, "Manhole 69," had appeared in the same issue as "Sector General") when his more traditionally-inclined work was claimed by Carnell—who was his agent as well as his editor—for *New Writings in S-F.*

When SF became briefly fashionable among respectable British publishers in the late 1960s and early 1970s five of White's novels appeared in hardcover, to some acclaim, but as the tide of fashion passed he was soon thrust back into the established mold of the genre paperback writer. He never won an award in Britain or America and toward the end of his life he could not get his books published in his native land. The novel that he and many others considered to be his *magnum opus, The Silent Stars Go By* (1991)—an alternative history in which Irish settlers establish a Hibernian Empire in the Americas long before Columbus, with the eventual happy result that Earth's first starship blasts off in 1492—never appeared there.

Ironically, it was only in the U.S.A., the homeland of militaristic SF, that he could find an adequate audience for his pacifist fiction in his later years, although *Underkill* (1979), a viscerally effective and brutal futuristic satire of life in Belfast, had earlier been considered too shocking for U.S. publication. White never complained about this indignity, and always seemed profoundly grateful to have any audience at all, but he was an exceedingly courteous man, soft-spoken and unusually generous of spirit. The development of the Sector General series was intimately bound up with his personal development as an exceptionally tolerant and compassionate human being.

*   *   *

The Sector General series eventually came to comprise twelve volumes; *Double Contact,* issued by Tor in 1999, was the last of them. It may seem odd that a narrative frame devised in 1957 could still be viable, without any significant modification, in 1999, but that persistence is a faithful reflection of the tenacity and artfulness with which the series clung to its basic principles. Its central characters do not simply spend all their time trying to heal people of many different biological types; they are always prepared to go to lengths so extraordinary as to be almost incredible to avoid killing *anyone,* no matter how extreme the temptation, provocation or apparent justification.

While his predecessors fitted their medical romances to a standardized "wandering vigilante" framework, White conceived of interplanetary medicine in terms of the staff of a vast hospital, further supported by an entire galactic bureaucracy committed to preventing war and cementing harmonious inter-species relationships. Even when Sector General sends out teams of paramedics in ambulance ships, and even when the quasi-military Monitor Corps is forced to involve its own personnel in their operations, the collective purpose of all the collaborators is to save as many lives as possible, without discrimination as to species. All other moral judgments are held in abeyance. The fact that White's characters are so often forced to do this in secret, carefully covering the tracks of their own altruism, is a revealing comment on the politics of everyday life in Northern Ireland in the latter part of the twentieth century.

As an ingenious designer of alien physiologies White is, of course, forced to rely on the logic of Darwinian evolution. His Diagnosticians solve novel problems in the only way available to them, by applying the logic of adaptation by natural selection to their knowledge of particular physical environments. He is always fully aware of the harsher implications of evolutionary theory: of the ceaseless struggle for existence that renders nature "red in tooth and claw." His interplanetary ambulancemen can hardly help being aware of the fact that any new species they encounter are likely to perceive them as dangerous monsters to be opposed with all available firepower. Their job is not merely to bring comfort and succour to the injured but to meet all paranoia with dutiful patience and all hostile fire with assiduous fortitude. Even under mortal threat, they make every possible effort to understand the behavior and thought processes of others, in the hope of establishing sufficient rapport to render any and all differences harmless.

Newly-encountered alien species, in this framework, usually have to be persuaded to set aside the preconceptions and habits of far more than a lifetime, and then to recognize the benefits that might accrue to them as a result of contact with hundreds of other species of whose existence and oft-exotic nature they had not previously dreamed. For the achievement of such an astonishing feat the only reward available to the heroes of the stories is promotion to a slightly higher rank, which entitles the promoted individuals to wrestle with even-more-complicated problems in the future. This restriction of available rewards is, however, an asset as well as a limitation. Sector General stories are replete with dramatic tension and narrative zest; they feature interesting ideas, cleverly extrapolated with charm and wit; they insist—very hard—that any attempt "to understand the behavior and thought processes of aliens" is *bound* to "illuminate the human condition," and that the project of "learning to adapt to a totally alien viewpoint" is the *only* intellectual exercise available to all of us that is guaranteed to place in their proper perspective "the very minor differences of skin pigmentation and politics which bedevil our own culture."

This is a job worth doing, and one that is not attempted frequently enough. The loss of a man prepared to do it and go on doing it, with all the skill and imagination available to him, in spite of all manner of adverse circumstances, is something to be mourned. Because James White died on 23 August 1999 he did not live to witness the devolution of political power from Westminster to Northern Ireland's first all-inclusive government a few months thereafter, but he would have been very glad to see it. Were he alive today he would be very well aware of the diplomatic mountain that still remains to be climbed, but he would have been hopeful that his countrymen would one day reach its summit. We know this, because he told us so in the Sector General stories, with all the vision, artistry and wit he could muster. The world would be a better place if there were more men in it willing and able to write stories like these.

HOSPITAL STATION

TO
BOB SHAW
IN APPRECIATION

CHAPTER 1

MEDIC

The alien occupying O'Mara's sleeping compartment weighed roughly half a ton, possessed six short, thick appendages which served both as arms or legs and had a hide like a flexible armor plate. Coming as it did from Hudlar, a four-G world with an atmospheric pressure nearly seven times Earth normal, such ruggedness of physique was to be expected. But despite its enormous strength the being was helpless, O'Mara knew, because it was barely six months old, it had just seen its parents die in a construction accident, and its brain was sufficiently well developed for the sight to have frightened it badly.

"I've b-b-brought the kid," said Waring, one of the section's tractor-beam operators. He hated O'Mara, and with good reason, but he was trying not to gloat. "C-C-Caxton sent me. He says your leg makes you unfit for normal duty, so you can look after the young one until somebody arrives from its home planet. He's on his way over n-now..."

Waring trailed off. He began checking the seals of his spacesuit, obviously in a hurry to get out before O'Mara could mention the accident. "I brought some of its food with me," he ended quickly. "It's in the airlock."

O'Mara nodded without speaking. He was a young man cursed with the kind of physique which ensured him winning every fight he had ever been in, and there had been a great many of them recently, and a face which was as square, heavy and roughly formed as was his over-muscled body. He knew that if he allowed himself to show how much that accident had affected him, Waring would think that he was simply putting on an act. Men who were put together as he was, O'Mara had long ago discovered, were not supposed to have any of the softer emotions.

Immediately Waring departed he went to the airlock for the glorified paint-sprayer with which Hudlarians away from their home planet were fed. While checking the gadget and its spare food tanks he tried to go over the story he would have to tell Caxton when the section chief arrived. Staring moodily through the airlock port at the bits and pieces of the gigantic jigsaw puzzle spread across fifty cubic miles of space outside, he tried to think. But his mind kept ducking away from the accident and slipping instead into generalities and events which were in the far past or future.

The vast structure which was slowly taking shape in Galactic Sector Twelve, midway between the rim of the parent galaxy and the densely populated systems of the Greater Magellanic Cloud, was to be a hospital—a hospital to end all hospitals. Hundreds of different environments would be accurately reproduced here, any extreme of heat, cold, pressure, gravity, radiation or atmosphere necessary for the patients and staff it would contain. Such a tremendous and complex structure was far beyond the resources of any one planet, so that hundreds of worlds had each fabricated sections of it and transported them to the assembly point.

But fitting the jigsaw together was no easy job.

Each of the worlds concerned had their copies of the master plan. But errors occurred despite this—probably through the plan having to be translated into so many different languages and systems of measurement. Sections which should have fitted snugly together very often had to be modified to make them join properly, and this necessitated moving the sections together and apart several times with massed tractor and pressor beams. This was very tricky work for the beam operators, because while the weight of the sections out in space was nil, their mass and inertia was tremendous.

And anyone unlucky enough to be caught between the joining faces of two sections in the process of being fitted became, no matter how tough a life-form they happened to be, an almost perfect representation of a two-dimensional body.

The beings who had died belonged to a tough species, physiological classification FROB to be exact. Adult Hudlarians weighed in the region of two Earth tons, possessed an incredibly hard but flexible tegument which, as well as protecting them from their own native and external pressures, allowed them to live and work comfortably in any atmosphere of lesser pressure down to and including the vacuum of space. In addition they had the highest radiation tolerance level known, which made them particularly invaluable during power pile assembly.

The loss of two such valuable beings from his section would, in any case, have made Caxton mad, quite apart from other considerations. O'Mara sighed heavily, decided that his nervous system demanded a more positive release than that, and swore. Then he picked up the feeder and returned to the bedroom.

Normally the Hudlarians absorbed food directly through their skin from the thick, soupy atmosphere of their planet, but on any other world or in space a concentrated food compound had to be sprayed onto the absorbent hides at certain intervals. The young e-t was showing large bare patches and in other places the previous food coating had worn very thin. Definitely, thought O'Mara, the infant was due for another feed. He moved as close as seemed safe and began to spray carefully.

The process of being painted with food seemed to be a pleasant one for the young FROB. It ceased to cower in the corner and began blundering excitedly about the small bedroom. For O'Mara it became a matter of trying to hit a rapidly moving object while practicing violent evasive maneuvers himself, which set his injured leg throbbing more painfully than ever. His furniture suffered, too.

Practically the whole interior surface of his sleeping compartment was covered with the sticky, sharp-smelling food compound, and also the exterior of the now-quiescent young alien, when Caxton arrived.

"What's going on?" said the Section Chief.

Space construction men as a class were simple, uncomplicated personalities whose reactions were easily predictable. Caxton was the type who always asked what was going on even when, as now, he knew—and especially when such unnecessary questions were meant simply to needle somebody. In the proper circumstances the section chief was probably a quite likeable individual, O'Mara thought, but between Caxton and himself those circumstances had yet to come about.

O'Mara answered the question without showing the anger he felt, and ended, ". . . After this I think I'll keep the kid in space, and feed it there . . ."

"You will not!" Caxton snapped. "You'll keep it here with you, all the time. But more about that later. At the moment I want to know about the accident. Your side of it, that is."

His expression said that he was prepared to listen, but that he already doubted every word that O'Mara would say in advance.

"Before you go any further," Caxton broke in after O'Mara had completed two sentences, "you know that this project is under Monitor Corps jurisdiction. Usually the Monitors let us settle any trouble that crops up in our own way, but this case involves extra-terrestrials and they'll have to be brought in on it. There'll be an investigation." He tapped the small, flat box hanging from his chest. "It's only fair to warn you that I'm taping everything you say."

O'Mara nodded and began giving his account of the accident in a low monotone. It was a very weak story, he knew, and stressing any particular incident so as to point it up in his favor would make it sound even more artificial. Several times Caxton opened his mouth to speak, but thought better of it. Finally he said:

"But did anyone *see* you doing these things? Or even see the two e-ts moving about in the danger area while the warning lights were burning? You have a neat little story to explain this madness on their part—which, incidentally, makes you quite a hero—but it could be that you switched on the lights *after* the accident, that it was your negligence regarding the lights which caused it, and that all this about the straying youngster is a pack of lies designed to get you out of a very serious charge—"

"Waring saw me," O'Mara cut in.

Caxton stared at him intently, his expression changing from suppressed anger to one of utter disgust and scorn. Despite himself O'Mara felt his face heating up.

"Waring eh?" said the section chief tonelessly. "A nice touch, that. You know, and we all know, that you have been riding Waring constantly, needling him and playing on his disability to such an extent that he must hate you like poison. Even if he did see you, the court would expect him to keep quiet about it. And if he did not see you, they would think that he had and was keeping quiet about it anyway. O'Mara, you make me sick."

Caxton wheeled and stamped toward the airlock. With one foot through the inner seal he turned again.

"You're nothing but a troublemaker, O'Mara," he said angrily, "a surly, quarrelsome lump of bone and muscle with just enough skill to make you worth keeping. You may think that it was technical ability which got you these quarters on your own. It wasn't, you're good but not that good! The truth is that nobody else in my section would share accommodation with you . . ."

The section chief's hand moved to the cut-off switch on his recorder. His voice, as he ended, became a quiet, deadly thing.

". . . And O'Mara if you let any harm come to that youngster, if anything happens to it at all, the Monitors won't even get the chance to try you."

The implications behind those final words were clear, O'Mara thought angrily as the section chief left; he was sentenced to live with this organic half-ton tank for a period that would feel like eternity no matter how short it was. Everybody knew that exposing Hudlarians to space was like putting a dog out for the night—there were no harmful effects at all. But what some people knew and what they felt were two vastly different things and O'Mara was dealing here with the personalities of simple, uncomplicated, over-sentimental and very angry construction men.

When he had joined the project six months before, O'Mara found that he was doomed again to the performance of a job which, while important in itself, gave him no satisfaction and was far below his capabilities. Since school his life had been a series of such frustrations. Personnel officers could not believe that a young man with such square, ugly features and shoulders so huge that his head looked moronically small by comparison could be interested in *subtle* subjects like psychology or electronics. He had gone into space in the hope of finding things different, but no. Despite constant efforts during interviews to impress people with his quite considerable knowledge, they were too dazzled by his muscle-power to listen, and his applications were invariably stamped "Approved Suitable for Heavy, Sustained Labor."

On joining this project he had decided to make the best of what promised to be another boring, frustrating job—he decided to become an unpopular character. As a result his life had been anything but boring. But now he was wishing that he had not been so successful at making himself disliked.

What he needed most at this moment was friends, and he hadn't a single one.

O'Mara's mind was dragged back from the dismal past to the even less pleasant present by the sharp all-pervading odor of the Hudlarian's food compound. Something would have to be done about that, and quickly. He hurriedly got into his lightweight suit and went through the lock.

II

His living quarters were in a tiny sub-assembly which would one day form the theater surgical ward and adjoining storage compartments of the hospital's low-gravity MSVK section. Two small rooms with a connecting section of corridor had been pressurized and fitted with artificial gravity grids for O'Mara's benefit, the rest of the structure remaining both airless and weightless. He drifted along short, unfinished corridors whose ends were open to space, staring into the bare, angular compartments which slid past. They were all full of trailing plumbing and half-built machinery the purpose of which it was impossible to guess without actually taking an MSVK educator tape. But all the compartments he examined were either too small to hold the alien or they were open in one direction to space. O'Mara swore with restraint but great feeling, pushed himself out to one of the ragged edges of his tiny domain and glared around him.

Above, below and all around him out to a distance of ten miles floated pieces of hospital, invisible except for the bright blue lights scattered over them as a warning to ship traffic in the area. It was a little like being at the center of a dense globular star cluster, O'Mara thought, and rather beautiful if you were in a mood to appreciate it. He wasn't, because on most of these floating sub-assemblies there were pressor-beam men on watch, placed there to fend off sections which threatened to collide. These men would see and report it to Caxton if O'Mara took his baby alien outside even for feeding.

The only answer apparently, he told himself disgustedly as he retraced his way, was nose-plugs.

Inside the lock he was greeted by a noise like a tinny foghorn. It blared out in long, discordant blasts with just enough interval in between to make him dread the arrival of the next one. Investigation revealed bare patches of hide showing through the last coat of food, so presumably his little darling was hungry again. O'Mara went for the sprayer.

When he had about three square yards covered there was an interruption. Dr. Pelling arrived.

The project doctor took off his helmet and gauntlets only, flexed the stiffness out of his fingers and growled, "I believe you hurt your leg. Let's have a look."

Pelling could not have been more gentle as he explored O'Mara's injured leg, but what he was doing was plainly a duty rather than an act of friendship. His voice was reserved as he said, "Severe bruising and a couple of pulled tendons is all—you were lucky. Rest. I'll give you some stuff to rub on it. Have you been redecorating?"

"What . . . ?" began O'Mara, then saw where the doctor was looking. "That's food compound. The little so-and-so kept moving while I was spraying it. But speaking of the youngster, can you tell me—"

"No, I can't," said Pelling. "My brain is overloaded enough with the ills and remedies of my own species without my trying to stuff it with FROB physiology tapes. Besides, they're tough—nothing *can* happen to them!" He sniffed loudly and made a face. "Why don't you keep it outside?"

"Certain people are too soft-hearted," O'Mara replied bitterly. "They are horrified by such apparent cruelties as lifting kittens by the scruff of the neck . . ."

"Humph," said the doctor, looking almost sympathetic. "Well, that's your problem. See you in a couple of weeks."

"Wait!" O'Mara called urgently, hobbling after the doctor with one empty trouser leg flapping. "What if something does happen? And there has to be rules about the care and feeding of these things, simple rules. You can't just leave me to . . . to . . ."

"I see what you mean," said Pelling. He looked thoughtful for a moment, then went on, "There's a book kicking around my place somewhere, a sort of Hudlarian first aid handbook. But it's printed in Universal . . ."

"I read Universal," said O'Mara.

Pelling looked surprised. "Bright boy. All right, I'll send it over." He nodded curtly and left.

O'Mara closed the bedroom door in the hope that this might cut down the intensity of the food smell, then lowered himself carefully into the living room couch for what he told himself was a well-deserved rest. He settled his leg so that it ached almost comfortably and began trying to talk himself into an acceptance of the situation. The best he could achieve was a seething, philosophical calm.

But he was so weary that even the effort of feeling angry became too much for him. His eyelids dropped and a warm deadness began creeping up from his hands and feet. O'Mara sighed, wriggled and prepared to sleep . . .

The sound which blasted him out of his couch had the strident, authoritative urgency of all the alarm sirens that ever were and a volume which threatened to blow the bedroom door off its runners. O'Mara grabbed instinctively for his spacesuit, dropped it with a curse as he realized what was happening, then went for the sprayer.

Junior was hungry again . . . !

During the eighteen hours which followed it was brought home to O'Mara how much he did not know about infant Hudlarians. He had spoken many times to its parents via Translator, and the baby had been mentioned often, but somehow they had not spoken of the important things. Sleep, for instance.

Judging from recent observation and experience, infant FROBs did not sleep. In the all too short intervals between feeds they blundered around the bedroom smashing all items of furniture which were not metal and bolted down—and these they bent beyond recognition or usefulness—or they huddled in a corner knotting and unknotting their tentacles. Probably this sight of a baby doing the equivalent of playing with its fingers would have brought coos of delight from an adult Hudlarian, but it merely made O'Mara sick and cross-eyed.

And every two hours, plus or minus a few minutes, he had to feed the brute. If he was lucky it lay quiet, but more often he had to chase it around with the sprayer. Normally FROBs of this age were too weak to move about—but that was under Hudlar's crushing gravity-pull and pressure. Here in conditions which were to it less than one quarter-G, the infant Hudlarian could move. And it was having fun.

O'Mara wasn't: his body felt like a thick, clumsy sponge saturated with fatigue. After each feed he dropped onto the couch and let his bone-weary body dive blindly into unconsciousness. He was so utterly and completely spent, he told himself after every spraying, that he could not possibly hear the brute the next time it complained—he would be too deeply out. But always that blaring, discordant foghorn jerked him at least half awake and sent him staggering like a drunken puppet through the motions which would end that horrible, mind-wrecking din.

After nearly thirty hours of it O'Mara knew he couldn't take much more. Whether the infant was collected in two days or two months the result as far as he was concerned would be the same; he would be a raving lunatic. Unless in a weak moment he took a walk outside without his suit. Pelling would never have allowed him to be subjected to this sort of punishment, he knew, but the doctor was an ignoramus where the FROB life-form was concerned. And Caxton, only a little less ignorant, was the simple, direct type who delighted in this sort of violent practical joke, especially when he considered that the victim deserved everything he got.

But just suppose the section chief was a more devious character than O'Mara had suspected? Suppose he knew exactly what he was sentencing him to by leaving the infant Hudlarian in his charge? O'Mara cursed tiredly, but he had been at it so constantly for the last ten or twelve hours that bad language had ceased to be an emotional safety valve. He shook his head angrily in a vain attempt to dispel the weariness which clogged his brain.

Caxton wasn't going to get away with it.

He was the strongest man on the whole project, O'Mara knew, and his reserves of strength must be considerable. All this fatigue and nervous twitching was simply in his mind, he told himself insistently, and a couple of days with practically no sleep meant nothing to his tremendous physique—even after the shaking up he'd received in the accident. And anyway, the present situation with the infant couldn't get any worse, so it must soon begin to improve. He would beat them yet, he swore. Caxton would not drive him mad, or even to the point of calling for help.

This was a challenge, he insisted with weary determination. Up to now he had bemoaned the fact that no job had fully exploited his capabilities. Well, this was a problem which would tax both his physical stamina and deductive processes to the limit. An infant had been placed in his charge and he intended taking care of it whether it was here for two weeks or two months. What was more, he was going to see that the kid was a credit to him when its foster parents arrived . . .

————

After the forty-eighth hour of the infant FROB's company and the fifty-seventh since he had had a good sleep, such illogical and somewhat maudlin thinking did not seem strange to O'Mara at all.

Then abruptly there came a change in what O'Mara had accepted as the order of things. The FROB after complaining, was fed and refused to shut up!

O'Mara's first reaction was a feeling of hurt surprise; this was against the *rules*. They cried, you fed them, they stopped crying—at least for a while. This was so unfair that it left him too shocked and helpless to react.

The noise was bedlam, with variations. Long, discordant blasts of sound beat over him. Sometimes the pitch and volume varied in an insanely arbitrary manner and at others it had a grinding, staccato quality as if broken glass had got into its vocal gears. There were intervals of quiet, varying between two seconds and half a minute, during which O'Mara cringed waiting for the next blast. He struck it out for as long as he could—a matter of ten minutes or so—then he dragged his leaden body off the couch again.

"What the blazes is *wrong* with you?" O'Mara roared against the din. The FROB was thoroughly covered by food compound so it couldn't be hungry.

Now that the infant had seen him the volume and urgency of its cries increased. The external, bellows-like flap of muscle on the infant's back—used for sound production only, the FROBs being non-breathers—continued swelling and deflating rapidly. O'Mara jammed the palms of his hands against his ears, an action which did no good at all, and yelled, *"Shut up!"*

He knew that the recently orphaned Hudlarian must still be feeling confused and frightened, that the mere process of feeding it could not possibly fulfill all of its emotional needs—he knew all this and felt a deep pity for the being. But these feelings were in some quiet, sane and civilized portion of his mind and divorced from all the pain and weariness and frightful onslaughts of sound currently torturing his body. He was really two people, and while one of him knew the reason for the noise and accepted it, the other—the purely physical O'Mara—reacted instinctively and viciously to stop it.

"Shut up! SHUT UP!" screamed O'Mara, and started swinging with his fists and feet.

Miraculously after about ten minutes of it, the Hudlarian stopped crying.

O'Mara returned to the couch shaking. For those ten minutes he had been in the grip of a murderous, uncontrollable rage. He had punched and kicked savagely until the pains from his hands and injured leg forced him to stop using those members, but he had gone on kicking and screeching invective with the only other weapons left to him, his good leg and tongue. The sheer viciousness of what he had done shocked and sickened him.

It was no good telling himself that the Hudlarian was tough and might not have felt the beating; the infant had stopped crying so he must have got through to it somehow. Admittedly Hudlarians were hard and tough, but this was a baby and babies had weak spots. Human babies, for instance, had a very soft spot on the top of their heads . . .

When O'Mara's utterly exhausted body plunged into sleep his last coherent thought was that he was the dirtiest, lowest louse that had ever been born.

Sixteen hours later he awoke. It was a slow, natural process which brought him barely above the level of unconsciousness. He had a brief feeling of wonder at the fact that the infant was not responsible for waking him before he drifted back to sleep again. The next time he wakened was five hours later and to the sound of Waring coming through the airlock.

"Dr. P-Pelling asked me to bring this," he said, tossing O'Mara a small book. "And I'm not doing you a favor, understand—it's just that he said it was for the good of the youngster. How is it doing?"

"Sleeping," said O'Mara.

Waring moistened his lips. "I'm-I'm supposed to check. C-C-Caxton says so."

"Ca-Ca-Caxton would," mimicked O'Mara.

He watched the other silently as Waring's face grew a deeper red. Waring was a thin young man, sensitive, not very strong, and the stuff of which heroes were made. On his arrival O'Mara had been over-whelmed with stories about this tractor-beam operator. There had been an accident during the fitting of a power pile and Waring had been trapped in a section which was inadequately shielded. But he had kept his head and, following instructions radioed to him from an engineer outside, had managed to avert a slow atomic explosion which nevertheless would have taken the lives of everyone in his section. He had done this while all the time fully convinced that the level of radiation in which he worked would, in a few hours time, certainly cause his death.

But the shielding had been more effective than had been thought and Waring did not die. The accident had left its mark on him, however, they told O'Mara. He had blackouts, he stuttered, his nervous system had been subtly affected, they said, and there were other things which O'Mara himself would see and was urged to ignore. Because Waring had saved all their lives and for that he deserved special treatment. That was why they made way for him wherever he went, let him win all fights, arguments and games of skill or chance, and generally kept him wrapped in a swathe of sentimental cottonwool.

And that was why Waring was a spoiled, insufferable, simpering brat.

Watching his white-lipped face and clenched fists, O'Mara smiled. He had never let Waring win at anything if he could possibly help it, and the first time the tractor-beam man had started a fight with him had also been the last. Not that he had hurt him, he had been just tough enough to demonstrate that fighting O'Mara was not a good idea.

"Go in and have a look," O'Mara said eventually. "Do what Ca-Ca-Caxton says."

They went in, observed the gently twitching infant briefly and came out. Stammering, Waring said that he had to go and headed for the airlock. He didn't often stutter these days, O'Mara knew; probably he was scared the subject of the accident would be brought up.

"Just a minute," said O'Mara. "I'm running out of food compound, will you bring—"

"G-get it yourself!"

O'Mara stared at him until Waring looked away, then he said quietly, "Caxton can't have it both ways. If this infant has to be cared for so thoroughly that I'm not allowed to either feed or keep it in airless conditions, it would be negligence on my part to go away and leave it for a couple of hours to get food. Surely you see that. The Lord alone knows what harm the kid might come to if it was left alone. I've been made responsible for this infant's welfare so I insist . . ."

"B-b-but it won't—"

"It only means an hour or so of your rest period every second or third day," said O'Mara sharply. "Cut the bellyaching. And stop sputtering at me, you're old enough to talk properly."

Waring's teeth came together with a click. He took a deep, shuddering breath then with his jaws still clenched furiously together he exhaled. The sound was like an airlock valve being cracked. He said:

"It . . . will . . . take . . . all of . . . my next two rest periods. The FROB quarters . . . where the food is kept . . . are being fitted to the main assembly the day after tomorrow. The food compound will have to be transferred before then."

"See how easy it is when you try," said O'Mara, grinning. "You were a bit jerky at first there, but I understood every word. You're doing fine. And by the way, when you're stacking the food tanks outside the airlock will you try not to make too much noise in case you wake the baby?"

For the next two minutes Waring called O'Mara dirty names without repeating himself or stuttering once.

"I said you were doing fine," said O'Mara reprovingly. "You don't have to show off."

III

After Waring left, O'Mara thought about the dismantling of the Hudlarian's quarters. With gravity grids set to four Gs and what few other amenities they required the FROBs had been living in one of the key sections. If it was about to be fitted to the main assembly then the completion of the hospital structure itself could only be five or six weeks off. The final stages, he knew, would be exciting. Tractor men at their safe positions—depressions actually on the joining faces—tossing thousand-ton loads about the sky, bringing them together gently while fitters checked alignment or adjusted or prepared the slowly closing faces for joining. Many of them would disregard the warning lights until the last possible moment, and take the most hair-raising risks imaginable, just to save the time and trouble of having their sections pulled apart and rejoined again for a possible re-fitting.

O'Mara would have liked to be in on the finish, instead of babysitting!

Thought of the infant brought back the worry he had been concealing from Waring. It had never slept this long before—it must be twenty hours since it had gone to sleep or he had kicked it to sleep. FROBs were tough, of course, but wasn't it possible that the infant was not simply asleep but unconscious through concussion . . . ?

O'Mara reached for the book which Pelling had sent and began to read.

It was slow, heavy going, but at the end of two hours O'Mara knew a little about the handling of Hudlarian babies, and the knowledge brought both relief and despair. Apparently his fit of temper and subsequent kicking had been a good thing—FROB babies needed constant petting and a quick calculation of the amount of force used by an adult of the species administering a gentle pat to its offspring showed that O'Mara's furious attack had been a very weak pat indeed. But the book warned against the dangers of over-feeding, and O'Mara was definitely guilty on this count. Seemingly the proper thing to do was to feed it every five or six hours during its waking period and use physical methods of soothing—patting, that was—if it appeared restless or still hungry. Also it appeared that FROB infants required, at fairly frequent intervals, a bath.

On the home planet this involved something like a major sandblasting operation, but O'Mara thought that this was probably due to the pressure and stickiness of the atmosphere. Another problem which he would have to solve was how to administer a hard enough consoling pat. He doubted very much if he could fly into a temper every time the baby needed its equivalent of a nursing.

But at least he would have plenty of time to work out something, because one of the things he had found out about them was that they were wakeful for two full days at a stretch, and slept for five.

During the first five-day period of sleep O'Mara was able to devise methods of petting and bathing his charge, and even had a couple of days free to relax and gather his strength for the two days of hard labor ahead when the infant woke up. It would have been a killing routine for a man of ordinary strength, but O'Mara discovered that after the first two weeks of it he seemed to make the necessary physical and mental adjustment to it. And at the end of four weeks the pain and stiffness had gone out of his leg and he had no worries regarding the baby at all.

Outside, the project neared completion. The vast, three-dimensional jigsaw puzzle was finished except for a few unimportant pieces around the edges. A Monitor Corps investigator had arrived and was asking questions—of everybody, apparently, except O'Mara.

He couldn't help wondering if Waring had been questioned yet, and if he had, what the tractor man had said. The investigator was a psychologist, unlike the mere Engineer officers already on the project, and very likely no fool. O'Mara thought that he, himself, was no fool either;

he had worked things out and by rights he should feel no anxiety over the outcome of the Monitor's investigations. O'Mara had sized up the situation here and the people in it, and the reactions of everyone were predictable. But it all depended on what Waring told that Monitor.

You're turning yellow! O'Mara thought in angry self-disgust. *Now that your pet theories are being put to the test you're scared silly they won't work. You want to crawl to Waring and lick his boots!*

And that course, O'Mara knew, would be introducing a wild variable into what should be a predictable situation, and it would almost certainly wreck everything. Yet the temptation was strong nevertheless.

It was at the beginning of the sixth week of his enforced guardianship of the infant, while he was reading up on some of the weird and wonderful diseases to which baby FROBs were prone, his airlock telltale indicated a visitor. He got off the couch quickly and faced the opening seal, trying hard to look as if he hadn't a worry in the world.

But it was only Caxton.

"I was expecting the Monitor," said O'Mara.

Caxton grunted. "Hasn't seen you yet, eh? Maybe he figures it would be a waste of time. After what we've told him he probably thinks the case is open and shut. He'll have cuffs with him when he comes."

O'Mara just looked at him. He was tempted to ask Caxton if the Corpsman had questioned Waring yet, but it was only a small temptation.

"My reason for coming," said Caxton harshly, "is to find out about the water. Stores department tells me you've been requisitioning treble the amount of water that you could conceivably use. You starting an aquarium or something?"

Deliberately O'Mara avoided giving a direct answer. He said, "It's time for the baby's bath, would you like to watch?"

He bent down, deftly removed a section of floor plating and reached inside.

"What are you doing?" Caxton burst out. "Those are the gravity grids, you're not allowed to touch—"

Suddenly the floor took on a thirty degree list. Caxton staggered against a wall, swearing. O'Mara straightened up, opened the inner seal of the airlock, then started up what was now a stiff gradient toward the bedroom. Still insisting loudly that O'Mara was neither allowed nor qualified to alter the artificial gravity settings, Caxton followed.

Inside, O'Mara said, "This is the spare food sprayer with the nozzle modified to project a high pressure jet of water." He pointed the instrument and began to demonstrate, playing the jet against a small area of the infant's hide. The subject of the demonstration was engaged in pushing what was left of one of O'Mara's chairs into even more unrecognizable shapes, and ignored them.

"You can see," O'Mara went on, "the area of skin where the food compound has hardened. This has to be washed at intervals because it clogs the being's absorption mechanism in those areas, causing the food intake to drop. This makes a young Hudlarian very unhappy and, ah, noisy . . ."

O'Mara trailed off into silence. He saw that Caxton wasn't looking at the infant but was watching the water which rebounded from its hide streaming along the now steeply slanted bedroom door, across the living room and into the open airlock. Which was just as well, because O'Mara's sprayer had uncovered a patch of the youngster's hide which had a texture and color he had never seen before. Probably there was nothing to worry about, but it was better not to have Caxton see it and ask questions.

"What's that up there?" said Caxton, pointing toward the bedroom ceiling.

In order to give the infant the petting it deserved O'Mara had had to knock together a system of levers, pulleys and counterweights and suspend the whole ungainly mass from the ceiling. He was rather proud of the gadget; it enabled him to administer a good, solid pat—a blow which would have instantly killed a human being—anywhere on that half-ton carcass. But he doubted if Caxton would appreciate the gadget. Probably the section chief would swear that he was torturing the baby and forbid its use.

O'Mara started out of the bedroom. Over his shoulder he said, "Just lifting tackle."

He dried up the wet patches of floor with a cloth which he threw into the now partly waterfilled airlock. His sandals and coveralls were wet so he threw them in, also, then he closed the inner seal and opened the outer. While the water was boiling off into the vacuum outside he readjusted the gravity grids so that the floor was flat and the walls vertical again, then he retrieved his sandals, coveralls and cloth which were now bone dry.

"You seem to have everything well organized," said Caxton grudgingly as he fastened his helmet. "At least you're looking after the youngster better than you did its parents. See it stays that way.

"The Monitor will be along to see you at hour nine tomorrow," he added, and left.

O'Mara returned quickly to the bedroom for a closer look at the colored patch. It was a pale bluish gray and in that area the smooth, almost steel-hard surface of the skin had taken on a sort of crackle finish. O'Mara rubbed the patch gently and the FROB wriggled and gave a blast of sound that was vaguely interrogatory.

"You and me both," said O'Mara absently. He couldn't remember reading about anything like this, but then he had not read all the book yet. The sooner he did so the better.

The chief method of communicating between beings of different species was by means of a Translator, which electronically sorted and classified all sense-bearing sounds and reproduced them in the native language of its user. Another method, used when large amounts of accurate data of a more subjective nature had to be passed on, was the Educator tape system. This transferred bodily all the sensory impressions, knowledge and personality of one being into the mind of another. Coming a long way third both in popularity and accuracy was the written language which was somewhat extravagantly called Universal.

Universal was of use only to beings who possessed brains linked to optical receptors capable of abstracting knowledge from patterns of markings on a flat surface—in short, the printed page. While there were many species with this ability, the response to color in each species was very rarely matched. What appeared to be a bluish-gray patch to O'Mara might look like anything from yellow-gray to dirty purple to another being, and the trouble was that the other being might have been the author of the book.

One of the appendices gave a rough color-equivalent chart, but it was a tedious, time-consuming job checking back on it, and his knowledge of Universal was not perfect anyway.

Five hours later he was still no nearer diagnosing the FROB's ailment, and the single blue-gray patch on its hide had grown to twice its original size and been joined by three more. He fed the infant, wondering anxiously whether that was the right thing to do in a case like this, then returned quickly to his studies.

According to the handbook there were literally hundreds of mild, short-lived diseases to which young Hudlarians were subject. This youngster had escaped them solely because it had been fed on tanked food compound and had avoided the air-borne bacteria so prevalent on its home planet. Probably this disease was nothing worse than the Hudlarian equivalent of a dose of measles, O'Mara told himself reassuringly, but it *looked* serious. At the next feeding the number of patches had grown to seven and they were a deeper, angrier blue, also the baby was continually slapping at itself with its appendages. Obviously the colored patches itched badly. Armed with this new datum O'Mara returned to the book.

And suddenly he found it. The symptoms were given as rough, discolored patches on the tegument with severe itching due to unabsorbed food particles. Treatment was to cleanse the irritated patches after each feed so as to kill the itching and let nature take care of the rest. The disease was a very rare one on Hudlar these days, the symptoms appeared with dramatic suddenness and it ran its course and disappeared equally quickly. Provided ordinary care was taken of the patient, the book stated, the disease was not dangerous.

O'Mara began converting the figures into his own time and size scale. As accurately as he could come to it the colored patches should grow to about eighteen inches across and he could expect anything up to twelve of them before they began to fade. This would occur, calculating from the time he had noticed the first spot, in approximately six hours.

He hadn't a thing to worry about.

IV

At the conclusion of the next feeding O'Mara carefully sprayed the blue patches clean, but still the young FROB kept slapping furiously at itself and quivering ponderously. Like a kneeling elephant with six angrily waving trunks, he thought. O'Mara had another look at the book, but it still maintained that under ordinary conditions the disease was mild and short-lived, and that the only palliative treatment possible was rest and seeing that the affected areas were kept clean.

Kids, thought O'Mara distractedly, *were a blasted worrisome thing . . . !*

All that quivering and slapping looked wrong, common sense told him, and should be stopped. Maybe the infant was scratching through sheer force of habit, though the violence of the process made this seem doubtful, and a distraction of some kind would make it stop. Quickly O'Mara chose a fifty-pound weight and used his lifting tackle to swing it to the ceiling. He began raising and dropping it rhythmically over the spot which he had discovered gave the infant the most pleasure—an area two feet back of the hard, transparent membrane which protected its eyes. Fifty pounds dropping from a height of eight feet was a nice gentle pat to a Hudlarian.

Under the patting the FROB grew less violent in its movements. But as soon as O'Mara stopped it began lashing at itself worse than ever, and even running full tilt into walls and what was left of the furniture. During one frenzied charge it nearly escaped into the living room, and the only thing which stopped it was the fact that it was too big to go through the door. Up to that moment O'Mara did not realize how much weight the FROB had put on in five weeks.

Finally sheer fatigue made him give up. He left the FROB threshing and blundering about in the bedroom and threw himself onto the couch outside to try to think.

According to the book it was now time for the blue patches to begin to fade. But they weren't fading—they had reached the maximum number of twelve and instead of being eighteen or less inches across they were nearly double that size. They were so large that at the next feeding the absorption area of the infant would have shrunk by a half, which meant that it would be further weakened by not getting enough food. And everyone knew that itchy spots should not be scratched if the condition was not to spread and become more serious . . .

A raucous foghorn note interrupted his thoughts. O'Mara had experience enough to know by the sound that the infant was badly frightened, and by the relative decrease in volume that it was growing weak as well.

He needed help badly, but O'Mara doubted very much if there was anyone available who could furnish it. Telling Caxton about it would be useless—the section chief would only call in Pelling and Pelling was much less informed on the subject of Hudlarian children than was O'Mara, who had been specializing in the subject for the past five weeks. That course would only waste time and not help the kid at all, and there was

a strong possibility that—despite the presence of a Monitor investigator—
Caxton would see to it that something pretty violent happened to O'Mara
for allowing the infant to take sick, for that was the way the section chief
would look at it.

Caxton didn't like O'Mara. Nobody liked O'Mara.

If he had been well-liked on the project nobody would have thought
of blaming him for the infant's sickness, or immediately and unanimously
assuming that he was the one responsible for the death of its parents. But
he had made the decision to appear a pretty lousy character, and he had
been too damned successful.

Maybe he really was a despicable person and that was why the role
had come so easy to him. Perhaps the constant frustration of never having
the chance to really use the brain which was buried in his ugly, muscle-
bound body had gradually soured him, and the part he thought he was
playing was the real O'Mara.

If only he had stayed clear of the Waring business. That was what
had them really mad at him.

But this sort of thinking was getting him nowhere. The solution of
his own problems lay—in part, at least—in showing that he was responsible, patient, kind and possessed the various other attributes which his
fellow men looked on with respect. To do that he must first show that
he could be trusted with the care of a baby.

He wondered suddenly if the Monitor could help. Not personally; a
Corps psychologist officer could hardly be expected to know about obscure diseases of Hudlar children, but through his organization. As the
Galaxy's police, maid-of-all-work and supreme authority generally, the
Monitor Corps would be able to find at short notice a being who would
know the necessary answers. But again, that being would almost certainly
be found on Hudlar itself, and the authorities there already knew of the
orphaned infant's position and help had probably been on the way for
weeks. It would certainly arrive sooner than the Monitor could bring it.
Help might arrive in time to save the infant. But again maybe it might
not.

The problem was still O'Mara's.

About as serious as a dose of measles.

But measles, in a human baby, could be very serious if the patient
was kept in a cold room or in some other environment which, although
not deadly in itself, could become lethal to an organism whose resistance
was lowered by disease or lack of food. The handbook had prescribed

rest, cleansing and nothing else. Or had it? There might be a large and well hidden assumption there. The kicker was that the patient under discussion was residing on its home world at the time of the illness. Under ordinary conditions like that the disease probably was mild and short-lived.

But O'Mara's bedroom was not, for a Hudlarian baby with the disease, anything like normal conditions.

With that thought came the answer, if only he wasn't too late to apply it. Abruptly O'Mara pushed himself out of the couch and hurried to the spacesuit locker. He was climbing into the heavy duty model when the communicator beeped at him.

"O'Mara," Caxton's voice brayed at him when he had acknowledged, "the Monitor wants to talk to you. It wasn't supposed to be until tomorrow but—"

"Thank you, Mr. Caxton," broke in a quiet, firmer voice. There was a pause, then, "My name is Craythorne, Mr. O'Mara. I had planned to see you tomorrow as you know, but I managed to clear up some other work which left me time for a preliminary chat . . ."

What, thought O'Mara fulminatingly, *a damned awkward time you had to pick!* He finished putting on the suit but left the gauntlets and helmet off. He began tearing into the panel which covered the air-supply controls.

". . . To tell you the truth," the quiet voice of the Monitor went on, "your case is incidental to my main work here. My job is to arrange accommodation and so on for the various life-forms who will shortly be arriving to staff this hospital, and to do everything possible to avoid friction developing between them when they do come. There are a lot of finicky details to attend to, but at the moment I'm free. And I'm curious about you, O'Mara. I'd like to ask some questions."

This is one smooth operator! thought one half of O'Mara's mind. The other half noted that the air-supply controls were set to suit the conditions he had in mind. He left the panel hanging loose and began pulling up a floor section to get at the artificial gravity grid underneath. A little absently he said, "You'll have to excuse me if I work while we talk. Caxton will explain—"

"I've told him about the kid," Caxton broke in, "and if you think you're fooling him by pretending to be the harassed mother type . . . !"

"I understand," said the Monitor. "I'd also like to say that forcing you to live with an FROB infant when such a course was unnecessary comes under the heading of cruel and unusual punishment, and that about ten years should be knocked off your sentence for what you've taken this past five weeks—that is, of course, if you're found guilty. And now, I always think it's better to see who one is talking to. Can we have vision, please?"

The suddenness with which the artificial gravity grids switched from one to two Gs caught O'Mara by surprise. His arms folded under him and his chest thumped the floor. A frightened bawl from his patient in the next room must have disguised the noise he made from his listeners because they didn't mention it. He did the great-grand-daddy of all press-ups and heaved himself to his knees.

He fought to keep from gasping. "Sorry, my vision transmitter is on the blink."

The Monitor was silent just long enough to let O'Mara know that he knew he was lying, and that he would disregard the lie for the moment. He said finally, "Well, at least you can see me," and O'Mara's vision plate lit up.

It showed a youngish man with close-cropped hair whose eyes seemed twenty years older than the rest of his features. The shoulder tabs of a Major were visible on the trim, dark-green tunic and the collar bone bore a caduceus. O'Mara thought that in different circumstances he would have liked this man.

"I've something to do in the next room," O'Mara lied again. "Be with you in a minute."

He began the job of setting the anti-gravity belt on his suit to two Gs repulsion, which would exactly counteract the floor's present attraction and allow him to increase the pull to four Gs without too much discomfort to himself. He would then reset the belt for three Gs, and that would give him back a normal gravity apparent of one G.

At least that was what should have happened.

Instead the G-belt or the floor grids or both started producing half-G fluctuations, and the room went mad. It was like being in an express elevator which was constantly being started and stopped. The frequency of the surges built up rapidly until O'Mara was being shaken up and down so hard his teeth rattled. Before he could react to this a new and more devastating complication occurred. As well as variations in strength the floor grids were no longer acting at right angles to their surface, but yawed erratically from ten to thirty degrees from the vertical. No storm-tossed ship had ever pitched and rolled as viciously as this. O'Mara staggered, grabbed frantically for the couch, missed and was flung heavily against the wall. The next surge sent him skidding against the opposite wall before he was able to switch off the G-belt.

The room settled down to a steady gravity-pull of two Gs again.

"Will this take long?" asked the Monitor suddenly.

O'Mara had almost forgotten the Major during the past hectic seconds. He did his best to make his voice sound both natural and as if it was coming from the next room as he replied, "It might. Could you call back later?"

"I'll wait," said the Monitor.

For the next few minutes O'Mara tried to forget the bruising he had received despite the protection given him by the heavy spacesuit, and concentrate on thinking his way out of this latest mess. He was beginning to see what must have happened.

When two anti-gravity generators of the same power and frequency were used close together, a pattern of interference was set up which affected the stability of both. The grids in O'Mara's quarters were merely a temporary job and powered by a generator similar to the one used in his suit, though normally a difference in frequency was built in against the chance of such instability occurring. But O'Mara had been fiddling with the grid settings constantly for the past five weeks—every time the infant had a bath, to be exact—so that he must have unknowingly altered the frequency.

He didn't know what he had done wrong and there wasn't enough time to try fixing it if he had known. Gingerly, O'Mara switched on his G-belt again and slowly began increasing power. It registered over three-quarters of a G before the first signs of instability appeared.

Four Gs less three-quarters made a little over three Gs. It looked, O'Mara thought grimly, like he was going to have to do this the hard way . . .

V

O'Mara closed his helmet quickly, then strung a cable from his suit mike to the communicator so that he would be able to talk without Caxton or the Monitor realizing that he was sealed inside his suit. If he was to have time to complete the treatment they must not suspect that there was anything out of the ordinary going on here. Next came the final adjustments to the air-pressure regulator and gravity grids.

Inside two minutes the atmosphere pressure in the two rooms had multiplied six times and the gravity apparent was four Gs—the nearest, in fact, that O'Mara could get to "ordinary conditions" for a Hudlarian. With shoulder muscles straining and cracking with the effort—for his under-powered G-belt took only three-quarters of a gravity off the four-G pull in the room—he withdrew the incredibly awkward and ponderous thing which his arm had become from the grid servicing space and rolled heavily onto his back.

He felt as if his baby was sitting on his chest, and large, black blotches hung throbbing before his eyes. Through them he could see a section of ceiling and, at a crazy angle, the vision panel. The face in it was becoming impatient.

"I'm back, Major," gasped O'Mara. He fought to control his breathing so that the words would not be squeezed out too fast. "I suppose you want to hear my side of the accident?"

"No," said the Monitor. "I've heard the tape Caxton made. What I'm curious about is your background prior to coming here. I've checked up and there is something which doesn't quite fit . . ."

A thunderous eruption of noise blasted into the conversation. Despite the deeper note caused by the increased air pressure O'Mara recognized the signal for what it was; the FROB was angry and hungry.

With a mighty effort O'Mara rolled onto his side, then propped himself up on his elbows. He stayed that way for a while gathering strength to roll over onto his hands and knees. But when he finally accomplished this he found that his arms and legs were swelling and felt as if they would burst from the pressure of blood piling up in them. Gasping, he eased himself down flat onto his chest. Immediately the blood rushed to the front of his body and his vision began to red out.

He couldn't crawl on hands and knees nor wriggle on his stomach. Most certainly, under three Gs, he could not stand up and walk. What else was there?

O'Mara struggled onto his side again and rolled back, but this time with his elbows propping him up. The neck-rest of his suit supported his head, but the insides of the sleeves were very lightly padded and his elbows hurt. And the strain of holding up even part of his three times heavier than normal body made his heart pound. Worst of all, he was beginning to black out again.

Surely there must be some way to equalize, or at least distribute, the pressures in his body so that he could stay conscious and move. O'Mara tried to visualize the layout of the acceleration chairs which had been used in ships before artificial gravity came along. It had been a not-quite-prone position, he remembered suddenly, with the knees drawn up . . .

Inching along on his elbows, bottom and feet, O'Mara progressed snail-like toward the bedroom. His embarrassment of riches where muscles were concerned was certainly of use now—in these conditions any ordinary man would have been plastered helplessly against the floor. Even so it took him fifteen minutes to reach the food sprayer in the bedroom, and during practically every second of the way the baby kept up its ear-splitting racket. With the increased pressure the noise was so tremendously loud and deep that every bone in O'Mara's body seemed to vibrate to it.

"I'm trying to talk to you!" the Monitor yelled during a lull. "Can't you keep that blasted kid shut up!"

"It's hungry," said O'Mara. "It'll quiet down when it's fed . . ."

The food sprayer was mounted on a trolley and O'Mara had fitted a pedal control so as to leave both hands free for aiming. Now that his patient was immobilized by four gravities he didn't have to use his hands. Instead he was able to nudge the trolley into position with his shoulders and depress the pedal with his elbow. The high-pressure jet tended to bend floorward owing to the extra gravity but he did finally manage to cover the infant with food. But cleaning the affected areas of food compound was another matter. The water jet, which handled very awkwardly from floor level, had no accuracy at all. The best he could manage was to wash down the wide, vivid blue patch—formed from three separate patches which had grown together—which covered nearly one quarter of its total skin area.

After that O'Mara straightened out his legs and lowered his back gently to the floor. Despite the three Gs acting on him, the strain of maintaining that half-sitting position for the last half hour made him feel almost comfortable.

The baby had stopped crying.

"What I was about to say," said the Monitor heavily when the silence looked like lasting for a few minutes, "was that your record on previous jobs does not fit what I find here. Previously you were, as you are now, a restless, discontented type, but you were invariably popular with your colleagues and only a little less so with your superiors—this last being because your superiors were sometimes wrong and you never were . . ."

"I was every bit as smart as they were," said O'Mara tiredly, "and proved it often. But I didn't *look* intelligent, I had mucker written all over me!"

It was strange, O'Mara thought, but he felt almost disinterested in his own personal trouble now. He couldn't take his eyes off the angry blue patch on the infant's side. The color had deepened and also the center of the patch seemed to have swelled. It was as if the super-hard tegument had softened and the FROB's enormous internal pressure had produced a swelling. Increasing the gravity and pressure to the Hudlarian normal should, he hoped, halt that particular development—if it wasn't a symptom of something else entirely.

O'Mara had thought of carrying his idea a step further and spraying the air around the patient with food compound. On Hudlar the natives' food was comprised of tiny organisms floating in their super-thick atmosphere, but then again the handbook expressly stated that food particles must be kept away from the affected areas of tegument, so that the extra gravity and pressure should be enough . . .

". . . Nevertheless," the Monitor was saying, "if a similar accident had happened on one of your previous jobs, your story would have been believed. Even if it had been your fault they would have rallied around to defend you from outsiders like myself.

"What caused you to change from a friendly, likeable type of personality to *this* . . . ?"

"I was bored," said O'Mara shortly.

There had been no sound from the infant yet, but he had seen the characteristic movements of the FROB's appendages which foretold of an outburst shortly to come. And it came. For the next ten minutes speech was, of course, impossible.

O'Mara heaved himself onto his side and rolled back onto his now raw and bleeding elbows. He knew what was wrong; the infant had missed its usual after-feed nursing. O'Mara humped his way slowly across to the two counterweight ropes of the gadget he had devised for petting the infant and prepared to remedy this omission. But the ends of the ropes hung four feet above the floor.

Lying propped by one elbow and straining to raise the dead weight of his other arm, O'Mara thought that the rope could just as easily have been four miles away. Sweat poured off his face and body with the intensity of the effort and slowly, trembling and wobbling so much that his gauntleted hand went past it first time, he reached up and grabbed hold. Still gripping it tightly he lowered himself gently back bringing the rope with him.

The gadget operated on a system of counterweights, so that there was no extra pull needed on the controlling ropes. A heavy weight dropped neatly onto the infant's back, administering a reassuring pat. O'Mara rested for a few minutes, then struggled up to repeat the process with the other rope, the pull on which would also wind up the first weight ready for use again.

After about the eighth pat he found that he couldn't see the end of the rope he was reaching for, though he managed to find it all the same. His head was being kept too high above the level of the rest of his body for too long a time and he was constantly on the point of blacking out. The diminished flow of blood to his brain was having other effects, too . . .

". . . There, there," O'Mara heard himself saying in a definitely maudlin voice. "You're all right now, pappy will take care of you. There now, shush . . ."

The funny thing about it was that he really did feel a responsibility and a sort of angry concern for the infant. He had saved it once only to let *this* happen! Maybe the three Gs which jammed him against the floor, making every breath a day's work and the smallest movement an operation which called for all the reserves of strength he possessed, was bringing back the memory of another kind of pressure—the slow, inexorable movement together of two large, inanimate and uncaring masses of metal.

The accident.

As fitter-in-charge of that particular shift O'Mara had just switched on the warning lights when he had seen the two adult Hudlarians chasing after their offspring on one of the faces being joined. He had called them through his translator, urging them to get to safety and leave him to chase the youngster clear—being much smaller than its parents the slowly closing faces would take longer to reach it, and during those extra few minutes O'Mara would have been able to herd it out of danger. But either their translators were switched off or they were reluctant to trust the safety of their child to a diminutive human being. Whatever the reason, they remained between the faces until it was too late. O'Mara had to watch helplessly as they were trapped and crushed by the joining structures.

The sight of the young one, still unharmed because of its smaller girth, floundering about between the bodies of its late parents sent O'Mara into belated action. He was able to chase it out of danger before the sections came close enough to trap it, and had just barely made it himself. For a few heart-stopping seconds back there O'Mara had thought he would have to leave a leg behind.

This was no place for kids anyway, he told himself angrily as he looked at the quivering, twitching body with the patches of vivid, scabrous blue. People shouldn't be allowed to bring kids out here, even tough people like the Hudlarians.

But Major Craythorne was speaking again.

". . . Judging by what I hear going on over there," said the Monitor acidly, "you're taking very good care of your charge. Keeping the youngster happy and healthy will definitely be a point in your favor . . ."

Happy and healthy, thought O'Mara as he reached toward the rope yet again. *Healthy . . . !*

". . . But there are other considerations," the quiet voice went on. "Were you guilty of negligence in not switching on the warning lights until after the accident occurred, which is what you are alleged to have done? And your previous record notwithstanding, here you have been a surly, quarrelsome bully and your behavior toward Waring especially . . . !"

The Monitor broke off, looked faintly disapproving, then went on, "A few minutes ago you said that you did all these things because you were bored. Explain that."

"Wait a minute, Major," Caxton broke in, his face appearing suddenly behind Craythorne's on the screen. "He's stalling for some reason, I'm sure of it. All those interruptions, this gasping voice he's using and this shush-a-bye-baby stuff is just an act to show what a great little nursemaid he is. I think I'll go over and bring him back here to answer you face to face—"

"That won't be necessary," said O'Mara quickly. "I'll answer any questions you want, right now."

He had a horrible picture of Caxton's reaction if the other saw the infant in its present state; the sight of it made O'Mara feel queasy and he was used to it now. Caxton wouldn't stop to think, or wait for explanations, or ask himself if it was fair to place an e-t in charge of a human who was completely ignorant of its physiology or weaknesses. He would just react. Violently.

And as for the Monitor . . .

O'Mara thought that he might get out of the accident part, but if the kid died as well he hadn't a hope. The infant had had a mild though uncommon disease which should have responded to treatment days ago, and instead had become progressively worse, so it would die anyway if O'Mara's last desperate try at reproducing its home planet's conditions did not come off. What he needed now was time. According to the book, about four to six hours of it.

Suddenly the futility of it all hit him. The infant's condition had not improved—it heaved and twitched and generally looked to be the most desperately ill and pitiable creature that had ever been born. O'Mara swore helplessly. What he was trying to do now should have been tried days ago, his baby was as good as dead, and continuing this treatment for another five or six hours would probably kill or cripple him for life. And it would serve him right!

VI

The infant's appendages curled in the way O'Mara knew meant that it was going to cry again, and grimly he began pushing himself onto his elbows for another patting session. That was the very least he could do. And even though he was convinced that going on was useless, the kid had to be given the chance. O'Mara had to have time to finish the treatment without interruptions, and to insure that he would have to answer this Monitor's questions in a full and satisfactory manner. If the kid started crying again he wouldn't be able to do that.

". . . For your kind cooperation," the Major was saying dryly. "First off, I want an explanation for your sudden change of personality."

"I was bored," said O'Mara. "Hadn't enough to do. Maybe I'd become a bit of a sorehead, too. But the main reason for setting out to be a lousy character was that there was a job I could do here which could not be done by a nice guy. I've studied a lot and think of myself as a pretty good rule-of-thumb psychologist . . ."

Suddenly came disaster. O'Mara's supporting elbow slipped as he was reaching for the counterweight rope and he crashed back to the floor from a distance of two-and-a-half feet. At three Gs this was equivalent to a fall of seven feet. Luckily he was in a heavy duty suit with a padded helmet so he did not lose consciousness. But he did cry out, and instinctively held onto the rope as he fell.

That was his mistake.

One weight dropped, the other swung up too far. It hit the ceiling with a crash and loosened the bracket which supported the light metal girder which carried it. The whole structure began to sag, and slip, then was suddenly yanked floorward by four Gs onto the infant below. In his dazed state O'Mara could not guess at the amount of force expended on the infant—whether it was a harder than usual pat, the equivalent of a sharp smack on the bottom, or something very much more serious. The baby was very quiet afterward, which worried him.

". . . For the third time," shouted the Monitor, "what the blazes is going on in there?"

O'Mara muttered something which was unintelligible even to himself. Then Caxton joined in.

"There's something fishy going on, and I bet it involves the kid! I'm going over to see—"

"No wait!" said O'Mara desperately. "Give me six hours . . ."

"I'll see you," said Caxton, "in ten minutes."

"Caxton!" O'Mara shouted, "if you come through my airlock you'll kill me! I'll have the inner seal jammed open and if you open the outer one you'll evacuate the place. Then the Major will lose his prisoner."

There was a sudden silence, then:

"What," asked the Monitor quietly, "do you want the six hours for?"

O'Mara tried to shake his head to clear it, but now that it weighed three times heavier than normal he only hurt his neck. What *did* he want six hours for? Looking around him he began to wonder, because both the food sprayer and its connecting water tank had been wrecked by the fall of tackle from the ceiling. He could neither feed, wash, nor scarcely see his patient for fallen wreckage, so all he could do for six hours was watch and wait for a miracle.

"I'm going over," said Caxton doggedly.

"You're not," said the Major, still polite but with a no-nonsense tone. "I want to get to the bottom of this. You'll wait outside until I've spoken with O'Mara alone. Now O'Mara, *what . . . is . . . happening?*"

Flat on his back again O'Mara fought to gain enough breath to carry on an extended conversation. He had decided that the best thing to do would be to tell the Monitor the exact truth, and then appeal to him to back O'Mara up in the only way possible which might save the infant—by leaving him alone for six hours. But O'Mara was feeling very low as he talked, and his vision was so poor that he couldn't tell sometimes whether his eyelids were open or shut. He did see someone hand the Major a note, but Craythorne didn't read it until O'Mara had finished speaking.

"You are in a mess," Craythorne said finally. He briefly looked sympathetic, then his tone hardened again. "And ordinarily I should be forced to do as you suggest and give you that six hours. After all, you have the book and so you know more than we do. But the situation has changed in the last few minutes. I've just had word that two Hudlarians have arrived, one of them a doctor. You had better step down, O'Mara. You tried, but now let some skilled help salvage what they can from the situation. For the kid's sake," he added.

It was three hours later. Caxton, Waring and O'Mara were facing the Major across the Monitor's desk. Craythorne had just come in.

He said briskly, "I'm going to be busy for the next few days so we'll get this business settled quickly. First, the accident. O'Mara, your case depends entirely on Waring's corroboration for your story. Now there seems to be some pretty devious thinking here on your part. I've already heard Waring's evidence, but to satisfy my own curiosity I'd like to know what *you* think he said?"

"He backed up my story," said O'Mara wearily. "He had no choice."

He looked down at his hands, still thinking about the desperate sick infant he had left in his quarters. He told himself again that he wasn't responsible for what had happened, but deep inside he felt that if he had shown more flexibility of mind and had started the pressure treatment sooner the kid would have been all right now. But the result of the accident enquiry didn't seem to matter now, one way or the other, and neither did the Waring business.

"*Why* do you think he had no choice?" prodded the Monitor sharply.

Caxton had his mouth open, looking confused. Waring would not meet O'Mara's eyes and he was beginning to blush.

"When I came here," O'Mara said dully, "I was looking out for a secondary job to fill my spare time, and hounding Waring was it. He is the reason for my being an obnoxious type, that was the only way I could go to work on him. But to understand that you have to go a bit further back. Because of that power pile accident," O'Mara went on, "all the men of his section were very much in Waring's debt—you've probably heard the details by now. Waring himself was a mess. Physically he was below par—had to get shots to keep his blood-count up, was just about strong enough to work his control console, and was fairly wallowing in self-pity. Psychologically he was a wreck. Despite all Pelling's assurances that the shots would only be necessary for a few more months he was convinced that he had pernicious anemia. He also believed that he had been made sterile, again despite everything the doctor told him, and this conviction made him act and talk in a way which would give any normal man the creeps—because that sort of thing is pathological and there wasn't anything like that wrong with him. When I saw how things were I started to ridicule him every chance I got. I hounded him unmercifully. So the way I see it he had no other choice but to support my story. Simple gratitude demanded it."

"I begin to see the light," said the Major. "Go on."

"The men around him were very much in his debt," O'Mara continued. "But instead of putting the brakes on, or giving him a good talking to, they smothered him with sympathy. They let him win all fights, card-games or whatever, and generally treated him like a little tin god. I did none of these things. Whenever he lisped or stuttered or was awkward about anything," O'Mara went on, "whether it was due to one of his mental and self-inflicted disabilities or a physical one which he honestly couldn't help, I jumped on him hard with both feet. Maybe I was too hard sometimes, but remember that I was one man trying to undo the harm that was being done by fifty. Naturally he hated my guts, but he always knew exactly where he was with me. And I never pulled punches. On the very few occasions when he was able to get the better of me, he knew that he had won despite everything I could do to stop him—unlike his friends who let him beat them at everything and in so doing made his winning meaningless. That was exactly what he needed for what ailed him, somebody to treat him as an equal and made no allowances at all. So when this trouble came," O'Mara ended, "I was pretty sure he would begin to see what I'd been doing for him—consciously as well as sub-consciously—and that simple gratitude plus the fact that basically he is a decent type would keep him from withholding the evidence which would clear me. Was I right?"

"You were," said the Major. He paused to quell Caxton who had jumped to his feet, protesting, then continued, "Which brings us to the FROB infant.

"Apparently your baby caught one of the mild but rare diseases which can only be treated successfully on the home planet," Craythorne went on. He smiled suddenly. "At least, that was what they thought until a few hours ago. Now our Hudlarian friends state that the proper treatment has already been initiated by you and that all they have to do is wait for a couple of days and the infant will be as good as new. But they're very annoyed with you, O'Mara," the Monitor continued. "They say that you've rigged special equipment for petting and soothing the kid and that you've done this much more often than is desirable. The baby has been overfed and spoiled shamelessly, they say, so much so that at the moment it prefers human beings to members of its own species—"

Suddenly Caxton banged the desk. "You're not going to let him get away with this," he shouted, red-faced. "Waring doesn't know what he's saying sometimes . . ."

"Mr. Caxton," said the Monitor sharply, "All the evidence available proves that Mr. O'Mara is blameless, both at the time of the accident and while he was looking after the infant later. However, I am not quite finished with him here, so perhaps you two would be good enough to leave . . ."

Caxton stormed out, followed more slowly by Waring. At the door the tractor-beam man paused, addressed one printable and three unprintable words to O'Mara, grinned suddenly and left. The Major sighed.

"O'Mara," he said sternly, "you're out of a job again, and while I don't as a rule give unasked for advice I would like to remind you of a few facts. In a few weeks time the staff and maintenance engineers for this hospital will be arriving and they will be comprised of practically every known species in the galaxy. My job is to settle them in and keep friction from developing between them so that eventually they will work together as a team. No text-book rules have been written to cover this sort of thing yet, but before they sent me here my superiors said that it would require a good rule-of-thumb psychologist with plenty of common sense who was not afraid to take calculated risks. I think it goes without saying that two such psychologists would be even better . . ."

O'Mara was listening to him all right, but he was thinking of that grin he'd got from Waring. Both the infant and Waring were going to be all right now, he knew, and in his present happy state of mind he could refuse nothing to anybody. But apparently the Major had mistaken his abstraction for something else.

"... Dammit I'm offering you a job! You *fit* here, can't you see that? This is a hospital, man, and you've cured our first patient ... !"

CHAPTER 2

SECTOR GENERAL

Like a sprawling, misshapen Christmas tree the lights of Sector Twelve General Hospital blazed against the misty backdrop of the stars. From its view-ports shone lights that were yellow and red-orange and soft, liquid green, and others which were a searing actinic blue. There was darkness in places also. Behind these areas of opaque metal plating lay sections wherein the lighting was so viciously incandescent that the eyes of approaching ships' pilots had to be protected from it, or compartments which were so dark and cold that not even the light which filtered in from the stars could be allowed to penetrate to their inhabitants.

To the occupants of the Telfi ship which slid out of hyper-space to hang some twenty miles from this mighty structure, the garish display of visual radiation was too dim to be detected without the use of instruments. The Telfi were energy-eaters. Their ship's hull shone with a crawling blue glow of radioactivity and its interior was awash with a high level of hard radiation which was also in all respects normal. Only in the stern section of the tiny ship were the conditions not normal. Here the active core of a power pile lay scattered in small, subcritical and unshielded masses throughout the ship's Planetary Engines room, and here it was too hot even for the Telfi.

The group-mind entity that was the Telfi spaceship Captain—*and* Crew—energized its short-range communicator and spoke in the staccato clicking and buzzing language used to converse with those benighted beings who were unable to merge into a Telfi gestalt.

"This is a Telfi hundred-unit gestalt," it said slowly and distinctly.

"We have casualties and require assistance. Our Classification to one group is VTXM, repeat VTXM ..."

"Details, please, and degree of urgency," said a voice briskly as the Telfi was about to repeat the message. It was translated into the same language used by the Captain. The Telfi gave details quickly, then waited. Around it and through it lay the hundred specialized units that were both its mind and multiple body. Some of the units were blind, deaf and perhaps even dead cells that received or recorded no sensory impressions whatever, but there were others who radiated waves of such sheer, excruciating agony that the group-mind writhed and twisted silently in sympathy. Would that voice never reply, they wondered, and if it did, would it be able to help them ... ?

"You must not approach the Hospital nearer than a distance of five miles," said the voice suddenly. "Otherwise there will be danger to unshielded traffic in the vicinity, or to beings within the establishment with low radiation tolerance."

"We understand," said the Telfi.

"Very well," said the voice. "You must also realize that your race is too hot for us to handle directly. Remote controlled mechanisms are already on the way to you, and it would ease the problem of evacuation if you arranged to have your casualties brought as closely as possible to the ship's largest entry port. If this cannot be done, do not worry—we have mechanisms capable of entering your vessel and removing them."

The voice ended by saying that while they hoped to be able to help the patients, any sort of accurate prognosis was impossible at the present time.

The Telfi gestalt thought that soon the agony that tortured its mind and wide-flung multiple body would be gone, but so also would nearly one quarter of that body ...

With that feeling of happiness possible only with eight hours sleep behind, a comfortable breakfast within and an interesting job in front of one, Conway stepped out briskly for his wards. They were not really his wards, of course—if anything went seriously wrong in one of them the most he would be expected to do would be to scream for help. But considering the fact that he had been here only two months he did not mind that, or knowing that it would be a long time before he could be trusted to deal with cases requiring other than mechanical methods of treatment.

Complete knowledge of any alien physiology could be obtained within minutes by Educator tape, but the skill to use that knowledge—especially in surgery—came only with time. Conway was looking forward with conscious pride to spending his life acquiring that skill.

At an intersection Conway saw an FGLI he knew—a Tralthan intern who was humping his elephantine body along on six spongy feet. The stubby legs seemed even more rubbery than usual and the little OTSB who lived in symbiosis with it was practically comatose. Conway said brightly, "Good morning," and received a translated—and therefore necessarily emotionless—reply of "Drop dead." Conway grinned.

There had been considerable activity in and about Reception last evening. Conway had not been called, but it looked as though the Tralthan had missed both his recreation and rest periods.

A few yards beyond the Tralthan he met another who was walking slowly alongside a small DBDG like himself. Not entirely like himself, though—DBDG was the one-group classification which gave the grosser physical attributes, the number of arms, heads, legs, etc., and their placement. The fact that the being had seven-fingered hands, stood only four feet tall and looked like a very cuddly teddy bear—Conway had forgotten the being's system of origin, but remembered being told that it came from a world which had suffered a sudden bout of glaciation which had caused its highest life-form to develop intelligence and a thick red fur coat—would not have shown up unless the Classification were taken to two or three groups. The DBDG had his hands clasped behind his back and was staring with vacant intensity at the floor. His hulking companion showed similar concentration, but favored the ceiling because of the different position of his visual organs. Both wore their professional insignia on golden armbands, which meant that they were lordly Diagnosticians, no less. Conway refrained from saying good morning to them as he passed, or from making undue noise with his feet.

Possibly they were deeply immersed in some medical problem, Conway thought, or equally likely, they had just had a tiff and were pointedly ignoring each other's existence. Diagnosticians were peculiar people. It wasn't that they were insane to begin with, but their job forced a form of insanity onto them.

At each corridor intersection annunciators had been pouring out an alien gabble which he had only half heard in passing, but when it switched suddenly to Terran English and Conway heard his own name being called, surprise halted him dead in his tracks.

"... To Admittance Lock Twelve at once," the voice was repeating monotonously. "Classification VTXM-23. Dr. Conway, please go to Admittance Lock Twelve at once. A VTXM-23 ..."

Conway's first thought was that they could not possibly mean him. This looked as if he was being asked to deal with a case—a big one, too, because the "23" after the classification code referred to the number of patients to be treated. And that Classification, VTXM, was completely new to him. Conway knew what the letters stood for, of course, but he had never thought that they could exist in that combination. The nearest he could make of them was some form of telepathic species—the V prefixing the classification showed this as their most important attribute, and that mere physical equipment was secondary—who existed by the direct conversion of radiant energy, and usually as a closely cooperative group or gestalt. While he was still wondering if he was ready to cope with a case like this, his feet had turned and were taking him toward Lock Twelve.

His patients were waiting for him at the lock, in a small metal box heaped around with lead bricks and already loaded onto a power stretcher carrier. The orderly told him briefly that the beings called themselves the Telfi, that preliminary diagnosis indicated the use of the Radiation Theater, which was being readied for him, and that owing to the portability of his patients he could save time by calling with them to the Educator room and leaving them outside while he took his Telfi physiology tape.

Conway nodded thanks, hopped onto the carrier and set it moving, trying to give the impression that he did this sort of thing every day.

In Conway's pleasurable but busy life with the high unusual establishment that was Sector General there was only one sour note, and he met it again when he entered the Educator room: there was a Monitor in charge. Conway disliked Monitors. The presence of one affected him rather like the close proximity of a carrier of a contagious disease. And while Conway was proud of the fact that as a sane, civilized and ethical being he could never bring himself actually to hate anybody or anything, he disliked Monitors intensely. He knew, of course, that there were people who went off the beam sometimes, and that there had to be somebody who could take the action necessary to preserve the peace. But with his abhorrence of violence in any form, Conway could not like the men who took that action.

And what were Monitors doing in a hospital anyway?

The figure in neat, dark green coveralls seated before the Educator control console turned quickly at his entrance and Conway got another shock. As well as a Major's insignia on his shoulder, the Monitor wore the Staff and Serpents emblem of a Doctor!

"My name is O'Mara," said the Major in a pleasant voice. "I'm the Chief Psychologist of this madhouse. You, I take it, are Dr. Conway." He smiled.

Conway made himself smile in return, knowing that it looked forced, and that the other knew it also.

"You want the Telfi tape," O'Mara said, a trifle less warmly. "Well, Doctor, you've picked a real weirdie this time. Be sure you get it erased as soon as possible after the job is done—believe me, this isn't one you'll want to keep. Thumb-print this and sit over there."

While the Educator head-band and electrodes were being fitted, Conway tried to keep his face neutral, and keep from flinching away from the Major's hard, capable hands. O'Mara's hair was a dull, metallic gray in color, cut short, and his eyes also had the piercing qualities of metal. Those eyes had observed his reactions, Conway knew, and now an equally sharp mind was forming conclusions regarding them.

"Well, that's it," said O'Mara when finally it was all over. "But before you go, Doctor, I think you and I should have a little chat; a re-orientation talk, let's call it. Not now, though, you've got a case—but very soon."

Conway felt the eyes boring into his back as he left.

He should have been trying to make his mind a blank as he had been told to do, so the knowledge newly impressed there could bed down comfortably, but all Conway could think about was the fact that a Monitor was a high member of the hospital's permanent staff—and a doctor, to boot. How could the two professions mix? Conway thought of the armband he wore which bore the Tralthan Black and Red Circle, the Flaming Sun of the chlorine-breathing Illensa and intertwining Serpents and Staff of Earth—all the honored symbols of Medicine of the three chief races of the Galactic Union. And here was this Dr. O'Mara whose collar said he was a healer and whose shoulder tabs said he was something else entirely.

One thing was now sure: Conway would never feel really content here again until he discovered why the Chief Psychologist of the hospital was a Monitor.

II

This was Conway's first experience of an alien physiology tape, and he noted with interest the mental double vision which had increasingly begun to affect his mind—a sure sign that the tape had "taken." By the time he had reached the Radiation Theater, he felt himself to be two people—an Earth-human called Conway and the great, five-hundred unit Telfi gestalt which had been formed to prepare a mental record of all that was known regarding the physiology of that race. That was the only disadvantage—if it was a disadvantage—of the Educator Tape system. Not only was knowledge impressed on the mind undergoing "tuition," the personalities of the entities who had possessed that knowledge was transferred as well. Small wonder then that the Diagnosticians, who held in their mind sometimes as many as ten different tapes, were a little bit queer.

A Diagnostician had the most important job in the hospital, Conway thought, as he donned radiation armor and readied his patients for the preliminary examination. He had sometimes thought in his more self-confident moments of becoming one himself. Their chief purpose was to perform original work in xenological medicine and surgery, using their tape-stuffed brains as a jumping-off ground, and to rally round, when a case arrived for which there was no physiology tape available, to diagnose and prescribe treatment.

Not for them were the simple, mundane injuries and diseases. For a Diagnostician to look at a patient that patient had to be unique, hopeless and at least three-quarters dead. When one did take charge of a case though, the patient was as good as cured—they achieved miracles with monotonous regularity.

With the lower orders of doctor there was always the temptation, Conway knew, to keep the contents of a tape rather than have it erased, in the hope of making some original discovery that would bring them fame. In practical, level-headed men like himself, however, it remained just that, a temptation.

———

Conway did not see his tiny patients even though he examined them individually. He couldn't unless he went to a lot of unnecessary trouble with shielding and mirrors to do so. But he knew what they were like, both inside and out, because the tape had practically made him one of them. That knowledge, taken together with the results of his examinations and the case history supplied him, told Conway everything he wanted to know to begin treatment.

His patients had been part of a Telfi gestalt engaged in operating an interstellar cruiser when there had been an accident in one of the power piles. The small, beetle-like and—individually—very stupid beings were radiation eaters, but that flare-up had been too much even for them. Their trouble could be classed as an extremely severe case of over-eating coupled with prolonged over-stimulation of their sensory equipment, especially of the pain centers. If he simply kept them in a shielded container and starved them of radiation—a course of treatment impossible on their highly radioactive ship—about seventy percent of them could be expected to cure themselves in a few hours. They would be the lucky ones, and Conway could even tell which of them came into that category. Those remaining would be a tragedy because if they did not suffer actual physical death their fate would be very much worse: they would lose the ability to join minds, and that in a Telfi was tantamount to being a hopeless cripple.

Only someone who shared the mind, personality and instincts of a Telfi, could appreciate the tragedy it was.

It was a great pity, especially as the case history showed that it was these individuals who had forced themselves to adapt and remain operative during that sudden flare of radiation for the few seconds necessary to scatter the pile and so save their ship from complete destruction. Now their metabolism had found a precarious balance based on three times the Telfi normal energy intake. If this intake of energy was interrupted for any lengthy period of time, say a few more hours, the communications centers of their brains would suffer. They would be left like so many dismembered hands and feet, with just enough intelligence to know that they had been cut off. On the other hand, if their upped energy-intake was continued they would literally burn themselves out within a week.

But there was a line of treatment indicated for these unfortunates, the only one, in fact. As Conway prepared his servos for the work ahead he felt that it was a highly unsatisfactory line—a matter of calculated risks, of cold, medical statistics which nothing he could do would influence. He felt himself to be little more than a mechanic.

Working quickly, he ascertained that sixteen of his patients were suffering from the Telfi equivalent of acute indigestion. These he separated into shielded, absorbent bottles so that re-radiation from their still "hot" bodies would not slow the "starving" process. The bottles he placed in a small pile furnace set to radiate at Telfi normal, with a detector in each which would cause the shielding to fall away from them as soon as their excess radioactivity had gone. The remaining seven would require special treatment. He had placed them in another pile, and was setting the controls to simulate as closely as possible the conditions which had obtained during the accident in their ship, when the nearby communicator beeped at him. Conway finished what he was doing, checked it, then said "Yes?"

"This is Enquiries, Dr. Conway. We've had a signal from the Telfi ship asking about their casualties. Have you any news for them yet?"

Conway knew that his news was not too bad, considering, but he wished intensely that it could be better. The breaking up or modification of a Telfi gestalt once formed could only be likened to a death trauma to the entities concerned, and with the empathy which came as a result of absorbing their physiology tape Conway felt for them. He said carefully, "Sixteen of them will be good as new in roughly four hours time. The other seven will be fifty percent fatalities, I'm afraid, but we won't know which for another few days. I have them baking in a pile at over double their normal radiation requirements, and this will gradually be reduced to normal. Half of them should live through it. Do you understand?"

"Got you." After a few minutes the voice returned. It said, "The Telfi say that is very good, and thank you. Out."

He should have been pleased at dealing successfully with his first case, but Conway somehow felt let down. Now that it was over his mind felt strangely confused. He kept thinking that fifty percent of seven was three and a half, and what would they do with the odd half Telfi? He hoped that four would pull through instead of three, and that they would not be mental cripples. He thought that it must be nice to be a Telfi, to soak up radiation all the time, and the rich and varied impressions of a corporate body numbering perhaps hundreds of individuals. It made his body feel somehow cold and alone. It was an effort to drag himself away from the warmth of the Radiation Theater.

Outside he mounted the carrier and left it back at the admittance lock. The right thing to do now was to report to the Educator room and have the Telfi tape erased—he had been ordered to do that, in fact. But

he did not want to go; the thought of O'Mara made him intensely uncomfortable, even a little afraid. Conway knew that all Monitors made
him feel uncomfortable, but this was different. It was O'Mara's attitude,
and that little chat he had mentioned. Conway had felt small, as if the
Monitor was his superior in some fashion, and for the life of him Conway
could not understand how he could feel small before a lousy Monitor!

The intensity of his feelings shocked him; as a civilized, well-
integrated being he should be incapable of thinking such thoughts. His
emotions had verged upon actual hatred. Frightened of himself this time,
Conway brought his mind under a semblance of control. He decided to
side-step the question and not report to the Educator room until after
he had done the rounds of his wards. It was a legitimate excuse if O'Mara
should query the delay, and the Chief Psychologist might leave or be
called away in the meantime. Conway hoped so.

His first call was on an AUGL from Chalderescol II, the sole occupant
of the ward reserved for that species. Conway climbed into the appropriate protective garment—a simple diving suit in this instance—and
went through the lock into the tank of green, tepid water which reproduced the being's living conditions. He collected the instruments from
the locker inside, then loudly signaled his presence. If the Chalder was
really asleep down there and he startled it the results could be serious.
One accidental flick of that tail and the ward would contain two patients
instead of one.

The Chalder was heavily plated and scaled, and slightly resembled a
forty-foot-long crocodile except that instead of legs there was an apparently haphazard arrangement of stubby fins and a fringe of ribbon-like
tentacles encircling its middle. It drifted limply near the bottom of the
huge tank, the only sign of life being the periodic fogging of the water
around its gills. Conway gave it a perfunctory examination—he was way
behind time due to the Telfi job—and asked the usual question. The
answer came through the water in some unimaginable form to Conway's
translator attachment and into his phones as slow, toneless speech.

"I am grievously ill," said the Chalder, "I suffer."

You lie, thought Conway silently, *in all six rows of your teeth!* Dr.
Lister, Sector General's Director and probably the foremost Diagnostician
of the day, had practically taken this Chalder apart. His diagnosis had
been hypochondria and the condition incurable. He had further stated
that the signs of strain in certain sections of the patient's body plating,
and its discomfort in those areas, were due simply to the big so-and-so's

laziness and gluttony. Anybody knew that an exoskeletal life-form could not put on weight except from inside! Diagnosticians were not noted for their bedside manners.

The Chalder became really ill only when it was in danger of being sent home, so the Hospital had acquired a permanent patient. But it did not mind. Visiting as well as Staff medics and psychologists had given it a going over, and continued to do so; also all the interns and nurses of all the multitudinous races represented on the hospital's staff. Regularly and at short intervals it was probed, pried into and unmercifully pounded by trainees of varying degrees of gentleness, and it loved every minute of it. The hospital was happy with the arrangement and so was the Chalder. Nobody mentioned going home to it anymore.

III

Conway paused for a moment as he swam to the top of the great tank; he felt peculiar. His next call was supposed to be on two methane-breathing life-forms in the lower temperature ward of his section, and he felt strongly loath to go. Despite the warmth of the water and the heat of his exertions while swimming around his massive patient he felt cold, and he would have given anything to have a bunch of students come flapping into the tank just for the company. Usually Conway did not like company, especially that of trainees, but now he felt cut-off, alone and friendless. The feelings were so strong they frightened him. A talk with a psychologist was definitely indicated, he thought, though not necessarily with O'Mara.

The construction of the hospital in this section resembled a heap of spaghetti—straight, bent and indescribably curved pieces of spaghetti. Each corridor containing an Earth-type atmosphere, for instance, was paralleled above, below and on each side—as well as being crossed above and below at frequent intervals—by others having different and mutually deadly variations of atmosphere, pressure and temperature. This was to facilitate the visiting of any given patient-species by any other species of doctor in the shortest possible time in case of emergency, because traveling the length of the hospital in a suit designed to protect a doctor against his patient's environment on arrival was both uncomfortable and slow. It had been found more efficient to change into the necessary protective suit outside the wards being visited, as Conway had done.

Remembering the geography of this section Conway knew that there was a shortcut he could use to get to his frigid-blooded patients—along the waterfilled corridor which led to the Chalder operating theater, through the lock into the chlorine atmosphere of the Illensan PVSJs and up two levels to the methane ward. This way would mean his staying in warm water for a little longer, and he was definitely feeling *cold*.

A convalescent PVSJ rustled past him on spiny, membraneous appendages in the chlorine section and Conway found himself wanting desperately to talk to it, about anything. He had to force himself to go on.

The protective suit worn by DBDGs like himself while visiting the methane ward was in reality a small mobile tank. It was fitted with heaters inside to keep its occupant alive and refrigerators outside so that the leakage of heat would not immediately shrivel the patients to whom the slightest glow of radiant heat—or even light—was lethal. Conway had no idea how the scanner he used in the examinations worked—only those gadget-mad beings with the Engineering armbands knew that—except that it wasn't by infrared. That also was too hot for them.

As he worked Conway turned the heaters up until the sweat rolled off him and still he felt cold. He was suddenly afraid. Suppose he had caught something? When he was outside in air again he looked at the tiny tell-tale that was surgically embedded on the inner surface of his forearm. His pulse, respiration and endocrine balance were normal except for the minor irregularities caused by his worrying, and there was nothing foreign in his bloodstream. What was wrong with him?

Conway finished his rounds as quickly as possible. He felt confused again. If his mind was playing tricks on him he was going to take the necessary steps to rectify the matter. It must be something to do with the Telfi tape he had absorbed. O'Mara had said something about it, though he could not remember exactly what at the moment. But he would go to the Educator room right away, O'Mara or no O'Mara.

Two Monitors passed him while he was on the way, both armed. Conway knew that he should feel his usual hostility toward them, also shock that they were armed inside a hospital, and he did, but he also wanted to slap their backs or even hug them: he desperately wanted to have people around, talking and exchanging ideas and impressions so that he would not feel so terribly alone. As they drew level with him Conway managed to get out a shaky "Hello." It was the first time he had spoken to a Monitor in his life.

One of the Monitors smiled slightly, the other nodded. Both gave him odd looks over their shoulders as they passed because his teeth were chattering so much.

His intention of going to the Educator room had been clearly formed, but now it did not seem to be such a good idea. It was cold and dark there with all those machines and shaded lighting, and the only company might be O'Mara. Conway wanted to lose himself in a crowd, and the bigger the better. He thought of the nearby dining hall and turned toward it. Then at an intersection he saw a sign reading "Diet Kitchen, Wards 52 to 68, Species DBDG, DBLF & FGLI." That made him remember how terribly cold he felt . . .

The Dietitians were too busy to notice him. Conway picked an oven which was fairly glowing with heat and lay down against it, letting the germ-killing ultraviolet which flooded the place bathe him and ignoring the charred smell given off by his light clothing. He felt warmer now, a little warmer, but the awful sense of being utterly and completely alone would not leave him. He was cut off, unloved and unwanted. He wished that he had never been born.

When a Monitor—one of the two he had recently passed whose curiosity had been aroused by Conway's strange behavior—wearing a hastily borrowed heat suit belonging to one of the Cook-Dietitians got to him a few minutes later, the big, slow tears were running down Conway's cheeks . . .

"You," said a well-remembered voice, "are a very lucky and very stupid young man."

Conway opened his eyes to find that he was on the Erasure couch and that O'Mara and another Monitor were looking down at him. His back felt as though it had been cooked medium rare and his whole body stung as if with a bad dose of sunburn. O'Mara was glaring furiously at him, he spoke again.

"Lucky not to be seriously burned and blinded, and stupid because you forgot to inform me on one very important point, namely that this was your first experience with the Educator . . ."

O'Mara's tone became faintly self-accusatory at this point, but only faintly. He went onto say that had he been thus informed he would have given Conway a hypno-treatment which would have enabled the doctor to differentiate between his own needs and those of the Telfi sharing his mind. He only realized that Conway was a first-timer when he filed the thumb-printed slip, and dammit how was he to know who was new and who wasn't in a place this size! And anyway, if Conway had thought more of his job and less of the fact that a Monitor was giving him the tape, this would never have happened.

Conway, O'Mara continued bitingly, appeared to be a self-righteous bigot who made no pretense at hiding his feelings of defilement at the touch of an uncivilized brute of a Monitor. How a person intelligent enough to gain appointment to this hospital could also hold those sort of feelings was beyond O'Mara's understanding.

Conway felt his face burning. It had been stupid of him to forget to tell the psychologist that he was a first-timer. O'Mara could easily bring charges of personal negligence against him—a charge almost as serious as carelessness with a patient in a multi-environment hospital—and have Conway kicked out. But that possibility did not weigh too heavily with him at the moment, terrible though it was. What got him was the fact that he was being told off by a *Monitor,* and before another Monitor!

The man who must have carried him here was gazing down at him, a look of half-humorous concern in his steady brown eyes. Conway found that harder to take even than O'Mara's abusiveness. How dare a Monitor feel sorry for *him!*

"... And if you're still wondering what happened," O'Mara was saying in withering tones, "you allowed—through inexperience, I admit—the Telfi personality contained in the tape to temporarily overcome your own. Its need for hard radiation, intense heat and light and above all the mental fusion necessary to a group-mind entity, became your needs—transferred into their nearest human equivalents, of course. For a while you were experiencing life as a single Telfi being, and an individual Telfi—cut off from all mental contact with the others of its group—is an unhappy beastie indeed."

O'Mara had cooled somewhat as his explanation proceeded. His voice was almost impersonal as he went on, "You're suffering from little more than a bad case of sunburn. Your back will be tender for a while and later it will itch. Serves you right. Now go away. I don't want to see you again until hour nine the day after tomorrow. Keep that hour free. That's an order—we have to have a little talk, remember?"

———

Outside in the corridor Conway had a feeling of complete deflation coupled with an anger that threatened to burst out of all control—an intensely frustrating combination. In all his twenty-three years of life he
could not remember being subjected to such extreme mental discomfort.
He had been made to feel like a small boy—a bad, maladjusted small
boy. Conway had always been a very good, well-mannered boy. It hurt.

He had not noticed that his rescuer was still beside him until the
other spoke.

"Don't go worrying yourself about the Major," the Monitor said sym-
pathetically. "He's really a nice man, and when you see him again you'll
find out for yourself. At the moment he's tired and a bit touchy. You see,
there are three companies just arrived and more coming. But they won't
be much use to us in their present state—they're in a bad way with
combat fatigue, most of 'em. Major O'Mara and his staff have to give
them some psychological first aid before—"

"Combat fatigue," said Conway in the most insulting tone of which
he was capable. He was heartily sick of people he considered his intellectual and moral inferiors either ranting at him or sympathizing with him.
"I suppose," he added, "that means they've grown tired of killing people?"

He saw the Monitor's young-old face stiffen and something that was
both hurt and anger burn in his eyes. He stopped. He opened his mouth
for an O'Mara-type blast of invective, then thought better of it. He said
quietly, "For someone who has been here for two months you have, to
put it mildly, a very unrealistic attitude toward the Monitor Corps. I can't
understand that. Have you been too busy to talk to people or something?"

"No," replied Conway coldly, "but where I come from we do not
discuss persons of your type, we prefer pleasanter topics."

"I hope," said the Monitor, "that all your friends—if you have
friends, that is—indulge in backslapping." He turned and marched off.

Conway winced in spite of himself at the thought of anything heavier
than a feather hitting his scorched and tender back. But he was thinking
of the other's earlier words, too. So his attitude toward Monitors was
unrealistic? Did they want him, then, to condone violence and murder
and befriend those who were responsible for it? And he had also mentioned the arrival of several companies of Monitors. Why? What for?
Anxiety began to eat at the edges of his hitherto solid block of self-
confidence. There was something here that he was missing, something
important.

When he had first arrived at Sector General the being who had given

Conway his original instructions and assignments had added a little pep-talk. It had said that Dr. Conway had passed a great many tests to come here and that they welcomed him and hoped he would be happy enough in his work to stay. The period of trial was now over, and henceforth nobody would be trying to catch him out, but if for any reason—friction with his own or any other species, or the appearance of some xenological psychosis—he became so distressed that he could no longer stay, then with great reluctance he would be allowed to leave.

He had also been advised to meet as many different entities as possible and try to gain mutual understanding, if not their friendship. Finally he had been told that if he should get into trouble through ignorance or any other reason, he should contact either of two Earth-human beings who were called O'Mara and Bryson, depending on the nature of his trouble, though a qualified being of any species would, of course, help him on request.

Immediately afterward he had met the Surgeon-in-Charge of the wards to which he had been posted, a very able Earth-human called Mannon. Dr. Mannon was not yet a Diagnostician, though he was trying hard, and was therefore still quite human for long periods during the day. He was the proud possessor of a small dog which stuck so close to him that visiting extra-terrestrials were inclined to assume a symbolic relationship. Conway liked Dr. Mannon a lot, but now he was beginning to realize that his superior was the only being of his own species toward whom he had any feeling of friendship.

That was a bit strange, surely. It made Conway begin to wonder about himself.

After that reassuring pep-talk Conway had thought he was all set— especially when he found how easy it was to make friends with the e-t members of the Staff. He had not warmed to his human colleagues— with the one exception—because of their tendency to be flippant or cynical regarding the very important and worthwhile work he, and they, were doing. But the idea of friction developing was laughable.

That was before today, though, when O'Mara had made him feel small and stupid, accused him of bigotry and intolerance, and generally cut his ego to pieces. This, quite definitely, was friction developing, and if such treatment at the hands of Monitors continued Conway knew that he would be driven to leave. He was a civilized and ethical human being—why were the Monitors in a position to tell him off? Conway just could not understand it at all. Two things he did know, however; he wanted to remain at the hospital, and to do that he needed help.

IV

The name "Bryson" popped into his mind suddenly, one of the names he had been given should he get into trouble. O'Mara, the other name, was out, but this Bryson now ...

Conway had never met anyone with that name, but by asking a passing Tralthan he received directions for finding him. He got only as far as the door, which bore the legend, "Captain Bryson, Monitor Corps, Chaplain," then he turned angrily away. Another Monitor! There was just one person left who might help him: Dr. Mannon. He should have tried him first.

But his superior, when Conway ran him down, was sealed in the LSVO theater where he was assisting a Tralthan Surgeon-Diagnostician in a very tricky piece of work. He went up to the observation gallery to wait until Mannon had finished.

The LSVO came from a planet of dense atmosphere and negligible gravity. It was a winged life-form of extreme fragility, which necessitated the theater being at almost zero gravity and the surgeons strapped to their position around the table. The little OTSB who lived in symbiosis with the elephantine Tralthan was not strapped down, but held securely above the operative field by one of its host's secondary tentacles—the OTSB life-form, Conway knew, could not lose physical contact with its host for more than a few minutes without suffering severe mental damage. Interested despite his own troubles, he began to concentrate on what they were doing.

A section of the patient's digestive tract had been bared, revealing a spongy, bluish growth adhering to it. Without the LSVO physiology tape Conway could not tell whether the patient's condition was serious or not, but the operation was certainly a technically difficult one. He could tell by the way Mannon hunched forward over it and by the tightly-coiled tentacles of the Tralthan not then in use. As was normal, the little OTSB with its cluster of wire-thin, eye- and sucker-tipped tentacles was doing the fine, exploratory work—sending infinitely detailed visual information of the field to its giant host, and receiving back instructions based on that data. The Tralthan and Dr. Mannon attended to the relatively crude work of clamping, tying-off and swabbing out.

Dr. Mannon had little to do but watch as the super-sensitive tentacles of the Tralthan's parasite were guided in their work by the host, but Conway knew that the other was proud of the chance to do even that. The Tralthan combination were the greatest surgeons the Galaxy had ever known. All surgeons would have been Tralthans had not their bulk and operating procedure made it impossible to treat certain forms of life.

Conway was waiting when they came out of the theater. One of the Tralthan's tentacles flicked out and tapped Dr. Mannon sharply on the head—a gesture which was a high compliment—and immediately a small bundle of fur and teeth streaked from behind a locker toward the great being who was apparently attacking its master. Conway had seen this game played out many times and it still seemed wildly ludicrous to him. As Mannon's dog barked furiously at the creature towering above both itself and its master, challenging it to a duel to the death, the Tralthan shrank back in mock terror and cried, "Save me from this fearsome beast!" The dog, still barking furiously, circled it, snapping at the leathery tegument protecting the Tralthan's six, blocky legs. The Tralthan retreated precipitously, the while calling loudly for aid and being very careful that its tiny attacker was not splattered under one of its elephantine feet. And so the sounds of battle receded down the corridor.

When the noise had diminished sufficiently for him to be heard, Conway said, "Doctor, I wonder if you could help me. I need advice, or at least information. But it's a rather delicate matter . . ."

Conway saw Dr. Mannon's eyebrows go up and a smile quirk the corners of his mouth. He said, "I'd be glad to help you, of course, but I'm afraid any advice I could give you at the moment would be pretty poor stuff." He made a disgusted face and flapped his arms up and down. "I've still got an LSVO tape working on me. You know how it is—half of me thinks I'm a bird and the other half is a little confused about it. But what sort of advice do you need?" he went on, his head perking to one side in an oddly bird-like manner. "If it's that peculiar form of madness called young love, or any other psychological disturbance, I'd suggest you see O'Mara."

Conway shook his head quickly; anybody but O'Mara. He said, "No. It's more of a philosophical nature, a matter of ethics, maybe . . ."

"Is *that* all!" Mannon burst out. He was about to say something more when his face took on a fixed, listening expression. With a sudden jerk of his thumb he indicated a nearby wall annunciator. He said quietly, "The solution to your weighty problems will have to wait—you're wanted."

". . . Dr. Conway," the annunciator was saying briskly, "Go to room 87 and administer pep-shots . . ."

"But 87 isn't even in our section!" Conway protested. "What's going on here . . . ?"

Dr. Mannon had become suddenly grim. "I think I know," he said, "and I advise you to keep a few of those shots for yourself because you are going to need them." He turned abruptly and hurried off, muttering something about getting a fast erasure before they started screaming for him, too.

Room 87 was the Casualty Section's staff recreation room, and when Conway arrived its tables, chairs and even parts of its floor were asprawl with green-clad Monitors, some of whom had not the energy to lift their heads when he came in. One figure pushed itself out of a chair with extreme difficulty and weaved toward him. It was another Monitor with a Major's insignia on his shoulders and the Staff and Serpents on his collar. He said, "Maximum dosage. Start with me," and began shrugging out of his tunic.

Conway looked around the room. There must have been nearly a hundred of them, all in stages of advanced exhaustion and their faces showing that tell-tale gray coloration. He still did not feel well disposed toward Monitors, but these were, after a fashion, patients, and his duty was clear.

"As a doctor I advise strongly against this," Conway said gravely. "It's obvious that you've had pep-shots already—far too many of them. What you need is sleep—"

"Sleep?" said a voice somewhere. "What's that?"

"Quiet, Teirnan," said the Major tiredly, then to Conway; "And as a doctor I understand the risks. I suggest we waste no more time."

Rapidly and expertly Conway set about administering the shots. Dull-eyed, bone-weary men lined up before him and five minutes later left the room with a spring in their step and their eyes too bright with artificial vitality. He had just finished when he heard his name over the annunciator again, ordering him to Lock Six to await instructions there. Lock

Six, Conway knew, was one of the subsidiary entrances to the Casualty section.

While he was hurrying in that direction Conway realized suddenly that he was tired and hungry, but he did not get the chance to think about it for long. The annunciators were giving out a call for all junior interns to report to Casualty, and directions for adjacent wards to be evacuated where possible to other accommodation. An alien gabble interspersed these messages as other species received similar instructions.

Obviously the Casualty section was being extended. But why, and where were all the casualties coming from? Conway's mind was a confused and rather tired question mark.

V

At Lock Six a Tralthan Diagnostician was deep in conversation with two Monitors. Conway felt a sense of outrage at the sight of the highest and the lowest being so chummy together, then reflected with a touch of bitterness that nothing about this place could surprise him anymore. There were two more Monitors beside the Lock's direct vision panel.

"Hello, Doctor," one of them said pleasantly. He nodded toward the viewport. "They're unloading at Locks Eight, Nine and Eleven. We'll be getting our quota any minute now."

The big transparent panel framed an awesome sight: Conway had never seen so many ships together at one time. More than thirty sleek, silver needles, ranging from ten-man pleasure yachts to the gargantuan transports of the Monitor Corps wove a slowly, complicated pattern in and around each other as they waited permission to lock-on and unload.

"Tricky work, that," the Monitor observed.

Conway agreed. The repulsion fields which protected ships against collision with the various forms of cosmic detritus required plenty of space. Meteorite screens had to be set up a minimum of five miles away from the ship they protected if heavenly bodies large and small were to be successfully deflected from them—further away if it was a bigger ship. But the ships outside were a mere matter of hundreds of yards apart, and had no collision protection except the skill of their pilots. The pilots would be having a trying time at the moment.

But Conway had little time for sight-seeing before three Earth-human interns arrived. They were followed quickly by two of the red-furred DBDGs and a caterpillar-like DBLF, all wearing medical insignia. There came a heavy scrape of metal against metal, the lock tell-tales turned from red to green indicating that a ship was properly connected up, and the patients began to stream through.

Carried in stretchers by Monitors they were of two kinds only: DBDGs of the Earth-human type and DBLF caterpillars. Conway's job, and that of the other doctors present, was to examine them and route them through to the proper department of Casualty for treatment. He got down to work, assisted by a Monitor who possessed all the attributes of a trained nurse except the insignia. He said his name was Williamson.

The sight of the first case gave Conway a shock—not because it was serious, but because of the nature of the injuries. The third made him stop so that his Monitor assistant looked at him questioningly.

"What sort of accident was this?" Conway burst out. "Multiple punctures, but the edge of the wounds cauterized. Lacerated punctures, as if from fragments thrown out by an explosion. How . . . ?"

The Monitor said, "We kept it quiet, of course, but I thought here at least the rumor would have got to everybody." His lips tightened and the look that identified all Monitors to Conway deepened in his eyes. "They decided to have a war," he went on, nodding at the Earth-human and DBLF patients around them. "I'm afraid it got a little out of control before we were were able to clamp down."

Conway thought sickly, *A war . . . !* Human beings from Earth, or an Earth-seeded planet, trying to kill members of the species that had so much in common with them. He had heard that there were such things occasionally, but had never really believed any intelligent species could go insane on such a large scale. So many *casualties . . .*

He was not so bound up in his thoughts of loathing and disgust at this frightful business that he missed noticing a very strange fact—that the Monitor's expression mirrored his own! If Williamson thought that way about war, too, maybe it was time he revised his thinking about the Monitor Corps in general.

A sudden commotion a few yards to his right drew Conway's attention. An Earth-human patient was objecting strenuously to the DBLF intern trying to examine him, and the language he was using was not nice. The DBLF was registering hurt bewilderment, though possibly the human had not sufficient knowledge of its physiognomy to know that, and trying to reassure the patient in flat, Translated tones.

It was Williamson who settled the business. He swung around on the loudly protesting patient, bent forward until their faces were only inches apart, and spoke in a low, almost conversational tone which nevertheless sent shivers along Conway's spine.

"Listen, friend," he said. "You say you object to one of the stinking crawlers that tried to kill you trying to patch you up, right? Well, get this into your head, and keep it there—this particular crawler is a doctor here. Also, in this establishment there are no wars. You all belong to the same army and the uniform is a nightshirt, so lay still, shut up and behave. Otherwise I'll clip you one."

Conway returned to work underlining his mental note about revising his thinking regarding Monitors. As the torn, battered and burnt life-forms flowed past under his hands his mind seemed strangely detached from it all. He kept surprising Williamson with expressions on his face that seemed to give the lie to some of the things he had been told about Monitors. This tireless, quiet man with the rock-steady hands—was he a killer, a sadist of low intelligence and nonexistent morals? It was hard to believe. As he watched the Monitor covertly between patients, Conway gradually came to a decision. It was a very difficult decision. If he wasn't careful he would very likely get clipped.

O'Mara had been impossible, so had Bryson and Mannon for various reasons, but Williamson now . . .

"Ah . . . er, Williamson," Conway began hesitantly, then finished with a rush, "have you ever killed anybody?"

The Monitor straightened suddenly, his lips a thin, bloodless line. He said tonelessly, "You should know better than to ask a Monitor that question, Doctor. Or should you?" He hesitated, his curiosity keeping check on the anger growing in him because of the tangle of emotion which must have been mirrored on Conway's face, then said heavily, "What's eating you, Doc?"

Conway wished fervently that he had never asked the question, but it was too late to back out now. Stammering at first, he began to tell of his ideals of service and of his alarm and confusion on discovering that Sector General—an establishment which he had thought embodied all his high ideals—employed a Monitor as its Chief Psychologist, and probably other members of the Corps in positions of responsibility. Conway knew now that the Corps was not all bad, that they had rushed units of their Medical Division here to aid them during the present emergency. But even so, *Monitors . . . !*

"I'll give you another shock," Williamson said dryly, "by telling you something that is so widely known that nobody thinks to mention it. Dr.

Lister, the Director, also belongs to the Monitor Corps.

"He doesn't wear uniform, of course," the Monitor added quickly, "because Diagnosticians grow forgetful and are careless about small things. The Corps frowns on untidiness, even in a Lieutenant-General."

Lister, a Monitor! "But, *why?*" Conway burst out in spite of himself. "Everybody knows what you are. How did you gain power here in the first place . . . ?"

"Everybody does not know, obviously," Williamson cut in, "because you don't, for one."

VI

The Monitor was no longer angry, Conway saw as they finished with their current patient and moved onto the next. Instead there was an expression on the other's face oddly reminiscent of a parent about to lecture an offspring on some of the unpleasant facts of life.

"Basically," said Williamson as he gently peeled back a field dressing of a wounded DBLF, "your trouble is that you, and your whole social group, are a protected species."

Conway said, "*What?*"

"A protected species," he repeated. "Shielded from the crudities of present-day life. From your social strata—on all the worlds of the Union, not only on Earth—come practically all the great artists, musicians and professional men. Most of you live out your lives in ignorance of the fact that you are protected, that you are insulated from childhood against the grosser realities of our interstellar so-called civilization, and that your ideas of pacifism and ethical behavior are a luxury which a great many of us simply cannot afford. You are allowed this luxury in the hope that from it may come a philosophy which may one day make every being in the Galaxy truly civilized, truly good."

"I didn't know," Conway stammered. "And . . . and you make us—me, I mean—look so useless . . ."

"Of course you didn't know," said Williamson gently. Conway wondered why it was that such a young man could talk down to him without giving offense; he seemed to possess *authority* somehow. Continuing, he said, "You were probably reserved, untalkative and all wrapped up in your high ideals. Not that there's anything wrong with them, understand, it's just that you have to allow for a little gray with the black and white. Our present culture," he went on, returning to the main line of discussion, "is based on maximum freedom for the individual. An entity may do anything he likes provided it is not injurious to others. Only Monitors forgo this freedom."

"What about the 'Normals' reservations?" Conway broke in. At last the Monitor had made a statement which he could definitely contradict. "Being policed by Monitors and confined to certain areas of country is not what I'd call freedom."

"If you think back carefully," Williamson replied, "I think you will find that the Normals—that is, the group on nearly every planet which thinks that, unlike the brutish Monitors and the spineless aesthetes of your own strata, it is truly representative of its species—are not confined. Instead they have naturally drawn together into communities, and it is in these communities of self-styled Normals that the Monitors have to be most active. The Normals possess all the freedom including the right to kill each other if that is what they desire, the Monitors being present only to see that any Normal not sharing this desire will not suffer in the process.

"We also, when a sufficiently high pitch of mass insanity overtakes one or more of these worlds, allow a war to be fought on a planet set aside for that purpose, generally arranging things so that the war is neither long nor too bloody." Williamson sighed. In tones of bitter self-accusation he concluded, "We underestimated them. This one was both."

Conway's mind was still balking at this radically new slant on things. Before coming to the hospital he'd had no direct contact with Monitors, why should he? And the Normals of Earth he had found to be rather romantic figures, inclined to strut and swagger a bit, that was all. Of course, most of the bad things he had heard about Monitors had come from them. Maybe the Normals had not been as truthful or objective as they could have been . . .

"This is all too hard to believe," Conway protested. "You're suggesting that the Monitor Corps is greater in the scheme of things than either the Normals or ourselves, the professional class!" He shook his head angrily. "And anyway, this is a fine time for a philosophical discussion!"

"You," said the Monitor, "started it."

There was no answer to that.

It must have been hours later that Conway felt a touch on his shoulder and straightened to find a DBLF nurse behind him. The being was holding a hypodermic. It said, "Pep-shot, Doctor?"

All at once Conway realized how wobbly his legs had become and how hard it was to focus his eyes. And he must have been noticeably slowing down for the nurse to approach him in the first place. He nodded and rolled up his sleeve with fingers which felt like thick, tired sausages.

"Yipe!" he cried in sudden anguish. "What are you using, a six-inch nail?"

"I am sorry," said the DBLF, "but I have injected two doctors of my own species before coming to you, and as you know our tegument is thicker and more closely grained than yours is. The needle has therefore become blunted."

Conway's fatigue dropped away in seconds. Except for a slight tingling in hands and feet and a grayish blotching which only others could see in his face he felt as clear-eyed, alert and physically refreshed as if he had just come out of a shower after ten hours sleep. He took a quick look around before finishing his current examination and saw that here at least the number of patients awaiting attention had shrunk to a mere handful, and the number of Monitors in the room was less than half what it had been at the start. The patients were being taken care of, and the Monitors had become patients.

He had seen it happening all around him. Monitors who had had little or no sleep on the transport coming here, forcing themselves to carry on helping the overworked medics of the hospital with repeated pep-shots and sheer, dogged courage. One by one they had literally dropped in their tracks and been taken hurriedly away, so exhausted that the involuntary muscles of heart and lungs had given up with everything else. They lay in special wards with robot devices massaging their hearts, giving artificial respiration and feeding them through a vein in the leg. Conway had heard that only one of them had died.

Taking advantage of the lull, Conway and Williamson moved to the direct vision panel and looked out. The waiting swarm of ships seemed only slightly smaller, though he knew that these must be new arrivals. He could not imagine where they were going to put these people—even the habitable corridors in the hospital were beginning to overflow now, and there was constant re-arranging of patients of all species to make more room. But that wasn't his problem, and the weaving pattern of ships was an oddly restful sight . . .

"Emergency," said the wall annunciator suddenly. "Single ship, one occupant, species as yet unknown requests immediate treatment. Occupant is in only partial control of its ship, is badly injured and communications are incoherent. Stand by at all admittance locks . . . !"

Oh, no, Conway thought, *not at a time like this!* There was a cold sickness in his stomach and he had a horrible premonition of what was going to happen. Williamson's knuckles shone white as he gripped the edge of the viewport. "Look!" he said in a flat, despairing tone, and pointed.

An intruder was approaching the waiting swarm of ships at an insane velocity and on a wildly erratic course. A stubby, black and featureless torpedo shape, it reached and penetrated the weaving mass of ships before Conway had time to take two breaths. In milling confusion the ships scattered, narrowly avoiding collision both with it and each other, and still it hurtled on. There was only one ship in its path now, a Monitor transport which had been given the all-clear to approach and was drifting in toward an admittance lock. The transport was big, ungainly and not built for fast acrobatics—it had neither the time nor the ability to get out of the way. A collision was certain, and the transport was jammed with wounded . . .

But no. At the last possible instant the hurtling ship swerved. They saw it miss the transport and its stubby torpedo shape foreshorten to a circle which grew in size with heart-stopping rapidity. Now it was headed straight at them! Conway wanted to shut his eyes, but there was a peculiar fascination about watching that great mass of metal rushing at him. Neither Williamson nor himself made any attempt to jump for a spacesuit— what was to happen was only split seconds away.

The ship was almost on top of them when it swerved again as its injured pilot sought desperately to avoid this greater obstacle, the hospital. But too late, the ship struck.

A smashing double-shock struck up at them from the floor as the ship tore through their double skin, followed by successively milder shocks as it bludgeoned its way into the vitals of the great hospital. A cacophony of screams—both human and alien—arose briefly, also whistlings, rustlings and gutteral jabberings as beings were maimed, drowned, gassed or decompressed. Water poured into sections containing pure chlorine. A blast of ordinary air rushed through a gaping hole in the compartment whose occupants had never known anything but trans-Plutonian cold and vacuum—the beings shriveled, died and dissolved horribly at the first touch of it. Water, air and a score of different atmospheric mixtures intermingled forming a sludgy, brown and highly corrosive mixture that steamed and bubbled its way out into space. But long before that had happened the air-tight seals had slammed shut, effectively containing the terrible wound made by that bulleting ship.

VII

There was an instant of shocked paralysis, then the hospital reacted. Above their heads the annunciator went into a quiet, controlled frenzy. Engineers and Maintenance men of all species were to report for assignment immediately. The gravity neutralizer grids in the LSVO and MSVK wards were failing—all medical staff in the area were to encase the patients in protective envelopes and transfer them to DBLF theater Two, where one-twentieth G conditions were being set up, before they were crushed by their own weight. There was an untraced leak in AUGL corridor Nineteen, and all DBDG's were warned of chlorine contamination in the area of their dining hall. Also, Dr. Lister was asked to report himself, please.

In an odd corner of his mind Conway noted how everybody else was ordered to their assignments while Dr. Lister was asked. Suddenly he heard his name being called and he swung around.

It was Dr. Mannon. He hurried up to Williamson and Conway and said, "I see you're free at the moment. There's a job I'd like you to do." He paused to receive Conway's nod, then plunged on breathlessly.

When the crashing ship had dug a hole half-way through the hospital, Mannon explained, the volume sealed off by the safety doors was not confined simply to the tunnel of wreckage it had created. The position of the doors was responsible for this—the result being analogous to a great tree of vacuum extending into the hospital structure, with the tunnel created by the ship as its trunk and the open sections of corridors leading off it the branches. Some of these airless corridors served compartments which themselves could be sealed off, and it was possible that these might contain survivors.

Normally there would be no necessity to hurry the rescue of these beings, they would be quite comfortable where they were for days, but in this instance there was an added complication. The ship had come to rest near the center—the nerve center, in fact—of the hospital, the section which contained the controls for the artificial settings of the entire structure. At the moment there seemed to be a survivor in that section somewhere—possibly a patient, a member of the Staff or even the occupant of the wrecked ship—who was moving around and unknowingly damaging the gravity control mechanisms. This state of affairs, if continued, could create havoc in the wards and might even cause deaths among the light-gravity life-forms.

Dr. Mannon wanted them to go in and bring the being concerned out before it unwittingly wrecked the place.

"A PVSJ has already gone in," Mannon added, "but that species is awkward in a spacesuit, so I'm sending you two as well to hurry things along. All right? Hop to it, then."

Wearing gravity neutralizer packs they exited near the damaged section and drifted along the Hospital's outer skin to the twenty-foot wide hole gouged in its side by the crashing ship. The packs allowed a high degree of maneuverability in weightless conditions, and they did not expect anything else along the route they were to travel. They also carried ropes and magnetic anchors, and Williamson—solely because it was part of the equipment issued with the service Standard suit, he said—also carried a gun. Both had air for three hours.

At first the going was easy. The ship had sheared a clean-edged tunnel through ward bulkheads, deck plating and even through items of heavy machinery. Conway could see clearly into the corridors they passed in their descent, and nowhere was there a sign of life. There were grisly remnants of a high-pressure life-form which would have blown itself apart even under Earth-normal atmospheric conditions. When subjected suddenly to hard vacuum the process had been that much more violent. And in one corridor there was disclosed a tragedy; a near-human DBDG nurse—one of the red, bear-like entities—had been neatly decapitated by the closing of an air-tight door which it had just failed to make in time. For some reason the sight affected him more than anything else he had seen that day.

Increasing amounts of "foreign" wreckage hampered their progress as they continued to descend—plating and structural members torn from the crashing ship—so that there were times when they had to clear a way through it with their hands and feet.

Williamson was in the lead—about ten yards below Conway that was—when the Monitor flicked out of sight. In the suit radio a cry of surprise was abruptly cut off by the clang of metal against metal. Conway's grip on the projecting beam he had been holding tightened instinctively in shocked surprise, and he felt it vibrate through his gauntlets. The wreckage was shifting! Panic took him for a moment until he realized that most of the movement was taking place back the way he had come, above his head. The vibration ceased a few minutes later without the debris around him significantly changing its position. Only then did Conway tie his line securely to the beam and look around for the Monitor.

Knees bent and arms in front of his head Williamson lay face downward partially embedded in a shelving mass of loose wreckage some twenty feet below. Faint, irregular sounds of breathing in his phones told Conway that the Monitor's quick thinking in wrapping his arms around his head had, by protecting his suit's fragile face-plate, saved his life. But whether or not Williamson lived for long or not depended on the nature of his other injuries, and they in turn depended on the amount of gravitic attraction in the floor section which had sucked him down.

It was now obvious that the accident was due to a square of deck in which the artificial gravity grid was, despite the wholesale destruction of circuits in the crash area, still operative. Conway was profoundly thankful that the attraction was exerted only at right angles to the grid's surface and that the floor section had been warped slightly. Had it been facing straight up then both the Monitor and himself would have dropped, and from a distance considerably greater than twenty feet.

Carefully paying out his safety line Conway approached the huddled form of Williamson. His grip tightened convulsively on the rope when he came within the field of influence of the gravity grid, then eased as he realized that its power was at most only one and a half Gs. With a steady attraction now pulling him downward toward the Monitor, Conway began lowering himself hand over hand. He could have used his neutralizer pack to counteract that pull, of course, and just drifted down, but that would have been risky. If he accidentally passed out of the floor section's area of influence, then the pack would have flung him upward again, with probably fatal results.

The Monitor was still unconscious when Conway reached him, and though he could not tell for sure, owing to the other wearing a spacesuit, he suspected multiple fractures in both arms. As he gently disengaged the limp figure from the surrounding wreckage it was suddenly borne on him that Williamson needed attention, immediate attention with all the resources the hospital could provide. He had just realized that the Monitor had been the recipient of a large number of pep-shots; his reserves of strength must be gone. When he regained consciousness, if he ever did, he might not be able to withstand the shock.

VIII

Conway was about to call through for assistance when a chunk of ragged-edged metal spun past his helmet. He swung around just in time to duck another piece of wreckage which was sailing toward him. Only then did he see the outlines of a nonhuman, spacesuited figure which was partially hidden in a tangle of metal about ten yards away. The being was throwing things at him!

The bombardment stopped as soon as the other saw that Conway had noticed it. With visions of having found the unknown survivor whose blundering about was playing hob with the hospital's artificial gravity system he hurried across to it. But he saw immediately that the being was incapable of doing any moving about at all, it was pinned down, but miraculously unhurt, by a couple of heavy structural members. It was also making vain attempts to reach around to the back of its suit with its only free appendage. Conway was puzzled for a moment, then he saw the radio pack which was strapped to the being's back, and the lead dangling loose from it. Using surgical tape he repaired the break and immediately the flat, Translated tones of the being filled his ear-phones.

It was the PVSJ who had left before them to search the wrecked area for survivors. Caught by the same trap which had snagged the unfortunate Monitor, it had been able to use its gravity pack to check its sudden fall. Overcompensating, it had crashed into its present position. The crash had been relatively gentle, but it had caused some loose wreckage to subside, trapping the being and damaging its radio.

The PVSJ—a chlorine-breathing Illensan—was solidly planted in the wreckage: Conway's attempts to free it were useless. While trying, however, he got a look at the professional insignia painted on the other's suit. The Tralthan and Illensan symbols meant nothing to Conway, but the third one—which was the nearest expression of the being's function in Earth-human terms—was a crucifix. The being was a padre. Conway might have expected that.

But now Conway had two immobilized cases instead of one. He thumbed the transmit switch of his radio and cleared his throat. Before he could speak the harsh, urgent voice of Dr. Mannon was dinning in his ears.

"Dr. Conway! Corpsman Williamson! One of you, report quickly, please!"

Conway said, "I was just going to," and gave an account of his troubles to date and requested aid for the Monitor and the PVSJ padre. Mannon cut him off.

"I'm sorry," he said hurriedly, "but we can't help you. The gravity fluctuations have been getting worse here, they must have caused a subsidence in your tunnel, because it's solidly plugged with wreckage all the way above you. Maintenance men have tried to cut a way through but—"

"Let me talk to him," broke in another voice, and there were the magnified, fumbling noises of a mike being snatched out of someone's hand. "Dr. Conway, this is Dr. Lister speaking," it went on. "I'm afraid that I must tell you that the well-being of your two accident cases is of secondary importance. Your job is to contact that being in the gravity control compartment and stop him. Hit him on the head if necessary, but stop him—he's wrecking the hospital!"

Conway swallowed. He said, "Yes, sir," and began looking for a way to penetrate further into the tangle of metal surrounding him. It looked hopeless.

Suddenly he felt himself being pulled sideways. He grabbed for the nearest solid looking projection and hung on for dear life. Transmitted through the fabric of his suit he heard the grinding, tearing jangle of moving metal. The wreckage was shifting again. Then the force pulling him disappeared as suddenly as it had come and simultaneously there came a peculiar, barking cry from the PVSJ. Conway twisted around to see that where the Illensan had been a large hole led downward into nothingness.

He had to force himself to let go of his handhold. The attraction which had seized him had been due, Conway knew, to the momentary activating of an artificial gravity grid somewhere below. If it returned while he was floating unsupported ... Conway did not want to think about that.

The shift had not affected Williamson's position—he still lay as Conway had left him—but the PVSJ must have fallen through.

"Are you all right?" Conway called anxiously.

"I think so," came the reply. "I am still somewhat numb."

Cautiously, Conway drifted across to the newly-created opening and looked down. Below him was a very large compartment, well-lit from a source somewhere off to one side. Only the floor was visible about forty feet below, the walls being beyond his angle of vision and this was thickly carpeted by a dark blue, tubular growth with bulbous leaves. The purpose of this compartment baffled Conway until he realized that he was looking at the AUGL tank minus its water. The thick, flaccid growth covering its floor served both as food and interior decoration for the AUGL patients. The PVSJ had been very lucky to have such a springy surface to land on.

The PVSJ was no longer pinned down by wreckage and it stated that it felt fit enough to help Conway with the being in the gravity control department. As they were about to resume the descent Conway glanced toward the source of light he had half-noticed earlier, and caught his breath.

One wall of the AUGL tank was transparent and looked out on a section corridor which had been converted into a temporary ward. DBLF caterpillars lay in the beds which lined one side, and they were by turns crushed savagely into the plastifoam and bounced upward into the air by it as violent and random fluctuations rippled along the gravity grids in the floor. Netting had been hastily tied around the patients to keep them in the beds, but despite the beating they were taking they were the lucky ones.

A ward was being evacuated somewhere and through his stretch of corridor there crawled, wriggled and hopped a procession of beings resembling the contents of some cosmic Ark. All the oxygen-breathing life-forms were represented together with many who were not, and human nursing orderlies and Monitors shepherded them along. Experience must have taught the orderlies that to stand or walk upright was asking for broken bones and cracked skulls, because they were crawling along on their hands and knees. When a sudden surge of three or four Gs caught them they had a shorter distance to fall that way. Most of them were wearing gravity packs, Conway saw, but had given them up as useless in conditions where the gravity constant was a wild variable.

He saw PVSJs in balloon-like chlorine envelopes being pinned against the floor, flattened like specimens pressed under glass, then bounced into the air again. And Tralthan patients in their massive, unwieldy harness— Tralthans were prone to injury internally despite their great strength—

being dragged along. There were DBDGs, DBLFs and CLSRs, also unidentifiable somethings in spherical, wheeled containers that radiated cold almost visibly. Strung out in a line, being pushed, dragged or manfully inching along on their own, the beings crept past, bowing and straightening up again like wheat in a strong wind as the gravity grids pulled at them.

Conway could almost imagine he felt those fluctuations where he stood, but knew that the crashing ship must have destroyed the grid circuits in its path. He dragged his eyes away from that grim procession and headed downward again.

"Conway!" Mannon's voice barked at him a few minutes later. "That survivor down there is responsible for as many casualties now as the crashed ship! A ward of convalescent LSVOs are dead due to a three-second surge from one-eighth to four gravities. What's happening now?"

The tunnel of wreckage was steadily narrowing, Conway reported, the hull and lighter machinery of the ship having been peeled away by the time it had reached their present level. All that could remain ahead was the massive stuff like hyperdrive generators and so on. He thought he must be very near the end of the line now, and the being who was the unknowing cause of the devastation around them.

"Good," said Mannon, "but hurry it up!"

"But can't the Engineers get through? Surely—"

"They can't," broke in Dr. Lister's voice. "In the area surrounding the gravity grid controls there are fluctuations of up to ten Gs. It's impossible. And joining up with your route from inside the hospital is out, too. It would mean evacuating corridors in the neighboring area, and the corridors are all filled with patients . . ." The voice dropped in volume as Dr. Lister apparently turned away from the mike, and Conway overhead him saying, "Surely an intelligent being could not be so panic-stricken that it . . . it . . . Oh, when I get my hands on it—"

"It may not be intelligent," put in another voice. "Maybe it's a cub, from the FGLI maternity unit . . ."

"If it is I'll tan its little—"

A sharp click ended the conversation at that point as the transmitter was switched off. Conway, suddenly realizing what a very important man he had become, tried to hurry it up as best he could.

IX

They dropped another level into a ward in which four MSVKs—fragile, tri-pedal storklike beings—drifted lifeless among loose items of ward equipment. Movements of the bodies and objects in the room seemed a little unnatural, as if they had been recently disturbed. It was the first sign of the enigmatic survivor they were seeking. Then they were in a great, metal-walled compartment surrounded by a maze of plumbing and unshielded machinery. On the floor in a bulge it had created for itself, the ship's massive hyper-drive generator lay with some shreds of control room equipment strewn around it. Underneath was the remains of a life-form that was now unclassifiable. Beside the generator another hole had been torn in the severely weakened floor by some other piece of the ship's heavy equipment.

Conway hurried over to it, looked down, then called excitedly, "There it is!"

They were looking into a vast room which could only be the grid control center. Rank upon rank of squat, metal cabinets covered the floor, walls and ceiling—this compartment was always kept airless and at zero gravity—with barely room for even Earth-human Engineers to move between them. But Engineers were seldom needed here because the devices in this all-important compartment were self-repairing. At the moment this ability was being put to a severe test.

A being which Conway classified tentatively as AACL sprawled across three of the delicate control cabinets. Nine other cabinets, all winking with red distress signals, were within range of its six, python-like tentacles which poked through seals in the cloudy plastic of its suit. The tentacles were at least twenty feet long and tipped with a horny substance which must have been steel-hard considering the damage the being had caused.

Conway had been prepared to feel pity for this hapless survivor, he had expected to find an entity injured, panic-stricken and crazed with pain. Instead there was a being who appeared unhurt and who was viciously smashing up gravity-grid controls as fast as the built-in self-repairing robots tried to fix them.

Conway swore and began hunting for the frequency of the other's suit radio. Suddenly there was a harsh, high-pitched cheeping sound in his ear-phones. "Got you!" Conway said grimly.

The cheeping sounds ceased abruptly as the other heard his voice and so did all movement of those highly destructive tentacles. Conway noted the wavelength, then switched back to the band used by the PVSJ and himself.

"It seems to me," said the chlorine-breather when he had told it what he had heard, "that the being is deeply afraid, and the noises it made were of fear—otherwise your Translator would have made you receive them as words in your own language. The fact that these noises and its destructive activity stopped when it heard your voice is promising, but I think that we should approach slowly and reassure it constantly that we are bringing help. Its activity down there gives me the impression that it has been hitting out at anything which moves, so a certain amount of caution is indicated, I think."

"Yes, Padre," said Conway with great feeling.

"We do not know in what direction the being's visual organs are directed," the PVSJ went on, "so I suggest we approach from opposite sides."

Conway nodded. They set their radios to the new band and climbed carefully down onto the ceiling of the compartment below. With just enough power in their gravity neutralizers to keep them pressing gently against the metal surface they moved away from each other onto opposite walls, down them, then onto the floor. With the being between them now, they moved slowly toward it.

The robot repair devices were busy making good the damage wrecked by those six anacondas it used for limbs but the being continued to lie quiescent. Neither did it speak. Conway kept thinking of the havoc this entity had caused with its senseless threshing about. The things he felt like saying to it were anything but reassuring, so he let the PSVJ padre do the talking.

"Do not be afraid," the other was saying for the twentieth time. "If you are injured, tell us. We are here to help you . . ."

But there was neither movement nor reply from the being.

On a sudden impulse Conway switched to Dr. Mannon's band. He said quickly, "The survivor seems to be an AACL. Can you tell me what it's here for, or any reason why it should refuse or be unable to talk to us?"

"I'll check with Reception," said Mannon after a short pause. "But are you sure of that classification? I can't remember seeing an AACL here, sure it isn't a Creppelian—"

"It isn't a Creppelian octopoid," Conway cut in. "There are *six* main appendages, and it is just lying here doing nothing . . ."

Conway stopped suddenly, shocked into silence, because it was no longer true that the being under discussion was doing nothing. It had launched itself toward the ceiling, moving so fast that it seemed to land in the same instant that it had taken off. Above him now, Conway saw another control unit pulverized as the being struck and others torn from their mounts as its tentacles sought anchorage. In his phones Mannon was shouting about gravity fluctuations in a hitherto stable section of the hospital, and mounting casualty figures, but Conway was unable to reply.

He was watching helplessly as the AACL prepared to launch itself again.

". . . We are here to help you," the PVSJ was saying as the being landed with a soundless crash four yards from the padre. Five great tentacles anchored themselves firmly, and a sixth lashed out in a great, curving blur of motion that caught the PVSJ and smashed it against the wall. Life-giving chlorine spurted from the PVSJ's suit, momentarily hiding in mist the shapeless, pathetic thing which rebounded slowly into the middle of the room. The AACL began making cheeping noises again.

Conway heard himself babbling out a report to Mannon, then Mannon shouting for Lister. Finally the Director's voice came in to him. It said thickly, "You've got to kill it, Conway."

You've got to kill it, Conway!

It was those words which shocked Conway back to a state of normality as nothing else could have done. How very like a Monitor, he thought bitterly, to solve a problem with a murder. And to ask a doctor, a person dedicated to the preserving of life, to do the killing. It did not matter that the being was insane with fear, it had caused a lot of trouble in the hospital, so kill it.

Conway had been afraid, he still was. In his recent state of mind he might have been panicked into using this kill-or-be-killed law of the jungle. Not now, though. No matter what happened to him or the hospital he would not kill an intelligent fellow being, and Lister could shout himself blue in the face . . .

It was with a start of surprise that Conway realized that both Lister and Mannon were shouting at him, and trying to counter his arguments. He must have been doing his thinking aloud without knowing it. Angrily he tuned them out.

But there was still another voice gibbering at him, a slow, whispering, unutterably weary voice that frequently broke off to gasp in pain. For a wild moment Conway thought that the ghost of the dead PVSJ was continuing Lister's arguments, then he caught sight of movement above him.

Drifting gently through the hole in the ceiling was the spacesuited figure of Williamson. How the badly injured Monitor had got there at all was beyond Conway's understanding—his broken arms made control of his gravity pack impossible, so that he must have come all the way by kicking with his feet and trusting that a still-active gravity grid would not pull him in a second time. At the thought of how many times those multiple fractured members must have collided with obstacles on the way down, Conway cringed. And yet all the Monitor was concerned with was trying to coax Conway into killing the AACL below him.

Close below him, with the distance lessening every second . . .

Conway felt the cold sweat break out on his back. Helpless to stop himself, the injured Monitor had cleared the rent in the ceiling and was drifting slowly floorward, *directly on top of the crouching AACL!* As Conway stared fascinated one of the steel-hard tentacles began to uncurl preparatory to making a death-dealing swipe.

Instinctively Conway launched himself in the direction of the floating Monitor, there was no time for him to feel consciously brave—or stupid—about the action. He connected with a muffled crash and hung on, wrapping his legs around Williamson's waist to leave his hands free for the gravity pack controls. They spun furiously around their common center of gravity, walls, ceilings and floor with its deadly occupant whirling around so fast that Conway could barely focus his eyes on the controls. It seemed years before he finally had the spin checked and he had them headed for the hole in the ceiling and safety. They had almost reached it when Conway saw the hawser-like tentacle come sweeping up at him . . .

X

Something smashed into his back with a force that knocked the breath out of him. For a heart-freezing moment he thought his air-tanks had gone, his suit torn open and that he was already sucking frenziedly at vacuum. But his gasp of pure terror brought air rushing into his lungs. Conway had never known canned air to taste so good.

The AACL's tentacle had only caught him a glancing blow—his back wasn't broken—and the only damage was a wrecked suit radio.

"Are you all right?" Conway asked anxiously when he had Williamson settled in the compartment above. He had to press his helmet against the other's—that was the only way he could make himself heard now.

For several minutes there was no reply, then the weary, pain-wrecked near-whisper returned.

"My arms hurt. I'm tired," it said haltingly. "But I'll be OK when . . . they take me . . . inside." Williamson paused, his voice seemed to gather strength from somewhere and he went on, "That is if there is anybody left alive in the hospital to treat me. If you don't stop our friend down there . . ."

Sudden anger flared in Conway. "Dammit, do you never give up?" he burst out. "Get this, I'm not going to kill an intelligent being! My radio's gone so I don't have to listen to Lister and Mannon yammering at me, and all I've got to do to shut you up is pull my helmet away from yours."

The Monitor's voice had weakened again. He said, "I can still hear Mannon and Lister. They say the wards in Section Eight have been hit now—that's the other low-gravity section. Patients and doctors are pinned flat to the floor under three Gs. A few more minutes like that and they'll never get up—MSVKs aren't at all sturdy, you know . . ."

"Shut up!" yelled Conway. Furiously, he pulled away from contact.

When his anger had abated enough for him to see again, Conway observed that the Monitor's lips were no longer moving. Williamson's eyes were closed, his face gray and sweaty with shock and he did not seem to be breathing. The drying chemicals in his helmet kept the face-plate from fogging, so that Conway could not tell for sure but the Monitor could very easily be dead. With exhaustion held off by repeated pep-shots, then his injuries on top of that, Conway had expected him to be dead long since. For some peculiar reason Conway felt his eyes stinging.

He had seen so much death and dismemberment over the last few hours that his sensitivity to suffering in others had been blunted to the point where he reacted to it merely as a medical machine. This feeling of loss, of bereavement, for the Monitor must be simply a resurgence of that sensitivity, and temporary. Of one thing he was sure, however, no-body was going to make this medical machine commit a murder. The Monitor Corps, Conway now knew, was responsible for a lot more good than bad, but he was not a Monitor.

Yet O'Mara and Lister were both Monitors and Doctors, one of them renowned throughout the Galaxy. Are you better than they are? a little voice nagged in his mind somewhere. And you're all alone now, it went on, with the hospital disorganized and people dying all over the place because of that being down there. What do you think your chances of survival are? The way you came is plugged with wreckage and nobody can come to your aid, so you're going to die, too. Isn't that so?

Desperately Conway tried to hang on to his resolution, to draw it tightly around him like a shell. But that insistent, that cowardly voice in his brain was putting cracks in it. It was with a sense of pure relief that he saw the Monitor's lips moving again. He touched helmets quickly.

"... Hard for you, a Doctor," the voice came faintly, "but you've got to. Just suppose you were that being down below, driven mad with fear and pain maybe, and for a moment you became sane and somebody told you what you had done—what you were doing, and the deaths you had caused ..." The voice wavered, sank, then returned. "Wouldn't you *want* to die rather than go on killing ...?"

"But I *can't* ...!"

"Wouldn't you *want* to die, in its place?"

Conway felt the defensive shell of his resolution begin to disintegrate around him. He said desperately, in a last attempt to hold firm, to stave off the awful decision, "Well, maybe, but I couldn't kill it even if I tried—it would tear me to pieces before I got near it ..."

"I've got a gun," said the Monitor.

Conway could not remember adjusting the firing controls, or even taking the weapon from the Monitor's holster. It was in his hand and trained on the AACL below, and Conway felt sick and cold. But he had not given in to Williamson completely. Near at hand was a sprayer of the fast-setting plastic which, when used quickly enough, could sometimes save a person whose suit had been holed. Conway planned to wound the being, immobilize it, then re-seal its suit with cement. It would be a close thing and risky to himself, but he could not deliberately kill the being.

Carefully he brought his other hand up to steady the gun and took aim. He fired.

When he lowered it there was not much left except shredded twitching pieces of tentacles scattered all over the room. Conway wished now that he had known more about guns, known that this one shot explosive bullets, and that it had been set for continuous automatic fire ...

Williamson's lips were moving again. Conway touched helmets out of pure reflex. He was past caring about anything anymore.

"...It's all right, Doctor," the Monitor was saying. "It isn't any-body..."

"It isn't anybody now," Conway agreed. He went back to examining the Monitor's gun and wished that it wasn't empty. If there had been one bullet left, just one, he knew how he would have used it.

"It was hard, we know that," said Major O'Mara. The rasp was no longer in his voice and the iron-gray eyes were soft with sympathy, and something akin to pride. "A doctor doesn't have to make a decision like that usually until he's older, more balanced, mature, if ever. You are, or were, just an over-idealistic kid—a bit on the smug and self-righteous side maybe—who didn't even know what a Monitor really was."

O'Mara smiled. His two big, hard hands rested on Conway's shoulders in an oddly fatherly gesture. He went on, "Doing what you forced yourself to do could have ruined both your career and your mental stability. But it doesn't matter, you don't have to feel guilty about a thing. Everything's all right."

Conway wished dully that he had opened his face-plate and ended it all before those Engineers had swarmed into the gravity grid control room and carried Williamson and himself off to O'Mara. O'Mara must be mad. He, Conway, had violated the prime ethic of his profession and killed an intelligent being. Everything most definitely was not all right.

"Listen to me," O'Mara said seriously. "The Communications boys managed to get a picture of the crashed ship's control room, with the occupant in it, before it hit. The occupant was not your AACL, understand? It was an AMSO, one of the bigger life-forms who are in the habit of keeping a non-intelligent AACL-type creature as pets. Also, there are no AACLs listed in the hospital, so the beastie you killed was simply the equivalent of a fear-maddened dog in a protective suit." O'Mara shook Conway's shoulder until his head wobbled. "Now do you feel better?"

Conway felt himself coming alive again. He nodded wordlessly.

"You can go," said O'Mara, smiling, "and catch up on your sleep. As for the reorientation talk, I'm afraid I haven't the time to spare. Remind me about it sometime, if you still think you need it..."

XI

During the fourteen hours in which Conway slept, the intake of wounded dropped to a manageable trickle, and news came that the war was over. Monitor engineers and maintenance men succeeded in clearing the wreckage and repairing the damaged outer hull. With pressure restored, the internal repair work proceeded rapidly, so that when Conway awoke and went in search of Dr. Mannon he found patients being moved into a section which only hours ago had been a dark, airless tangle of wreckage.

He tracked his superior down in a side ward off the main FGLI Casualty section. Mannon was working over a badly burned DBLF whose caterpillar-like body was dwarfed by a table which was designed to take the more massive Tralthan FGLIs. Two other DBLFs, under sedation, showed as white mounds on a similarly outsize bed against the wall, and another lay twitching slightly on a stretcher-carrier near the door.

"Where the blazes have you been?" Mannon said in a voice too tired to be angry. Before Conway could reply he went on impatiently, "Oh, don't tell me. Everybody is grabbing everybody else's staff, and junior interns have to do as they're told . . ."

Conway felt his face going red. Suddenly he was ashamed of that fourteen hours sleep, but was too much of a coward to correct Mannon's wrong assumption. Instead he said, "Can I help, sir?"

"Yes," said Mannon, waving toward his patients. "But these are going to be tricky. Punctured and incised wounds, deep. Metallic fragments still within the body, abdominal damage and severe internal hemorrhage. You won't be able to do much without a tape. Go get it. And come straight back, mind!"

A few minutes later he was in O'Mara's office absorbing the DBLF physiology tape. This time he didn't flinch from the Major's hands. While the headband was being removed he asked, "How is Corpsman Williamson?"

"He'll live," said O'Mara dryly. "The bones were set by a Diagnostician. Williamson won't dare die . . ."

Conway rejoined Mannon as quickly as possible. He was experiencing the characteristic mental double-vision and had to resist the urge to crawl on his stomach, so he knew that the DBLF tape was taking. The caterpillar-like inhabitants of Kelgia were very close to Earth-humans both in basic metabolism and temperament, so there was less of the confusion he had encountered with the earlier Telfi tape. But it gave him an affinity for the beings he was treating which was actually painful.

The concept of gun, bullet and target was a very simple one—just point, pull the trigger, and the target is dead or disabled. The bullet didn't think at all, the pointer didn't think enough, and the target . . . suffered.

Conway had seen too many disabled targets recently, and lumps of metal which had plowed their way into them leaving red craters in torn flesh, bone splinters and ruptured blood vessels. In addition there was the long, painful process of recovery. Anyone who would inflict such damage on a thinking, feeling entity deserved something much more painful than the Monitor corrective psychiatry.

A few days previously Conway would have been ashamed of such thoughts—and he was now, a little. He wondered if recent events had initiated in him a process of moral degeneration, or was it that he was merely beginning to grow up?

Five hours later they were through. Mannon gave his nurse instructions to keep the four patients under observation, but told her to get something to eat first. She was back within minutes carrying a large pack of sandwiches and bearing the news that their dining hall had been taken over by Tralthan Male Medical. Shortly after that Dr. Mannon went to sleep in the middle of his second sandwich. Conway loaded him onto the stretcher-carrier and took him to his room. On the way out he was collared by a Tralthan Diagnostician who ordered him to a DBDG casualty section.

This time Conway found himself working on targets of his own species and his maturing, or moral degeneration, increased. He had begun to think that the Monitor Corps was too damned soft with some people.

Three weeks later Sector General was back to normal. All but the most seriously wounded patients had been transferred to their local planetary hospitals. The damage caused by the colliding spaceship had been repaired. Tralthan Male Medical had vacated the dining hall, and Conway no longer had to snatch his meals off assorted instrument trolleys. But if things were back to normal for the hospital as a whole, such was not the case with Conway personally.

He was taken off ward duty completely and transferred to a mixed group of Earth-humans and e-ts—most of whom were senior to himself—taking a course of lectures in Ship Rescue. Some of the difficulties experienced in fishing survivors out of wrecked ships, especially those which contained still-functioning power sources, made Conway open his eyes. The course ended with an interesting, if back-breaking, practical which he managed to pass, and was followed by a more cerebral course in e-t comparative philosophy. Running at the same time was a series on contamination emergencies: what to do if the methane section sprung a leak and the temperature threatened to rise above minus one-forty, what to do if a chlorine-breather was exposed to oxygen, or a water-breather was strangling in air, or vice-versa. Conway had shuddered at the idea of some of his fellow students trying to give him artificial respiration—some of whom weighed half a ton!—but luckily there was no practical at the end of that course.

Every one of the lecturers stressed the importance of rapid and accurate classification of incoming patients, who very often were in no condition to give this information themselves. In the four-letter classification system the first letter was a guide to the general metabolism, the second to the number and distribution of limbs and sense organs, and the rest to a combination of pressure and gravity requirements, which also gave an indication of the physical mass and form of protective tegument a being possessed. A, B and C first letters were water-breathers. D and F warm-blooded oxygen-breathers into which classification most of the intelligent races fell. G to K were also oxygen-breathing, but insectile, light-gravity beings. L and M were also light-gravity, but bird-like. The chlorine-breathers were contained in the O and P classifications. After that came the weirdies—radiation-eaters, frigid-blooded or crystalline beings, entities capable of changing physical shape at will, and those possessing various forms of extra-sensory powers. Telepathic species such as the Telfi were given the prefix V. The lecturers would flash a three-second picture of an e-t foot or a section of tegument onto the screen, and if Conway could not rattle off an accurate classification from this glimpse, sarcastic words would be said.

It was all very interesting stuff, but Conway began to worry a little when he realized that six weeks had passed without him even seeing a patient. He decided to call O'Mara and ask what for—in a respectful, roundabout way, of course.

"Naturally you want back to the wards," O'Mara said, when Conway finally arrived at the point. "Dr. Mannon would like you back, too. But I may have a job for you and don't want you tied up anywhere else. But don't feel that you are simply marking time. You are learning some useful stuff, Doctor. At least, I hope you are. Off."

As Conway replaced the intercom mike he was thinking that a lot of the things he was learning had regard to Major O'Mara himself. There wasn't a course of lectures on the Chief Psychologist, but there might well have been, because every lecture had O'Mara creeping into it somewhere. And he was only beginning to realize how close he had come to being kicked out of the hospital for his behavior during the Telfi episode.

O'Mara bore the rank of Major in the Monitor Corps, but Conway had learned that within the hospital it was difficult to draw a limiting line to his authority. As Chief Psychologist he was responsible for the mental health of all the widely varied individuals and species on the staff, and the avoidance of friction between them.

Given even the highest qualities of tolerance and mutual respect in its personnel, there were still occasions when friction occurred. Potentially dangerous situations arose through ignorance or misunderstanding, or a being could develop a xenophobic neurosis which might affect its efficiency, or mental stability, or both. An Earth-human doctor, for instance, who had a subconscious fear of spiders would not be able to bring to bear on an Illensan patient the proper degree of clinical detachment necessary for its treatment. So it was O'Mara's job to detect and eradicate such signs of trouble—or if all else failed—remove the potentially dangerous individual before such friction became open conflict. This guarding against wrong, unhealthy or intolerant thinking was a duty which he performed with such zeal that Conway had heard him likened to a latterday Torquemada.

E-ts on the staff whose home-planet histories did not contain an equivalent of the Inquisition likened him to other things, and often called him them to his face. But in O'Mara's book Justifiable Invective was not indicative of wrong thinking, so there were no serious repercussions.

O'Mara was *not* responsible for the psychological shortcomings of patients in the hospital, but because it was so often impossible to tell when a purely physical pain left off and a psychosomatic one began, he was consulted in these cases also.

The fact that the Major had detached him from ward duty could mean either promotion or demotion. If Mannon wanted him back, however, then the job which O'Mara had in mind for him must be of greater importance. So Conway was pretty certain that he was not in any trouble with O'Mara, which was a very nice way to feel. But curiosity was killing him.

Then next morning he received orders to present himself at the office of the Chief Psychologist . . .

CHAPTER 3

TROUBLE WITH EMILY

It must have been one of the big colonial transports of the type which had carried four generations of colonists between the stars before the hyper-drive made such gargantuan ships obsolete, Conway thought, as he stared at the great tear-drop shape framed in the direct vision port beside O'Mara's desk. With the exception of the pilot's greenhouse, its banks of observation galleries and viewports were blocked off by thick metal plating, and braced solidly from the outside to withstand considerable internal pressure. Even beside the tremendous bulk of Sector General it looked huge.

"You are to act as liaison between the hospital here and the doctor and patient from that ship," said Chief Psychologist O'Mara, watching him closely. "The doctor is quite a small life-form. The patient is a dinosaur."

Conway tried to keep the astonishment he felt from showing in his face. O'Mara was analyzing his reactions, he knew, and perversely he wanted to make the other's job as difficult as possible. He said simply, "What's wrong with it?"

"Nothing," said O'Mara.

"It must be psychological, then . . . ?"

O'Mara shook his head.

"Then what is a healthy, sane and intelligent being doing in a hos—"

"It isn't intelligent."

Conway breathed slowly in and out. O'Mara was obviously playing guessing games with him again—not that Conway minded that, provided he was given a sporting chance to guess the right answers. He looked again at the great mass of the converted transport, and meditated.

Putting hyper-drive engines into that great sow of a ship had cost money, and the extensive structural alterations to the hull a great deal more. It seemed an awful lot of trouble to go to for a . . .

"I've got it!" said Conway grinning. "It's a new specimen for us to take apart and investigate . . ."

"Good Lord, *no!*" cried O'Mara, horrified. He shot a quick, almost frightened look at a small sphere of plastic which was half hidden by some books on his desk, then went on seriously, "This whole business has been arranged at the highest level—a sub-assembly of the Galactic Council, no less. As to what exactly it is all about neither I nor anyone else in Sector General knows. Possibly the doctor who accompanied the patient and who has charge of it may tell you sometime . . ."

O'Mara's tone at that point implied that he very much doubted it.

". . . However, all that the hospital and yourself are required to do is cooperate."

Apparently the being who was the doctor in the case came from a race which had been only recently discovered, O'Mara went on to explain, which had tentatively been given the classification VUXG: that was, they were a life-form possessing certain psi faculties, had the ability to convert practically any substance into energy for their physical needs and could adapt to virtually any environment. They were small and well-nigh indestructible.

The VUXG doctor was telepathic, but ethics and the privacy taboo forbade it using this faculty to communicate with a non-telepathic life-form, even if its range included the Earth-human frequency. For that reason the Translator would be used exclusively. This doctor belonged to a species long-lived both as individuals and in recorded history, and in all that vast sweep of time there had been no war.

They were an old, wise and humble race, O'Mara concluded; intensely humble. So much so that they tended to look down on other races who were not so humble as they. Conway would have to be very tactful because this extreme, this almost overbearing humility might easily be mistaken for something else.

Conway looked closely at O'Mara. Was there not a faintly sardonic gleam in those keen, iron-gray eyes and a too carefully neutral expression on that square-chiseled competent face? Then with a feeling of complete bafflement he saw O'Mara wink.

Ignoring it, Conway said, "This race, they sound stuck up to me."

He saw O'Mara's lips twitch, then a new voice broke in on the proceedings with dramatic suddenness. It was a flat, toneless, Translated voice which boomed, "The sense of the preceding remark is not clear to me. We are stuck—adhering—up where?" There was a short pause, then, "While I admit that my own mental capabilities are very low, at the same time I would suggest in all humility that the fault may not altogether lie with me, but be due in part to the lamentable tendency for you younger and more impractical races to make sense-free noises when there is no necessity for a noise to be made at all."

It was then that Conway's wildly searching eyes lit on the transparent plastic globe on O'Mara's desk. Now that he was really looking at it he could see several lengths of strapping attached to it, together with the unmistakable shape of a Translator pack. Inside the container there floated a *something* . . .

"Dr. Conway," said O'Mara dryly, "meet Dr. Arretapec, your new boss." Mouthing silently, he added, "You and your big mouth!"

The thing in the plastic globe, which resembled nothing so much as a withered prune floating in a spherical gob of syrup, was the VUXG doctor! Conway felt his face burning. It was a good thing that the Translator dealt only with words and did not also transfer their emotional— in this instance sarcastic—connotations, otherwise he would have been in a most embarrassing position.

"As the closest cooperation is required," O'Mara went on quickly, "and the mass of the being Arretapec is slight, you will *wear* it while on duty." O'Mara deftly suited actions to his words and strapped the container onto Conway's shoulder. When he had finished he added, "You can go, Dr. Conway. Detailed orders, when and where necessary, will be given to you direct by Dr. Arretapec."

It could only happen here, Conway thought wryly as they left. Here he was with an e-t doctor riding on his shoulder like a quivering, transparent dumpling, their patient a healthy and husky dinosaur, and the purpose of the whole business was something which his colleague was reluctant to clarify. Conway had heard of blind obedience but blind cooperation was a new—and he thought, rather stupid—concept.

On the way to Lock Seventeen, the point where the hospital was joined to the ship containing their patient, Conway tried to explain the organization of Sector Twelve General Hospital to the extra-terrestrial doctor.

Dr. Arretapec asked some pertinent questions from time to time, so presumably he was interested.

Even though he had been expecting it, the sheer size of the converted transport's interior shocked Conway. With the exception of the two levels nearest the ship's outer skin, which at the moment housed the artificial gravity generators, the Monitor Corps engineer had cut away everything to leave a great sphere of emptiness some two thousand feet in diameter. The inner surface of this sphere was a wet and muddy shambles. Great untidy heaps of uprooted vegetation were piled indescriminately about, most of it partially trampled into the mud. Conway also noticed that quite a lot of it was withered and dying.

After the gleaming, aseptic cleanliness which he was used to Conway found that the sight was doing peculiar things to his nervous system. He began looking around for the patient.

His gaze moved out and upward across the acres of mud and tumbled vegetation until, high above his head on the opposite side of the sphere the swamp merged into a small, deep lake. There were shadowy movements and swirlings below its surface. Suddenly a tiny head mounted on a great sinuous neck broke the surface, looked around, then submerged again with a tremendous splash.

Conway surveyed the distance to the lake and the quality of the terrain between it and himself. He said, "It's a long way to walk, I'll get an antigravity belt . . ."

"That will not be necessary," said Arretapec. The ground abruptly flung itself away from them and they were hurtling toward the distant lake.

Classification VUXG, Conway reminded himself when he got his breath back; *possessing certain psi faculties . . .*

II

They landed gently near the edge of the lake. Arretapec told Conway that it wanted to concentrate its thinking processes for a few minutes and requested him to keep both quiet and still. A few seconds later an itching started deep inside his ear somewhere. Conway manfully refrained from poking at it with his finger and instead kept all his attention on the surface of the lake.

Suddenly a great gray-brown, mountainous body broke the surface, a long tapering neck and tail slapping the water with explosive violence. For an instant Conway thought that the great beast had simply bobbed to the surface like a rubber ball but then he told himself that the bed of the lake must have shelved suddenly under the monster, giving an optically similar effect. Still threshing madly with neck, tail and four massive columnar legs the giant reptile gained the lake's edge and floundered onto, or rather *into*, the mud, because it sank over its knee joints. Conway estimated that the said knee-joints were at least ten feet from ground level, that the thickest diameter of the great body was about eighteen feet and that from head to tail the brute measured well over one hundred feet. He guessed its weight at about 80,000 pounds. It possessed no natural body armor but the extreme end of its tail, which showed surprising mobility for such a heavy member, had an osseous bulge from which spouted two wicked, forward-curving bony spikes.

As Conway watched, the great reptile continued to churn up the mud in obvious agitation. Then abruptly it fell onto its knees and its great neck curved around and inward until its head muzzled underneath its own underbelly. It was a ridiculous but oddly pathetic posture.

"It is badly frightened," said Arretapec. "These conditions do not adequately simulate its true environment."

Conway could understand and sympathize with the beast. The ingredients of its environment were no doubt accurately reproduced but rather than being arranged in a lifelike manner they had just been thrown together into a large muddy stew. Probably not deliberately, he thought, there must have been some trouble with the artificial gravity grids on the way out to account for this jumbled landscape. He said:

"Is the mental state of the patient of importance to the purpose of your work?"

"Very much so," said Arretapec.

"Then the first step is to make it a little more happy with its lot," said Conway, and went down on his haunches. He took a sample of the lake water, the mud and several of the varieties of vegetation nearby. Finally he straightened up and said, "Is there anything else we have to do here?"

"I can do nothing at present," Arretapec replied. The Translated voice was toneless and utterly without emotion, naturally, but from the spacing of the words Conway thought that the other sounded deeply disappointed.

Back at the entry lock Conway made determined tracks toward the dining hall reserved for warm-blooded, oxygen-breathing life-forms. He was hungry.

Many of his colleagues were in the hall—DBLF caterpillars who were slow everywhere but in the operating theater, Earth-human DBDGs like himself and the great, elephantine Tralthan—classification FGLI—who, with the little OTSB life-form who lived in symbiosis with it, was well on the way to joining the ranks of the lordly Diagnosticians. But instead of engaging in conversation all around, Conway concentrated on gaining all the data possible on the planet of origin of the reptilian patient.

For greater ease of conversation he had taken Arretapec out of its plastic container and placed it on the table in a space between the potatoes and gravy dish. At the end of the meal Conway was startled to find that the being had dissolved—ingested—a two inch hole in the table!

"When in deep cogitation," Arretapec replied when Conway rather exasperatedly wanted to know why, "the process of food-gathering and ingestion is automatic and unconscious with us. We do not indulge in eating as a pleasure as you obviously do, it dilutes the quality of our thinking. However, if I have caused damage . . . ?"

Conway hastily reassured him that a plastic tablecloth was relatively valueless in the present circumstances, and beat a quick retreat from the place. He did not try to explain how catering officers could feel rather peeved over their relatively valueless property.

After lunch Conway picked up the analysis of his test samples, then headed for the Maintenance Chief's office. This was occupied by one of the Nidian teddy bears wearing an armband with gold edging, and an Earth-human in Monitor green whose collar bore a Colonel's insignia over an Engineering flash. Conway described the situation and what he wanted done, if such a thing was possible.

"It is possible," said the red teddy bear after they had gone into a huddle of Conway's data sheets, "but—"

"O'Mara told me expense is no object," Conway interrupted, nodding toward the tiny being on his shoulder. "Maximum cooperation, he said."

"In that case we can do it," the Monitor Colonel put in briskly. He was regarding Arretapec with an expression close to awe. "Let's see, transports to bring the stuff from its home planet—quicker and cheaper in the long run than synthesizing its food here. And we'll need two full companies of the Engineers' Division with their robots to make its house a happy home, instead of the twenty-odd men responsible for bringing it here." His eyes became unfocused as rapid calculations went on behind them, then: "Three days."

Even allowing for the fact that hyper-drive travel was instantaneous, Conway thought that that was very fast indeed. He said so.

The Colonel acknowledged the compliment with the thinnest of smiles. He said, "What is all this in aid of, you haven't told us yet?"

Conway waited for a full minute to give Arretapec plenty of time to answer the question, but the VUXG kept silent. He could only mumble "I don't know" and leave quickly.

The next door they entered was boldly labeled "Dietitian-in-Chief—Species DBDG, DBLF and FGLI. Dr. K. W. HARDIN." Inside, the white-haired and distinguished head of Dr. Hardin raised itself from some charts he was studying and bawled, "And what's biting *you* . . . ?"

While Conway was impressed by and greatly respected Dr. Hardin, he was no longer afraid of him. The Chief Dietitian was a man who was quite charming to strangers, Conway had learned; with acquaintances he tended to be a little on the abrupt side, and toward his friends he was downright rude. As briefly as possible Conway tried to explain what was biting him.

"You mean I have to go around replanting the stuff it's eaten, so that it doesn't know but that it grew naturally?" Hardin interrupted at one point. "Who the blazes do you think I am? And how much does this dirty great cow eat, anyway?"

Conway gave him the figures he had worked out.

"Three and a half *tons* of palm fronds a day!" Hardin roared, practically climbing his desk. "And tender green shoots of . . . Ye Gods! And they tell me dietetics is an exact science. Three and a half tons of shrubbery, exact! *Hah . . . !*"

They left Hardin at that point. Conway knew that everything would be all right because the dietitian had shown no signs of becoming charming.

To the VUXG Conway explained that Hardin had not been non-cooperative, but had just sounded that way. He was keen to help as had been the other two. Arretapec replied to the effect that members of such immature and short-lived races could not help behaving in an insane fashion.

A second visit to their patient followed. Conway brought a G-belt along with him this time and so was independent of Arretapec's teleportive ability. They drifted around and above the great, ambulating mountain of flesh and bone, but not once did Arretapec so much as touch the creature. Nothing whatever happened except that the patient once again showed signs of agitation and Conway suffered a periodic itch deep inside his ear. He sneaked a quick look at the tell-tale which was surgically embedded in his forearm to see if there was anything foreign in his blood-stream, but everything was normal. Maybe he was just allergic to dinosaurs.

Back in the hospital proper Conway found that the frequency and violence of his yawns was threatening to dislocate his jaw, and he realized that he had had a hard day. The concept of sleep was completely strange to Arretapec, but the *being* raised no objections to Conway indulging in it if it was necessary to his physical well-being. Conway gravely assured it that it was, and headed for his room by the shortest route.

What to do with Dr. Arretapec bothered him for a while. The VUXG was an important personage; he could not very well leave it in a storage closet or in a corner somewhere, even though the being was tough enough to be comfortable in much more rugged surroundings. Nor could he simply put it out for the night without gravely hurting its feelings—at least, if the positions had been reversed *his* feelings would have been hurt. He wished O'Mara had given instructions to cover this contingency. Finally he placed the being on top of his writing desk and forgot about it.

Arretapec must have thought deeply during the night, because there was a three inch hole in the desktop next morning.

III

During the afternoon of the second day a row started between the two doctors. At least Conway considered it a row; what an entirely alien mind like Arretapec's chose to think of it was anybody's guess.

It started when the VUXG requested Conway to be quiet and still while it went into one of its silences. The being had gone back to the old position on Conway's shoulder, explaining that it could concentrate more

1LD2 · JAMES WHITE

effectively while at rest rather than with part of its mind engaged in levitating. Conway had done as he was told without comment though there were several things he would have liked to say: What was wrong with the patient? What was Arretapec doing about it? And *how* was it being done when neither of them so much as touched the creature? Conway was in the intensely frustrating position of a doctor confronted with a patient on whom he is not allowed to practice his craft: he was eaten up with curiosity and it was bothering him. Yet he did his best to stand still.

But the itching started inside his ear again, worse than ever before. He barely noticed the geysers of mud and water flung up by the dinosaur as it threshed its way out of the shallows and onto the bank. The gnawing, unlocalized itch built up remorselessly until with a sudden yell of fright he slapped at the side of his head and began poking frantically at his ear. The action brought immediate and blessed relief, but . . .

"I cannot work if you fidget," said Arretapec, the rapidity of the words the only indication of their emotional content. "You will therefore leave me at once."

"I wasn't fidgeting," Conway protested angrily. "My ear itched and I—"

"An itch, especially one capable of making you move as this one has done, is a symptom of a physical disorder which should be treated," the VUXG interrupted. "Or it is caused by a parasitic or symbiotic life-form dwelling, perhaps unknown to you, on your body.

"Now, I expressly stated that my assistant should be in perfect physical health and not a member of a species who either consciously or unconsciously harbored parasites—a type, you must understand, which are particularly prone to fidget—so that you can understand my displeasure. Had it not been for your sudden movement I might have accomplished something, therefore go."

"Why you supercilious—"

The dinosaur chose that moment to stagger into the shallow water again, lose its footing and come the great grand-daddy of all bellyflops. Falling mud and spray drenched Conway and a small tidal wave surged over his feet. The distraction was enough to make him pause, and the pause gave him time to realize that he had not been personally insulted. There were many intelligent species who harbored parasites—some of them actually necessary to the health of the host body, so that in their case the slang expression being lousy also meant being in tiptop condition. Maybe Arretapec had meant to be insulting, but he could not be sure. And the VUXG was, after all, a very important person . . .

"What exactly might you have accomplished?" Conway asked sarcastically. He was still angry, but had decided to fight on the professional rather than the personal level. Besides, he knew that the Translator would take the insulting edge off his words. "What are you *trying* to accomplish, and how do you expect to do it merely by—from what I can see, anyway—just looking at the patient?"

"I cannot tell you," Arretapec replied after a few seconds. "My purpose is . . . is vast. It is for the future. You would not understand."

"How do you know? If you told me what you were doing maybe I could help."

"You cannot help."

"Look," said Conway exasperated, "you haven't even tried to use the full facilities of the hospital yet. No matter what you are trying to do for your patient, the first step should have been a thorough examination— immobilisation, followed by X rays, biopsies, the lot. This would have given you valuable physiological data upon which to work—"

"To state the matter simply," Arretapec broke in, "you are saying that in order to understand a complicated organism or mechanism, one must first be broken down into its component parts that they might be understood individually. My race does not believe that an object must be destroyed—even in part—before it can be understood. Your crude methods of investigation are therefore worthless to me. I suggest that you leave."

Seething, Conway left.

His first impulse was to storm into O'Mara's office and tell the Chief Psychologist to find somebody else to run errands for the VUXG. But O'Mara had told him that his present assignment was important, and O'Mara would have unkind things to say if he thought that Conway was throwing his hand in simply out of pique because his curiosity had not been satisfied or his pride hurt. There were lots of doctors—the assistants to Diagnosticians, particularly—who were not allowed to touch their superior's patients, or was it just that Conway resented a being like Arretapec being his superior . . . ?

If Conway went to O'Mara in his present frame of mind there was real danger of the psychologist deciding that he was temperamentally unsuited for his position. Quite apart from the prestige attached to a post at Sector General, the work performed in it was both stimulating and very much worthwhile. Should O'Mara decide that he was unfit to remain here and pack him off to some planetary hospital, it would be the greatest tragedy of Conway's life.

But if he could not go to O'Mara, where could he go? Ordered off one job and not having another, Conway was at loose ends. He stood at a corridor intersection for several minutes thinking, while beings representing a cross-section of all the intelligent races of the galaxy strode undulated or skittered past him, then suddenly he had it. There was something he could do, something which he would have done anyway if everything had not happened with such a rush.

The hospital library had several items on the prehistoric periods of Earth, both taped and in the old-fashioned and more cumbersome book form. Conway heaped them on a reading desk and prepared to make an attempt to satisfy his professional curiosity about the patient in this roundabout fashion.

The time passed very quickly.

Dinosaur, Conway discovered at once, was simply a general term applied to the giant reptiles. The patient, except for its larger size and bony enlargement of the tip of the tail, was identical in outward physical characteristics to the brontosaurus which lived among the swamps of the Jurassic Period. It also was herbiverous, but unlike their patient had no means of defense against the carnivorous reptiles of its time. There was a surprising amount of physiological data available as well, which Conway absorbed greedily.

The spinal column was composed of huge vertebrae, and with the exception of the caudal vertebrae all were hollow—this saving of osseous material making possible a relatively low body weight in comparison with its tremendous size. It was oviparous. The head was small, the brain case one of the smallest found among the vertebrates. But in addition to this brain there was a well-developed nerve center in the region of the sacral vertebrae which was several times as large as the brain proper. It was thought that the brontosaur grew slowly, their great size being explained by the fact that they could live two hundred or more years.

Their only defense against contemporary rivals was to take to and remain in the water—they could pasture under water and required only brief mouthfuls of air, apparently. They became extinct when geologic changes caused their swampy habitats to dry up and leave them at the mercy of their natural enemies.

One authority stated that these saurians were nature's biggest failure. Yet they had flourished, said another, through three geologic periods— the Triassic, Jurassic and Cretaceous—which totalled 140 million years, a long time indeed for a "failure" to be around, considering the fact that Man had existed only for approximately half a million years . . . !

Conway left the library with the conviction that he had discovered something important, but what exactly it was he could not say; it was an intensely frustrated feeling. Over a hurried meal he decided that he badly needed more information and there was only one person who might be able to give it to him. He would see O'Mara again.

"Where is our small friend?" said the psychologist sharply when Conway entered his office a few minutes later. "Have you had a fight or something?"

Conway gulped and tried to keep his voice steady as he replied, "Dr. Arretapec wished to work with the patient alone for a while, and I've been doing some research on dinosaurs in the library. I wondered if you had anymore information for me?"

"A little," O'Mara said. He looked steadily at Conway for several very uncomfortable seconds, then grunted, "Here it is . . ."

The Monitor Corps survey vessel which had discovered Arretapec's home planet had, after realizing the high stage of civilization reached by the inhabitants, given them the hyper-drive. One of the first planets visited had been a raw, young world devoid of intelligent life, but one of its life-forms had interested them—the giant saurian. They had told the Galactic powers-that-be that given the proper assistance they might be able to do something which would benefit civilization as a whole, and as it was impossible for any telepathic race to tell a lie or even understand what a lie is, they were given the assistance asked for and Arretapec and his patient had come to Sector General. There was one other small item as well, O'Mara told Conway. Apparently the VUXG's psi faculties included a sort of precognitive ability. This latter did not appear to be of much use because it did not work with individuals but only with populations, and then so far in the future and in such a haphazard manner that it was practically useless.

Conway left O'Mara feeling more confused than ever.

He was still trying to make the odd bits and pieces of information add up to something which made sense, but either he was too tired or too stupid. And definitely he was tired; these past two days his brain had been just so much thick, weary fog . . .

There must be an association between the two factors, Arretapec's coming and this unaccountable weariness, Conway thought: he was in good physical condition and no amount of muscular or mental exertion had left him feeling this way before. And had not Arretapec said something about the itching sensations he had felt being symptomatic of a disorder?

All of a sudden his job with the VUXG doctor was no longer merely frustrating or annoying. Conway was beginning to feel anxiety for his own personal safety. Suppose the itching was due to some new type of bacteria which did not show up on his personal tell-tale? He had thought something like this when his fidgeting had caused Arretapec to send him away, but for the rest of the day he had been subconsciously trying to convince himself that it was nothing because the intensity of the sensations had diminished to practically zero. Now he knew that he should have had one of the senior physicians look into it. He should, in fact, do it now.

But Conway was very tired. He promised himself that he would get Dr. Mannon, his previous superior, to give him a going over in the morning. And in the morning he would have to get on the right side of Arretapec again. He was still worrying about the strange new disease he might have caught and the correct method of apologizing to a VUXG life-form when he fell asleep.

IV

Next morning there was another two-inch hollow eaten in the top of his desk and Arretapec was nestling inside it. As soon as Conway demonstrated that he was awake by sitting up, the being spoke:

"It had occurred to me since yesterday," the VUXG said, "that I have perhaps been expecting too much in the way of self-control, emotional stability, and the ability to endure or to discount minor physical irritants in a member of a species which is—relatively, you understand—of low mentality. I will therefore do my utmost to bear these points in mind during our future relations together."

It took a few seconds for Conway to realize that Arretapec had apologized to him. When he did he thought that it was the most insulting apology he had ever had tendered to him, and that it spoke well for his self-control that he did not tell the other so. Instead he smiled and insisted that it was all his fault. They left to see their patient again.

The interior of the converted transport had changed out of all recognition. Instead of a hollow sphere covered with a muddy shambles of soil, water and foliage, three-quarters of the available surface was now a perfect representation of a Mesozoic landscape. Yet it was not exactly the same as the pictures Conway had studied yesterday, because they had been of a distant age of Earth and this flora had been transplanted from the patient's own world, but the differences were surprisingly small. The greatest change was in the sky.

Where previously it had been possible to look up at the opposite side of the hollow sphere, now one looked up into a blue-white mist in which burned a very lifelike sun. The hollow center of the ship had been almost filled with this semi-opaque gas so that now it would take a keen eye and a mind armed with foreknowledge for a person to know that he was not standing on a real planet with a real sun in the foggy sky above him. The engineers had done a fine job.

"I had not thought such an elaborate and lifelike reconstruction possible here," said Arretapec suddenly. "You are to be commended. This should have a very good effect on the patient."

The life-form under discussion—for some peculiar reason the engineers insisted on calling it Emily—was contentedly shredding the fronds from the top of a thirty foot high palm-like growth. The fact of its being on dry land instead of pasturing under water was indicative of its state of mind, Conway knew, because the old-time brontosaur invariably took to the water when threatened by enemies, that being its only defense. Apparently this neo-brontosaurus hadn't a care in the world.

"Essentially it is the same as fitting up a new ward for the treatment of any extra-terrestrial patient," said Conway modestly, "the chief difference here being the scale of the work undertaken."

"I am nevertheless impressed," said Arretapec.

First apologies and now compliments, Conway thought wryly. As they moved closer and Arretapec once again warned him to keep quiet and still, Conway guessed that the VUXG's change of manner was due to the work of the engineers. With the patient now in ideal surroundings the treatment, whatever form it was taking, might have an increased chance of success . . .

Suddenly Conway began to itch again. It started in the usual place deep inside his right ear, but this time it spread and built up in intensity until his whole brain seemed to be crawling with viciously biting insects. He felt cold sweat break on him, and remembered his fears of the previous evening when he had resolved to go to Mannon. This wasn't imagination, this was serious, perhaps deadly serious. His hands flew to his head with a panicky, involuntary motion, knocking the container holding Arretapec to the ground.

"You are fidgeting again . . ." began the VUXG.

"I . . . I'm sorry," Conway stammered. He mumbled something incoherent about having to leave, that it was important and couldn't wait, then fled in disorder.

Three hours later he was sitting in Dr. Mannon's DBDG examination room while Mannon's dog alternately growled fiercely at him or rolled on its back and looked appealing in vain attempts to entice him to play with it. But Conway had no inclination for the ritual pummeling and wrestling that the dog and himself enjoyed when he had the time for it. All his attention was focused on the bent head of his former superior and on the charts lying on Mannon's desk. Suddenly the other looked up.

"There's nothing wrong with you," he said in the peremptory manner reserved for students and patients suspected of malingering. A few seconds later he added, "Oh, I've no doubt you've felt these sensations—tiredness, itching, and so on—but what sort of case are you working on at the moment?"

Conway told him. A few times during the narration Mannon grinned.

"I take it this is your first long-term—er—exposure to a telepathic life-form and that I am the first you've mentioned this trouble to?" Mannon's tone was of one making a statement rather than of asking a question. "And, of course, although you feel this itching sensation intensely when close to the VUXG and the patient, it continues in a weaker form at other times."

Conway nodded. "I felt it for a while just five minutes ago."

"Naturally, there is attenuation with distance," Mannon said. "But as regards yourself, you have nothing to worry about. Arretapec is—all un-knowingly, you understand—simply trying to make a telepath out of you. I'll explain . . ."

Apparently prolonged contact with some telepathic life-forms stim-ulated a certain area in the human brain which was either the beginnings of a telepathic function that would evolve in the future, or the atrophied remnant of something possessed in the primitive past and since lost.

The result was troublesome but a quite harmless irritation. On very rare occasions however, Mannon added, this proximity produced in the human a sort of artificial telepathic faculty—that was, he could some-times receive thoughts from the telepath to whom he had been exposed, but of no other being. The faculty was in all cases strictly temporary, and disappeared when the being responsible for bringing it about left the human.

"But these cases of induced telepathy are extremely rare," Mannon concluded, "and obviously you are getting only the irritant by-product, otherwise you might know what Arretapec is playing at simply by reading his mind . . ."

While Dr. Mannon had been talking, and relieved of the worry that he had caught some strange new disease, Conway's mind had been working furiously. Vaguely, as odd events with Arretapec and the brontosaurus returned to his mind and were added to scraps of the VUXG's conver-sations and his own studying of the life—and extinction—of Earth's long-gone race of giant reptiles, a picture was forming in his mind. It was a crazy—or at least cockeyed—picture, and it was still incomplete, but what else *could* a being like Arretapec be doing to a patient like the bronto-saurus, a patient who had nothing at all wrong with it?

"Pardon?" Conway said. He had become aware that Mannon had said something which he had not caught.

"I said if you find out what Arretapec is doing, let me know," Man-non repeated.

"Oh, I know what it's doing," said Conway. "At least I think I do—and I understand why Arretapec does not want to talk about it. The ridicule if it tried and failed, why even the idea of its trying is ridiculous. What I don't know is *why* it is doing it . . ."

"Dr. Conway," said Mannon in a deceptively mild voice, "if you don't tell me what you're talking about I will, as our cruder-minded interns so succinctly put it, have your guts for garters."

Conway stood up quickly. He had to get back to Arretapec without further delay. Now that he had a rough idea of what was going on there were things he must see to—urgent safety precautions that a being such as the VUXG might not think of. Absently, he said, "I'm sorry, sir, I can't tell you. You see, from what you've told me there is a possibility that my knowledge derives directly from Arretapec's mind, telepathically, and is therefore privileged information. I've got to rush now, but thanks very much."

Once outside Conway practically ran to the nearest communicator and called Maintenance. The voice which answered he recognized as belonging to the engineer Colonel he had met earlier. He said quickly, "Is the hull of that converted transport strong enough to take the shock of a body of approximately eight thousand pounds moving at, uh, anything between twenty and one hundred miles an hour, and what safety measures can you take against such an occurrence?"

There was a long, loaded silence, then, "Are you kidding? It would go through the hull like so much plywood. But in the event of a major puncture like that the volume of air inside the ship is such that there would be plenty of time for the maintenance people to get into suits. Why do you ask?"

Conway thought quickly. He wanted a job done but did not want to tell why. He told the Colonel that he was worried about the gravity grids which maintained the artificial gravity inside the ship. There were so many of them that if one section should accidentally reverse its polarity and fling the brontosaurus away from it instead of holding it down . . .

Rather testily the Colonel agreed that the gravity grids could be switched to repulsion, also focused into pressor or attractor beams, but that the changeover did not occur simply because somebody breathed on them. There were safety devices incorporated which . . .

"All the same," Conway broke in, "I would feel much safer about things if you could fix all the gravity grids so that at the approach of a heavy falling body they would automatically switch over to repulsion— just in case the worst happens. Is that possible?"

"Is this an order?" said the Colonel, "or are you just the worrying type?"

"It's an order, I'm afraid," said Conway.

"Then it's possible." A sharp click put a full stop to the conversation.

Conway set out to rejoin Arretapec again to become an ideal assistant to his chief in that he would have answers ready before the questions were asked. Also, he thought wryly, he would have to maneuver the VUXG into asking the proper questions so that he could answer them.

V

On the fifth day of their association, Conway said to Arretapec, "I have been assured that your patient is not suffering from either a physical condition or one requiring psychiatric correction, so that I am led to the conclusion that you are trying to effect some change in the brain structure by telepathic, or some related means. If my conclusions are correct, I have information which might aid or at least interest you:

"There was a giant reptile similar to the patient which lived on my own planet in primitive times. From remains unearthed by archaeologists we know that it possessed, or required, a second nerve center several times as big as the brain proper in the region of the sacral vertebrae, presumably to handle movements of the hind legs, tail and so on. If such was the case here you might have two brains to deal with instead of one."

As he waited for Arretapec to reply Conway gave thanks that the VUXG belonged to a highly ethical species which did not hold with using their telepathy on non-telepaths, otherwise the being would have known that Conway *knew* that their patient had two nerve-centers—that he knew because while Arretapec had been slowly eating another hole in his desk one night and Conway and the patient had been asleep, a colleague of Conway's had surreptitiously used an X-ray scanner and camera on the unsuspecting dinosaur.

"Your conclusions are correct," said Arretapec at last, "and your information is interesting. I had not thought it possible for one entity to possess two brains. However this would explain the unusual difficulty of communication I have with this creature. I will investigate."

Conway felt the itching start inside his head again, but now that he knew what it was he was able to take it without "fidgeting." The itch died away and Arretapec said, "I am getting a response. For the first time I am getting a response." The itching sensation began inside his skull again and slowly built up, and up . . .

It wasn't just like ants with red-hot pincers chewing at his brain cells, Conway thought agonizedly as he fought to keep from moving and distracting Arretapec now that the being appeared to be getting somewhere;

it felt as though somebody was punching holes in his poor, quivering brain with a rusty nail. It had never been like this before, this was sheer torture.

Then suddenly there was a subtle change in the sensations. Not a lessening, but of something added. Conway had a brief, blinding glimpse of something—it was like a phrase of great music played on a damaged recording, or the beauty of a masterpiece that is cracked and disfigured almost beyond recognition. He knew that for an instant, through the distorting waves of pain, he had actually seen into Arretapec's mind.

Now he knew *everything* . . .

The VUXG continued to have responses all that day, but they were erratic, violent and uncontrolled. After one particular dramatic response had caused the panicky dinosaur to level a couple of acres of trees, then sent it charging into the lake in terror, Arretapec called a halt.

"It is useless," said the doctor. "The being will not use what I am trying to teach it for itself, and when I force the process it becomes afraid."

There was no emotion in the flat, Translated tones, but Conway who had had a glimpse of Arretapec's mind knew the bitter disappointment that the other felt. He wished desperately that he could help, but he knew that he could do nothing directly of assistance—Arretapec was the one who had to do the real work in this case, he could only prod things along now and then. He was still wracking his brain for an answer to the problem when he turned in that night, and just before he went to sleep he thought he found it.

Next morning they tracked down Dr. Mannon just as he was entering the DBLF operating theater. Conway said, "Sir, can we borrow your dog?"

"Business or pleasure?" said Mannon suspiciously. He was very attached to his dog, so much so that non-human members of the staff suspected a symbiotic relationship.

"We won't hurt it at all," said Conway reassuringly.

"Thanks." He took the lead from the appendage of the Tralthan intern holding it, then said to Arretapec, "Now back to my room . . ."

Ten minutes later the dog, barking furiously, was dashing around Conway's room while Conway himself hurled cushions and pillows at it. Suddenly one connected fairly, bowling it over. Paws scrabbling and skidding on the plastic flooring it erupted into frantic burst of high-pitched yelps and snarls.

Conway found himself whipped off his feet and suspended eight feet up in mid-air.

"I did not realize," boomed the voice of Arretapec from his position on the desk, "that you had intended this to be a demonstration of Earth-human sadism. I am shocked, horrified. You will release this unfortunate animal at once."

Conway said, "Put me down and I'll explain..."

On the eighth day they returned the dog to Dr. Mannon and went back to work on the dinosaur. At the end of the second week they were still working and Arretapec, Conway and their patient were being talked, whistled, cheeped and grunted about in every language in use at the hospital. They were in the dining hall one day when Conway became aware that the annunciator which had been droning out messages in the background was now calling his name.

"... O'Mara on the intercom," it was saying monotonously, "Doctor Conway, please. Would you contact Major O'Mara on the intercom as soon as possible..."

"Excuse me," Conway said to Arretapec, who was nestling on the plastic block which the catering superintendent had rather pointedly placed at Conway's table, and headed for the nearest communicator.

"It isn't a life-and-death matter," said O'Mara when he called and asked what was wrong. "I would like to have some things explained to me. For instance:

"Dr. Hardin is practically frothing at the mouth because the food-vegetation which he plants and replenishes so carefully has now got to be sprayed with some chemical which will render it less pleasant to taste, and why is a certain amount of the vegetation kept at its full flavor but in storage? What are you doing with a tri-di projector? And where does Mannon's dog fit into this?" O'Mara paused, reluctantly, for breath, then went on, "And Colonel Skempton says that his engineers are run ragged setting up tractor and pressor beam mounts for you two—not that he minds that so much, but he says that if all that gadgetry was pointed outward instead of inward that hulk you're messing around in could take on and lick a Federation cruiser.

"And his men, well..." O'Mara was holding his tone to a conversational level, but it was obvious that he was having trouble doing so. ". . . Quite a few of them are having to consult me professionally. Some of them, the lucky ones perhaps, just don't believe their eyes. The others would *much* prefer pink elephants."

There was a short silence, then O'Mara said, "Mannon tells me that you climbed onto your ethical high horse and wouldn't say a thing when he asked you. I was wondering—"

"I'm sorry, sir," said Conway awkwardly.

"But what the blinding blue blazes are you *doing*?" O'Mara erupted, then, "Well, good luck with it anyway. Off."

Conway hurried to rejoin Arretapec and take up the conversation where it had been left off. As they were leaving a little later, Conway said, "It was stupid of me not to take the size factor into consideration. But now that we have—"

"Stupid of us, friend Conway," Arretapec corrected in its toneless voice. "Most of your ideas have worked out successfully so far. You have been of invaluable assistance to me, so that I sometimes think that you have guessed my purpose. I am hoping that this idea, also, will work."

"We'll keep our fingers crossed."

On this occasion Arretapec did not, as it usually did, point out that firstly it did not believe in luck and secondly that it possessed no fingers. Arretapec was definitely growing more understanding of the ways of humans. And Conway now wished that the high-minded VUXG would read his mind, just so that the being would know how much he was with it in this, how much he wanted Arretapec's experiment to succeed this afternoon.

Conway could feel the tension mounting in him all the way to the ship. When he was giving the engineers and maintenance men their final instructions and making sure that they knew what to do in any emergency, he knew that he was joking a bit too much and laughing a little too heartily. But then everyone was showing signs of strain. A little later, however, as he stood less than fifty yards from the patient and with equipment festooning him like a Christmas tree—an anti-gravity pack belted around his waist, a tri-di projector locus and viewer strapped to his chest and his shoulders hung with a heavy radio pack—his tension had reached the point of immobility and outward calm of the spring which can be wound no tighter.

"Projector crew ready," said a voice.

"The food's in place," came another.

"All tractor and pressor beam men on top line," reported a third.

"Right, Doctor," Conway said to the hovering Arretapec, and ran a suddenly dry tongue around drier lips. "Do your stuff."

He pressed a stud on the locus mechanism on his chest and immediately there sprang into being around and above him the immaterial image of a Conway who was fifty feet high. He saw the patient's head go up, heard the low-pitched whinnying sound that it made when agitated or afraid and which contrasted so oddly with its bulk, and saw it backing ponderously toward the water's edge. But Arretapec was radiating furiously at the brontosaur's two small, almost rudimentary brains—sending out great waves of calm and reassurance—and the great reptile grew quiet. Very slowly so as not to alarm it, Conway went through the motions of reaching behind him, picking something up and placing it well in front of him. Above and around him his fifty-foot image did the same.

But where the image's great hand came down there was a bundle of greenery, and when the solid-seeming but immaterial hand moved upward the bundle followed it, kept in position at the apex of three delicately manipulated pressor beams. The fresh, moist bundle of plants and palm fronds was placed close to the still uneasy dinosaur, apparently by the hand which then withdrew. After what seemed like an eternity to the waiting Conway the massive, sinuous neck arched downward. It began poking at the greenery. It began to nibble . . .

Conway went through the same motions again, and again. All the time he and his fifty-foot image kept edging closer.

The brontosaur, he knew, could at a pinch eat the vegetation which grew around it, but since Dr. Hardin's sprayer had gone into operation it wasn't very nice stuff. But it could tell that these titbits were the real, old stuff; the fresh, juicy, sweet-smelling food that it used to know which had so unaccountably disappeared of late. Its nibbles became hungry gobblings.

Conway said, "All right. Stage Two . . ."

VI

Using the tiny viewer which showed his image's relationship to the dinosaur as a guide, Conway reached forward again. High up and invisible on the opposite wall of the hull another pressor beam went into operation, synchronizing its movements with the hand which was now apparently stroking the patient's great neck, and administering a firm but gentle pressure. After an initial instant of panic the patient went back to eating, and occasionally shuddering a little. Arretapec reported that it was enjoying the sensation.

"Now," said Conway, "We'll start playing rough."

Two great hands were placed against its side and massed pressors toppled it over with a ground-shaking crash. In real terror now it threshed and heaved madly in a vain attempt to get its ponderous and ungainly body upright on its feet. But instead of inflicting mortal damage, the great hands continued only to stroke and pat. The brontosaur had quieted and was showing signs of enjoying itself again when the hands moved to a new position. Tractor and pressor beams both seized the recumbent body, yanked it upright and toppled it onto the opposite side.

Using the anti-gravity belt to increase his mobility, Conway began hopping over and around the brontosaur, with Arretapec, who was in rapport with the patient, reporting constantly on the effects of the various stimuli. He stroked, patted, pummeled and pushed at the giant reptile with blown-up, immaterial hands and feet. He yanked its tail and he slapped its neck, and all the time the tractor and pressor crews kept perfect time with him . . .

Something like this had occurred before, not to mention other things which, it was rumored, had driven one engineer to drink and at least four off it. But it was not until the size factor had been taken into consideration as it had today with this monster tri-di projection that there had been such promising results. Previously it had been as if a mouse were manhandling a St. Bernard during the past week or so—no wonder the brontosaurus had been in a frenzy of panic when all sorts of inexplicable things had been happening to it and the only reason it could see for them was two tiny creatures that were just barely visible to it!

But the patient's species had roamed its home planet for a hundred million years, and it personally was immensely long-lived. Although its two brains were tiny it was really much smarter than a dog, so that very soon Conway had it trying to sit and beg.

And two hours later the brontosaurus took off.

It rose rapidly from the ground, a monstrous, ungainly and indescribable object with its massive legs making involuntary walking movements and the great neck and tail hanging down and waving slowly. Obviously it was the brain in the sacral area and not the cranium which was handling the levitation, Conway thought, as the great reptile approached the bunch of palm fronds which were balanced tantalizingly two hundred feet above its head. But that was a detail, it was levitating, that was the main thing. Unless—

"Are you helping?" Conway said sharply to Arretapec.

"No."

The reply was flat and emotionless by necessity, but had the VUXG been human it would have been a yell of sheer triumph.

"Good old Emily!" somebody shouted in Conway's phones, probably one of the beam operators, then, "Look, she's passing it!"

The brontosaur had missed the suspended bundle of foliage and was still rising fast. It made a clumsy, convulsive attempt to reach it in passing, which had set up a definite spin. Further wild movements of neck and tail were aggravating it...

"Better get her down out of there," said a second voice urgently. "That artificial sun could scorch her tail off."

"...And that spin is making it panicky," agreed Conway. "Tractor beam men...!"

But he was too late. Sun, earth and sky were careening in wild, twisting loops around a being which had been hitherto accustomed to solid ground under its feet. It wanted down or up, or *somewhere*. Despite Arretapec's frantic attempts to soothe it, it teleported again.

Conway saw the great mountain of flesh and bone go hurtling off at a tangent, at least four times faster than its original speed. He yelled, "H-sector men! Cushion it down, *gently*."

But there was neither time nor space for the pressor beam men to slow it down gently. To keep it from crashing fatally to the surface—also through the underlying plating and out into space outside—they had to slow it down steadily but firmly, and to the brontosaurus that necessarily sharp braking must have felt like a physical blow. It teleported again.

"C-sector, it's coming at you!"

But at C it was a repetition of what happened with H, the beast panicked and shot off in another direction. And so it went on, with the great reptile rocketing from one side of the ship's interior to the other until...

"Skempton here," said a brisk authoritative voice. "My men say the pressor beam mounts were not designed to stand this sort of thing. Insufficiently braced. The hull plating has sprung in eight places."

"Can't you—"

"We're sealing the leaks as fast as we can," Skempton cut in, answering Conway's question before he could ask it. "But this battering is shaking the ship apart . . ."

Dr. Arretapec joined in at that point.

"Doctor Conway," the being said, "while it is obvious that the patient has shown a surprising aptitude with its new talent, its use is uncontrolled because of its fear and confusion. This traumatic experience will cause irreparable damage, I am convinced, to the being's thinking processes . . ."

"Conway, *look out!*"

The reptile had come to a halt near ground level a few hundred yards away, then shot off at right angles toward Conway's position. But it was traveling a straight line inside a hollow sphere, and the surface was curving up to meet it. Conway saw the hurtling body lurch and spin as the beam operators sought desperately to check its velocity. Then suddenly the mighty body was ripping through the low, thickly-growing trees, then it was plowing a wide, shallow furrow through the soft, swampy ground and with a small mountain of earth-uprooted vegetation piling up in front of it, Conway was right in its path.

Before he could adjust the control of his anti-gravity pack the ground came up and fell on him. For a few minutes he was too dazed to realize why it was he couldn't move, then he saw that he was buried to the waist in a sticky cement of splintered branches and muddy earth. The heavings and shudderings he felt in the ground were the brontosaurus climbing to its feet. He looked up to see the great mass towering over him, saw it turn awkwardly and heard the sucking and crackling noises as the massive, pile-driver legs drove almost knee deep into the soil and underbrush.

Emily was heading for the lake again, and between the water and it was Conway . . .

He shouted and struggled in a frenzied attempt to attract attention, because the anti-grav and radio were smashed and he was stuck fast. The great reptilian mountain rolled up to him, the immense, slowly-waving neck was cutting off the light and one gigantic forefoot was poised to both kill and bury him in one operation, then Conway was yanked suddenly upward and to the side to where a prune in a gob of syrup was floating in the air.

"In the excitement of the moment," Arretapec said, "I had forgotten that you require a mechanical device to teleport. Please accept my apologies."

"Q-quite all right," said Conway shakily. He made an effort to steady his jumping nerves, then caught sight of a pressor beam crew on the surface below him. He called suddenly, "Get another radio and projector locus here, quick!"

Ten minutes later he was bruised, battered but ready to continue again. He stood at the water's edge with Arretapec hovering at his shoulder and his fifty-foot image again rising above him. The VUXG doctor, in rapport with the brontosaur under the surface of the lake, reported that success or failure hung in the balance. The patient had gone through what was to it a mind-wrecking experience, but the fact that it was now in what it felt to be the safety of underwater—where it had hitherto sought refuge from hunger and attacks of its enemies—was, together with the mental reassurances of Arretapec, exerting a steadying influence.

At times hopefully, at others in utter despair, Conway waited. Sometimes the strength of his feelings made him swear. It would not have been so bad, meant so much to him, if he hadn't caught that glimpse of what Arretapec's purpose had been, or if he had not grown to like the rather prim and over-condescending ball of goo so much. But any being with a mind like that who intended doing what it hoped to do had a right to be condescending.

Abruptly the huge head broke surface and the enormous body heaved itself onto the bank. Slowly, ponderously, the hind legs bent double and the long, tapering neck stretched upward. The brontosaurus wanted to play again.

Something caught in Conway's throat. He looked to where a dozen bundles of succulent greenery lay ready for use, with one already being maneuverd toward him. He waved his arm abruptly and said, "Oh, give it the whole lot, it deserves them . . ."

". . . So that when Arretapec saw the conditions on the patient's world," Conway said a little stiffly, "and its precognitive faculty told him what the brontosaur's most likely future would be, it just had to try to change it."

Conway was in the Chief Psychologist's office making a preliminary, verbal report and the intent faces of O'Mara, Hardin, Skempton and the hospital's Director encircled him. He felt anything but comfortable as, clearing his throat, he went on, "But Arretapec belongs to an old, proud race, and being telepathic added to its sensitivity—telepaths really *feel* what others think about them. What Arretapec proposed doing was so radical, it would leave itself and its race open to such ridicule if it failed, that it just had to be secretive. Conditions on the brontosaur's planet indicated that there would be no rise of an intelligent life-form after the great reptiles became extinct, and geologically speaking that extinction would not be long delayed. The patient's species had been around for a long time—that armored tail and amphibious nature had allowed it to survive more predatory and specialized contemporaries—but climatic changes were imminent and it could not follow the sun toward the equator because the planetary surface was composed of a large number of island continents. A brontosaurus could not cross an ocean. But if these giant reptiles could be made to develop the psi faculty of teleportation, the ocean barrier would disappear and with it the danger from the encroaching cold and shortage of food. It was this which Dr. Arretapec succeeded in doing."

O'Mara broke in at that point: "If Arretapec gave the brontosaurus the teleportive ability by working directly on its brain, why can't the same be done for us?"

"Probably because we've managed fine without it," replied Conway. "The patient, on the other hand, was shown and made to understand that this faculty was necessary for its survival. Once this is realized the ability will be used and passed on, because it is latent in nearly all species. Now that Arretapec has proved the idea possible his whole race will want to get in on it. Fostering intelligence on what would otherwise be a dead planet is the sort of *big* project which appeals to those high-minded types . . ."

Conway was thinking of that single, precognitive glimpse he had had into Arretapec's mind, of the civilization which would develop on the brontosaur's world and the monstrous yet strangely graceful beings that it would contain in some far, far, future day. But he did not mention these thoughts aloud. Instead he said, "Like most telepaths Arretapec was both squeamish and inclined to discount purely physical methods of investigation. It was not until I introduced him to Dr. Mannon's dog, and pointed out that a good way to get an animal to use a new ability was to teach it tricks with it, that we got anywhere. I showed that trick where I throw cushions at the dog and after wrestling with them for a while it arranges them in a heap and lets me throw it on top of them, thus demonstrating that simple-minded creatures don't mind—within limits, that is—a little roughhousing—"

"So that," said O'Mara, gazing reflectively at the ceiling, "is what you do in your spare time . . ."

Colonel Skempton coughed. He said, "You're playing down your own part in this. Your foresight in stuffing that hulk with tractor and pressor beams . . ."

"There's just one other thing before I see it off," Conway broke in hastily. "Arretapec heard some of the men calling the patient Emily. It would like to know why."

"It would," said O'Mara disgustedly. He pursed his lips then went on, "Apparently one of the maintenance men with an appetite for early fiction—the Brontë sisters, Charlotte, Emily and Anne to be exact—dubbed our patient Emily Brontosaurus. I must say that I feel a pathological interest in a mind which thinks like that . . ." O'Mara looked as though there was a bad smell in the room.

Conway groaned in sympathy. As he turned to go, he thought that his last and hardest job might be in explaining what a pun was to the high-minded Dr. Arretapec.

Next day Arretapec and the dinosaur left, the Monitor transport officer whose job it was to keep the hospital supplied heaved a great sigh of relief, and Conway found himself on ward duty again. But this time he was something more than a medical mechanic. He had been placed in charge of a section of the Nursery, and although he had to use data, drugs and case-histories supplied by Thornnastor, the Diagnostician-in-Charge of Pathology, there was nobody breathing directly down his neck. He could walk through his section and tell himself that these were *his* wards. And O'Mara had even promised him an assistant . . . !

". . . It has been apparent since you first arrived here," the Major had told him, "that you mix more readily with e-ts than with members of your own species. Saddling you with Dr. Arretapec was a test, which you passed with honors, and the assistant I'll be giving you in a few days might be another."

O'Mara had paused then, shook his head wonderingly and went on, "Not only do you get on exceptionally well with e-ts, but I don't hear a single whisper on the grapevine of you chasing the females of our species . . ."

"I don't have the time," said Conway seriously. "I doubt if I ever will."

"Oh, well, misogyny is an allowable neurosis," O'Mara had replied, then had gone onto discuss the new assistant. Subsequently Conway had returned to his wards and worked much harder than if there had been a Senior Physician breathing down his neck. He was too busy to hear the rumors which began to go around regarding the odd patient who had been admitted to Observation Ward Three.

CHAPTER 4

VISITOR AT LARGE

Despite the vast resources of medical and surgical skill available, resources which were acknowledged second to none anywhere in the civilized Galaxy, there had to be times when a case arrived in Sector General for which nothing whatever could be done. This particular patient was of classification SRTT, which was a physiological type never before encountered in the hospital. It was amoebic, possessed the ability to extrude any limbs, sensory organs or protective tegument necessary to the environment in which it found itself, and was so fantastically adaptable that it was difficult to imagine how one of these beings could ever fall sick in the first place.

The lack of symptoms was the most baffling aspect of the case. There was in evidence none of the visually alarming growths of malfunctionings to which so many of the extraterrestrial species were prone, nor were there any bacteria present in what could be considered harmful quantities. Instead the patient was simply *melting*—quietly, cleanly and without fuss or bother, like a piece of ice left in a warm room, its body was literally turning to water. Nothing that was tried had any effect in halting the process and, while they continued their attempts at finding a cure with even greater intensity, the Diagnosticians and lesser doctors in attendance had begun to realize a little sadly that the run of medical miracles produced with such monotonous regularity by Sector Twelve General Hospital was due to be broken.

And it was for that reason alone that one of the strictest rules of the hospital was temporarily relaxed.

"I suppose the best place to start is at the beginning," said Dr. Conway, trying hard not to stare at the iridescent and not quite atrophied wings of his new assistant. "At Reception, where the problems of admittance are dealt with."

Conway waited to see if the other had any comments, and continuing to walk in the direction of the stated objective while doing so. Rather than walk beside his companion he maintained a two-yard lead—not out of any wish to give offense but for the simple reason that he was afraid of inflicting severe physical damage on his assistant if he strayed any closer than that.

The new assistant was a GLNO—six-legged, exoskeletal and insect-like, with the empathic faculty—from the planet Cinruss. The gravity-pull of its home world was less than one-twelfth Earth-normal, which was the reason for an insect species growing to such size and becoming dominant, so that it wore two anti-G belts to neutralize the attraction which would otherwise have mashed it into ruin against the corridor floor. One neutralizer belt would have been adequate for this purpose, but Conway did not blame the being one bit for wanting to play safe. It was a spindly, awkward-looking and incredibly fragile life-form, and its name was Dr. Prilicla.

Prilicla had previous experience both in planetary and in the smaller multi-environment hospitals and so was not completely green, Conway had been told, but it would naturally feel at a loss before the size and complexity of Sector General. Conway was to be its guide and mentor for a while and then, when his present period of duty in charge of the nursery was complete, he would hand over Prilicla. Apparently the hospital's Director had decided that light-gravity life-forms with their extreme sensitivity and delicacy of touch would be particularly suited to the care and handling of the more fragile e-t embryos.

It was a good idea, Conway thought as he hastily interposed himself between Prilicla and a Tralthan intern who lumbered past on six elephantine feet, if the low-gravity life-form in question could survive the association with its more massive and clumsy colleagues.

"You understand," said Conway as he guided the GLNO toward Reception's control room, "that getting some of the patients into the place is a problem in itself. It isn't so bad with the small ones, but Tralthans, or a forty-foot-long AUGL from Chalderescol . . ." Conway broke off suddenly and said, "Here we are."

Through a wide, transparent wall section could be seen a room containing three massive control desks, only one of which was currently occupied. The being before it was a Nidian, and a group of indicator lights showed that it had just made contact with a ship approaching the hospital.

Conway said, "Listen . . ."

"Identify yourself, please," said the red teddy bear in its staccato, barking speech, which was filtered through Conway's Translator as flat and toneless English and which came to Prilicla as equally unemotionless Cinrusskin. "Patient, visitor or Staff, and species?"

"Visitor," came the reply, "and Human."

There was a second's pause, then: "Give your physiological classification please," said the red-furred receptionist with a wink toward the two watchers. "All intelligent races refer to their own species as human and think of all others as being nonhuman, so that what you call yourself has no meaning . . ."

Conway only half heard the conversation after that because he was so engrossed in trying to visualize what a being with that classification could look like. The double-T meant that both its shape and physical characteristics were variable, R that it had high heat and pressure tolerance, and the S in that combination . . . ! If there had not actually been one waiting outside, Conway would not have believed such a weird beastie could exist.

And the visitor was an important person, apparently, because the receptionist was now busily engaged in passing on the news of its arrival to various beings within the hospital—most of whom were Diagnosticians, no less. All at once Conway was intensely curious to see this highly unusual being, but thought that he would not be showing a very good example to Prilicla if he dashed off on a rubbernecking expedition when they had work to do elsewhere. Also, his assistant was still very much an unknown quantity where Conway was concerned—Prilicla might be one of those touchy individuals who held that to look at a member of another species for no other reason than to satisfy mere curiosity was a grievous insult . . .

"If it would not interfere with more urgent duties," broke in the flat, translated voice of Prilicla, "I would very much like to see this visitor."

Bless you! thought Conway, but outwardly pretended to mull over the latter. Finally he said, "Normally I could not allow that, but as the lock where the SRTT is entering is not far from here and there is some time to spare before we are due at our wards, I expect it will be all right to indulge your curiosity just this once. Please follow me, Doctor."

As he waved goodbye to the furry receptionist, Conway thought that it was a very good thing that Prilicla's Translator was incapable of transferring the strongly ironic content of those last words, so that the other was not aware what a rise Conway was taking out of him. And then suddenly he stopped in his mental tracks. Prilicla, he realized uncomfortably, was an empath. The being had not said very much since they had met a short time ago, but everything that it had said had backed up Conway's feelings in the particular matter under discussion. His new assistant was not a telepath—it could not read thoughts—but it was sensitive to feelings and emotions and would therefore have been aware of Conway's curiosity.

Conway felt like kicking himself for forgetting that empathic faculty, and wryly wondered just who had been taking the rise out of which.

He had to console himself with the thought that at least he was agreeable, and not like some of the people he had been attached to recently like Dr. Arretapec.

Lock Six, where the SRTT was to be admitted, could have been reached in a few minutes if Conway had used the shortcut through the water-filled corridor leading to the AUGL operating room and across the surgical ward of the chlorine-breathing PVSJs. But it would have meant donning one of the lightweight diving suits for protection, and while he could climb in and out of such a suit in no time at all, he very much doubted if the ultra-leggy Prilicla could do so. They therefore had to take the long way round, and hurry.

At one point a Tralthan wearing the gold-edged armband of a Diagnostician and an Earth-human maintenance engineer overtook them, the FGLI charging along like a runaway tank and the Earthman having to trot to keep up. Conway and Prilicla stood aside respectfully to allow the Diagnostician to pass—as well as to avoid being flattened—and then continued. A scrap of overheard conversation identified the two beings as part of the arriving SRTT's reception committee, and from the somewhat caustic tone of the Earth-human's remarks it was obvious that the visitor had arrived earlier than expected.

When they turned a corner a few seconds later and came within sight of the great entry lock Conway saw a sight which made him smile in spite of himself. Three corridors converged on the antechamber of Lock Six on this level as well as two others on upper and lower levels which reached it via sloping ramps, and figures were hurrying along each one. As well as the Tralthan and Earthman who had just passed them there was another Tralthan, two of the DBLF caterpillars and a spiny, membranous Illensan in a transparent protective suit—who had just emerged from the adjacent chlorine-filled corridor of the PVSJ section—all heading for the inner seal of the big Lock, already swinging open on the expected visitor. To Conway it seemed to be a wildly ludicrous situation, and he had a sudden mental picture of the whole crazy menagerie of them coming together with a crash in the same spot at the same time . . .

Then while he was still smiling at the thought, comedy changed swiftly and without warning to tragedy.

II

As the visitor entered the antechamber and the seal closed behind it Conway saw something that was a little like a crocodile with horn-tipped tentacles and a lot like nothing he had ever seen before. He saw the being shrink away from the figures hurrying to meet it, then suddenly dart toward the PVSJ—who was, Conway was to remember later, both the nearest and the smallest. Everybody seemed to be shouting at once then, so much so that Conway's and presumably everyone else's Translators went into an ear-piercing squeal of oscillation through sheer overload.

Faced by the teeth and hard-tipped tentacles of the charging visitor the Illensan PVSJ, no doubt thinking of the flimsiness of the envelope which held its life-saving chlorine around it, fled back into the intercorridor lock for the safety of its own section. The visitor, its way suddenly blocked by a Tralthan booming unheard reassurances at it, turned suddenly and scuttled for the same airlock . . .

All such locks were fitted with rapid action controls in case of emergency, controls which caused one door to open and the other to shut simultaneously instead of waiting for the chamber to be evacuated and refilled with the required atmosphere. The PVSJ, with the berserk visitor close behind it and its suit already torn by the SRTT's teeth so that it was in imminent danger of dying from oxygen poisoning, rightly considered his case to be an emergency and activated the rapid-action controls. It was perhaps too frightened to notice that the visitor was not completely into the lock, and that when the inner door opened the outer one would neatly cut the visitor in two . . .

There was so much shouting and confusion around the lock that Conway did not see who the quick-thinking person was who saved the visitor's life by pressing yet another emergency button, the one which caused both doors to open together. This action kept the SRTT from being cut in two, but there was now a direct opening into the PVSJ section from which billowed thick, yellow clouds of chlorine gas. Before Conway could react, contamination detectors in the corridor walls touched off the alarm siren and simultaneously closed the air-tight doors in the immediate vicinity, and they were all neatly trapped.

For a wild moment Conway fought the urge to run to the air-tight doors and beat on them with his fists. Then he thought of plunging through that poisonous fog to another intersection lock which was on the other side of it. But he could see a maintenance man and one of the DBLF caterpillars in it already, both so overcome with chlorine that Conway doubted if they could live long enough to put on the suits. Could he, he wondered sickly, get over there? The lock chamber also contained helmets good for ten minutes or so—that was demanded by the safety regulations—but to do it he would have to hold his breath for at least three minutes and keep his eyes jammed shut, because if he got a single whiff of that gas or it got at his eyes he would be helplessly disabled. But how could he pass that heaving, struggling mass of Tralthan legs and tentacles spread across the corridor floor while groping about with his eyes shut . . . ?

The fear-filled chaos of his thoughts was interrupted by Prilicla, who said, "Chlorine is lethal to my species. Please excuse me."

Prilicla was doing something peculiar to itself. The long, many-jointed legs were waving and jerking about as though performing some weird ritual dance and two of the four manipulatory appendages—whose possession was the reason for its species' fame as surgeons—were doing complicated things with what looked like rolls of transparent plastic sheeting. Conway did not see exactly how it happened but suddenly his GLNO assistant was swathed in a loose, transparent cover through which protruded its six legs and two manipulators—its body, wings and other two members, which were busily engaged in spraying sealing solution on the leg openings, were completely covered by it. The loose covering bellied out and became taut, proving that it was air-tight.

"I didn't know you had..." Conway began, then with a surge of hope bursting up within him he gabbled, "Listen. Do exactly as I tell you. You've got to get me a helmet, *quickly* ..."

But the hope died just as suddenly before he finished giving the GLNO his instructions. Prilicla could doubtless find a helmet for him, but how could the being ever hope to make it to the lock where they were kept through that struggling mass on the floor between. One blow could tear off a leg or cave in that flimsy exoskeleton like an eggshell. He couldn't ask the GLNO to do it, it would be murder.

He was about to cancel all previous instructions and tell the GLNO to stay put and save itself when Prilicla dashed across the corridor floor, ran diagonally up the wall and disappeared into the chlorine fog traveling along the ceiling. Conway reminded himself that many insect life-forms possessed sucker-tipped feet and began to feel hopeful again, so much so that other sensations began to register.

Close beside him the wall annunciator was informing everyone in the hospital that there was contamination in the region of Lock Six, while below it the intercom unit was emitting red light and harsh buzzing sounds as somebody in Maintenance Division tried to find out whether or not the contaminated area was occupied. The drifting gas was almost on him as Conway snatched at the intercom mike.

"Quiet and listen!" he shouted. "Conway here, at Lock Six. Two FGLIs, two DBLFs, one DBDG all with chlorine poisoning not yet fatal. One PVSJ in damaged protective suit with oxy-poisoning and possibly other injuries, and one up there—"

A sudden stinging sensation in the eyes made Conway drop the mike hurriedly. He backed away until stopped by the airtight door and watched the yellow mist creep nearer. He could see practically nothing of what was going on down the corridor now, and an agonizing eternity seemed to go by before the spindly shape of Prilicla came swinging along the ceiling above him.

III

The helmet which Prilicla brought was in a reality a mask, a mask with a self-contained air supply which, when in position, adhered firmly along the edge of the hair line, cheeks and lower jaw. Its air was good only for a very limited time—ten minutes or so—but with it on and the danger of death temporarily removed, Conway discovered that he could think much more clearly.

His first action was to go through the still open intersection lock. The PVSJ inside it was motionless and with the gray blush, the beginning of a type of skin cancer, spreading over its body. To the PVSJ life-form oxygen was vicious stuff. As gently as possible he dragged the Illensan into its own section and to a nearby storage compartment which he remembered being there. Pressure in this section was slightly greater than that maintained for warm-blooded oxygen-breathers so that where the PVSJ was concerned the air here was reasonably pure. Conway shut it in the compartment, after first grabbing an armful of the woven plastic sheets, in this section the equivalent of bed linen. There was no sign of the SRTT.

Back in the other corridor he explained to Prilicla what he wanted done—the Earth-human he had seen earlier had succeeded in donning his suit, but was blundering about, eyes streaming and coughing violently and was obviously incapable of giving any assistance. Conway picked his way around the weakly moving or unconscious bodies to the seal of Lock Six and opened it. There was a neatly racked row of air-bottles on the wall inside. He lifted down two of them and staggered out.

Prilicla had one unconscious form already covered with a sheet. Conway cracked the valve of an air-bottle and slid it under the covering, then watched as the plastic sheet bellied and rippled slightly with the air being released underneath it. It was the crudest possible form of oxygen tent, Conway thought, but the best that could be done at the moment. He left for more bottles.

After the third trip Conway began to notice the warning signs. He was sweating profusely, his head was splitting and big black splotches were beginning to blot out his vision—his air supply was running out. It was high time he took off the emergency helmet, stuck his own head under a sheet like the others and waited for the rescuers to arrive. He took a few steps toward the nearest sheeted figure, and the floor hit him. His heart was banging thunderously in his chest, his lungs were on fire and all at once he didn't even have the strength to pull off the helmet . . .

Conway was forced from his state of deep and oddly comfortable unconsciousness by pain: something was making strong and repeated attempts to cave in his chest. He stuck it just as long as he could, then opened his eyes and said, "Get off me, dammit, I'm all right!"

The hefty intern who had been enthusiastically engaged in giving Conway artificial respiration climbed to his feet. He said, "When we arrived, daddy-longlegs here said you had ceased to emote. I was worried about you for a moment—well, slightly worried." He grinned and added, "If you can walk and talk, O'Mara wants to see you."

Conway grunted and rose to his feet. Blowers and filtering apparatus had been set up in the corridor and were rapidly clearing the air of the last vestiges of chlorine and the casualties were being removed, some on tented stretcher-carriers and others being assisted by their rescuers. He fingered the raw area of forehead caused by the hurried removal of his helmet and took a few great gulps of air just to reassure himself that the nightmare of a few minutes ago was really over.

"Thank you, Doctor," he said feelingly.

"Don't mention it, Doctor," said the intern.

They found O'Mara in the Educator Room. The Chief Psychologist wasted no time on preliminaries. He pointed to a chair for Conway and indicated a sort of surrealistic wastepaper basket to Prilicla and barked, "What happened?"

The room was in shadow except for the glow of indicator lights on the Educator equipment and a single lamp on O'Mara's desk. All Conway could see of the psychologist as he began his story was two hard, competent hands projecting from the sleeves of a dark green uniform and a pair of steady gray eyes in a shadowed face. The hands did not move and the eyes never left him while Conway was speaking.

When he was finished O'Mara sighed and was silent for several seconds, then he said, "There were four of our top Diagnosticians at Lock Six just then, beings this hospital could ill afford to lose. The prompt action you took certainly saved at least three of their lives, so you're a couple of heroes. But I'll spare your blushes and not belabor that point. Neither," he added dryly, "will I embarrass you by asking what you were doing there in the first place."

Conway coughed. He said, "What I'd like to know is why the SRTT ran amok like that. Because of the crowd running to meet it, I'd say, except that no intelligent, civilized being would behave like that. The only visitors we allow here are either government people or visiting specialists, neither of which are the type to be scared at the sight of an alien life-form. And why so many Diagnosticians to meet it in the first place?"

"They were there," replied O'Mara, "because they were anxious to see what an SRTT looked like when it was not trying to look like something else. This data might have aided them in a case they are working on. Also, with a hitherto unknown life-form like that it is impossible to guess at what made it act as it did. And finally, it is not the type of visitor which we allow here, but we had to break the rules this time because its parent is in the hospital, a terminal case."

Conway said softly, "I see."

A Monitor Lieutenant came into the room at that point and hurried across to O'Mara. "Excuse me, sir," he said. "I've been able to find one item which may help us with the search for the visitor. A DBLF nurse reports seeing a PVSJ moving away from the area of the accident at about the right time. To one of the DBLF caterpillars the PVSJs are anything but pretty, as you know, but the nurse says that this one looked worse than usual, a real freak. So much so that the DBLF was sure that it was a patient suffering from something pretty terrible—"

"You checked that we have no PVSJ suffering from the malady described?"

"Yes, sir. There is no such case."

O'Mara looked suddenly grim. He said, "Very good, Carson, you know what to do next," and nodded dismissal.

Conway had been finding it hard to contain himself during the conversation, and with the departure of the Lieutenant he burst out, "The thing I saw come out of the air-lock had tentacles and . . . and . . . Well, it wasn't anything like a PVSJ. I know that an SRTT is able to modify its physical structure, of course, but so radically and in such a short time . . . !"

Abruptly O'Mara stood up. He said, "We know practically nothing about this life-form—its needs, capabilities or emotional response patterns—and it is high time we found out. I'm going to build a fire under Colinson in Communications to see what he can dig up; environment, evolutionary background, cultural and social influences and so on. We can't have a visitor running around loose like this, it's bound to make a nuisance of itself through sheer ignorance.

"But what I want you two to do is this," he went on. "Keep an eye open for any odd-looking patients or embryos in the Nursery sections. Lieutenant Carson has just left to get on the PA and make these instructions general. If you do find somebody who may be our SRTT approach them *gently*. Be reassuring, make no sudden moves and be sure to avoid confusing it, that only one of you talks at once. And contact me immediately."

When they were outside again Conway decided that nothing further could be done in the current work period, and postponing the rounds of their wards for another hour, led the way to the vast room which served as a dining hall for all the warm-blooded oxygen-breathers on the hospital's Staff. The place was, as usual, crowded, and although it was divided up into sections for the widely variant life-forms present, Conway could see many tables where three or four different classifications had come together—with extreme discomfort for some—to talk shop.

Conway pointed out a vacant table to Prilicla and began working toward it, only to have his assistant—aided by its still functional wings— get there before him and in time to foil two maintenance men making for the same spot. A few heads turned during this fifty yard flight, but only briefly—the diners were used to much stranger sights than that.

"I expect most of our food is suited to your metabolism," said Conway when he was seated, "but do you have any special preferences?"

Prilicla had, and Conway nearly choked when he heard them. But it was not the combination of well-cooked spaghetti and raw carrots that was so bad, it was the way the GLNO set about eating the spaghetti when it arrived. With all four eating appendages working furiously Prilicla wove it into a sort of rope which was passed into the being's beak-like mouth. Conway was not usually affected by this sort of thing, but the sight was definitely doing things to his stomach.

Suddenly Prilicla stopped. "My method of ingestion is disturbing you," it said. "I will go to another table—"

"No, no," said Conway quickly, realizing that his feelings had been picked up by the empath. "That won't be necessary, I assure you. But it is a point of etiquette here that, whenever it is possible, a being dining in mixed company uses the same eating tools as its host or senior at the table. Er, do you think you could manage a fork?"

Prilicla could manage a fork. Conway had never seen spaghetti disappear so fast.

From the subject of food the talk drifted not too unnaturally to the hospital's Diagnosticians and the Educator Tape system without which these august beings—and indeed the whole hospital—could not function.

Diagnosticians deservedly had the respect and admiration of everyone in the hospital—and a certain amount of the pity as well. For it was not simply knowledge which the Educator gave them, the whole personality of the entity who had possessed that knowledge was impressed on their brains as well. In effect the Diagnostician subjected himself or itself voluntarily to the most drastic type of multiple schizophrenia, and with the alien other components sharing their minds so utterly *different* in every respect that they often did not even share the same system of logic.

Their one and only common denominator was the need of all doctors, regardless of size, shape or number of legs, to cure the sick.

There was a DBDG Earth-human Diagnostician at a table nearby who was visibly having to force himself to eat a perfectly ordinary steak. Conway happened to know that this man was engaged on a case which necessitated using a large amount of the knowledge contained in the Tralthan physiology tape which he had been given. The use of this knowledge had brought into prominence within his mind the personality of the Tralthan who had furnished the brain record, and Tralthans abhorred meat in all its forms . . .

IV

After lunch Conway took Prilicla to the first of the wards to which they were assigned, and on the way continued to reel off more statistics and background information. The Hospital comprised three hundred and eighty-four levels and accurately reproduced the environments of the sixty-eight different forms of intelligent life currently known to the Galactic Federation. Conway was not trying to cow Prilicla with the vastness of the great hospital nor to boast, although he was intensely proud of the fact that he had gained a post in this very famous establishment. It was simply that he was uneasy about his assistant's means of protecting itself against the conditions it would shortly meet, and this was his way of working around to the subject.

But he need not have worried, for Prilicla demonstrated how the light, almost diaphanous, suit which had saved it at Lock Six could be strengthened from inside by a scaled-down adaptation of the type of force-field used as meteorite protection of interstellar ships. When necessary its legs could be folded so as to be within the protective covering as well, instead of projecting outside it as they had done at the lock.

While they were changing prior to entering the AUGL Nursery Ward, which was their first call, Conway began filling in his assistant on the case history of the occupants.

The fully-grown physiological type AUGL was a forty foot long, oviparous, armored fish-like life-form native of Chalderescol II, but the beings now in the ward for observation had been hatched only six weeks ago and measured only three feet. Two previous hatchings by the same mother had, as had this one, been in all respects normal and with the offspring seemingly in perfect health, yet two months later they had all died. A PM performed on their home world gave the cause of death as extreme calcification of the articular cartilage in practically every joint in the body, but had been unable to shed any light on the cause of death. Now Sector General was keeping a watchful eye on the latest hatching, and Conway was hoping that it would be a case of third time lucky.

"At present I look them over every day," Conway went on, "and on every third day take an AUGL tape and give them a thorough checkup. Now that you are assisting me this will also apply to you. But when you take this tape I'd advise you to have it erased immediately after the examination, unless you would *like* to wander around for the rest of the day with half of your brain convinced that you are a fish and wanting to act accordingly . . ."

"That would be an intriguing but no doubt confusing hybrid," agreed Prilicla. The GLNO was now enclosed completely—with the exception of two manipulators—in the bubble of its protective suit, which it had weighted sufficiently for it not to be hampered by too much buoyancy. Seeing that Conway was also ready, it operated the lock controls, and as they entered the great tank of warm, greenish water that was the AUGL ward it added, "Are the patients responding to treatment?"

Conway shook his head. Then realizing that the gesture probably meant nothing to the GLNO he said, "We are still at the exploratory stage—treatment has not yet begun. But I've had a few ideas, which I can't properly discuss with you until we both take the AUGL tape tomorrow and am fairly certain that two of our three patients will come through—in effect, one of them will have to be used as a guinea-pig in order to save the others. The symptoms appear and develop very quickly," he continued, "which is why I want such a close watch kept on them. Now that the danger point is so close I think I'll make it three-hourly, and we'll work out a timetable so's neither of us will miss too much sleep. You see, the quicker we spot the first symptoms the more time we have to act and the greater the possibility of saving all three of them. I'm very keen to do the hat-trick."

Prilicla wouldn't know what a hat-trick was either, Conway thought, but the being would quickly learn how to interpret his nods, gestures and figures of speech—Conway had had to do the same in his early days with e-t superiors, sometimes wondering fulminating why somebody did not make a tape on Alien Esoterics to aid junior interns in his position. But these were only surface thoughts. At the back of his mind, so steady and so sharp that it might have been painted there, was the picture of a young, almost embryonic life-form whose developing exoskeleton—the hundred or so flat, bony plates normally free to slide or move on flexible hinges of cartilage so as to allow mobility and breathing—was about to become a petrified fossil imprisoning, for a very short time, the frantic consciousness within . . .

"How can I assist you at the moment?" asked Prilicla, bringing Conway's mind back from near future to present time with a rush. The GLNO was eyeing the three thin, streamlined shapes darting about the great tank and obviously wondering how it was going to stop one long enough to examine it. It added, "They're fast, aren't they?"

"Yes, and very fragile," said Conway. "Also they are so young that for present purposes they can be considered mindless. They frighten easily and any attempt to approach them closely sends them into such a panic that they swim madly about until exhausted or injure themselves against the tank walls. What we have to do is lay a minefield . . ."

Quickly Conway explained and demonstrated how to place a pattern of anesthetic bulbs which dissolved in the water and how, gently and at a distance, to maneuver their elusive patients through it. Later, while they were examining the three small, unconscious forms and Conway saw how sensitive and precise was the touch of Prilicla's manipulators and the corresponding sharpness of the GLNO's mind, his hopes for all three of the infant AUGLs increased.

They left the warm and to Conway rather pleasant environment of the AUGLs for the "hot" ward of their section. This time the checking of the occupants was done with the aid of remote-controlled mechanisms from behind twenty feet of shielding. There was nothing of an urgent nature in this ward, and before leaving Conway pointed out the complicated masses of plumbing surrounding it. The maintenance division he explained, used the "hot" ward as a stand-by power pile to light and heat the hospital.

Constantly in the background the wall annunciators kept droning out the progress of the search for the SRTT visitor. It had not been found yet, and cases of mistaken identity and of beings seeing things were mounting steadily. Conway had not thought much about the SRTT since leaving O'Mara, but now he was beginning to feel a little anxious at the thought of what the runaway visitor might do in this section especially—not to mention what some of the infant patients might do to it. If only he knew more about it, had some idea of its militations. He decided to call O'Mara.

In reply to Conway's request the Chief Psychologist said, "Our latest information is that the SRTT life-form evolved on a planet with an eccentric orbit around its primary. Geologic, climatic and temperature changes were such that a high degree of adaptability was necessary for survival. Before they attained a civilization their means of defense was either to assume as frightening an aspect as possible or to copy the physical form of their attackers in the hope that they would escape detection in this way—protective mimicry being the favorite method of avoiding danger, and so often used that the process had become almost involuntary. There are some other items regarding mass and dimensions at different ages. They are a very long-lived species—and this not particularly helpful collection of data, which was digested from the report of the survey ship which discovered the planet, ends by saying that all the foregoing is for our information only and that these beings do not take sick."

O'Mara paused briefly, then added, "Hah!"

"I agree," said Conway.

"One item we have which might explain its panicking on arrival," O'Mara went on, "is that it is their custom for the very youngest to be present at the death of a parent rather than the eldest—there is an unusually strong emotional bond between parent and last-born. Estimates of mass place our runaway as being very young. Not a baby, of course, but definitely nowhere near maturity."

Conway was still digesting this when the Major continued, "As to its limitations, I'd say that the Methane section is too cold for it and the radioactive wards too hot—also that glorified turkish bath on level Eighteen where they breathe super-heated steam. Apart from those, your guess is as good as mine where it may turn up."

"It might help a little if I could see this SRTT's parent," Conway said. "Is that possible?"

There was a lengthy pause, then: "Just barely," said O'Mara dryly. "The immediate vicinity of that patient is literally crawling with Diagnosticians and other high-powered talent... But come up after you've finished your rounds and I'll try to fix it."

"Thank you, sir," said Conway and broke the circuit.

He still felt a vague uneasiness about the SRTT visitor, a dark premonition that he had not yet finished with this e-t juvenile delinquent who was the ultimate in quick-change artists. Maybe, he thought sourly, his current duties had brought out the mother in him, but at the thought of the havoc which that SRTT could cause—the damage to equipment and fittings, the interruption of important and closely-timed courses of treatment and the physical injury, perhaps even death, to the more fragile life-forms through its ignorant blundering about—Conway felt himself go a little sick.

For the failure to capture the runaway had made plain one very disquieting fact, and that was that the SRTT was not too young and immature not to know how to work the intersection locks...

Half angrily, Conway pushed these useless anxieties to the back of his mind and began explaining to Prilicla about the patients in the ward they were going to visit next, and the protective measures and examinative procedures necessary when handling them.

This ward contained twenty-eight infants of the FROB classification—low, squat, immensely strong beings with a horny covering that was like flexible armor plate. Adults of the species with their increased mass tended to be slow and ponderous, but the infants could move surprisingly fast despite the condition of four times Earth-normal gravity and pressure in which they lived. Heavy-duty suits were called for in these conditions and the floor level of the ward was never used by visiting physicians or nursing staff except in cases of the gravest emergency. Patients for examination were raised from the floor by a grab and lifting apparatus to the cupola set in the ceiling for this purpose, where they were anesthetized before the grab was released. This was done with a long, extremely strong needle which was inserted at the point where the inner side of the foreleg joined the trunk—one of the very few soft spots on the FROB's body.

"... I expect you to break a lot of needles before you get the hang of it," Conway added, "but don't worry about that, or think that you are hurting them. These little darlings are so tough that if a bomb went off beside them they would hardly blink."

Conway was silent for a few seconds while they walked briskly toward the FROB ward—Prilicla's six, multi-jointed and pencil-thin legs seeming to spread out all over the place, but somehow never actually getting underfoot. He no longer felt that he was walking on eggs when he was near the GLNO, or that the other would crumple up and blow away if he so much as brushed against it. Prilicla had demonstrated its ability to avoid all contacts likely to be physically harmful to it in a way which, now that Conway was becoming accustomed to it, was both dexterous and strangely graceful.

A man, he thought, could get used to working with anything.

"But to get back to our thick-skinned little friends," Conway resumed, "physical toughness in that species—especially in the younger age groups—is not accompanied by resistance to germ or virus infections. Later they develop the necessary antibodies and as adults are disgustingly healthy, but in the infant stage . . ."

"They catch everything," Prilicla put in. "And as soon as a new disease is discovered they get that, too."

Conway laughed. "I was forgetting that most e-t hospitals have their quota of FROBs and that you may already have had experience with them. You will know also that these diseases are rarely fatal to the infants, but that their cure is long, complicated, and not very rewarding, because they straightaway catch something else. None of our twenty-eight cases here are serious, and the reason that they are here rather than at a local hospital is that we are trying to produce a sort of shotgun serum which will artificially induce in them the immunity to infection which will eventually be theirs in later life and so . . . Stop!"

The word was sharp, low and urgent, a shouted whisper. Prilicla froze, its sucker-tipped legs gripping the corridor floor, and stared along with Conway at the being who had just appeared at the intersection ahead of them.

At first glance it looked like an Illensan. The shapeless, spiny body with the dry, rustling membrane joining upper and lower appendages belonged unmistakably to the PVSJ chlorine-breathers. But there were two eating tentacles which seemed to have been transplanted from an FGLI, a furry breast pad which was pure DBLF and it was breathing, as they were, an atmosphere rich in oxygen.

It could only be the runaway.

All the laws of physiology to the contrary Conway felt his heart battering at the back of his throat somewhere as, remembering O'Mara's strict orders not to frighten the being, he tried to think of something friendly and reassuring to say. But the SRTT took off immediately it caught sign of them, and all Conway could find to say was, "Quick, after it!"

At a dead run they reached the intersection and turned into the corridor taken by the fleeing SRTT, Prilicla scuttling along the ceiling again to keep out of the way of Conway's pounding feet. But the sight in front of them caused Conway to forget all about being gentle and reassuring, and he yelled, "Stop, you fool! Don't go in there . . . !"

The runaway was at the entrance to the FROB ward.

They reached the entry lock just too late and watched helplessly through the port as the SRTT opened the inner seal and, gripped by the four times normal gravity pull of the ward, was flung down out of sight. The inner door closed automatically then, allowing Prilicla and Conway to enter the lock and prepare for the environment within the ward.

Conway struggled frantically into the heavy duty suit which he kept in the lock chamber and quickly set the repulsion of its anti-gravity belt to compensate for the conditions inside. Prilicla, meanwhile, was doing similar things to its own equipment. While checking the seals and fastenings of the suit, and swearing at this very necessary waste of time, Conway could see through the inner inspection window a sight which made him shudder.

The pseudo-Illensan shape of the SRTT lay plastered against the floor. It was twitching slightly, and already one of the larger FROB infants was coming pounding up to investigate this odd-looking object. One of the great, spatulate feet must have trod on the recumbent SRTT, because it jerked away and began rapidly and incredibly to *change*. The weak, membranous appendages of the PVSJ seemed to dissolve into the main body which became the bony, lizard-like form with the wicked, horn-tipped tentacles which they had seen first at Lock Six. This was obviously the SRTT's most frightening manifestation.

But the infant FROB possessed nearly five times the other's mass and so could hardly be expected to be frightened. It put down its massive head and butted, sending the SRTT crashing against the wall plating twenty feet across the ward. The FROB wanted to play.

Both doctors were out of the lock and onto the ceiling catwalk now, where the view was much clearer. The SRTT was changing again, fast. The tentacled lizard shape had not worked at all well for it in four-G conditions against these infant behemoths and it was trying something else.

The FROB had closed in on it again and was watching fascinated.

V

Conway said urgently, "Doctor, can you handle the grab apparatus? Good! Then go to it . . ." As Prilicla scurried along the catwalk to the control cupola Conway set his anti-gravity controls to zero and called, "I'll direct you from below." Weightless now, he kicked himself toward the floor.

But Conway was no stranger to the FROB infant—very probably it disliked or was bored by this diminutive figure whose only game was that of sticking big needles in it while something big and strong held it still, and despite all of Conway's frantic shouting and arm-waving he found himself being ignored. But the other occupants of the ward were taking an interest, and their attention was being drawn to the still-changing SRTT . . .

"*No!*" Conway shouted, aghast at what the visitor was changing into. "No! Stop! *Change back . . . !*"

But it was too late. The whole ward seemed to be stampeding toward the SRTT, giving vent to a thunderous bedlam of excited growls and yelps which, from the older infants, were Translated into shouts of "Dolly! Dolly! Nice dolly . . . !"

Springing upward to avoid being trampled, Conway looked down on the milling mass of FROBs and felt the strong and sickening conviction that the luckless SRTT had departed this life. But no. The being had somehow managed to run—or squeeze—the gauntlet of stamping feet and eager, bludgeoning heads by keeping low and tightly pressed against the wall. It emerged battered but still in the shape which it had, chameleon-like, adopted in the mistaken idea that a tiny version of an FROB would be safe.

Conway called, "Quickly! Grab!"

But Prilicla was not sleeping on its job. The massive jaws of the grab were already hanging open above the dazed and slow-moving SRTT, and as Conway shouted they dropped and crashed shut. Conway sprang for one of the lifting cables and as they rose from the floor together he said hurriedly, "You're safe now. Relax. I'm here to help you . . ."

His reply was a sharp convulsion of the SRTT which nearly shook him loose, and suddenly the being had become a thing of lithe, oily convolutions which slipped between the fingers of the grab and slapped onto the floor. The FROBs hooted excitedly and charged again.

It could not possibly survive this time, Conway thought with a mixture of horror, pity and impatience; this being who had had one fright on arrival and who had not stopped running since, and who was still too utterly terrified even to be helped. The grab was useless but there was one other possibility. O'Mara would probably skin him alive for it, but he would at least be saving SRTT's life for the time being if he allowed it to escape.

On the wall opposite the entry lock which Prilicla and himself had used was the door through which the FROB patients were brought to the ward. It was a simple door because the corridor outside it, which led to the FROB operating theater, was maintained at the same level of gravity and pressure as was the ward. Conway dived across the intervening space to the controls and slid it open, watching the SRTT—who was not so insensible with fear that it missed seeing this way of escape—as it slithered through. He closed it again just in time to prevent some of the patients from getting out as well, then made for the control cupola to report the whole ghastly mess to O'Mara.

For the situation was now much worse than they all had thought. While he had been at the other end of the ward he had seen something which increased the difficulties of catching and pacifying the runaway many, many times, and which explained the visitor's lack of response to him while in the grab. It had been the shattered, trampled ruin of the SRTT's Translator pack.

Conway's hand was on the intercom switch when Prilicla said, "Excuse me, sir, but does my ability to detect your emotions cause you mental distress? Or does mentioning aloud what I may have found trouble you?"

"Eh? What?" said Conway. He thought that he must be radiating impatience at a furious rate at the moment, because his assistant had picked a great time to start asking questions like *that*! His first impulse was to cut the other off, but then he decided that delaying his report to O'Mara by a few seconds would not make any difference, and possibly Prilicla considered the matter important. Aliens were funny.

"No to both questions," Conway replied shortly. "Though in the sec-

ond instance I might be embarrassed if you made known your findings
to a third party in certain circumstances. Why do you ask?"

"Because I have been aware of your deep anxiety regarding the possible depredations of this SRTT among your patients," Prilicla said, "and
I am loath to further increase that anxiety by telling you of the type and
intensity of the emotions which I detected just now in the being's mind."

Conway sighed. "Spit it out, things couldn't be much worse than they
are now . . ."

But they could and were.

When Prilicla finished speaking Conway pulled his hand away from the
intercom switch as though it had grown teeth and bit him. "I can't tell
him *that* over the intercom!" he burst out. "It would be sure to leak to
the patients and if they, or even some of the Staff knew about it, there
would be a panic." He dithered for a moment, then cried, "Come on,
we've got to see O'Mara!"

But the Chief Psychologist was not in his office or in the nearby
Educator room. However, information supplied by one of his assistants
sent them hurrying to the forty-seventh level and Observation Ward
Three.

This was a vast, high-ceilinged room maintained at a pressure and
temperature suited to warm-blooded oxygen-breathers. DBDG, DBLF
and FGLI doctors carried out preliminary examinations here on the more
puzzling or exotic cases—the patients, if these atmospheric conditions
did not suit them, being housed in large, transparent cubicles spaced at
intervals around the walls and floor. It was known irreverently as the
Punch and Ponder department and Conway could see a group of medics
of all shapes and species gathered around a glass-walled tank in the middle
of the ward. This must be the older and dying SRTT he had heard about,
but he had no attention to spare for anything until he had spoken to
O'Mara.

He caught sight of the psychologist at a communications desk beside
the wall and hurried over.

While he talked O'Mara listened stolidly, several times opening his
mouth as though to interrupt, then each time closing it in a grimmer,
tighter line. But when Conway reached the point where he had seen the
broken Translator, O'Mara waved him to silence and hit the intercom
switch with the same jerky motion of his hand.

"Get me Engineering Division, Colonel Skempton," he barked. Then: "Colonel, our runaway is in the FROB nursery area. But there is a complication, I'm afraid—it has lost its Translator . . ." There was a short pause, then: "Neither do I know how I expect you to pacify it when you can't communicate, but do what you can in the meantime—I'm going to work on the communication angle now."

He snapped the switch off and then on again, and said, "Colinson, in Communications . . . hello, Major. I want a relay between here and the Monitor Survey team on the SRTT's home planet—yes, the one I had you collecting about a few hours ago. Will you arrange that? And have them prepare a sound tape in the SRTT native language—I'll give you the wording I want in a moment—and have them relay it here. The substance of the speech, which must be obtained from an adult SRTT, will have to be roughly as follows—"

He broke off as Major Colinson's voice erupted from the speaker. The communications man was reminding a certain desk-bound head-shrinker that the SRTT planet was halfway across the Galaxy, that subspace radio was susceptible to interference just like any other kind and that by the time every sun in the intervening distance had splattered the signal with their share of static it would be virtually unintelligible.

"Have them repeat the signal," O'Mara said. "There are sure to be usable words and phrases which we can piece together to reconstruct the original message. We need this thing badly, and I'll tell you why . . ."

The SRTT species were an extremely long-lived race, O'Mara explained quickly, who reproduced hermaphroditically at very great intervals and with great pain and effort. There was therefore a bond of great affection and—what was more important in the present circumstances—discipline between the adults and children of the species. There was also the belief, so strong as to be almost a certainty, that no matter what changes a member of this species worked it would always try to retain the vocal and aural organs which allowed it to communicate with its fellows.

Now if one of the adults on the home planet could prepare a few general remarks directed toward youths who misbehaved when they ought to have known better, and these were relayed to Sector General and in turn played over the PA to their runaway visitor, then the young SRTT's ingrained obedience to its elders would do the rest.

". . . And that," said O'Mara to Conway as he switched off, "should take care of that little crisis. With any luck we'll have our visitor quieted down within a few hours. So your troubles are over, you can relax ..."

The psychologist broke off at the expression on Conway's face, then he said softly, "There's more?"

Conway nodded. Indicating his assistant he said, "Dr. Prilicla detected it, by empathy. You must understand that the runaway is in a very bad way psychologically—grief for its dying parent, the fright it received at Lock Six when everyone came charging at it, and now the mauling it has undergone in the FROB nursery. It is young, immature, and these experiences have thrown it back to the stage where its responses are purely animal and ... well ..." Conway licked dry lips, "... has anyone calculated how long it has been since that SRTT has eaten?"

The implications of the question were not lost on O'Mara either. He paled suddenly and snatched up the mike again. "Get me Skempton again, quickly! ... Skempton? ... Colonel, I am not trying to sound melodramatic but would you use the scrambler attached to your set, there is another complication ..."

Turning away, Conway debated with himself whether to go over for a brief look at the dying SRTT or hurry back to his section. Back in the FROB nursery Prilicla had detected in the runaway's mind strong hunger radiation as well as the expected fear and confusion, and it had been the communication of these findings which had caused first Conway, then O'Mara and Skempton to realize just what a deadly menace the visitor had become. The youths of any species are notoriously selfish, cruel and uncivilized, Conway knew, and driven by steadily increasing pangs of hunger this one would certainly turn cannibal. In its present confused mental state the young SRTT would probably not know that it had done so, but that fact would make no difference at all to the patients concerned.

If only the majority of Conway's charges were not so small, defenseless and ... tasty.

On the other hand a look at the elder being might suggest some method of dealing with the younger—his curiosity regarding the SRTT terminal case having nothing to do with it, of course ...

He was maneuvering for a closer look at the patient inside the tank and at the same time trying not to jostle the Earth-human doctor who was blocking his view, when the man turned irritably and asked, "Why the blazes don't you climb up my back? ... Oh, hello, Conway. Here to contribute another uninformed wild guess, I suppose?"

It was Mannon, the doctor who had at one time been Conway's superior and was now a Senior Physician well on the way to achieving Diagnostician status. He had befriended Conway on his arrival at the hospital, Mannon had several times explained within Conway's hearing, because he had a soft spot for stray dogs, cats and interns. Currently he was allowed to retain permanently in his brain just three Educator tapes— that of a Tralthan specialist in micro-surgery and two belonging to surgeons of the low-gravity LSVO and MSVK species—so that for long periods of each day his reactions were quite human. At the moment he was eyeing Prilicla, who was skittering about on the fringe of the crowd, with raised eyebrows.

Conway began to give details regarding the character and accomplishments of his new assistant, but was interrupted by Mannon saying loudly, "That's enough, lad, you're beginning to sound like an unsolicited testimonial. A light touch and the empathic faculty will be a big help in your current line of work. I grant that. But then you always did pick odd associates; levitating balls of goo, insects, dinosaurs, and such like—all pretty peculiar people, you must admit. Except for that nurse on the twenty-third level, now I admire your taste there—"

"Are they making any headway with this case, sir?" Conway said, determinedly shunting the conversation back onto the main track again. Mannon was the best in the world, but he had the painful habit sometimes of pulling a person's leg until it threatened to come off at the hip.

"None," said Mannon. "And what I said about wild guesses is a fact. We're all making them here, and getting nowhere—ordinary diagnostic techniques are completely useless. Just look at the thing!"

Mannon moved aside for Conway, and a sensation as of a pencil being laid across his shoulder told him that Prilicla was behind him craning to see, too.

VI

The being in the tank was indescribable for the simple reason that it had obviously been trying to become several different things at once when the dissolution had begun. There were appendages both jointed and tentacular, patches of scales, spines and leathery, wrinkled tegument together with the suggestion of mouth and gill openings, all thrown together in a gruesome hodge-podge. Yet none of the physiological details were clear because the whole flaccid mass was softened, eroded away, like a wax model left too long in the heat. Moisture oozed from the patient's body continuously and trickled to the floor of the tank, where the water level was nearly six inches deep.

Conway swallowed and said, "Bearing in mind the adaptability of this species, its immunity to physical damage and so on, and considering the wildly mixed-up state of its body, I should say that there may be a strong possibility that the trouble stems from psychological causes."

Mannon looked him up and down slowly with an expression of awe on his face, then said, witheringly, "Psychological causes, hey? Amazing! Well, what else *could* cause a being who is immune both to physical damage and bacterial infection to get into this state except something wrong with its think tank? But perhaps you were going to be more specific?"

Conway felt his neck and ears getting warm. He said nothing.

Mannon grunted, then went on, "The water that it is melting into is just that, plus a few harmless organisms which are suspended in it. We've tried every method of physical and psychological treatment that we could think of, without results. At the moment someone is suggesting that we quick-freeze the patient, both to halt the melting and to give us more time to think of something else. This has been vetoed because in its present state such a course might kill the patient outright. We've had a couple of our telepathic life-forms try to tune to its mind with a view to straightening it out that way, and O'Mara has gone back to the dark ages to such a point that he has tried crude electro-shock therapy, but nothing works. Altogether we have brought, singly and acting in concert, the viewpoints of very nearly every species in the Galaxy, and still we can't get a line on what ails it . . ."

"If the trouble was psychological," put in Conway, "I should have thought that the telepaths—"

"No," said Mannon. "In this life-form the mind and memory function is evenly distributed throughout the whole body and not housed in a permanent brain casing, otherwise it could not accomplish such marked changes in its physical structure. At present the being's mind is withdrawing, draining away, into smaller and smaller units—so small that the telepaths cannot work them.

"This SRTT is a real weirdie," Mannon continued thoughtfully. "It evolved out of the sea, of course, but later its world saw outbreaks of volcanic activity, earthquakes—the surface being coated with sulfur and who knows what else—and finally a minor instability in their sun converted the planet into the desert which it now is. They had to be adaptable to survive all that. And their method of reproduction—a budding and splitting-off process which causes the loss of a sizable portion of the parent's mass—is interesting, too, because it means that the embryo is born with part of the body-and-brain cell structure of the parent. No conscious memories are passed to the newly-born but it retains unconsciously the memories which enable it to adapt—"

"But that means," Conway burst out, "that if the parent transfers a section of its body-and-mind to the offspring, then each individual's unconscious memory must go back—"

"And it is the unconscious which is the seat of all psychoses," interrupted O'Mara, who had come up behind them at that point. "Don't say any more, I have nightmares at the very idea. Imagine trying to analyze a patient whose subconscious mind goes back fifty thousand years . . . !"

The conversation dried up quickly after that and Conway, still anxious about the younger SRTT's activities, hurried back to the nursery section. The whole area was infested with maintenance men and green-uniformed Monitors, but the runaway had not been sighted again. Conway placed a DBDG nurse—the one Mannon was so fond of pulling his leg about, strangely enough—on duty in a diving suit at the AUGL ward, because he was expecting developments there at any time, and prepared with Prilicla to pay a call on the methane nursery.

Their work among the frigid-blooded beings in that ward was also routine, and during it Conway pestered Prilicla with questions about the emotional state of the elder SRTT they had just left. But the GLNO was very little help; all it would say was that it had detected an urge toward dissolution which it could not describe more fully to Conway because there was nothing in its own previous experience which it could relate the feeling to.

Outside again they discovered that Colinson had wasted no time. From the wall annunciators there poured out a staccato howl of static through which could be dimly heard an alien gobbling which was presumably the SRTT sound tape. Conway thought that if positions were reversed and he was a frightened small boy listening to a voice striving to speak to him through that incredible uproar, he would feel anything but reassured. And the atmosphere of the SRTT's home planet would almost certainly be of a different density to this one, which would further increase the distortion of the voice. He did not say anything to Prilicla, but Conway thought that it would be nothing less than a miracle if this cacophony produced the result which O'Mara had intended.

The racket cut off suddenly, was replaced by a voice in English which droned out, "Would Dr. Conway please go to the intercom," then it returned unabated. Conway hurried to the nearest set.

"This is Murchison in the AUGL lock, Doctor," said a worried female voice. "Somebody—I mean something—just went past me into the main ward. I thought it was you at first until it began opening the inner seal without putting on a suit, then I knew it must be the runaway SRTT." She hesitated, then said, "Considering the state of the patients inside I didn't give the alarm until checking with you, but I can call—"

"No, you did quite right, Nurse," Conway said quickly. "We'll be down at once."

When they arrived at the lock five minutes later, the nurse had a suit ready for Conway, and the combination of physiological features which made it impossible for the Earth-human members of the Staff to regard Murchison with anything like a clinical detachment were rendered slightly less distracting by her own protective suit. But Conway had eyes at the moment only for the inner inspection window and the thing which floated just inside it.

It was, or had been, very like Conway. The hair coloring was right, also the complexion, and it was in whites. But the features were out of proportion and ran together in a way that was quite horrible, and the neck and hands did not go into the tunic, they *became* the collar and sleeves of the garment. Conway was reminded of a lead figure that had been crudely fashioned and carelessly painted.

At the moment Conway knew that it was not a threat to the lives of the ward's tiny patients, but it was changing. There was a slow growing together of the arms and legs, a lengthening out and the sprouting of long, narrow protuberences which could only be the beginnings of fins. The AUGL patients might be difficult for an Earth-human DBDG to catch, but the SRTT was adapting to water also, and speed.

"Inside!" said Conway urgently. "We've got to herd it out of here before it—"

But Prilicla was making no attempt to begin the bodily contortions which would bring it inside its protective envelope. "I have detected an interesting change in the quality of its emotional radiation," the GLNO said suddenly. "There is still fear and confusion present, and an over-riding hunger . . ."

"Hunger . . . !" Murchison had not realized until then just what deadly danger the patients were in.

". . . But there is something else," Prilicla continued, disregarding the interruption. "I can only describe it as a background pleasure sensation coupled with that same urge toward dissolution which I detected a short time ago in its parent. But I am puzzled to account for this sudden change."

Conway's mind was on his three tiny patients, and the predatory form the SRTT was beginning to take. He said impatiently, "Probably because recent events have affected its sanity also, the pleasure trace being due possibly to a liking for the water—"

Abruptly he stopped, his mind racing too fast for words or even ordered logical thought. Rather it was a feverish jumble of facts, experiences and wild guesswork which boiled chaotically through his brain, then incredibly became still and cool and very, very clear as . . . the answer.

And yet none of the tremendous intellects in the observation ward could have found it, Conway was sure, because they were not present with an empathic assistant when a young SRTT close to insanity through fear and grief had been immersed suddenly in the tepid, yellow depths of the AUGL tank . . .

When an intelligent, mature and mentally complex being encounters unpleasant and hurtful facts of sufficient numbers and severity the result is a retreat from reality. First a striving to return to the simple, unwor-risome days of childhood and then, when that period turns out to be not nearly so carefree and uncomplicated as remembered, the ultimate retreat into the womb and the motionless, mindless condition of the catatonic. But to a mature SRTT the fetal position of catatonia could not be simple to attain, because its reproductive system was such that instead of the unborn offspring being in a state of warm, mindless comfort, it found itself part of its parent's mature adult body and called upon to share in the decisions and adjustments its parent had to make. Because the SRTT body, every single cell of it, was the mind and any sort of separation was impossible to a life-form whose every cell was interchangeable.

How divide a glass of water without pouring some off into another container?

The diseased intellect would be forced to retreat again and again, only to find that it had become involved in endless changes and adaptations in its efforts to return to this nonexistent womb. It would go back—far, far back—until it eventually did find the mindless state which it craved and its mind, which was inseparable from its body, became the warm water teeming with unicellular life from which it had originally evolved.

Now Conway knew the reason for the slow, melting dissolution of the terminal case upstairs. More, he thought he saw a way of solving the whole horrible mess. If he could only bank on the fact that, as was the case with most other species, a complex, mature mind tended to go insane faster than an undeveloped and youthful one . . .

He was only vaguely aware of going to the intercom again and calling O'Mara, and of Murchison and Prilicla drawing closer to him as he talked. Then he was waiting for what seemed like hours for the Chief Psychologist to absorb the information and react. Finally:

"An ingenious theory, Doctor," said O'Mara warmly. "More than that—I would say that that is exactly what has happened here, and no theorizing about it. The only pity is the understanding what has happened does nothing to aid the patient—"

"I've been thinking about that, too," Conway broke in eagerly, "and the way I see it the runaway is the most urgent problem now—if it isn't caught and pacified soon there are going to be serious casualties among the Staff and patients, in my section anyway, if nowhere else. Unfortunately, for technical reasons, your idea of calming it by means of a sound tape in its own language is not very successful up to now . . ."

"That's putting it kindly," said O'Mara dryly.

". . . But," went on Conway, "if this idea was modified so that the runaway was spoken to, reassured, by its parent upstairs. If we first cured the elder SRTT—"

"Cured the elder! What the blazes do you think we've been trying to do this past three weeks?" O'Mara demanded angrily. Then as the realization came that Conway was not trying to be funny or willfully stupid, that he sounded in deadly earnest, he said flatly, "Keep talking, Doctor."

Conway kept talking. When he had finished the intercom speaker registered the sound of a great, explosive sigh, then; "I think you've got the answer all right, and we've certainly got to try it despite the risks you mentioned," O'Mara said excitedly. Then abruptly his tones became clipped and efficient. "Take charge down there, Doctor. You know what you want done better than anyone else does. And use the DBLF recreation room on level fifty-nine—it's close to your section and can be evacuated quickly. We're going to tap in on the existing communications circuits so there will be no delay here, and the special equipment you want will be in the DBLF recreation room inside fifteen minutes. So you can start anytime, Conway . . ."

Before he was cut off he heard O'Mara begin issuing instructions to the effect that all Monitor Corps personnel and Staff in the nursery section were to be placed at the disposal of Doctors Conway and Prilicla, and he had barely turned away from the set before green-uniformed Monitors began crowding into the lock.

VII

The SRTT youth had somehow to be forced into the DBLF recreation room which was rapidly being booby-trapped for its benefit, and the first step was to get it out of the AUGL ward. This was accomplished by twelve Monitors swimming, sweating and cursing furiously in their heavy issue suits who chased awkwardly after it until they had it hemmed in at the point where the entry lock gave it the only avenue of escape.

Conway, Prilicla and another bunch of Monitors were waiting in the corridor outside when it came through, all garbed against any one of half a dozen environments through which the chase might lead them. Murchison had wanted to go, too—she had wanted to be in at the kill, she had stated—but Conway had told her sharply that her job was watching over the three AUGL patients and that she had better do just that.

He had not meant to lose his temper with Murchison like that, but he was on edge. If the idea he had been so enthusiastic about to O'Mara did not pan out there was a very good chance that there would be two incurable SRTT patients instead of one, and "in at the kill" had been an unfortunate choice of words.

The runaway had changed again—a semi-involuntary defense mechanism triggered off by the shapes of its pursuers—into a vaguely Earth-human form. It ran soggily along the corridor on legs which were too rubbery and which bent in the wrong places, and the scaly, dun-colored tegument it had worn in the AUGL tank was twitching and writhing and smoothing out into the pink and white of flesh and medical tunic. Conway could look on the most alien beings imaginable suffering from the most horrible maladies without inward distress, but the sight of the SRTT trying to become a human being as it ran made him fight to retain his lunch.

A sudden sideways dash into an MSVK corridor took them unawares and resulted in a kicking, floundering pile-up of pursuers beyond the inner seal of the connecting lock. The MSVK life-forms were tri-pedal, vaguely stork-like beings who required an extremely low gravity pull, and the DBDGs like Conway could not adjust to it immediately. But while Conway was still slowly falling all over the place the Monitors' space training enabled them to find their feet quickly. The SRTT was headed off into the oxygen section again.

It had been a bad few minutes while it lasted, Conway thought with relief, because the dim lighting and the opacity of the fog which the MSVKs called an atmosphere would have made the SRTT difficult to find if it had been lost to sight. If that had happened at this stage . . . Well, Conway preferred not to think about that.

But the DBLF recreation room was only minutes away now, and the SRTT was heading straight for it. The being was changing again, into something low and heavy which was moving on all fours. It seemed to be drawing itself in, condensing, and there was a suggestion of a carapace forming. It was still in that condition when two Monitors, yelling and waving their arms wildly, dashed suddenly out of an intersection and stampeded it into the corridor which contained the recreation room . . .

. . . And found it empty!

Conway swore luridly. There should have been half a dozen Monitors strung across that corridor to bar its way, but he had made such good time getting here that they were not in position yet. They were probably still inside the rec room placing their equipment, and the SRTT would go right past the doorway.

But he had not counted on the quick mind and even more agile body of Prilicla. His assistant must have realized the position in the same instant that he did. The little GLNO ran clicking down the corridor, rapidly overtaking the SRTT, then swinging up onto the ceiling until it had passed the runaway before dropping back. Conway tried to yell a warning, tried to shout that a fragile GLNO had no chance of heading off a being who was now the characteristics of an outsize and highly mobile armored crab, and that Prilicla was committing suicide. Then he saw what his assistant was aiming at.

There was a powered stretcher-carrier in its alcove about thirty feet ahead of the fleeing SRTT. He saw Prilicla skid to a halt beside it, hit the starter, then charge on. Prilicla was not being stupidly brave, it was being brainy and fast which was much better in these circumstances.

The stretcher-carrier, uncontrolled, lurched into motion and went wobbling across the corridor—right into the path of the charging SRTT. There was a metallic crash and a burst of dense yellow and black smoke as its heavy batteries shattered and shorted across. Before the fans could quite clear the air the Corpsmen were able to work around the stunned and nearly motionless runaway and herd it into the recreation room.

A few minutes later a Monitor officer approached Conway. He gave a jerk of his head which indicated the weird assortment of gadgetry which had been rushed to the compartment only minutes ago and which lay in neat piles around the room, and included the green-clad men ranged solidly against the walls—all facing toward the center of the big compartment where the SRTT rotated slowly in the exact center of the floor, seeking a way of escape. Quite obviously he was eaten up with curiosity, but his tone was carefully casual as he said, "Dr. Conway, I believe? Well, Doctor, what do you want us to do now?"

Conway moistened his lips. Up to now he had not thought much about this moment—he had thought that it would be easy to do this because the young SRTT had been such a menace to the hospital in general and caused so much trouble in his own section in particular. But now he was beginning to feel sorry for it. It was, after all, only a kid who had been sent out of control by a combination of grief, ignorance and panic. If this thing did not turn out right . . .

He shook off the feelings of doubt and inadequacy and said harshly, "You see that beastie in the middle of the room. I want it scared to death."

He had to elaborate, of course, but the Monitors got the idea very quickly and began using the equipment which had been sent them with great fervor and enthusiasm. Watching grimly, Conway identified items from Air Supply, Communications and the various diet kitchens, all being used for a purpose for which they had never been designed. There were things which emitted shrill whistles, siren howls of tremendous volumes and others which consisted simply of banging two metal trays together. To this fearful racket was added the whoops of the men wielding those noise-makers.

And there was no doubt that the SRTT was scared—Prilicla reported its emotional reactions constantly. But it was not scared enough.

"Quiet!" yelled Conway suddenly. "Start using the silent stuff!"

The preceding din had only been a primer. Now would come the really vicious stuff—but silent, because any noise made by the SRTT had to be heard.

Flares burst around the shaking figure in the middle of the floor, blindingly incandescent but of negligible heat. Simultaneously tractor and pressor beams pushed and pulled at it, sliding it back and forth across the floor, occasionally tossing it into mid-air or flattening it against the ceiling. The beams worked on the same principle as the gravity neutralizer belts, but were capable of much finer control and focus. Other beam operators began flinging lighted flares at the suspended, wildly struggling figure, only yanking them back or turning them aside at the last possible moment.

The SRTT was really frightened now, so frightened that even non-empaths could feel it. The shapes it was taking were going to give Conway nightmares for many weeks to come.

Conway lifted a hand mike to his lips and flicked the switch. "Any reaction up there yet?"

"Nothing yet," O'Mara's voice boomed from the speakers which had been set up around the room. "Whatever you're doing at the moment you'll have to step it up."

"But the being is in a condition of extreme distress . . ." began Prilicla.

Conway rounded on his assistant. "If you can't take it, leave!" he snapped.

"Steady, Conway," O'Mara's voice came sharply. "I know how you must feel, but remember that the end result will cancel all this out . . ."

"But if it doesn't work." Conway protested, then: "Oh never mind." To Prilicla he said, "I'm sorry." To the officer beside him he asked, "Can you think of any way of putting on more pressure?"

"I'd hate anything like that being done to me," said the Monitor tightly, "but I would suggest adding spin. Some species are utterly de-moralized by spin when they can take practically anything else . . ."

Spin was added to the pummeling which the SRTT was already under-going with the pressors—not a simple spin, but a wild, rolling, pitching movement which made Conway's stomach feel queasy just by looking at it, and the flares dived and swooped around it like insane moons around their primary. Quite a few of the men had lost their first enthusiasm, and Prilicla swayed and shook on its six pipe-stem legs, in the grip of an emotional gale which threatened to blow it away.

It had been wrong to bring Prilicla in on this, Conway told himself angrily; no empath should have to go through this sort of hell by proxy. He had made a mistake from the very first, because the whole idea was cruel and sadistic and *wrong*. He was worse than a monster...

High in the center of the room the twisting, spinning blur that was the younger SRTT began to emit a high-pitched and terrified gobbling noise.

A crashing bedlam erupted from the wall speakers; shouts, cries, breaking noises and the sounds of running feet over-laying that of something slower and infinitely heavier. They could hear O'Mara's voice shouting out some sort of explanation to somebody at the top of his lungs, then an unidentified voice yelled at them, "For Pete's sake stop it down there! Buster's papa has woke up and is wrecking the joint...!"

Quickly but gently they checked the spinning SRTT and lowered it to the floor, then they waited tensely while the shouting and crashing being relayed to them from Observation Ward Three reached a crescendo and began gradually to die down. Around the room men stood motionless watching each other, or the whimpering being on the floor, or the wall speakers, waiting. And then it came.

The sound was similar to the alien gobbling which had been relayed through the annunciators some hours previously, but without the accompanying roar of static, and because everyone had their Translators switched on the words also came through as English.

It was the elder SRTT, incurable no longer because it was physically whole again, speaking both reassuringly and chidingly to its erring offspring. In effect it was saying that junior had been a bad boy, that he must cease forthwith running around and getting himself and everyone else into a state, and that nothing else unpleasant would happen to him if he did as he was told by the beings now surrounding him. The sooner it did these things, the elder SRTT ended, the sooner they could both go home.

Mentally, the runaway had taken a terrible beating, Conway knew. Maybe it had taken too much. Tense with anxiety he watched it—still in a shape that was neither fish, flesh or fowl—begin humping its way across the floor. When it began gently and submissively to butt one of the watching Monitors in the knees, the cheer that went up very nearly gave it a relapse.

"When Prilicla here gave me the clue to what was troubling the elder SRTT, I was sure that the cure would have to be drastic," Conway said to the Diagnosticians and Senior Physicians ranged around and behind O'Mara's desk.

The fact that he was seated in such august company was a sure sign of the approval in which he was held, but despite that he still felt nervous as he went on. "Its regression toward the—to it—fetal state—complete dissolution into individual and unthinking cells floating in the primeval ocean—was far advanced, perhaps too far judging by its physical state. Major O'Mara had already tried various shock treatments which it, with its fantastically adaptable cell structure, was able to negate or ignore. My idea was to use the close physical and emotional bond which I discovered existed between the SRTT adult and its last-born offspring, and get at it that way."

Conway paused, his eyes drifting sideways briefly to take in the shambles around them. Observation Ward Three looked as though a bomb had hit it, and Conway knew that there had been a rather hectic few minutes here between the time the elder SRTT had come out of its catatonic state and explanations had been given it. He cleared his throat and went on:

"So we trapped the young one in the DBLF recreation room and tried to frighten it as much as possible, piping the sounds it made up here to the parent. It worked. The elder SRTT could not lie doing nothing while its latest and most loved offspring was apparently in frightful danger, and parental concern and affection overcame and destroyed the psychosis and forced it back to present time and reality. It was able to pacify the young one, and so all concerned were left happy."

"A nice piece of deductive reasoning on your part, Doctor," O'Mara said warmly. "You are to be commended..."

At that moment the intercom interrupted him. It was Murchison reporting that the three AUGLs were showing the first signs of stiffening up, and would he come at once. Conway requested an AUGL tape for Prilicla and himself, and explained the urgency of the matter. While they were taking them the Diagnosticians and Senior Physicians began to leave. A little disappointedly Conway thought that Murchison's call had spoiled what might have been his greatest moment.

"Don't worry about it, Doctor," O'Mara said cheerfully, reading his mind again. "If that call had come five minutes later your head would have been too swollen to take a physiology tape . . ."

Two days later Conway had his first and only disagreement with Dr. Prilicla. He insisted that without the aid of Prilicla's empathic faculty— an incredibly accurate and useful diagnostic tool—and Murchison's vigilance, the cure of all three AUGLs would not have been possible. The GLNO stated that, much as it was against its nature to oppose his superior's wishes, on this occasion Dr. Conway was completely mistaken. Murchison said that she was glad that she had been able to help, and could she please have some leave?

Conway said yes, then continued the argument with Prilicla, even though he knew he had no hope of winning it.

Conway honestly *knew* that he would not have been able to save the infant AUGLs without the little empath's help—he might not have saved any of them, in fact. But he was the Boss, and when a Boss and his assistants accomplish something the credit invariably goes to the Boss.

The argument, if that was the proper word for such an essentially friendly disagreement, raged for days. Things were going well in the Nursery and they hadn't anything of a serious nature to think about. They were not aware of the wreck which was then on its way to the hospital, or of the survivor it contained.

Nor did Conway know that within the next two weeks the whole Staff of the hospital would be despising him.

CHAPTER 5

OUT-PATIENT

The Monitor Corps cruiser *Sheldon* flicked into normal space some five hundred miles from Sector Twelve General Hospital, the wreck which was its reason for coming held gently against the hull within the field of its hyperdrive generators. At this distance the vast, brilliantly lit structure which floated in interstellar space at the galactic rim was only a dim blur of light, but that was because the Monitor Captain had had a close decision to make. Buried somewhere inside the wreck which he had brought in was a survivor urgently in need of medical attention. But like any good policeman his actions were constrained by possible effects on innocent bystanders—in this case the Staff and patients of the Galaxy's largest multi-environment hospital.

Hurriedly contacting Reception he explained the situation, and received their reassurances that the matter would be taken care of at once. Now that the welfare of the survivor was in competent hands, the Captain decided that he could return with a clear conscience to his examination of the wreck, which just might blow up in his face at any moment.

In the office of the hospital's Chief Psychologist, Dr. Conway sat uneasily on a very easy chair and watched the square, craggy features of O'Mara across an expanse of cluttered desk.

"Relax, Doctor," O'Mara said suddenly, obviously reading his thoughts. "If you were here for a carpeting I'd have given you a harder chair. On the contrary, I've been instructed to administer a hefty pat on the back. You've been up-graded, Doctor. Congratulations. You are now, Heaven help us all, a Senior Physician."

Before Conway could react to the news, the psychologist held up a large, square hand.

"In my own opinion a ghastly mistake has been made," he went on, "but seemingly your success with that dissolving SRTT and your part in the levitating dinosaur business has impressed the people upstairs—they think it was due to ability instead of sheer luck. As for me," he ended, grinning, "I wouldn't trust you with my appendix."

"You're too kind, sir," said Conway dryly.

O'Mara smiled again. "What do you expect, praise? My job is to shrink heads, not swell 'em. And now I suppose I'll have to give you a minute to adjust to your new glory..."

Conway was not slow in appreciating what this advance in status was going to mean to him. It pleased him, definitely—he had expected to do another two years before making Senior Physician. But he was a little frightened, too.

Henceforth he would wear an armband trimmed with red, have the right-of-way in corridors and dining halls over everyone other than fellow Seniors and Diagnosticians, and all the equipment or assistance he might need would be his for the asking. He would bear full responsibility for any patient left in his charge, with no possibility of ducking it or passing the buck. His personal freedom would be more constrained. He would have to lecture nurses, train junior interns, and almost certainly take part in one of the long-term research programs. These duties would necessitate his being in permanent possession of at least one physiology tape, probably two. *That* side of it, he knew, was not going to be pleasant.

Senior Physicians with permanent teaching duties were called on to retain one or two of these tapes continuously. That, Conway had heard, was no fun. The only thing which could be said for it was that he would be better off that a Diagnostician, the hospital's *elite*, one of the rare beings whose mind was considered stable enough to retain permanently six, seven or even ten Educator tapes simultaneously. To their data-crammed minds were given the job of original research in xenological medicine, and the diagnosis and treatment of new diseases in the hitherto unknown life-forms.

There was a well-known saying in the hospital, reputed to have originated with the Chief Psychologist himself, that anyone sane enough to want to be a Diagnostician was mad.

For it was not only physiological data which the Educator tapes imparted, but the complete memory and personality of the entity who had possessed that knowledge was impressed on their brains as well. In effect, a Diagnostician subjected himself or itself voluntarily to the most drastic form of multiple schizophrenia . . .

Suddenly O'Mara's voice broke in on his thoughts. ". . . And now that you feel three feet taller and are no doubt raring to go," the psychologist said, "I have a job for you. A wreck has been brought in which contains a survivor. Apparently the usual procedures for extricating it cannot be used. Physiological classification unknown—we haven't been able to identify the ship so have no idea what it eats, breathes or looks like. I want you to go over there and sort things out, with a view to transferring the being here as quickly as possible for treatment. We're told that its movements inside the wreckage are growing weaker," he ended briskly, "so treat the matter as urgent."

"Yes, sir," said Conway, rising quickly. At the door he paused. Later he was to wonder at his temerity in saying what he did to the Chief Psychologist, and decided that promotion must have gone to his head. As a parting shot he said exultantly, "I've *got* your lousy appendix. Kellerman took it out three years ago. He pickled it and put it up as a chess trophy. It's on my bookcase . . ."

O'Mara's only reaction was to incline his head, as if receiving a compliment.

Outside in the corridor Conway went to the nearest communicator and called Transport. He said, "This is Dr. Conway. I have an urgent outpatient case and need a tender. Also a nurse able to use an analyzer and with experience of fishing people out of wrecks, if possible. I'll be at Admission Lock Eight in a few minutes . . ."

Conway made good time to the lock, all things considered. Once he had to flatten himself against a corridor wall as a Tralthan Diagnostician lumbered absently past on its six, elephantine feet, the diminutive and nearly mindless OTSB life-form which lived in symbiosis with it clinging to its leathery back. Conway didn't mind giving way to a Diagnostician, and the Tralthan FGLI-OTSB combination were the finest surgeons in the Galaxy. Generally, however, the people he encountered—nurses of the DBLF classification mostly, and a few of the low-gravity, bird-like LSVOs—made way for him. Which showed what a very efficient grapevine the hospital possessed, because he was still wearing his old armband.

His swelling head was rapidly shrunk back to size by the entity waiting for him at Lock Eight. It was another of the furry, multi-pedal DBLF nurses, and it began hooting and whining immediately when he came into sight. The DBLF's own language was unintelligible, but Conway's Translator pack converted the sounds which it made—as it did all the other grunts, chirps and gobblings heard in the hospital—into English.

"I have been awaiting you for over seven minutes," it said. "They told me this was an emergency, yet I find you ambling along as if you had all the time in the world..."

Like all Translated speech the words had been flat and strained free of all emotional content. So the DBLF *could* have been joking, or half joking, or even making a simple statement of fact as it saw them with no disrespect intended. Conway doubted the last very strongly, but knew that losing his temper at this stage would be futile.

He took a deep breath and said, "I might have shortened your waiting period if I had run all the way. But I am against running for the reason that undue haste in a being in my position gives a bad impression— people tend to think I am in a panic over something and so feel unsure of my capabilities. So for the record," he ended dryly, "I wasn't ambling, I was walking with a confident, unhurried tread."

The sound which the DBLF made in reply was not Translatable.

Conway went through the boarding tube ahead of the nurse, and seconds later they shot away from the lock. In the tender's rear vision screen the sprawling mass of lights which was Sector General began to crawl together and shrink, and Conway started worrying.

This was not the first time he had been called to a wreck, and he knew the drill. But suddenly it was brought home to him that he would be solely responsible for what was to happen—he couldn't scream for help if something went wrong. Not that he had ever done that, but it had been comforting to know that he could have done so if necessary. He had an urgent desire to share some of his newly-acquired responsibility with someone—Dr. Prilicla, for instance, the gentle, spidery, emotion-sensitive who had been his assistant in the Nursery, or any of his other human and non-human colleagues.

During the trip to the wreck the DBLF, who told him that its name was Kursedd, tried Conway's patience sorely. The nurse was completely without tact, and although Conway knew the reason for this failing, it was still a little hard to take.

As a race Kursedd's species were not telepathic, but among themselves they could read each other's thoughts with a high degree of accuracy by the observation of expression. With four extensible eyes, two hearing antenna, a coat of fur which could lie silky smooth or stick out in spikes like a newly-bathed dog, plus various other highly flexible and expressive features—all of which they had very little control over—it was understandable that this caterpillar-like race had never learned diplomacy. Invariably they said exactly what they thought, because to another member of their race those thoughts were already plain anyhow, so that saying something different would have been stupid.

Then all at once they were sliding up to the Monitor cruiser and the wreck which hung beside it.

Apart from the bright orange coloring it looked pretty much like any other wreck he had seen, Conway thought; ships resembled people in that respect—a violent end stripped them of all individuality. He directed Kursedd to circle a few times, and moved to the forward observation panel.

At close range the internal structure of the wreck was revealed by the mishap which had practically sheered it in two, it was of dark and fairly normal-looking metal, so that the garish coloration of the hull must be due simply to paint. Conway filed that datum away carefully in his mind, because the shade of paint a being used could give an accurate guide to the range of its visual equipment, and the opacity or otherwise of its atmosphere. A few minutes later he decided that nothing further could be abstracted from an external examination of the ship, and signaled Kursedd to lock onto *Sheldon*.

The lock antechamber of the cruiser was small and made even more cramped by the crowd of green-uniformed Corpsmen staring, discussing and cautiously poking at an odd-looking mechanism—obviously something salvaged from the wreck—which was lying on the deck. The compartment buzzed with the technical jargon of half a dozen specialities and nobody paid any attention to the doctor and nurse until Conway cleared his throat loudly twice. Then an officer with Major's insignia, a thin-faced, graying man, detached himself from the crowd, and came toward them.

"Summerfield, Captain," he said crisply, giving the thing on the floor a fond backward glance as he spoke. "You, I take it, will be the high-powered medical types from the hospital?"

Conway felt irritated. He could understand these people's feelings, of course—a wrecked interstellar ship belonging to an unknown alien culture was a rare find indeed, a technological treasure trove on whose value no limit could be set. But Conway's mind was oriented differently; alien artifacts came a long way second in importance to the study, investigation and eventual restoration of alien life. That was why he got right down to business.

"Captain Summerfield," he said sharply, "we must ascertain and reproduce this survivor's living conditions as quickly as possible, both at the hospital and in the tender which will take it there. Could we have someone to show us over the wreck please. A fairly responsible officer, if possible, with a knowledge of—"

"Surely," Summerfield interrupted. He looked as if he was going to say something else, then he shrugged, turned, and barked, "Hendricks!" A Lieutenant wearing the bottom half of a spacesuit and a rather harassed expression joined them. The Captain performed brief introductions, then returned to the enigma on the floor.

Hendricks said, "We'll need heavy-duty suits. I can fit you Dr. Conway, but Dr. Kursedd is a DBLF . . ."

"There is no problem," Kursedd put in. "I have a suit in the tender. Give me five minutes."

The nurse wheeled and undulated toward the airlock, its fur rising and falling in slow waves which ran from the sparse hair at its neck to the bushier growth on the tail. Conway had been on the point of correcting Hendrick's mistake regarding Kursedd's status, but he suddenly realized that being called "Doctor" had elicited an intense emotional response from the DBLF—that rippling fur was certainly an expression of *something*! Not being a DBLF himself Conway could not tell whether the expression registered was one of pleasure or pride at being mistaken for a Doctor, or if the being was simply laughing one of its thirty-four legs off at the error. It wasn't a vital matter, so Conway decided to say nothing.

II

The next occasion that Hendricks addressed "Doctor" Kursedd was when they were entering the wreck, but this time the DBLF's expression was hidden by the casing of its spacesuit.

"What happened here?" Conway asked as he looked around curiously. "Accident, collision or what?"

"Our theory," Lieutenant Hendricks replied, "is that one of the two pairs of generators which maintained the ship in hyperspace during faster-than-light velocities failed for some reason. One half of the vessel was suddenly returned to normal space, which automatically meant that it was braked to a velocity far below that of light. The result was that the ship was ripped in two. The section containing the faulty generators was left behind," Hendricks went on, "because after the accident the remaining pair of generators must have remained functional for a second or so. Various safety devices must have gone into operation to seal off the damage, but the shock had practically shaken the whole ship to pieces so they weren't very successful. But an automatic distress signal was emitted which we were fortunate enough to hear, and obviously there is still pressure somewhere inside because we heard the survivor moving about. But the thing I can't help wondering about," he ended soberly, "is the condition of the other half of the wreck. It didn't, or couldn't, send out a distress signal or we would have heard it also. Someone might have survived in that section, too."

"A pity if they did," said Conway. Then, in a firmer voice, "But we're going to save this one. How do I get close to it?"

Hendricks checked their suits' anti-gravity belts and air tanks, then said, "You can't, at least not for some time. Follow me and I'll show you why."

O'Mara had made reference to difficulties in reaching the alien, Conway remembered, and he had assumed it was the normal trouble of wreckage blocking the way. But from the competent look of this Lieutenant in particular and the known efficiency of the Corps in general, he was sure that their troubles would not be ordinary.

Yet when they penetrated further into the wreck the ship's interior seemed remarkably clear. There was the usual loose stuff floating about, but no solid blockage. It was only when Conway looked closely at his surroundings that he was able to see the full extent of the damage. There was not one fitting, wall support or section of plating which was not either loose, cracked or sprung at the seams. And at the other end of the compartment they had just entered he could see where a heavy door had been burned through, with traces of the rapid-sealing goo used in setting up a temporary airlock showing all around it.

"That is our problem," Hendricks said, as Conway looked questioningly at him. "The disaster very nearly shook the ship apart. If we weren't in weightless conditions it would fall to pieces around us."

He broke off to go to the aid of Kursedd, who was having trouble getting through the hole in the door, then resumed, "All the air-tight doors must be closed automatically, but with the ship in this condition the fact of an air-tight door being closed does not necessarily mean that there is pressure on the other side of it. And while we think we have figured out the manual controls, we cannot be absolutely sure that opening one by this method will not cause every other door in the ship to open at the same time, with lethal results for the survivor."

In Conway's phones there was the sound of a short, heavy sigh, then the Lieutenant went on;

"We've been forced to set up locks outside every bulkhead we came to so that if there *should* be an atmosphere on the other side when we burn through, the pressure drop will be only fractional. But it's a very time-wasting business, and no short cuts are possible which would not risk the safety of the alien."

"Surely more rescue teams would be the answer," Conway said. "If there aren't enough on your ship we can bring them from the hospital. That would cut down the time required—"

"*No,* Doctor!" Hendricks said emphatically. "Why do you think we parked five hundred miles out? There is evidence of considerable power storage in this wreck and until we know exactly how and where, we have to go easy. We want to save the alien, you understand, but we don't want to blow it and ourselves up. Didn't they tell you about this at the hospital?"

Conway shook his head. "Maybe they didn't want me to worry."

Hendricks laughed. "Neither do I. Seriously, the chance of a blow-up is vanishingly small provided we take proper precautions. But with men swarming all over the wreck, burning and pulling it apart, it would be a near-certainty."

While the Lieutenant had been talking they passed through two other compartments and along a short corridor. Conway noticed that the interior of each room had a different color scheme. The survivor's race, he thought, must have highly individual notions regarding interior decoration.

He said, "When do you expect to get through to it?"

This was a simple question which required a long, complicated answer, Hendricks explained ruefully. The alien had made its presence known by noise—or more accurately, by the vibrations set up in the fabric of the ship by its movements. But the condition of the wreck plus the fact that its movements were of irregular duration and weakening made it impossible to judge its position with certainty. They were cutting a way toward the center of the wreck on the assumption that that was where an undamaged, air-tight compartment was most likely to be. Also, they were missing any later movements it made, which might have given them a fix on its position, because of the noise and vibration set up by the rescue team.

Boiled down, the answer was between three and seven hours.

And after they made contact with it, thought Conway, he had to sample, analyze and reproduce its atmosphere, ascertain its pressure and gravity requirements, prepare it for transfer to the hospital and do whatever he could for its injuries until it could be treated properly.

"Far too long," said Conway, aghast. The survivor could not be expected, in its steadily weakening state, to survive indefinitely. "We'll have to prepare accommodation without actually seeing our patient—there's nothing else for it. Now this is what we'll do . . ."

Rapidly, Conway gave instruction for tearing up sections of floor plating so as to bare the artificial gravity grids beneath. This sort of thing was not in his line, he told Hendricks, but no doubt the Lieutenant could make a fair guess at their output. There was only one known way of neutralizing gravity used by all the space-going races of the Galaxy; if the survivor's species had a different way of doing it then they might as well give up there and then.

". . . The physical characteristics of any life-form," he went on, "can be deduced from specimens of their food supply, the size and power demands of their artificial gravity grids, and air trapped in odd sections of piping. Enough data of this sort would enable us to reproduce its living conditions—"

"Some of the loose objects floating around must be food containers," Kursedd put in suddenly.

"That's the idea," Conway agreed. "But obtaining and analyzing a sample of air must come first. That way we'll have a rough idea of its metabolism, which should help you to tell which cans hold paint and which syrup . . . !"

Seconds later the search to detect and isolate the wreck's air-supply system was under way. The quantity of plumbing in any compartment of a space-ship was necessarily large, Conway knew, but the amount of piping which ran through even the smallest rooms in this ship left him feeling aston-ished by its complexity. The sight caused a vague stirring at the back of his mind, but either his association centers were not working properly or the stimulus was too weak for him to make anything out of it.

Conway and the others were working on the assumption that if a compartment could be sealed by air-tight bulkheads, then the pipelines supplying air to that section would be interrupted by cut-off valves where they entered and left it. The finding of a section of piping containing atmosphere was therefore only a matter of time. But the maze of plumb-ing all around them included control and power lines, some of which must still be live. So each section of piping had to be traced back to a break or other damage which allowed them to identify it as *not* belonging to the air-supply system. It was a long, exhausting process of elimination, and Conway raged inwardly at this sheerly mechanical puzzle on whose quick solution depended his patient's life. Furiously he wished that the team cutting into the wreck would contact the survivor, just so he could go back to being a fairly capable doctor instead of acting like an engineer with ten thumbs.

Two hours slipped by and they had the possibilities narrowed down to a single heavy pipe which was obviously the outlet, and a thick bundle of metal tubing which just had to bring the air in.

Apparently there were seven air inlets!

"A being that needs seven different chemical . . ." began Hendricks, and lapsed into a baffled silence.

"Only one line carries the main constituent," Conway said. "The others must contain necessary trace elements or inert components, such as the nitrogen in our own air. If those regulator valves you can see on each tube had not closed when the compartment lost pressure we could tell by the settings the proportions involved."

He spoke confidently, but Conway was not feeling that way. He had premonitions.

Kursedd moved forward. From its kit the nurse produced a small cutting torch, focused the flame to a six-inch, incandescent needle, then gently brought it into contact with one of the seven inlet pipes. Conway moved closer, an open sample flask held at the ready.

Yellowish vapor spurted suddenly and Conway pounced. His flask now held little more than a slightly soft vacuum, but there was enough of the gas caught inside for analysis purposes. Kursedd attacked another section of tubing.

"Judging by sight alone I would say that is chlorine," the DBLF said as it worked. "And if chlorine is the main constituent of its atmosphere then a modified PVSJ ward could take the survivor."

"Somehow," said Conway, "I don't think it will be as simple as that."

He had barely finished speaking when a high-pressure jet-white vapor filled the room with fog. Kursedd jerked back instinctively, pulling the flame away from the holed pipe, and the vapor changed to a clear liquid which bubbled out to hang as shrinking, furiously steaming globes all around them. They looked and acted like water, Conway thought, as he collected another sample.

With the third puncture the cutting flame, held momentarily in the jet of escaping gas, swelled and brightened visibly. That reaction was unmistakable.

"Oxygen," said Kursedd, putting Conway's thoughts into words, "or a high oxygen content."

"The water doesn't bother me," Hendricks put in, "but chlorine and oxy is a pretty unbreathable mixture."

"I agree," said Conway. "Any being who breathes chlorine finds oxygen lethal in a matter of seconds, and vice versa. But one of the gases might form a very small percentage of the whole, a mere trace. It is also possible that both gases are trace constituents and the main component hasn't turned up yet."

The four remaining lines were pierced and samples taken within a few minutes, during which Kursedd had obviously been pondering over Conway's statement. Just before it left for the tender and the analysis equipment therein the nurse paused.

"If these gases are in trace quantity only," it said in its toneless, Translated voice, "why are not all the trace and inert elements, even the oxidizer or its equivalent, pre-mixed and pumped in together as we and most other races do it? They all leave by one pipe."

Conway harrumphed. Precisely the same question had been bothering him, and he couldn't even begin to answer it. He said sharply, "Right now I want those samples analyzed, get moving on that. Lieutenant Hendricks and I will try to work out the physical size and pressure requirements of the being. And don't worry," he ended dryly, "all things will eventually become plain."

"Let us hope the answers come during curative surgery," Kursedd gave out as a parting shot, "and not at the post-mortem."

Without further urging Hendricks began lifting aside the buckled floor plating to get at the artificial gravity grids. Conway thought that he looked like a man who knew exactly what he was doing, so he left him to it and went looking for furniture.

III

The disaster had not been as other shipwrecks, where all movable objects together with a large number normally supposed to be immovable were lifted and hurled toward the point of impact. Here, instead, there had been a brief, savage shock which had disrupted the binding powers of practically every bolt, rivet and weld in the ship. Furniture, which was about the most easily damaged item in any ship, had suffered worst.

From a chair or bed could be told the shape, carriage and number of limbs of its user with fair accuracy, or if it possessed a hard tegument or required artificial padding for comfort. And a study of materials and design could give the gravity-pull which the being considered normal. But Conway was dead out of luck.

Some of the bits and pieces floating weightless in every compartment were almost certainly furniture, but they were so thoroughly mixed together that it was like trying to make sense of the scrambled parts of sixteen jigsaw puzzles. He thought of calling O'Mara, then decided against it. The Major would not be interested in how well he wasn't getting on.

He was searching the ruins of what might have been a row of lockers, hoping wistfully to strike a bonanza in the shape of clothing or an e-t pin-up picture, when Kursedd called.

"The analysis is complete," the nurse reported. "There is nothing unusual about the samples when considered separately. As a mixture they would be lethal to any species possessing a respiratory system. Mix them any way you want the result is a sludgy, poisonous mess."

"Be more explicit," said Conway sharply. "I want data, not opinions."

"As well as the gases already identified," Kursedd replied, "there is ammonia, CO_2, and two inerts. Together, and in any combination of which I can conceive, they form an atmosphere which is heavy, poisonous and highly opaque . . ."

"It can't be!" Conway snapped back. "You saw their interior paintwork, they used pastels a lot. Races living in an opaque atmosphere would not be sensitive to subtle variations of color—"

"Doctor Conway," Hendricks' voice broke in apologetically, "I've finished checking that grid. So far as I can tell it's rigged to pull five Gs."

A pull of five times Earth-normal gravity meant a proportionately high atmospheric pressure. The being must breathe a thick, poisonous soup—but a clear soup, he added hastily to himself. And there were other more immediate, and perhaps deadly, implications as well.

To Hendricks he said quickly, "Tell the rescue team to watch their step—without slowing down, if possible. Any beastie living under five Gs is apt to have muscles, and people in the survivor's position have been known to run amuck."

"I see what you mean," said Hendricks worriedly, and signed off. Conway returned to Kursedd.

"You heard the Lieutenant's report," he resumed in a quieter voice. "Try combinations under high pressure. And remember, we want a *clear* atmosphere!"

There was a long pause, then: "Very well. But I must add that I dislike wasting time, even when I am ordered to do so."

For several seconds Conway practiced savage self-restraint until a click in his phones told him that the DBLF had broken contact. Then he said a few words which, even had they been subjected to the emotion-filtering process of Translation, would have left no doubt in any e-t's mind that he was angry.

But slowly his rage toward this stupid, conceited, downright impertinent nurse he had been given began to fade. Perhaps Kursedd wasn't stupid, no matter what else it might be. Suppose it was right about the opacity of that atmosphere, where did that leave them? The answer was with yet another piece of contradictory evidence.

The whole wreck was stuffed with contradictions, Conway thought wearily. The design and construction did not suggest a high-G species, yet the artificial gravity grids could produce up to five Gs. And the interior color schemes pointed to a race possessing a visual range close to Conway's own. But the air they lived in, according to Kursedd, would need radar to see through. Not to mention a needlessly complex air-supply system and a bright orange outer hull . . .

For the twentieth time Conway tried to form a meaningful picture from the data at his disposal, in vain. Maybe if he attacked the problem from a different direction . . .

Abruptly he snapped on his radio's transmit switch and said, "Lieutenant Hendricks, will you connect me with the hospital, please. I want to talk to O'Mara. And I would like Captain Summerfield, yourself and Kursedd in on it, too. Can you arrange that?"

Hendricks made an affirmative noise and said, "Hang on a minute."

Interspersed by clicks, buzzes and bleeps, Conway heard the chopped-up voices of Hendricks, a Monitor radio officer on *Sheldon* calling up the hospital and requesting Summerfield to come to the radio room, and the flat, Translated tones of an e-t operator in the hospital itself. In a little under the stipulated minute the babble subsided and the stern, familiar voice of O'Mara barked, "Chief Psychologist here. Go ahead."

As briefly as possible Conway outlined the situation at the wreck, his lack of progress to date and the contradictory data they had uncovered. Then he went on, ". . . The rescue team is working toward the center of the wreck because that is the most likely place for the survivor to be. But it may be in a pocket off to one side somewhere and we may have to search every compartment in the ship to be sure of finding it. This could take many days. The survivor," he went on grimly, "if not already dead must be in a very bad way. We don't have that much time."

"You have a problem, Doctor. What are you going to do about it?"

"Well," Conway replied evasively, "a more general picture of the situation might help. If Captain Summerfield could tell me about the finding of the wreck—its position, course, or any personal impressions he can remember. For instance, would the extension each way of its direction of flight help us find its planet of origin? That would solve—"

"I'm afraid not, Doctor," Summerfield's voice came in. "Sighting backward we found that its course passed through a not-too-distant solar system. But this system had been mapped by us over a century previous and listed as a future possibility for colonization, which as you know means that it was devoid of intelligent life. No race can rise from nothing to a spaceship technology in one hundred years, so the wreck could not have originated in that system. Extending the line forward led nowhere—into intergalactic space, to be exact. In my opinion, the accident must have caused a violent change in course, so that the wreck's position and course when found will tell you nothing."

"So much for that idea," said Conway sadly, then in a more determined voice he went on, "But the other half of the wreck is out there somewhere. If we could find that, especially if it contained the body or bodies of other members of its crew, that would solve everything! I admit that it's a roundabout way to do it, but judging by our present rate of progress it might be the fastest way. I want a search made for the other half of the wreck," Conway ended, and waited for the storm to break.

Captain Summerfield demonstrated that he had the fastest reaction time by getting in the first blast.

"Impossible! You don't know what you're asking! It would take two hundred units or more—a whole Sector sub-fleet!—to cover that area in the time necessary to do you any good. And all this is just to find a dead specimen so you can analyze it and maybe help another specimen, which by that time might be dead as well. I know that life is more valuable in your book than any material considerations," Summerfield continued in a somewhat quieter voice, "but this verges on the ridiculous. Besides, I haven't the authority to order, or even suggest, such an operation—"

"The Hospital has," O'Mara broke in gruffly, then to Conway: "You're sticking your neck out, Doctor. If as a result of the search the survivor is saved, I don't think much will be said regarding the fuss and expense caused. The Corps might even give you a pat on the back for putting them on to another intelligent species. But if this alien dies, or it turns out that it was already dead before the search was begun, you, Doctor, are for it."

Looking at the thing honestly, Conway could not say that he was more than normally concerned about his patient, and definitely not enough to want to throw away his career in the faint hope of saving the being. It was more an angry curiosity which drove him, and a vague feeling that the conflicting data they possessed formed part of a picture which included much more than just a wreck and its lone survivor. Aliens did not build ships for the sole purpose of bewildering Earth-human doctors, so the apparently contradictory evidence had to mean something.

For a moment Conway thought he had the answer. Growing at the fringes of his mind was a dim, still-formless picture . . . which was obliterated, violently and completely, by the excited voice of Hendricks in his phones:

"Doctor, we've found the alien!"

When Conway joined him a few minutes later he found a portable airlock in position. Hendricks and the men of the rescue team had their helmets together talking, so as not to tie up the radio circuit. But the most wonderful sight of all to Conway was the tightly-stretched fabric of the lock.

There was pressure inside.

Hendricks switched suddenly to radio and said, "You can go in, Doctor. Now that we've found it we can open the door instead of melting through." He indicated the taut fabric beside him and added, "Pressure in there is about twelve pounds."

That wasn't a lot, thought Conway soberly, considering that the survivor's normal environment was supposed to be five-Gs, with the tremendous air-pressure which went with such a killing gravity. He hoped that it was enough to sustain life. There must have been a slow leakage of air since the accident, he thought. Maybe the being's internal pressure had equalized sufficiently to save it.

"Get an air sample to Kursedd, quickly!" Conway said. Once they knew the composition it used it would be a simple matter to increase pressure when they had the being in the tender. He added quickly, "And I want four men to stand by at the tender. We'll need special equipment to get the survivor out of here and I might need it in a hurry."

With Hendricks he entered the tiny lock. The Lieutenant checked the seals, worked the manual control beside the door, and straightened up. A creaking in Conway's suit told of mounting pressure as air from the compartment beyond rushed in. It was clear air, he noted with some satisfaction, and not the super-thick fog which Kursedd had predicted. The air-tight door slid aside, hesitated as the still-hot section moved into its recess, then came fully open with a rush.

"Don't come in unless I call you," Conway said quietly, and stepped through. In his phones there was a grunt of assent from Hendricks, followed closely by the voice of Kursedd announcing that it was recording.

The first glimpse of the new physiological type was always a confused blur to Conway. His mind insisted on trying to relate its physical features to others in his experience, and whether it was successful or not in this the process took a little time.

"Conway!" O'Mara's voice came sharply. "Have you gone to sleep?"

Conway had forgotten about O'Mara, Summerfield and the assorted radio operators who were still linked up with him. He cleared his throat and hastily began to talk:

"The being is ring-shaped, rather like a large balloon tire. Overall diameter of the ring is about nine feet, with the thickness between two and three feet. Mass appears to be about four times my own. I can see no movements, nor indications of gross physical injury."

He took a deep breath and went on, "Tegument is smooth, shiny and gray in color where it is not covered with a thick, brownish encrustation. The brown stuff, which covers more than half of the total skin area, looks cancerous but may be some type of natural camouflage. Or it might be the result of severe decompression.

"The outer surface of the ring contains a double row of short, tentacular limbs at present folded flat against the body. There are five pairs, and no evidence of specialization. Neither can I see any visual organs or means of ingestion. I'm going to have a closer look."

There was no visible reaction as he approached the creature, and he began to wonder if they had reached it too late. There was still no sign of eyes or mouth, but he could see small gill-like openings and something which looked like an ear. He reached out and gently touched one of the tightly-folded limbs.

The being seemed to explode.

Conway was sent spinning backward against the floor, his whole right arm numb from the blow which, had he not been wearing a heavy-duty suit, would have smashed his wrist. Frantically he worked the G-belt controls to hold him against the deck, then began inching backward toward the door. The babble of questions in his phones gradually sorted itself into two main ones: Why had he shouted, and what were the banging noises currently going on?

Conway said shakily, "Uh . . . I have established that the survivor is alive . . ."

The watching Hendricks made a choking sound. "I don't believe," said the Lieutenant in an awed voice, "that I have ever seen anything more so."

"Talk sense, you two!" O'Mara snapped. "What is happening?"

That was a difficult question to answer, Conway thought as he watched the tire-like being half-rolling, half-bouncing about the compartment. Physical contact with the survivor had triggered off a panic reaction, and while Conway had without doubt been the cause the first time, now contact with *anything*—walls, floor, or loose debris floating about the room—had the same result. Five pairs of strong, flexible limbs lashed out in a vicious, two-foot radius arc, the force of which sent the being skidding across the room again. And no matter which part of the massive ring body it was it struck out blindly in all directions at once.

Conway made it to the shelter of the portable lock just as a fortunate combination of circumstances left the alien floating helpless in the middle of the compartment, spinning slowly and bearing a remarkable resemblance to one of the old-time space stations. But it was drifting toward one of the walls again, and he had to get things organized before it started bouncing around a second time.

Ignoring O'Mara for the moment, Conway said quickly, "We'll need a fine-mesh net, size five, a plastic envelope to go over it, and a set of pumps. In its present state we can expect no cooperation from the being. When it is under restraint and encased in the envelope we can pump in its own air, which should keep it going until it reaches the tender. By that time Kursedd should be ready for it. But hurry with that net!"

How a high-pressure life-form could display such violent activity in what must be to it extremely rarified air was something Conway could not understand.

"Kursedd, how is the analysis going?" he asked suddenly.

The answer was so long in coming that Conway had almost decided that the nurse had broken contact, but eventually the slow, necessarily emotionless voice replied, "It is complete. The composition of the air in the survivor's compartment is such that, if you were to take off your helmet, Doctor, you could breathe it yourself."

And that, thought Conway, stunned, *was the wildest contradiction of all.* Kursedd must be equally flabbergasted, he knew. Suddenly he laughed, thinking of what the nurse's fur must be doing *now* . . .

IV

Six hours later, after struggling furiously forevery minute of the way, the survivor had been transferred to Ward 310B, a small observation room with theater off the main DBLF Surgical ward. By now Conway wasn't sure whether he wanted to restore the alien to health or murder it, and judging by the comments, during the transfer, of Kursedd and the Corpsmen, they were similarly confused. Conway made a preliminary examination—as thorough as possible considering the restraining net—and finished off by taking blood and skin samples. These he sent to Pathology, plastered with red Most Urgent labels. Kursedd took them up personally rather than commit them to the pneumo tube, because the pathological staff were notoriously color blind where priority labels were concerned. Finally he ordered X rays to be taken, left Kursedd to keep the patient under observation, then went to see O'Mara.

When he had finished, O'Mara said, "The hardest part is over now. But I expect you want to follow through on this case?"

"I . . . I don't think so," Conway replied.

O'Mara frowned heavily. "If you don't want to go on with it, say so. I don't approve of dithering."

Conway breathed through his nose, then slowly and with exaggerated distinctness said, "I want to continue with the case. The doubt which I expressed was not due to an inability to make up my mind on this point, but was with regard to your mistaken assumption that the hardest part is over. It isn't. I have made a preliminary examination and when the results of the tests are in I intend making a more detailed one tomorrow. When I do so, I would like to have present, if it is possible, Doctors Mannon and Prilicla, Colonel Skempton and yourself."

O'Mara's eyebrows went up. He said, "An odd selection of talent, Doctor. Mind telling me what you need us for?"

Conway shook his head. "I'd rather not, just yet."

"Very well, we'll be there," O'Mara said with forced gentleness. "And I apologize for suggesting that you were a ditherer, when all you did was mumble and yawn in my face so much that I could only make out one word in three. Now go away and get some sleep, Doctor, before I brain you with something."

It was only then that Conway realized how tired he was. His gait on the way to his room must be closer to a weary shuffle, he thought, than an unhurried, confident tread.

Next morning Conway spent two hours with his patient before calling for the consultation he had requested from O'Mara. Everything which he had discovered, and that wasn't a great deal, made it plain that nothing constructive could be done for the being without bringing in some highly-specialized help.

Dr. Prilicla, the spidery, low-gravity and extremely fragile being of physiological classification GLNO, arrived first. O'Mara and Colonel Skempton, the hospital's senior engineering officer, came together. Dr. Mannon, because of a job in the DBLF theater, arrived late at a near run, braked, then walked slowly around the patient twice.

"Looks like a doughnut," he said, "with barnacles."

Everyone looked at him.

"They aren't anything so simple and harmless," Conway said, wheeling the X-ray scanner forward, "but a growth which the pathological boys say shows every indication of being malignant. And if you'll look through here you'll see that it isn't a doughnut, but possesses a fairly normal anatomy of the DBLF type—a cylindrical, lightly-boned body with heavy musclature. The being is not ring-shaped, but gives that impression because for some reason known best to itself it has been trying to swallow its tail."

Mannon stared intently into the scanner, gave an incredulous grunt, then straightened up. "A vicious circle if ever I saw one," he muttered, then added: "Is this why O'Mara is here? You suspect marbles missing?"

Conway did not think the question serious, and ignored it. He went on, "The growth is thickest where the mouth and tail of the patient come together, in fact it is so widespread in that area that it is nearly impossible to see the joint. Presumably this growth is painful or at least highly irritant, and an intolerable itch might explain why it is apparently biting its own tail. Alternatively, its present physical posture might be due to an involuntary muscular contraction brought about by the growth, a type of epileptic spasm . . ."

"I like the second idea best," Mannon broke in. "For the condition to spread from mouth to tail, or vice-versa, the jaws must have locked in that position for a considerable time."

Conway nodded. He said, "Despite the artificial gravity equipment in the wreck I've established that the patient's air, pressure and gravity requirements are very similar to our own. Those gill openings back of the head and not yet reached by the growth are breathing orifices. The smaller openings, partly covered by flaps of muscle, are ears. So the patient can hear and breathe, but not eat. You all agree that freeing the mouth would be the first step?"

Mannon and O'Mara nodded. Prilicla spread four manipulators in a gesture which meant the same thing, and Colonel Skempton stared woodenly at the ceiling, very obviously wondering what *he* was doing here? Without further delay, Conway began to tell him.

While Mannon and he decided on the operative procedure, the Colonel and Dr. Prilicla were to handle the communications angle. By using its empathic faculty the GLNO could listen for a reaction while a couple of Skempton's Translator technicians ran sound tests. Once the patient's audio range was known a Translator could be modified to suit it, and the being would be able to help them in the diagnosis and treatment of its complaint.

"This place is crowded enough already," the Colonel said stiffly. "I'll handle this myself." He strode across to the intercom to order the equipment he needed. Conway turned to O'Mara.

"Don't tell me, let me guess," the psychologist began before Conway could speak. "I'm to have the easiest bit—that of reassuring the patient once we're able to talk to it, and convincing it that your pair of butchers mean it no harm."

"That's it exactly," Conway said, grinning, and returned all his attention to the patient.

Prilicla reported that the survivor was unaware of them and that the emotional radiation was so slight that it suggested the being was both unconscious and close to physical exhaustion. Despite this, Conway warned them all against touching the patient.

Conway had seen malignant growths in his time, both terrestrial and otherwise, but this one took a lot of beating.

Like a tough, fibrous bark of a tree it completely covered the joint between the patient's mouth and tail. And to add to their trouble the bone structure of the jaw, with which they would be chiefly concerned during the operation, could not be seen plainly with the scanner because of the fact that the growth itself was nearly opaque to X rays. The being's eyes were also somewhere under the thick, obscuring shell, which was another reason for going carefully.

Mannon indicated the blurred picture in the scanner and said vehemently, "It wasn't scratching to relieve an itch. Those teeth are really locked on, it has practically bitten its tail off! Definitely an epileptic condition, I'd say. Or such self-inflicted punishment could mean mental unbalance . . ."

"Oh, *great!*" said O'Mara disgustedly from behind them.

Skempton's equipment arrived then, and Prilicla and the Colonel began calibrating a Translator for the patient. Being practically unconscious, the test sounds had to be of a mind-wrecking intensity to get through to it, and Mannon and Conway were driven out to the main ward to finish their discussion.

Half an hour later Prilicla came out to tell them that they could talk to the patient, but that the being's mind still seemed to be only partly conscious. They hurried in.

O'Mara was saying that they were all friends, that they liked and felt sympathy for the patient, and that they would do everything in their power to help it. He spoke quietly into his own Translator, and a series of alien clicks and gobbles roared out from the other which had been placed near the patient's head. In the pauses between sentences Prilicla reported on the being's mental state.

"Confusion, anger, great fear," the GLNO's voice came tonelessly through its own Translator. And for several minutes the intensity and type of emotional radiation remained constant. Conway decided to take the next step.

"Tell it I am going to make physical contact," he said to O'Mara. "That I apologize for any discomfort this may cause, but that I intend no harm."

He took a long, needle-pointed probe and gently touched the area where the growth was thickest. The GLNO reported no reaction. Apparently it was only on an area unaffected by the growth where a touch could send the patient wild. Conway felt that at least he was beginning to get somewhere.

Switching off the patient's Translator, he said, "I was hoping for this. If the affected areas are dead to pain we should be able, with the patient's cooperation, to cut the mouth free without using an anesthetic. As yet we don't know enough about its metabolism to anesthetize without risk of killing the patient. Are you sure," he asked Prilicla suddenly, "that it hears and understands what we're saying?"

"Yes, Doctor," the GLNO replied, "so long as you speak slowly and without ambiguity."

Conway switched the Translator on again and said quietly. "We are going to help you. First we will enable you to resume your natural posture by freeing your mouth, and then we will remove this growth . . ."

Abruptly the restraining net bulged as five pairs of tentacles whipped furiously back and forward. Conway jumped away cursing, angry with the patient and angrier with himself for having rushed things too much.

"Fear and anger," said Prilicla, and added: "The being . . . it seems to have reasons for these emotions."

"But *why*? I'm trying to *help* it . . . !"

The patient's struggles increased to a violence that was incredible. Prilicla's fragile, pipestem body trembled under the impact of the emotional gale from the survivor's mind. One of its tentacles, a member which projected from the growth area, became entangled in a fold of net and was torn off.

Such blind, unreasoning panic, Conway thought sickly. But Prilicla had said that there were reasons for this reaction on the alien's part. Conway swore: even the workings of the survivor's mind were contradictory.

"Well!" said Mannon explosively, when the patient had quietened down again.

"Fear, anger, hatred," the GLNO reported. "I would say, most definitely, that it does not want your help."

"We have here," O'Mara put in grimly, "a very sick beastie indeed."

The words seemed to echo back and forth in Conway's brain, growing louder and more insistent every time. They had significance. O'Mara had, of course, been alluding to the mental condition of the patient, but that didn't matter. *A very sick beastie*—that was the key-piece of the puzzle, and the picture was beginning to fall into place around it. As yet it was incomplete, but there was enough of it there to make Conway feel more horribly afraid than he had ever been before in his life.

When he spoke he hardly recognized his own voice.

"Thank you, gentlemen. I'll have to think of another approach. When I do I'll let you know . . ."

Conway wished that they would all go away and let him think this thing out. He also wanted to run away and hide somewhere, except that there was probably nowhere in the whole Galaxy safe from what he was afraid.

They were all staring at him now, their expressions reflecting a mixture of surprise, concern and embarrassment. Lots of patients resisted treatment aimed at helping them, but that didn't mean the doctor ceased treating such a case at the first sign of resistance. Obviously they thought he had taken cold feet over what promised to be a highly unpleasant and technically strenuous operation, and in their various ways they tried to reassure him. Even Skempton was offering suggestions.

". . . If a safe anesthetic is your chief problem," the Colonel was saying, "isn't it possible for Pathology to develop one, from a dead or damaged, er, specimen. I have in mind the search you requested earlier. It seems to me you have ample reason to order it now. Shall I—"

"No!"

They were really staring at him now. O'Mara in particular wore a decidedly clinical expression. Conway said hurriedly, "I forgot to tell you that Summerfield contacted me again. He says that current investigations now show that the wreck, instead of being the most nearly intact half of the original ship, is the half which came off worst in the accident. The other part, he says, instead of being scattered all over space, was probably in good enough shape to make it home under its own steam. So you can see that the search would be pointless."

Conway hoped desperately that Skempton was not going to be difficult about this, or insist on checking the information himself. Summerfield had reported again from the wreck, but the Captain's findings had not been nearly so definite as Conway had just made out. The thought of a Monitor search force blundering about in that area of space, in the light of what he knew now, made Conway break into a cold sweat.

But the Colonel merely nodded and dropped the subject. Conway relaxed, a little, and said quickly, "Dr. Prilicla, I would like a discussion with you on the patient's emotional state during the past few minutes, but later. Thank you again, gentlemen, for your advice and assistance . . ."

He was practically kicking them out, and their expressions told him that they knew it—there was going to be some very searching questions asked about his behavior in this affair by O'Mara, but at the moment Conway didn't care. When they had gone he told Kursedd to make a visual check on the patient's condition every half-hour, and to call him if there was any change. Then he headed for his room.

V

Conway often groused at the tininess of the place where he slept, kept his few personal possessions, and infrequently entertained colleagues, but now its very smallness was comforting. He sat down as there was no room to pace about. He began to extend and fill in the picture which had come in a single flash of insight back in the ward.

Really, the thing had been staring him in the face from the very beginning. First there had been the wreck's artificial gravity grids— Conway had stupidly overlooked the fact that they did not have to be operated at full power, but could be turned to any point between zero and five-Gs. Then there had been the air-supply layout—confusing only because he had not realized that it had been designed to many different forms of life instead of only one. And there had been the physical condition of the survivor, and the color of the outer hull—a nice, urgent, dramatic orange. Earth ships of that type, even surface vessels, were traditionally painted white.

The wreck was an ambulance ship.

But interstellar vessels of any kind were products of an advanced technical culture which must cover, or shortly hope to cover, many solar systems. And when a culture progressed to the point where such ships reached the stage of simplification and specialization which had been reached here, then that race was highly advanced indeed. In the Galactic Federation only the cultures of Illensa, Traltha and Earth had reached that stage, and their spheres of influence were tremendous. How could a culture of that size have remained hidden for so long?

Conway squirmed uneasily in his couch: he had the answer to that question, too.

Summerfield had said that the wreck was the worst damaged section of a ship, the other half of which could be presumed to have continued under its own power to the nearest repair base. So the section containing the survivor had been torn from the ship during the original accident, which meant that the course constants of this unpowered fragment had to be the same as that of the ship as a whole before the disaster.

The ship had been coming, then, from a planet which was listed as uninhabited. But in a hundred years someone could have set up a base there, or even a colony. And the ambulance ship had been heading away from that world and into intergalactic space . . .

A culture which had crossed from one Galaxy to plant a colony on the fringes of this one, Conway thought grimly, had to be treated with great respect. And caution. Especially since its only representative so far could not, by any stretch of toleration or semantic work-juggling, be considered nice. And the survivor's race, probably highly advanced medically might not take kindly to news that someone was botching the treatment of one of their sick. On the present evidence Conway thought that they would not take kindly to anything or anybody.

Interstellar wars of conquest were logistically impossible, Conway knew. But the same did not apply to simple wars of annihilation, where planetary atmospheres were exploded or otherwise rendered useless forever with no thought of eventual occupation or assimilation. Remembering his last contact with the patient, Conway wondered if at last they had encountered a completely vicious and inimical race.

The communicator buzzed suddenly. It was Kursedd reporting that the patient had been quiet for the last hour, but that the growth seemed to be spreading rapidly and threatened to cover one of the being's breathing openings. Conway said he would be along presently. He put out a call for Dr. Prilicla, then sat down again.

He dare not tell anyone of his discovery, Conway told himself as he resumed his interrupted thought. To do so would mean a force of Monitors swarming out there to make premature contact—premature, that was, so far as Conway was concerned. For he was afraid that that first meeting between cultures would be in the nature of an ideological head-on collision, and the only possibility of cushioning the shock would be if the Federation could show that they had rescued, taken care of, and *cured* one of the intergalactic colonists.

Of course there was the possibility that the patient was atypical of its race, that it was mentally ill as O'Mara had suggested. But Conway doubted if the aliens would consider that an excuse for not curing it. And against that idea was the fact that the patient had had logical—to it—reasons for being afraid and hating the person trying to help it. For a moment Conway wondered wildly if there was such a thing as a contra-terrene mind, a mentality wherein assistance produced feelings of hate instead of gratitude. Even the fact of its being found in an ambulance was no reassurance. To people like himself the concept of an ambulance had altruistic implications, errands of mercy, and so on. But many races, even within the Federation, tended to look upon illness as mere physical inefficiency and corrected it as such.

As he left his room Conway did not have the faintest idea of how to go about curing his patient. Neither, he knew, did he have much time to do it in. At the moment, Captain Summerfield, Hendricks and the others investigating the wreck were too dazzled by a multiplicity of puzzles to think about anything else. But it was only a matter of time before they got around to it, a matter of days or even hours, and then they would come to the same conclusions as had Conway.

Shortly thereafter the Monitor Corps would make contact with the aliens, who would naturally want to know about their ailing brother, who by that time would have to be either cured or well on the way to recovery.

Or else.

The thought which Conway tried desperately to keep from thinking was: *What if the patient died...?*

Before beginning the next examination he questioned Prilicla regarding the patient's emotional state, but learned nothing new. The being was now motionless and practically unconscious. When Conway spoke to it via the Translator it emoted fear, even when Prilicla assured him that it understood what he was saying.

"I will not harm you," Conway said slowly and distinctly into the Translator, moving closer as he spoke, "but it is necessary that I touch you. Please believe me, I mean no harm..." He looked enquiringly at Prilicla.

The GLNO said, "Fear and... and helplessness. Also acceptance mixed with threats... no, warnings. Apparently it believes what you say, but is trying to warn you about something."

This was more promising, Conway thought. It was warning him, but it didn't mind him touching it. He moved closer and gently touched the being with his gloved hand on one of the unaffected areas of tegument.

He grunted with the violence of the blow which knocked his arm aside. He backed away hurriedly, rubbing his arm, then switched off the Translator so as to give vent to his feelings.

After a respectful pause, the GLNO said, "We have obtained a very important datum, Dr. Conway. Despite the physical reaction, the patient's feelings toward you are exactly the same as they were before you touched it."

"So what?" said Conway irritably.

"So that the reaction must be involuntary."

Conway digested that for a moment, then said disgustedly, "It also means we can't risk a general anesthetic, even if we had one, because the heart and lungs use involuntary muscles, too. That's another complication. We can't knock it out and it won't cooperate..." He moved to the ward control panel and pushed buttons. The clamps holding the net opened and the net itself was whisked away by a grab. He went on, "It keeps injuring itself on that net, you can see where it has nearly lost another appendage."

Prilicla objected to the removal of the net, saying that if the patient was free to move about it was more likely than ever to injure itself. Conway pointed out that in its present posture—head to tail and underbelly, which contained its five sets of tentacles, facing outward—it could do little moving about. And now that he thought of it, that position looked like the perfect defensive stance for the creature. It reminded him of the way an Earth cat lies on its side during a fight, so as to bring all four of its claws to bear. This was a ten-legged cat who could defend itself from all directions at once.

Built-in involuntary reactions of that order were the product of evolution. But why should the being adopt this defensive position and make itself completely unapproachable at the time when it needed help the most . . . ?

Suddenly, like a great light bursting in his mind, Conway knew the answer. Or, he amended with cautious excitement, he was near ninety percent sure that he did.

They had all been making wrong assumptions about this case from the start. His new theory hinged on the fact that they had made a further wrong assumption, single, simple and basic. Given that then the patient's hostility, physical posture and mental state could all be explained. It even indicated the only possible line of treatment to be taken. Best of all, it gave Conway reason for thinking that the patient might not belong to the type of vicious and implacably hostile race which its behavior had led him to believe.

The only trouble with the new theory was that it, also, might be wrong.

His first wild enthusiasm waned and his degree of certainty dropped to the mid-eighties. Another trouble was that he could not possibly discuss his intended line of treatment with anyone. To do so might mean demotion, and to insist on carrying through with it would mean his dismissal from the hospital should the patient die. What he contemplated was as serious as that.

Conway approached the patient again and switched on the Translator. He knew before he spoke what the reaction would be so it was probably an act of wanton cruelty to say the words, but he had to test this theory once more for his own reassurance. He said, "Don't worry, young fellow, we'll have you back the way you were in no time . . ."

The reaction was so violent that Dr. Prilicla, whose empathic faculty made it feel everything which the patient felt at full intensity, had to leave the ward.

It was only then that Conway finally made his decision.

During the three days which followed, Conway visited the ward regularly. He took careful notes on the rate of growth of the thick, fibrous encrustation which now covered two thirds of the patient's body. There could be no doubt that it was both accelerating and growing thicker. He sent specimens to Pathology, which reported that the patient appeared to be suffering from a peculiar and particularly virulent form of skin cancer and asked if curative radiation or surgery was possible. Conway replied that in this opinion neither were possible without grave danger to the patient.

About the most constructive thing he did during that time was to post instructions that anyone contacting the patient via Translator was to avoid trying to reassure it at all costs. The being had suffered too much already from that form of well-meaning stupidity. If Conway could have forbidden entrance to the ward to everyone but Kursedd, Prilicla and himself he would have done so.

But the greater part of his time was spent in trying to convince himself that he was doing the right thing.

Conway had been deliberately avoiding Dr. Mannon since the original examination. He did not want his old friend discussing the case with him, because Mannon was too smart to be foisted off with double talk, and Conway could not tell even him the truth. He thought longingly that the ideal situation would be for Captain Summerfield to be kept too busy at the wreck to put two and two together, for O'Mara and Skempton to forget his existence, and for Mannon to keep his nose completely out of the affair.

But that was not to be.

Dr. Mannon was waiting for him in the ward when he made his second morning visit on the fifth day. Properly he requested Conway's permission to look at the patient. Then with this polite formality over he said, "... Listen, you young squirt, I'm getting fed up with you gazing abstractedly at your boots or the ceiling every time I come near you—if I hadn't got the hide of a Tralthan I'd feel slighted. I know, of course, that newly-appointed Seniors take their responsibilities very heavily for the first few weeks, but your recent behavior has been downright rude."

He held up his hand before Conway could speak, and went on, "I accept your apology, and now to business. I've been talking to Prilicla and the people up in Pathology. They tell me that the growth now completely covers the body, that it is opaque to X rays of safe intensities and that the replacement and workings of the patient's internal organs can now only be guessed at. You can't cut the stuff away under anesthetic because paralyzing the appendages might knock out the heart, too. Yet an operation is impossible with those limbs whipping about. At the same time the patient is weakening and will continue to do so unless given food, which can't be done unless its mouth is freed. To complicate matters further your later specimens show that the growth is extending inward rapidly as well, and there are indications that if the operation isn't done quickly the mouth and tail will have fused together. Is that, in a rather large nutshell, it?"

Conway nodded.

Mannon took a deep breath, then plunged on, "Suppose you amputate the limbs and remove the covering growth from head and tail, replacing the tegument with a suitable synthetic. With the patient able to take nourishment it would shortly be strong enough for the process to be repeated over the rest of its body. It is a drastic procedure, I admit. But in the circumstances it seems to be the only one which could save the patient's life. And there is always the possibility of successful grafting or artificial members—"

"*No!*" said Conway violently, and he knew from the way Mannon looked at him that he had gone pale. If his theory concerning the patient was correct, then any sort of operation at this stage would prove fatal. And if not, and the patient was the type of entity which it appeared to be—vicious, warped, and implacably hostile—and its friends came looking for it . . .

In a quieter voice Conway said, "Suppose a friend of yours with a bad skin condition was picked up by an e-t doctor, and the only thing it could think of doing was to skin him alive and lop his arms and legs off. If or when you found him you would be annoyed. Even taking into account the fact that you are civilized, tolerant and prepared to make allowances— qualities which we cannot safely ascribe to the patient as yet—I would venture to suggest that there would be merry hell to play."

"That's not a true analogy and you know it!" Mannon said heatedly. "Sometimes you have to take chances. This is one of those times."

"No," said Conway again.

"Maybe you have a better suggestion?"

Conway was silent for a moment, then he said carefully, "I do have an idea which I'm trying out, but I don't want to discuss it just yet. If it works out you'll be the first to know, and if it doesn't you'll know anyhow. Everybody will."

Mannon shrugged and turned away. At the door he paused to say awkwardly, "Whatever you're doing it must be pretty hair-brained for you to be so secretive about it. But remember that if you call me in and the thing goes sour on us, the blame gets halved . . ."

And there speaks a true friend, thought Conway. He was tempted to unburden himself completely to Mannon then. But Dr. Mannon was a nosy, kindly and very able Senior Physician who always had, and always would, take his profession as a healer very seriously, despite the cracks he often made about it. He might not be able to do what Conway would ask, or keep his mouth shut while Conway was doing it.

Regretfully, Conway shook his head.

VI

When Mannon had gone, Conway returned to his patient. Visually it still resembled a doughnut, he thought, but a doughnut which had become wrinkled and fossilized with the passage of eons. He had to remind himself that only a week had passed since the patient had been admitted. The five pairs of limbs, all beginning to show signs of being affected by the growth, projected stiffly and at odd angles from the body, like petrified twigs on a rotten tree. Realizing that the growth would cover the breathing openings, Conway had inserted tubes to keep the respiratory passages clear. The tubes were having the desired effect, but despite this the respiration had slowed and become shallow. The stethoscope indicated that the heartbeats were fainter but had increased in frequency.

Sheer indecision made Conway sweat.

If only it was an ordinary patient, Conway thought angrily; one that could be treated openly and its treatment discussed freely. But this one was complicated by the fact that it was a member of a highly advanced and possibly inimical race, and he could not confide in anyone lest he be pulled off the case before his theory was proven. And the trouble was that the theory might be all wrong. It was quite possible that he was engaged in slowly killing his patient.

Noting the heart and respiration rates on the chart, Conway decided
that it was time he increased the periodicity of his visits, and also arranged
the times so that Prilicla, who was busy these days in the Nursery, could
accompany him.

Kursedd was watching him intently as he left the ward, and its fur
was doing peculiar things. Conway did not waste his breath telling the
nurse to keep quiet about what he was doing to his patient because that
would have made the being gossip even more. It was he who was being
talked about already by the nursing staff, and he had begun to detect a
certain coldness toward him from some of the senior nurses in this section. But with any luck, word of what he was doing would not filter up
to his seniors for several days.

Three hours later he was back in 310B with Dr. Prilicla. He checked
heart and respiration again while the GLNO probed for emotional radiation.

"It is very weak," Prilicla reported slowly. "Life is present, but so
faintly that it is not even conscious of itself. Considering the almost nonexistent respiration and weak, rapid pulse-rate . . ." The thought of death
was particularly distressing to an empath, and the sensitive little being
could not bring itself to finish the sentence.

"All these scares we gave it, trying to reassure it, didn't help," Conway
said, half to himself. "It hadn't been able to eat and we caused it to use
up reserves of energy which it badly needed to keep. But it had to protect
itself . . ."

"But why? We were helping the patient."

"Of course we were," Conway said in a bitingly sarcastic tone which
he knew would not carry through the other's Translator. He was about
to continue with the examination when there was a sudden interruption.

The being whose vast bulk scraped both sides and the top of the ward
door on its way in was a Tralthan, physiological classification FGLI. To
Conway the natives of Traltha were as hard to tell apart as sheep, but he
knew this one. This was no less than Thornnastor, Diagnostician-in-
Charge of Pathology.

The Diagnostician curled two of its eyes in Prilicla's direction and
boomed, "Get out of here, please. You too, Nurse." Then it turned all
four of them on Conway.

"I am speaking to you alone," Thornnastor said when they had gone, "because some of my remarks have bearing on your professional conduct during this case, and I have no wish to increase your discomfort by public censure. However, I will begin by giving you the good news that we have produced a specific against this growth. Not only does it inhibit the condition spreading but it softens up the areas already affected and regenerates the tissues and blood-supply network involved."

Oh, *blast!* thought Conway. Aloud he said, "A splendid accomplishment." Because it really was.

"It would not have been possible had we not sent out a doctor to the wreck with instructions to send us anything which might throw light on the patient's metabolism," the Diagnostician continued. "Apparently you overlooked this source of data completely, Doctor, because the only specimens you furnished were those taken from the wreck during the time you were there, a very small fraction indeed of the quantity which was available. This was sheer negligence, Doctor, and only your previous good record has kept you from being demoted and taken off this case . . .

"But our success was due mainly to the finding of what appears to be a very well-equipped medical chest," Thornnastor continued. "Study of the contents together with other information regarding the fittings in the wreck led to the conclusion that it must have been some kind of ambulance ship. The Monitor Corps officers were very excited when we told them—"

"When?" said Conway sharply. The bottom had dropped out of everything and he felt so cold that he might have been in shock. But there might be a chance to make Skempton delay making contact. "*When* did you tell them about it being an ambulance ship?"

"That information can be only of secondary interest to you," said Thornnastor, removing a large, padded flask from its satchel. "Your primary concern is, or should be, the patient. You will need a lot of this stuff, and we are synthesizing it as quickly as we can, but there is enough here to free the head and mouth area. Inject according to instructions. It takes about an hour to show effect."

Conway lifted the flask carefully. Stalling for time, he said, "What about long-term effects? I wouldn't like to risk—"

"Doctor," Thornnastor interrupted, "it seems to me that you are taking caution to foolish, even criminal lengths." The Diagnostician's voice in Conway's Translator was emotionless, but he did not have to be an empath to know that the other was extremely angry. The way Thornnastor charged out the door made that more than plain.

Conway swore luridly. The Monitors were about to contact the alien colony, if they had not done so already, and very soon the aliens would be swarming all over the hospital demanding to know what he was doing for the patient. If it wasn't doing well by that time there would be trouble, no matter what sort of people they were. And much sooner than that would come trouble from inside the hospital, because he had not impressed Thornnastor with his professional ability at all.

In his hand was the flask whose contents would certainly do all that the Head Pathologist claimed—in short, cure what seemed to ail the patient. Conway dithered for a moment, then stuck grimly to the decision which he had made several days back. He managed to hide the flask before Prilicla returned.

"Listen to me carefully," Conway said savagely, "before you say anything at all. I don't want any arguments regarding the conduct of this case, Doctor. I think I know what I'm doing, but if I should be wrong and you were in on it, your professional reputation would suffer. Understand?"

Prilicla's six, pipe-stem legs had been quivering as he talked, but it was not the words which were affecting the little creature, it was the feelings behind them. Conway knew that his emotional radiation just then was not a pleasant thing.

"I understand," said Prilicla.

"Very well," Conway said. "Now we'll get back to work. I want you to check me with the pulse and respiration, as well as the emotional radiation. There should be a variation soon and I don't want to miss it."

For two hours they listened and observed closely with no detectable change in the patient. At one point Conway left the being with Prilicla and Kursedd while he tried to contact Colonel Skempton. But he was told that the Colonel had left the hospital hurriedly three days ago, that he had given the spatial coordinates of his destination, but that it was impossible to contact a ship over interstellar distances while it was in motion. They were sorry but the Doctor's message would have to wait until the Colonel got where he was going.

So it was too late to stop the Corps making contact with the aliens. The only course now was for him to "cure" the patient.

If he was allowed . . .

The wall annunciator clicked, coughed and said, "Dr. Conway, report to Major O'Mara's office immediately." He was thinking bitterly that Thornnastor had lost no time in registering a complaint when Prilicla said, "Respiration almost gone. Irregular heartbeat."

Conway snatched up the ward intercom mike and yelled, "Conway, here. Tell O'Mara I'm busy!" Then to Prilicla he said, "I caught it, too. How about emotion?"

"Stronger during the erratic pulse, but both back to normal now. Registration is still fading."

"Right. Keep your ears and mind open."

Conway took a sample of expelled air from one of the breathing orifices and ran it through the analyzer. Even considering the shallowness of the being's respiration this result, like the others he had taken during the past twelve hours, left no possibility for doubt. Conway began to feel a little more confident.

"Respiration almost gone," said Prilicla.

Before Conway could reply, O'Mara burst through the door. Stopping about six inches from Conway he said in a dangerously quiet voice. "Just what are you busy *at*, Doctor?"

Conway was practically dancing with impatience. He asked pleadingly, "Can't this wait?"

"No."

He would not be able to get rid of the psychologist without some sort of explanation for his recent conduct, Conway knew, and he desperately wanted to have the next hour free from interference. He moved quickly to the patient and over his shoulder gave O'Mara a hasty *résumé* of his deductions regarding the alien ambulance ship and the colony from which it had come. He ended by urging the psychologist to call Skempton to delay the first contact until something more definite was known about the patient's condition.

"So you knew all this a week ago and didn't tell us," O'Mara said thoughtfully, "and I can understand your reasons for keeping quiet. But the Corps had made a great many first contacts and managed them very well, thank you. We have people specially trained for this sort of thing. You, however, have been reacting like an ostrich—doing nothing and hoping that the problem would go away. This problem, involving a culture advanced enough to have crossed intergalactic space, is too big to be dodged. It has to be solved quickly and positively. Ideally it would involve us showing proof of good feeling by producing the survivor alive and well . . ."

O'Mara's voice hardened suddenly into an angry rasp, and he was so close behind Conway that the doctor could feel his breath on his neck.

". . . Which brings us back to the patient here, the being which you are supposed to be treating.

"Look at me, Conway!"

Conway turned around, but only after ensuring that Prilicla was still keeping a close watch. Angrily he wondered why everything had come to the boil at once instead of happening in a nice, consecutive fashion.

"At the first examination," O'Mara resumed quietly, "you fled to your room before we could make any headway. This looked like professional cold feet to me, but I was inclined to make allowances. Later, Dr. Mannon suggested a line of treatment which although drastic was not only allowable but definitely indicated in the patient's condition. You refused to move. Then Pathology developed a specific which could have cured the patient in a matter of hours, and you balked at using even *that*!

"Ordinarily I discount rumors and gossip in this place," O'Mara continued, his voice rising again, "but when they become both widespread and insistent, especially among the nursing staff who generally know what they're talking about medically, I have to take notice. It has become plain that despite the constant watch you have kept on the patient, the frequent examinations and the numerous samples you have sent to Pathology, you have done absolutely nothing for the being.

"It has been dying while you *pretended* to treat it. You've been so afraid of the consequences of failure that you were incapable of making the simplest decision—"

"No!" Conway protested. That had stung even though O'Mara's accusation was based on incomplete information. And much worse than the words was the look on the Major's face, an expression of anger and scorn and a deep hurt that someone he had trusted both professionally and as a friend could have failed him so horribly. O'Mara was blaming himself almost as much as Conway for his business.

"Caution can be taken to extremes, Doctor," O'Mara said almost sadly. "You have to be bold, sometimes. If a close decision is necessary you should make it, and stick to it no matter what . . ."

"And what the blazes," asked Conway furiously, "do you *think* I'm doing?"

"Nothing!" shouted O'Mara. "Absolutely nothing!"

"That's right!" Conway yelled back.

"Respiration has ceased," Prilicla said quietly.

Conway swung around and thumbed the buzzer for Kursedd. He said, "Heart action? Mind?"

"Pulse faster. Emoting a little more strongly."

Kursedd arrived then and Conway began rattling out instructions. He needed instruments from the adjoining DBLF theater and detailed his requirements. Aseptic procedure was unnecessary, likewise anesthetics— he wanted only a large selection of cutting instruments. The nurse disappeared and Conway called Pathology, asking if they could suggest a safe coagulant for the patient should extensive surgery be necessary. They could and said he would have it within minutes. As he was turning from the intercom, O'Mara spoke:

"All this frantic activity, this window-dressing, proves nothing. The patient has stopped breathing. If it isn't dead it is as near to it as makes no difference, and you're to blame. Heaven help you, Doctor, because nobody here will."

Conway shook his head distractedly. "Unfortunately you may be right, but I'm hoping that it won't die," he said. "I can't explain just now, but you could help me by contacting Skempton and telling him to go easy on that alien colony. I need time, just how much of it I still don't know."

"You don't know when to give up," said O'Mara angrily, but went to the intercom nevertheless. While he was arranging a link-up, Kursedd undulated in with an instrument trolley. Conway placed it convenient to the patient, then said over his shoulder to O'Mara, "Here is something you might think about. For the past twelve hours the air expelled from the patient's lungs has been free from impurities. It has been breathing but apparently not using its breath . . ."

He bent quickly, adjusted his stethoscope and listened. The heartbeats were a little faster, he thought, and stronger. But there was a jarring irregularity to them. Through the thick, almost solid growth which enclosed it the sounds were both magnified and distorted. Conway could not tell if the heart alone was responsible for the noise or if other organic movements were contributing. This worried him because he didn't know what was normal for a patient like this. The survivor had, after all, been in an ambulance ship, which meant that there might have been something wrong with it in addition to its present condition . . .

"What are you raving about?" O'Mara broke in roughly, making Conway realize that he had been thinking aloud. "Are you saying now that the patient isn't sick . . . ?"

Absently, Conway said, "An expectant mother can be suffering, yet not be technically ill."

He wished that he knew more of what was going on inside his patient. If the being's ears had not been completely covered by the growth he would have tried the Translator again. The sucking, bumping, gurgling noises could mean anything.

"Conway . . . !" began O'Mara, and took a breath which could be heard all over the ward. Then he forced his voice down to a conversational level and went on, "I'm in touch with Skempton's ship. Apparently they made good time and have already contacted the aliens. They're fetching the Colonel now . . ." He broke off, then added, "I'll turn up the volume so you can hear what he says."

"Not too loud," said Conway, then to Prilicla, "How is it emoting?"

"Much stronger. I detect separate emotions again. Feelings of urgency, distress and fear—probably claustrophobic—approaching the point of panic."

Conway gave the patient a long, careful appraisal. There was no visible movement. Abruptly he said, "I can't risk waiting any longer. It must be too weak to help itself. Screens, Nurse."

The screens were meant only to exclude O'Mara. Had the psychologist seen what was to come without fully knowing what was going on he would doubtless have jumped to more wrong conclusions, probably to the extent of forcibly restraining Conway.

"Its distress is increasing," Prilicla said suddenly. "There is no actual pain, but there are intense feelings of constriction . . ."

Conway nodded. He motioned for a scalpel and began cutting into the growth, trying to establish its depth. It was now like soft, crumbling cork which offered little resistance to the knife. At a depth of eight inches he bared what looked like a grayish, oily and faintly irridescent membrane, but there was no rush of body fluid into the operative field. Conway heaved a sigh of relief, withdrew, then repeated the process in another area. This time the membrane revealed had a greenish tinge and was twitching slightly. He moved on again.

Apparently the average depth of the growth was eight inches. Working with furious speed Conway opened the covering growth in a total of nine places, spaced out at roughly equal intervals around the ring-like body, then he looked a question at Prilicla.

"Much worse now," said the GLNO. "Extreme mental distress fear, feelings of . . . of stangulation. Pulse is up, and irregular—there is considerable strain on the heart. Also it is losing consciousness again . . ."

Before the empath had finished speaking Conway was hacking away. With long, sawing, savage strokes he linked together the openings already made with deep, jagged incisions. *Everything* was sacrificed for speed. By no stretch of the imagination could what he was doing be called surgery, because a lumberjack with a blunt axe could have performed neater work.

Finished, he stood looking at the patient for three whole seconds, but there was still no sign of movement. Conway dropped the scalpel and began tearing at the growth with his hands.

Suddenly the voice of Skempton filled the ward, excitedly describing his landing on the alien colony and the opening of communications with them. He went on, ". . . And O'Mara, the sociological set-up is weird, I've never heard of anything like it, or them! There are two distinct life-forms—"

"But belonging to the same species," Conway put in loudly as he worked. The patient was showing definite signs of life and was beginning to help itself. He felt like yelling with sheer exhultation, but instead he went on, "One form is the ten-legged type of our friend here, but without their tails sticking in their mouths. That is a transition-stage position only.

"The other form is . . . is . . ." Conway paused to give the being now revealed before him a searching, analytical stare. The remains of the growth which had covered it lay about the floor, some thrown there by Conway and the rest which it had shaken off itself. He continued, "Let's see, oxygen-breathing, of course. Oviparous. Long, rod-like but flexible body possessing four insectile legs, manipulators, the usual sense organs, and three sets of wings. Classification GKNM. Visual aspect something like a dragonfly.

"I would say that the first form, judging by the crudely-developed appendages we noticed, performed most of the hard labor. Not until it passed the 'Chrysalis' stage to become the more dexterous, and beautiful, dragonfly form would it be considered mature and capable of doing responsible work. This would, I suppose, make for a complicated society..."

"I had been about to say," Colonel Skempton broke in, his voice reflecting the chagrin of one whose thunder has just been stolen, "that a couple of the beings are on their way to take care of the survivor. They urge that nothing whatever be done to the patient..."

At that point O'Mara pushed through the screen. He stood gaping at the patient who was now engaged in shaking out its wings, then with a visible effort pulled himself together. He said, "I suppose apologies are in order, Doctor. But why didn't you *tell* someone...?"

"I had no clear proof that my theory was right," Conway said seriously. "When the patient went into a panic several times when I suggested helping it, I suspected that the growth might be normal. A caterpillar could be expected to object to anyone trying to remove its chrysalis prematurely, for the good reason that such a course would kill it. And there were other pointers. The lack of food intake, the ring-like position with the appendages facing outward—obviously a defense mechanism from a time when natural enemies threatened the new being inside the slowly hardening shell of the old, and finally the fact that its expelled breath during the later stages showed no impurities, proving that the lungs and heart we were listening to had no longer a direct connection."

Conway went on to explain that in the early stages of the treatment he had been unsure of his theory, but still not doubtful enough in his mind to allow Mannon or Thornnastor to have their way. He had made the decision that the patient's condition was normal, or fairly normal, and the best course would be to do absolutely nothing. Which was what he had done.

"...But this is a hospital which believes in doing everything possible for a patient," Conway went on, "and I can't imagine Dr. Mannon, yourself or any of the other people I know just standing by and doing nothing while their patient was apparently dying on them. Maybe someone would have accepted my theory and agreed to act on it, but I couldn't be sure. And we just *had* to cure this patient, because its friends at that time were rather an unknown quantity..."

"All right, all right," O'Mara broke in, holding up his hands. "You're a genius, Doctor, or something. Now what?"

Conway rubbed his chin, then said thoughtfully, "We must remember that the patient was in a hospital ship, so there must have been something wrong with it in addition to its condition. It was too weak to break out of its own chrysalis and had to have help. Maybe this weakness was its only trouble. But if it was something else, Thornnastor and his crowd will be able to cure it now that we can communicate and get its cooperation."

"Unless," he said, suddenly worried, "our earlier and misguided attempts to reassure it have caused mental damage." He switched on the Translator, chewed at his lips for a moment, then addressed the patient; "How do you feel?"

The reply was short and to the point, but in it were contained all the implications which gladden a worried doctor's heart.

"I'm hungry," said the patient.

STAR
SURGEON

TO
GEORGE L. CHARTERS
FOR LOTS OF REASONS . . .

CHAPTER 1

F ar out on the galactic Rim, where star systems were sparse and the
darkness nearly absolute, Sector Twelve General Hospital hung in
space. In its three hundred and eighty-four levels were reproduced in the
environments of all the intelligent life-forms known to the Galactic Federation, a biological spectrum ranging from the ultra-frigid methane life-
forms through the more normal oxygen- and chlorine-breathing types up
to the exotic beings who existed by the direct conversion of hard radiation. Its thousands of viewports were constantly ablaze with light—light
in the dazzling variety of color and intensity necessary for the visual
equipment of its extra-terrestrial patients and staff—so that to approaching ships the great hospital looked like a tremendous, cylindrical Christmas tree.

Sector General represented a two-fold miracle of engineering and
psychology. Its supply and maintenance was handled by the Monitor
Corps—the Federation's executive and law enforcement arm—who also
saw to its administration, but the traditional friction between the military
and civilian members of its staff did not occur. Neither were there any
serious squabbles among its ten-thousand-odd medical personnel, who
were composed of over sixty different life-forms with sixty differing sets
of mannerisms, body odors and ways of looking at life. Perhaps their one
and only common denominator was the need of all doctors, regardless
of size, shape or number of legs, to cure the sick.

The staff of Sector General was a dedicated, but not always serious,
group of beings who were fanatically tolerant of all forms of intelligent
life—had this not been so they would not have been there in the first
place. And they prided themselves that no case was too big, too small or

too hopeless. Their advice or assistance was sought by medical authorities from all over the Galaxy. Pacifists all, they waged a constant, all-out war against suffering and disease whether it was in individuals or whole planetary populations.

But there were times when the diagnosis and treatment of a diseased interstellar culture, entailing the surgical removal of deeply-rooted prejudice and unsane moral values without either the patient's cooperation or consent could, despite the pacifism of the doctors concerned, lead to the waging of war. Period.

*   *   *

The patient being brought into the observation ward was a large specimen—about one thousand pounds mass, Conway estimated—and resembled a giant, upright pear. Five thick, tentacular appendages grew from the narrow head section and a heavy apron of muscle at its base gave evidence of a snail-like, although not necessarily slow, method of locomotion. The whole body surface looked raw and lacerated, as though someone had been trying to take its skin off with a wire brush.

To Conway there was nothing very unusual about the physical aspect of the patient or its condition, six years in space Sector General Hospital having accustomed him to much more startling sights, so he moved forward to make a preliminary examination. Immediately the Monitor Corps lieutenant who had accompanied the patient's trolley into the ward moved closer also. Conway tried to ignore the feeling of breath on the back of his neck and took a closer look at the patient.

Five large mouths were situated below the root of each tentacle, four being plentifully supplied with teeth and the fifth housing the vocal apparatus. The tentacles themselves showed a high degree of specialization at their extremities; three of them were plainly manipulatory, one bore the patient's visual equipment and the remaining member terminated in a horn-tipped, boney mace. The head was featureless, being simply an osseous dome housing the patient's brain.

There wasn't much else to be seen from a superficial examination. Conway turned to get his deep probe gear, and walked on the Monitor officer's feet.

"Have you ever considered taking up medicine seriously, Lieutenant?" he said irritably.

The lieutenant reddened, his face making a horrible clash of color against the dark green of his uniform collar. He said stiffly, "This patient is a criminal. It was found in circumstances which indicate that it killed and ate the other member of its ship's crew. It has been unconscious during the trip here, but I've been ordered to stand guard on it just in case. I'll try to stay out of your way, Doctor."

Conway swallowed, his eyes going to the vicious-looking, horny bludgeon with which, he had no doubt, the patient's species had battered their way to the top of their evolutionary tree. He said dryly, "Don't try too hard, Lieutenant."

Using his eyes and a portable X-ray scanner Conway examined his patient thoroughly inside and out. He took several specimens, including sections of the affected skin, and sent them off to Pathology with three closely-written pages of covering notes. Then he stood back and scratched his head.

The patient was warm-blooded, oxygen-breathing, and had fairly normal gravity and pressure requirements which, when considered with the general shape of the beastie, put its physiological classification as EPLH. It seemed to be suffering from a well-developed and widespread epithelioma, the symptoms being so plain that he really should have begun treatment without waiting for the Path report. But a cancerous skin condition did not, ordinarily, render a patient deeply unconscious.

That could point to psychological complications, he knew, and in that case he would have to call in some specialized help. One of his telepathic colleagues was the obvious choice, if it hadn't been for the fact that telepaths could only rarely work minds that were not already telepathic and of the same species as themselves. Except for the very odd instance, telepathy had been found to be a strictly closed circuit form of communication. Which left his GLNO friend, the empath Dr. Prilicla . . .

Behind him the Lieutenant coughed gently and said, "When you've finished the examination, Doctor, O'Mara would like to see you."

Conway nodded. "I'm going to send someone to keep an eye on the patient," he said, grinning, "guard them as well as you've guarded me."

Going through to the main ward Conway detailed an Earth-human nurse—a very good-looking Earth-human nurse—to duty in the observation ward. He could have sent in one of the Tralthan FGLIs, who belonged to a species with six legs and so built that beside one of them an Earthly elephant would have seemed a fragile, sylph-like creature, but he felt that he owed the Lieutenant something for his earlier bad manners.

Twenty minutes later, after three changes of protective armor and a trip through the chlorine section, a corridor belonging to the AUGL water-breathers and the ultra-refrigerated wards of the methane life-forms, Conway presented himself at the office of Major O'Mara.

As Chief Psychologist of a multi-environment hospital hanging in frigid blackness at the Galactic rim, he was responsible for the mental well-being of a Staff of ten thousand entities who were composed of eighty-seven different species. O'Mara was a very important man at Sector General. He was also, on his own admission, the most approachable man in the hospital. O'Mara was fond of saying that he didn't care who approached him or when, but if they hadn't a very good reason for pestering him with their silly little problems then they needn't expect to get away from him again unscathed. To O'Mara the medical staff were patients, and it was the generally held belief that the high level of stability among that variegated and often touchy bunch of e-ts was due to them being too scared of O'Mara to go mad. But today he was in an almost sociable mood.

"This will take more than five minutes so you'd better sit down, Doctor," he said sourly when Conway stopped before his desk. "I take it you've had a look at our cannibal?"

Conway nodded and sat down. Briefly he outlined his findings with regard to the EPLH patient, including his suspicion that there might be complications of a psychological nature. Ending, he asked, "Do you have any other information on its background, apart from the cannibalism?"

"Very little," said O'Mara. "It was found by a Monitor patrol vessel in a ship which, although undamaged, was broadcasting distress signals. Obviously it became too sick to operate the vessel. There was no other occupant, but because the EPLH was a new species to the rescue party they went over its ship with a fine-tooth comb, and found that there should have been another person aboard. They discovered this through a sort of ship's log cum personal diary kept on tape by the EPLH, and by study of the airlock tell-tales and similar protective gadgetry the details of which don't concern us at the moment. However, all the facts point to there being two entities aboard the ship, and the log tape suggests pretty strongly that the other one came to a sticky end at the hands, and teeth, of your patient."

O'Mara paused to toss a slim sheaf of papers onto his lap and Conway saw that it was a typescript of the relevant sections of the log. He had time only to discover that the EPLH's victim had been the ship's doctor, then O'Mara was talking again.

"We know nothing about its planet of origin," he said morosely, "except that it is somewhere in the other galaxy. However, with only one quarter of our own Galaxy explored, our chances of finding its home world are negligible—"

"How about the Ians," said Conway, "maybe they could help?"

The Ians belonged to a culture originating in the other galaxy which had planted a colony in the same sector of the home galaxy which contained the Hospital. They were an unusual species—classification GKNM—which went into a chrysalis stage at adolescence and metamorphosized from a ten-legged crawler into a beautiful, winged life-form. Conway had had one of them as a patient three months ago. The patient had been long since discharged, but the two GKNM doctors, who had originally come to help Conway with the patient, had remained at Sector General to study and teach.

"A Galaxy's a big place," said O'Mara with an obvious lack of enthusiasm, "but try them by all means. However, to get back to your patient, the biggest problem is going to come *after* you've cured it.

"You see, Doctor," he went on, "this particular beastie was found in circumstances which show pretty conclusively that it is guilty of an act which every intelligent species we know of considers a crime. As the Federation's police force among other things the Monitor Corps is supposed to take certain measures against criminals like this one. They are supposed to be tried, rehabilitated or punished as seems fit. But how can we give this criminal a fair trial when we know nothing at all about its background, a background which just might contain the possibility of extenuating circumstances? At the same time we can't just let it go free . . ."

"Why not?" said Conway. "Why not point it in the general direction from whence it came and administer a judicial kick in the pants?"

"Or why not let the patient die," O'Mara replied, smiling, "and save trouble all around?"

Conway didn't speak. O'Mara was using an unfair argument and they both knew it, but they also knew that nobody would be able to convince the Monitor enforcement section that curing the sick and punishing the malefactor were not of equal importance in the Scheme of Things.

"What I want you to do," O'Mara resumed, "is to find out all you can about the patient and its background after it comes to and during treatment. Knowing how soft-hearted, or soft-headed you are, I expect you will side with the patient during the cure and appoint yourself an unofficial counsel for the defense. Well, I won't mind that if in so doing you obtain the information which will enable us to summon a jury of its peers. Understood?"

Conway nodded.

O'Mara waited precisely three seconds, then said, "If you've nothing better to do than laze about in that chair . . ."

Immediately on leaving O'Mara's office Conway got in touch with Pathology and asked for the EPLA report to be sent to him before lunch. Then he invited the two Ian GKNMs to lunch and arranged for a consultation with Prilicla regarding the patient shortly afterward. With these arrangements made he felt free to begin his rounds.

During the two hours which followed Conway had no time to think about his newest patient. He had fifty-three patients currently in his charge together with six doctors in various stages of training and a supporting staff of nurses, the patients and medical staff comprising eleven different physiological types. There were special instruments and procedures for examining these extra-terrestrial patients, and when he was accompanied by a trainee whose pressure and gravity requirements differed both from those of the patient to be examined and himself, then the "routine" of his rounds could become an extraordinarily complicated business.

But Conway looked at all his patients, even those whose convalescence was well advanced or whose treatment could have been handled by a subordinate. He was well aware that this was a stupid practice which only served to give him a lot of unnecessary work, but the truth was promotion to a resident Senior Physician was still too recent for him to have become used to the large-scale delegation of responsibility. He foolishly kept on trying to do everything himself.

After rounds he was scheduled to give an initial midwifery lecture to a class of DBLF nurses. The DBLFs were furry, multipedal beings resembling outsize caterpillars and were native to the planet Kelgia. They also breathed the same atmospheric mixture as himself, which meant that he was able to do without a pressure suit. To this purely physical comfort was added the fact that talking about such elementary stuff as the reason for Kelgian females conceiving only once in their lifetime and then producing quads who were invariably divided equally in sex, did not call for great concentration on his part. It left a large section of his mind free to worry about the alleged cannibal in his observation ward.

CHAPTER 2

Half an hour later he was with the two Ian doctors in the Hospital's main dining hall—the one which catered for Tralthan, Kelgian, human and the various other warm-blooded, oxygen-breathers on the Staff—eating the inevitable salad. This in itself did not bother Conway unduly, in fact, lettuce was downright appetizing compared with some of the things he had had to eat while playing host to other e-t colleagues, but he did not think that he would ever get used to the gale they created during lunch.

The GKNM denizens of Ia were a large, delicate, winged life-form who looked something like a dragonfly. To their rod-like but flexible bodies were attached four insectile legs, manipulators, the usual sensory organs and three tremendous sets of wings. Their table manners were not actually unpleasant—it was just that they did not sit down to dine, they hovered. Apparently eating while in flight aided their digestions as well as being pretty much a conditioned reflex with them.

Conway set the Path report on the table and placed the sugar bowl on top of it to keep it from blowing away. He said, ". . . You'll see from what I've just been reading to you that this appears to be a fairly simple case. Unusually so, I'd say, because the patient is remarkably clear of harmful bacteria of any type. Its symptoms indicate a form of epithelioma, that and nothing else, which makes its unconsciousness rather puzzling. But maybe some information on its planetary environment, sleeping periods and so on, would clarify things, and that is why I wanted to talk to you.

"We know that the patient comes from your galaxy. Can you tell me anything at all about its background?"

The GKNM on Conway's right drifted a few inches back from the table and said through its Translator, "I'm afraid I have not yet mastered the intricacies of your physiological classification system, Doctor. What does the patient look like?"

"Sorry, I forgot," said Conway. He was about to explain in detail what an EPLH was, then he began sketching on the back of the Path report instead. A few minutes later he held up the result and said, "It looks something like that."

Both Ians dropped to the floor.

Conway who had never known the GKNMs to stop either eating or flying during a meal was impressed by the reaction.

He said, "You know about them, then?"

The GKNM on the right made noises which Conway's Translator reproduced as a series of barks, the e-t equivalent of an attack of stuttering. Finally it said, "We know of them. We have never seen one of them, we do not know their planet of origin, and before this moment we were not sure that they had actual physical existence. They . . . they are gods, Doctor."

Another VIP . . . ! thought Conway, with a sudden sinking feeling. His experience with VIP patients was that their cases were *never* simple. Even if the patient's condition was nothing serious there were invariably complications, none of which were medical.

"My colleague is being a little too emotional," the other GKNM broke in. Conway had never been able to see any physical difference between the two Ians, but somehow this one had the air of being a more cynical, world-weary dragonfly. "Perhaps I can tell you what little is known, and deduced, about them rather than enumerate all the things which are not . . ."

The species to which the patient belonged was not a numerous one, the Ian doctor went onto explain, but their sphere of influence in the other galaxy was tremendous. In the social and psychological sciences they were very well advanced, and individually their intelligence and mental capacity was enormous. For reasons known only to themselves they did not seek each other's company very often, and it was unheard of for more than one of them to be found on any planet at the same time for any lengthy period.

They were always the supreme ruler on the worlds they occupied.

Sometimes it was a beneficient rule, sometimes harsh—but the harshness, when viewed with a century or so's hindsight, usually turned out to be beneficence in disguise. They used people, whole planetary populations, and even interplanetary cultures, purely as a means to solve the problems which they set themselves, and when the problem was solved they left. At least this was the impression received by not quite unbiased observers.

In a voice made flat and emotionless only because of the process of Translation the Ian went on, ". . . Legends seem to agree that one of them will land on a planet with nothing but its ship and a companion who is always of a different species. By using a combination of defensive science, psychology and sheer business acumen they overcome local prejudice and begin to amass wealth and power. The transition from local authority to absolute planetary rule is gradual, but then they have plenty of time. They are, of course, immortal."

Faintly, Conway heard his fork clattering onto the floor. It was a few minutes before he could steady either his hands or his mind.

There were a few extra-terrestrial species in the Federation who possessed very long life spans, and most of the medically advanced cultures—Earth's included—had the means of extending life considerably with rejuvenation treatments. Immortality, however, was something they did *not* have, nor had they ever had the chance to study anyone who possessed it. Until now, that was. Now Conway had a patient to care for, and cure and, most of all, investigate. Unless . . . but the GKNM was a doctor, and a doctor would not say immortal if he merely meant long-lived.

"Are you sure?" croaked Conway.

The Ian's answer took a long time because it included the detailing of a great many facts, theories and legends concerning these beings who were satisfied to rule nothing less than a planet apiece. At the end of it Conway was still not sure that his patient was immortal, but everything he had heard seemed to point that way.

Hesitantly, he said, "After what I've just heard perhaps I shouldn't ask, but in your opinion are these beings capable of committing an act of murder and cannibalism—"

"No!" said one Ian.

"Never!" said the other.

There was, of course, no hint of emotion in the Translated replies,

STAR SURGEON · 215

but their sheer volume was enough to make everyone in the dining hall look up.

A few minutes later Conway was alone. The Ians had requested permission to see the legendary EPLH and then dashed off full of awe and eagerness. Ians were nice people, Conway thought, but at the same time it was his considered opinion that lettuce was fit only for rabbits. With great firmness he pushed his slightly mussed salad away from him and dialed for steak with double the usual accessories.

This promised to be a long, hard day.

When Conway returned to the observation ward the Ians had gone and the patient's condition was unchanged. The Lieutenant was still guarding the nurse on duty—closely—and was beginning to blush for some reason. Conway nodded gravely, dismissed the nurse and was giving the Path report a rereading when Dr. Prilicla arrived.

Prilicla was a spidery, fragile, low-gravity being of classication GLNO who had to wear G-nullifiers constantly to keep from being mashed flat by a gravity which most other species considered normal. Besides being a very competent doctor Prilicla was the most popular person in the hospital, because its empathic faculty made it nearly impossible for the little being to be disagreeable to anyone. And, although it also possessed a set of large, iridescent wings it sat down at mealtimes and ate spaghetti with a fork. Conway liked Prilicla a lot.

Conway briefly described the EPLH's condition and background as he saw it, then ended, ". . . I know you can't get much from an unconscious patient, but it would help me if you could—"

"There appears to be a misunderstanding here, Doctor," Prilicla broke in, using the form of words which was the nearest it ever came to telling someone they were wrong. "The patient is conscious . . ."

"Get back!"

Warned as much by Conway's emotional radiation at the thought of what the patient's boney club could do to Prilicla's eggshell body as his words, the little GLNO skittered backward out of range. The Lieutenant edged closer, his eyes on the still motionless tentacle which ended in that monstrous bludgeon. For several seconds nobody moved or spoke, while outwardly the patient remained unconscious. Finally Conway looked at Prilicla. He did not have to speak.

Prilicla said, "I detect emotional radiation of a type which emanates only from a mind which is consciously aware of itself. The mental processes themselves seem slow and, considering the physical size of the patient, weak. In detail, it is radiating feelings of danger, helplessness and confusion. There is also an indication of some overall sense of purpose."

Conway sighed.

"So it's playing 'possum," said the Lieutenant grimly, talking mostly to himself.

The fact that the patient was feigning unconsciousness worried Conway less than it did the Corpsman. In spite of the mass of diagnostic equipment available to him he subscribed firmly to the belief that a doctor's best guide to any malfunction was a communicative and cooperative patient. But how did one open a conversation with a being who was a near deity . . . ?

"We . . . we are going to help you," he said awkwardly. "Do you understand what I'm saying?"

The patient remained motionless as before.

Prilicla said, "There is no indication that it heard you, Doctor."

"But if it's conscious . . ." Conway began, and ended the sentence with a helpless shrug.

He began assembling his instruments again and with Prilicla's help examined the EPLH again, paying special attention to the organs of sight and hearing. But there was no physical or emotional reaction while the examination was in progress, despite the flashing lights and a considerable amount of ungentle probing. Conway could see no evidence of physical malfunction in any of the sensory organs, yet the patient remained completely unaware of all outside stimulus. Physically it was unconscious, insensible to everything going on around it, except that Prilicla insisted that it wasn't.

What a crazy, mixed-up demi-god, thought Conway. Trust O'Mara to send him the weirdies. Aloud he said, "The only explanation I can see for this peculiar state of affairs is that the mind you are receiving has severed or blocked off contact with all its sensory equipment. The patient's condition is not the cause of this, therefore the trouble must have a psychological basis. I'd say the beastie is urgently in need of psychiatric assistance.

"However," he ended, "the head-shrinkers can operate more effectively on a patient who is physically well, so I think we should concentrate on clearing up this skin condition first . . ."

A specific had been developed at the hospital against epithelioma of the type affecting the patient, and Pathology had already stated that it was suited to the EPLH's metabolism and would produce no harmful side-effects. It took only a few minutes for Conway to measure out a test dosage and inject subcutaneously. Prilicla moved up beside him quickly to see the effect. This, they both knew, was one of the rare, rapid-action miracles of medicine—its effect would be apparent in a matter of seconds rather than hours or days.

Ten minutes later nothing at all had happened.

"A tough guy," said Conway, and injected the maximum safe dose.

Almost at once the skin in the area darkened and lost its dry, cracked look. The dark area widened perceptibly as they watched, and one of the tentacles twitched slightly.

"What's its mind doing?" said Conway.

"Much the same as before," Prilicla replied, "but with mounting anxiety apparent since the last injection. I detect feelings of a mind trying to make a decision . . . of making a decision . . ."

Prilicla began to tremble violently, a clear sign that the emotional radiation of the patient had intensified. Conway had his mouth open to put a question when a sharp, tearing sound dragged his attention back to the patient. The EPLH was heaving and throwing itself against its restraining harness. Two of the anchoring straps had parted and it had worked a tentacle free. The one with the club . . .

Conway ducked frantically, and avoided having his head knocked off by a fraction of an inch—he felt that ultimate in blunt instruments actually touch his hair. But the Lieutenant was not so lucky. At almost the end of its swing the boney mace thudded into his shoulder, throwing him across the tiny ward so hard that he almost bounced off the wall. Prilicla, with whom cowardice was a prime survival characteristic, was already clinging with its sucker-tipped legs to the ceiling, which was the only safe spot in the room.

From his position flat on the floor Conway heard other straps go and saw two more tentacles begin feeling about. He knew that in a few minutes the patient would be completely free of the harness and able to move about the room at will. He scrambled quickly to his knees, crouched, then dived for the berserk EPLH. As he hung on tightly with his arms around its body just below the roots of the tentacles Conway was nearly deafened by a series of barking roars coming from the speaking orifice beside his ear. The noise translated as "Help me! Help me!" Simultaneously he saw the tentacle with the great, boney bludgeon at its tip swing downward. There was a crash and a three inch hollow appeared on the floor at the point where he had been lying a few seconds previously.

Tackling the patient the way he had done might have seemed foolhardy, but Conway had been trying to keep his head in more ways than one. Clinging tightly to the EPLH's body below the level of those madly swinging tentacles, Conway knew, was the next safest place in the room.

Then he saw the Lieutenant . . .

The Lieutenant had his back to the wall, half lying and half sitting up. One arm hung loosely at his side and in the other hand he held his gun, steadying it between his knees, and one eye was closed in a diabolical wink while the other sighted along the barrel. Conway shouted desperately for him to wait, but the noise from the patient drowned him out. At every instant Conway expected the flash and shock of exploding bullets. He felt paralyzed with fear, he couldn't even let go.

Then suddenly it was all over. The patient slumped onto its side, twitched and became motionless. Holstering his unfired weapon the Lieutenant struggled to his feet. Conway extricated himself and Prilicla came down off the ceiling.

Awkwardly, Conway said, "Uh, I suppose you couldn't shoot with me hanging on there?"

The Lieutenant shook his head. "I'm a good shot, Doctor, I could have hit it and missed you all right. But it kept shouting 'Help me' all the time. That sort of thing cramps a man's style . . ."

CHAPTER 3

I t was some twenty minutes later, after Prilicla had sent the Lieutenant away to have a cracked humerus set and Conway and the GLNO were fitting the patient with a much stronger harness, that they noticed the absence of the darker patch of skin. The patient's condition was now exactly the same as it had been before undergoing treatment. Apparently the hefty shot which Conway had administered had had only a temporary effect, and that was decidedly peculiar. It was in fact downright impossible.

From the moment Prilicla's empathetic faculty had been brought to bear on the case Conway had been sure that the root of the trouble was psychological. He also knew that a severely warped mind could do tremendous damage to the body which housed it. But this damage was on a purely physical level and its method of repair—the treatment developed and proved time and time again by Pathology—was a hard, physical fact also. And no mind, regardless of its power or degree of malfunction, should be able to ignore, to completely negate, a physical fact. The Universe had, after all, certain fixed laws.

So far as Conway could see there were only two possible explanations. Either the rules were being ignored because the Being who had made them had also the right to ignore them or somehow, someone—or some combination of circumstances or mis-read data—was pulling a fast one. Conway infinitely preferred the second theory because the first one was altogether too shattering to consider seriously. He desperately wanted to go on thinking of his patient with a small P . . .

———

Nevertheless, when he left the ward Conway paid a visit to the office of Captain Bryson, the Monitor Corps Chaplain, and consulted that officer at some length in a semi-professional capacity—Conway believed in carrying plenty of insurance. His next call was on Colonel Skempton, the officer in charge of Supply, Maintenance and Communications at the Hospital. There he requested complete copies of the patient's log—not just the sections relevant to the murder—together with any other background data available to be sent to his room. Then he went to the AUGL theater to demonstrate operative techniques on submarine life-forms, and before dinner he was able to work in two hours in the Pathology department during which he discovered quite a lot about his patient's immortality.

When he returned to his room there was a pile of typescript on his desk that was nearly two inches thick. Conway groaned, thinking of his six-hour recreation period and how he was going to spend it. The thought obtruded of how he would have *liked* to spend it, bringing with it a vivid picture of the very efficient and impossibly beautiful Nurse Murchison whom he had been dating regularly of late. But Murchison was currently with the FGLI Maternity Section and their free periods would not coincide for another two weeks.

In the present circumstances perhaps it was just as well, Conway thought, as he settled down for a good long read.

The Corpsmen who had examined the patient's ship had been unable to convert the EPLH's time units into the Earth-human scale with any accuracy, but they had been able to state quite definitely that many of the taped logs were several centuries old and a few of them dated back to two thousand years or more. Conway began with the oldest and sifted carefully through them until he came to the most recent. He discovered almost at once that they were not so much a series of taped diaries—the references to personal items were relatively rare—as a catalog of memoranda, most of which was highly technical and very heavy going. The data relevant to the murder, which he studied last, was much more dramatic.

... *My physician is making me sick,* the final entry read, *it is killing me. I must do something. It is a bad physician for allowing me to become ill. Somehow I must get rid of it* ...

Conway replaced the last sheet on its pile, sighed, and prepared to adopt a position more conducive to creative thinking; i.e. with his chair tipped far back, feet on desk and practically sitting on the back of his neck.

What a mess, he thought.

The separate pieces of the puzzle—or most of them, anyway—were available to him now and required only to be fitted together. There was the patient's condition, not serious so far as the Hospital was concerned but definitely lethal if not treated. Then there was the data supplied by the two Ians regarding this God-like, power-hungry but essentially beneficent race and the companions—who were never of the same species— who always traveled or lived with them. These companions were subject to replacement because they grew old and died while the EPLHs did not. There were also the Path reports, both the first written one he had received before lunch and the later verbal one furnished during his two hours with Thornnastor, the FGLI Diagnostician-in-Charge of Pathology. It was Thornnastor's considered opinion that the EPLH patient was not a true immortal, and the Considered Opinion of a Diagnostician was as near to being a rock-hard certainty as made no difference. But while immortality had been ruled out for various physiological reasons, the tests had shown evidence of longevity or rejuvenation treatments of the un-selective type.

Finally there had been the emotion readings furnished by Prilicla before and during their attempted treatment of the patient's skin condition. Prilicla had reported a steady radiation pattern of confusion, anxiety and helplessness. But when the EPLH had received its second injection it had gone berserk, and the blast of emotion exploding from its mind had, in Prilicla's own words, nearly fried the little empath's brains in their own ichor. Prilicla had been unable to get a detailed reading on such a violent eruption of emotion, mainly because it had been tuned to the earlier and more gentle level on which the patient had been radiating, but it agreed that there was evidence of instability of the schizoid type.

Conway wriggled deeper into his chair, closed his eyes and let the pieces of the puzzle slide gently into place.

It had begun on the planet where the EPLHs had been the dominant life-form. In the course of time they had achieved civilization which included interstellar flight and an advanced medical science. Their life span, lengthy to begin with, was artificially extended so that a relatively short-lived species like the Ians could be forgiven for believing them to be immortal. But a high price had had to be paid for their longevity: reproduction of their kind, the normal urge toward immortality of race in a species of mortal individuals, would have been the first thing to go; then their civilization would have dissolved—been forced apart, rather—into a mass of star-traveling, rugged individualists; and finally there would have been the psychological rot which set in when the risk of purely physical deterioration had gone.

Poor demi-gods, thought Conway.

They avoided each other's company for the simple reason that they'd already had too much of it—century after century of each other's mannerisms, habits of speech, opinions and the sheer, utter boredom of looking at each other. They had set themselves vast, sociological problems— taking charge of backward or errant planetary cultures and dragging them up by their bootstraps, and similar large-scale philanthropies—because they had tremendous minds, they had plenty of time, they had constantly to fight against boredom and because basically they must have been nice people. And because part of the price of such longevity was an ever-growing fear of death, they had to have their own personal physicians— no doubt the most efficient practitioners of medicine known to them— constantly in attendance.

Only one piece of the puzzle refused to fit and that was the odd way in which the EPLH had negated his attempts to treat it, but Conway had no doubt that that was a physiological detail which would soon become clear as well. The important thing was that he now knew how to proceed.

Not every condition responded to medication, despite Thornnastor's claims to the contrary, and he would have seen that surgery was indicated in the EPLH's case if the whole business had not been so be-fogged with considerations of who and what the patient was and what it was supposed to have done. The fact that the patient was a near-deity, a murderer and generally the type of being not to be trifled with were details which should not have concerned him.

Conway sighed and swung his feet to the floor. He was beginning to feel so comfortable that he decided he had better go to bed before he fell asleep.

Immediately after breakfast next day Conway began setting up things for the EPLH's operation. He ordered the necessary instruments and equipment sent to the observation ward, gave detailed instructions regarding its sterilization—the patient was supposed to have killed one doctor already for allowing it to become sick, and a dim view would be taken if another one was the cause of it catching something else because of faulty aseptic procedures—and requested the assistance of a Tralthan surgeon to help with the fine work. Then half an hour before he was due to start Conway called on O'Mara.

The Chief Psychologist listened to his report and intended course of action without comment until he had finished, then he said, "Conway, do you realize what could happen to this hospital if that thing got loose? And not just physically loose, I mean. It is seriously disturbed mentally, you say, if not downright psychotic. At the moment it is unconscious, but from what you tell me its grasp of the psychological sciences is such that it could have us eating out of its manipulatory appendage just by talking at us.

"I'm concerned as to what may happen when it wakes up."

It was the first time Conway had heard O'Mara confess to being worried about anything. Several years back when a runaway spaceship had crashed into the hospital, spreading havoc and confusion through sixteen levels, it was said that Major O'Mara had expressed a feeling of concern on that occasion also . . .

"I'm trying not to think about that," said Conway apologetically. "It just confuses the issue."

O'Mara took a deep breath and let it out slowly through his nose, a mannerism of his which could convey more than twenty scathing sentences. He said coldly, "Somebody should think about these things, Doctor. I trust you will have no objection to *me* observing the coming operation . . . ?"

To what was nothing less than a politely worded order there could be no reply other than an equally polite, "Glad to have you, sir."

When they arrived in the observation ward the patient's "bed" had been raised to a comfortable operating height and the EPLH itself was strapped securely into position. The Tralthan had taken its place beside the recording and anesthetizing gear and had one eye on the patient, one on its equipment and the other two directed toward Prilicla with whom it was discussing a particularly juicy piece of scandal which had come to light the previous day. As the two beings concerned were PVSJ chlorine-breathers the affair could have only an academic interest for them, but apparently their academic interest was intense. At the sight of O'Mara, however, the scandal-mongering ceased forthwith. Conway gave the signal to begin.

The anesthetic was one of several which Pathology had pronounced safe for the EPLH life-form, and while it was being administered Conway found his mind going off at a tangent toward his Tralthan assistant.

Surgeons of that species were really two beings instead of one, a combination of FGLI and OTSB. Clinging to the leathery back of the lumbering, elephantine Tralthan was a diminutive and nearly mindless being who lived in symbiosis with it. At first glance the OTSB looked like a furry ball with a long ponytail sprouting from it, but a closer look showed that the ponytail was composed of scores of fine manipulators most of which incorporated sensitive visual organs. Because of the *rapport* which existed between the Tralthan and its symbiote the FGLI-OTSB combination were the finest surgeons in the Galaxy. Not all Tralthans chose to link up with a symbiote, but FGLI medics wore them like a badge of office.

Suddenly the OTSB scurried along its host's back and huddled atop the dome-like head between the eye-stalks, its tail hanging down toward the patient and fanning out stiffly. The Tralthan was ready to begin.

"You will observe that this is a surface condition only," Conway said, for the benefit of the recording equipment, "and that the whole skin area looks dead, dried-up and on the point of flaking off. During the removal of the first skin samples no difficulty was encountered, but later specimens resisted removal to a certain extent and the reason was discovered to be a tiny rootlet, approximately one quarter of an inch long and invisible to the naked eye. My naked eye, that is. So it seems clear that the condition is about to enter a new phase. The disease is beginning to dig in rather than remain on the surface, and the more promptly we act the better."

Conway gave the reference numbers of the Path reports and his own preliminary notes on the case, then went on, ". . . As the patient, for reasons which are at the moment unclear, does not respond to medication I propose surgical removal of the affected tissue, irrigation, cleansing and replacement with surrogate skin. A Tralthan-guided OTSB will be used to ensure that the rootlets are also excised. Except for the considerable area to be covered, which will make this a long job, the procedure is straightforward—"

"Excuse me, Doctors," Prilicla broke in, "the patient is still conscious."

An argument, polite only on Prilicla's side, broke out between the Tralthan and the little empath. Prilicla held that the EPLH was thinking thoughts and radiating emotions and the other maintained that it had enough of the anesthetic in its system to render it completely insensible to everything for at least six hours. Conway broke in just as the argument was becoming personal.

"We've had this trouble before," he said irritably. "The patient has been physically unconscious except for a few minutes yesterday, since its arrival, yet Prilicla detected the presence of rational thought processes. Now the same effect is present while it is under anesthetic. I don't know how to explain this, it will probably require a surgical investigation of its brain structure to do so, and that is something which will have to wait. The important thing at the moment is that it is physically incapable of movement or of feeling pain. Now shall we begin?"

To Prilicla he added, "Keep listening just in case . . ."

CHAPTER 4

For about twenty minutes they worked in silence, although the procedure did not require a high degree of concentration. It was rather like weeding a garden, except that everything which grew was a weed and had to be removed one plant at a time. He would peel back an affected area of skin, the OTSB's hair-thin appendages would investigate, probe and detach the rootlets, and he would peel back another tiny segment. Conway was looking forward to the most tedious operation of his career.

Prilicla said, "I detect increasing anxiety linked with a strengthening sense of purpose. The anxiety is becoming intense . . ."

Conway grunted. He could think of no other comment to make.

Five minutes later the Tralthan said, "We will have to slow down, Doctor. We are at a section where the roots are much deeper . . ."

Two minutes later Conway said, "But I can *see* them! How deep are they now?"

"Four inches," replied the Tralthan. "And Doctor, they are visibly lengthening as we work."

"But that's impossible!" Conway burst out; then, "We'll move to another area."

He felt the sweat begin to trickle down his forehead and just beside him Prilicla's gangling, fragile body began to quiver—but not at anything the patient was thinking. Conway's own emotional radiation just then was not a pleasant thing, because in the new area and in the two chosen at random after that the result was the same. Roots from the flaking pieces of skin were burrowing deeper as they watched.

"Withdraw," said Conway harshly.

For a long time nobody spoke. Prilicla was shaking as if a high wind was blowing in the ward. The Tralthan was fussing with its equipment, all four of its eyes focused on one unimportant knob. O'Mara was looking intently at Conway, also calculatingly and with a large amount of sympathy in his steady gray eyes. The sympathy was because he could recognize when a man was genuinely in a spot and the calculation was due to his trying to work out whether the trouble was Conway's fault or not.

"What happened, Doctor?" he said gently.

Conway shook his head angrily. "I don't know. Yesterday the patient did not respond to medication, today it won't respond to surgery. Its reactions to anything we try to do for it are crazy, impossible! And now our attempt to relieve its condition surgically has triggered off—something—which will send those roots deep enough to penetrate vital organs in a matter of minutes if their present rate of growth is maintained, and you know what that means . . ."

"The patient's sense of anxiety is diminishing," Prilicla reported. "It is still engaged in purposeful thinking."

The Tralthan joined in then. It said, "I have noticed a peculiar fact about those root-like tendrils which join the diseased flakes of skin with the body. My symbiote has extremely sensitive vision, you will understand, and it reports that the tendrils seem to be rooted at each end, so that it is impossible to tell whether the growth is attacking the body or the body is deliberately holding onto the growth."

Conway shook his head distractedly. The case was full of mad contradictions and outright impossibilities. To begin with no patient, no matter how fouled up mentally, should be able to negate the effects of a drug powerful enough to bring about a complete cure within half an hour, and all within a few minutes. And the natural order of things was for a being with a diseased area of skin to slough it off and replace it with new tissue, not hang onto it grimly no matter what. It was a baffling, hopeless case.

Yet when the patient had arrived it had seemed a simple, straightforward case—Conway had felt more concern regarding the patient's background than its condition, whose cure he had considered a routine matter. But somewhere along the way he had missed something, Conway was sure, and because of this sin of omission the patient would probably die during the next few hours. Maybe he had made a snap diagnosis, been too sure of himself, been criminally careless.

It was pretty horrible to lose a patient at any time, and at Sector General losing a patient was an extremely rare occurrence. But to lose one whose condition no hospital anywhere in the civilized galaxy would have considered as being serious . . . Conway swore luridly, but stopped because he hadn't the words to describe how he felt about himself.

"Take it easy, son."

That was O'Mara, squeezing his arm and talking like a father. Normally O'Mara was a bad-tempered, bull-voiced and unapproachable tyrant who, when one went to him for help, sat making sarcastic remarks while the person concerned squirmed and shamefacedly solved his own problems. His present uncharacteristic behavior proved something, Conway thought bitterly. It proved that Conway had a problem which Conway could not solve himself.

But in O'Mara's expression there was something more than just concern for Conway, and it was probably that deep down the psychologist was a little glad that things had turned out as they did. Conway meant no reflection on O'Mara's character, because he knew that if the Major had been in his position he would have tried as hard if not harder to cure the patient, and would have felt just as badly about the outcome. But at the same time the Chief Psychologist must have been desperately worried about the possibility of a being of great and unknown powers, who was also mentally unbalanced, being turned loose on the Hospital. In addition O'Mara might also be wondering if, beside a conscious and alive EPLH, he would look like a small and untutored boy . . .

"Let's try taking it from the top again," O'Mara said, breaking in on his thoughts. "Is there anything you've found in the patients's background that might point to it wanting to destroy itself?"

"*No!*" said Conway vehemently. "To the contrary! It would want desperately to live. It was taking unselective rejuvenation treatments, which means that the complete cell-structure of its body was regenerated periodically. As the process of storing memory is a product of aging in the brain cells, this would practically wipe its mind clean after every treatment . . ."

"That's why those taped logs resembled technical memoranda,"

O'Mara put in. "That's exactly what they were. Still, I prefer our own method of rejuvenation even though we won't live so long, regenerating damaged organs only and allowing the brain to remain untouched..."

"I know," Conway broke in, wondering why the usually taciturn O'Mara had become so talkative. Was he trying to simplify the problem by making him state it in non-professional terms? "But the effect of continued longevity treatments, as you know yourself, is to give the possessor an increasing fear of dying. Despite loneliness, boredom and an altogether unnatural existence, the fear grows steadily with the passage of time. That is why it always traveled with its own private physician, it was desperately afraid of sickness or an accident befalling it between treatments, and that is why I can sympathize to a certain extent with its feelings when the doctor who was supposed to keep it well allowed it to get sick, although the business of eating it afterward—"

"So you are on its side," said O'Mara dryly.

"It could make a good plea of self-defense," Conway retorted. "But I was saying that it was desperately afraid of dying, so that it would be constantly trying to get a better, more efficient doctor for itself... Oh!"

"Oh, what?" said O'Mara.

It was Prilicla, the emotion sensitive who replied. It said, "Doctor Conway has just had an idea."

"What is it, you young whelp? There's no need to be so damn secretive..!" O'Mara's voice had lost its gentle fatherly tone, and there was a gleam in his eye which said that he was glad that gentleness was no longer necessary. "What *is* wrong with the patient?"

Feeling happy and excited and at the same time very much unsure of himself, Conway stumbled across to the intercom and ordered some very unusual equipment, checked again that the patient was so thoroughly strapped down that it would be unable to move a muscle, then he said, "My guess is that the patient is perfectly sane and we've been blinding ourselves with psychological red herrings. Basically, the trouble is something it ate."

"I had a bet with myself you would say that sometime during this case," said O'Mara. He looked sick.

The equipment arrived—a slender, pointed wooden stake and a mechanism which would drive it downward at any required angle and controlled speeds. With the Tralthan's help Conway set it up and moved it into position. He chose a part of the patient's body which contained several vital organs which were, however, protected by nearly six inches of musculature and adipose, then he set the stake in motion. It was just touching the skin and descending at the rate of approximately two inches per hour.

"What the blazes is going on?" stormed O'Mara. "Do you think the patient is a vampire or something!"

"Of course not," Conway replied. "I'm using a wooden stake to give the patient a better chance of defending itself. You wouldn't expect it to stop a steel one, would you." He motioned the Tralthan forward and together they watched the area where the stake was entering the EPLH's body. Every few minutes Prilicla reported on the emotional radiation. O'Mara paced up and down, occasionally muttering to himself.

The point had penetrated almost a quarter of an inch when Conway noticed the first coarsening and thickening of the skin. It was taking place in a roughly circular area, about four inches in diameter, whose center was the wound created by the stake. Conway's scanner showed a spongy, fibrous growth forming under the skin to a depth of half an inch. Visibly the growth thickened and grew opaque to his scanner's current setting, and within ten minutes it had become a hard, boney plate. The stake had begun to bend alarmingly and was on the point of snapping.

"I'd say the defenses are now concentrated at this one point," Conway said, trying to keep his voice steady, "so we'd better have it out."

Conway and the Tralthan rapidly incised around and undercut the newly-formed bony plate, which was immediately transferred into a sterile, covered receptacle. Quickly preparing a shot—a not quite maximum dose of the specific he had tried the previous day—Conway injected, then went back to helping the Tralthan with the repair work on the wound. This was routine work and took about fifteen minutes, and when it was finished there could be no doubt at all that the patient was responding favorably to treatment.

Over the congratulations of the Tralthan and the horrible threats of O'Mara—the Chief Psychologist wanted some questions answered, fast—Prilicla said, "You have effected a cure, Doctor, but the patient's anxiety level has markedly increased. It is almost frantic."

Conway shook his head, grinning. "The patient is heavily anesthetized and cannot feel anything. However, I agree that at this present moment . . ." He nodded toward the sterile container. ". . . its personal physician must be feeling pretty bad."

In the container the excised bone had begun to soften and leak a faintly purplish liquid. The liquid was rippling and sloshing gently about at the bottom of the container as if it had a mind of its own. Which was, in fact, the case ...

Conway was in O'Mara's office winding up his report on the EPLH and the Major was being highly complimentary in a language which at times made the compliments indistinguishable from insults. But this was O'Mara's way, Conway was beginning to realize, and the Chief Psychologist was polite and sympathetic only when he was professionally concerned about a person.

He was still asking questions.

"... An intelligent, amoebic life-form, a organized collection of sub-microscopic, virus-type cells, would make the most efficient doctor obtainable," said Conway in reply to one of them. "It would reside within its patient and, given the necessary data, control any disease or organic malfunction from the inside. To a being who is pathologically afraid of dying it must have seemed perfect. And it was, too, because the trouble which developed was not really the doctor's fault. It came about through the patient's ignorance of its own physiological background.

"The way I see it," Conway went on, "the patient had been taking its rejuvenation treatments at an early stage of its biological lifetime. I mean that it did not wait until middle or old age before regenrating itself. But on this occasion, either because it forgot or was careless or had been working on a problem which took longer than usual, it aged more than it had previously and acquired this skin condition. Pathology says that this was probably a common complaint with this race, and the normal course would be for the EPLH to slough off the affected skin and carry on as usual. But our patient, because the type of its rejuvenation treatment caused memory damage, did not know this, so its personal physician did not know it either."

Conway continued, "This, er, resident physician knew very little about the medical background of its patient-host's body, but its motto must have been to maintain the *status quo* at all costs. When pieces of its patient's body threatened to break away it held onto them, not realizing that this could have been a normal occurrence like losing hair or a reptile periodically shedding its skin, especially as its master would have insisted that the occurrence was not natural. A pretty fierce struggle must have developed between the patient's body processes and its doctor, with the patient's mind also ranged against its doctor. Because of this the doctor had to render the patient unconscious the better to do what it considered to be the right thing.

"When we gave it the test shots the doctor neutralized them. They were a foreign substance being introduced into its patient's body, you see. And you know what happened when we tried surgical removal. It was only when we threatened underlying vital organs with that stake, forcing the doctor to defend its patient at that one point . . ."

"When you began asking for wooden stakes," said O'Mara dryly, "I thought of putting *you* in a tight harness."

Conway grinned. He said, "I'm recommending that the EPLH takes his doctor back. Now that Pathology has given it a fuller understanding of its employer's medical and physiological history it should be the ultimate in personal physicians, and the EPLH is smart enough to see that."

O'Mara smiled in return. "And I was worried about what it might do when it became conscious. But it turned out to be a very friendly, likeable type. Quite charming, in fact."

As Conway rose and turned to go he said slyly, "That's because it's such a good psychologist. It is pleasant to people *all* the time . . ."

He managed to get the door shut behind him before the explosion.

CHAPTER 5

I n time the EPLH patient, whose name was Lonvellin, was discharged and the steady procession of ailing e-ts who came under his care made the memory of Lonvellin's fade in Conway's mind. He did not know whether the EPLH had returned to its home galaxy or was still wandering this one in search of good deeds to do, and he was being kept too busy to care either way. But Conway was not quite finished with the EPLH.

Or more accurately, Lonvellin was not quite finished with Conway . . .

"How would you like to get away from the hospital for a few months, Doctor?" O'Mara said, when Conway had presented himself in the Chief Psychologist's office in answer to an urgent summons over the PA. "It would be in the nature of a holiday, almost."

Conway felt his initial unease grow rapidly into panic. He had urgent personal reasons for *not* leaving the hospital for a few months. He said, "Well . . ."

The psychologist raised his head and fixed Conway with a pair of level gray eyes which saw so much and which opened into a mind so keenly analytical that together they gave O'Mara what amounted to a telepathic faculty. He said dryly, "Don't bother to thank me, it is your own fault for curing such powerful, influential patients."

He went on briskly, "This is a large assignment, Doctor, but it will consist mainly of clerical work. Normally it would be given to someone at Diagnostician level, but that EPLH, Lonvellin, has been at work on a planet which it says is urgently in need of medical aid. Lonvellin has requested Monitor Corps as well as hospital assistance in this, and has asked that you personally should direct the medical side. Apparently a

Great Intellect isn't needed for the job, just one with a peculiar way of looking at things . . ."

"You're too kind, sir," said Conway.

Grinning, O'Mara said, "I've told you before, I'm here to shrink heads, not inflate them. And now, this is the report on the situation there at the moment . . ." He slid the file he had been reading across to Conway, and stood up. ". . . You can brief yourself on it when you board ship. Be at Lock Sixteen to board *Vespasian* at 2130, meanwhile I expect you have loose ends to tidy up. And Conway, try not to look as if all your relatives had died. Very probably she'll wait for you. If she doesn't, why you have two hundred and seventeen other female DBDGs to chase after. Goodbye and good luck, Doctor."

Outside O'Mara's office Conway tried to work out how best to tidy up his loose ends in the six hours remaining before embarkation time. He was scheduled to take a group of trainees through a basic orientation lecture in ten minutes from now, and it was too late to foist that job onto someone else. That would kill three of the six hours, four if he was unlucky and today he felt unlucky. Then an hour to tape instructions regarding his more serious ward patients, then dinner. He might just do it. Conway began hurrying toward Lock Seven on the one hundred and eighth level.

He arrived at the lock antechamber just as the inner seal was opening, and while catching his breath began mentally checking off the trainees who were filing past him. Two Kelgian DBLFs who undulated past like giant, silver-furred caterpillars; then a PVSJ from Illensa, the outlines of its spiny, membranous body softened by the chlorine fog inside its protective envelope; a water-breathing Creppelian octopoid, classification AMSL, whose suit made loud bubbling noises. These were followed by five AACPs, a race whose remote ancestors had been a species of mobile vegetable. They were slow moving, but the CO_2 tanks which they wore seemed to be the only protection they needed. Then another Kelgian . . .

When they were all inside and the seal closed behind them Conway spoke. Quite unnecessarily and simply as a means of breaking the conversational ice, he said, "Is everyone present?"

Inevitably they all replied in chorus, sending Conway's Translator into a howl of oscillation. Sighing, he began the customary procedure of introducing himself and bidding his new colleagues welcome. It was only at the end of these polite formalities that he worked in a gentle reminder regarding the operating principles of the Translator, and the advisability of speaking one at a time so as not to overload it . . .

On their home worlds these were all very important people, medically speaking. It was only at Sector General that they were new boys, and for some of them the transition from acknowledged master to lowly pupil might be difficult, so that large quantities of tact were necessary when handling them at this stage. Later, however, when they began to settle in, they could be bawled out for their mistakes like anyone else.

"I propose to start our tour at Reception," Conway went on, "where the problems of admittance and initial treatment are dealt with. Then, providing the environment does not require complex protective arrangements for ourselves and the patient's condition is not critical, we will visit the adjacent wards to observe examination procedures on newly-arrived patients. If anyone wants to ask questions at any time, feel free to do so.

"On the way to Reception," he continued, "we will use corridors which may be crowded. There is a complicated system of precedence governing the rights of way of junior and senior medical staff, a system which you will learn in time. But for the present there is just one simple rule to remember. If the being coming at you is bigger than you are, get out of its way."

He was about to add that no doctor in Sector General would *deliberately* trample a colleague to death, but thought better of it. A great many e-ts did not have a sense of humor and such a harmless pleasantry, if taken literally, could lead to endless complications. Instead he said, "Follow me, please."

Conway arranged for the five AACPs, who were the slowest-moving of the group, to follow himself and set the pace for the others. After them came the two Kelgians whose undulating gait was only slightly faster than the vegetable life-forms preceding them. The chlorine-breather came next and the Creppelian octopoid brought up the rear, the bubbling noise from its suit giving Conway an audible indication that his fifty-yard long tail was all in one piece.

Strung out as they were there was no point in Conway trying to talk, and they negotiated the first stage of the journey in silence—three ascending ramps and a couple of hundred yards of straight and angled corridors. The only person they met coming in the opposite direction was a Nidian wearing the armband of a two-year intern. Nidians averaged four feet in height so that nobody was in any danger of being trampled to death. They reached the internal lock which gave access to the water-breather's section.

In the adjoining dressing room Conway supervised the suiting-up of the two Kelgians, then climbed into a light-weight suit himself. The AACPs said that their vegetable metabolism enabled them to exist under water for long periods without protection. The Illensan was already sealed against the oxygen-laden air so that the equally poisonous water did not worry it. But the Creppelian was a water-breather and wanted to take its suit off—it had eight legs which badly needed stretching, it said. But Conway vetoed this on the grounds that it would only be in the water for fifteen minutes at most.

The lock opened into the main AUGL ward, a vast, shadowy tank of tepid green water two hundred feet deep and five hundred feet across. Conway quickly discovered that moving the trainees from the lock to the corridor entrance on the other side was like trying to drive a three dimensional herd of cattle through green glue. With the single exception of the Creppelian they all lost their sense of direction in the water within the first few minutes. Conway had to swim frantically around them, gesticulating and shouting directions, and despite the cooling and drying elements in his suit the interior soon became like an overheated turkish bath. Several times he lost his temper and directed his charges to a place other than the corridor entrance.

And during one particularly chaotic moment an AUGL patient—one of the forty-foot, armored, fish-like natives of Chalderescol II—swam ponderously toward them. It closed to within five yards, causing a near-panic among the AACPs, said "Student!" and swam away again. Chalders were notoriously antisocial during convalescence, but the incident did not help Conway's temper any.

It seemed much longer than fifteen minutes later when they were assembled in the corridor at the other side of the tank. Conway said, "Three hundred yards along this corridor is the transfer lock into the oxygen section of Reception, which is the best place to see what is going on there. Those of you who are wearing protection against water only will remove their suits, the others will go straight through . . ."

As he was swimming with them toward the lock the Creppelian said to one of the AACPs, "Ours is supposed to be filled with superheated steam, but you have to have done something very bad to be sent there."

To which the AACP replied, "Our Hell is hot, too, but there is no moisture in it at all . . ."

Conway had been about to apologize for losing his temper back in the tank, fearing that he might have hurt some sensitive extra-terrestrial feelings, but obviously they hadn't taken what he'd said very seriously.

CHAPTER 6

Through the transparent wall of its observation gallery, Reception showed as a large, shadowy room containing three large control desks, only one of which was currently occupied. The being seated before it was another Nidian, a small humanoid with seven-fingered hands and an overall coat of tight, curly red fur. Indicator lights on the desk showed that it had just made contact with a ship approaching the hospital.

Conway said, "Listen . . ."

"Identify yourself, please," said the red teddy bear in its staccato, barking speech—which was filtered through Conway's Translator as flat, toneless English and which came to the others as equally toneless Kelgian, Illensan or whatever. "Patient, visitor or staff, and species?"

"Pilot, with one passenger-patient aboard," came the reply. "Both human."

There was a short pause, then; "Give your physiological classification, please, or make full-vision contact," said the Nidian with a very Earth-human wink toward the watchers in the gallery. "All intelligent races refer to their own species as human and think of all others as being non-human. What you call yourself has no meaning so far as preparing accommodation for the patient is concerned . . ."

Conway muted the speaker which carried the conversation between ship and receptionist into the gallery and said, "This is as good a time as any to explain our physiological classification system to you. Briefly, that is, because later there will be special lectures on this subject."

Clearing his throat, he began, "In the four-letter classification system the first letter indicates the level of physical evolution, the second denotes the type and distribution of limbs and sense organs and the other two the combination metabolism and pressure and gravity requirements, which in turn give an indication of the physical mass and form of protective tegument possessed by the being. I must mention here, in case any of you might feel inferior regarding your classification, that the level of physical evolution has no relation to the level of intelligence . . ."

Species with the prefix A, B and C, he went onto explain, were water-breathers. On most worlds life had originated in the sea and these beings had developed high intelligence without having to leave it. D through F were warm-blooded oxygen-breathers, into which group fell most of the intelligence races in the galaxy, and the G and K types were also oxygen-breathing but insectile. The Ls and Ms were light-gravity, winged beings.

Chlorine-breathing life-forms were contained in the O and P groups, and after that came the more exotic, the more highly-evolved physically and the downright weird types. Radiation-eaters, frigid-blooded or crystalline beings, and entities capable of modifying their physical structure at will. Those possessing extra-sensory powers sufficiently well-developed to make walking or manipulatory appendages unnecessary were given the prefix V, regardless of size or shape.

Conway admitted to anomalies in the system, but these could be blamed on the lack of imagination by its originators. One of the species present in the observation gallery was a case in point—the AACP type with its vegetable metabolism. Normally the A prefix denoted a water-breather, there being nothing lower in the system than the piscatorial life-forms. But the AACPs were vegetables and plants had come before fish.

". . . Great stress is laid on the importance of a rapid and accurate classification of incoming patients, who very often are in no condition to furnish this information themselves," Conway went on. "Ideally, you should reach a stage of proficiency which will enable you to rattle off a classification after a three-second glimpse of an e-t foot or section of tegument.

"But look there," he said, pointing.

Over the control desk three screens were alight, and adjacent indicators added detail to the information contained in the pictures. The first showed the interior of Lock Three, which contained two Earth-human orderlies and a large stretcher-carrier. The orderlies wore heavy duty suits and anti-gravity belts, which didn't surprise Conway at all because Lock Three and its associated levels were maintained at five Gs with pressure to match. Another screen showed the exterior of the lock with its transfer servo-mechanisms and the ship about to make contact, and the third picture was being relayed from inside the ship and showed the patient.

Conway said, "You can see that it is a heavy, squat life-form possessing six appendages which serve both as arms and legs. Its skin is thick, very tough and pitted all over, and is also encrusted in places with a dry, brownish substance which sometimes flakes off when the patient moves. Pay particular attention to this brown substance, and to features which seem to be missing from the body. The tell-tales show a warm-blooded, oxygen-breathing metabolism adapted to a gravity pull of four Gs. Would one of you like to classify it for me?"

There was a long silence, then the Creppelian AMSL twitched a tentacle and said, "FROL, sir."

"Very close," said Conway approvingly. "However, I happen to know that this being's atmosphere is a dense, nearly opaque soup, the resemblance to soup being increased by the fact that its lower reaches are alive with small airborne organisms which it feeds upon. You missed the fact that it has no eating mouth but absorbs food directly via the pittings in its skin. When traveling in space, however, the food has to be sprayed on, hence the brownish encrustation—"

"FROB," said the Creppelian quickly.

"Correct."

Conway wondered whether this AMSL was a little brighter than the others or just less shy. He made a mental note to keep an eye on this particular batch of trainees. He could use a bright assistant in his own wards.

Waving goodbye to the furry receptionist, Conway gathered his flock about him again and headed them toward the FGLI ward five levels below. After that came other wards until Conway decided to introduce them to the complex, far flung department of the Hospital without whose constant and efficient working the tremendous establishment of Sector General could not have functioned and the vast multitude of its patients, staff and maintenance personnel could not have lived.

Conway was feeling hungry, and it was time he showed them where they all ate.

AACPs did not eat in the normal manner but planted themselves during their sleep period in specially prepared soil and absorbed nutriment in that way. After seeing them settled he deposited the PVSJ in the dim, noisome depths of the hall where the chlorine-breathers ate, and this left him with the two DBLFs and the AMSL to dispose of.

The largest dining hall in the hospital, the one devoted to oxygen-breathers, was close by. Conway saw the two Kelgians placed with a group of their own species, then with a look of hungry yearning toward the Senior's enclosure he hurried out again to take care of the Creppelian.

To reach the section catering for the water-breathers necessitated a fifteen minute walk along some of the busiest corridors of the hospital. Entities of all shapes and sizes flapped, undulated and sometimes walked past them. Conway had become inured to being jostled by elephantine Tralthans and having to step carefully around the fragile, diminutive LSVOs, but the Creppelian was like an armor plated octopus walking on eggs—there were times when the AMSL seemed afraid to move. The bubbling sounds from its suit had increased noticably, too.

Conway tried to make it relax by getting it to talk about its previous hospital experience, but without much success. Then suddenly they turned a corner and Conway saw his old friend Prilicla coming from a side ward . . .

The AMSL went "Wheep!" and its eight legs threshed frantically into reverse. One of them swung heavily into the back of Conway's knees and he sat down violently. The octopoid took off down the corridor, still wheeping.

"What the blazes . . . !" said Conway, with what he thought later was commendable restraint.

"This is my fault entirely, I frightened it," said Prilicla as it hurried up. "Are you hurt, Doctor?"

"*You* frightened it . . . !"

The gentle, spider-like creature from Cinruss apologized, "Yes, I'm afraid so. The combination of surprise and what seems to be a deeply-rooted xenophobic neurosis caused a panic reaction. It is badly frightened but not completely out of control. Are you hurt, Doctor?"

"Just my feelings," Conway growled, scrambling to his feet and going after the fleeing Creppelian, who was now out of sight and very nearly out of earshot.

His progress in the wake of the AMSL became a rapid zigzag that was half sprint and half waltz. To his superiors he called "Excuse me!" and to equals and inferiors he bawled "Gangway!" Almost at once he began to overtake the AMSL, proving once again that as an efficient means of locomotion two feet were much better than eight, and he was just drawing level when the being trapped itself neatly by turning into a linen storeroom. Conway skidded to a halt outside the still open door, went in and closed it firmly behind him.

As calmly as shortage of breath would allow he said, "Why did you run away?"

Words poured suddenly from the AMSL. The Translator filtered out all the emotional overtones but from the sheer rapidity of its speech he knew that the Creppelian was having the equivalent of hysterics, and as he listened he knew that Prilicla's emotional reading had been right. Here was a xenophobic neurosis and no mistake.

O'Mara will get you if you don't watch out, he thought grimly.

Given even the highest qualities of tolerance and mutual respect, there were still occasions when inter-racial friction occurred in the hospital. Potentially dangerous situations arose through ignorance or misunderstanding, or a being could develop xenophobia to a degree which affected its professional efficiency, mental stability, or both. An Earth-human doctor, for instance, who had a subconscious fear of spiders would not be able to bring to bear on a Cinrusskin patient the proper degree of clinical detachment necessary for its treatment. And if one of the Cinrusskins, like Prilicla, were to treat such an Earth-human patient . . .

It was O'Mara's job as Chief Psychologist to detect and eradicate such trouble—or if all else failed, to remove the potentially dangerous individuals—before such friction developed into open conflict. Conway did not know how O'Mara would react to a hulking great AMSL who fled in panic from such a fragile creature as Dr. Prilicla.

When the Creppelian's outburst began to ease off Conway raised his hand for attention and said, "I realize now that Dr. Prilicla bears a physical resemblance to a species of small, amphibious predator native to your home world, and that in your youth you experienced an extremely harrowing incident with these animals. But Doctor Prilicla is not an animal and the resemblance is purely visual. Far from being a threat you could kill Prilicla if you were to touch it carelessly.

"Knowing this," Conway ended seriously, "would you be frightened into running if you were to meet this being again?"

"I don't know," said the AMSL. "I might."

Conway sighed. He could not help remembering his own first weeks at Sector General and the horrible, nightmare creatures which had haunted his sleep. What had made the nightmares particularly horrifying had been the fact that they were not figments of his imagination but actual, physical realities which in many cases were only a few bulkheads away.

He had never fled from any of these nightmares who had later become his teachers, colleagues and eventually friends. But to be honest with himself this was not due so much to intestinal fortitude as the fact that extreme fear had a tendency to paralyze Conway rather than to make him run away.

"I think you may need psychiatric assistance, Doctor," he told the Creppelian gently, "and the hospital's Chief Psychologist will help you. But I would advise you not to consult him at once. Spend a week or so trying to adapt to the situation before going to him. You will find that he will think more highly of you for doing this..."

... *And less likely,* he added silently, *to send you packing as unsuited for duty in a multi-environment hospital.*

The Creppelian left the storeroom with very little persuasion, after Conway told it that Prilicla was the only GLNO in the hospital at the moment and that their paths were very unlikely to cross twice in the same day. Ten minutes later the AMSL was settled in its dining tank and Conway was making for his own dinner by the fastest possible route.

CHAPTER 7

By a stroke of luck he saw Dr. Mannon at an otherwise empty table in the Senior's enclosure. Mannon was an Earth-human who had once been Conway's superior and was now a Senior Physician well on the way to achieving Diagnostician status. Currently he was allowed to retain three physiology tapes—those of a Tralthan specialist in microsurgery and two which had been made by surgeons of the low-gravity LSVO and MSVK species—but despite this his reactions were reasonably human. At the moment he was working through a salad with his eyes turned toward Heaven and the dining hall ceiling in an effort not to look at what he was eating. Conway sat down facing him and made a sympathetic, querying noise.

"I've had a Tralthan *and* a LSVO on my list this afternoon, both long jobs," Mannon said grumpily. "You know how it is, I've been thinking like them too much. If only these blasted Tralthans weren't vegetarians, or the LSVOs weren't sickened by anything which doesn't look like bird seed. Are you anybody else today?"

Conway shook his head. "Just me. Do you mind if I have steak?"

"No, just don't talk about it."

"I won't."

Conway knew only too well the confusion, mental double vision and the severe emotional disturbance which went with a physiology tape that had become too thoroughly keyed in to the operating physician's mind. He could remember a time only three months ago when he had fallen hopelessly—but *hopelessly*—in love with one of a group of visiting specialists from Melf IV. The Melfans were ELNTs—six-legged, amphibious, vaguely crab-like beings—and while one half of his mind had insisted that the whole affair was ridiculous the other half thought lovingly of that gorgeously marked carapace and generally felt like baying at the moon.

Physiology tapes were decidedly a mixed blessing, but their use was necessary because no single being could hope to hold in its brain all the physiological data needed for the treatment of patients in a multi-environment hospital. The incredible mass of data required to take care of them was furnished by means of Educator tapes, which were simply the brain recordings of great medical specialists of the various species concerned. If an Earth-human doctor had to treat a Kelgian patient he took one of the DBLF physiology tapes until treatment was complete, after which he had it erased. But Senior Physicians with teaching duties were often called onto retain these tapes for long periods, which wasn't much fun at all.

The only good thing from their point of view was that they were better off than the Diagnosticians.

They were the hospital's *elite*. A Diagnostician was one of those rare beings whose mind was considered stable enough to retain permanently up to ten physiology tapes simultaneously. To their data-crammed minds was given the job of original research in xenological medicine and the diagnosis and treatment of new diseases in hitherto unknown life-forms. There was a well-known saying in the hospital, reputed to have originated with O'Mara himself, that anyone sane enough to want to be a Diagnostician was mad.

For it was not only physiological data which the tapes imparted, the complete memory and personality of the entity who had possessed that knowledge was impressed on the receiving brain as well. In effect a Diagnostician subjected himself or itself voluntarily to the most drastic form of multiple schizophrenia, with the alien personality sharing his mind so utterly *different* that in many cases they did not have even a system of logic in common.

Conway brought his thoughts back to the here and now. Mannon was speaking again.

"A funny thing about the taste of salad," he said, still glaring at the ceiling as he ate, "is that none of my alter egos seem to mind it. The sight of it yes, but not the taste. They don't particularly like it, mind, but neither does it completely revolt them. At the same time there are few species with an overwhelming passion for it, either. And speaking of over-whelming passions, how about you and Murchison?"

246 · JAMES WHITE

One of these days Conway expected to hear gears clashing, the way Mannon changed subjects so quickly.

"I'll be seeing her tonight if I've time," he replied carefully. "However, we're just good friends."

"Haw," said Mannon.

Conway make an equally violent switch of subjects by hurriedly breaking the news about his latest assignment. Mannon was the best in the world, but he had the painful habit of pulling a person's leg until it threatened to come off at the hip. Conway managed to keep the conversation off Murchison for the rest of the meal.

As soon as Mannon and himself split up he went to the intercom and had a few words with the doctors of various species who would be taking over the instruction of the trainees, then he looked at his watch. There was almost an hour before he was due aboard *Vespasian*. He began to walk a little more hurriedly than befitted a Senior Physician . . .

The sign over the entrance read "Recreation Level, Species DBDG, DBLF, ELNT, GKNM & FGLI." Conway went in, changed his whites for shorts and began searching for Murchison.

Trick lighting and some really inspired landscaping had given the recreation level the illusion of tremendous spaciousness. The overall effect was of a small, tropical beach enclosed on two sides by cliffs and open to the sea, which stretched out to a horizon rendered indistinct by heat haze. The sky was blue and cloudless—realistic cloud effects were difficult to reproduce, a maintenance engineer had told him—and the water of the bay was deep blue shading to turquoise. It lapped against the golden, gently sloping beach whose sand was almost too warm for the feet. Only the artificial sun, which was too much on the reddish side for Conway's taste, and the alien greenery fringing the beach and cliff's kept it from looking like a tropical bay anywhere on Earth.

But then space was at a premium in Sector General and the people who worked together were expected to play together as well.

The most effective, yet completely unseen, aspect of the place was the fact that it was maintained at one-half normal gravity. A half-G meant that people who were tired could relax more comfortably and the ones who were feeling lively could feel livelier still, Conway thought wryly as a steep, slow-moving wave ran up the beach and broke around his knees. The turbulence in the bay was not produced artificially, but varied in proportion to the size, number and enthusiasm of the bathers using it.

Projecting from one of the cliffs were a series of diving ledges connected by concealed tunnels. Conway climbed to the highest, fifty-foot ledge and from this point of vantage tried to find a DBDG female in a white swimsuit called Murchison.

She wasn't in the restaurant on the other cliff, or in the shallows adjoining the beach, or in the deep green water under the diving ledges. The sand was thickly littered with reclining forms which were large, small, leathery, scaley and furry—but Conway had no difficulty separating the Earth-human DBDGs from the general mass, they being the only intelligent species in the Federation with a nudity taboo. So he knew that anyone wearing clothing, no matter how abbreviated, was what *he* considered a human being.

Suddenly he caught a glimpse of white which was partly obscured by two patches of green and one of yellow standing around it. That would be Murchison, all right. He took a quick bearing and retraced his steps.

When Conway approached the crowd around Murchison, two Corpsmen and an intern from the eighty-seventh level dispersed with obvious reluctance. In a voice which, much to his disgust, had gone up in pitch, he said, "Hi. Sorry I'm late."

Murchison shielded her eyes to look up at him. "I just arrived myself," she said, smiling. "Why don't you lie down?"

Conway dropped onto the sand but remained propped on one elbow, looking at her.

Murchison possessed a combination of physical features which made it impossible for any Earth-human male member of the staff to regard her with anything like clinical detachment, and regular exposure to the artificial but UV-rich sun had given her a deep tan made richer by the dazzling contrast of her white swimsuit. Dark auburn hair stirred restively in the artificial breeze, her eyes were closed again and her lips slightly parted. Her respiration was slow and deep, that of a person either perfectly relaxed or asleep, and the things it was doing to her swimsuit was also doing things to Conway. He thought suddenly that if she was telepathic at this moment she would be up and running for dear life . . .

"You look," she said, opening one eye, "like somebody who wants to growl deep in his throat and beat his manly, clean-shaven chest—"

"It isn't clean-shaven," Conway protested, "it's just naturally not hairy. But I want you to be serious for a moment. I'd like to talk to you, alone, I mean . . ."

"I don't care either way about chests," she said soothingly, "so you don't have to feel bad about it."

"I don't," said Conway, then doggedly; "Can't we get away from this menagerie and . . . Oops, stampede!"

He reached across quickly and clapped his hand over her eyes, simultaneously closing his own.

Two Tralthans on a total of twelve, elephantine feet thundered past within a few yards of them and plowed into the shallows, scattering sand and spray over a radius of fifty yards. The half-G conditions which allowed the normally slow and ponderous FGLIs to gambol like lambs also kept the sand they had kicked up airborne for a considerable time. When Conway was sure that the last grains had settled he took his hand away from Murchison's eyes. But not completely.

Hesitantly, a little awkwardly, he slid his hand over the soft warm contour of her cheek until he was cupping the side of her jaw in his palm. Then gently he pushed his fingers into the soft tangle of curls behind her ear. He felt her stiffen, then relax again.

"Uh, see what I mean," he said dry-mouthed. "Unless you *like* half-ton bullies kicking sand in your face . . ."

"We'll be alone later," said Murchison, laughing, "when you take me home."

"And then what happens!" Conway said disgustedly. "Just the same as last time. We'll sneak up to your door, being very careful not to wake your roommate who has to go on early duty, and then that damned servo will come trundling up . . ." Angrily, Conway began to mimic the taped voice of the robot as he went on, ". . . I perceive that you are beings of classification DBDG and are of differing genders, and note further that you have been in close juxtaposition for a period of two minutes forty-eight seconds. In the circumstances I must respectfully remind you of Regulation Twenty-one, Sub-section Three regarding the entertaining of visitors in DBDG Nurses' Quarters . . ."

Almost choking, Murchison said, "I'm sorry, it must have been very frustrating for you."

Conway thought sourly that the expression of sorrow was rather spoiled by the suppressed laughter preceeding it. He leaned closer and took her gently by the shoulder. He said, "It was and is. I want to talk to you and I won't have time to see you home tonight. But I don't want to talk here, you always head for the water when I get you cornered. Well, I want to get you in a corner, both literally and conversationally, and ask some serious questions. This being friends is killing me . . ."

STAR SURGEON • 249

Murchison shook her head. She took his hand away from her shoulder, squeezed it and said, "Let's swim."

Seconds later as he chased her into the shallows he wondered if perhaps she wasn't a little telepathic after all. She was certainly running fast enough.

In half-G conditions swimming was an exhilarating experience. The waves were high and steep and the smallest splash seemed to hang in the air for seconds, with individual drops sparkling red and amber in the sun. A badly executed dive by one of the heavier life-forms—the FGLIs especially had an awful lot of belly to flop—could cause really spectacular effects. Conway was threshing madly after Murchison on the fringe of just such a titanic upheaval when a loudspeaker on the cliff roared into life.

"Doctor Conway," it boomed. "Will Doctor Conway report at Lock Sixteen for embarkation, please . . ."

They were walking rapidly up the beach when Murchison said, very seriously for her, "I didn't know you were leaving. I'll change and see you off."

There was a Monitor Corps officer in the lock antechamber. When he saw Conway had company he said, "Doctor Conway? We leave in fifteen minutes, sir," and disappeared tactfully. Conway stopped beside the boarding tube and so did Murchison. She looked at him but there was no particular expression on her face, it was just beautiful and very desirable. Conway went on telling her about his important new assignment although he didn't want to talk about that at all. He talked rapidly and nervously until he heard the Monitor officer returning along the tube, then he pulled Murchison tightly against him and kissed her hard.

He couldn't tell if she responded. He had been too sudden, too ungentle . . .

"I'll be gone about three months," he said, in a voice which tried to explain and apologize at the same time. Then with forced lightness he ended, "And in the morning I won't feel a bit sorry."

CHAPTER 8

Conway was shown to his cabin by an officer wearing a medic's caduceus over his insignia who introduced himself as Major Stillman. Although he spoke quietly and politely Conway got the impression that the Major was not a person who would be overawed by anything or anybody. He said that the Captain would be pleased to see Conway in the control room after they had made the first jump, to welcome him aboard personally.

A little later Conway met Colonel Williamson, the ship's Captain, who gave him the freedom of the ship. This was a courtesy rare enough on a government ship to impress Conway, but he soon discovered that although nobody said anything he was simply in everyone's way in the control room, and twice he lost himself while trying to explore the ship's interior. The Monitor heavy cruiser *Vespasian* was much larger than Conway had realized. After being guided back by a friendly Corpsman with a too-expressionless face he decided that he would spend most of the trip in his cabin familiarizing himself with his new assignment.

Colonel Williamson had given him copies of the more detailed and recent information which had come in through Monitor Corps channels, but he began by studying the file which O'Mara had given him.

The being Lonvellin had been on the way to a world, about which it had heard some very nasty rumors, in a practically unexplored section of the Lesser Megellanic Cloud, when it had been taken ill and admitted to Sector General. Shortly after being pronounced cured it had resumed the journey and a few weeks later it had contacted the Monitor Corps. It had stated that conditions on the world it had found were both sociologically complex and medically barbaric, and that it would need advice on the medical side before it could begin to act effectively against the many social ills afflicting this truly distressed planet. It had also asked if some beings of physiological classification DBDG could be sent along to act as information gatherers as the natives were of that classification and were violently hostile to all off-planet life, a fact which seriously hampered Lonvellin's activities.

The fact of Lonvellin asking for help of any sort was surprising in itself in view of the enormous intelligence and experience of his species in solving vast sociological problems. But on this occasion things had gone disastrously wrong, and Lonvellin had been kept too busy using its defensive science to do anything else . . .

According to Lonvellin's report it had begun by observing the planet from space during many rotations, monitoring the radio transmissions through its Translator, and taking particular note of the low level of industrialization which contrasted so oddly with the single, still functioning space port. When all the information which it had thought necessary had been collected and evaluated it chose what it considered to be the best place to land.

From the evidence at hand Lonvellin judged the world—the native's name for it was Etla—to have been a once-prosperous colony which had regressed for economic reasons until now it had very little contact with outside. But it did have some, which meant that Lonvellin's first and usually most difficult job, that of making the natives trust an alien and perhaps visually horrifying being who had dropped out of the sky, was greatly simplified. These people would know about e-ts. So it took the role of a poor, frightened, slightly stupid extra-terrestrial who had been forced to land to make repairs to its ship. For this it would require various odd and completely worthless chunks of metal or rock, and it would pretend great difficulty in making the Etlans understand exactly what it needed. But for these valueless pieces of rubbish it could exchange items of great value, and soon the more enterprising natives would get to know about it.

At this stage Lonvellin expected to be exploited shamelessly, but it didn't mind. Gradually things would change. Rather than give items of value it would offer to perform even more valuable services. It would let it be known that it now considered its ship to be irreparable, and gradually it would become accepted as a permanent resident. After that it would be just a matter of time, and time was something with which Lonvellin was particularly well supplied.

It landed close to a road which ran between two small towns, and soon had the chance to reveal itself to a native. The native, despite Lonvellin's careful contact and many reassurances via the Translator, fled. A few hours later small, crude projectiles with chemical warheads began falling on his ship and the whole area, which was densely wooded, had been saturated with volatile chemicals and deliberately set alight.

Lonvellin had been unable to proceed without knowing why this race with experience of space-travel should be so blindly hostile to e-ts, and not being in a position to ask questions himself it had called for Earth-human assistance. Shortly afterward Alien Contact specialists of the Monitor Corps had arrived, sized up the situation for themselves and gone in.

Quite openly, as it happened.

They discovered that the natives were terrified of e-ts because they believed them to be disease carriers. What was even more peculiar was the fact that they were not worried by off-planet visitors of their own species or a closely similar race, members of which would have been more likely to be carriers of disease: because it was a well-known medical fact that diseases which affected extra-terrestrials were not communicable to members of other planetary species. Any race with a knowledge of space travel should know *that,* Conway thought. It was the first thing a star-traveling culture learned.

He was trying to make some sense out of this strange contradiction, using a tired brain and some hefty reference works on the Federation's colonization program, when Major Stillman's arrival made a very welcome interruption.

"We'll arrive in three days time, Doctor," the Major began, "and I think it's time you had some cloak and dagger training. By that I mean getting to know how to wear Etlan clothes. It's a very fetching costume, although personally I don't have the knees for a kilt . . ."

Etla had been contacted on two levels by the Corps, Stillman went onto explain. On one they had landed secretly using the native language and dress, no other disguise being necessary because the physiological resemblance had been so close. Most of their later information had been gained in this way and so far none of the agents had been caught. On the other level the Corpsmen admitted their extra-terrestrial origin, conversed by Translator, and their story was that they had heard of the plight of the native population and had come to give medical assistance. The Etlans had accepted this story, revealing the fact that similar offers of help had been made in the past, that an Empire ship was sent every ten years loaded with the newest drugs, but despite all this the medical situation continued to worsen. The Corpsmen were welcome to try to relieve the situation if they could, but the impression given by the Etlans was that they were just another party of well-intentional bunglers.

Naturally when the subject of Lonvellin's landing came up the Corps had to pretend complete ignorance, and their expressed opinions leaned heavily toward the middle of the road.

It was a very complex problem, Stillman told him, and became more so with every new report sent in by undercover agents. But Lonvellin had a beautifully simple plan for clearing up the whole mess. When Conway heard it he wished suddenly that he hadn't tried to impress Lonvellin with his skill as a doctor. He would much rather have been back in the hospital right now. This being made responsible for organizing the cure of an entire planetary population gave him an unpleasantly gone feeling in the region of his transverse colon . . .

Etla was beset with much sickness and suffering and narrow, superstitious thinking, their reaction to Lonvellin being a shocking illustration of their intolerance toward species which did not resemble themselves. The first two conditions increased the third, which in turn worsened the first two. Lonvellin hoped to break this vicious circle by causing a marked improvement in the health of the population, one that would be apparent to even the least intelligent and bigoted natives. It would then have the Corpsmen admit publicly that they had been acting under Lonvellin's instructions all along, which should make the e-t hating natives feel somewhat ashamed of themselves. Then during the perhaps temporary increase of e-t tolerance which would follow, Lonvellin would set about gaining their trust and eventually return to its original long-term plan for making them a sane, happy and thriving culture again.

Conway told Stillman that he wasn't an expert in these matters but it sounded like a very good plan.

Stillman said, "I am, and it is. If it works."

On the day before they were due to arrive the Captain asked if Conway would like to come to Control for a few minutes. They were computing their position in preparation for making the final jump and the ship had emerged relatively close to a binary system, one star of which was a short-term variable.

Awed, Conway thought it was the sort of spectacle which makes people feel small and alone, makes them feel the urge to huddle together and the need to talk so that they might re-establish their puny identities amid all the magnificence. Conversational barriers were down and all at once Captain Williamson was speaking in tones which suggested three things to the listening Conway—that the Captain might be human after all, that he had hair and that he was about to let it down a little.

"Er, Doctor Conway," he began apologetically, "I don't want to sound as if I'm criticizing Lonvellin. Especially as it was a patient of yours and may also have been a friend. Neither do I want you to think that I'm annoyed because it has a Federation cruiser and various lesser units running errands for it. That isn't so . . ."

Williamson took off his cap and smoothed a wrinkle from the head-band with his thumb. Conway had a glimpse of thinning gray hair and a forehead whose deep worry lines had been concealed by the cap's visor. The cap was replaced and he became the calm, efficient senior officer again.

". . . To put it bluntly, Doctor," he went on, "Lonvellin is what I would call a gifted amateur. Such people always seem to stir up trouble for us professionals, upsetting schedules and so on. But this doesn't bother me either, because the situation Lonvellin uncovered here most definitely needs something done about it. The point I'm trying to make is that, as well as our survey, colonization and enforcement duties, we have experience at sorting out just such sociological tangles as this one, although at the same time I admit that there is no individual within the Corps with anything like Lonvellin's ability. Nor can we suggest any plan at the moment better than the one put forward by Lonvellin . . ."

Conway began to wonder if the Captain was getting at something or merely blowing off steam. Williamson had not struck him as being the complaining type.

". . . As the person with most responsibility next to Lonvellin on this project," the Captain finished with a rush, "it is only fair that you know what we think as well as what we are doing. There are nearly twice as many of our people working on Etla than Lonvellin knows about, and more are on the way. Personally I have the greatest respect for our long-lived friend, but I can't help feeling that the situation here is more complex than even Lonvellin realizes."

Conway was silent for a moment, then he said, "I've wondered why a ship like *Vespasian* was being used on what is basically a cultural study project. Do you think that the situation is more, ah, dangerous as well?"

"Yes," said the Captain.

At that moment the tremendous double-star system pictured in the view-screen dissolved and was replaced by that of a normal G-type sun and, within a distance of ten million miles, the tiny sickle shape of the planet which was their destination. Before Conway could put any of the questions he was suddenly itching to ask, the Captain informed him that they had completed their final jump, that from now until touchdown he would be a very busy man, and ended by politely throwing him out of the control room with the advice that he should catch as much sleep as possible before landing.

Back in his cabin Conway undressed thoughtfully and, a part of his mind was pleased to note, almost automatically. Both Stillman and he had been wearing Etlan costume—blouse, kilt and a waist-sash with pockets, a beret and a dramatic calf-length cloak being added for outdoor use—continually for the past few days, so that now he felt comfortable in it even while dining with *Vespasian*'s officers. At the moment, however, his discomfort was caused solely by the Captain's concluding remarks to him in the control room.

Williamson thought that the Etlan situation was dangerous enough to warrant using the largest type of law enforcement vessel possessed by the Monitor Corps. Why? Where was the danger?

Certainly there was nothing resembling a military threat on Etla. The very worst that the Etlans could do they had done to Lonvellin's ship and that had hurt the being's feelings and nothing else. Which meant that the danger had to come from somewhere outside.

Suddenly Conway thought he knew what was worrying the Captain. *The Empire* . . .

Several of the reports had contained references to the Empire. It was the great unknown quantity so far. The Monitor Corps survey vessels had not made contact with it, which wasn't surprising because this sector of the galaxy was not scheduled for mapping for another fifty years, and would not have been entered if Lonvellin's project had not come unstuck. All that was known about the Empire was that Etla was part of it and that it sent medical aid at regular if lengthy intervals.

To Conway's mind the quality of that aid and the intervals between its arrival told an awful lot about the people responsible for sending it. They could not be medically advanced, he reasoned, or the drugs they sent would have checked, if only temporarily, some of the epidemics which had been sweeping Etla at the time. And they were almost certainly poor or the ships would have come at shorter intervals. Conway would not be surprised if the mysterious Empire turned out to be a mother world and a few struggling colonies like Etla. But most important of all, an Empire which regularly sent aid to its distressed colony, whether it was large, medium or small as Empires went, did not seem to Conway to be a particularly evil or dangerous entity. To the contrary, on the evidence available he rather approved of this Empire.

Captain Williamson, he thought as he rolled into bed, was inclined to worry too much.

CHAPTER 9

Vespasian landed. On the main screen in the Communications room Conway saw a cracked white expanse of concrete which stretched to the half-mile distant periphery, where the fine details of vegetation and architecture which would have made the scene alien were lost in the heat haze. Dust and dried leaves littered the concrete and small heaps of cloud were scattered untidily about a very Earth-like sky. The only other ship on the field was a Monitor courier vessel which was grounded close to the block of disused offices that had been loaned by the Etlan authorities for use as the visitor's surface base.

Behind Conway the Captain said, "You understand, Doctor, that Lonvellin is unable to leave its ship, and that any physical contact between us at this stage would wreck our present good relations with the natives. But this is a big screen. Excuse me . . ."

There was a click and Conway was looking into the control room of Lonvellin's ship, with a life-size image of Lonvellin itself sprawling across most of the picture.

"Greetings, friend Conway," the EPLH's voice boomed from the speaker. "It is a great pleasure to see you again."

"A pleasure to be here, sir," Conway replied, "I trust you are in good health . . . ?"

The enquiry was not merely a polite formality. Conway wanted to know if there had been anymore "misunderstandings" on the cellular level between Lonvellin and its personal physician, the intelligent, organized virus-colony which dwelt within its patient-host's body. Lonvellin's doctor had caused quite a stir at Sector General, where they were still arguing as to whether it should be classified as a doctor or a disease . . .

"My health is excellent, Doctor," Lonvellin replied, then straightaway got down to the business in hand. Conway hastily returned his mind to present time and concentrated on what the EPLH was saying.

Conway's own instructions were general. He was to coordinate the work of data-gathering Corps medical officers on Etla and, because the sociological and medical aspects of the problem were so closely connected, he was advised to keep abreast of the developments outside his specialty. With the arrival of the latest reports the sociological problem seemed more confusing, and it was Lonvellin's hope that a mind trained for the complexities of a multi-environment hospital would be able to establish a sensible pattern among this welter of contradictory facts. Dr. Conway would no doubt appreciate the urgency of the matter, and wish to begin work immediately . . .

". . . And I would like data on the Earth-human Clarke who is operating in District Thirty-five," Lonvellin went on without a pause, "so that I may properly evaluate the reports of this being . . ."

As Captain Williamson was giving the required information Stillman tapped Conway's arm and nodded for them to leave. Twenty minutes later they were in the back of a covered truck on the way to the perimeter. Conway's head and one ear had been swathed in bandages, and he felt anxious and a little stupid.

"We'll stay hidden until we're clear of the port," Stillman said reassuringly, "then we'll sit with the driver. Lots of Etlans travel with our people these days, but it might arouse suspicion for us to be seen coming from the ship. And we'll head straight for town instead of calling at ground headquarters. I think you should see some of your patients as soon as possible."

Seriously, Conway said, "I know the symptoms are purely psychosomatic, but both my feet seem to be in an advanced stage of frostbite . . ."

Stillman laughed. "Don't worry, Doctor," he said. "The translator bandaged to your ear will let you know everything that goes on, and you won't have to speak because I'll explain that your head injury has temporarily affected your speech centers. Later, however, when you begin to pick up a little of the language a good tip is to develop a stutter. An impediment of this kind disguises the fact that the sufferer does not have the local idiom or accent, the large fault concealing all the smaller ones.

"Not all our undercover people have advanced linguistic training," he added, "and such ruses are necessary. But the main thing to remember is not to stay in any one place long enough for the more definite oddities of behavior to be noticed . . ."

At that point the driver remarked that they were coming level with a blond whom he could cheerfully stay near for the rest of his life. Stillman went on, "Despite the coarse suggestions of Corpsman Briggs here, perhaps our best protection lies in our mental approach to the work, to the fact that our intentions toward these people are completely honorable. If we were hostile agents intent on sabotage, or gathering intelligence for a future act of war, we would be much more likely to be caught. We should be tensed up, trying too hard to be natural, too suspicious and are more inclined to make mistakes because of this."

Conway said dryly, "You make it sound too easy." But he felt reassured nevertheless.

The truck left them in the center of town and they began to walk around. The first thing Conway noticed was that there were very few large or new-looking buildings, but that even the oldest were very well kept, and that the Etlans had a very attractive way of decorating the outside of their houses with flowers. He saw the people, the men and women working, shopping or going about businesses which at the present moment he could not even guess at. He *had* to think of them as men and women, as being he and she rather than a collection of coldly alien its.

He saw the twisted limbs, the crutches, the disease scarred faces, his analytical eye detecting and isolating conditions which had been stamped out among the Federation citizenship over a century ago. And everywhere he saw a sight familiar to anyone who had ever been to or worked in a hospital, that of the less sick patient freely and unselfishly giving all the aid possible to those who were worse off than himself.

The sudden realization that he was not in a hospital ward where such sights were pleasantly normal but in a city street brought Conway physically and mentally to a halt.

"What gets me," he said when he could speak again, "is that so many of these conditions are curable. Maybe all of them. We haven't had epilepsy for one hundred and fifty years . . ."

"And you feel like running amuck with a hypo," Stillman put in grimly, "injecting all and sundry with the indicated specifics. But you have to remember that the whole planet is like this, and that curing a few would not help at all. You are in charge of a very big ward, Doctor."

"I've read the reports," Conway said shortly. "It's just that the printed figures did not prepare me for the actuality . . ."

He stopped with the sentence incomplete. They had paused at a busy intersection and Conway noticed that both pedestrian and vehicular traffic had either slowed or come to a halt. Then he saw the reason.

There was a large wagon coming along the street. Painted and draped completely in red it was, unlike the other vehicle around it, unpowered. Short handles projected at intervals along each side and at every handle an Etlan walked or limped or hobbled, pushing it along. Even before Stillman took his beret off and Conway followed suit he knew that he was seeing a funeral.

"We'll visit the local hospital now," Stillman said when it had gone past. "If asked, my story is that we are looking for a sick relative called Mennomer who was admitted last week. On Etla that is a name like Smith. But we're not likely to be questioned, because practically everybody does a stint of hospital work and the staff are used to the part-time help coming and going all the time. And should we run into a Corps medical officer, as well we might, don't recognize him.

"And in case you're worried about your Etlan colleagues wanting to look under your bandages," Stillman went on practically reading Conway's mind, "they are far too busy to be curious about injuries which have already been treated . . ."

They spent two hours in the hospital without once having to tell their story about the ailing Mennomer. It was obvious from the start that Stillman knew his way about the place, that he had probably worked there. But there were always too many Etlans about for Conway to ask if it had been as a Corpsman observer or an undercover part-time nurse. Once he caught a glimpse of a Corpsman medic watching an Etlan doctor draining a pleural cavity of its empyema, his expression showing how dearly he would have liked to roll up his dark green sleeves and wade in himself.

The surgeons wore bright yellow instead of white, some of the operative techniques verged on the barbaric and the concept of isolation wards or barrier nursing had never occurred to them—or perhaps it had occurred to them, Conway thought in an effort to be fair, but the utterly fantastic degree of overcrowding made it impracticable. Considering the facilities at their disposal and the gigantic problem it had to face, this was a very good hospital. Conway approved of it and, judging from what he had seen of its staff, he approved of them, too.

"These are nice people," Conway said rather inadequately at one point. "I can't understand them jumping Lonvellin the way they did, somehow they don't seem to be the type."

"But they did it," Stillman replied grimly. "Anything which hasn't two eyes, two ears, two arms and two legs, or which has these things but happens to have them in the wrong places, gets jumped. It's something drummed into them at a very early age, with their ABCs, practically. I wish we knew why."

Conway was silent. He was thinking that the reason he had been sent here was to organize medical aid for this planet, and that wandering in fancy dress over one small piece of the jigsaw was not going to solve the big puzzle. It was time he got down to some serious work.

As if reading Conway's mind again Stillman said, "I think we should go back now. Would you prefer to work in the office block or the ship, Doctor?"

Stillman, Conway thought, was going to be a very good *aide*. Aloud he said, "The office block, please. I get lost too easily in the ship."

And so Conway was installed in a small office with a large desk, a button for calling Stillman and some other less-vital communications equipment. After his first lunch in the officers dining quarters he ate all his meals in the office with Stillman. Sometimes he slept in the office and sometimes he didn't sleep at all. The days passed and his eyes began to feel like hot, gritty marbles in his head from reading reports and more reports. Stillman always kept them coming. Conway reorganized the medical investigation, bringing in some of the Corps doctors for discussion or flying out to those who could not for various reasons get in.

A large number of the reports were outside his province, being copies of information sent in by Williamson's men on purely sociological problems. He read them on the off-chance of their having a bearing on his own problem, which many of them did, But they usually added to his puzzlement.

Blood samples, biopsies, specimens of all kinds began to flow in. They were immediately loaded onto a courier—the Corps had put three of them at his disposal now—and rushed to the Diagnostician-in-Charge of Pathology at Sector General. The results were sub-radioed back to *Vespasian*, taped, and the reels dumped on Conway's desk within a few days. The ship's main computer, or rather the section of it which wasn't engaged on Translator relay, was also placed at his disposal, and gradually the vaguest suggestion of a pattern seemed to be emerging out of the

262 · JAMES WHITE

flood of related and unrelated facts. But it was a pattern which made no sense to anyone, least of all Conway. He was nearing the end of his fifth week on Etla and there was still very little progress to report to Lonvellin.

But Lonvellin wasn't pushing for results. It was a very patient being who had all the time in the world. Sometimes Conway found himself wondering if Murchison would be as patient as Lonvellin.

CHAPTER 10

In answer to his buzz Major Stillman, red-eyed and with his usually crisp uniform just slightly rumpled, stumbled in and sat down. They exchanged yawns, then Conway spoke.

"In a few days I'll have the supply and distribution figures needed to begin curing this place," he said. "Every serious disease has been listed together with information on the age, sex and geographical location of the patient, and the quantities of medication calculated. But before I give the go ahead for flooding the place with medical supplies I'd feel a lot easier in my mind if we knew exactly how this situation came about in the first place.

"Frankly, I'm worried," he went on. "I think we may be guilty of replacing the broken crockery while the bull is still loose in the china shop."

Stillman nodded, whether in agreement or with weariness Conway couldn't say.

On a planet which was an absolute pest-hole why were infant mortality figures, or deaths arising from complications or infections during childbirth so low? Why was there a marked tendency for infants to be healthy and the adults chronically ill? Admittedly a large proportion of the infant population were born blind or were physically impaired by inherited diseases, but relatively few of them died young. They carried their deformities and disfigurements through to late middle age where, statistically, most of them succumbed.

And there was also statistical evidence that the Etlans were guilty of gross exhibitionism in the matter of their diseases. They ran heavily to unpleasant skin conditions, maladies which caused gradual wasting or deformity of the limbs, and some pretty horrible combinations of both. And their costume did nothing to conceal their afflictions. To the contrary, Conway had the feeling sometimes that they were like so many small boys showing off their sore knees to their friends . . .

Conway realized that he had been thinking aloud when Stillman interrupted him suddenly.

"You're wrong, Doctor!" he said, sharply for him. "These people aren't masochists. Whatever went wrong here originally, they've been trying to fight it. They've been fighting, with very little assistance, for over a century and losing all the time. It surprises me they have a civilization left at all. And they wear an abbreviated costume because they believe fresh air and sunlight is good for what ails them, and in most cases they are quite right.

"This belief is drilled into them from an early age," Stillman went on, his tone gradually losing its sharpness, "like their hatred of e-ts and the belief that isolating infectious diseases is unnecessary. Is dangerous, in fact, because they believe that the germs of one disease fight the germs of another so that both are weakened . . ."

Stillman shuddered at the thought and fell silent.

"I didn't mean to belittle our patients, Major," Conway said. "I have no sensible answers to this thing so my mind is throwing up stupid ones. But you mentioned the lack of assistance which the Etlans receive from their Empire. I would like more details on that, especially on how it is distributed. Better still, I'd like to ask the Imperial Representative on Etla about it. Have you been able to find him yet?"

Stillman shook his head and said dryly, "This aid doesn't come like a batch of food parcels. There are drugs, of course, but most of it would be in the form of the latest medical literature relevent to the conditions here. How it reaches the people is something we are just now finding out . . ."

Every ten years an Empire ship would land and be met by the Imperial Representative, Stillman went on to explain, and after unloading and handing over what were presumably dispatches it left again within a matter of hours. Apparently no citizen of the Empire would stay on Etla for a second longer than was necessary, which was understandable. Then the Imperial Representative, a personage called Teltrenn, set about distributing the medical aid.

But instead of using the mass distribution media to bring local medical authorities up to date on these new methods, and allow local GPs time to familiarize themselves with the theory and procedures before the medication arrived, Teltrenn sat tight on all the information until such times as he could pay them a personal visit. Then he handed everything over as being a personal gift from their glorious Emperor, accruing no small measure of glory himself by being the middleman, and the data which could have been in the hands of every doctor on the planet within three months reached them piecemeal in anything up to six years . . .

"Six *years!*" said Conway, startled.

"Teltrenn isn't, so far as we've been able to find out, a very energetic person," Stillman said. "What makes matters worse is that little or no original medical research is being done on Etla, due to the absence of the researcher's most vital tool, the microscope. Etla can't make precision optical equipment and apparently no Empire ship has thought to bring them.

"It all boils down to the fact," Stillman ended grimly, "that the Empire does all of Etla's medical thinking for her, and the evidence suggests that medically the Empire is not very smart."

Conway said firmly, "I'd like to see the correlation between the arrival of this aid and the incidence of disease immediately thereafter. Can you help me in that?"

"There's a report just in which might help you," Stillman replied. "It's a copy of the records of a North Continent hospital which go back past Teltrenn's last visit to them. The records show that he brought on that occasion some useful data on obstetrics and a specific against what we have called B-Eighteen. The incidence of B-Eighteen dropped rapidly within a few weeks there, although the overall figures remained much the same because F-Twenty-one began to appear about that time . . ."

B-Eighteen was analogous to a severe influenza, fatal to children and young adults in four cases out of ten. F-Twenty-one was a mild, non-fatal fever which lasted three to four weeks during which large, crescentric weals appeared all over the face, limbs and body. When the fever abated the weals darkened to a livid purple and remained for the rest of the patient's life.

Conway shook his head angrily. He said, "One of the main things wrong with Etla is its Imperial Representative!"

Standing up, Stillman said, "We want to ask him a few questions, too. We've advertised that fact widely by radio and print, so much so that we are now fairly certain that Teltrenn is hiding from us deliberately. Probably the reason is a guilty conscience over his mismanagement of affairs here. But a psych report, based on what hearsay evidence we have been able to gather about him, has been prepared for Lonvellin. I'll have them send a copy from the ship."

"Thank you," said Conway.

Stillman nodded, yawned and left. Conway thumbed his communicator switch, contacted *Vespasian* and asked for an audio link with the fifty miles distant Lonvellin. He was still worried and wanted to get it off his chest, the only trouble being he did not know exactly what "it" was.

". . . You have done very well, friend Conway," Lonvellin said when he had finished speaking, "in fulfilling your part of the project so quickly, and I am fortunate indeed in the quality and eagerness of my assistants. We have now gained the trust of the Etlan doctors in most areas and the way will shortly be open to begin full-scale instruction in your latest curative techniques. You will therefore be returning to your hospital within a few days, and I urge that you do not leave with the feeling that you have not performed your assigned task in a completely satisfactory manner. These anxieties you mention are groundless.

"Your suggestion that the being Teltrenn should be removed or replaced as part of the re-education program is sound," Lonvellin continued ponderously, "and I already had this step in mind. An added reason for removing it from office being the well-documented fact that it is the being largely responsible for keeping alive the widespread intolerance of off-planet life-forms. Your other suggestion that these harmful ideas may originate, not with Teltrenn but in the Empire, may or may not be correct. This does not, however, call for an immediate search for and investigation of the Empire which you urge."

Lonvellin's Translated voice was slow and necessarily emotionless, but Conway seemed to detect a hardening in its tone as it went on, "I perceive Etla as an isolated world kept in quarantine. The problem can therefore be solved without bringing in considerations of Empire influences or understanding fully the various inconsistencies which puzzle us both. These will become plain after its cure has been effected, and the answers we seek are of secondary importance to the planet-wide relief of suffering.

"Your contention that the visits of the Imperial ship," it went on, "which occur every ten years and last only a few hours, is a major factor in this problem is invalid. I might even suggest that, unconsciously perhaps, you are laying too much stress on this point merely that your curiosity regarding this Empire might be satisfied."

You're so right, Conway thought. But before he could reply the EPLH went on, "I wish to treat Etla as an isolated problem. Bringing in the Empire, which itself may or may not be in need of medical aid also, would enlarge the scope of the operation beyond managable limits.

"However, and purely to remove your evident anxiety," Lonvellin ended, "you may tell the being Williamson that it has my permission to scout for this Empire and report on conditions within it. In the event of it being found, however, no mention of what we are doing here on Etla is to be made until the operation is completed."

"I understand, sir," Conway said, and broke the connection. He thought it decidedly odd that Lonvellin had pinned his ears back for being curious, then almost with the same breath given him permission to indulge that curiosity. Was Lonvellin more concerned about the Empire's influence here than it cared to admit, or was the big beastie just going soft in its old age?

He called Captain Williamson.

The Captain hemmed a coupled of times when Conway had finished speaking and there was a distinctly embarrassed note in his voice when he replied. He said, "We've had a number of officers, both medical and cultural contact people, searching for the Empire for the last two months, Doctor. One of them has been successful and sent in a preliminary report. It comes from a medical officer who was not attached to the Etla project, and knows very little of what has been happening here, so it may not be as informative as you might wish. I'll send you a copy with the material on Teltrenn."

Coughing slightly, Williamson ended, "Lonvellin will have to be informed of this, naturally, but I must leave it to your discretion *when* you tell it."

Suddenly Conway laughed out loud. "Don't worry, Colonel, I'll sit on the information for a while. But if you *are* found out you can always remind Lonvellin that the function of a good servant is to anticipate the wishes of his master."

He continued laughing softly after Williamson signed off, then all at once the reaction set in.

Conway hadn't laughed much since coming to Etla. And he had not been guilty of over-identifying with his patients—no half-way decent doctor with the good of his charges at heart would commit that crime. It was just that nobody laughed very much on Etla. There was something in the atmosphere of the place, a feeling comprised both of urgency and hopelessness which seemed to intensify with each day that passed. It was rather like the atmosphere in a ward where a patient was going to die, Conway thought, except that even in those circumstances people found time to make cracks and relax for a few minutes between crises . . .

Conway was beginning to miss Sector General. He was glad that in a few days he would be going back, despite his feeling of dissatisfaction over all the loose ends he was leaving untied. He began to think about Murchison.

That was something he had not done very often on Etla, either. Twice he had sent messages to her with the Elan specimens. He knew that Thornnastor in Pathology would see that she got them, even though Thornnastor was an FGLI with only the barest of passing interests in the emotional involvements of Earth-human DBDGs. But Murchison was the undemonstrative type. She might consider that going to the trouble of smuggling back a reply would be giving him too much encouragement, or maybe that kiss and run episode at the airlock had soured her on him completely. She was a peculiar girl. Very serious-minded, extremely dedicated, absolutely no time for men.

The first time she agreed to date him it had been because Conway had just pulled off a slick op and wanted to celebrate, and that previously he had worked with her on a case without once making a pass. Since then he had dated Murchison regularly and had been the envy of all the male DBDGs in the hospital. The only trouble was that they had nothing to be envious about . . .

His lugubrious train of thought was interrupted by the arrival of a Corpsman who dropped a folder onto his desk and said, "The material on Teltrenn, Doctor. The other report was confidential to Colonel Williamson and has to be copied by his Writer. We'll have it for you in fifteen minutes."

"Thank you," said Conway. The Corpsman left and he began to read.

Being a colony world which had not had the chance to grow naturally, Etla did not have national boundaries or the armed forces which went with them, but the police force enforcing the law on the planet were technically soldiers of the Emperor and under the command of Teltrenn. It had been a force of these policemen-soldiers who had attacked, and were still attacking, Lonvellin's ship. At first appraisal, the report stated, the evidence pointed to Teltrenn having a personality which was proud and power-hungry, but the cruelty usually found in such personalities was absent. In his relations with the native population—the Imperial Representative had not been born on Etla—Teltrenn showed fairness and consideration. It was plain that he looked down on the natives—way down, almost as if they were members of a lower species. But he did not, openly, despise them, and he was never cruel to them.

Conway threw down the report; this was another stupid piece of an already senseless puzzle, and all at once he was sick of the whole silly business. He rose and stamped into the outer office, sending the door crashing against the wall. Stillman twitched slightly and looked up.

"Dump that paperwork until morning!" Conway snapped. "Tonight we are going to indulge shamelessly in pleasures of the flesh. We're going to sleep in our own cabins . . ."

"Sleep?" said Stillman, grinning suddenly. "What's that?"

"I don't know," said Conway, "I thought you might. I hear it's a new sensation, unutterable bliss and very habit-forming. Shall we live danger-ously . . . ?"

"After you," said Stillman.

Outside the office block the night was pleasantly cool. There was broken cloud on the horizon but above them the stars seemed to crowd down, bright and thick and cold. This was a dense region of space, a fact further proved by the meteorites which made white scratches across the sky every few minutes. Altogether it was an inspiring and calming sight, but Conway could not stop worrying. He was convinced that he was missing something, and his anxiety was much worse out here under the sky than it had been at any time in the office. Suddenly he wanted to read that report on the Empire as quickly as possible.

To Stillman, he said, "Do you ever think of something, then feel horribly ashamed for having the kind of dirty mind which thinks thoughts like that?"

Stillman grunted, treating it as a rhetorical question, and they con-tinued walking toward the ship. Abruptly they stopped.

On the Southern horizon the sun seemed to be rising. The sky had become a pale, rich blue which shaded through turquoise into black, and the bases of the distant clouds burned pink and gold. Then before they could appreciate, or even react to this glorious, misplaced sunrise it had faded to an angry red smudge on the horizon. They felt a tiny shock transmitted through the soles of their shoes, and a little later they heard a noise like distant thunder.

"Lonvellin's ship!" said Stillman.

They began to run.

CHAPTER 11

The communications room on *Vespasian* was a whirlwind of activity with the Captain forming its calm and purposeful center. When Stillman and Conway arrived orders had gone out to the courier ship and all available helicopters to load decontamination and rescue gear and proceed to the blast area to render all possible aid. There was, of course, no hope for the Etlan force which had been surrounding Lonvellin's ship, but there were isolated farms and at least one small village on the fringe area. The rescuers would have to deal with panic as well as radiation casualties, because the Etlans had no experience of nuclear explosions and would almost certainly resist evacuation.

Out on the field, when Conway had seen Lonvellin's ship go up and had realized what it meant, he had felt physically ill. And now, listening to Williamson's urgent but unhurried orders going out, he felt cold sweat trickle down his forehead and spine. He licked his lips and said, "Captain, I have an urgent suggestion to make . . ."

He did not speak loudly, but there was something in his tone which made Williamson swing around immediately.

"This accident to Lonvellin means that you are in charge of the project, Doctor," Williamson said impatiently. "There is no need for such diffidence."

"In that case," said Conway in the same low, tense voice, "I have orders for you. Call off the rescue attempts and order everyone back to the ship. Take off before we are bombed, too . . ."

Conway saw them all looking at him, at his white, sweating face and frightened eyes, and he could see them all jumping to wrong conclusions. Williamson looked angry, embarrassed and completely at a loss for a few seconds, then his expression hardened. He turned to an officer beside him, snapped an order, then swung to face Conway again.

"Doctor," he began stiffly, "I have just put out our secondary meteor shield. Any solid object greater than one inch in diameter approaching from any direction whatever will be detected at a distance of one hundred miles and automatically deflected by pressors. So I can assure you, Doctor, that we are in no danger from any hypothetical attack with atomic missiles. The idea of a nuclear bombardment here is ridiculous, anyway. There is no atomic power on Etla, none whatever. We have instruments . . . You must have read the report.

"My *suggestion*," the Captain went on, in exactly the tone he used to suggest that the junior astrogator make an alteration in course, "is that we rush all possible help to the survivors of the blow-up, which must have been caused by a fault in Lonvellin's power pile . . ."

"Lonvellin wouldn't have a faulty pile!" Conway said harshly. "Like many long-lived beings it suffered from a constant and increasing fear of death the longer its life went on. It had the ultimate in personal physicians so that illness would not shorten its already tremendous life span, and it follows that it would not have endangered itself by using a ship which was anything but mechanically perfect.

"Lonvellin was killed," Conway went on grimly, "and the reason they hit its ship first is probably because they dislike e-ts so much. And it's nice to know that you can protect the ship, but if we leave now they might not launch another missile at all, and our people out there and a lot more Etlans would not have to die . . ."

It was no good, Conway thought sickly. Williamson looked angry and embarrassed and stubborn—angry at being given apparently senseless orders, embarrassed because it looked as though Conway was behaving like a frightened old woman and stubborn because he thought he and not Conway was right. *Get the lead out of your pants, you unprintable fool!* Conway raged at him, but under his breath. He could not address such words to a Monitor Colonel surrounded by junior officers, and for the added reason that Williamson was not nor ever had been a fool. He was a reasonable, intelligent, highly competent officer. It was just that he had not had the chance to put the facts together properly. He didn't have any medical training, nor did he have a nasty, suspicious mind like Conway . . .

"You have a report on the Empire for me," he said instead. "Can I read it?"

Williamson's eyes flickered toward the battery of view-screens surrounding them. All showed scenes of frantic activity—a helicopter being readied for flight, another staggering off the ground with a load obviously in excess of the safety limit, and a stream of men and decontamination equipment being rushed through the lock of the courier ship. He said, "You want to read it *now* . . . ?"

"Yes," said Conway, then quickly shook his head as another idea struck him. He had been trying desperately to make Williamson take off immediately and leave the explanations until later when there was time to give them, but it was obvious now that he would have to explain first, and fast. He said, "I've a theory which explains what has been going on here and the report should verify it. But if I can tell you what I think is in that report before reading it, will you give my theory enough credence to do what I tell you and take off at once?"

Outside the ship both 'copters were climbing into the night sky, the courier boat was sealing her lock and a collection of surface transport, both Etlan and Monitor, was dispersing toward the perimeter. More than half of the ship's crew were out there, Conway knew, together with all the land-based Corpsmen who could possibly be spared—all heading for the scene of the blow-up and all piling up the distance between themselves and *Vespasian* with every second which passed.

Without waiting for Williamson's reply, Conway rushed on, "My guess is that it is an Empire in the strict sense of the word, not a loose Federation like ours. This means an extensive military organization to hold it together and implement the laws of its Emperor, and the government on individual worlds would also be an essentially military one. All the citizens would be DBDGs like the Etlans and ourselves, and on the whole pretty average people except for their antipathy toward extra-terrestrials, who they have had little opportunity of getting to know so far."

Conway took a deep breath and went on, "Living conditions and level of technology should be similar to our own. Taxation might be high, but this would be negated by government controlled news channels. My guess is that this Empire has reached the unwieldy stage, say about forty to fifty inhabited systems . . ."

"Forty-three," said Williamson in a surprised voice.

". . . And I would guess that everyone in it knows about Etla and are sympathetic toward its plight. They would consider it a world under constant quarantine, but they do everything they can to help it . . ."

"They certainly do!" Williamson broke in. "Our man was on one of the outlying planets of the Empire for only two days before he was sent to the Central world for a audience with the Big Chief. But he had time to see what the people thought of Etla. There are pictures of the suffering Etlans practically everywhere he looked. In places they out-numbered commercial advertising, and it is a charity to which the Imperial Government gives full support! These look like being very nice people, Doctor."

"I'm sure they are, Captain," Conway said savagely. "But don't you think it a trifle odd that the combined charity of forty-three inhabited systems can only run to sending one ship every ten years . . . ?"

Williamson opened his mouth, closed it, and looked thoughtful. The whole room was silent except for the muted, incoming messages. Then suddenly, from behind Conway, Stillman swore and said thickly, "I see what he's getting at, sir. We've got to take off at once . . . !"

Williamson's eyes flicked from Conway to Stillman and back again. He murmured, "One could be temporary insanity, but two represents a trend . . ."

Three seconds later recall instructions were going out to all personnel, their urgency emphasized by the ear-splitting howl of the General Alarm siren. When every order which had been issued only minutes ago had been reversed, Williamson turned to Conway again.

"Go on, Doctor," he said grimly. "I think I'm beginning to see it, too."

Conway sighed thankfully and began to talk.

Etla had begun as a normal colony world, with a single spacefield to land the initial equipment and colonists, then towns had been set up convenient to natural resources and the planetary population had increased nicely. But then they must have been hit by a wave of disease, or a succession of diseases, which had threatened to wipe them out. Hearing of their plight the citizens of the Empire had rallied round, as people do when their friends are in trouble, and soon help began to arrive.

It must have started in a small way but built up quickly as news of the colony's distress got around. But so far as the Etlans were concerned the assistance stayed small.

The odd, un-missed pennies of a whole planetary population added up to a respectable amount, and when scores of worlds were contributing the amount was something which could not be ignored by the Imperial government, or by the Emperor himself. Because even in those days the

Empire must have grown too big and the inevitable rot had set in at its core. More and more revenue was needed to maintain the Empire, and/ or to maintain the Emperor and his court in the luxury to which they felt entitled. It was natural to assume that they might tell themselves that charity began at home, and appropriate a large part of these funds for their own use. Then gradually, as the Etlan charity was publicized and encouraged, these funds became an essential part of the administration's income.

That was how it had begun.

Etla was placed in strict quarantine, even though nobody in their right mind would have wanted to go there anyway. But then a calamity threatened, the Etlans through their own unaided efforts must have begun to cure themselves. The lucrative source of revenue looked like drying up. Something had to be done, quickly.

From withholding the aid which would have cured them it was only a small matter ethically, the administration must have told itself, to keep the Etlans sick by introducing a few relatively harmless diseases from time to time. The diseases would have to be photogenic, of course, to have the maximum effect on the kind-hearted citizenry—disfiguring diseases, for the most part, or those which left the sufferer crippled or deformed. And steps had to be taken to ensure that the supply of suffering natives did not fall off, so that the techniques of gynecology and child care on Etla were well advanced.

At a fairly early stage an Imperial Representative, psychologically tailored to fit his post, was installed to ensure that the level of health on the planet was held at the desired point. Somehow the Etlans had ceased to be people and had become valuable sick animals, which was just how the Imperial Representative seemed to regard them.

Conway paused at that point. The Captain and Stillman were looking ill, he thought; which was exactly how he had felt since the destruction of Lonvellin's ship had caused all the pieces of the puzzle to fall into place.

He said, "A native force sufficient to drive off or destroy chance visitors is always at Teltrenn's disposal. Because of the quarantine all visitors are likely to be alien, and the natives have been taught to hate aliens regardless of shape, number or intentions . . ."

"But how could they be so . . . so cold-blooded?" Williamson said, aghast.

"It probably started as simple misappropriation of funds," Conway said tiredly, "then it gradually got out of hand. But now we, by our interference, have threatened to wreck a very profitable Imperial racket. So now the Empire is trying to wreck us."

Before Williamson could reply the Chief Communications officer reported both helicopter crews back in the ship, also all personnel who had been within earshot of the siren, which meant everyone in town. The remainder could not make it back to *Vespasian* for several hours at least and had been ordered to go under cover until a scoutship sneaked in later to pick them up. Almost before the officer had finished speaking the Captain snapped "Lift ship" and Conway felt a moment's dizziness as the ship's anti-gravity grids compensated for full emergency thrust. *Vespasian* climbed frantically for space, with the courier vessel only ten seconds behind her.

"You must have thought me pretty stupid back there . . ." Williamson began, then was interrupted by reports from the returned crew-men. One of the helicopters had been fired on and the men from town had been ordered to stay there by the local police. These orders had come directly from the Imperial Representative, with instructions to kill anyone who tried to escape. But the local police and Corpsmen had come to know each other very well, and the Etlans had aimed well above their heads . . .

"This is getting dirtier by the minute," said Stillman suddenly. "You know, I think we are going to be blamed for what happened around Lonvellin's ship, for all the casualties in the area. Everything we have done here is going to be twisted so that *we* will be the villians. And I bet a lot of new diseases will be introduced immediately we leave, for which *we* will be blamed!"

Stillman swore, then went on, "You know how the people of the Empire think of this planet. Etla is their poor, weak, crippled sister, and we are going to be the dirty aliens who cold-bloodedly assaulted her . . ."

As the Major had been talking Conway had begun to sweat again. His deductions regarding the Empire's treatment of Etla had been from medical evidence, and it had been the medical aspect which had most concerned him, so that the larger implications of it all had not yet occurred to him. Suddenly he burst out, "But this could mean a *war!*"

"Yes indeed," said Stillman savagely, "and that is probably just what the Imperial government wants. It has grown too big and fat and rotten at the core, judging by what has been happening here. Within a few decades it would probably fall apart of its own accord, and a good thing, too. But there is nothing like a good war, a Cause that everybody can feel strongly about, to pull a crumbling Empire together again. If they play it right *this* war could make it stand for another hundred years."

Conway shook his head numbly. "I should have seen what was happening sooner," he said. "If we'd had time to tell the Etlans the truth—"

"You saw it sooner than anyone else," the Captain broke in sharply, "and telling the natives would not have helped them or us if the ordinary people of the Empire could not have been told also. You have no reason to blame yourself for—"

"Ordinance Officer," said a voice from one of the twenty-odd speaker grills in the room. "We have a trace at Green Twelve Thirty-one which I'm putting on your repeater screen Five. Trace is putting out patterned interference against missile attack and considerable radar window, suggesting that it has a guilty conscience and is smaller than we are. Instructions, sir?"

Williamson glanced at the repeater screen. "Do nothing unless it does," he said, then turned to Stillman and Conway again. When he spoke it was with the calming, confidence-inspiring tone of the senior officer who bears, *and* accepts, full responsibility, a tone which insisted that they were not to worry because he was there to do it for them.

He said, "Don't look so distressed, gentlemen. This situation, this threat of interstellar war, was bound to come about sometime and plans have been devised for dealing with it. Luckily we have plenty of time to put these plans into effect.

"Spatially the Empire is a small, dense association of worlds," he went on reassuringly, "otherwise we could not have made contact with them so soon. The Federation, however, is spread thinly across half the Galaxy. We had a star cluster to search where one sun in five possessed an inhabited planet. Their problem is nowhere near as simple. If they were *very* lucky they might find us in three years, but my own estimate is that it would be nearer twenty. So you can see that we have plenty of time."

Conway did not feel reassured and he must have shown it, but the Captain was trying to meet his objections before he could make them.

"The agent who made the report may help them," Williamson went on quickly. "Willingly, because he doesn't know the truth about the Empire yet, he may give information regarding the Federation and the organization and strength of its Monitor Corps. But because he is a doctor this information is unlikely to be either complete or accurate, and would be useless anyway unless the Empire knows where we are. They won't find that out unless they capture an astrogator or a ship with its charts intact, and that is a contingency which we will take very great precautions to guard against from this moment on.

"Agents are trained in linguistics, medicine or the social sciences," Williamson ended confidently. "Their knowledge of interstellar navigation is nil. The scoutship which lands them returns to base immediately, this being standard precautionary procedure in operations of this sort. So you can see that we have a serious problem but that it is not an immediate one."

"Isn't it?" said Conway.

He saw Williamson and Stillman looking at him—intently and cautiously as if he was some kind of bomb which, having exploded half an hour ago was about to do so again. In a way Conway was sorry that he had to explode on them again and make them share the fear and horrible, gnawing anxiety which up to now had been his alone. He wet his lips and tried to break it to them as gently as possible.

"Speaking personally," he said quietly, "I don't have the faintest idea of the coordinates of Traltha, or Illensa or Earth, or even the Earth-seeded planet where I was born. But there is one set of figures which I do know, and any other doctor on space service in this Sector is likely to know them also. They are the coordinates of Sector General.

"I don't think we have any time at all."

CHAPTER 12

T he only constructive thing which Conway did during the trip back to Sector General was to catch up on his sleep, but very often the sleep was made so hideous by nightmares of the coming war that it was more pleasant to stay awake, and his waking time he spent in discussions with Williamson, Stillman and the other senior officers on *Vespasian*. Since he had called the shots right during that last half hour on Etla Williamson seemed to value any ideas he might have, even though problems of espionage, logistics and fleet maneuvers were hardly within the specialty of a Senior Physician.

The discussions were interesting, informative and, like his dreams, anything but pleasant.

According to Colonel Williamson an interstellar war of conquest was logistically impossible, but a simple war of extermination could be fought by anyone with sufficient force and stomachs strong enough to withstand the thought of slaughtering other intelligent beings by the planet-load. The Empire had more than enough force, and the strength of its collective stomach was dependent on factors over which the Monitor Corps had no control, *as yet*.

Given enough time agents of the Corps could have infiltrated the Empire. They already knew the position of one of its inhabited worlds and, because there was traffic between it and the other planets of the Empire, they would soon know the positions of others. The first step then would be to gather intelligence and eventually . . . Well, the Corps were no mean propagandists themselves and in a situation like this where the enemy was basing their campaign on a series of Big Lies, some method of striking at this weak spot could be devised. The Corps was primarily a police organization, a force intended not so much to wage war as to maintain peace. And like any good police force its actions were constrained by the possible effects on innocent bystanders—in this case the citizens of the Empire as well as the people of the Federation.

That was why the plan for undermining the Empire would be set in motion, even though it could not possibly take effect before the first clash occurred. Williamson's fondest hope—or prayer might be a more accurate word—was that the Corpsman who was now in Empire hands would not know, and so would not be able to tell, the coordinates of Sector General. The Colonel was realist enough to know that if the agent knew anything the enemy would get it out of him one way or another. But failing this ideal solution the hospital would be defended in such a way that it would be the only Federation position that the enemy would know—unless they diverted a large proportion of their force to the time-wasting job of searching the main body of the Galaxy, which was just what the Corps wanted.

Conway tried not to think of what it would be like at Sector General when the entire mobile force of the Empire was concentrated there . . .

A few hours before emergence they received another report from the agent who was now on the Empire's Central World. The first one had taken nine days to reach Etla, the second was relayed with top priority coding in eighteen hours.

The report stated that the Central World did not seem to be as hostile toward extra-terrestrials as Etla and the other worlds of the Empire. The people there seemed much more cosmopolitan and occasionally e-ts could be seen in the streets. There were subtle indications, however, that beings had diplomatic status and were natives of worlds with which the Empire had made treaties with the purpose of holding them off as a group until such times as it could annex them individually. So far as the agent personally had been treated, things could not have been nicer, and in a few days time he was due for an audience with the Emperor himself. Nevertheless, he was beginning to feel uneasy.

It was nothing that he could put his finger on—he was a doctor who had been yanked off Survey and pre-Colonization duty, he reminded them, and not one of the Cultural Contact hot-shots. He got the impression that on certain occasions and among certain people, all mention of the Federation's aims and constitution by himself was discouraged, while at other times, usually when there were only a few people present, they encouraged him to talk at great length. Another point which worried him was the fact that none of the newscasts he had seen made any mention of his arrival. Had the position been reversed and a citizen of the Empire made contact with the Federation, the event would have been top-line news for weeks.

He wondered sometimes if he was talking too much, and wished that a subspace receiver could be built as small as a sender so that he could ask for instructions . . .

That was the last they ever heard from that agent.

Conway's return to Sector General was not as pleasant as he had thought it would be a few weeks previously. Then he had expected to return as a near-heroic personage with the biggest assignment of his career successfully accomplished, the plaudits of his colleagues ringing in his ears and with Murchison waiting to receive him with open arms. The latter had been a very slim probability indeed, but Conway liked to dream sometimes. Instead he was returning from a job which had blown up most horribly in his face, hoping that his colleagues would not stop him to ask how or what he had been doing, and with Murchison standing inside the lock with a friendly smile on her face and both arms hanging correctly by her sides.

Meeting him after a long absence, Conway thought sourly, was the sort of thing one *friend* did for another—there could be nothing more to it than that. She said it was nice to see him back and he said it was nice to be back, and when she started to ask questions he said he had a lot of things to do now but would it be all right if he called her later, and he smiled as if calling her to arrange a date was the most important thing in his mind. But his smile had suffered through lack of use and she must have seen that there was something definitely insincere about it. She went all Doctor-and-Nurse on him, said that *of course* he had more important things to attend to, and left quickly.

Murchison had looked as beautiful and desirable as ever and he had undoubtedly hurt her feelings, but somehow none of these things mattered to Conway at the moment. His mind would not think of anything but his impending meeting with O'Mara. And when he presented himself in the office of the Chief Psychologist shortly afterward it seemed that his worst forebodings were to be realized.

"Sit down, Doctor," O'Mara began. "So you finally succeeded in involving us in an interstellar war . . . ?"

"That isn't funny," said Conway.

O'Mara gave him a long, steady look. It was a look which not only

noted the expression on Conway's face but such other factors as his posture in the chair and the position and movements of his hands. O'Mara
did not set much store by correct modes of address, but the fact that
Conway had omitted to say "Sir" was also being noted as a contributory
datum and given its proper place in his analysis of the situation. The
process took perhaps two minutes and during that time the Chief Psychologist did not move an eyelid. O'Mara had no irritating mannerisms;
his strong, blunt hands never twitched or fiddled with things, and when
he desired it his features could be as expressive as a lump of rock.

On this occasion he let his face relax into an expression of almost
benign disfavor, and finally he spoke.

"I agree," he said quietly, "it isn't a bit funny. But you know as well
as I do that there is always the chance of some well-intentioned doctor
in a place like this stirring up trouble on a large scale. We have often
brought in some weird beastie of a hitherto unknown species who requires treatment urgently, and there is no time to search for its friends
to discover if what we propose to do is the right procedure in the circumstances. A case in point was that Ian chrysalis you had a few months
ago. That was before we made formal contact with the Ians, and if you
hadn't correctly diagnosed the patient's condition as a growing chrysalis
instead of a malignant growth requiring instant removal, a procedure
which would have killed the patient, we would have been in serious trouble with the Ians."

"Yes, sir," said Conway.

O'Mara went on, "My remark was in the nature of a pleasantry, and
had a certain aptness considering your recent experience with that Ian.
Perhaps it was in questionable taste, but if you think I'm going to apologize then you obviously believe in miracles. Now tell me about Etla.

"And," he added quickly before Conway could speak, "my desk and
wastebasket are full of reports detailing the implications and probable
dire consequences of the Etla business. What I want to know is how you
handled your assignment as originally given."

As briefly as possible Conway did as he was told. While he talked he
felt himself begin to relax. He still had a confused and very frightening
picture in the back of his mind of what the war would mean to countless
millions of beings, to the hospital and to himself, but he no longer felt
that he was partly responsible for bringing it about. O'Mara had begun
the interview by accusing him of the very thing he had felt guilty of, then
without saying so in so many words had made him see how ridiculous

it had been to feel guilty. But as he neared the point where Lonvellin's ship had been destroyed, the feeling returned full strength. If he had put the pieces together sooner, Lonvellin would not have died . . .

O'Mara must have detected the change of feeling, but allowed him to finish before he said, "It surprises me that Lonvellin didn't see it before you did, it being the brain behind the operation. And while we're on the subject of brains, yours does not seem to be thrown into complete disorder by problems involving large numbers of people requiring differing forms of treatment. So I have another job for you. It is smaller than the Etla assignment, you won't have to leave the hospital, and with any luck it won't blow up in your face.

"I want you to organize the evacuation of Sector General."

Conway swallowed, then swallowed again.

"Stop looking as though you'd been sandbagged!" O'Mara said testily, "or I *will* hit you with something! You must have thought this thing through far enough to see that we can't have patients here when the Empire force arrives. Or any non-military staff who have not volunteered to stay. Or *any* person, regardless of position or rank, who has in his mind detailed information regarding the whereabouts of any Federation planets. And surely the idea of telling people nominally your superiors what to do doesn't frighten you, not after ordering a Corps Colonel around . . ."

Conway felt his neck getting warm. He let the dig about Williamson pass and said, "I thought we might leave the place empty for them."

"No," said O'Mara dryly. "It has too much sentimental, monetary and strategic value. We hope to keep a few levels operating for the treatment of casualties sustained by the defending force. Colonel Skempton is already at work on the evacuation problem and will help you all he can. What time is it by you, Doctor?"

Conway told him that when he had left *Vespasian* it had been two hours after breakfast.

"Good," said O'Mara. "You can contact Skempton and go to work at once. With me it is long past bedtime, but I'll sleep here in case you or the Colonel want something. Goodnight, Doctor."

So saying he took off and folded his tunic, stepped out of his shoes and lay down. Within seconds his breathing became deep and regular. Suddenly Conway laughed.

"Seeing the Chief Psychologist lying on his own couch," Conway said through his laughter, "is something of a traumatic experience. I very much doubt, sir, if our relationship will ever be quite the same . . ."

As he was leaving O'Mara murmured sleepily, "I'm glad. For a while there I thought you were going all melancholy on me . . ."

CHAPTER 13

Seven hours later Conway surveyed his littered desk wearily but with a measure of triumph, rubbed his eyes and looked across at the desk facing his. For a moment he felt that he was back on Etla and that a red-eyed Major Stillman would look up and ask what he wanted. But it was a red-eyed Colonel Skempton who looked up when he spoke.

"The breakdown of patients to be evacuated is complete," Conway said tiredly. "There are divided first into species, which will indicate the number of ships required to move them and the living conditions which must be reproduced in each ship. With some of the weirder types this will necessitate structural alterations to the vessels, which will take time. Then each species is sub-divided into degrees of seriousness of the patient's condition, which will determine the order of their going . . ."

Except, thought Conway sourly, when a patient's condition was such that to move it would endanger its life. In which case it would have to be evacuated last instead of first so that treatment could be prolonged as much as possible, which meant that specialized medical staff who themselves should have been evacuated by that time would be held back to treat it, and by that time its life might be endangered by missiles from an Empire warship anyway. *Nothing* seemed to happen in a tidy, consecutive fashion anymore.

". . . Then it will take a few days for Major O'Mara's department to process the medical and maintenance staff," Conway went on, "even though he just has to ask them a few questions under scop. When I arrived I expected the hospital to be under attack already. At the moment I don't know whether to plan for a panic evacuation within forty-eight hours, which is the absolute minimum time for it and which would probably kill more patients than it would save, or take my time and plan for a merely hurried evacuation."

"I couldn't assemble the transport in forty-eight hours," said Skempton shortly, and lowered his head again. As Chief of Maintenance and the Hospital's ranking Monitor officer the job of assembling, modifying and routing the transports devolved on him, and he had an awful lot of work to do.

"What I'm trying to say," Conway said insistently, "is how much time do you think we've got?"

The Colonel looked up again. "Sorry, Doctor," he said. "I have an estimate which came in a few hours ago . . ." He lifted one of the top layer of papers on his desk and began to read.

Subjecting all the known factors to a rigid analysis, the report stated, it appeared likely that a short time-lag would occur between the point at which the Empire discovered the exact position of Sector General and the time when they acted on this information. The initial action was likely to be an investigation by a scoutship or a small scouting force. Monitor units at present stationed around Sector General would attempt to destroy this force. Whether they were successful or not the Empire's next move would be more decisive, probably a full-scale offensive which would require many days to mount. By that time additional units of the Monitor Corps would have reached the area . . .

". . . Say eight days," Skempton concluded, "or three weeks if we're lucky. But I don't think we'll be lucky."

"Thank you," said Conway, and returned to work.

First he prepared an outline of the situation for distribution to the medical staff within the next six hours. In it he laid as much stress as possible on the necessity for a quick, orderly evacuation without overdoing it to the extent of causing a panic, and recommended that patients be informed via their physicians so as to cause the minimum distress. In the case of seriously ill patients the doctors in charge should use their discretion whether the patient should be told or evacuated under sedation. He added that an at present unspecified number of medical staff would be evacuated with the patients and that everyone should be prepared to leave the hospital at a few hours notice. This document he sent to Publications for copying in print and tape so that everyone would be in possession of the information at roughly the same time.

At least that was the theory, Conway thought dryly. But if he knew his hospital grapevine the essential data would be circulating ten minutes after it left his desk.

Next he prepared more detailed instructions regarding the patients. The warm-blooded oxygen-breathing life-forms could leave by any of several levels, but the heavy-G, high-pressure species would pose special problems, not to mention the light-gravity MSVKs and LSVOs, the giant, water-breathing AUGLs, the ultra-frigid types and the dozen or so beings on Level Thirty-eight who breathed superheated steam. Conway was planning on the operation taking five days for the patients and an additional two for the staff, and for this rapid clearing of the wards he would have to send people through levels foreign to them to reach their embarkation points. There would be possible oxygen contamination of chlorine environments, danger of chlorine leaking into the AUGL wards, or of water flooding all over the place. Precautions would have to be taken against failure of the methane life-forms' refrigerators, breakdown of the anti-gravity equipment of the fragile, bird-like LSVOs and rupture of Illensan pressure envelopes.

Contamination was the greatest danger in a multi-environment hospital—contamination by oxygen, chlorine, methane, water, cold, heat or radiation. During the evacuation the safety devices usually in operation—airtight doors, double, inter-level locks, the various detection and alarm systems—would have to be overridden in the interests of a quick getaway.

Then staff would have to be detailed to inspect the transport units to ensure that their passenger space accurately reproduced the environment of the patients they were to carry . . .

All at once Conway's mind refused to take any more of it. He closed his eyes, sank his head into the palms of his hands and watched the after-image of his desktop fade slowly into redness. He was sick of paperwork. Since being given the Etla job his whole life had been paperwork; reports, summaries, charts, instructions. He was a doctor currently planning a complicated operation, but it was the sort of operation performed by a high-level clerk rather than a surgeon. Conway had not studied and trained for the greater part of his life to be a clerk.

He stood up, excused himself hoarsely to the Colonel and left the office. Without really thinking about it he was moving in the direction of his wards.

A new shift was just coming on duty and to the patients it was half an hour before the first meal of the day, which made it a very unusual time for a Senior Physician to do his rounds. The mild panic he caused would, in other circumstances, have been funny. Conway greeted the intern on duty politely, felt mildly surprised to find that it was the Creppelian octopoid he had met as a trainee two months previously, then felt annoyed when the AMSL insisted on following him around at a respectful distance. This was the proper procedure for a junior intern, but at that moment Conway wanted to be alone with his patients and his thoughts.

Most strongly of all he felt the need to see and speak to the sometimes weird and always wonderful extra-terrestrial patients who were technically under his care—all the beings he had come to know before leaving for Etla having been long since discharged. He did *not* look at their charts, however, because he had an allergy toward the abstraction of information via the printed word at the moment. Instead he questioned them closely, almost hungrily, regarding their symptoms and condition and background. He left some of the minor cases pleased and flabbergasted by such attention from a Senior Physician, and some might have been annoyed by his prying. But Conway had to do it. While he still had patients left he wanted to be a doctor.

An *e-t* doctor ...

Sector General was breaking up. The vast, complex structure dedicated to the relief of suffering and the advance of xenological medicine was dying, succumbing like any terminal patient to a disease too powerful for it to resist. Tomorrow or the next day these wards would begin to empty. The patients with their exotic variations of physiology, metabolism and complaints would drain away. In darkened wards the weird and wonderful fabrications which constituted the alien idea of a comfortable bed would crouch like surrealistic ghosts along the walls. And with the departure of the e-t patients and staff would go the necessity for maintaining the environments which housed them, the Translators which allowed them to communicate, the physiology tapes which made it possible for one species to treat another ...

But the Galaxy's greatest e-t hospital would not die completely, not for another few days or weeks. The Monitor Corps had no experience of interstellar wars, this being their first, but they thought they knew what to expect. Casualties among the ship's crews would be heavy and with a very high proportion of them fatal. The still-living casualties brought in would be of three types; decompression, bone-fractures and radiation poisoning. It was expected that two or three levels would be enough to take care of them, because if the engagement was fought with nuclear weapons, and there was no reason to suppose otherwise, most of the decompression and fracture cases would be radiation-terminal also—there would be no danger of overcrowding.

Then the internal break-up began with the evacuation would continue on the structural level as the Empire forces attacked. Conway was no military tactician, but he could not see how the vast, nearly-empty hospital could be protected. It was a sitting duck, soon to be a dead one. A great, fused and battered metal graveyard . . .

All at once a tremendous wave of feeling washed through Conway's mind—bitterness, sadness and a surge of sheer anger which left him shaking. As he stumbled out of the ward he didn't know whether he wanted to cry or curse or knock somebody down. But the decision was taken away from him when he turned the corner leading to the PVSJ section and collided solidly with Murchison.

The impact was not painful, one of the colliding bodies being well endowed with shock-absorbing equipment, but it was sharp enough to jolt his mind of a very somber train of thought onto one infinitely more pleasant. Suddenly he wanted to watch and talk to Murchison as badly as he had wanted to visit his patients, and for the same reason. This might be the last time he would see her.

"I—I'm sorry," he stammered, backing off. Then remembering their last meeting, he said, "I was a bit rushed at the lock this morning, couldn't say much. Are you on duty?"

"Just coming off," said Murchison in a neutral voice.

"Oh," said Conway, then; "I wondered if . . . that is, would you mind . . ."

"I wouldn't mind going for a swim," she said.

"Fine," said Conway.

They went up to the recreation level, changed and met inside on the simulated beach. While they were walking toward the water she said suddenly, "Oh, Doctor. When you were sending me those letters, did you ever think of putting them in envelopes with my name and room number on them?"

"And let everybody know I was writing to you?" Conway said. "I didn't think you wanted that."

Murchison gave a lady-like snort. "The system you devised was not exactly secret," she said with a hint of anger in her tone. "Thornnastor in Pathology has three mouths and it can't keep any of them shut. They were nice letters, but I don't think it was fitting for you to write them on the back of sputum test reports . . . !"

"I'm sorry," said Conway. "It won't happen again."

With the words the dark mood which the sight of Murchison had pushed from his mind came rushing back. It certainly wouldn't happen again, he thought bleakly, not ever. And the hot, artificial sun did not seem to be warming his skin as he remembered it and the water was not so stingingly cold. Even in the half-G conditions the swim was wearying rather than exhilarating. It was as if some deep layer of tiredness swathed his body, dulling all sensation. After only a few minutes he returned to the shallows and waded onto the beach. Murchison followed him, looking concerned.

"You've got thinner," she said when she had caught up with him.

Conway's first impulse was to say "You haven't," but the intended compliment could have been taken another way, and he was lousy enough company already without running the risk of insulting her. Then he had an idea and said quickly, "I forgot that you're just off duty and haven't eaten yet. Will we go to the restaurant?"

"Yes, *please*," said Murchison.

The restaurant was perched high on the cliff facing the diving ledges and boasted a continuous transparent wall which allowed a full view of the beach while keeping out the noise. It was the only place in the recreation level where quiet conversation was possible. But the quietness was wasted on them because they hardly spoke at all.

Until half way through the meal when Murchison said, "You aren't eating as much, either."

Conway said, "Have you ever owned, or navigated, a space vessel?"

"*Me?* Of course not!"

"Or if you were wrecked in a ship whose astrogator was injured and unconscious," he persisted, "and the ship's drive had been repaired, could you give the coordinates for reaching some planet within the Federation?"

"No," said Murchison impatiently. "I'd have to stay there until the astrogator woke up. What sort of questions are these?"

"The sort I'll be asking all my friends," Conway replied grimly. "If you had answered 'Yes' to one of them it would have taken a load off my mind."

Murchison put down her knife and fork, frowning slightly. Conway thought that she looked lovely when she frowned, or laughed, or did anything. Especially when she was wearing a swimsuit. That was one thing he liked about this place, they allowed you to dine in swimsuits. And he wished that he could pull himself out of his dismal mood and be sparkling company for a couple of hours. On his present showing he doubted if Murchison would let him take her home, much less cooperate in the clinch for the two minutes, forty-eight seconds it took for the robot to arrive . . .

"Something is bothering you," Murchison said. She hesitated, then went on, "If you need a soft shoulder, be my guest. But remember it is only for crying on, nothing else."

"What else could I use it for?" said Conway.

"I don't know," she said, smiling, "but I'd probably find out."

Conway did not smile in return. Instead he began to talk about the things that were worrying him—and the people, including her. When he had finished she was quiet for a long time. Sadly Conway watched the faintly ridiculous picture of a young, dedicated, very beautiful girl in a white swimsuit coming to a decision which would almost certainly cost her her life.

"I think I'll stay behind," she said finally, as Conway knew she would. "You're staying too, of course?"

"I haven't decided yet," Conway said carefully. "I can't leave until after the evacuation anyway. And there may be nothing to stay for . . ." He made a last try to make her change her mind. ". . . and all your e-t training would be wasted. There are lots of other hospitals that would be glad to have you . . ."

Murchison sat up straight in her seat. When she spoke it was in the brisk, competent, no-nonsense tone of a nurse prescribing treatment to a possibly recalcitrant patient. She said, "From what you tell me you're going to have a busy day tomorrow. You should get all the sleep you can. In fact, I think you should go to your room right away."

Then in a completely different tone she added, "But if you'd like to take me home first . . ."

CHAPTER 14

On the day after instructions to evacuate the hospital had been issued, everything went smoothly. The patients gave no trouble at all, the natural order of things being for patients to leave hospital and in this instance their discharge was just a little bit more dramatic than usual. Discharging the medical staff, however, was a most unnatural thing. To a patient Hospital was merely a painful, or at least not very pleasant, episode in his life. To the staff of Sector General the hospital *was* their life.

Everything went smoothly with the staff on the first day also. Everyone did as they were told, probably because habit and their state of shock made that the easiest thing to do. But by the second day the shock had worn off and they began to produce arguments, and the person they most wanted to argue with was Dr. Conway.

On the third day Conway had to call O'Mara.

"What's the trouble!" Conway burst out when O'Mara replied. "The trouble is making this . . . this gaggle of geniuses see things sensibly! And the brighter a being is the more stupid it insists on acting. Take Prilicla, a beastie who is so much eggshell and matchsticks that it would blow away in a strong draft, *it* wants to stay. And Doctor Mannon, who is as near being a Diagnostician as makes no difference. Mannon says treating exclusively human casualties would be something of a holiday. And the reasons some of the others have thought up are fantastic.

"You've got to make them see sense, sir. You're the Chief Psychologist . . ."

"Three quarters of the medical and maintenance staff," O'Mara said sharply, "are in possession of information likely to help the enemy in the event of their capture. They will be leaving, regardless of whether they are Diagnosticians, computermen or junior ward orderlies, for reasons of security. They will have no choice in the matter. In addition to these there will be a number of specialist medical staff who will feel obliged, because of their patient's condition, to travel with their charges. So far as the remainder are concerned there is very little I can do, they are sane, intelligent, mature beings capable of making up their own minds."

Conway said, "Hah."

"Before you impugn other people's sanity," O'Mara said dryly, "answer me one question. Are *you* going to stay?"

"Well . . ." began Conway.

O'Mara broke the connection.

Conway stared at the handset a long time without reclipping it. He still had not made up his mind if he was going to stay or not. He knew that he wasn't the heroic type, and he badly wanted to leave. But he didn't want to leave without his friends, because if Murchison and Prilicla and the others stayed behind, he couldn't have borne the things they would think about him if he was to run away.

Probably they all thought that he meant to stay but was being coy about it, while the truth was that he was too cowardly and at the same time too much of a hypocrite to admit to them that he was afraid . . .

The sharp voice of Colonel Skempton broke into his mood of self-loathing, dispelling it for the moment.

"Doctor, the Kelgian hospital ship is here. And an Illensan freighter. Locks Five and Seventeen in ten minutes."

"Right," said Conway. He left the office at a near run, heading for Reception.

All three control desks were occupied when he arrived, two by Nidians and the other by a Corps Lieutenant on stand-by. Conway positioned himself between and behind the Nidians where he could study both sets of repeater screens and began hoping very hard that he could deal with the things which would inevitably go wrong.

The Kelgian vessel already locked on at Five was a brute, one of the latest interstellar liners which had been partially converted into a hospital ship on the way out. The alterations were not quite complete, but a team of maintenance staff and robots were already boarding it together with senior ward staff who would arrange for the disposition of their patients. At the same time the occupants of the wards were being readied for the transfer and the equipment necessary for treating them was being dismantled, rapidly and with little regard for the subsequent condition of the ward walls. Some of the smaller equipment, heaped onto powered stretcher-carriers, was already on the way to the ship.

Altogether it looked like being a fairly simple operation. The atmosphere, pressure and gravity requirement of the patients were exactly those of the ship, so that no complicated protective arrangements were necessary, and the vessel was big enough to take all of the Kelgian patients with room to spare. He would be able to clear the DBLF levels completely *and* get rid of a few Tralthan FGLIs as well. But even though the first job was relatively uncomplicated, Conway estimated that it would take at least six hours for the ship to be loaded and away. He turned to the other control desk.

Here the picture was in many respects similar. The environment of the Illensan freighter matched perfectly that of the PVSJ wards, but the ship was smaller and, considering its purpose, did not have a large crew. The preparations for receiving patients aboard were, for this reason, not well advanced. Conway directed extra maintenance staff to the Illensan freighter, thinking that they would be lucky to get away with sixty PVSJs in the same time as it took the other ship to clear three whole levels.

He was still trying to find shortcuts in the problem when the Lieutenant's screen lit up.

"A Tralthan ambulance ship, Doctor," he reported. "Fully staffed and with provision for six FROBs and a Chalder as well as twenty of their own species. No preparation needed at their end, they say just load 'em up."

The AUGL denizens of Chalderescol, a forty-foot long, armored fish-like species were water-breathers who could not live in any other medium for more than a few seconds and live. On the other hand the FROBs were squat, immensely massive and thick-skinned beings accustomed to the crushing gravity and pressure of Hudlar. Properly speaking Hudlarians did not breathe at all, and their incredibly strong tegument allowed them to exist for long periods in conditions of zero gravity and pressure, so that the water in the AUGL section would not bother them . . .

Conway said quickly, "Lock Twenty-eight for the Chalder. While they're loading it send the FROBs through the ELNT section into the main AUGL tank and out by the same Lock. Then tell them to move to Lock Five and we'll have their other patients waiting . . ."

Gradually the evacuation got under way. Accommodations was prepared for the first convalescent PVSJs aboard the Illensan freighter and the slow trek of patients and staff through the noisome yellow fog of the chlorine section commenced. Simultaneously the other screen was showing a long, undulating file of Kelgians moving toward their ship, with medical and engineering staff carrying equipment charging up and down the line.

To some it might have seemed callous to evacuate the convalescent patients first, but there were very good reasons for doing so. With these walking wounded out of the way the wards and approaches to the locks would be less congested, which would allow the complicated frames and harnesses containing the more seriously ill patients to be moved more easily, as well as giving them a little more time in the optimum conditions of the wards.

"Two more Illensan ships, Doctor," the lieutenant said suddenly. "Small jobs, capacity about twenty patients each."

"Lock Seventeen is still tied up," said Conway. "Tell them to orbit."

The next arrival was a small passenger ship from the Earth-human world of Gregory, and with it came the lunch trays. There were only a few Earth-human patients at Sector General, but at a pinch the Gregorian ship could take any warm-blooded oxygen-breather below the mass of a Tralthan. Conway dealt with both arrivals at the same time, not caring if he *did* have to speak or even shout, with his mouth full . . .

Then suddenly the sweating, harassed face of Colonel Skempton flicked onto the internal screen. He said sharply, "Doctor, there are two Illensan ships hanging about in orbit. Don't you have work for them?"

"Yes!" said Conway, irritated by the other's tone. "But there is a ship already loading chlorine-breathers at Seventeen, and there is no other lock suitable on that level. They'll have to wait their turn . . ."

"That won't do," Skempton cut in harshly. "While they're hanging about out there they are in danger should the enemy attack suddenly. Ether you start loading them at once or we send them away to come back later. Probably much later. Sorry."

Conway opened his mouth and then shut it with a click over what he had been about to say. Hanging grimly onto his temper he tried to think.

He knew that the build-up of the defense fleet had been going on for days and that the astrogation officers responsible for bringing those units in would leave again as soon as possible—either on their own scout-ships or with the patients leaving Sector General. The plan devised by the Monitor Corps called for no information regarding the whereabouts of the Federation being available in the minds of the defending forces or the non-combatants who remained in the hospital. The defense fleet was deployed to protect the hospital and the ships locked onto it, and the thought of two other ships swinging around loose, ships which contained fully qualified astrogators aboard, must have made the Monitor fleet commander start biting his nails.

"Very well, Colonel," Conway said. "We'll take the ships at Fifteen and Twenty-one. This will mean chlorine-breathers traveling through the DBLF maternity ward and a part of the AUGL section. Despite these complications we should have the patients aboard in three hours . . ."

Complications was right . . . ! Conway thought grimly as he gave the necessary orders. Luckily both the DBLF ward and that section of the AUGL level would be vacant by the time the chlorine-breathing Illensans in their pressure tents came through. But the ship from Gregory was at an adjoining lock taking on ELNTs who were being shepherded through the area by DBLF nurses in protective suits. Also there were some of the low-G, bird-like MSVKs being brought to the same vessel through the chlorine ward which he was hoping to clear . . .

There weren't enough screens in Reception to keep properly in touch with what was going on down there, Conway decided suddenly. He had the horrible feeling that a most awful snarl-up would occur if he wasn't careful. But he couldn't be careful if he didn't know what was going on. The only course was for him to go there and direct the traffic himself.

He called O'Mara, explained the situation quickly and asked for a relief.

CHAPTER 15

D r. Mannon arrived, groaned piteously at the battery of screens and flashing lights, then smoothly took over the job of directing the evacuation. As a replacement Conway could not have hoped for anyone better. He was turning to go when Mannon pushed his face within three inches of one of the screens and said "Harrumph."

Conway stopped. "What's wrong?"

"Nothing, nothing," said Mannon, without turning round. "It's just that I'm beginning to understand why you want to go down there."

"But I told you why!" said Conway impatiently. He stamped out, telling himself angrily that Mannon was indulging in senseless conversation at a time when unnecessary talk of any kind was criminal. Then he wondered if the aging Dr. Mannon was tired, or had a particularly confusing tape riding him, and felt suddenly ashamed. Snapping at Skempton or the receptionists hadn't worried him unduly, but he did not want to begin biting the heads off his friends—even if he was harassed and tired and the whole place was rapidly going to Hell on horseback. Then very soon he was being kept too busy to feel ashamed.

Three hours later the state of confusion around him seemed to have doubled, although in actual fact it was simply that twice as much was being accomplished twice as fast. From his position at one of the high-level entrances to the main AUGL ward Conway could look down on a line of ELNTs—six-legged, crab-like entities from Melf IV—scuttling or being towed across the floor of the great tank. Unlike their amphibious patients, the thickly-furred, air breathing Kelgians attending them had to wear protective envelopes which were sweltering hot inside. The scraps of Translated conversation which drifted up to him, although necessarily emotionless, verged on the incandescent. But the work was being done, and much faster than Conway had ever hoped for.

In the corridor behind him a slow procession of Illensans, some in protective suits and the more seriously ill in pressure tents which enclosed their beds, moved past. They were being attended by Earth-human and Kelgian nurses. The transfer was going smoothly now, but there had been a time only half an hour back when Conway had wondered if it would go at all . . .

When the large pressure tents came through into the water-filled AUGL section they had risen like giant chlorine bubbles and stuck fast against the ceiling. Towing them along the corridor ceiling had been impossible because outgrowths of plumbing might have ruptured the thin envelopes, and getting five or six nurses to weigh them down was impractical. And when he brought in powered stretcher carriers from the level above—vehicles not designed for but theoretically capable of operating under water—with the idea of both holding his super-buoyant patients down and moving them quickly, a battery casing had split and the carrier became the center of a mass of hissing, bubbling water which had rapidly turned black.

Conway would not be surprised to hear that the patient on that particular carrier had a relapse.

He had solved the problem finally with a magnificent flash of inspiration which, he told himself disgustedly, should have come two seconds after he had seen the problem. He had quickly switched the artificial gravity grids in the corridor to zero attraction and in the weightless condition the pressure tents had lost their buoyancy. It meant that the nurses had to swim instead of walk with their patients, but that was a small thing.

It was during the transfer of these PVSJs that Conway learned the reason for Mannon's "Harrumph" up in Reception—Murchison was one of the nurses on that duty. She hadn't recognized him, of course, but he knew there was only one person who could fill a nurse's lightweight suit the way she did. He didn't speak to her, however—it didn't seem to be the proper time or place.

Time passed rapidly without another major crisis developing. At Lock Five the Kelgian hospital ship was ready to go, waiting only for some of the hospital's senior staff to go aboard and for a Monitor ship to escort them out to a safe jump distance. Remembering some of the beings who were scheduled to leave on that ship, many of them friends of long standing, Conway decided the chance offered by the quiet spell to say a quick good-bye to some of them. He called Mannon to tell him where he was going, then headed for Five.

But by the time he arrived the Kelgian ship had gone. In one of the big direction vision panels he could see it drawing away with a Monitor cruiser in close attendance; and beyond them, hanging like newly-formed constellations in the blackness, lay the Monitor defense fleet. The buildup of units around the hospital was proceeding as planned and had increased visibly since Conway had looked at it yesterday. Reassured, and not a little awed by the sight, he hurried back to the AUGL section.

And arrived to find the corridor almost plugged by an expanding sphere of ice.

The ship from Gregory contained a specially refrigerated compartment for beings of the SNLU classification. These were fragile, crystalline, methane-based life-forms who would be instantly cremated if the temperature rose above minus one-twenty. Sector General was currently treating seven of these ultra-frigid creatures, and all of them had been packed into a ten-foot refrigerated sphere for the transfer. Because of the difficulties expected in handling them they were the last patients for the Gregorian ship.

If there had been a direct opening to space from the cold section they would have been moved to the ship along the outer hull, but as this was not possible they had to be brought through fourteen levels from the methane ward to their loading point at Lock Sixteen. In all the other levels the corridors had been spacious and filled with air or chlorine, so that all that the protective sphere had done was to collect a coating of frost and chill the surrounding atmosphere. But in the AUGL section it was growing ice. Fast.

Conway had known this would happen but had not considered it important because the sphere should not have been in the water-filled corridor long enough to cause a problem. But one of the towing lines had snapped and pulled it against some projecting conduit and within seconds they were welded together with ice. Now the sphere was encased in an icy shell four feet thick and there was barely room to pass above or below it.

"Get cutting torches down here," Conway bawled up to Mannon, "quick!"

Three Corpsmen arrived just before the corridor was completely blocked. With the cutting flames of their torches set to maximum dispersal they attacked the icy mass, melting it free of the projection and trying to reduce it to a more managable size. In the confined space of the corridor the heat being applied to the ice-ball sent the water temperature soaring up, and none of their suits had cooling units. Conway began to feel a distinct empathy toward boiled lobsters. And the great, awkward mass of ice was a danger to life and limb—danger from being crushed between it and the corridor wall, and the scalding, nearly opaque water which made it so easy to put an arm or leg between the ice and a cutting flame.

But finally the job was done. The container with its SNLU occupants was maneuvered through the inter-level lock into another air-filled section. Conway rubbed a hand across the outside of his helmet in an unconscious attempt to wipe the sweat from his forehead and wondered what else would go wrong.

The answer, according to Dr. Mannon up in Reception was not a thing.

All three levels of DBLF patients had left with the Kelgian ship, Mannon told him enthusiastically, the only caterpillars remaining in the hospital being a few of the nursing staff. Between them the three Illensan freighters had cleared the PVSJ wards of their chlorine-breathers, except for a few stragglers who would be aboard within a few minutes. Among the water-breathing types the AUGLs and ELNTs were clear, and the SNLUs in their baby iceberg were just going aboard. In all fourteen levels had been cleared and that was not a bad day's work. Dr. Mannon suggested that Dr. Conway might take this opportunity of applying a pillow to his head and going into a state of voluntary unconsciousness in preparation for an equally busy day tomorrow.

Conway was swimming tiredly toward the inter-level lock, his mind revolving around the infinitely alluring concepts of a large steak and a long sleep, when it happened.

Something which he did not see struck him a savage, disabling blow. It bit simultaneously in the abdomen, chest and legs—the places where his suit was tightest. Agony burst inside him like a red explosion that was just barely contained by his tortured body. He doubled up and began to black out, he wanted to die and he desperately wanted to be sick. But some tiny portion of his brain unaffected by the pain and nausea insisted that he did not allow himself to be sick, that being sick inside his helmet was a very *nasty* way to die . . .

Gradually the pain receded and became bearable. Conway still felt as if a Tralthan had kicked him in the groin with all six feet, but other things were beginning to register. Loud, insistent, gurgling noises and the extremely odd sight of a Kelgian drifting in the water without its protective suit. A second look told him that it was wearing a suit, but that it was ruptured and full of water.

Further down in the AUGL tank two more Kelgians floated, their long, soft, furry bodies burst open from head to tail, the ghastly details mercifully obscured by an expanding red fog. And against the opposite wall of the tank there was an area of turbulence around a dark, irregular hole through which the water seemed to be leaving.

Conway swore. He thought he knew what had happened. Whatever had made that ragged-edged hole had, because of the non-compressibility of water, also expended its force on the unfortunate occupants of the AUGL tank. But because the other Kelgian and himself had been up here in the corridor they had escaped the worst effects of it.

Or maybe only one of them had escaped . . .

It took three minutes for him to drag the Kelgian nurse into the lock ten yards along the corridor. Once inside he set the pumps going to clear the chamber of water, simultaneously cracking an air valve. While the last of the water was draining away he struggled to lay the sodden, inert body on its side against one wall. The being's silvery pelt was a mass of dirty gray spikes, and he could detect no pulse or respiration. Conway quickly lay down on his side on the floor, moved the third and fourth set of legs apart so that he could put his shoulder into the space between them, then with his own feet braced firmly against the opposite wall he began to push rhythmically. Sitting on top of it and pressing down with the palms was not, Conway knew, an effective method of applying artificial respiration to one of the massive DBLFs. After a few seconds water began trickling out of its mouth.

He broke off suddenly as he heard somebody trying to open the lock from the AUGL corridor side. Conway tried his radio, but one or the other of their sets was not working. Taking off his helmet quickly he put his mouth up against the seal, cupped his hands around it and yelled, "I've an air-breather in here without its suit, don't open the seal or else you'll drown us! Come in from the other side . . . !"

A few minutes later the seal on the air-filled side opened and Murchison was looking down at him. She said, "D-Doctor Conway . . ." in a peculiar voice.

Conway straightened his legs sharply, ramming his shoulder into the area of the Kelgian's underbelly nearest its lungs and said, "What?"

"I . . . You . . . the explosion . . ." she began. Then after the brief false start her tone became firm and purposeful as she went on, "There's been an explosion, Doctor. One of the DBLF nurses is injured, severe lacerated wounds caused by a piece of floor plating spinning against it. We coagulated at once but I don't think its holding. And the corridor where its lying is being flooded, the explosion must have opened a way into the AUGL section. The air-pressure is dropping slightly so we must be open to space somewhere, too, and there is a distinct smell of chlorine . . ."

Conway groaned and ceased his efforts with the Kelgian, but before he could speak Murchison went on quickly, "All the Kelgian doctors have been evacuated and the only DBLFs left are this one and a couple who should be around here somewhere, but they're just nursing staff . . ."

Here was a proper mess, Conway thought as he scrambled to his feet; contamination *and* threatening decompression. The injured being would have to be moved quickly, because if the pressure dropped too much the airtight doors would drop and if the patient was on the wrong side of them when they did it would be just too bad. And the absence of a qualified DBLF meant that he would have to take a Kelgian physiology tape and do the job himself, which meant a quick trip to O'Mara's office. But first he would have to look at the patient.

"Take over this one, please Nurse," he said, indicating the sodden mass on the floor, "I think it's beginning to breath for itself, but will you give it another ten minutes . . ." He watched while Murchison lay down on her side, knees bent and with both feet planted against the opposite wall. This was definitely neither the time nor the place, but the sight of her lying there in that demoralizingly tight suit made the urgency of patients, evacuations and physiology tapes diminish for just an instant. Then the tight, moisture beaded suit made him remember that Murchison had been in the AUGL tank, too, just a few minutes before the explosion, and he had an awful vision of her lovely body burst open like those of the two hapless DBLFs . . .

"Between the third and fourth pair of legs, not the fifth and sixth!" Conway said harshly as he turned to go.

Which wasn't what he had meant to say at all.

CHAPTER 16

For some reason Conway's mind had been considering the effects of the explosion rather than its cause. Or perhaps he had been deliberately trying not to think along that line, trying to fool himself that there had been some sort of accident rather than that the hospital was under attack. But the yammering PA reminded him of the truth at every intersection and on the way to O'Mara's office everyone was moving twice as fast as usual and, as usual, all in a direction opposite to Conway's. He wondered if they all felt as he did, scared, unprotected, momentarily expecting a second explosion to rip the floor apart under their hurrying feet. Yet it was stupid of him to hurry because he might be rushing toward the spot where the next explosion would occur . . .

He had to force himself to walk slowly into the Chief Psychologist's office, detail his requirements and ask O'Mara quietly what had happened.

"Seven ships," O'Mara replied, motioning Conway onto the couch as he lowered the Educator helmet into position. "They seem to have been small jobs, with no evidence of unusual armament or defenses. There was quite a scrap. Three got away and one of the four which didn't launched a missile at us before it was clobbered. A small missile with a chemical warhead.

"Which is very odd," O'Mara went on thoughtfully, "because if it had been a nuclear warhead there would be no hospital here now. We weren't expecting them just as soon as this and were taken by surprise a little. Do you have to take this patient?"

"Eh? Oh, yes," said Conway. "You know DBLF. Any incised wound is an emergency with them. By the time another doctor had a look at the patient and came up here for a tape it might be too late."

O'Mara grunted. His hard, square, oddly gentle hands checked the fitting of the helmet, then pressed Conway down onto the couch. He went on, "They tried to press that attack home, it was really vicious. A clear indication, I would say, of their feelings toward us. Yet they used a chemical head when they could have destroyed us completely. Peculiar. One thing, though, it has made the ditherers make up their minds. Anybody who wants to stay here now really wants to stay and the ones who are leaving are going to leave fast, which is a good thing from Dermod's point of view . . ."

Dermod was the fleet commander.

". . . Now make your mind a blank," he ended sourly, "or at least make it blanker than usual."

Conway did not have to try to make his mind a blank, a process which aided the reception of an alien physiology tape. O'Mara's couch was wonderfully soft and comfortable. He had never appreciated it properly before, he seemed to be sinking right into it . . .

A sharp tap on the shoulder made him jump. O'Mara said caustically, "Don't go to sleep! And when you finish with your patient go to bed. Mannon can handle things in Reception and the hospital won't go to pieces without you unless we get hit with an atomic bomb . . ."

With the first evidence of double-mindedness already becoming apparent, Conway left the office. Basically the tape was a brain recording of one of the great medical minds of the species of the patient to be treated. But the doctor taking such a tape had, literally, to share his mind with a completely alien personality. That was how it felt, because *all* the memories and experience of the being who had donated the tape were impressed on the receiving mind, not just selected pieces of medical data. Physiology tapes could not be edited.

But the DBLFs were not as alien as some of the beings Conway had had to share his mind with. Although physically they resembled giant, silvery caterpillars they had a lot in common with Earth-humans. Their emotional reactions to such stimuli as music, a piece of scenic grandeur, or DBLFs of the opposite sex were very nearly identical. This one even liked meat, so that Conway would not have to starve on salad if he had to keep the tape for any length of time.

What matter if he *did* feel unsafe walking on just two legs, or found himself humping his back rhythmically as he walked. Or even, when he reached the abandoned DBLF section and the small theater where the patient had been brought, that a part of his mind thought of Murchison as just another one of those spindly DBDGs from Earth . . .

Although Murchison had everything ready for him, Conway did not start at once. Because of the mind and personality of the great Kelgian doctor sharing his brain he really *felt* for the patient now. He appreciated the seriousness of its condition and knew that there were several hours of delicate, exacting work ahead of him. At the same time he knew that he was very tired, that he could barely keep his eyes open. It was an effort even to move his feet, and his fingers, when he was checking over the instruments, felt like thick, tired sausages. He knew that he couldn't work in this condition unless he wanted to kill the patient.

"Fix me a pep-shot, will you please?" he said, biting down on a yawn.

For an instant Murchison looked as if she might give him an argument. Pep-shots were frowned on in the hospital—their use was sanctioned only in cases of the gravest emergency, and for very good reasons. But she prepared and injected the shot without saying anything, using a blunt needle and quite unnecessary force to jab it home. Even though half his mind wasn't his own, Conway could see that she was mad at him.

Then suddenly the shot took effect. Except for a slight tingling sensation in his feet and a blotchiness which only Murchison could see in his face Conway felt as clear-eyed, alert and physically refreshed as if he had just come out of a shower after ten hours sleep.

"How's the other one?" he asked suddenly. He had been so tired he had forgotten the Kelgian he had left with Murchison in the lock.

"Artificial respiration brought it round," she replied, then with more enthusiasm, "but it was still in shock. I sent it up to the Tralthan section, they still have a few senior staff there . . ."

"Good," said Conway warmly. He wanted to say more, to be more personally complimentary, but he knew that there was no time to stand and chat. He ended, "Let's begin, shall we . . . ?"

Except for the thin-walled, narrow casing which housed the brain the DBLF species had no boney structure. Their bodies were composed of an outer cylinder of musclature which, in addition to being its primary means of locomotion, served to protect the vital organs within it. To the mind of a being more generously reinforced with bones this protection was far from adequate. Another severe disadvantage in the event of injury was its complex and extremely vulnerable circulatory system; the blood-supply network which had to feed the tremendous bands of muscle encircling its body ran close under the skin. The thick fur of the pelt gave some protection here, but not against chunks of jagged-edged, flying metal.

An injury which many other species would consider superficial could cause a DBLF to bleed to death in minutes.

Conway worked slowly and carefully, dissolving away the coagulant so hastily applied by Murchison, repairing or partially replacing damaged major blood vessels and sealing off the minor branches which were too fine for him to do anything else. This part of the operation worried him— not because it endangered the life of the patient but because he knew that the beautiful silvery fur would never grow properly in these areas again, that if it grew at all it would be yellowed and visually repulsive to a male Kelgian. The injured nurse was a remarkably handsome young female and such a disfiguration could be a real tragedy. Conway hoped she wouldn't be too proud to keep the area covered with surrogate fur. Admittedly it did not have the rich, deep luster of living fur and would be immediately recognizable for what it was, but neither would it be so visually distressing . . .

An hour ago this would have been just another caterpillar, Conway thought dryly, an "it" about whom he felt only clinical concern. Now he had reached the stage of worrying about the patient's marriage prospects. A physiology tape certainly made one *feel* for one's e-t patients.

When he had finished Conway called Reception, described the patient's condition and urged that it should be evacuated as quickly as possible. Mannon told him that there was half a dozen small vessels loading at the moment, most of them with provision for taking oxy-breathers, and gave him a choice of two Locks in the vicinity. Mannon added that, with the exception of a few patients on the critically ill list, all patients of classifications A through G had either gone or were on the point of going, along with staff members of the same classifications who had been ordered to go by O'Mara for security reasons.

Some of them had displayed extreme reluctance to leave. One in particular, a hoary old Tralthan Diagnostician who was unfortunate enough to own a personal space yacht—something which in normal conditions would *not* have been considered a misfortune!—had had to be formally charged with attempted treason, disturbing the peace and incitement to mutiny and arrested, that being the only way to get it aboard ship.

As he broke the connection Conway thought that they wouldn't have to go to such lengths to get him to leave the hospital. He shook his head, angry and ashamed of himself, and gave Murchison instructions for transfering the patient to the ship.

The injured Kelgian had to be enclosed in a pressure tent for the initial stage of its trip through the AUGL ward, which was now open to space. There were no water-breathers left in the big tank and no water, there being more urgent things to do than repairing and refilling a section which would very likely never be used again. The sight of the great tank, empty now, with its walls vacuum dry and the lush, underwater vegetation which had been designed to make the ward seem more homelike to its occupants hanging like pieces of brittle, discolored parchment made Conway feel horribly depressed. The depression remained with him while they negotiated the three empty chlorine levels below it and came to another air-filled section.

Here they had to pause to allow a procession of TLTUs to pass. Conway was glad of the chance to stop for a while because, although the pep-shot had him still feeling full of artificial beans, Murchison was beginning to droop. As soon as their patient was aboard he thought he would order her off to bed.

Seven TLTUs filed slowly past, their protective spheres anchored to stretcher-carriers driven by sweating, tense-faced orderlies. Unlike those of the methane life-forms these spheres did not collect frost. Instead they emitted a high-pitched, shuddering whine as their generators labored to maintain the internal temperature at a comfortable, for their occupants, five hundred degrees. Each one of them passed in a wave of heat which Conway could feel six yards away.

If another warhead was to strike here and now, and one of those globes was opened . . . Conway didn't think there was a worse way to die than to have the flesh boiled off his bones in a blast of super-heated steam.

By the time they had handed the patient over to the ship's medical officer at the Lock, Conway was having difficulty focusing his eyes and his legs had a definite rubbery feel to them. Bed was indicated, he thought, or another pep-shot. He had just decided on the former course of treatment when he was collared respectfully by a Monitor officer wearing a heavy-duty suit which was still radiating the cold of space.

"The casualties are here, sir," the officer said urgently. "We brought them in on a supply ship because Reception is tied up with the evacuation. We're locked onto the DBLF section, but the place is empty and

STAR SURGEON · 307

you're the first doctor I've seen. Will you take care of them?"

Conway almost asked what casualties, but stopped himself in time. There had been an attack, he remembered suddenly, the attack had been beaten off and the ensuing casualties, whether great or small, were obviously of prime concern to this officer. If he had known that Conway had been too busy to think about the battle and its casualties . . .

"Where did you put them?" said Conway.

"They're still in the ship," the officer replied, relaxing slightly. "We thought it better for someone to look at them before they were moved. Some of them . . . I mean . . . Uh, will you follow me, sir?"

There were eighteen of them, the wreckage of men who had been fished out of the wreckage of a ship, whose suits were still cold to the touch. Only their helmets had been taken off, and that had been to ascertain whether or not they still lived. Conway counted three decompressions, the rest being fractures of varying degrees of complication one of which was quite definitely a depressed fracture of the skull. There were no radiation cases. So far it had been a clean war, if any war could have been described as clean . . .

Conway felt himself getting angry, but fought it back. This was no time to become emotional over broken, bleeding and asphyxiated patients or the reasons for them being in that condition. Instead he straightened and turned to Murchison.

"I'll take another pep-shot," he said briskly, "this will be a long session. But first I'll have the DBLF tape erased and try to around up some help. While I'm gone you might see to getting these men out of their suits and moved to DBLF Theater Five, then you can catch up on your sleep.

"And thank you," he added awkwardly, not wanting to say too much because the Corpsman was still at his elbow. If he had tried to say the things he wanted to say to Murchison with eighteen urgent cases lying around their feet the officer would have been scandalized, and Conway would not have blamed him. But dammit the Corpsman hadn't been working beside Murchison for the last three hours, with a pep-shot heightening all his senses . . .

"If it would help you," said Murchison suddenly, "I could take a pep-shot, too."

Gratefully, Conway said, "You're a very silly girl, but I was hoping you would say that . . ."

CHAPTER 17

By the eighth day all the extra-terrestrial patients had been evacuated and with them had gone nearly four-fifths of the hospital's staff. On the levels which maintained extremes of temperature, pressure or gravity the power was withdrawn causing the ultra-frigid solids to melt and gasify and the dense or superheated atmospheres to condense into a sludgy liquid mess on the floors. Then as the days passed more and more Corpsmen of the Engineering Division arrived, converting the one-time wards into barracks and tearing out large sections of the outer hull so that they could erect projector bases and launching platforms. Dermod's idea now was that Sector General should defend itself instead of relying completely on the fleet, which had already shown that it wasn't capable of stopping everything. By the twenty-fifth day Sector General had made the transition from being a defenseless hospital into what amounted to a heavily armed military base.

Because of its tremendous size and vast reserves of power—several times greater than that of the mobile forces defending it—the weapons were many and truly formidable. Which was as well because on the twenty-ninth day they were tested to the utmost in the first major attack by the enemy.

It lasted for three days.

Conway knew that there were sound, logical reasons for the Corps fortifying the hospital as they had done, but he didn't like it. Even after that fantastic, three-day long attack when the hospital had been hit four times—again with chemical warheads, luckily—he still felt wrong about it. Every time he thought of the tremendous structure which had been dedicated to the highest ideals of humanity and medicine being made into an engine of destruction, geared to a hellish and unnatural ecology wherein it produced its own casualties, Conway felt angry and sad and not a little sickened by the whole ghastly mess. Sometimes he was apt to give vent to his opinions . . .

It was five weeks after the beginning of the evacuation and he was lunching with Mannon and Prilicla. The main dining hall was no longer crowded at mealtimes and green uniformed Corpsmen heavily outnumbered the e-ts at the tables, but there were still upward of two hundred extra-terrestrials in the place and this was what Conway was currently objecting to.

". . . I still say it's a waste," he said angrily, "a waste of lives, of medical talent, everything! All the cases are, and will continue to be, Monitor casualties. Every one an Earth-human. So there are no juicy e-t cases for them to work on. The e-t staff should be sent home!

"Present company included," he ended, with a glare at Prilicla before he turned to face Mannon.

Dr. Mannon made an incision in his steak and hefted a generous forkful mouthward. Since the disappearance of all his light-gravity patients he had had his LSVO and MSVK tapes erased and so had no mental restrictions placed on his diet. In the five weeks since the evacuation he had noticeably put on weight.

"To an e-t," he said reasonably, "we *are* juicy e-ts."

"You're quibbling," said Conway. "What I'm objecting to is senseless heroics."

Mannon raised his eyebrows. "But heroics are nearly always senseless," he said dryly, "and highly contagious as well. In this case I'd say the Corps started it by wanting to defend this place, and because of that we felt obliged to stay also to look after the wounded. At least a few of us feel like that, or we *think* a few of us feel like that.

"The sane, logical thing to do would have been to get while the going was good," Mannon continued, not quite looking at Conway, "and not a word would have been said to those who got. But then these sane, logical people have colleagues or, uh, friends who they suspect might be in the true hero category, and they won't leave because of what they imagine their friends will think of them if they run away. So they'd sooner *die* than have their friends think they were cowards, and they stay."

Conway felt his face getting warm, but he didn't say anything.

Mannon grinned suddenly and went on, "But this is a form of heroism, too. A case of Death before Dishonor, you might say. And before you can turn around twice everybody is a hero of one kind or the other. And no doubt the e-ts . . ." He gave a sly glance at Prilicla. ". . . are staying for similar reasons. And also, I suspect, because they don't want it thought that Earth-human DBDGs have a monopoly on heroism."

"I see," said Conway. He knew that his face was flaming red. It was now quite obvious that Mannon knew that the only reason he had stayed in the hospital was because Murchison, O'Mara and Mannon himself might have been disappointed in him if he'd left. And at the other side of the table Prilicla, the emotion sensitive, would be reading him like a book. Conway thought that he had never felt worse in his whole life.

"You are so right," said Prilicla suddenly, deftly inserting its fork into the plate of spaghetti before it and using two mandibles to twist. "If it had not been for the heroic example of you DBDGs I would have been on the second ship out."

"The second?" asked Mannon.

"I am not," said Prilicla, waving spaghetti for emphasis, "completely without valor."

Listening to the by-play Conway thought that the honest thing would have been for him to admit his cowardice to them, but he also knew that to do so would be to cause embarrassment all round. It was plain that they both knew him for the coward he was and were telling him in their separate fashions that it didn't matter. And looking at it objectively it really did not matter, because there would be no more ships leaving Sector General and its remaining staff were going to be heroes whether they liked it or not. But Conway still did not think it right that he should be given credit for being a brave, selfless, dedicated man of medicine when he was nothing of the sort.

Before he could say anything, however, Mannon switched subjects abruptly. He wanted to know where Conway and Murchison had been during the fourth, fifth and sixth days of the evacuation. He said that it was highly suggestive that both of them were out of circulation at exactly the same time and he began to list some of the suggestions which occurred to him—which were colorful, startling and next to physically impossible. Soon Prilicla joined in, although the sexual mores of two Earth-human DBDGs could have at most only an academic interest to a sexless GLNO, and Conway was defending himself strenuously from both sides.

Both Prilicla and Mannon knew that Murchison and himself, along with about forty other members of the staff, had been keeping at peak operating efficiency by means of pep-shots for nearly sixty hours. Pep-shots did not give something for nothing, and Conway and the others had been forced to adopt the horizontal position of the patient for three days while they recovered from an advanced state of exhaustion. Some of them had literally dropped in their tracks and been taken away hurriedly, so exhausted that the involuntary muscles of heart and lungs were threatening to give up with everything else. They had been taken to special wards where robot devices massaged their hearts, gave artificial respiration and fed them intraveneously.

Still, it *did* look bad that Conway and Murchison had not been seen around together, or separately, or *at all* for three whole days . . .

The alarm siren saved Conway just as the counsels for the prosecution were having it all their own way. He swung out of his seat and sprinted for the door with Mannon pounding along behind him and Prilicla, its not quite atrophied wings aided by its anti-gravity devices, whirring away in front.

Come Hell, high water or interstellar war, Conway thought warmly as he headed for his wards, while there was a reputation to blacken or a leg to pull, Mannon would be there with the latest scandal and prepared to exert traction on the limb in question until it threatened to come off at the acetabulum. In the circumstance all this scandal-mongering had irritated Conway at first, but then he had begun to realize that Mannon was making him see that the whole word hadn't come to an end yet, that this was still Sector General—a frame of mind rather than a place—and that it would continue to be Sector General until the last one of its dedicated and often wacky staff had gone.

When he reached his ward the siren, a constant reminder of the probable manner of their going, had stopped.

Pressure tents hung slackly over all twenty-eight occupied beds, already sealed and with their self-contained air units operating against the possibility of the ward being opened suddenly to space. The nurses on duty, a Tralthan, a Nidian and four Earth-humans, were struggling into their suits. Conway did the same, sealing everything as the others had done with the exception of the faceplate. He made a quick around of his patients, expressed approval to the Tralthan Senior Nurse, then opened the switch which cut off the artificial gravity grids in the floor.

Irregularities in the power supply, and that was no rare occurrence when the hospital's defensive screens were under attack or its weapons went into action, could cause the artificial gravity grid to vacillate between one half and two Gs, which was not a good thing when the patients were mainly fracture cases. It was better to have no gravity at all.

Once patients and staff were protected so far as was possible there was nothing to do but wait. To keep his mind off what was going on outside Conway insinuated himself into an argument between a Tralthan nurse and one of the red-furred Nidians about the modifications currently going on in the giant Translator computer. This vast electronic brain—the Translator packs which everyone wore were merely extensions of it, just sending and receiving units—which handled all the e-t translations in the hospital was, since the evacuation, operating at only a small fraction of its full potential. Hearing this Dermod, the fleet commander, had ordered the unused sections to be reprogrammed to deal with tactical and supply problems. But despite the Corps' reassurances that they were allowing ample circuits for Translation the two nurses were not quite happy. Suppose, they said, there should be an occasion when all the e-ts were talking at once?

Conway wanted to tell them that in his opinion the e-ts, especially the nurses, were always talking period so that there was really no problem, but he couldn't think of a tactful way of phrasing it.

An hour passed without anything happening so far as the hospital was concerned; no hits and no indication that its massive armament had been used. The nurses on duty were relieved by the next shift, three Tralthans and three Earth-humans this time, the senior nurse being Murchison. Conway was just settling down to a very pleasant chat when the siren sounded a steady, low-pitched, faintly derisive note. The attack was over.

Conway was helping Murchison out of her suit when the PA hummed into life.

"Attention, please," it said urgently. "Will Doctor Conway go to Lock Five at once, please . . ."

Probably a casualty, Conway thought, *one they are not sure how to move* . . . But then the PA shifted without a break into another message.

". . . Will Doctor Mannon and Major O'Mara go to Lock Five immediately, please . . ."

What, Conway wondered, could be at Lock Five which required the services of two Senior Physicians and the Chief Psychologist. He began to hurry.

O'Mara and Mannon had been closer to Five to begin with and so were there ahead of him by a few seconds. There was a third person in the lock antechamber, clad in a heavy-duty suit with its helmet thrown back. The newcomer was graying, had a thin, lined face and a mouth which was like a tired gray line, but the overall harshness was offset by a pair of the softest brown eyes Conway had ever seen in a man. The insignia on his collar was more ornate than Conway had ever seen before, the highest ranking Corps officer he'd had dealings with being a Colonel, but he knew instinctively that this was Dermod, the fleet commander.

O'Mara tore off a salute which was returned as punctiliously as it had been given, and Mannon and Conway received handshakes with apologies for the gauntlets being worn. Then Dermod got straight down to business.

"I am not a believer in secrecy when it serves no useful purpose," he began crisply. "You people have elected to stay here to look after our casualties, so you have a right to know what is happening whether the news is good or bad. Being the senior Earth-human medical staff remaining in the hospital, and having an understanding of the probable behavior of your staff in various contingencies, I must leave it up to you whether this information should or should not be made public."

He had been looking at O'Mara. His eyes moved quickly to Mannon, then Conway, then back to O'Mara again. He went on, "There has been an attack, a completely surprising attack in that it was totally abortive. We did not lose a single man and the enemy force was completely wiped out. They didn't seem to know the first thing about deployment or . . . or anything. We were expecting the usual sort of attack, vicious, pressed home regardless of cost, that previously has taken everything we've got to counter. This was a massacre . . ."

Dermod's voice and the look in his eyes, Conway noted, did not reflect any joy at the victory.

". . . Because of this we were able to investigate the enemy wreckage quickly enough to have a chance of finding survivors. Usually we're too busy licking our own wounds to have time for this. We didn't find any survivors, but . . ."

He broke off as two Corpsmen came through the inner seal carrying a covered stretcher. Dermod was looking straight at Conway when he went on.

He said, "You were on Etla, Doctor, and will see the implications behind this. And at the same time you might think about the fact that we are under attack by an enemy who refuses either to communicate or negotiate, fights as though driven by a fanatical hatred, and yet uses only limited warfare against us. But first you'd better take a look at this."

When the cover was pulled off the stretcher nobody said anything for a long time. *It* was the tattered, grisly remnant of a once-living, thinking and feeling entity who was now too badly damaged even to classify with any degree of accuracy. But enough remained to show that *it* was not and never had been a human being.

The war, Conway thought sickly, was spreading.

CHAPTER 18

"Since *Vespasian* left Etla we have been trying to infiltrate the Empire with our agents," Dermod resumed quietly, "and have been successful in planting eight groups including one on the Central World itself. Our intelligence regarding public opinion, and through it the propaganda machinery used to guide it, is fairly dependable.

"We know that feeling against us is high over the Etla business," he continued, "or rather what we are supposed to have done to the Etlans, but I'll come to that later. This latest development will make things even worse for us . . ."

According to the Imperial government, Dermod explained, Etla had been invaded by the Monitor Corps. Its natives, under the guise of being offered medical assistance, had been callously used as guinea-pigs to test out various types of bacteriological weapons. As proof of this hadn't the Etlans suffered a series of devastating plagues which had commenced within days of the Monitors leaving? Such callous and inhuman behavior could not go unpunished, and the Emperor was sure that every citizen was behind him in the decision he had taken.

But information received—again according to Imperial sources—from a captured agent of the invaders made it plain that their behavior on Etla was no isolated instance of wanton brutality. On that luckless planet the invaders had been preceded by an extra-terrestrial—a stupid, harmless being sent to test the planet's defenses before landing themselves, a mere tool about which they had denied any connection or knowledge when later they contacted the Etlan authorities. It was now plain that they made wide use of such extra-terrestrial life-forms. That they used them as servants, as experimental animals, probably as food . . .

There was a tremendous structure maintained by the invaders, a combination military base and laboratory, where atrocities similar to those practiced on Etla were carried on as a matter of course. The invader agent, who had been tricked into giving the spatial coordinates of this base, had confessed to what went on there. It appeared that the invaders ruled over a large number of differing extra-terrestrial species, and it was here that the methods and weapons were developed which held them in bondage.

The Emperor stated that he was quite willing, indeed he considered it his duty, to use his forces to stamp out this foul tyranny. He also felt that he should use only Imperial forces, because he had to confess with shame that relations between the Empire and the extra-terrestrials within its sphere of influence had not always been as warm as they should have been. But if any of these species who may have been slighted in the past were to offer their aid, he would not refuse it . . .

". . . And this explains many of the puzzling aspects of these enemy attacks," Dermod went on. "They are restricting themselves to vibratory and chemical weapons, and in the confined space of our defense globe we must do the same, because this place must be captured rather than destroyed. The Emperor must find out the positions of the Federation planets to keep the war going. The fact that they fight viciously and to the death can be explained by their being afraid of capture, because to them the hospital is nothing but a space-going torture chamber.

"And the completely ineffectual recent attack," he continued, "must have been mounted by some of the hot-headed e-t friends of the Empire, who were probably allowed to come here without proper training or information about our defenses. They were wiped out, and *that* will cause a lot of e-ts on their side who are wavering to make up their minds.

"In the Empire's favor," he ended bitterly.

When the fleet commander stopped speaking Conway remained silent; he had had access to the Empire reports sent to Williamson and knew that Dermod was not exaggerating the situation. O'Mara had had similar information and maintained the same grim silence. But Dr. Mannon was not the silent type.

"But this is ridiculous!" he burst out. "They're twisting things! This is a hospital, not a torture chamber. And they're accusing us of the things they are doing themselves . . . !"

Dermod ignored the outburst, but in such a way as not to give offense. He said soberly, "The Empire is unstable politically. With enough time we could replace their present government with something more desirable. The Imperial citizens would do it themselves, in fact. But we need time. And we also have to stop the war from spreading too much, from gaining too much momentum. If too many extra-terrestrial allies join the Empire against us the situation will become too complex to control, the original reasons for fighting, or the truth or otherwise of these accusations, will cease to matter.

"We can gain time by holding out here as long as possible," he ended grimly, "but there isn't much we can do about restricting the war. Except hope."

He swung his helmet forward and began to fasten it, although his face-plate was still open for conversation. It was then that Mannon asked the question which Conway had wanted to ask for a long time, but fear of being thought a coward had stopped him from asking it.

"Do we have any chance, really, of holding out?"

Dermod hesitated a moment, obviously wondering whether to be reassuring or to tell the truth. Then he said, "A well-supported and supplied defensive globe is the ideal tactical position. It can also, if the enemy outnumbers it sufficiently, be a perfect trap . . ."

When Dermod left, the specimen he had brought with him was claimed by Thornnastor, the Tralthan Diagnostician-in-Charge of Pathology, who would no doubt be happy with it for days. O'Mara went back to bullying his charges into remaining sane, and Mannon and Conway went back to their wards. The reaction of the staff to the possibility of e-ts attacking them was about equally divided between concern over the war spreading and interest regarding the possible methods necessary to treat casualties belonging to a brand new species.

But two weeks passed without the expected attack developing. The Monitor Corps warships continued to arrive, shoot their astrogators back in life-ships, and take up their positions. From the hospital's direct vision ports they seemed to cover the sky, as if Sector General was the center of a vast, tenuous star cluster with every star a warship. It was an awesome and tremendously reassuring sight, and Conway tried to visit one of the direct vision panels at least once every day.

Then on the way back from one of these visits he ran across a party of Kelgians.

For a moment he couldn't believe his eyes. *All* the Kelgian DBLFs had been evacuated, he had watched the last of them go himself, yet here were twenty-odd of the outsize caterpillars humping along in single file. A closer look showed that they were not wearing the usual brassard with engineering or medical emblems on it—instead their silvery fur was dyed with circular and diamond patterns of red, blue and black. This was Kelgian military insignia. Conway went storming off to O'Mara.

"... I was about to ask the same question, Doctor," the Chief Psychologist said gruffly, indicating his vision screen, "although in much more respectful language. I'm trying to get the fleet commander now, so stop shouting and sit down!"

Dermod's face appeared a few minutes later. His tone was polite but hurried when he said, "This is not the Empire, gentlemen. We are obliged to inform the Federation government and through it the people of the true state of affairs as we see them, although the item about our being attacked by an enemy e-t force has not yet been made public.

"But you must give the e-ts within the Federation credit for having the same feelings as ourselves," he went on, "Extra-terrestrials have stayed behind at Sector General, and on their various home worlds their friends are beginning to feel that they should come out here and help defend them. It is as simple as that."

"But you said that you didn't want the war to spread," Conway protested.

"I didn't ask them to come here, Doctor," Dermod said sharply, "but now they're here I can certainly use them. The latest intelligence reports indicate that the next attack may be decisive ..."

Later over lunch Mannon received the news about the e-t defenders with the deepest gloom. He was beginning to enjoy being only himself and guzzling steak at dinner, he told Conway sadly, and now with the likelihood of e-t casualties coming in it looked as if they were all going to be tape-ridden again. Prilicla ate spaghetti and observed how lucky it was that the e-t staff hadn't left the hospital after all, not looking at Conway when it said it, and Conway said very little.

The next attack, Dermod had said, *may be decisive ...*

It began three weeks later after a period during which nothing happened other than the arrival of a volunteer force of Tralthans and a single ship whose crew and planet of origin Conway had never heard of before, and whose classification was QLCL. He learned that Sector General had never had the opportunity of meeting these beings professionally because they were recent, and very enthusiastic, members of the Federation. Conway prepared a small ward to receive possible casualties from this race, filling it with the horribly corrosive fog they used for an atmosphere and stepping up the lighting to the harsh, actinic blue which QLCLs considered restful.

The attack began in an almost leisurely fashion, Conway thought as he watched it through the observation panel. The main defense globe seemed barely disturbed by the three minor attacks launched at widely separate points on its surface. All that was visible was three tiny, confused swirls of activity—moving points of light that were ships, missiles, counter-missiles and explosions—which looked too slow to be dangerous. But the slowness was only apparent, because the ships were maneuvering at a minimum of five Gs, with automatic anti-gravity devices keeping their crews from being pulped by the tremendous accelerations in use, and the missiles were moving at anything up to fifty Gs. The wide-flung repulsion screens which sometimes deflected the missiles were invisible as were the pressors and rattlers which nearly always stopped those which the screens missed. Even so this was merely an initial probing at the hospital's defenses, a series of offensive patrols, the curtain-raiser . . .

Conway turned away from the view-port and began moving toward his post. Even the unimportant skirmishes produced casualties and he really had no business being up here sightseeing. Besides, he would get a much truer picture of how the battle was going down in the wards.

For the next twelve hours casualties arrived in a steady trickle, then the light, probing attacks changed to heavy, feinting thrusts and the wounded came in an irregular stream. Then the attack proper began and they became a flood.

He lost all sense of time, of who his assistants were, of the number of cases he dealt with. There were many times when he needed a pep-shot to clear the fatigue from his mind and hands, but pep-shots were now forbidden regardless of circumstances—the medical staff were hard-pressed enough without some of them becoming patients. Instead he had to work tired, knowing that he was not bringing everything he had to the treatment of his patients, and he ate and slept when he reached the point of not being able to hold his instruments properly. Sometimes it was the towering bulk of a Tralthan at his side, sometimes a Corpsman medical orderly, sometimes Murchison. *Mostly* it was Murchison, he thought. Either she didn't need to sleep, or she snatched a catnap the same times as he did, or even at a time like this he was more inclined to notice her. It was usually Murchison who pushed food at his unresisting face and told him when he really ought to lie down.

By the fourth day the attack showed no signs of diminishing. The rattlers on the outer hull were going almost constantly, their power drain making the lights flicker.

The principle which furnished artificial gravity for the floor and compensated for the killing accelerations used by the ships also lay behind the weapons of both sides—the repulsion screen, originally a meteor protection device, the tractor and pressor beams, and the rattler which was a combination of both. The rattler pushed and pulled—vibrated—depending on how narrowly it was focused, at up to eighty Gs. A push of eighty gravities then a pull of eighty gravities, several times a minute. Naturally it was not always focused accurately on target, both ships were moving and taking counter-measures, but it was still tight enough to tear the plating off a hull or, in the case of a small ship, to shake it until the men inside rattled.

There was a lot of rattler work going on now. The Empire forces were attacking savagely, compressing the Monitor defense globe down against the hospital's outer hull. The infighting which was taking place was with rattler only, space being too congested to fling missiles about indiscriminately. This applied only to the warring ships, however—there were still missiles being directed at the hospital, probably hundreds of them, and some of them were getting through. At least five times Conway felt the tell-tale shock against the soles of his shoes where his feet were strapped to the operating room floor.

There was no fine diagnostic skill required in the treatment of these rattled men. It was all too plain that they suffered from multiple and complicated fractures, some of them of nearly every bone in their bodies. Many times when he had to cut one of the smashed bodies out of its suit Conway wanted to yell at the men who had brought it in, "What do you expect me to do with *this* . . . ?"

But *this* was alive, and as a doctor he was supposed to do everything possible to make it stay that way.

He had just finished a particularly bad one, with both Murchison and a Tralthan nurse assisting, when Conway became aware of a DBLF in the room. Conway had become familiar with the dyed patterns of color used by the Kelgian military to denote rank, and he saw that this one bore an additional symbol which identified it as a doctor.

"I am to relieve you, Doctor," the DBLF said in a flat, Translated, hurried voice. "I am experienced in treating beings of your species. Major O'Mara wants you to go to Lock Twelve at once."

Conway quickly introduced Murchison and the Tralthan—there was another casualty being floated in and they would be working on it within minutes—then said, "Why?"

"Doctor Thornnastor was disabled when the last missile hit us," the Kelgian replied, spraying its manipulators with the plastic its race used instead of gloves. "Someone with e-t experience is required to take over Thornnastor's patients and the FGLIs which are coming in now at Lock Twelve. Major O'Mara suggests you look at them as soon as possible to see what tapes you need.

"And take a suit, Doctor," the DBLF added as Conway turned to go. "The level above this one is losing pressure . . ."

There had been little for Pathology to do since the evacuation, Conway thought as he propelled himself along the corridors leading to Twelve, but the Diagnostician in charge of that department had demonstrated its versatility by taking over the largest casualty section. In addition to FGLIs of its own species Thornnastor had taken DBLFs and Earth-humans, and the patients who had that lumbering, irascible, incredibly brilliant Tralthan to care for them were lucky indeed. Conway wondered how badly it was injured, the Kelgian doctor hadn't been able to tell him.

He passed a view-port and took a quick look outside. It reminded him of a cloud of angry fireflies. The stanchion he was gripping slapped his hand, telling him that another missile had struck not too far away.

There were two Tralthans, a Nidian and a space-suited QCQL in the antechamber when he arrived as well as the ever present Corpsmen. The Nidian explained that a Tralthan ship had been nearly pulled apart by enemy rattlers but that many of its crew had survived. The tractor beams mounted on Sector General itself had whisked the damaged vessel down to the lock and . . .

The Nidian began to bark at him.

"Stop that!" said Conway irritably.

The Nidian looked startled, then it started to bark again. A few seconds later the Tralthan nurses came over and began to deafen him with their modulated fog-horn blasts, and the QCQL was whistling at him through its suit radio. The Corpsmen, engrossed in bringing the casualties through the boarding tube, were merely looking puzzled. Suddenly Conway began to sweat.

They had been hit again, but because he had not been holding onto anything he had not felt it—but he knew exactly where they had been hit. Conway fumbled with his Translator, rapped it sharply with his knuckles—a completely futile gesture—and kicked himself toward the intercom.

On every circuit he tried things howled and trumpeted and moaned and made gutteral barking sounds, a mad cacaphony that set Conway's teeth on edge. A picture of the theater he had just left flashed before his mind, with Murchison and the Tralthan and the Kelgian doctor working on that casualty *and not one of them knowing what the other was saying*. Instructions, vital directions, demands for instruments or information on the patient's condition—all would be given in an alien gabble incomprehensible to the theater staff. He was seeing the picture repeated all over the hospital. Only beings of the same species could make themselves understood to each other, and even that did not hold true in every case. There were Earth-humans who did not speak Universal, who spoke languages native to areas on their home planets and who had to rely on Translators even when speaking to other Earth-humans . . .

From the alien babel Conway's straining ears were able to isolate words and a voice which he could understand. It was intelligence battling through a high level of background noise, and all at once his ears seemed to tune out the static and hear only the voice, the voice which was saying, ". . . Three torps playing follow-my-leader, sir. They blasted a way right through. We *can't* jury-rig a Translator, there's nothing of it left to do it with. The last torp went off inside the computer room . . ."

Outside the intercom niche the e-t nurses were whistling and growling and moaning at him and at each other. He should be giving instructions for the preliminary examination of his casualties, arranging for ward accommodation, checking on the readiness of the FGLI theater. But he could not do any of these things because his nursing staff would not understand a word he said.

CHAPTER 19

For a long time, although it might have only been a few seconds, Conway could not bring himself to leave the alcove which contained the intercom unit, and the Chief Psychologist would have been clinically concerned about the thoughts which were going through his mind just then. But slowly he fought down the panic that made him want to run away and hide somewhere, by reminding himself savagely that there was nowhere to run to and by forcing himself to look at the FGLIs drifting about in the antechamber. The place was literally filled with them.

Conway himself knew only the rudiments of Tralthan physiology, but that was the least of his worries because he could easily take an FGLI tape. What he had to do was to start things moving for them *now*. But it was hard to think of each other and the Corpsmen shouting to know what was the matter and the casualties, many of whom were conscious, making pitiful, frantic noises that were muffled only slightly by their pressure envelopes.

"Sergeant!" Conway bawled suddenly at the senior orderly, waving at the casualties. "Ward Four-B, Two-Hundred and Seventh level. Know where it is?"

The NCO bobbed his head, and Conway turned to the nurses.

He got nowhere with the Nidian and QCQL despite all his efforts at sign language, and it was only when he wrapped his legs around one of the FGLI's forelimbs and by brute force twisted the appendage containing its visual equipment until the cluster of eyes pointed at where the casualities were going that he got anywhere at all. Finally he made the Tralthans understand—he hoped—that they were to accompany the injured and do what they could for them when they arrived.

Four-B had been given over almost entirely to FGLI casualties and most of the staff were Tralthan also, which meant that some of the patients could be reassured by nurses speaking their own language. Conway refused to think of the other casualties who did not have this advantage. He had been assigned Thornnastor's wards. One thing at a time.

When he reached O'Mara's office the Major wasn't there. Carrington, one of his assistants, explained that O'Mara was busy trying to match up patients and staff into species wherever possible, and that he wanted to see Conway immediately the Doctor was finished in the Tralthan wards. Carrington added that as communications were either dead or tied up with e-ts yelling gibberish at each other would he mind either reporting back here or remaining where he was so that the Major could find him. Ten minutes later Conway had the tape he wanted and was on his way to Four-B.

He had taken FGLI tapes before and they weren't too bad. There was a tendency for him to feel awkward at having to walk on only two feet instead of six, and he wanted to move his head and neck about to follow moving objects instead of merely swiveling his eyes. But it was not until he reached the ward that he realized how fully his Tralthan mind partner had settled in. The rows of Tralthan patients became his most immediate and pressing concern, while only a small part of his mind was engaged with the problem of the Tralthan nurses who were obviously close to panic and whose words, for some odd reason, he could not understand. For the Earth-human nurses—puny, shapeless and unlovely bags of dough—he felt only impatience.

Conway went over to the group of shapeless and unlovely bags, although to the human portion of his mind a couple of them looked very shapely indeed, and said, "Give me your attention, please. I have a Tralthan tape which will enable me to treat these FGLIs, but the Translator breakdown means I can't talk to them or the Tralthan staff. You girls will have to help with the preliminary examinations and in the theater."

They were all staring at him and losing their fear at being told what to do again by someone in authority, even though they were being told to do the impossible. There were forty-seven FGLI patients in the ward, which included eight new arrivals needing immediate attention. There were only three Earth-human nurses.

"The FGLI staff and yourselves can't talk now," he went on after a moment's hesitation, "but you use the same system of medical notation. Some method of communication can be worked out. It will be slow and roundabout, of course, but you must let them know what we are doing and get their help.

"Wave your arms," he ended, "draw pictures. Above all, use your pretty little heads."

Soft soap at a time like this, he thought ashamedly. But it was all he could think of at the moment, he wasn't a psychologist like O'Mara . . .

He had dealt with four of the most urgent cases when Mannon arrived with another FGLI in a stretcher held to the floor with magnets. The patient was Thornnastor and it was immediately obvious that the Diagnostician would be immobilized for a long time to come.

Mannon gave details of Thornnastor's injuries and what he had done about them, then went on, ". . . Seeing that you have the monopoly on Tralthans you'd better handle its post-op nursing. And this is the sanest and quietest ward in the hospital, dammit. What's your secret? Boyish charm, a bright idea, or have you access to a bootleg Translator?"

Conway explained what he was trying to do about the mixed species nurses.

"Ordinarily I don't hold with nurses and doctors passing notes during an op," Mannon said. His face was gray with fatigue, his attempt at humor little more than a conditioned reflex. "But it seemed to work for you. I'll pass the idea on."

They maneuverd Thornnastor's vast body into one of the padded frameworks used as beds for FGLIs in weightless conditions, then Mannon said, "I've got an FGLI tape, too. Needed it for Thorny, here. Now I've got two QCQLs lined up. Didn't know there was any such beastie until today, but O'Mara has the tape. It's a suit job, that gunk they breathe would kill anything that walks, crawls or flies, excluding them. They're both conscious, too, and I can't talk to them. I can see I'm going to have fun."

Suddenly his shoulders drooped and the muscles holding up the corners of his mouth gave up the fight. He said dully, "I wish you'd think of something, Conway. In wards like this where the patients and some nurses are of the same classification it isn't too bad. Relatively, that is. But other places where the casualties and staff are completely mixed, and where singletons among the e-t staff have become casualties in the bombardment, things are rough."

Conway had heard the bombardment, a continuous and irregular series of crashes that had been transmitted through the metal of the hospital as if someone was beating on a discordant gong. He had heard them and tried not to think about them, for he knew that the staff were becoming casualties and the casualties that the staff had been taking care of were becoming casualties twice over.

"I can imagine," Conway said grimly. "But with Thornnastor's wards to look after I've plenty to do—"

"Everybody has plenty to do!" Mannon said sharply, "but someone will have to come up with something quick!"

What do you want me to do about it? Conway thought angrily at Mannon's receding back, then he turned to his next patient.

For the past few hours something distinctly odd had been happening in Conway's mind. It had begun with an increasingly strong feeling that he almost knew what the Tralthan nurses in the ward were saying. This he put down to the fact that the FGLI tape he had taken—the complete memory record of an eminent physiologist of that race—had given him a lot of data on Tralthan attitudes and expressions and tones of voice. He had never noticed the effect before—probably, he supposed, because he had never had to deal with so many Tralthans in so short a time before, and he had always had a Translator anyway. But working with mainly Tralthan patients had caused the FGLI recorded personality to gain greater than usual prominence at the expense of the human personality.

There was no struggle for possession of his mind, no conflict in the process. It happened naturally because he was being forced to do so much FGLI type thinking. When he did have occasion to speak to an Earth-human nurse or patient, he had to concentrate hard if the first few words they spoke were not to sound like gibberish to him.

And now he was beginning to hear and understand Tralthan talking.

It was far from perfect, of course. For one thing the elephantine hootings and trumpetings were being filtered through human rather than Tralthan ears to the FGLI within his mind, and suffered distortion and change of pitch accordingly. The words tended to be muffled and growly, but he did get some of them, which meant that he possessed a Translator of sorts. It was a strictly one-way affair, of course. Or was it?

When he was preparing the next case for the theater he decided to try talking back.

His FGLI alter ego knew how the words should sound, he knew how to work his own vocal cords, and the Earth-human voice was reputed to be one of the most versatile instruments in the Galaxy. Conway took a deep breath and gave forth.

The first attempt was disastrous. It ended in an uncontrollable fit of coughing on his part and spread alarm and consternation for the length and breadth of the ward. But with the third attempt he got through— one of the Tralthan nurses answered him! After that it was just a matter of time until he had enough of the more important directions off pat, and subsequent operations proceeded more quickly, efficiently and with enormously increased chances for the patient.

The Earth-human nurses were greatly impressed by the odd noises issuing from Conway's overworked throat. At the same time they seemed to see an element of humor in the situation . . .

"Well, well," said a familiar, irascible voice behind him, "a ward full of happy, smiling patients, with the Good Doctor keeping up morale by doing animal impressions. What the blazes do you think you're doing?"

O'Mara, Conway saw with a shock, was really angry—not just playing his usual, short-tempered self. In the circumstances it would be better to answer the question and ignore the rhetoric.

"I'm looking after Thornnastor's patients, plus some new arrivals," Conway said quietly. "The Corpsmen and FGLI patients have been taken care of, and I was about to ask you for a DBLF tape for the Kelgians who have just come in."

O'Mara snorted. "I'll send down a Kelgian doctor to take care of that," he said angrily, "and your nurses can take care of the others for the time being. You don't seem to realize that this is one level out of three-hundred eighty-four, Doctor Conway. That there are ward patients urgently in need of the simplest treatment or medication, and they won't get it because the staff concerned whistle while they cheep. That the casualties are piling up around the locks, some of them in corridors which have been opened to space. Those pressure litters won't supply air forever, you know, and the people in them can't be feeling very happy . . ."

"What do you want me to do?" said Conway.

For some reason this made O'Mara angrier. He said bitingly, "I don't know, Doctor Conway. I am a psychologist. I can no longer act effectively because most of my patients no longer speak the same language. Those who do I've tried to chivvy into thinking of something to get us out of this mess. But they're all too busy treating the sick in their own neighborhood to think of the hospital as a whole. They want to leave it to the Big Brains . . ."

"In these circumstances," Conway put in, "a Diagnostician seems to be the logical person to come up with a bright idea."

O'Mara's anger was being explained, Conway thought. It must be pretty frustrating for a psychologist who could neither listen or talk to his patients. But the anger seemed almost personal, as if Conway himself had fallen down on the job in some fashion.

"Thornnastor is out of the picture," O'Mara said, lowering his voice slightly. "You were probably too busy to know that the other two Diagnosticians who stayed behind were killed earlier today. Among the Senior Physicians, Harkness, Irkultis, Mannon—"

"Mannon! Is he . . . ?"

"I thought you might have known about him," O'Mara said almost gently, "since it happened just two levels away. He was working on two QCQLs when the theater was opened up. A piece of flying metal ruptured his suit. He's decompressed, and before that poison they use for air escaped completely he breathed some of it. But he'll live."

Conway found that he had been holding his breath. He said, "I'm glad."

"Me, too," said O'Mara gruffly. "But what I started to say was that there are no Diagnosticians left and no Senior Physicians other than yourself, and the place is in a mess. As the senior surviving medical officer in the hospital, what do you plan to do about it?"

He stood watching Conway, and waiting.

CHAPTER 20

Conway had thought that nothing could make him feel worse than the realization some hours previously that the Translator system had broken down. He didn't want this responsibility, the very thought of it scared him to death. Yet there had been times when he'd dreamed of being Sector General's director and having absolute control over all things medical within the gigantic organization. But in those dreams the hospital had not been a dying, war-torn behemoth that was virtually paralyzed by the breakdown of communications between its separate and vital organs, nor had it bristled with death-dealing weapons, nor had it been criminally understaffed and horribly overcrowded with patients.

Probably these were the only circumstances which would allow someone like himself to become Director of a hospital like this, Conway told himself sadly. He wasn't the best available, he was the only one available. Even so it gave him a quite indescribable feeling, compounded of fear, anger and pride, that he was to be its head for the remaining days or weeks of its life.

Conway gave a quick look around his ward, at the orderly if uneven rows of Tralthan and Earth-human beds and at the quietly efficient staff. He had made it this way. But he was beginning to see that he had been hiding himself down here, that he had been running away from his responsibilities.

"I do have an idea," he said suddenly to O'Mara. "It isn't a good idea, and I think we ought to go to your office to talk about it, because you'll probably object to it, loudly, and that might disturb the patients."

O'Mara looked at him sharply. When he spoke the anger had gone from his voice so that it was merely normally sarcastic again. He said, "I find all your ideas objectionable, Doctor. It's because I've got such an orderly mind."

On the way to O'Mara's office they passed a group of high-ranking Monitor officers and the Major told him that they were part of Dermod's staff who were preparing to shift tactical command into the hospital. At the moment Dermod was commanding from *Vespasian*. But even the capital ships were taking a beating now, and the fleet commander had already had *Domitian* not quite shot from under him . . .

When they arrived Conway said, "It isn't such a hot idea, and seeing those Corpsmen on the way up here has given me a better one. Suppose we ask Dermod to let us use his ship Translators . . . ?"

O'Mara shook his head. "It won't work," he said. "I thought of that idea, too. It seems the only Translator computers of any use to us are on the big ships, and they are such an integral part of the structure that it would practically wreck the ship to take one out. Besides, for our absolute minimum needs we would require twenty capital ship computers. We haven't got twenty capital ships left, and what we do have Dermod says he has a much better use for.

"Now what was your other not very good idea?"

Conway told him.

When he had finished, O'Mara looked at him steadily for nearly a minute. Finally he said, "Consider your idea objected to, but strongly. Consider, if you like, that I jumped up and down and pounded the desk, because that is what I'd be doing if I wasn't so blasted tired. Don't you realize what you'd be letting yourself in for?"

From somewhere below them came a tearing crash with ridiculous, gong-like overtones. Conway jerked involuntarily, then said, "I think so. There will be a lot of mental confusion and discomfort, but I hope to avoid most of it by letting the tape entity take over almost completely until I have what I need, then I partly suppress it and do the translation. That was how it worked with the Tralthan tape and there's no reason why it shouldn't work with DBLFs or any of the others. The DBLF language should be a cinch, it being easier to moan like a Kelgian than hoot like a Tralthan . . ."

He would not have to stay in any one place for very long, Conway hoped, only long enough to sort out the local translation problems. Some of the e-t sounds would be difficult to reproduce orally, but he had an idea for modifying certain musical instruments which might take care of that. And he would not be the only walking Translator, there were still

STAR SURGEON · 331

e-t and human doctors who could help by taking one or two tapes. Some of them might have done so already, but had not thought of using them for translation yet. As he talked Conway's tongue was having a hard job to keep up with his racing mind.

"Just a minute," said O'Mara at one point. "You keep talking about letting one personality come to the fore, then suppressing it, then bringing out two together and so on. You might find that you haven't that much control. Multiple physiology tapes are tricky, and you've never had more than two before at any one time. I have your records."

O'Mara hesitated for a moment, then went on seriously, "What you get is the recorded memories of an e-t high in the medical profession on its home planet. It *isn't* an alien entity fighting for possession of your mind, but because its memory and personality are impressed alongside your own you may be panicked into thinking that it is trying to take over. Some of our tapes were taken from very aggressive individuals, you see.

"Odd things happen to doctors who take a number of longterm tapes for the first time," O'Mara went on. "Pains, skin conditions, perhaps organic malfunctionings develop. All have a psychosomatic basis, of course, but to the person concerned they hurt just as much as the real thing. These disturbances can be controlled, even negated, by a strong mind. Yet a mind with strength alone will break under them in time. Flexibility allied with strength is required, also something to act as a mental anchor, something that you must find for yourself . . .

"Suppose I agree to this," he ended abruptly, "how many will you need?"

Conway thought quickly. Tralthan, Kelgian, Melfan, Nidian, the ambulating plants he had met before going to Etla, who also had remained behind, and the beasties Mannon had been treating when he was knocked out of it. He said, "FGLI, DBLF, ELNT, Nidian-DBDG, AACP and QCQL. Six."

O'Mara compressed his lips. "I wouldn't mind if it was a Diagnostician doing this," he objected, "because they are used to splitting their minds six ways. But you are just—"

"The senior medical officer of the hospital," Conway finished for him, grinning.

"Hm," said O'Mara.

In the silence they could hear human voices and a peculiar, alien gabbling go past in the corridor outside. Whoever was making the noise must have been shouting very loud because the Major's office was supposed to be soundproof.

"All right," said O'Mara suddenly, "you can try it. But I don't want to have deal with you in my professional capacity, and that is a much stronger possibility than you seem to think. We're too short of doctors to have you immobilizing yourself in a straight-jacket, so I'm going to set a watchdog on you. We'll add GLNO to your list."

"Prilicla!"

"Yes. Being an empath it has had a hard time with the sort of emotional radiation that is going around recently, and I've had to keep it under sedation. But it will be able to keep a mental eye on you, and probably help you, too. Move over to the couch."

Conway moved to the couch and O'Mara fitted the helmet. Then the Major began to talk softly, sometimes asking questions, sometimes just talking. Conway should be unconscious for a multiple transfer, he said, he should in fact sleep for at least four hours for the best results, and he needed sleep anyway. Probably, O'Mara said, he had thought up this whole, harebrained scheme just to have a legitimate excuse to sleep. He had a big job ahead, the psychologist told him quietly, and he would really need to be in seven places as well as being seven people at once, so that a sleep would do him good ...

"It won't be too bad," Conway said, struggling to keep his eyes open. "I'll stay in any one place only long enough to learn a few basic words and phrases that I can teach to the nursing staff. Just enough so they'll understand when an e-t surgeon says 'Scalpel,' or 'Forceps' or 'Stop breathing down the back of my neck, Nurse ...' "

The last words that Conway heard clearly were O'Mara saying, "Hang onto your sense of humor, lad. You're going to need it ..."

He awoke in a room that was too large and too small, alien in six different ways and at the same time completely familiar. He did not feel rested. Clinging to the ceiling by six pipestem legs was a tiny, enormous, fragile, beautiful, disgustingly insectile creature that reminded him of his worst nightmares the amphibious *cllels* he used to hunt at the bottom of his private lake for breakfast, and many other things including a perfectly ordinary GLNO Cinrusskin like himself. It was beginning to quiver slightly in reaction to the emotional radiation he was producing. All of him knew that the GLNOs from Cinruss were empaths.

Fighting his way to the surface of a maelstrom of alien thoughts, memories and impressions Conway decided that it was time to go to work. Prilicla was immediately available for the first test of his idea. He began searching for and bringing up the GLNO memories and experiences, sifting through a welter of alien data for the type of information which is not consciously remembered but is constantly in use—data on the Cinrusskin language.

No, *not* the Cinrusskin language, he reminded himself sharply, *his* language. He had to think and feel and listen like a GLNO. Gradually he began to do it . . .

And it was not pleasant.

He was a Cinrusskin, a member of a fragile, low-gravity, insect race of empaths. The handsome, delicately marked exoskeleton and the youthful, iridescent sheen of Prilicla's not quite atrophied wings were now things which he could properly appreciate, and the way Prilicla's mandibles quivered in sudden concern at his distress. For Conway was a member of an empathic race, all the memories and experience of his GLNO life were those of a normally happy and healthy empath, but now he was an empath no more. He could see Prilicla, but the faculty which let him share the other's emotions, and subtly colored every word, gesture and expression so that for two Cinrusskins to be within visual range was to be unalloyed pleasure for both, was missing. He could remember having empathetic contact, remember having it all his life, but now he was little more than a deaf mute.

His human brain did not possess the empathetic faculty, and it was not bestowed by filling his mind with memories of having had it.

Prilicla made a series of clicking, buzzing sounds. Conway, who had never spoken with the GLNO other than by means of the toneless and emotion-filtering process of Translation, heard it say "I'm sorry" in a voice full of concern and pity.

In return Conway tried to make the soft trill and click which was Prilicla's name, the true sound of the Earth-human word "Prilicla" being only a clumsy approximation. On the fifth attempt he succeeded in making something which was close to the sound he wanted.

"That is very good, friend Conway," Prilicla said warmly. "I had not considered this idea of yours possible. Can you understand me?"

Conway sought the word-sounds he needed, then carefully began to form them. "Thank you," he said, "and yes."

They tried more difficult phrases then, technical words to put across obtuse medical and physiological details. Sometimes Conway was able to do it, sometimes not. His was at best only the crudest of pidgin Cinrusskin, but he persevered. Then suddenly there was an interruption.

"O'Mara here," said a voice from his room communicator. "You should be awake now so here is the latest position, Doctor. We are still under attack, but this has eased off somewhat since more volunteer e-ts arrived to reinforce us. These are Melfans, some more Tralthans and a force of Illensan chlorine-breathers. So you're going to have PVSJs to worry about, too. Then inside the hospital . . ."

There followed a detailed breakdown of casualties and available staff into species, location and numbers, with further data on problems peculiar to each section and their degree of urgency.

". . . It's for you to decide where to start," O'Mara went on, "and the sooner the better. But in case you are still feeling confused I'll repeat—"

"No need," said Conway, "I got it."

"Good. How do you feel?"

"Awful. Horrible. And very peculiar."

"That," said O'Mara dryly, "is in all respects a normal reaction. Off."

Conway released the strapping which held him to the bed and swung his legs out. Immediately he stiffened, unable to let go. Many of the beings inhabiting his mind were terrified by weightless conditions and the reaction was instinctive. Because of this it was very difficult to counter, and he had a moment of sheer panic when he discovered that his feet would not stick to the ceiling the way Prilicla's did. And when he did relax his grip on the edge of the bed he found that he had been holding on with an appendage that was pallid and flabby and horribly different to the clean, hard outlines of the mandible he had expected to see. But somehow he managed to cross his room into the corridor and traverse it for a distance of fifty yards.

Then he was stopped.

An irate medical orderly in Corps green wanted to know why he was out of bed and what ward he had come from. The Corpsman's language was colorful and not at all respectful.

Conway became aware of his large, gross, fragile, loathsome pink body. A perfectly good body, part of his mind insisted, if a little on the skinny side. And this shapeless, puny, monstrosity was encircled, where it was joined by its two lower appendages, by a piece of white fabric which served no apparent purpose. The body looked ridiculous as well as alien.

Oh damn! thought Conway, struggling up through a smother of alien impressions, *I forgot to dress.*

CHAPTER 21

Conway's first act was to install one representative from each species in the Communications room. A semblance of order had already been restored to the network by posting Corpsmen at every intercom unit to forbid their use—if the would-be user was not too persistent and well-muscled—to e-ts. This meant that Earth-human personnel could talk to each other. But with e-ts on the switchboard, calls by other species could be answered and redirected. Conway spent nearly two hours, more time than he ever spent anywhere else, putting himself *en rapport* with the e-t operators and devising a list of synonyms which would allow them to pass simple—*very* simple—messages to each other. He had two Monitor language experts with him on it, and it was they who suggested that he made a taped record of this seven-way Rosetta stone, and make others to fit the conditions he would find in the wards.

Wherever he went after that Prilicla, the language experts and a Corps radio technician trailed behind, in addition to the nursing staff he accumulated from time to time. It was an impressive procession, but Conway was in no mood to appreciate it just then.

Earth-human medical staff made up more than half of the present complement, but Earth-human Monitor casualties outnumbered the e-ts by thirty to one. On some levels one nurse had a whole ward of Corpsmen in her charge, with a few Tralthans or Kelgians trying to assist her. In such cases Conway's job was simply that of arranging a minimum of communication between the human and e-t nurses. But there were other instances when the staff were ELNTs and FGLIs and the patients in their charge were DBLF, QCQL and Earth-human, or Earth-humans in charge of ELNTs, or the plant-like AACPs looking after a mixed bag of practically everything. The simple answer would have been to move the patients into the charge of staff of their own species—except that they could not be moved for the reason that they were too ill, that there was no staff available to move them, or that there were no nurses of that particular species. In these cases Conway's job was infinitely more complex.

The shortage of nursing staff of all species was chronic. With regard to doctors the position was desperate. He called O'Mara.

"We haven't enough doctors," he said. "I think nurses should be given more discretion in the diagnosis and treatment of casualties. They should do as they think best without waiting for authority from a doctor who is too busy to supervise anyway. The casualties are still coming in and I can't see any other way of—"

"Do it, you're the boss," O'Mara broke in harshly.

"Right," said Conway, nettled. "Another thing. I've had offers by a lot of the doctors to take two or three tapes for translation purposes in addition to the tape they draw for current ops. And some of the girls have volunteered to do the same—"

"*No!*" said O'Mara. "I've had some of your volunteers up here and they aren't suitable. The doctors left to us are either very junior interns or Corps medical officers and e-ts who came with the volunteer forces. None of them have experience with multiple physiology tapes. It would render them permanently insane within the first hour.

"As for the girls," he went on, a sardonic edge in his voice, "you have noticed by this time that the female Earth-human DBDG has a rather peculiar mind. One of its peculiarities is a deep, sex-based mental fastidiousness. No matter what they *say* they will not, repeat not, allow alien beings to apparently take over their pretty little brains. If such should happen, severe mental damage would result. No again. Off."

Conway resumed his tour. It was beginning to get him down now. Even though his technique was improving the process of Translation was an increasing strain. And in the relatively easy periods between translations he felt as if there were seven different people all arguing and shouting inside his brain, and his own was very rarely the loudest voice. His throat was raw from making noises that it had never been designed for, and he was hungry.

All seven of him had different ideas for assuaging that hunger, revoltingly different ideas. Since the hospital's catering arrangement had suffered as badly as everything else there was no wide selection from which he could have picked neutral items that would not have offended, or at least not completely nauseated, his alter egos. He was reduced to eating sandwiches with his eyes shut, in case he would find out what was in them, and drinking water and glucose. None of him objected to water.

Eventually an organization for the reception and treatment of casualties was operating again in all the habitable levels—it was slow, but it was operating. And now that there were facilities for treating them Conway's next job was to move the patients who were currently jamming the approaches to the airlocks. There were actually pressure-litters anchored to the outer hull, he had been told.

Prilicla objected.

For a few minutes he tried to find out why. One of Prilicla's objections was that Conway was tired, which he countered by telling it that everybody in the hospital, including Prilicla itself, was tired. The other objections were either too weak or too subtle for the limited communications available. Conway ignored them and headed for the nearest lock.

The problems here were very similar to those inside the hospital— the major disadvantage being his spacesuit radio which hampered translation considerably. But to offset this he could get around much more quickly. The tractor beam men who handled the wrecks and wreckage around the hospital could whisk his whole party from point to point within seconds.

But he discovered that the Melfan segment of his mind, which had been seriously troubled by the weightless conditions inside the hospital, was utterly terrified outside it. The Melfan ELNT who had produced the tape had been an amphibious, crab-like being who lived mainly under water and had had no experience whatever of space. Conway had to fight down the panic which threatened his whole, multi-tenanted mind as well as the fear which all of him felt at the battle going on above his head.

O'Mara had told him that the attack was easing off, but Conway could not imagine anything more savage than what he was seeing.

Between the warring ships no missiles were being used—the attackers and defenders were too condensed, too inextricably tangled up. Like tiny, fast-moving models, so sharply defined that he felt he could reach up and grab one, the ships wheeled through their wild, chaotic dance. Singly and in groups they lunged, whirled, took frantic evasive action, broke formation or had their formations broken, reformed and attacked again. It was endless, implacable and almost hypnotic. There was, of course, no noise. What missiles were launched were directed at the hospital, a target too big to miss, and they were felt rather than heard.

Between the ships, tractor and pressor beams jabbed out like solid, invisible fingers, slowing or deflecting the target ship so that a rattler could be focused. Sometimes three or more vessels would converge on a single target and tear it apart within seconds. Sometimes a well-directed rattler would rip apart the artificial gravity system an instant before it disrupted the drive. With the crew hammered flat by high acceleration the ship would go tumbling out of the fight, unless someone put another rattler on it or a tractor man on Sector General's hull pulled it down to look for survivors.

Whether or not there were any survivors the wreck could be used . . .

The once smooth and shining hull was a mass of deep, jagged-edged craters and buckled plating. And because the missile lighting did strike twice, or even three times, in the same place—that was how the Translator computer had been destroyed—the craters were being plugged with wreckage in an effort to keep the missiles from exploding deeper inside the hospital. Any type of wreckage served, the tractor men weren't choosy.

Conway was on a tractor-beam mount when one of the wrecks was pulled in. He saw the rescue team shooting from the shelter of the airlock, circle the hulk carefully, then enter. About ten minutes later they came out towing . . . something.

"Doctor," said the NCO in charge of the installation, "I think I goofed. My men say the beastie they've pulled out of that wreck is new to them and want you to have a look. I'm sorry, but one wreck is like any other wreck. I don't think it is one of ours . . ."

Six parts of Conway's mind contained personalities whose memories did not contain data on the war and they did not think it mattered. As the minority opinion Conway didn't think it mattered either, but he knew that neither the sergeant nor himself had time to start an ethical debate on it. He had a quick look, then said, "Take it inside. Level Two-forty, Ward Seven."

Since being given the tapes Conway had been forced to watch helplessly while patients—casualties whose condition was such that they merited a fully qualified Senior Physician at least to perform the surgery—were operated on by tired, harassed, but well-intentioned beings who just did not have the required skill. They had done the job as best they could because there was nobody else to do it. Conway had wanted to step in many times, but had reminded himself and been reminded by Prilicla and the rest of his entourage, that he had to consider the Big Picture. Reorganizing the hospital then had been more important than any one patient. But now he felt that he could stop being an organizer and go back to being a doctor.

This was a new species to the hospital. O'Mara would not have a tape on its physiology, and even if the patient recovered consciousness it would not be able to cooperate because the Translators were dead. Conway had got to take this one and nobody was going to talk him out of it.

Ward Seven was adjacent to the section where a Kelgian military doctor and Murchison had been working wonders with a mixed bag of FGLI, QCQL and Earth-human patients, so he asked them both to assist. Conway put the new arrival's classification as TRLH, being aided in this by the fact that the patient's spacesuit was transparent as well as flexible. Had the suit been less flexible the being's injuries would have been less severe, but then the suit would have cracked instead of bending with the force which had smashed against it.

Conway bored a tiny hole in the suit, drew off a sample of the internal atmosphere and resealed it. He put the sample in the analyzer.

"And I thought the QCQLs were bad," said Murchison when he showed her the result. "But we can reproduce it. You will need to replace the air here, I expect?"

Conway said, "Yes, please."

They climbed into their operating suits—regulation light-weight pattern except that the arms and hands sections ended in a fine, tight-fitting sheath that was like a second skin. The air was replaced by the patient's atmosphere and they began cutting it out of its suit.

The TRLH had a thin carapace which covered its back and curved down and inward to protect the central area of its underside. Four thick, single-jointed legs projected from the uncovered sections and a large, but again lightly boned head contained four manipulatory appendages, two recessed but extensible eyes and two months, one of which had blood coming from it. The being must have been hurled against several metal projections. Its shell was fractured in six places and in one area it had been almost shattered, the pieces being severely depressed. In this area it was losing blood rapidly. Conway began charting the internal damage with the X-ray scanner, then a few minutes later he signaled that he was ready to start.

He wasn't ready, but the patient was bleeding to death.

The internal arrangement of organs was different from anything he had previously encountered, and different from anything in the experience of the six personalities sharing his mind. But from the QCQL he received pointers on the probable metabolism of beings who breathed such highly corrosive air, from the Melfan data on the possible methods of exploring the damaged carapace, and the FGLI, DBLF, GLNO and AACP contributed their experience. But it was not always helpful—at every stage they literally shrieked warnings to be careful, so much so that for seconds at a time Conway stood with his hands shaking, unable to go on. He was probing the recorded memories deeply now, hitherto it had only been for data on language, and *everything* was coming up.

The private nightmares and neuroses of the individuals, triggered off by being so inextricably mixed with the similar alien nightmares around them, and all mounting, growing worse by the minutes. The beings who had produced the tapes did not all have e-t hospital experience, they were not accustomed to alien points of view. The proper thing was to keep reminding himself that they were not separate personalities, Conway told himself, but merely a mass of alien data of different types. But he was horribly, stupidly tired and he was beginning to lose control of what was going on in his mind. And still the memories welled up in a dark, turgid flood. Petty, shameful, secret memories mostly concerned with sex—and that, in e-ts, was *alien,* so alien that he wanted to scream. He found suddenly that he was bent over, sweating, as if there was a heavy weight on his back.

He felt Murchison gripping his arm. "What's wrong, Doctor?" she said urgently. "Can I help?"

He shook his head, because for a second he didn't know how to form words in his own language, but he kept looking at her for all of ten seconds. When he turned back he had a picture of her in his mind as she was to him, not as a Tralthan or a Melfan or a Kelgian saw her. The concern in her eyes had been for him alone. At times Conway had had secret thoughts of his own about Murchison, but they were normal, human thoughts. He hugged them to him tightly and for a time he was in control again. Long enough to finish with the patient.

Then suddenly his mind was tearing itself apart into seven pieces and he was falling into the deepest, darkest pits of even different Hells. He did not know that his limbs stiffened or bent or twisted as if something alien had separate possession of each one. Or that Murchison dragged him out and held him while Prilicla, at great danger to life and its fragile, spidery limbs, gave him the shot which knocked him out.

CHAPTER 22

The intercom buzzer awakened Conway, instantly but without confusion in the pleasant, familiar, cramped surroundings of his own room. He felt rested and alert and ready for breakfast, and the hand he used to push back the sheets had five pink fingers on it and felt just right that way. But then he became aware of a certain strangeness which made him hesitate for a moment. The place was *quiet* . . . !

"To save you the where-am-I-what-time-is-it? routine," O'Mara's voice came wearily, "you have not been consciously with us for two days. During that time, early yesterday, to be exact, the attack ceased and has not yet been resumed and I did a lot of work on you. For your own good you were given a hypno treatment to forget everything, so you will not be eternally grateful for what I've done for you. How do you feel now?"

"Fine," said Conway enthusiastically. "I can't feel any . . . I mean, there seems to be plenty of *room* in my head . . ."

O'Mara grunted. "The obvious retort is that your head is empty, but I won't make it."

The Chief Psychologist, despite his attempt to maintain his usual dry, sardonic manner, sounded desperately tired—his words were actually slurred with weariness. But O'Mara, Conway knew, was not the type who became tired—he might, if driven long and hard enough, succumb to mental fatigue . . .

"The fleet commander wants a meeting with us in four hours time," O'Mara went one, "so don't get involved with any cases between now and then. Things are running fairly smoothly now, anyway, so you can afford to play hooky for a while. *I'm* going to sleep. Off."

But it was very difficult to spend four hours doing nothing, Conway found. The main dining hall was jammed with Corpsmen—projector crews engaged on hull defense, replacements for the defending ships, maintenancemen and Medical Division personnel who were supplementing the civilian medical staff. Conversation was loud and nervous and too cheerful, and revolved around the past and possible future aspects of the attack.

Apparently the Monitor force had practically been pushed down onto the outer hull when an e-t force of volunteer Illensans had emerged from hyperspace just outside the enemy globe. Illensan ships were big and badly designed and looked like capital ships even though they only had the armament of a light cruiser, and the sight of ten of them popping out of nowhere had put the enemy off his stride. The attacking force had pulled back temporarily to regroup and the Monitors, with nothing to regroup with, were concentrating on increasing the armament of their last line of defense, the hospital itself. But even though it concerned him as closely as anyone else in the room, Conway felt averse to joining in the cheerfully morbid conversations.

Since O'Mara had erased all the physiology tapes and indulged in some curative tinkering with his mind, the nightmare of two days ago and the e-t language data he had gained had faded, so he could not indulge in polite conversation with the e-ts scattered about the hall. And the Earth-human nurses were being monopolized by Corpsmen, usually at the rate of ten or twelve to one, with an obvious improvement in morale in both directions. Conway ate quickly and left, feeling that his own morale was in need of improvement, too.

Which made him wonder suddenly if Murchison was on duty, off duty or asleep. If she was asleep there was nothing he could do, but if she was on duty he could very soon take her off it, and when she was off . . .

Strangely he felt only the slightest pricklings of conscience over this shameless abuse of his authority for his own selfish ends. In time of war, he thought, people became less bound by their professional and moral codes. Ethically he was going to the dogs.

But Murchison was just going off duty when he arrived in her ward, so he did not have to openly commit the crime he had been intent on committing. In the same loud, too-cheerful tone that he had considered so artificial when he had heard it in the dining hall he asked if she had any previous engagement, suggested a date, and muttered something horribly banal about all work and no play . . .

"Previous engage ... *play* ... ! But I want to *sleep!*" she protested; then in more reasonable tones, "You can't ... I mean, where would we go, what would we do? The place is a wreck. Would I have to change?"

"The recreation level is still there," Conway said, "and you look fine."

The regulation nurses uniform of blue, tight-fitting tunic and slacks—very tight-fitting so as to ease the problem of climbing in and out of protective suits—flattered Murchison, but she looked worn out. As she unhooked the broad white belt and instrument pouches and removed her cap and hairnet Conway growled deep in his throat, and immediately burst into a fit of coughing because it was still tender from making e-t noises.

Murchison laughed, shaking out her hair and rubbing her cheeks to put some color into them. She said brightly, "Promise you won't keep me out too late ... ?"

On the way to the recreation level it was difficult not to talk shop. Many sections of the hospital had lost pressure so that in the habitable levels overcrowding was severe—there was scarcely an air-filled corridor which was not also filled with casualties. And this was a situation which none of them had foreseen. They had not expected the enemy to use limited warfare on them. Had atomic weapons been used there would not have been any overcrowding, or, possibly, any hospital. Most of the time Conway was not listening to Murchison, but she didn't seem to notice. Perhaps because she wasn't listening to him.

The recreation level was the same in detail as they remembered it, but the details had been dramatically changed around. With the hospital's center of gravity being above the recreation level what little attraction there was was upward, and all the loose material normally on the ground or in the bay had collected against the roof, where it made a translucent chaos of sand-veined water, air-pockets and trailing watery globes through which the submerged sun shone a deep, rich purple.

"Oh, this is *nice!*" said Murchison. "And restful, sort of."

The lighting gave her skin a warm, dusky coloration that was wholly indescribable, Conway thought, but nice. Her lips—soft purple, verging on black—were parted slightly to reveal teeth which seemed almost iridescent, and her eyes were large and mysterious and glowing.

"The word," he said, "is romantic."

They launched themselves gently into the vast room in the direction of the restaurant. Below them the tree tops drifted past and they ran through a wisp of fog—cooling steam produced by the warm, underwater sun—which beaded their faces and arms with moisture. Conway caught her hand and held it gently, but their velocities were not exactly matching and they began to spin around their center of gravity. Conway bent his elbow slowly, drawing her toward him, and their rate of spin increased. Then he slid his other arm around her waist and pulled her closer still.

She started to protest and then suddenly, gloriously, she was kissing him and clinging to him as fiercely as he was to her, and the empty bay, cliffs, and purple, watery sky was whirling madly around them.

In a calm, impersonal corner of his mind Conway thought that his head would have been spinning anyway even if his body hadn't, it was that sort of kiss. Then they spun gently into the cliff-top at the other side of the bay and broke apart, laughing.

They used the artificial greenery to pull themselves toward the one-time restaurant. It was dim inside, and during its slow fall ceilingward a lot of water had collected under the transparent roof and on the undersides of the table canopies. Like some fragile, alien fruit it hung in clusters which stirred gently at their passage or burst into hundreds of tiny silvery globes when they blundered against a table. With the low ceiling and dim light it was difficult to keep from knocking into things and soon the globes were all around them, seeming to crowd in, throwing back a hundred tiny, distorted reflections of Murchison and himself. It was like an alien dream world, Conway thought; and it was a wish-fulfillment dream. The dark, lovely shape of Murchison drifting beside him left no doubt about that.

They sat down at one of the tables, but carefully so as not to dislodge the water in the canopy above them. Conway took her hand in his, the others being needed to hold them onto their chairs, and said, "I want to talk to you."

She smiled, a little warily.

Conway tried to talk. He tried to say the things that he had rehearsed to himself many times, but what came out was a disjointed hodge-podge. She was beautiful, he said, and he didn't want to be friends and she was a stupid little fool for staying behind. He loved her and wanted her and he would have been happy spending months—not too many months, maybe—getting her in a corner where she couldn't say anything but yes. But now there wasn't time to do things properly. He thought about her all the time and even during the TRLH operation it had been thinking about her that let him hang on until the end. And all during the bombardment he had worried in case . . .

"I worried about you, too," Murchison broke in softly. "You were all over the place and every time there was a hit . . . And you always knew exactly what to do and . . . and I was afraid you would get yourself killed."

Her face was shadowed, her uniform clung damply. Conway felt his mouth dry.

She said warmly, "You were wonderful that day with the TRLH. It was like working with a Diagnostician. *Seven* tapes, O'Mara said. I . . . I asked him to give me one, earlier, to help you out. But he said no because . . ." She hesitated, and looked away. ". . . because he said girls are very choosy who they let take possession of them. Their minds, I mean . . ."

"How choosy?" said Conway thickly. "Does the choice exclude . . . friends?"

He leaned forward involuntarily as he spoke, letting go his hold on the chair with his other hand. He drifted heavily up from the table, jarred the canopy and touched one of the floating globes with his forehead. With the surface tension broken it collapsed wetly all over his face. Spluttering he brushed it away, knocking it into a cloud of tiny, glowing marbles. Then he saw it.

It was the only harsh note in this dream world, a pile of unarmed missiles occupying a dark corner of the room. They were held to the floor by clamps and further secured with netting in case the clamps were jarred free by an explosion. There was plenty of slack in the netting. Still holding onto Murchison, he kicked himself over to it, searched until he found the edge of the net, and pulled it up from the floor.

"We can't talk properly if we keep floating into the air," he said quietly. "Come into my parlor . . ."

Maybe the netting was too much like a spider's web, or his tone resembled too closely that of a predatory spider. He felt her hesitate. The hand he was holding was trembling.

"I . . . I know how you feel," she said quickly, not looking at him. "I like you, too. Maybe more than that. But this isn't right. I know we don't have any time, but sneaking down here like this and . . . it's selfish. I keep thinking about all those men in the corridors, and the other casualties still to come. I know it sounds stuffy, but we're supposed to think about other people first. That's why—"

"Thank you," said Conway furiously. "Thank you for reminding me of my duty."

"Oh, please!" she cried, and suddenly she was clinging to him again, her head against his chest. "I don't want to hurt you, or make you hate me. I didn't think the war would be so horrible. I'm frightened. I don't want you to be killed and leave me all alone. Oh, please, hold me tight and . . . and tell me what to do . . ."

Her eyes were glittering and it was not until one of the tiny points of light floated away from them that he realized she was crying silently. He had never imagined Murchison crying, somehow. He held her tightly for a long time, then gently pushed her away from him.

Roughly, he said, "I don't hate you, but I don't want you to discuss my exact feelings at the moment, either. Come on, I'll take you home."

But he didn't take her home. The alarm siren went a few minutes later and when it stopped a voice on the PA was asking Doctor Conway to come to the intercom.

CHAPTER 23

Once it had been Reception, with three fast-talking Nidians to handle the sometimes complex problems of getting patients out of their ambulances and into the hospital. Now it was Command Headquarters and twenty Monitor officers murmuring tensely into throat mikes, their eyes glued to screens which showed the enemy at all degrees of magnification from nil to five hundred. Two of the three main screens showed sections of the enemy fleet, the images partly obliterated by the ghostly lines and geometrical figures that was a tactical officer trying to predict what they would do next. The other screen gave a wide-angle view of the outer hull.

A missile came down like a distant shooting star, making a tiny flash and throwing up in minute fountain of wreckage. The tearing, metallic crash which reverberated through the room was out of all proportion to the image.

Dermod said, "They've withdrawn out of range of the heavy stuff mounted on the hospital and are sending in missiles. This is the softening up process designed to wear us down prior to the main attack. A counterattack by our remaining mobile force would result in its destruction, they are so heavily outnumbered that they can operate effectively only if backed by the defenses of the hospital. So we have no choice but to soak up this stage as best we can and save our strength for—"

"What strength?" said Conway angrily. Beside him O'Mara made a disapproving noise, and across the desk the Fleet commander looked coldly at him. When Dermod spoke it was to Conway, but he didn't answer the question.

"We can also expect small raids by fast, maneuverable units designed to further unsettle us," he went on. "Your casualties will come from Corpsmen engaged on hull defense, personnel from the defending ships, and perhaps enemy casualties. Which brings me to a point which I would like cleared up. You seem to be handling a lot of enemy wounded, Doctor, and you've told me that your facilities are already strained to the limit . . ."

"How the blazes can you tell?" said Conway. Dermod's expression became more frigid, but this time he answered the question.

"Because I have reports of patients lying beside each other finding that the other one is talking gibberish, patients of the same physological type, that is. What steps are you taking to—"

"None!" said Conway, so angry suddenly that he wanted to take this cold, unfeeling martinet by the throat and shake some humanity into him.

At the beginning he had liked Dermod. He had thought him a thoughtful and sensitive as well as a competent Fleet commander, but during the past few days he had become the embodiment of the blind, coldly implacable forces which had Conway and everyone else in the hospital trapped. Daily conferences between the military and medical authorities in the hospital had been ordered since the last attack had begun, and at all three of them Conway had found himself running across the fleet commander with increasing frequency.

But when Conway snapped, the Fleet commander did not snap back. Dermod merely looked at him with his eyes so bleak and distant that Conway felt that the commander wasn't seeing him at all. And it did no good at all when O'Mara advised him quietly to hold his tongue and not be so all-fired touchy—that Dermod had a war to fight and he was doing the best he could, and that the pressures he was under excused a certain lack of charm in his personality.

"Surely," said Dermod coldly, just as Conway had decided that he really ought to be more patient with this cold-blooded, military creature, "you are not treating enemy casualties the same as our own . . . ?"

"It is difficult," said Conway, speaking so quietly that O'Mara looked suddenly worried, "to tell the difference. Subtle variations in spacesuit design mean nothing to the nursing staff and myself. And when, as frequently happens, the suit and underlying uniform is cut away the latter may be unidentifiable due to the bleeding. Between the injection of antipain and unconsciousness the oral noises they make are not easily translatable. And if there is any way to tell the difference between a Corpsman and one of the enemy screaming, I don't want to know about it . . ."

He had started quietly, but when he ended he was close to shouting.

". . . I won't make any such distinction between casualties and neither will my staff! This is a *hospital,* damn you! Well *isn't* it?"

"Take it easy, son. It's still a hospital," said O'Mara gently.

"It is also," Dermod snapped, "a military base!"

"What I don't understand," O'Mara put in quickly, trying desperately to pour on the oil, "is why the hell they don't finish us with atomic warheads . . . ?"

Another hit, more distant this time, sent its tinny echoes through the room.

"The reason they don't finish us off with an atomic bomb, Major," he replied, with his eyes still locked with Conway's, "is because they must make a conquest. The political forces involved demand it. The Empire must take and occupy this outpost of the hated enemy, the Emperor's general must have a triumph and not a pyrrhic victory, and subjugating the enemy and capturing his territory, no matter how few or how little, can be made to look like a triumph to the citizens of the Empire.

"Our own casualties are heavy," Dermod went on coldly. "A space battle being what it is only ten percent of the casualties survive to be hospitalized and we are fortunate both in having medical facilities immediately available and in occupying a strong defensive position. The number of enemy casualties is much higher than ours, my estimate would be twenty to one, so that if they were to knock us out with an atomic missile now, when they could have done the same thing at the very beginning without losing a man, some very awkward questions will be asked within the Empire. If the Emperor can't answer them he might find that the war, and all the fine, martial fervor he has built up, will backfire on him . . ."

"Why don't you communicate with them?" Conway interrupted harshly. "Tell them the truth about us, and tell them about the wounded here. You surely don't expect to win this battle now. Why don't we surrender . . . ?"

"We cannot communicate with them, Doctor," the commander said bitingly, "because they won't listen to us. Or if they do listen they don't believe what we say. They know, or think they know, what we did on Etla and what we are supposed to be doing here. Telling them that we were really helping the Etlan natives and that we have been forced to defend our hospital is no good. A series of plagues swept Etla soon after we left and this establishment no longer behaves, outwardly, that is, like a hospital. What we say to them has no importance, it is what we *do* that counts. And we are doing exactly what their Emperor has lead them to expect of us.

"If they were really thinking," he continued savagely, "they would wonder at the large number of our e-ts who are helping us. According to them our e-ts are downtrodden, subject races who are little more than slaves. The volunteers who have come out to help us do not fight like slaves, but at the present stage that is too subtle a thing to make any impression. They are thinking emotionally instead of logically . . ."

"And *I'm* thinking emotionally, too!" Conway broke in sharply. "I'm thinking of my patients. The wards are full. They are lying in odd corners and along corridors all over the place, with inadequate protection against pressure loss . . ."

"You've lost the ability to think about anything *but* your patients, Doctor!" Dermod snapped back. "It might surprise you to know that I think about them, too, but I try not to be so mauldin about it. If I did think that way I would begin to feel angry, begin to hate the enemy. Before I knew it I would want revenge . . ."

Another hit rang like a loud, discordant gong through the hospital. The commander raised his voice, and kept on raising it.

". . . You must know that the Monitor Corps is the police force for most of the inhabited Galaxy, and keeping the peace within the Federation calls for the constant application of the psychological and social sciences. In short, guiding and molding opinion both on the individual and planetary population levels. So the situation we have here, a gallant band of Corpsmen and doctors holding out against the savage, unceasing attacks of an overwhelmingly superior enemy, is one I could use. Even so it would take the Federation a long time to become angry enough to mobilize for war, far too long to do us personally any good, but think how we would be avenged, Doctor . . . !"

His voice was shaking now, his face white and tight with fury. He was shouting.

"In an interstellar war planets cannot be captured, Doctor. They can only be detonated. That stinking little Empire with its forty planets would be stamped out, destroyed, completely obliterated . . . !"

O'Mara did not speak. Conway couldn't, nor could he take his eyes off Dermod to see how the psychologist was reacting to this outburst. He hadn't thought it possible for the commander to blow up like this and it was suddenly frightening. Because Dermod's sanity and self-control, like O'Mara's, was something Conway had depended on even though he hated it.

"But the Corps is a police force, remember?" he raged on. "We are trying to think of this as a disturbance, a riot on an interstellar scale where as usual the casualties among the rioters outnumber those of the police. Personally I think it is past the time when *anything* will make them see the truth and a full-scale war is inevitable, but I do not want to hate them. This is the difference, Doctor, between maintaining peace and waging war.

"And I don't want any sniveling, narrow-minded doctors, who have nothing to worry about except their patients, reminding me of all the horrible ways my men are dying. Trying to make me lose my perspective, making me hate people who are no different to us except that they are being fed wrong information.

"And I don't care if you treat enemy and Corps wounded alike," he yelled, trying to bring his voice down but not succeeding, "but you will listen when I give orders concerning them. This is a military base and they are enemy casualties. The ones who are in a condition to move must be guarded against the possibility of them committing acts of sabotage. Now do you understand, Doctor?"

"Yes, sir," said Conway in a small voice.

When he left Reception with O'Mara a few minutes later Conway still had the feeling of being charred around the edges. It was plain now that he had gravely misjudged the fleet commander, and he should apologize for the hard things he had been thinking about Dermod. Underneath all the ice Dermod was a good man.

Beside him O'Mara said suddenly, "I like to see these cold, controlled types blow off steam occasionally. Psychologically it is desirable, considering the pressures he is under at the present time. I'm glad you finally made him angry."

"What about *me*?" said Conway.

"You, Doctor, are not controlled at all," O'Mara replied sternly. "Despite your new authority, which should make you set an example of tolerance and good behavior at least, you are fast becoming a bad-tempered brat. Watch it, Doctor."

Conway had been looking for sympathy for the tongue-lashing Dermod had given him, and a little consideration for the pressures he himself was under, not criticism from another quarter. When O'Mara turned off toward his office a few minutes later, Conway was still too angry to speak.

CHAPTER 24

Next day Conway did not get the chance to apologize to the Fleet commander—the rioters launched their most vicious attack yet and both the Station Inspector and the Police Surgeon were much too busy to talk. But calling the battle a riot, Conway thought cynically, made no difference to the nature and number of the casualties which flooded suddenly in, because it began with a near-catastrophe for both sides.

The enemy force closed in, stepping up the missile bombardment to a fantastic rate and englobing the hospital so tightly that there were times when they came within a few hundred feet of the outer hull. Dermod's ships—*Vespasian,* a Tralthan capital ship and the other smaller units remaining to him—dropped back to anchor with tractors against the hospital, there being no space to maneuver without obstructing the heavy armament below them. They settled and with their lighter weapons strengthened the fixed defenses wherever possible.

But this must have been the move which the enemy commander had been waiting for. With the rapidity possible only to a well-planned maneuver the ranks of the attacking globe thinned, scattered and reformed over one small area of the hull. On this area was concentrated the total firepower of three-quarters of the entire enemy force.

A storm of missiles tore into the heavy plating, blasting away the wreckage which plugged earlier damage and gouging into the more fragile inner hull. Tractors and rattlers seized the still-settling wreckage, shaking it viciously apart and pulling it away so that the missiles could gouge deeper still. Monitor defenses took a frightful toll of the tightly packed ships, but only for minutes. The tremendous concentration of fire battered them down, hammered them flat, ripped and worried at them until they were one with the other shifting masses of savaged men and metal. They left a section of the outer hull completely undefended, and suddenly it became plain that this was not only an attack but an invasion.

Under the covering fire of the massed attackers, three, giant, unarmed ships were dropping ponderously toward the undefended section. Transports . . .

At once *Vespasian* was directed to fill the gap in the defenses. It shot toward the point where the first transport was about to touch down, running the gauntlet of Monitor as well as enemy fire and throwing everything it had as soon as the target appeared above the curve of the hull . . .

There were several excuses given for what happened then. An error in judgment by its pilot, a hit by one of the enemy—or even its own people's—missiles which deflected it from course at exactly the wrong moment. But it was never suggested that Captain Williamson deliberately rammed the enemy transport, because Williamson was known to be a clear-headed, competent officer and a one-to-one swap, even at this desperate stage of the battle, was a tactically stupid move considering how the enemy outnumbered them.

Vespasian struck the larger but more lightly constructed transport near its stern and seemed to go right through it before grinding silently to a halt. Inside the wreckage a single, small explosion lit the fog of escaping air but the two ships remained locked together, spinning slowly.

For a second everything seemed to stop. Then the Monitor fixed defenses lashed out, ignoring all other targets if their projectors would bear on the second descending transport. Within minutes rattlers had torn off plating in three areas of its hull and were biting deeper. The transport withdrew ponderously, losing air. The third one was already pulling back. The whole enemy force was pulling back, but not very far. Only slightly diminished in intensity the bombardment continued.

It was not by any stretch of the imagination a victory for the Monitor Corps. The enemy had merely made an error of judgment, been a little premature. The hospital required further softening up.

Tractor beams reached out and gently brought the spinning wreckage to a halt and lowered it onto the ravaged hull. Corpsmen jetted out to look for survivors and soon the casualties were coming in. But by roundabout routes, because under the wrecked ships there now stretched other wreckage and other rescue teams working to free patients who were casualties for the second and third time . . .

Dr. Prilicla was with the rescue teams. The GLNO life-form was the most fragile known to the Federation, cowardice being acknowledged as one of their prime survival characteristics. But Prilicla was guiding his thin-walled pressure bubble over jagged plating and through wreckage which shifted visibly all around it, seeking life. Living minds radiated even when unconscious and the little GLNO was pointing out unerringly the living from the dead. With casualties bleeding to death inside their suits or the suits themselves losing pressure, such identification directed effort to where it did the most good, and Prilicla was saving many, many lives. But for an empath, an emotion sensitive, it was a hellish job in every horrible and painful sense of the word . . .

Major O'Mara was everywhere. If there hadn't been weightless conditions the Chief Psychologist would have been dragging himself from place to place, but as it was his extreme fatigue showed only in the way he misjudged distances and collided with doors and people. But when he talked to Earth-human patients, nurses and Corpsmen his voice was never tired. His mere presence had a steadying effect on the e-t staff as well, for although they could not understand him they remembered the person he had been when there were Translators and he could lift off their hides with a few pungent words.

The e-t staff—the massive, awkward Tralthan FGLIs, the crab-like Melfan ELNTs and all the others—were everywhere, on some levels directing Earth-human staff and on others aiding the nurses and Corpsmen orderlies. They were tired and harried and all too often they did not know what was being said to them, but between them they saved a great many lives.

And every time a missile struck the hospital, they lost a little ground . . .

Dr. Conway never left the dining hall. He had communication with most of the other levels, but the corridors leading to them were in many cases airless or blocked with wreckage, and it was the general opinion that the hospital's last remaining Senior Physician should stay in a reasonably safe place. He had plenty of human casualties to look after and the difficult e-t cases, whether combatants or casualties among his own staff, were sent to him.

In a way he had the biggest and most compact ward in the hospital. Since nobody had time to gather for meals anymore and relied on packaged food sent to the wards, the main dining hall had been converted. Beds and theater equipment had been clamped to the floor, walls and ceiling of the great room and the patients, being space personnel, were not troubled either by the weightlessness or the sight of other patients hanging a few yards above them. It was convenient for the patients who were able to talk.

Conway had reached the stage of tiredness where he no longer felt tired. The tinny crash and clangor of missiles striking had become a monotonous background noise. He knew that the bombardment was steadily eating through the outer and inner hulls, a deadly erosion which must soon open every corridor and ward to space, but his brain had ceased to react to the sound. When casualties arrived he did what was indicated, but his reactions then were simply the conditioned reflexes of a doctor. He had lost much of his capacity to think or feel or remember, and when he did remember he had no sense of time. The last e-t case— which had required him taking four physiology tapes—stood out amid the weary, bloody, noisy monotony, as did the arrival of *Vespasian*'s injured. But Conway did not know whether that had been three days of three weeks ago, or which incident had occurred first.

He remembered the *Vespasian* incident often. Cutting Major Stillman out of his battered suit, stripping it off and pushing away the pieces which persisted in floating around the bed. Stillman had two cracked ribs, a shattered humerus and a minor decompression which was temporarily affecting his eyesight. Until the hypo took hold he kept asking about the Captain.

And Captain Williamson kept asking about his men. Williamson was in a cast from neck to toes, had very little pain and had remembered Conway immediately. It had been a large crew and he must have known them all by their names. Conway didn't.

"Stillman is three beds away on your right," Conway had told him, "and there are others all over the place."

Williamson's eyes had moved along the patients hanging above him. He couldn't move anything else. "There's some of them I don't recognize," he had said.

Looking at the livid bruises around Williamson's right eye, temple and jaw where his face had struck the inside of his helmet, Conway had dragged up his mouth into the semblance of a smile and said, "Some of them won't recognize you."

He remembered the second TRLH . . .

It had arrived strapped to a pressure litter whose atmosphere unit had already filled it with the poison which the occupant called air. Through the twin transparencies of the litter wall and the TRLH's suit its injuries were plainly apparent—a large, depressed fracture of the carapace which had cut underlying blood vessels. There was no time to take the tapes he had used during the previous TRLH case because the patient was obviously bleeding to death. Conway nodded for the litter to be clamped into the cleared area in the center of the floor and quickly changed his suit gauntlets for litter gloves. From the beds attached to the ceiling, eyes watched his every move.

He charged the gloves and pushed his hands against the sagging, transparent fabric of the tent. Immediately the thin, tough material became rubbery and pliable without losing any of its strength. It clung to the charged gloves, if not like a second skin at least like another pair of thin gloves. Carefully so as not to strain the fabric which separated the two mutually poisonous atmospheres, Conway removed the patient's suit with instruments clipped to the inside of the litter.

Quite complex procedures were possible while operating a flexible tent—Conway had a couple of PVSJs and a QCQL a few beds away to prove it—but they were limited by the instruments and medication available inside the tent, and the slight hampering effect of the fabric.

He had been removing the splinters of carapace from the damaged area when the crash of a missile striking nearby made the floor jump. The alarm bell which indicated a pressure drop sounded a few minutes later and Murchison and the Kelgian military doctor—the entire ward staff—had hurried to check the seals on the tents of patients who were not able to check their own. The drop was slight, probably a small leak caused by sprung plating, but to Conway's patient inside the tent it could be deadly. He had begun working with frantic speed.

But while he had striven to tie off the severed blood vessels the thin, tough fabric of the pressure litter began to swell out. It had become difficult to hold instruments, virtually impossible to guide them accurately, and his hands were actually pushed away from the operative field. The difference in pressure between the interior of the tent and the ward was only a few pounds per square inch at most, barely enough to have made Conway's ears pop, but the fabric of the litter had continued to balloon out. He had withdrawn helplessly, and half an hour later when the leak had been sealed and normal pressure restored, he had started again. By then it had been too much.

He remembered a sudden impairment of vision then, and a shock of surprise when he realized that he was crying. Tears weren't a conditioned medical reflex, he knew, because doctors just did not cry over patients.

Probably it had been a combination of anger at losing the patient—who really should not have been lost—and his extreme fatigue. And when he'd seen the expressions of all the patients watching him, Conway had felt horribly embarrassed.

Now the events around him had taken on a jerky, erratic motion. His eyes kept closing and several seconds, or minutes, passed before he could force them open again even though to himself no time at all went by. The walking wounded—patients with injuries which allowed them to move about the ward and return quickly to their tents in the event of a puncture—were moving from bed to bed doing the small, necessary jobs, or chatting with patients who couldn't move, or hanging like ungainly shoals of fish while they talked among themselves. But Conway was always too busy with the newly-arrived patients, or too confused with a multiplicity of tapes, to chat with the older ones. Mostly, however, his eyes went to the sleeping figures of Murchison and the Kelgian who floated near the entrance to the ward.

The Kelgian hung like a great, furry question mark, now and then emitting the low moaning sound which some DBLFs made when they were asleep. Murchison floated at the end of a snaking, ten-foot safety line, turning slowly. It was odd how sleepers in the weightless condition adopted the fetal position, Conway thought tenderly as he watched his beautiful, adult girl baby swaying at the end of an impossibly thin umbilical cord. He desperately wanted to sleep himself, but it was his spell on duty and he would not be relieved for a long time—five minutes maybe, or five hours, but an eternity in either case. He would have to keep doing something.

Without realizing he had made a decision he found himself moving into the empty storeroom which housed the terminal and probable terminal cases. It was only here that Conway spared himself the time to chat, or if talking was not possible to do the essential and at the same time useless things which help to comfort the dying. With the e-ts he could only stand by and hope that the shattered, bloody wreckage of the Tralthan or Melfan or whatever would be given a tiny flash of Prilicla's emphathetic faculty so that they would know he was a friend and how he felt.

It was only gradually that Conway became aware that the walking wounded had followed him into the room, together with patients who had no business being outside their tents who were being towed by the others. They gathered slowly around and above him, their expression grim, determined and respectful. Major Stillman pushed his way to the front, awkwardly, because in his one good hand he carried a gun.

"The killing has got to stop, Doctor," Stillman said quietly. "We've all talked it over and that's what we decided. And it's got to be stopped right now." He reversed the weapon suddenly, offering it to Conway. "You might need this, to point at Dermod to keep him from doing anything foolish while we're telling him what has been going on . . ."

Close behind Stillman hung the mummified shape of Captain Williamson and the man who had towed him in. They were talking to each other in low voices and the language was both foreign and familiar to Conway. Before he could place it the patients all began moving out again and he noticed how many of them were armed. The weapons had been part of the spacesuits they had worn, and Conway had not thought about guns when he had piled the suits into a ward storage space. Dermod, he thought, would be very annoyed with him. Then he followed the patients out to the main ward entrance, and the corridor which led to Reception.

Stillman talked nearly all the time, telling him what had been happening. When they were almost there he said anxiously, "You don't think I'm . . . I'm a traitor for doing this, Doctor?"

There were so many different emotions churning inside Conway that all he could say was *"No!"*

CHAPTER 25

He felt ridiculous pointing the gun at the Fleet commander, but that had seemed to be the only way to do this thing. Conway had entered Reception, threaded his way through the officers around the control desks until he had reached Dermod, then he had held the gun on the Fleet commander, while the others came in. He had also tried to explain things, but he wasn't doing a very good job.

". . . So you want me to surrender, Doctor," said Dermod wearily, not looking at the gun. His eyes went from Conway's face to those of some of the Corpsmen patients who were still floating into the room. He looked hurt and disappointed, as if a friend had done a very shameful thing.

Conway tried again.

"Not surrender, sir," he said, pointing at the man who was still guiding Williamson's stretcher. "We . . . I mean, that man over there needs a communicator. He wants to order a cease fire . . ."

Stammering in his eagerness to explain what had happened, Conway started with the influx of casualties after the collision between *Vespasian* and the enemy transport. The interiors of both ships were a shambles and, while it was known that there were enemy as well as Corpsmen injured, there had never been time or the staff available to separate them. Then later, when the less seriously injured began to move around, talking to or helping to nurse the other patients, it became plain that almost half of the casualties were from the other side. Oddly this did not seem to matter much to the patients, and the staff were too busy to notice. So the patients went on doing the simpler, necessary and not very pleasant jobs for each other, jobs which just had to be done in a ward so drastically understaffed, and talking . . .

For these were Corpsmen from *Vespasian,* and *Vespasian* had been to Etla. Which meant that its crew were variously proficient in the Etlan language, and the Etlans spoke the same language as that used all over the Empire—a general purpose language similar to the Federation's Universal. They talked to each other a lot and one of the things they learned, after the initial caution and distrust had passed, was that the enemy transport had contained some very high officers. One of the ones who had survived the collision was third in line of command of the Empire forces around Sector General . . .

". . . And for the last few days peace talks have been going on among my patients," Conway ended breathlessly. "Unofficial, perhaps, but I think Colonel Williamson and Heraltnor here have enough rank to make them binding."

Heraltnor, the enemy officer, spoke briefly and vehemently to Williamson in Etlan, then gently tilted the plaster encased figure of the Captain until he could look at the fleet commander. Heraltnor watched Dermod, too. Anxiously.

"He's no fool, sir," said Williamson painfully. "From the sound of the bombardment and the glimpses he's had of your screens he knows our defenses are hammered flat. He says that his people could land now and we couldn't do a thing to stop them. That is true, sir, and we both know it. He says his chief will probably order the landing in a matter of hours, but he still wants a cease fire, sir, not a surrender.

"He doesn't want his side to win," the Captain ended weakly. "He just wants the fighting to stop. There are some things he has been told about this war and us which need straightening out, he says . . ."

"He's been saying a lot," said Dermod angrily. His face had a tortured look, as if he was wanting desperately to hope but did not dare let himself do so. He went on, "And you men have been doing a lot of talking! Why didn't you let me know about it . . . ?"

"It wasn't what we *said,*" Stillman broke in sharply, "it was what we *did*! They didn't believe a word we told them at first. But this place wasn't at all what they had been told to expect, it looked more like a hospital than a torture chamber. Appearances could have been deceptive, and they were a very suspicious bunch, but they saw human and e-t doctors and nurses working themselves to death over them, and they saw *him*. Talking didn't do anything, at least not until later. It was what we did, what *he* did . . . !"

Conway felt his ears getting warm. He protested, "But the same thing was happening in every ward of the hospital!"

"Shut up, Doctor," Stillman said respectfully, then went on, "He never seemed to sleep. He hardly ever spoke to us once we were out of danger, but the patients in the side ward he never let up on, even though they were the hopeless cases. A couple of them he proved not to be hopeless, and moved them out to us in the main ward. It didn't matter what side they were on, he worked as hard foreverybody . . ."

"Stillman," said Conway sharply, "you're dramatizing things . . . !"

". . . Even then they were wavering a bit," Stillman went on regardless. "But it was the TRLH case which clinched things. The TRLHs were enemy e-t volunteers, and normally the Empire people don't think much of e-ts and expected us to feel the same. Especially as this e-t was on the other side. But he worked just as hard on it, and when the pressure drop made it impossible for him to go on with the operation and the e-t died, they saw his reaction—"

"*Stillman!*" said Conway furiously.

But Stillman did not go into details. He was silent, watching Dermod anxiously. Everybody was watching Dermod. Except Conway, who was looking at Heraltnor.

The Empire officer did not look very impressive at that moment, Conway thought. He looked like a very ordinary, graying, middle-aged man with a heavy chin and worry-lines around his eyes. In comparison to Dermod's trim green uniform with its quietly impressive load of insignia the shapeless, white garment issued to DBDG patients put Heraltnor at somewhat of a disadvantage. As the silence dragged on Conway wondered whether they would salute each other or just nod.

But they did better than either, they shook hands.

* * *

There was an initial period of suspicion and mistrust, of course. The Empire commander-in-chief was convinced that Heraltnor had been hypnotized at first, but when the investigating party of Empire officers landed on Sector General after the cease fire the distrust diminished rapidly to zero. For Conway the only thing which diminished was his worries regarding wards being opened to space. There was still too much for his staff and himself to do, even though engineers and medical officers from the Empire fleet were doing all they could to put Sector General together again. While they worked the first trickle of the evacuated staff began to return, both medical and maintenance, and the Translator computer went back into operation. Then five weeks and six days after the cease fire the Empire fleet left the vicinity of the hospital. They left their wounded behind them, the reasons being that they were getting the best possible treatment where they were, and that the fleet might have more fighting to do.

In one of the daily meetings with the hospital authorities—which still consisted of O'Mara and Conway since nobody more senior to them had come with the recent arrivals—Dermod tried to put a complex situation into very simple terms.

"... Now that the Imperial citizens know the truth about Etla among other things," he said seriously, "the Emperor and his administration are virtually extinct. But things are still very confused in some sectors and a show of force will help stabilize things. I'd like it to be just a show of force, which is why I talked their commander into taking some of our cultural contact and sociology people with him. We want rid of the Emperor, but not at the price of a civil war.

"Heraltnor wanted you to go along, too, Doctor. But I told him that ..."

Beside him O'Mara groaned. "Besides saving hundreds of lives," the Chief Psychologist said, "and averting a galaxy-wide war, our miracle-working, brilliant young doctor is being called on to—"

"Stop needling him, O'Mara!" Dermod said sharply. "Those things are literally true, or very nearly so. If he hadn't ..."

"Just force of habit, sir," said O'Mara blandly. "As a head-shrinker I consider it my bounden duty to keep his from swelling ..."

At that moment the main screen behind Dermod's desk, manned by a Nidian Receptionist now instead of a Monitor officer, lit with a picture of a furry Kelgian head. It appeared that there was a large DBLF transport coming in with FGLI and ELNT staff aboard in addition to the Kelgians, eighteen of which were Senior Physicians. Bearing in mind the damaged state of the hospital and the fact that just three locks were in operable condition, the Kelgian on the screen wanted to discuss quarters and assignments *before* landing with the Diagnostician-in-Charge ...

"Thornnastor's still unfit and there are no other ..." Conway began to say when O'Mara reached across to touch his arm.

"Seven tapes, remember," he said gruffly. "Let us not quibble, Doctor."

Conway gave O'Mara a long, steady look, a look which went deeper than the blunt, scowling features and the sarcastic, hectoring voice. Conway was not a Diagnostician—what he had done two months ago had been forced on him, and it had nearly killed him. But what O'Mara was saying—with the touch of his hand and the expression in his eyes, not the scowl on his face and the tone of his voice—was that it would be just a matter of time.

Coloring with pleasure, which Dermod probably put down to embarrassment at O'Mara's ribbing, he dealt quickly with the quartering and duties of the staff on the Kelgian transport, then excused himself. He was supposed to meet Murchison at the recreation level in ten minutes, and she had asked *him* . . .

As he was leaving he heard O'Mara saying morosely, ". . . And in addition to saving countless billions from the horrors of war, I bet he gets the girl, too . . ."

MAJOR
OPERATION

INVADER

Far out on the Galactic Rim, where star systems were widely scattered and the darkness nearly absolute, the tremendous structure which was Sector Twelve General Hospital hung in space. Inside its three hundred and eighty-four levels were reproduced the environments of all the intelligent life-forms known to the Galactic Federation, a biological spectrum ranging from the ultrafrigid methane species through the more normal oxygen- and chlorine-breathing types up to the exotic beings who existed by the direct conversion of hard radiation. In addition to the patients, whose number and physiological classification was a constant variable, there was a medical and maintenance staff who were composed of sixty-odd differing life-forms with sixty different sets of mannerisms, body odors and ways of looking at life.

The staff of Sector General was an extremely able, dedicated, but not always serious group of people who were fanatically tolerant of all forms of intelligent life—had this not been so they could never have served in such a multienvironment hospital in the first place. They prided themselves that no case was too big, too small or too hopeless, and their facilities and professional reputation were second to none. It was unthinkable that one of their number should be guilty of nearly killing a patient through sheer carelessness.

"Obviously the thought isn't unthinkable," O'Mara, the Chief Psychologist, said dryly. "I'm thinking it, reluctantly, and you are also thinking it—if only momentarily. Far worse, Mannon himself is convinced of his own guilt. This leaves me with no choice but to—"

"No!" said Conway, strong emotion overriding his usual respect for authority. "Mannon is one of the best Seniors we have—you know that!

368 · JAMES WHITE

He wouldn't . . . I mean, he isn't the type to . . . He's . . ."

"A good friend of yours," O'Mara finished for him, smiling. When Conway did not reply he went on, "My liking for Mannon may not equal yours, but my professional knowledge of him is much more detailed and objective. So much so that two days ago I would not have believed him capable of such a thing. Now, dammit, uncharacteristic behavior bothers me . . ."

Conway could understand that. As Chief Psychologist, O'Mara's prime concern was the smooth and efficient running of the hospital's medical staff, but keeping so many different and potentially antagonistic life-forms working in harmony was a big job whose limits, like those of O'Mara's authority, were difficult to define. Given even the highest qualities of tolerance and mutual respect in its personnel, there were still occasions when friction occurred.

Potentially dangerous situations arose through ignorance or misunderstanding, or a being could develop a xenophobic neurosis which might affect its efficiency, mental stability, or both. An Earth-human doctor, for instance, who had a subconscious fear of spiders would not be able to bring to bear on one of the insectile Cinrusskin patients the proper degree of clinical detachment necessary for its treatment. It was O'Mara's duty to detect and eradicate such trouble, or to remove the potentially troublesome individuals. This guarding against wrong, unhealthy or intolerant thinking was a duty which he performed with such zeal that Conway had heard him likened to a latter-day Torquemada.

Now it looked as if this paragon of psychologists had been something less than alert. In psychology there were no effects without prior cause and O'Mara must now be thinking that he had missed some small but vital warning signal—a slightly uncharacteristic word or expression or display of temper, perhaps—which should have warned him of trouble developing for Senior Physician Mannon.

The psychologist sat back and fixed Conway with a pair of gray eyes which saw so much and which opened into a mind so keenly analytical that together they gave O'Mara what amounted to a telepathic faculty. He said, "No doubt you are thinking that I have lost my grip. You feel sure that Mannon's trouble is basically psychological and that there is an explanation other than negligence for what happened. You may decide that the recent death of his dog has caused him to go to pieces from sheer grief, and other ideas of an equally uncomplicated and ridiculous nature will occur to you. In my opinion, however, any time spent investigating the psychological aspects of this business will be completely wasted. Doctor Mannon has been subjected to the most exhaustive tests. He is physically sound and as sane as we are. As sane as I am anyway . . ."

"Thank you," said Conway.

"I keep telling you, Doctor," O'Mara said sourly, "my job here is to shrink heads, not swell them. Your assignment, if we can call it that, is strictly unofficial. Since there is no excuse for Mannon's error so far as health and psychoprofile are concerned I want you to look for some other reason—some outside influence, perhaps, of which the Doctor is unaware. Doctor Prilicla observed the incident in question and may be able to help you.

"You have a peculiar mind, Doctor," O'Mara concluded, rising from his seat, "and an odd way of looking at problems. We don't want to lose Doctor Mannon, but if you *do* get him out of trouble the surprise will probably kill me. I mention this so that you will have an added incentive . . ."

Conway left the office, fuming slightly. O'Mara was always flinging his allegedly peculiar mind in his face when the simple truth was that he had been so shy when he had first joined the hospital, especially with nurses of his own species, that he had felt more comfortable in extraterrestrial company. He was no longer shy, but still he numbered more friends among the weird and wonderful denizens of Traltha, Illensa and a score of other systems than beings of his own species. This might be peculiar, Conway admitted, but to a doctor living in a multi-environment hospital it was also a distinct advantage.

Outside in the corridor Conway contacted Prilicla in the other's ward, found that the little empath was free and arranged a meeting for as soon as possible on the Forty-sixth Level, which was where the Hudlar operating theater was situated. Then he devoted a part of his mind to the problem of Mannon while the rest of it guided him toward Forty-six and kept him from being trampled to death en route.

His Senior Physician's armband automatically cleared the way so far as nurses and subordinate grades of doctors were concerned, but there were continual encounters with the lordly and absentminded Diagnosticians who plowed their way through everyone and everything regardless, or with junior members of the staff who happened to belong to a more massive species. Tralthans of physiological classification FGLI—warmblooded oxygen breathers resembling a sort of low-slung, six-legged elephant. Or the Kelgian DBLFs who were giant, silver-furred caterpillars who hooted like a siren when they were jostled whether they were out-ranked or not, or the crab-like ELNTs from Melf IV . . .

The majority of the intelligent races in the Federation were oxygen breathers even though their physiological classifications varied enor-mously, but a much greater hazard to navigation on foot was the entity traversing a foreign level in protective armor. The protection required by a TLTU doctor, who breathed superheated steam and whose gravity and pressure requirements were three times those of the oxygen levels, was a great, clanking juggernaut which was to be avoided at all costs.

At the next intersection lock he donned a lightweight suit and let himself into the yellow, foggy world of the chlorine-breathing Illensans. Here the corridors were crowded with the spiny, membraneous and un-adorned denizens of Illensa while it was the Tralthans, Kelgians and Earth-humans like himself who wore, or in some cases drove, protective armor. The next leg of his journey took him through the vast tank where the thirty-foot long, water-breathing entities from Chalderescol II swam pon-derously through their warm, green world. The same suit served him here and, while the traffic was less dense, he was slowed down considerably through having to swim instead of walk. Despite this he was on the Forty-sixth Level observation gallery, his suit still streaming Chalder water, just fifteen minutes after leaving O'Mara's office, and Prilicla arrived close behind him.

"Good morning, friend Conway," said the little empath as it swung itself deftly onto the ceiling and hung by six fragile, sucker-tipped legs. The musical trills and clicks of its Cinrusskin speech were received by Conway's Translator pack, relayed down to the tremendous computer at the center of the hospital and transmitted back to his earpiece as flat, emotionless English. Trembling slightly, the Cinrusskin went on, "I feel you needing help, Doctor."

"Yes indeed," said Conway, his words going through the same process of Translation and reaching Prilicla as equally toneless Cinrusskin. "It's about Mannon. There was no time to give details when I called you . . ."

"No need, friend Conway," said Prilicla. "On the Mannon incident the grapevine is more than usually efficient. You want to know what I saw and felt, of course."

"If you don't mind," said Conway apologetically.

Prilicla said that it didn't mind. But the Cinrusskin was, in addition to being the nicest entity in the whole hospital, its greatest liar.

Of physiological classification GLNO—insectile, exoskeletal with six pipestem legs and a pair of iridescent and not quite atrophied wings, and possessing a highly developed empathic faculty, only on Cinruss with its one-eighth Earth gravity could a race of insects have grown to such dimensions and in time developed intelligence and a high civilization. But in Sector General Prilicla was in deadly danger for most of its working day. It had to wear gravity nullification devices everywhere outside its quarters because the gravity pull which most beings considered normal would instantly have crushed it flat, and when Prilicla held a conversation with anyone it swung itself out of reach of any thoughtless movement of arm or tentacle which would have caved in its fragile body or snapped off a leg. While accompanying anyone on rounds it usually kept pace with them along the corridor walls or ceiling so as to avoid the same fate.

Not that anyone would have wanted to hurt Prilicla in any way—it was too well liked for that. Prilicla's empathic faculty saw to it that the little being always said and did the right thing to people—being an emotion-sensitive to do otherwise would mean that the feelings of anger or sorrow which its thoughtless action caused would bounce back and figuratively smack it in the face. So the little empath was forced constantly to lie and to always be kind and considerate in order to make the emotional radiation of the people around it as pleasant for itself as possible.

Except when its professional duties exposed it to pain and violent emotion in a patient, or it wanted to help a friend.

Just before Prilicla began its report Conway said, "I'm not sure myself what exactly it is I'm looking for, Doctor. But if you can remember anything unusual about Mannon's actions or emotions, or those of his staff . . ."

With its fragile body trembling with the memory of the emotional gale which had emanated from the now empty Hudlar theater two days ago, Prilicla set the scene as it had been at the beginning of the operation. The little GLNO had not taken the Hudlar physiology tape and so had not been able to view the proceedings with any degree of involvement with the patient's condition, and the patient itself was anesthetized and scarcely radiating at all. Mannon and his staff had been concentrating on their duties with only a small part of their minds free to think or emote about anything else. And then Senior Physician Mannon had his . . . accident. In actual fact it was five separate and distinct accidents.

Prilicla's body began to quiver violently and Conway said, "I . . . I'm sorry."

"I know you are," said the empath, and resumed its report.

The patient had been partially decompressed so that the operative field could be worked more effectively. There was some danger in this considering the Hudlar pulse rate and blood pressure, but Mannon himself had evolved this procedure and so was best able to weigh the risks. Since the patient was decompressed he had had to work quickly, and at first everything seemed to be going well. He had opened a flap of the flexible armor-plating which the Hudlars used for skin and had controlled the subcutaneous bleeding when the first mistake occurred, followed in quick succession by two more. Prilicla could not tell by observation that they were mistakes, even though there was considerable bleeding—it was Mannon's emotional reactions, some of the most violent the empath had ever experienced, which told it that the surgeon had committed a serious and stupid blunder.

There were longer intervals between the two others which followed—Mannon's work had slowed drastically, his technique resembling the first fumblings of a student rather than that of one of the most skillful surgeons in the hospital. He had become so slow that curative surgery was impossible, and he had barely time to withdraw and restore pressure before the patient's condition deteriorated beyond the point of no return.

". . . It was very distressing," Prilicla said, still trembling violently. "He wanted to work quickly, but the earlier mistakes had wrecked his self-confidence. He was thinking twice about doing even the simplest things, things which a surgeon of his experience would do automatically, without thinking."

Conway was silent for a moment, thinking about the horrible situation Mannon had been in. Then he said, "Was there anything else unusual about his feelings? Or those of the theater staff?"

Prilicla hesitated, then said, "It is difficult to isolate subtle nuances of emotion when the source is emoting so . . . so violently. But I received the impression of . . . the effect is hard to describe . . . of something like a faint emotional echo of irregular duration . . ."

"Probably the Hudlar tape," said Conway. "It's not the first time a physiology tape gave me mental double vision."

"That might possibly be the case," said Prilicla. Which, in a being who was invariably and enthusiastically in agreement with whatever was said to it, was as close as the empath could come to a negative reply. Conway began to feel that he might be getting onto something important.

"How about the others?"

"Two of them," said Prilicla, "were radiating the shock-worry-fear combination indicative of a mildly traumatic experience in the recent past. I was in the gallery when both incidents occurred, and one of them gave me quite a jolt..."

One of the nurses had almost had an accident while lifting a tray of instruments. One of them, a long, heavy, Hudlar Type Six scalpel used for opening the incredibly tough skin of that species, had slipped off the tray for some reason. Even a small punctured or incised wound was a very serious matter for a Kelgian, so that the Kelgian nurse had a bad fright when it saw that vicious blade dropping toward its unprotected side. But somehow it had struck in such a way—it was difficult to know how, considering its shape and lack of balance—that it had not penetrated the skin or even damaged the fur. The Kelgian had been relieved and thankful for its good fortune, but still a little disturbed.

"I can imagine," said Conway. "Probably the Charge Nurse read the riot act. Minor errors become major crimes where theater staff are concerned..."

Prilicla's legs began to tremble again, a sign that it was nerving itself for the effort of being slightly disagreeable. It said, "The entity in question was the Charge Nurse. That was why, when the other nurse goofed on an instrument count—there was one too many or too few—the ticking off was relatively mild. And during both incidents I detected the echo effect radiated by Mannon, although in these cases the echo was from the respective nurses."

"We may have something there!" said Conway excitedly. "Did the nurses have any physical contact with Mannon?"

"They were assisting him," said Prilicla, "and they were all wearing protective suits. I don't see how any form of parasitic life or bacteria could have passed between them, if that is the idea which is making you feel so excited and hopeful just now. I am very sorry, friend Conway, but this echo effect, while peculiar, does not seem to me to be important."

"It's something they had in common," said Conway.

"Yes," Prilicla said, "but the something did not have self identity, it was not an individual. Just a very faint emotional echo of the feelings of the people concerned."

"Even so," said Conway.

Three people had made mistakes or had had accidents in this theater two days ago, all of whom had radiated an odd emotional echo which Prilicla did not consider important. The presence of an accident-prone Conway ruled out because O'Mara's screening methods were too efficient in that respect. But suppose Prilicla was wrong and something had got in the theater or into the hospital, some form of life which was difficult to detect and outside their present experience. It was well known that when odd things happened in Sector General the reasons very often were found outside the hospital. At the moment, however, he hadn't enough evidence to form even a vague theory and the first job should be to gather some—even though he might not recognize it if he tripped over it with both feet.

"I'm hungry and it's high time we talked to the man himself," said Conway suddenly. "Let's find him and invite him to lunch."

The dining hall for the oxygen-breathing Medical and Maintenance staff occupied one complete level, and at one time it had been sectioned off into physiological types with low dividing ropes. But this had not worked out too well because the diners very often wanted to talk shop with other-species colleagues or they found that there were no vacant places in their own enclosure and space going to waste in that of another life-form. So it was no surprise when they arrived to find that they had the choice of sitting at an enormous Tralthan table with benches which were a shade too far from the table's edge and one in the Melfan section which was cozier but whose chairs resembled surrealistic wastepaper baskets. They insinuated themselves into three of the latter and began the usual preliminaries to ordering.

"I'm just myself today," said Prilicla in answer to Conway's question. "The usual, if you please."

Conway dialed for the usual, which was a triple helping of Earth-type spaghetti, then looked at Mannon.

"I've an FROB *and* an MSVK beastie riding me," the other Senior said gruffly. "Hudlars aren't persnickity about food, but those blasted MSVKs are offended by anything which doesn't look like birdseed! Just get me something nutritious, but don't tell me what it is and put it in about three sandwiches so's I won't see what it is. . . ."

While they were waiting for the food to arrive Mannon spoke quietly, the normality of his tone belied by the fact that his emotional radiation was making Prilicla shake like a leaf. He said, "The grapevine has it that you two are trying to get me out of this trouble I'm in. It's nice of you, but you're wasting your time."

"We don't think so and neither does O'Mara," said Conway, shading the truth considerably. "O'Mara gives you a clean bill of mental and physical health, and he said that your behavior was most uncharacteristic. There must be some explanation, some environmental influence, perhaps, or something whose presence or absence would make you behave, if only momentarily, in an uncharacteristic fashion . . ."

Conway outlined what little they knew to date, trying to sound more hopeful than he really felt, but Mannon was no fool.

"I don't know whether to feel grateful for your efforts or concerned for your respective mental well-beings," Mannon said when he had finished. "These peculiar and rather vague mental effects are . . . are . . . at the risk of offending Daddy-longlegs here I would suggest that any peculiarities there are lie in your own minds—your attempts to find excuses for me are becoming ridiculous!"

"Now *you're* telling me I have a peculiar mind," said Conway.

Mannon laughed quietly, but Prilicla was trembling worse than ever.

"A circumstance, person or thing," Conway repeated, "whose presence or absence might effect your—"

"Ye Gods!" Mannon burst out. "You're not thinking of the dog!"

Conway had been thinking about the dog, but he was too much of a moral coward to admit it right then. Instead he said, "Were you thinking about it during that op, Doctor?"

"No!" said Mannon.

There was a long, awkward silence after that, during which the service panels slid open and their orders rose into view. It was Mannon who spoke first.

"I liked that dog," he said carefully, "when I was myself, that is. But for the past four years I've had to carry MSVK and LSVO tapes permanently in connection with my teaching duties, and recently I've needed the Hudlar and Melfan tapes for a project Thornnastor invited me to join. They were in permanent occupation as well. With my brain thinking that it was five different people, five *very* different people . . . Well, you know how it is . . ."

Conway and Prilicla knew how it was only too well.

The Hospital was equipped to treat every known form of intelligent life, but no single person could hold in his brain even a fraction of the physiological data necessary for this purpose. Surgical dexterity was a matter of ability and training, but the complete physiological knowledge of any patient was furnished by means of an Educator Tape, which was simply the brain record of some great medical genius belonging to the same or a similar species to that of the patient being treated. If an Earth-human doctor had to treat a Kelgian patient he took a DBLF physiology tape until treatment was completed, after which it was erased. The sole exceptions to this rule were Senior Physicians with teaching duties and the Diagnosticians.

A Diagnostician was one of the élite, a being whose mind was considered stable enough to retain permanently six, seven or even ten physiology tapes simultaneously. To their data-crammed minds was given the job of original research in xenological medicine and the treatment of new diseases in hitherto unknown life-forms.

But the tapes did not impart only physiological data, the complete memory and personality of the entity who had possessed that knowledge was transferred as well. In effect a Diagnostician subjected himself or itself voluntarily to the most drastic form of schizophrenia. The entities apparently sharing one's mind could be unpleasant, aggressive individuals—geniuses were rarely charming people—with all sorts of peeves and phobias. These did not become apparent only at mealtimes. The worst period was when the possessor of the tapes was relaxing prior to sleeping.

Alien nightmares were really nightmarish and alien sexual fantasies and wish-fulfillment dreams were enough to make the person concerned wish, if he were capable of wishing coherently for anything, that he was dead.

". . . Within the space of a few minutes," Mannon continued, "she would change from being a ferocious, hairy beast intent on tearing out my belly feathers to a brainless bundle of fur which would get squashed by one of my six feet if it didn't get to blazes out of the way, to a perfectly ordinary dog wanting to play. It wasn't fair to the mutt, you know. She was a very old and confused dog toward the end, and I'm more glad than sorry that she died.

"And now let's talk and emote about some other subject," Mannon ended briskly. "Otherwise we will completely ruin Prilicla's lunch . . ."

He did just that for the remainder of the meal, discussing with apparent relish a juicy piece of gossip originating in the SNLU section of the methane wards. How anything of a scandalous nature could occur between two intelligent crystalline life-forms living at minus one hundred and fifty degrees Centigrade was something which puzzled Conway, or for that matter why their moral shortcomings were of such interest to a warm-blooded oxygen-breather. Unless this was one of the reasons why

Senior Physician Mannon was so far on the way to becoming a Diagnostician himself.

Or had been.

If Mannon was assisting Thornnastor, the Diagnostician-in-Charge of Pathology (and as such the hospital's senior Diagnostician) in one of that august being's projects, then Mannon *had* to be in good physical and mental shape—Diagnosticians were terribly choosy about their assistants. And everything the Chief Psychologist had told him pointed the same way. But then what *had* got into Mannon two days ago to make him behave as he had?

As the others talked Conway began to realize that the sort of evidence he needed might be difficult to gather. The questions he had to ask would require tact and some sort of theory to explain his line of investigation. His mind was still miles away when Mannon and Prilicla began rising to go. As they were leaving the table Conway moved closer to Prilicla and asked softly, "Any echoes, Doctor?"

"Nothing," said Prilicla, "nothing at all."

Within seconds their places at the table were taken by three Kelgians who draped their long, silvery, caterpillar bodies over the backs of the ELNT chairs so that their forward manipulators hung over the table at a comfortable distance for eating. One of the three was Naydrad, the Charge Nurse on Mannon's theater staff. Conway excused himself to his friends and returned quickly to the table.

When he had finished talking it was Naydrad who spoke first. It said, "We would like to help, sir, but this is an unusual request. It involves, at very least, the wholesale betrayal of confidence . . ."

"We don't want names," said Conway urgently. "The mistakes are required for statistical purposes only and no disciplinary action will be taken. This investigation is unofficial, an idea of my own. Its only purpose is to help Doctor Mannon."

They were all keen to help their Chief, naturally, and Conway went on, "To summarize, if we accept that Senior Physician Mannon is incapable of gross professional misconduct—which we all do—then we must assume that his error was caused by an outside influence. Since there is strong evidence that the Doctor was mentally stable and free from all disease or physical malfunction it follows that we are looking for an outside influence—or more accurately, indications of the presence of an outside influence—which may be nonphysical.

"Mistakes by a person in authority are more noticeable, and serious, than those of a subordinate," Conway went on, "but if these errors are being caused by an outside agency they should not be confined only to senior staff, and it is here that we need data. There are bound to be mistakes, especially among trainee staff—we all realize this. What we must know is whether there has been an overall or local increase in the number of these minor errors and, if so, exactly where and when they occurred."

"Is this matter to be kept confidential?" one of the Kelgians asked.

Conway nearly choked at the idea of anything being kept confidential in this place, but the sarcasm was, fortunately, filtered out of his tone by the process of Translation.

"The more people gathering data on this the better," he said. "Just use your discretion . . ."

A few minutes later he was at another table saying much the same thing, then another and another. He would be late back to his wards today, but fortunately he had a couple of very good assistants—the type who just loved it when they had a chance to show how well they could do without him.

During the remainder of the day there was no great response, nor had he expected any, but on the second day nursing staff of all shapes and species began approaching him with elaborate secrecy to tell of incidents which invariably had happened to a third party. Conway noted times and places carefully while showing no curiosity whatever regarding the identities of the persons concerned. Then on the morning of the third day Mannon sought him out during his rounds.

"You're really working at this thing, aren't you, Conway," Mannon said harshly, then added, "I'm grateful. Loyalty is nice even when it's misplaced. But I wish you would stop. You're heading for serious trouble."

Conway said, "You're the one in trouble, Doctor, not me."

"That's what you think," said Mannon gruffly. "I've just come from O'Mara's office. He wants to see you. Forthwith."

A few minutes later Conway was being waved into the inner sanctum by one of O'Mara's assistants, who was trying hard to warn him of impending doom with his eyebrows while commiserating with him by turning down the corners of his mouth. The combination of expressions looked so ridiculous that Conway found himself inside before he realized it, facing a very angry O'Mara with what must have been a stupid grin on his face.

The psychologist stabbed a finger in the direction of the least comfortable chair and shouted, "What the blazes do you mean by infesting the hospital with a disembodied intelligence?"

"What . . . ?" began Conway.

". . . Are you trying to make a fool of yourself?" O'Mara stormed on, disregarding him. "Or make a fool out of *me*? Don't interrupt! Granted you're the youngest Senior in the place and your colleagues—none of whom specialize in applied psychology, let me add—think highly of you. But such idiotic and irresponsible behavior is worthy only of a patient in the psychiatric wards!

"Junior staff discipline is going to pot, thanks to you," O'Mara went on, a little more quietly. "It is now becoming the done thing to make mistakes! Practically every Charge Nurse in the place is screaming for me—me!—to get rid of the thing! All *you* did was invent this invisible, undetectable, insubstantial monster—apparently the job of getting rid of it is the responsibility of the Chief Psychologist!"

O'Mara paused to catch his breath, and when he continued his tone had become quiet and almost polite. He said, "And don't think that you are fooling anyone. Boiled down to its simplest terms, you are hoping that if enough other mistakes are made your friend's will pass relatively unnoticed. And stop opening and closing your mouth—your turn to talk will come! One of the aspects of this whole situation which really troubles me is that I share responsibility for it in that I gave you an insoluble problem hoping that you might attack it from a new angle—an angle which might give a partial solution, enough to let our friend off the hook. Instead you created a new and perhaps worse problem!

"I may have exaggerated things a little because of excusable annoyance, Doctor," O'Mara went on quietly, "but the fact remains that you may be in serious trouble over this business. I don't believe that the nursing staff will deliberately make mistakes—at least, not of the order which would endanger their patients. But *any* relaxation of standards is dangerous, obviously. Do you begin to see what you've been doing, Doctor?"

"Yes, sir," said Conway.

"I see that you do," O'Mara said with uncharacteristic mildness. "And now I would like to know why you did it. Well, Doctor?"

Conway took his time about answering. This was not the first time he had left the Chief Psychologist's office with his ego singed around the edges, but this time it looked serious. The generally held opinion was that when O'Mara was not unduly concerned over, or in some cases when he actually liked an individual, the psychologist felt able to relax with them and be his bad-tempered, obnoxious self, but when O'Mara became quiet and polite and not at all sarcastic, when he began treating a person as a patient rather than a colleague in other words, that person was in trouble up to his or its neck.

Finally, Conway said, "At first it was simply a story to explain why I was being so nosy, sir. Nurses don't tell tales and it might have looked as if that was what I wanted them to do. All I did was suggest that as Doctor Mannon was in all respects fit, outside physical agencies such as e-t bacteria or parasites and the like were ruled out because of the thoroughness of our aseptic procedures. You, sir, had already reassured us regarding his mental condition. I postulated an . . . an outside, nonmaterial cause which might or might not be consciously directed.

"I haven't anything so definite as a theory about it," Conway went on quickly. "Nor did I mention disembodied intelligences to anyone, but something odd happened in that theater, and not only during the time of Mannon's operation . . ."

He described the echo effect Prilicla had detected while monitoring Mannon's emotional radiation, and the similar effect when Naydrad had had the accident with the knife. There was also the later incident of the Melfan intern whose sprayer wouldn't spray—their mandibles weren't suited to surgical gloves so that they painted them with plastic before an op. When the intern had tried to use the sprayer it oozed what the Melfan described as metallic porridge. Later the sprayer in question could not be found. Perhaps it had never existed. And there were other peculiar incidents. Mistakes which seemed a little too simple for trained staff to make—errors in instrument counts, dropping things, and all seeming to involve a certain amount of temporary mental confusion and perhaps outright hallucination.

". . . So far there has not been enough to make a statistically meaningful sample," Conway went on, "but they are enough to make me curious. I'd give you their names if I wasn't sworn to keep them confidential, because I think *you* would be interested in the way they describe some of these incidents."

"Possibly, Doctor," said O'Mara coldly. "On the other hand I might not want to lend my professional support to a figment of your imagination by investigating such trivia. As for the near-accidents with scalpels and the other mistakes, it is my opinion that some people are lucky, others a little bit stupid at times, while others are fond of pulling other peoples' legs. Well, Doctor?"

Conway took a firmer grip on the arms of his chair and said doggedly, "The dropped scalpel was an FROB Type Six, a very heavy, unbalanced instrument. Even if it had struck handle first it would have spun into Naydrad's side a few inches below the point of impact and caused a deep and serious wound—if the blade had any actual physical existence at all! This is something I'm beginning to doubt. That is why I think we should widen the scope of this investigation. May I have permission to see Colonel Skempton and if necessary contact the Corps survey people, to check on the origins of recent arrivals?"

The expected explosion did not come. Instead O'Mara's voice sounded almost sympathetic as he said, "I cannot decide whether you are honestly convinced that you're onto something or simply that you've gone too far to back down without looking ridiculous. So far as I'm concerned you couldn't look anymore ridiculous at the moment. You should not be afraid to admit you were wrong, Doctor, and begin repairing some of the damage to discipline your irresponsibility has caused."

O'Mara waited precisely ten seconds for Conway's reply, then he said, "Very well, Doctor. See the Colonel. And tell Prilicla I'm rearranging its schedule—it may be helpful to have your emotional echo-detector available at all times. Since you insist on making a fool of yourself you might as well do it properly. Afterward—well, we will be very sorry to see Mannon go, and in all honesty I suppose I must say the same about you. Both of you are likely to be on the same ship out . . ."

A few seconds later he was dismissed very quietly.

Mannon himself had accused Conway of misguided loyalty and now O'Mara had suggested that his present stand was the result of not wanting to admit to a mistake. He had been given an out, which he had refused to take, and now the thought of service in the smaller multienvironment hospital, or even a planet-side establishment where the arrival of an e-t patient would be considered a major event, was beginning to come home to him. It gave him an unpleasantly gone feeling in the abdominal area. Maybe he *was* basing his theory on too little evidence and refusing to admit it. Maybe the odd errors were part of an entirely different puzzle, with no connection whatever with Mannon's trouble. As he strode along the corridors, taking evading action or being evaded every few yards, the impulse grew in him to rush back to O'Mara, say yes to everything, apologize abjectly and promise to be a good boy. But by the time he was ready to give into it he was outside Colonel Skempton's door.

Sector General was supplied and to a large extent maintained by the Monitor Corps, which was the Federation's executive and law-enforcement arm. As the senior Corps officer in the hospital, Colonel Skempton handled traffic to and from the hospital in addition to a horde of other administrative details. It was said that the top of his desk had never been visible since the day it arrived. When Conway was shown in he looked up, said "Good morning," looked down at his desk and said, "Ten minutes . . ."

It took much longer than ten minutes. Conway was interested in traffic from odd points of origin, or ships which had called at such places. He wanted data on the level of technology, medical science and physiological classification of their inhabitants—especially if the psychological sciences or psionics were well-developed or if the incidence of mental illness was unusually high. Skempton began excavating among the papers on his desk.

But the supply ship, ambulances and ships pressed into emergency service as ambulances which had arrived during the past few weeks had originated from Federation worlds which were well known and medically innocuous. All except one, that was—the Cultural Contact and Survey vessel *Descartes*. It had landed, very briefly, on a most unusual planet. She was on the ground, if it could be called that, for only a few minutes. None of the crew had left the ship, the air-locks had remained sealed and the samples of air, water and surface material were drawn in, analyzed and declared interesting but harmless. The pathology department of the hospital had made a more thorough analysis and had had the same thing to say. *Descartes* had called briefly to leave the samples and a patient . . .

"A *patient*!" Conway almost shouted when the Colonel reached that point in his report. Skempton would not need an empathic faculty to know what he was thinking.

"Yes, Doctor, but don't get your hopes up," said the Colonel. "He had nothing more exotic than a broken leg. And despite the fact e-t bugs find it impossible to live on beings of another species, a fact which simplifies the practice of extraterrestrial medicine no end, ship medics are constantly on the lookout for the exception which is supposed to prove the rule. In short, he was suffering only from a broken leg."

"I'd like to see him anyway," said Conway.

"Level Two-eighty-three, Ward Four, name of Lieutenant Harrison," said Skempton. "Don't slam the door."

But the meeting with Lieutenant Harrison had to wait until late that evening, because Prilicla's schedule needed time to rearrange and Conway himself had duties other than the search for hypothetical disembodied intelligences. The delay, however, was fortunate because much more information was made available to him, gathered during rounds and at mealtimes, even though the data was such that he did not quite know what to do with it.

The number of boobs, errors and mistakes was surprising, he suspected, only because he had not interested himself in such things before now. Even so, the silly, stupid mistakes he encountered, especially among the highly trained and responsible OR staff, were definitely uncharacteristic, he thought. And they did not form the sort of pattern he had expected. A plot of times and places should have shown an early focal point of this hypothetical mental contagion becoming more widespread as the disease progressed. Instead the pattern indicated a single focus moving within a certain circumscribed area—the Hudlar theater and its immediate surroundings. Whatever the thing was, if there was anything there at all, it was behaving like a single entity rather than a disease.

". . . Which is ridiculous!" Conway protested. "Even *I* didn't seriously believe in a disembodied intelligence—it was a working hypothesis only. I'm not *that* stupid!"

He had been filling Prilicla in on the latest developments while they were on the way to see the Lieutenant. The empath kept pace with him along the ceiling for a few minutes in silence, then said inevitably, "I agree."

Conway would have preferred some constructive objections for a change, so he did not speak again until they had reached 283-Four. This was a small private ward off a larger e-t compartment and the Lieutenant seemed glad to see them. He looked, and Prilicla said that he felt, bored.

"Apart from some temporary structural damage you are in very good shape, Lieutenant," Conway began, just in case Harrison was worried by the presence of two Senior Physicians at his bed. "What we would like to talk about is the events leading up to your accident. If you wouldn't mind, that is."

"Not at all," said the Lieutenant. "Where do you want me to start? With the landing, or before that?"

"If you were to tell us a little about the planet itself first," suggested Conway.

The Lieutenant nodded and moved his headrest to a more comfortable angle for conversation, then began, "It was a weirdie. We had been observing it for a long time from orbit . . ."

Christened Meatball because Captain Williamson of the cultural contact and survey vessel *Descartes* had declined, very forcibly, to have such an odd and distasteful planet named after him, it had to be seen to be believed—and even then it had been difficult for its discoverers to believe what they were seeing.

Its oceans were a thick, living soup and its land masses were almost completely covered by slow-moving carpets of animal life. In many areas there were mineral outcroppings and soil which supported vegetable life, and other forms of vegetation grew in the water, on the sea bed, or rooted itself on the organic land surface. But the greater part of the land surface was covered by a layer of animal life which in some places was half a mile thick.

This vast organic carpet was subdivided into strata which crawled and slipped and fought their way through each other to gain access to necessary topsurface vegetation or subsurface minerals or simply to choke off and cannibalize each other. During the course of this slow, gargantuan struggle these living strata heaved themselves into hills and valleys, altering the shapes of lakes and coastlines and changing the whole topography of their world from month to month.

It had been generally agreed by the specialists on *Descartes* that if the planet possessed intelligent life it should take one of two forms, and both were a possibility. The first type would be large—one of the tremendous, living carpets which might be capable of anchoring itself to the underlying rock while pushing extensions toward the surface for the purpose of breathing, ingestion, and the elimination of wastes. It should also possess a means of defense around its far-flung perimeter to keep less intelligent strata creatures from insinuating themselves between it and the ground below or from slipping over it and cutting off light, food, and air as well as discouraging sea predators large and small who seemed to nibble at it around the clock.

The second possibility might be a fairly small life-form, smooth-skinned, flexible, and fast enough to allow them to live inside or between the strata creatures and avoid the ingestive processes of the strata beasts whose movements and metabolism were slow. Their homes, which would have to be safe enough to protect their young and develop their culture and science, would probably be in caves or tunnel systems in the underlying rock.

If either life-form existed on the planet it was unlikely that they would possess an advanced technology. Certainly the larger, complex type of industrial machinery was impossible on this heaving world. Tools, if they developed them at all, would be small, handy and unspecialized, but the chances were that it would be a very primitive society with no roots.

"They might be strong in the philosophical sciences," Conway broke in at that point. Prilicla moved closer, trembling with Conway's excitement as well as its own.

Harrison shrugged. "We had a Cinrusskin with us," he said, looking at Prilicla. "It reported no indication of the more subtle type of emoting usually radiated by intelligent life, but the aura of hunger and raw, animal ferocity emanating from the whole planet was such that the empath had to be kept under sedation most of the time. This background radiation might well have concealed intelligent emoting. The proportion of intelligent life on any given world is only a small proportion of its total life . . ."

"I see," said Conway, disappointed. "How about the landing?"

The Captain had chosen an area composed of some thick, dry, leathery material. The stuff looked dead and insensitive so that the ship's tail-flare should not cause pain to any life in the area, intelligent or otherwise. They landed without incident and for perhaps ten minutes nothing happened. Then gradually the leathery surface below them began to sag, but slowly and evenly so that the ship's gyros had no trouble keeping them level. They began to sink into what was at first a shallow depression and then a low-walled crater. The lips of the crater curled toward them, pressing against the landing legs. The legs were designed to retract telescopically, not fold toward the center line of the ship. The extension mechanism and leg housings began to give, with a noise like somebody tearing sheet metal into small pieces.

Then somebody or something began throwing rocks. To Harrison it had sounded almost as if *Descartes* was sitting atop a volcano in process of erupting. The din was unbelievable and the only way to transmit orders was through the suit radios with the volume turned way up. Harrison was ordered to make a quick damage check of the stern prior to take-off . . .

". . . I was between the inner and outer skin close to the venturi orifice level when I found the hole," the Lieutenant went on quickly. "It was about three inches across and when I started to patch it I found the edges to be slightly magnetized. Before I could finish the Captain decided to take off at once. The crater wall was threatening to trap one of the landing legs. He *did* give us five seconds' warning . . ."

Harrison paused at that point as if to clarify something in his own mind. He said carefully, "There wasn't much danger in this, you understand. We were taking off at about one-and-a-half Gs because we weren't sure whether the crater was a manifestation of intelligence, even hostile intelligence, or the involuntary movement of some dirty great beastie closing its mouth, so we wanted to avoid unnecessary destruction in the area. If I hung onto a couple of supporting struts and had somewhere to brace my feet I'd be all right. But long-duration suits are awkward and five seconds isn't long. I had two good hand-holds and was looking for a bracket which should have been there to brace my foot. Then I saw it, and actually felt my boot touch it, but . . . but . . ."

"You were confused and misjudged the distance," Conway finished for him softly. "Or perhaps you simply imagined it was there."

On the other side of the Lieutenant, Prilicla began to tremble again. It said, "I'm sorry, Doctor. No echoes."

"I didn't expect any," said Conway. "It must have moved on by now."

Harrison looked from one to the other, his expression puzzled and a little hurt. He said, "Maybe I did imagine it was there. Anyhow, it didn't hold me and I fell. The landing leg on my side tore free during the take-off and the wreckage of its housing plugged the interskin space so tightly that I couldn't get out. The engine room control lines passed too close to me for them to risk cutting me out, and our medic said it would be better to come here and let your heavy-rescue people cut a way in. We were coming here with the samples anyway."

Conway looked quickly at Prilicla, then said, "At any time during the trip back did your Cinrusskin empath monitor your emotional radiation?"

Harrison shook his head. "There was no need—I was having pain despite the suit's medication and it would have been unpleasant for an empath. Nobody could get within yards of me . . ."

The Lieutenant paused, then in the tone of one who wished to change an unpleasant subject he said brightly, "We'll send down an unmanned ship next, packed with communications equipment. If that thing is just a big mouth connected with a bigger belly and with no brains at all, at worst we'll lose a drone and it will get indigestion. But if it is intelligent or if there are smaller intelligent beings on the planet who maybe use, or have trained, the bigger beasties to serve them—that is a strong possibility, our cultural contact people say—then they are bound to be curious and try to communicate . . ."

"The imagination boggles," said Conway, smiling. "At the present moment I'm trying hard not to think about the medical problems a beastie the size of a subcontinent would have. But to return to the here and now, Lieutenant Harrison, we are both very much obliged for the information you've given us, and we hope you won't mind if we come again to—"

"Any time," said Harrison. "Glad to help. You see, most of the nurses here have mandibles or tentacles or too many feet . . . No offense, Doctor Prilicla . . ."

"None taken," said Prilicla.

". . . And my ideas regarding ministering angels are rather old-fashioned," he ended as they turned to go. His expression looked decidedly woebegone.

In the corridor Conway called Murchison's quarters. By the time he had finished explaining what he wanted her to do she was fully awake.

"I'm on duty in two hours and don't have any free time for another six," she said, yawning. "And normally I do not spend my precious time off doing a Mata Hari on lonely patients. But if this one has information which might help Doctor Mannon I don't mind at all. I'd do anything for that man."

"How about *me*?"

"For you, dear, almost anything. 'Bye."

Conway racked the handset and said to Prilicla, "*Something* gained entrance to that ship. Harrison suffered the same type of mild hallucination or mental confusion that the OR staff experienced. But I keep thinking about that hole in the outer skin—a disembodied intelligence shouldn't have to make a hole to get in. And those rocks hitting the stern. Suppose this was only a side-effect of the major, nonmaterial influence—a disturbance analogous to the poltergeist phenomena. Where does that leave us?"

Prilicla didn't know.

"I'll probably regret it," said Conway, "but I think I'll call O'Mara . . ."

But it was the Chief Psychologist who did all the talking at first. Mannon had just left his office after having told O'Mara that the Hudlar patient's condition had deteriorated suddenly, necessitating a second operation not later than noon tomorrow. The Senior Physician, it had been obvious, held no hopes for the patient's survival, but had said that what little chance it did have would be fractionally increased if they operated quickly.

O'Mara ended, "This doesn't give you much time to prove your theory, Conway. Now, what did you want to say to me?"

The news about Mannon had put Conway badly off his stride, so that he was woefully aware that his report on the Meatball incident and his ideas regarding it sounded weak and, what was worse where O'Mara was concerned, incoherent. The psychologist had little patience with people who did not think clearly and say exactly what they meant.

"... And the whole affair is so peculiar," he concluded awkwardly, "that I'm almost convinced now that the Meatball business has nothing to do with Mannon's trouble, except that ..."

"Conway!" said O'Mara sharply. "You're talking in circles, dithering! You must realize that if two peculiar events occur with only a small separation in time then the probability is high that they have a common cause. I don't mind too much if your theory is downright ridiculous— at least you arrived at it by a tortuous form of logic—but I *do* mind you ceasing to think at all. Being wrong, Doctor, is infinitely preferable to being stupid!"

For a few seconds Conway breathed heavily through his nose, trying to control his anger enough to reply. But O'Mara saved him the trouble by breaking the connection.

"He was not very polite to you, friend Conway," said Prilicla. "Toward the end he sounded quite bad-tempered. This is a significant improvement over his feelings for you this morning ..."

Conway laughed in spite of himself. He said, "One of these days you will forget to say the right thing, Doctor, and everyone in the hospital will drop dead!"

The galling part of the whole affair was that they did not know what exactly they were looking for, and now their time for finding it had been cut in half. All they could do was to continue gathering information and hope that something would emerge from it. But even the questions sounded nonsensical—variations of "Have you done or omitted to do something during the past few days which might lead you to suspect that something was influencing your mind?" They were loosely worded, silly, almost meaningless questions, but they went on asking them until Prilicla's pencil-thin legs were rubbery with fatigue—the empath's stamina was proportional to its strength, which was practically nonexistent—and it had to retire. Doggedly Conway went on asking them, feeling more tired, angrier and more stupid with every hour which passed.

Deliberately he refrained from contacting Mannon again—the Doctor at that time would, if anything, be a demoralizing influence. He called Skempton to ask if *Descartes'* medical officer had made a report, and was sworn at horribly because it was the middle of the Colonel's night. But he did find out that the Chief Psychologist had called seeking the same information, saying that he preferred his facts to come from the official report rather than through an emotionally involved Doctor with a disembodied ax to grind. Then the totally unexpected happened in that Conway's sources of information went suddenly dry on him.

Apparently O'Mara was bringing in certain operating room staff for their periodic testing before their psych tests were due, and most of them had been people who had been very helpful about admitting their mistakes to Conway. It was not suggested in so many words that Conway had broken confidence and blabbed to O'Mara, but at the same time nobody would talk about anything.

Conway felt weary and discouraged and stupid, but mostly weary. It was too near breakfast time, however, to go to bed.

After his rounds Conway had an early lunch with Mannon and Prilicla, then accompanied the doctor to O'Mara's office while the empath left for the Hudlar theater to monitor the emotional radiation of the staff during their preparations. The Chief Psychologist looked a little tired, which was unusual, and rather grumpy, which was usually a good sign.

"Are you assisting Senior Physician Mannon in this operation, Doctor?"

"No, sir, observing," Conway replied. "But from inside the theater. If anything funny is going on—I mean, the Hudlar tape might confuse me and I want to be as alert as possible—"

"Alert, he says." O'Mara's tone was scathing. "You look asleep on your feet." To Mannon he said, "You will be relieved to know that I, too, am beginning to suspect something funny is going on, and this time I'll be observing from the observation blister. And now if you'll lie on the couch, Mannon, I'll give you the Hudlar tape myself . . ."

Mannon sat on the edge of the low couch. His knees were nearly

level with his chin and he had half-folded his arms across his chest so
that his posture was almost a fetal position, sitting up. When he spoke
his tone was pleading, desperate. He said, "Look. I've worked with empaths and telepaths before. Empaths receive but do not project emotion,
and telepaths can only communicate with other telepaths of their own
species—they've tried occasionally, but all they did was give me a slight
mental itch. But that day in the theater I was in complete mental control
of myself—I am absolutely sure of this! Yet you all keep trying to tell me
that something unsubstantial, invisible and undetectable influenced my
judgment. It would be much simpler if you admitted that this thing you're
looking for is nonexistent as well, but you're all too damned—"

"Excuse me," said O'Mara, pushing Mannon backward and lowering
the massive helmet into position. He spent a few minutes positioning the
electrodes, then switched on. Mannon's eyes began to glaze as the memories and experience of one of the greatest Hudlar physicians who had
ever lived flooded into his brain.

Just before he lost consciousness completely he muttered, "My trouble is that no matter what I say or do, you believe only the best about
me . . ."

Two hours later they were in the theater. Mannon wore a heavy operating suit and Conway a lighter type which relied only on its gravity
neutralizers for protection. The G-plates under the floor were set for a
pull of five gravities, the Hudlar normal, but the pressure was only a
fraction higher than the Earth norm—Hudlars were not unduly bothered
by low pressure and could, in fact, work quite without protection in the
vacuum of space. But if something went disastrously wrong and the patient needed full, home-planet pressure, Conway would have to leave in
a hurry. Conway had a direct line to Prilicla and O'Mara in the observation blister and another, and completely separate, channel linking him
with Mannon and the operating staff.

O'Mara's voice crackled suddenly in his ear-piece. "Prilicla is getting
emotional echoes, Doctor. Also the radiation indicative of a minor error
having been made—minor level anxiety and confusion . . ."

"Yehudi is here," said Conway softly.

"What?"

"The little man who isn't there," Conway replied, and went on, mis-
quoting slightly, "The little man upon the stair. He isn't there again today,
Oh, gee I wish he'd go away . . ."

O'Mara grunted, then said, "Despite what I told Mannon in my office there is still no real proof that anything untoward is happening. My remarks then were designed to help both Doctor and patient by bolstering Mannon's weakening self-confidence—something which they failed to do. So it would be better for Mannon and yourself if your little man came in and introduced himself."

The patient was brought in at that moment and transferred to the table. Mannon's hands, projecting from the heavy arms of the suit, were encased only in thin, transparent plastic, but should full Hudlar pressure become necessary he could snap on heavy gauntlets within a few seconds. But to open a Hudlar at all in these conditions was to cause an immediate decompression, so that the subsequent procedures had to be done quickly.

Physiological classification FROB, the Hudlar was a low, squat, immensely powerful being somewhat reminiscent of an armadillo with a tegument like flexible armor plate. Inside and out the Hudlars were tough—so much so that Hudlar medical science was a almost complete stranger to surgery. If a patient could not be cured by medication very often it could not be cured at all, because surgery on that planet was impracticable if not downright impossible. But in Sector General, where pressure and gravity of any desired combination could be produced at a few minutes notice, Mannon and a few others had been nibbling at the edges of the hitherto impossible.

Conway watched him make a triangular incision in the incredibly tough tegument and clamp back the flap. Immediately a bright yellow, inverted cone of mist flicked into being above the operative field—a fine spray of blood under pressure escaping from the severed capillaries. A nurse quickly interposed a sheet of plastic between the opening and Mannon's visor while another positioned a mirror which gave him an indirect view of the operative field. In four and a half minutes he had controlled the bleeding. He should have done it in two.

Mannon seemed to be reading Conway's mind, because he said, "The first time was faster than this—I was thinking two or three moves ahead, you know how it is. But I found I was making incisions *now* that I shouldn't have made until several seconds later. If it had happened once it would have been bad enough, but five times . . . ! I had to withdraw before I killed the patient there and then.

"And now," he added in a voice thick with self-loathing, "I'm trying to be careful and the result will be the same."

Conway remained silent.

"Such a piddling little growth, too," Mannon went on. "So near the

392 • JAMES WHITE

surface and a natural for the first attempt at Hudlar surgery. Simply cut away the growth, encase the three severed blood vessels in the area with plastic tubing, and the patient's blood pressure and our special clamps should make a perfect seal until the veins regenerate in a few months. But *this* . . . ! Have you ever seen such a botched-up *mess* . . . !"

More than half of the growth, a grayish, spongy mass which seemed to be more than half vegetable, remained in position. Five major blood vessels in the area had been severed—two of necessity, the rest by "accident"—and encased in tubing. But these lengths of artificial vein were too short or insecurely clamped—or perhaps the movement of the heart had pulled one of the vessels partially out of its tube. The only thing which had saved the patient's life had been Mannon's insistence that it was not to be allowed to regain consciousness since the first operation. The slightest physical effort could have pulled one of those vessels free of its tubing and caused a massive internal hemorrhage and, with the tremendous pulse rate and pressure of the Hudlar species, death within a few minutes.

On O'Mara's channel Conway said harshly, "Any echoes? Anything at all?"

"Nothing," said O'Mara.

"This is ridiculous!" Conway burst out. "If there is an intelligence, disembodied or otherwise, it should possess the attributes—curiosity, the ability to use tools, and so on. Now this hospital is a large and interesting place, with no barriers we know of to the movements of the entity we are trying to find. Why then had it stayed in one place? Why didn't it go prowling around *Descartes*? What makes it stay in this area? Is it frightened, or stupid, or disembodied even?

"There is little likelihood of finding a complex technology on Meatball," Conway went on quickly, "but a good chance of them being well advanced in the philosophical sciences. If something physical boarded *Descartes*, there is a definite lower limit to the mass of an intelligent being . . ."

"If you want to ask questions of anyone, Doctor," O'Mara said quietly, "I will throw a little of my weight behind them. But there isn't much time."

Conway thought for a moment, then said, "Thank you, sir. I'd like you to get Murchison for me. She's in—"

"At a time like this," said O'Mara in a dangerous voice, "he wants to call his . . ."

"She's with Harrison at the moment," said Conway. "I want to establish a physical connection between the Lieutenant and this theater, even though he has never been within fifty levels of the place. Would you ask her to ask him..."

It was a long, involved, many-sided question, designed to tell him how a small, intelligent life-form had reached this area without detection. It was also a stupid question because any intelligence which affected the minds of Earth-humans and e-ts alike could not have remained undetected with an empath like Prilicla around. Which left him back where he started with a nonmaterial something which refused, or was incapable of, moving beyond the environs of the theater.

"Harrison says he had lots of delusions during the trip back," O'Mara's voice sounded suddenly. "He says the ship's doctor said this was normal considering all the dope he had in him. He also says he was completely out when he arrived here and doesn't know how or where he came in. And now I suppose we contact Reception, Doctor. I'm patching you in, just in case I ask the wrong questions..."

Seconds later a slow, flat, translated voice which could have belonged to anything said, "Lieutenant Harrison was not processed in the usual way. Being a corpsman whose medical background was known in detail he was admitted to Service Lock Fifteen into the charge of Major Edwards..."

Edwards was not available, but his office promised O'Mara that they would have him in a few minutes.

All at once Conway felt like giving up. Lock Fifteen was too far away—a difficult, complicated journey involving three major changes of environment. For their hypothetical invader, who was also a stranger to the hospital, to find its way to this theater would have necessitated it taking mental control of someone and being carried. But if that was the case Prilicla would have detected its presence. Prilicla could detect *anything* which thought—from the smallest insect to the slow emanations of a mind deeply and totally unconscious. No living thing could shut its mind down completely and still be alive.

Which meant that the invader might not be alive!

A few feet distant Mannon had signaled for a nurse to stand by the pressure cock. A sudden return to Hudlar normal pressure would diminish the violence of any bleeding which might occur, but it would also make it impossible for Mannon to operate without heavy gloves. Not only that, the pressure increase would cause the operative field to subside within the opening, where movement transmitted from the nearby heart would make delicate work impossible. At present, despite the danger of a wrong incision, the complex of blood vessels was distended, separate and relatively motionless.

Suddenly it happened. Bright yellow blood spurted out, so violently that it hit Mannon's visor with an audible slap. Driven by the patient's enormous blood pressure and pulse rate the severed vein whipped about like a miniature unheld hose-pipe. Mannon got to it, lost it, tried again. The spurting became a thin, wavering spray and stopped. The nurse at the pressure cock relaxed visibly while the one at Mannon's side cleaned his visor.

Mannon moved back slightly while the field was sucked clear. Through the visor his eyes glittered oddly in the sweating white mask of his face. Time was important now. Hudlars were tough, but there were limits—they could not stand decompression indefinitely. There would be a gradual movement of body fluid toward the opening in the tegument, a strain on vital organs in the vicinity and an even greater increase in blood pressure. To be successful the operation could not last for much more than thirty minutes and more than half the time had gone merely in opening up the seat of the trouble. Even if the growth was removed, its removal entailed damage to underlying blood vessels which had to be repaired with great care before Mannon withdrew.

They all knew that speed was essential, but to Conway it seemed suddenly as if he was watching a film which was steadily being speeded up. Mannon's hands were moving faster than Conway had ever seen them move before. And faster still . . .

"I don't like this," said O'Mara harshly. "It looks like he's regained his confidence, but more likely that he's ceased caring—about himself, that is. He still cares about the patient, obviously, even though he knows it hasn't much chance. And the tragic thing about it is that it never did have much chance, Thornnastor tells me. If it hadn't been for your hypothetical friend's interference Mannon wouldn't have worried too much about losing this patient—it would have been one of his very few failures. When he made that first slip it wrecked his self-confidence and now he's—"

"Something *made* him slip," said Conway firmly.

"You've tried convincing him of that, with what result?" the psychologist snapped back. He went on, "Prilicla is seriously agitated and its shakes are getting worse by the minute. But Mannon is, or was, a pretty stable type—I don't think he'll crack until after the operation. Though with these serious, dedicated types whose profession is their whole life it's hard to say what might happen."

"Edwards here," said a new voice. "What is it?"

"Go ahead, Conway," said the psychologist. "You ask the questions. Right now I've other things on my mind."

The spongy growth had been lifted clear, but a great many small blood vessels had been severed to accomplish this and the job of repairing them would be much more difficult than anything which had gone before. Insinuating the severed ends into the tubing, far enough so that they would not simply squirm out again when circulation was restored, was a difficult, repetitious, nerve-wracking procedure.

There were only eighteen minutes left.

"I remember Harrison well," the distant Edwards replied when Conway had explained what he wanted to know. "His suit was damaged in the leg section only, so we couldn't write it off—those things carry a full set of tools and survival gear and are expensive. And naturally we decontaminated it! The regulations expressly state that—"

"It still may have been a carrier of some kind, Major," Conway said quickly. "How thoroughly did you carry out this decon—"

"Thoroughly," said the Major, beginning to sound annoyed. "If it was carrying any kind of bug or parasite it is defunct now. The suit together with all its attachments was sterilized with high-pressure steam and irradiated—it went through the same sterilization procedure as your surgical instruments, in fact. Does that satisfy you, Doctor?"

"Yes," said Conway softly. "Yes indeed."

He now had the link-up between Meatball and the operating theater, via Harrison's suit and the sterilization chamber. But that wasn't all he had. He had Yehudi!

Beside him Mannon had stopped. The surgeon's hands were trembling as he said desperately, "I need eight pairs of hands, or instruments that can do eight different operations at once. This isn't going well, Conway. Not well at all . . ."

"Don't do *anything* for a minute, Doctor," Conway said urgently, then began calling out instructions for the nurses to file past him carrying their instrument trays. O'Mara started shouting to know what was going on, but Conway was concentrating too hard to answer him. Then one of the Kelgian nurses made a noise like a foghorn breathing in, the DBLF equivalent of a shriek of surprise, because suddenly there was a medium-sized box spanner among the forceps on her tray.

"You won't believe this," said Conway joyfully as he carried the—thing—to Mannon and placed it in the surgeon's hands, "but if you'll just listen for a minute and then do as I tell you . . ."

Mannon was back at work in less than a minute.

Hesitantly at first, but then with growing confidence and speed, he resumed the delicate repair work. Occasionally he whistled through his teeth or swore luridly, but this was normal behavior for Mannon during a difficult op which was promising to go well. In the observation blister Conway could see the happily scowling, baffled face of the Chief Psychologist and the fragile, spidery body of the empath. Prilicla was still trembling, but very slowly. It was a type of reaction not often seen in a Cinrusskin off its native planet, indicating a nearby source of emotional radiation which was intense and altogether pleasant.

After the operation they had all wanted to question Harrison about Meatball, but before they could do so Conway had first to explain what had happened again to the Lieutenant.

". . . And while we still have no idea what they look like," Conway was saying, "we do know that they are highly intelligent and in their own fashion technically advanced. By that I mean they fashion and use tools . . ."

"Indeed yes," said Mannon dryly, and the thing in his hand became a metallic sphere, a miniature bust of Beethoven and a set of Tralthan dentures. Since it had become certain that the Hudlar would be another one of Mannon's successes rather than a failure he had begun to regain his sense of humor.

". . . But the tool-making stage must have followed a long way after the development of the philosophical sciences," Conway went on. "The imagination boggles at the conditions in which they evolved. These tools are not designed for manual use, the natives may not possess hands as we know them. But they have *minds* . . . !"

Under the mental control of its owner the "tool" had cut a way into *Descartes* beside Harrison's station, but during the sudden takeoff it had been unable to get back and a new source of mental control, the Lieutenant, had unwittingly taken over. It had become the foothold which Harrison had needed so badly, only to give under his weight because it had not really been part of the ship's structure. When the attachments of Harrison's suit had been sterilized in the same room as the surgical instruments and when a nurse had come looking for a certain instrument for the theater, it again became what was wanted.

From then on there was confusion over instrument counts and falling scalpels which did not cut and sprayers which behaved oddly indeed, and Mannon had used a knife which had followed his mind instead of his hands, with near-fatal results for the patient. But the second time it happened Mannon knew that he was holding a small, unspecialized, all-purpose tool which was subject to mental as well as manual control, and some of the shapes he had made it take and the things he had made it do would make Conway remember that operation for the rest of his life.

"... This ... gadget ... is probably of great value to its owner," Conway finished seriously. "By rights we should return it. But we need it here, many more of them if possible! Your people have got to make contact and set up trade relations. There's bound to be something we have or can do that they want ..."

"I'd give my right arm for one," said Mannon, then added, grinning, "My right leg, anyway."

The Lieutenant returned his smile. He said, "As I remember the place, Doctor, there was no shortage of raw meat."

O'Mara, who had been unusually silent until then, said very seriously, "Normally I am not a covetous man. But consider the things this hospital could *do* with just ten of those things, or even five. We have one and, if we were doing the right thing, we would put it back where we found it—obviously a tool like this is of enormous value. This means that we will have to buy or conduct some form of trade for them, and to do this we must first learn to communicate with their owners."

He looked at each of them in turn, then went on sardonically. "One hesitates to mention such sordid commercial matters to pure-minded, dedicated medical men like yourselves, but I must do so to explain why, when *Descartes* eventually makes contact with the beings who use the tools, I want Conway and whoever else he may select to investigate the medical situation on Meatball.

"Our interest will not be entirely commercial, however," he added quickly, "but it seems to me that if we have to go in for the practice of barter and exchange, the only thing we have to trade is our medical knowledge and facilities."

VERTIGO

I t was perhaps inevitable that when the long-awaited indication of intelligent life at last appeared the majority of the ship's observers were looking somewhere else, that it did not appear in the batteries of telescopes that were being trained on the surface or on the still and cine films being taken by *Descartes'* planetary probes, but on the vessel's close-approach radar screens.

In *Descartes'* control room the Captain jabbed a button on his console and said sharply, "Communications . . . ?"

"We have it, sir," came the reply. "A telescope locked onto the radar bearing—the image is on your repeater screen Five. It is a two- or three-stage chemically fueled vehicle with the second stage still firing. This means we will be able to reconstruct its flight path and pinpoint the launch area with fair accuracy. It is emitting complex patterns of radio-frequency radiation indicative of high-speed telemetry channels. The second stage has just cut out and is falling away. The third stage, if it is a third stage, has not ignited . . . It's in trouble!"

The alien spacecraft, a slim, shining cylinder pointed at one end and thickened and blunt at the other, had begun to tumble. Slowly at first but with steadily increasing speed it swung and whirled end over end.

"Ordnance?" asked the Captain.

"Apart from the tumbling action," said a slower, more precise voice, "the vessel seems to have been inserted into a very neat circular orbit. It is most unlikely that this orbit was taken up by accident. The lack of sophistication—relative, that is—in the vehicle's design and the fact that its nearest approach to us will be a little under two hundred miles all point to the conclusion that it is either an artificial satellite or a manned orbiting vehicle rather than a missile directed at this ship.

"If it is manned," the voice added with more feeling, "the crew must be in serious trouble . . ."

"Yes," said the Captain, who treated words like nuggets of some rare and precious metal. He went on, "Astrogation, prepare intersecting and matching orbits, please. Power Room, stand by."

As the tremendous bulk of *Descartes* closed with the tiny alien craft it became apparent that, as well as tumbling dizzily end over end, the other vessel was leaking. The rapid spin made it impossible to say with certainty whether it was a fuel leak from the unfired third stage or air escaping from the command module if it was, in fact, a manned vehicle.

The obvious procedure was to check the spin with tractor beams as gently as possible so as to avoid straining the hull structure, then defuel the unfired third stage to remove the fire hazard before bringing the craft alongside. If the vessel was manned and the leak was of air rather than fuel, it could then be taken into *Descartes'* cargo hold where rescue and first contact proceedings would be possible—at leisure since Meatball's air was suited to human beings and the reverse, presumably, also held true.

It was expected to be a fairly simple rescue operation, at first . . .

"Tractor stations Six and Seven, sir. The alien spacecraft won't stay put. We've slowed it to a stop three times and each time it applies steering thrust and recommences spinning. For some reason it is deliberately fighting our efforts to bring it to rest. The speed and quality of the reaction suggests direction by an on-the-spot intelligence. We can apply more force, but only at the risk of damaging the vessel's hull—it is incredibly fragile by present-day standards, sir."

"I suggest using all necessary force to immediately check the spin, opening its tanks and jettisoning all fuel into space then whisking it into the cargo hold. With normal air pressure around it again there will be no danger to the crew and we will have time to . . ."

"Astrogation, here. Negative to that, I'm afraid, sir. Our computation shows that the vessel took off from the sea—more accurately, from beneath the sea, because there is no visible evidence of floating gantries or other launch facilities in the area. We can reproduce Meatball air because it is virtually the same as our own, but not that animal and vegetable soup they use for water, and all the indications point toward the crew being water breathers."

For a few seconds the Captain did not reply. He was thinking about the alien crew member or members and their reasons for behaving as they were doing. Whether the reason was technical, physiological, psychological or simply alien was, however, of secondary importance. The main thing was to render assistance as quickly as possible.

If his own ship could not aid the other vessel directly it could, in a matter of days, take it to a place which possessed all the necessary facilities for doing so. Transportation itself posed only a minor problem—the spinning vehicle could be towed without checking its spin by attaching a magnetic grapple to its center of rotation, and with the shipside attachment point also rotating so that the line would not twist-shorten and bring the alien craft crashing into *Descartes'* side. During the trip the larger ship's hyper-drive field could be expanded to enclose both vessels.

His chief concern was over the leak and his complete ignorance of how long a period the alien spacecraft had intended to stay in orbit. He had also, if he wanted to establish friendly relations with the people on Meatball, to make the correct decision quickly.

He knew that in the early days of human space flight leakage was a quite normal occurrence, for there had been many occasions when it had been preferable to carry extra air supplies rather than pay the severe weight penalty of making the craft completely airtight. On the other hand the leak and spinning were more likely to be emergency conditions with the time available for their correction strictly limited. Since the alien astronaut or astronauts would not, for some odd reason, let him immobilize their ship to make a more thorough investigation of its condition and because he could not reproduce their environment anyway, his duty was plain. Probably his hesitancy was due to misplaced professional pride because he was passing responsibility for a particularly sticky one to others.

Quickly and with his usual economy of words the Captain issued the necessary orders and, less than half an hour after it had first been sighted, the alien spacecraft was on its way to Sector General.

With quiet insistence the PA was repeating, "Will Senior Physician Conway please contact Major O'Mara . . ."

Conway quickly sized up the traffic situation in the corridor, jumped across the path of a Tralthan intern who was lumbering down on him on six elephantine feet, rubbed fur briefly with a Kelgian caterpillar who was moving in the opposite direction and, while squeezing himself against the wall to avoid being run over by something in a highly refrigerated box on wheels, unracked the hand-set of the communicator.

As soon as he had established contact the PA began insisting quietly that somebody else contact somebody else.

"Are you doing anything important at the moment, Doctor?" asked the Chief Psychologist without preamble. "Engaged on vital research, perhaps, or in performing some life-or-death operation?" O'Mara paused, then added dryly, "You realize, of course, that these questions are purely rhetorical . . ."

Conway sighed and said, "I was just going to lunch."

"Fine," said O'Mara. "In that case you will be delighted to know that the natives of Meatball have put a spacecraft into orbit—judging by its looks it may well be their first. It got into difficulties—Colonel Skempton can give you the details—and *Descartes* is bringing it here for us to deal with. It will arrive in just under three hours and I suggest you take an ambulance ship and heavy rescue gear out to it with a view to extricating its crew. I shall also suggest that Doctors Mannon and Prilicla be detached from their normal duties to assist you, since you three are going to be our specialists in Meatball matters."

"I understand," said Conway eagerly.

"Right," said the Major. "And I'm glad, Doctor, that you realize that there are things more important than food. A less enlightened and able psychologist than myself might wonder at this sudden hunger which develops whenever an important assignment is mentioned. I, of course, realize that this is not an outward symptom of a sense of insecurity but sheer, blasted greed!

"You will have arrangements to make, Doctor," he concluded pleasantly. "Off."

Skempton's office was fairly close so that Conway needed just fifteen minutes—which included the time taken to don a protective suit for the two hundred yards of the journey which lay through the levels of the Illensan chlorine breathers—to reach it.

"Good morning," said Skempton while Conway was still opening his mouth. "Tip the stuff off that chair and sit down. O'Mara has been in touch. I've decided to return *Descartes* to Meatball as soon as it leaves the distressed spacecraft. To native observers it might appear that the vehicle was taken—one might almost say kidnaped—and *Descartes* should be on hand to note reactions, make contact if possible and give reassurances. I'd be obliged if you would extricate, treat and return this patient to Meatball as quickly as possible—you can imagine the boon this would be to our cultural contact people.

"This is a copy of the report on the incident radioed from *Descartes*," the Colonel went on without, apparently, even pausing for breath. "And you will need this analysis of water taken from the sea around the take-off—the actual samples will be available as soon as *Descartes* arrives. Should you need further background information on Meatball or on contact procedures call on Lieutenant Harrison, who is due for discharge now and who will be glad to assist. Try not to slam the door, Doctor."

The Colonel began excavating deeply in the layer of paperwork covering his desk and Conway closed his mouth again and left. In the outer office he asked permission to use the communicator and got to work.

An unoccupied ward in the Chalder section was the obvious place to house the new patient. The giant denizens of Chalderescol II were water breathers, although the tepid, greenish water in which they lived was almost one hundred percent pure compared with the soupy environment of Meatball's seas. The analysis would allow Dietetics and Environmental Control to synthesize the food content of the water—but not to reproduce the living organisms it contained. That would have to wait until the samples arrived and they had a chance to study and breed these organisms, just as the E.C. people could reproduce the gravity and water pressure, but would have to wait for the arrival of the spacecraft to add the finishing touches to the patient's quarters.

Next he arranged for an ambulance ship with heavy rescue equipment, crew and medical support to be made available prior to *Descartes'* arrival. The tender should be prepared to transfer a patient of unknown physiological classification who was probably injured and decompressed and close to terminal by this time, and he wanted a rescue team experienced in the rapid emergency transfer of shipwreck survivors.

Conway was about to make a final call, to Thornnastor, the Diagnostician-in-Charge of Pathology, when he hesitated.

He was not quite sure whether he wanted to ask a series of specific questions—even a series of hypothetical questions—or to indulge in several minutes worrying out loud. It was vitally important that he treat and cure this patient. Quite apart from it being his and the hospital's job to do so, successful treatment would be the ideal way of opening communications with the natives of Meatball and ultimately laying hands on more of those wonderful, thought-controlled surgical instruments.

But what were the owners of those fabulous tools really like? Were they small and completely unspecialized with no fixed physical shape like the tools they used or, considering the mental abilities needed to develop the tools in the first place, were they little more than physically helpless brains dependent on their thought-controlled instruments to feed them, protect them and furnish all their physical needs? Conway badly wanted to know what to expect when the ship arrived. But Diagnosticians, as everyone knew, were unpredictable and even more impatient of muddy or confused thinking than was the Chief Psychologist.

He would be better advised, Conway told himself, to let his questions wait until he had actually seen his patient, which would be in just over an hour from now. The intervening period he would spend studying *Descartes'* report.

And having lunch.

The Monitor Survey cruiser popped into normal space, the alien space-craft spinning like an unwieldy propeller astern, then just as quickly reentered hyperspace for the return trip to Meatball. The rescue tender closed in, snagged the towline which had been left by *Descartes* and fixed the free end to a rotating attachment point of its own.

Spacesuited Doctors Mannon and Prilicla, Lieutenant Harrison and Conway watched from the tender's open airlock.

"It's still leaking," said Mannon. "That's a good sign—there is still pressure inside . . ."

"Unless it's a fuel leak," Harrison said.

"What do you feel?" asked Conway.

Prilicla's fragile, eggshell body and six pipe-stem legs were beginning to quiver violently so it was obvious that it was feeling something.

"The vessel contains one living entity," said Prilicla slowly. "Its emotional radiation is comprised chiefly of fear and feelings of pain and suffocation. I would say that these feelings have been with it for many days—the radiation is subdued and lacking in clarity due to developing unconsciousness. But the quality of that entity's mentation leaves no doubt that it is intelligent and not simply an experimental animal . . ."

"It's nice to know," said Mannon dryly, "that we're not going to all this trouble for an instrument package or a Meatball space puppy . . ."

"We haven't much time," said Conway.

He was thinking that their patient must be pretty far gone by now. It's fear was understandable, of course, and its pain, suffocation and diminished consciousness were probably due to injury, intense hunger and foul breathing water. He tried to put himself in the Meatball astronaut's position.

Even though the pilot had been badly confused by the apparently uncontrollable spinning, the being had deliberately sought to maintain the spin when *Descartes* tried to take it aboard because it must have been smart enough to realize that a tumbling ship could not be drawn into the cruiser's hold. Possibly it could have checked its own spin with steering power if *Descartes* had not been so eager to rush to its aid—but that was simply a possibility, of course, and the spacecraft had been leaking badly as well. Now it was still leaking and spinning and, with its occupant barely conscious, Conway thought he could risk frightening it just a little more by checking the spin and moving the vehicle into the tender and the patient as quickly as possible into the water-filled compartment where they could work on it.

But as soon as the immaterial fingers of the tractor beams reached out an equally invisible force seemed to grip Prilicla's fragile body and shake it furiously.

"Doctor," said the empath, "the being is radiating extreme fear. It is forcing coherent thought from a mind which is close to panic. It is losing consciousness rapidly, perhaps dying . . . Look! It is using steering thrust!"

"*Cut!*" shouted Conway to the tractor beamers. The alien spacecraft, which had almost come to rest, began to spin slowly as vapor jetted from lateral vents in the nose and stern. After a few minutes the jets became irregular, weaker and finally ceased altogether, leaving the vehicle spinning at approximately half its original speed. Prilicla still looked as if its body was being shaken by a high wind.

"Doctor," said Conway suddenly, "considering the kind of tools these people use I wonder if some kind of psionic force is being used against you—you are shaking like a leaf."

When it replied Prilicla's voice was, of course, devoid of all emotion. "It is not thinking directly at anyone, friend Conway," said the empath. "Its emotional radiation is composed chiefly of fear and despair. Perceptions are diminishing and it seems to be struggling to avoid a final catastrophe . . ."

"Are you thinking what I'm thinking?" said Mannon suddenly.

"If you mean am I thinking of setting the thing spinning at full speed again," Conway replied. "The answer is yes. But there's no logical reason for doing so, is there?"

A few seconds later the tractor beam men reversed polarity to increase the vessel's spin. Almost immediately Prilicla's trembling ceased and it said, "The being feels much better now—relatively, that is. Its vitality is still very low."

Prilicla began to tremble again and this time Conway knew that his own feelings of angry frustration were affecting the little being. He tried to make his thinking cooler and more constructive, even though he knew that the situation was essentially the same as it had been when *Descartes* had first tried to aid the Meatball astronaut, that they were making no progress at all.

But there were a few things he could do which would help the patient, however indirectly.

The vapor escaping from the vehicle should be analyzed to see if it was fuel or simply water from the being's life-support system. Much valuable data could be gained from a direct look at the patient—even if it was only possible to see it through the wrong end of a periscope, since the vessel did not possess a direct-vision port. They should also seek means of entering the vessel to examine and reassure the occupant before transferring it to the ambulance and the wards.

Closely followed by Lieutenant Harrison, Conway pulled himself along the towing cable toward the spinning ship. By the time they had gone a few yards both men were turning with the rotating cable so that when they reached the spacecraft it seemed steady while the rest of creation whirled around them in dizzying circles. Mannon stayed in the airlock, insisting that he was too old for such acrobatics, and Prilicla approached the vessel drifting free and using its spacesuit propulsors for maneuvering.

Now that the patient was almost unconscious the Cinrusskin had to be close to detect subtle changes in its emotional radiation. But the long, tubular hull was hurtling silently past the little being like the vanes of some tremendous windmill.

Conway did not voice his concern, however. With Prilicla one did not need to.

"I appreciate your feelings, friend Conway," said Prilicla, "but I do not think that I was born, despite my physiological classification, to be swatted."

At the hull they transferred from the towing cable and used wrist and boot magnets to cling to the spinning ship, noting that the magnetic grapple placed there by *Descartes* had seriously dented the hull plating and that the area was obscured by a fog of escaping vapor. Their own suit magnets left shallow grooves in the plating as well. The metal was not much thicker than paper, and Conway felt that if he made a too-sudden movement he would kick a hole in it.

"It isn't quite as bad as that, Doctor," said the Lieutenant. "In our own early days of spaceflight—before gravity control, hyperspatial travel and atomic motors made considerations of weight of little or no importance—vehicles had to be built as light as possible. So much so that the fuel contents were sometimes used to help stiffen the structure . . ."

"Nevertheless," said Conway, "I feel as if I am lying on very thin ice—I can even hear water or fuel gurgling underneath. Will you check the stern, please. I'll head forward."

They took samples of the escaping vapor from several points and they tapped and sounded and listened carefully with sensitive microphones to the noises coming from inside the ship. There was no response from the occupant, and Prilicla told them that it was unaware of their presence. The only signs of life from the interior were mechanical. There seemed to be an unusually large amount of machinery, to judge from the sounds they could hear, in addition to the gurgling of liquid. And as they moved toward the extremities of the vessel, centrifugal force added another complication.

The closer they moved toward the bow or stern, the greater was the force tending to fling them off the spinning ship.

Conway's head was pointing toward the ship's bow so that the centrifugal force was imposing a negative G on his body. It was not really uncomfortable as yet, however—he felt a little pop-eyed but there was no redding out of vision. His greatest discomfort came from the sight of the ambulance ship, Prilicla and the vast, tubular Christmas tree which was Sector General sweeping around the apparently steady ship's bows. When he closed his eyes the feeling of vertigo diminished, but then he could not see what he was doing.

The farther forward he went the more power his suit magnets needed to hold him against the smooth metal of the ship's hull, but he could not increase the power too much because the thin plating was beginning to ripple under the magnets and he was afraid of tearing open the hull. But a few feet ahead there was a stubby, projecting pipe which was possibly some kind of periscope and he began to slide himself carefully toward it. Suddenly he began to slip forward and grabbed instinctively for the pipe as he slithered past.

The projection bent alarmingly in his hand and he let go hurriedly, noticing the cloud of vapor which had formed around it, and he felt himself being flung away like a stone from a slingshot.

"Where the blazes are you, Doctor?" said Mannon. "Last time around you were there, now you aren't . . ."

"I don't know, Doctor," Conway replied angrily. He lit one of his suit's distress flares and added, "Can you see me now?"

As he felt the tractor beams focus on him and begin to draw him back to the tender, Conway went on, "This is ridiculous! We're taking far too long over what should be a simple rescue job. Lieutenant Harrison and Doctor Prilicla, go back to the tender, please. We'll try another approach."

While they were discussing it Conway had the spacecraft photographed from every angle and had the tender's lab begin a detailed analysis of the samples Harrison and himself had gathered. They were still trying to find another approach when the prints and completed analyzes reached them several hours later.

It had been established that all the leaks in the alien spacecraft were of water rather than fuel, that the water was for breathing purposes only since it did not contain the usual animal and vegetable matter found in the Meatball ocean samples and that, compared with these local samples, its CO_2 content was rather high—the water was, in brief, dangerously stale.

A close study of the photographs by Harrison, who was quite an authority on early spaceflight, suggested that the flared-out stern of the ship contained a heat shield to which was mounted a solid fuel retro pack. It was now plain that, rather than an unignited final stage, the long cylindrical vehicle contained little more than the life-support equipment which, judging by its size, must be pretty crude. Having made this statement the Lieutenant promptly had second, more charitable thoughts and added that while air-breathing astronauts could carry compressed air with them a water breather could not very well compress its water.

The point of the nose cone contained small panels which would probably open to release the landing parachutes. About five feet astern of this was another panel which was about fifteen inches wide and six feet deep. This was an odd shape for an entry and exit hatch for the pilot, but Harrison was convinced that it could be nothing else. He added that the lack of sophistication shown in the vehicle's construction made it unlikely that the exit panel was the outer seal of an airlock, that it was almost certainly a simple hatch opening into the command module.

If Doctor Conway was to open this hatch, he warned, centrifugal force would empty the ship of its water—or to be quite accurate, of half its water—within a few seconds. The same force would see to it that the water in the stern section remained there, but it was almost certain that the astronaut was in the nose cone.

Conway yawned furiously and rubbed his eyes. He said, "I have to see the patient to get some idea of its injuries and to prepare accommodation, Lieutenant. Suppose I cut a way in amidships at the center of rotation. An appreciable quantity of its water has already leaked away and centrifugal force has caused the remainder to be pushed toward the nose and stern, so that the middle of the ship would be empty and the additional loss of water caused by my entry would be slight."

"I agree, Doctor," said Harrison. "But the structure of the ship might be such that you would open a seam into the water-filled sections—it's so fragile there is even the danger that centrifugal force might pull it apart."

Conway shook his head. "If we put a wide, thin-metal band around the waist section, and if the band included a hinged, airtight hatch big enough for a man, we can seal the edges of the band to the ship with fast-setting cement—no welding, of course, as the heat might damage the skin—and rig a temporary airlock over the hatch. That would allow me to get in without—"

"That would be a very tricky job," said Mannon, "on a spinning ship."

Harrison said, "Yes. But we can set up a light, tubular framework anchored to the hull by magnets. The band and airlock could be set up working from that. It will take a little time, though."

Prilicla did not comment. Cinrusskins were notoriously lacking in physical stamina and the little empath had attached itself to the ceiling with six, sucker-tipped legs and had gone to sleep.

Mannon, the Lieutenant and Conway were ordering material and specialized assistance from the Hospital and beginning to organize a work party when the tender's radioman said, "I have Major O'Mara for you on Screen Two."

"Doctor Conway," said the Chief Psychologist, when he was able to see and be seen. "Rumors have reached me that you are trying—and may have already succeeded, in fact—to set up a new record for the length of time taken to transfer a patient from ship to ward. I have no need to remind you of the urgency and importance of this matter, but I will anyway. It is urgent, Doctor, and important. Off."

"You sarcastic . . ." began Conway angrily to the already fading image, then quickly controlled his feelings because they were beginning to make Prilicla twitch in its sleep.

"Maybe," said the Lieutenant, looking speculatively at Mannon, "my leg isn't properly healed since I broke it during that landing on Meatball. A friendly, cooperative doctor might decide to send me back to Level Two-eighty-three, Ward Four."

"The same friendly, helpful doctor," said Mannon dryly, "might decide a certain Earth-human nurse in 283-Four had something to do with your relapse, and he might send you to . . . say, 241-Seven. There is nothing like being fussed over by a nurse with four eyes and far too many legs to cure a man of baying at the moon."

Conway laughed. "Ignore him, Harrison. At times his mind is even nastier than O'Mara's. Right now there isn't anything more we can do and it has been a long, hard day. Let's go to bed before we go to sleep."

Another day went by without any significant progress being made. Because of the need for urgency the team setting up the framework tried to hurry the job, with the result that they lost tools, sections of framework and on several occasions men overboard. The men could be retrieved easily enough by tractor beams, but the tools and framework sections were not equipped with signal flares and were usually lost. Cursing the necessity for having to perform a tricky job of construction on a space-going merry-go-round, the men went back to work.

Progress became much slower but a little more certain, the number of dents and furrows put in the spacecraft's hull by tools and spaceboots had become uncountable, and the fog of water vapor escaping from the vessel continued to increase.

In a desperate attempt to speed things up, and much against Prilicla's wishes, Conway tried slowing the craft's rate of spin again. There were no signs of panic from the occupant this time, the empath reported, because it was too deeply unconscious to care. It added that it could not describe the patient's emotional radiation to anyone but another empath, but that it was its considered professional opinion that if full spin was not restored the patient would die very shortly.

Next day the framework was completed and work started on fitting the metal band which would take the temporary airlock. While the lock structure was going up Conway and Harrison attached safety lines to the framework and examined the hull. The Lieutenant discovered quite a lot about the steering jets and the circuits to the retro pack, while Conway could only stare baffled at the long, narrow exit hatch or stare through the tiny glass port—it was only a few inches in diameter—which showed little more than a shutter which opened and closed rapidly. And it was not until the following day that the Lieutenant and himself were able to enter the alien spacecraft.

Its occupant was still alive, Prilicla said, but only just.

As expected the waist section of the spacecraft was almost empty of water. Centrifugal force had caused it to collect toward the extremities of the ship, but their spotlights reflected off a dazzling fog of water vapor and droplets which, a quick investigation showed, were being stirred up by the operation of a system of sprocket wheels and chain drives that ran the length of the ship.

Moving carefully so as not to snag a hand between a gear wheel and its chain or inadvertently stick a boot through the fragile hull into space, the Lieutenant moved aft while Conway went forward. They did this so as to ensure that the vessel's center of gravity stayed as closely as possible to its center of rotation, for any imbalance introduced now would shake loose the framework and probably tear holes in the sides of the ship.

"I realize that the circulation and purification of water requires heavier hardware than an air recycling system," said Conway, speaking to Harrison and the tender, "but surely there should be a higher proportion of electrical to mechanical systems? I can't move more than a few yards forward and all I can see are gear wheels and chains drives. The circulation system sets up a strong current, as well, and I'm in danger of being drawn into the works."

The fine, ever-present mist of bubbles made it difficult to see clearly, but for a moment he caught a glimpse of something which was not part of the machinery—something that was brown and convoluted and with a suggestion of fronds or short tentacles sprouting from it, something organic. The being was hemmed in on all sides by revolving machinery, and it also seemed to be rotating, but there was so little of its body visible that he could not be sure.

"I see it," said Conway. "Not enough for accurate classification, though. It doesn't seem to be wearing a pressure suit so this must be its equivalent of shirt-sleeve conditions. But we can't get at the brute without tearing its ship apart and killing it in the process." He swore, then went on furiously, "This is ridiculous, insane! I'm supposed to come out here, immobilize the patient, transfer it to a ward and give treatment. But this blasted thing *can't* be immobilized without..."

"Suppose there is something wrong with its life-support system," the Lieutenant broke in. "Something which requires gravity, or artificial gravity in the form of centrifugal force, to restore proper function. If we could somehow repair this malfunctioning equipment..."

"But why?" said Conway suddenly, as a vague idea that had been lurking at the back of his mind began to creep out into the light. "I mean, why should we assume that it is malfunctioning..." He paused, then said, "We'll open the valves of a couple of oxygen tanks in here to freshen up the beastie's air—I mean water. It's only a first-aid measure, I'm afraid, until we're in a position to do something more positive. Then back to the tender, I'm beginning to get some odd ideas about this astronaut and I'd like to test them."

They returned to the control room without taking off their suits, and were met by Prilicla who told them that the patient's condition seemed a little better although it was still unconscious. The empath added that the reason for this might be that the being was injured and in an advanced state of malnutrition as well as having been close to death through asphyxiation. Conway began telling them about his idea and sketching the alien ship as he talked.

"If this is the center of spin," he said when the drawing was complete, "and the distance from that point to the pilot's position is this, and the rate of rotation is this, can you tell me how closely does the apparent gravity in the pilot's position approach that of Meatball itself?"

"Just a minute," said Harrison as he took Conway's pen and began to scribble. A few minutes later—he had taken extra time to double check his calculations—he said, "Very close, Doctor. Identical, in fact."

"Which means," said Conway thoughtfully, "that we have here a beastie which can't, for some very good physiological reason no doubt, live without gravity, for whom weightless conditions are fatal..."

"Excuse me, Doctor," the quiet voice of the radioman cut in. "I have Major O'Mara for you on Screen Two..."

Conway felt the idea which was beginning to take shape at the back of his mind being blown into tatters. *Spin,* he thought furiously, trying to draw it back; *centrifugal force, wheels within wheels!* But the square, craggy features of the Chief Psychologist were filling the screen and it was impossible to think of anything else.

O'Mara spoke pleasantly—a very bad sign. He said, "Your recent activity has been impressive, Doctor—especially when it took the form of man-made meteorite activity in the shape of dropped tools and structural material. But I'm concerned about your patient. We all are—even, and especially, the Captain of *Descartes* who has recently returned to Meatball.

"The Captain has run into trouble," the psychologist continued, "in the shape of three missiles with nuclear warheads which were directed at his ship. One of them went off course and dirtied up a large area of Meatball ocean, and the other two came so close that he had to use full emergency thrust to avoid them. He says that establishing communications and friendly contact with the inhabitants in these circumstances is impossible, that they obviously think he has kidnaped their astronaut for some ghastly purpose of his own, and that the return of the being in a happy and healthy condition is the only means there is of retrieving the situation . . . Doctor Conway, your mouth is open. Either say something or close it!"

"Sorry, sir," said Conway absently. "I was thinking. There is something I would like to try, and perhaps you could help me with it—by getting Colonel Skempton's support, I mean. We're wasting time out here, I realize that now, and I want to bring the spacecraft inside the hospital. Still spinning, of course—at first, anyway. Cargo Lock Thirty is big enough to take it and is close enough to the water-filled corridor leading to the ward we are preparing for this patient. But I'm afraid the Colonel will be a bit sticky about allowing the spacecraft into the hospital."

The Colonel was very sticky indeed, despite Conway's arguments and the support given by O'Mara. Skempton, for the third time, gave a firm and unequivocal negative.

He said, "I realize the urgency of this matter. I fully appreciate its importance to our future hopes of trading with Meatball and I sympathize with your technical problems. But you are not, repeat not, going to bring a chemically powered spacecraft with a live retro pack inside this hospital! If it accidentally ignited we might have a hole blown in the hull which would cause a lethal pressure drop on a dozen levels, or the vehicle might go bulleting into the central computer or gravity-control sections!"

"Excuse me," said Conway angrily, and turned to the Lieutenant. He asked, "Can you ignite that retro pack, working from the ambulance ship, or disconnect it?"

"I probably couldn't disconnect it without inadvertently setting it off and burning myself to a crisp," Harrison replied slowly, "but I know enough to be able to set up a relay which . . . Yes, we could ignite it from this control room."

"Go to it, Lieutenant," said Conway, and returned to the image of Skempton. "I take it, sir, that you have no objection to taking the vessel aboard after its retro pack has been fired? Or to furnishing the special equipment I will need in the cargo lock and ward?"

"The maintenance officer on that level has orders to cooperate," said Skempton. "Good luck, Doctor. Off."

While Harrison set up his relay, Prilicla kept an emotional eye on the patient while Mannon and himself worked out the being's approximate size and weight based on the brief look Conway had had of the astronaut and on the dimensions of its ship. This information would be needed quickly if the special transporter and the rotating operating theater were to be ready in time.

"I'm still here, Doctor," said O'Mara sharply, "and I have a question. Your idea that the being needs gravity, either normal or artificial, to live I can understand, but strapping it onto an elaborate merry go-round . . ."

"Not a merry-go-round, sir," said Conway. "It will be mounted vertically, like a ferris wheel."

O'Mara breathed heavily through his nose. "I suppose you are quite sure that you know what you're doing, Doctor?"

"Well . . ." began Conway.

"Ask a stupid question," said the psychologist, and broke the connection.

It took longer than the Lieutenant had estimated to set up his relay—*everything* took longer than estimated on this assignment!—and Prilicla reported that the patient's condition was rapidly worsening. But at last the spacecraft's retros flared out for the number of seconds necessary to have brought it out of its original orbit and the ambulance ship kept pace with it, spinning it with opposing tractors as soon as thrust disappeared so that the occupant would still have the gravity it needed. There were complications even so. Immediately the retros cut out, panels opened in the nose cone and the landing parachute tumbled out and within seconds the spinning ship had wound the parachute untidily around itself.

The short period of thrust had added to the hull damage as well.

"It's leaking like a sieve!" Conway burst out. "Shoot another magnetic grapple to it. Keep it spinning and get us to Lock Thirty quick! How is the patient?"

"Conscious now," said Prilicla, trembling. "Just barely conscious and radiating extreme fear . . ."

Still spinning, the vehicle was maneuvered into the enormous mouth of Lock Thirty. Inside the lock chamber the artificial gravity grids under the deck were set at neutral so that the weightless conditions of space were duplicated there. Conway's feeling of vertigo, which had been with him since he had first seen the ship, was intensified by the sight of the alien vessel whirling ponderously in the enclosed space, flinging out streamers of coldly steaming water as it spun.

Then suddenly the lock's outer seal clanged shut, the tractors smoothly checked the ship's spin as, simultaneously, the artificial gravity of the deck was brought up to Meatball normal. Within a few seconds the spacecraft was resting horizontally on the deck.

"How is it?" began Conway anxiously.

Prilicla said, "Fear . . . no, extreme anxiety. The radiation is quite strong now—otherwise the being seems all right, or at least improved . . ." The empath gave the impression of not believing its own feelings.

The spacecraft was lifted gently and a long, low trolley mounted on balloon wheels rolled under it. Water began pouring into the lock chamber from the seal which had opened into the adjacent water-filled section. Prilicla ran up the wall and across the ceiling until it was in position a few yards above the nose of the vessel, and Mannon, Harrison and Conway waded, then swam, in the same direction. When they reached it they clustered around the forward section, ignoring the team which was throwing straps around the hull and fastening it to the trolley prior to moving it into the nearby corridor of the water-breathers, while they cut into the thin hull plating and carefully peeled it away.

Conway insisted on extreme care during this operation so as to avoid damaging the life-support machinery.

Gradually the nose section became little more than a skeleton and the astronaut lay revealed, like a leathery, brown caterpillar with its tail in its mouth that was caught on one of the innermost gear wheels of a giant clock. By this time the vessel was completely submerged, oxygen was being released into the water all around it, and Prilicla was reporting the patient's feelings as being extremely anxious and confused.

"*It's* confused . . ." said a familiar, irascible voice and Conway discovered O'Mara swimming beside him. Colonel Skempton was dog-paddling along on his other side, but silently. The psychologist went on, "This is an important one, Doctor, in case you've forgotten—hence our close personal interest. But now why don't you pull that glorified alarm clock apart and get the patient out of there? You've proved your theory that it needed gravity to live, and we're supplying that now . . ."

"No, sir," said Conway, "not just yet . . ."

"Obviously the rotation of the being inside the capsule," Colonel Skempton broke in, "compensates for the ship's spin, thus allowing the pilot a stationary view of the outside world."

"I don't know," said Conway doggedly. "The ship's rotation does not quite match that of the astronaut inside it. In my opinion we should wait until we can transfer it quickly to the ferris wheel, which will almost exactly duplicate module conditions. I have an idea—it may be a pretty wild one—that we aren't out of the woods yet."

"But transferring the whole ship into the ward when the patient alone could be moved there in a fraction of the time . . ."

"No," said Conway.

"He's the Doctor," said O'Mara, before the argument could develop further, and smoothly directed the Colonel's attention to the system of paddle-wheels which kept the water-breathing astronaut's "air" circulating.

The enormous trolley, its weight supported in the water to a large extent by air-filled balloon tires, was manhandled along the corridor and into the tremendous tank which was one of the combined theater/wards of the hospital's water-breathing patients. Suddenly there was another complication.

"*Doctor!* It's coming out!"

One of the men swarming around the nose section must have accidentally pushed the astronaut's ejection button, because the narrow hatch had swung open and the system of gears, sprocket wheels and chain drives was sliding into new positions. Something which looked like three five-foot diameter tires was rolling toward the opening.

The innermost tire of the three was the astronaut while the two on each side of it had a metallic look and a series of tubes running from them into the central, organic tire—probably food storage tanks, Conway thought. His theory was borne out when the outer sections stopped just inside the hatch and the alien, still trailing one of the feeding tubes, rolled out of its ship. Still turning it began to fall slowly toward the floor eight feet below.

Harrison, who was nearest, tried to break its fall but could only get one hand to it. The being tipped over and hit the floor flat on its side. It bounced slowly just once and came to rest, motionless.

"*It is unconscious again, dying! Quickly, friend Conway!*"

The normally polite and self-effacing empath had turned the volume of its suit radio to maximum so as to attract attention quickly. Conway acknowledged with a wave—he was already swimming toward the fallen astronaut as fast as he could—and yelled at Harrison, "Get it upright, man! Turn it!"

"What . . ." began Harrison, but he nevertheless got both hands under the alien and began to lift.

Mannon, O'Mara and Conway arrived together. With four of them working on it they quickly lifted the being into an upright position, but when Conway tried to get them to roll it, it wobbled like a huge, soggy hoop and tended to fold in on itself. Prilicla, at great danger to life and its extremely fragile limbs, landed beside them and deafened everyone with details of the astronaut's emotional radiation—which was now virtually nonexistent.

Conway yelled directions to the other three to lift the alien to waist height while keeping it upright and turning. Within a few seconds he had O'Mara pulling down on his side, Mannon lifting on his and the Lieutenant and himself at each flank turning and steadying the great, flaccid, ring-shaped body.

"Cut your volume, Prilicla!" O'Mara shouted. Then in a quieter, furious voice he snarled, "I suppose one of us knows what we're doing?"

"I think so," said Conway. "Can you speed it up—it was rotating much faster than this inside its ship. Prilicla?"

"It . . . it is barely alive, friend Conway."

They did everything possible to speed the alien's rotation while at the same time moving it toward the accommodation prepared for it. This contained the elaborate ferris wheel which Conway had ordered and a watery atmosphere which duplicated the soup of Meatball's oceans. It was not an exact duplicate because the material suspended in the soup was a nonliving synthetic rather than the living organisms found in the original, but it had the same food value and, because it was nontoxic so far as the other water breathers who were likely to use the ward were concerned, the astronaut's quarters were contained by a transparent plastic film rather than metal plating and a lock chamber. This also helped speed the process of getting the patient into its ward and onto the wheel.

Finally it was in position, strapped down and turning in the direction and at the same velocity as its "couch" on the spacecraft. Mannon, Prilicla and Conway attached themselves as close to the center of the wheel and their rotating patient as possible and, as their examination proceeded, theater staff, special instruments, diagnostic equipment and the very special, thought-controlled "tool" from Meatball added themselves or were attached to the framework of the wheel and whirled up and over and around through the nearly opaque soup.

The patient was still deeply unconscious at the end of the first hour.

For the benefit of O'Mara and Skempton, who had relinquished their places on the wheel to members of the theater staff, Conway said, "Even at close range it is difficult to see through this stuff, but as the process of breathing is involuntary and includes ingestion, and as the patient has been short of food and air for a long time, I'd prefer not to work in clear, food-free water at this time."

"My favorite medicine," said Mannon, "is food."

"I keep wondering how such a life-form got started," Conway went on. "I suppose it all began in some wide, shallow, tidal pool—so constituted that the tidal effects caused the water to wash constantly around it instead of going in and out. The patient might then have evolved from some early beastie which was continually rolled around in the shallows by the circular tides, picking up food as it went. Eventually this prehistoric creature evolved specialized internal musculature and organs which allowed it to do the rolling instead of trusting to the tides and currents, also manipulatory appendages in the form of this fringe of short tentacles sprouting from the inner circumference of its body between the series of gill mouths and eyes. Its visual equipment must operate like some form of coeleostat since the contents of its field of vision are constantly rotating.

"Reproduction is probably by direct fission," he went on, "and they keep rolling forevery moment of their lives, because to stop is to die."

"But why?" O'Mara broke in. "Why must it roll when water and food can be sucked in without it having to move?"

"Do you know what is wrong with the patient, Doctor?" Skempton asked sharply, then added worriedly, "Can you treat it?"

Mannon made a noise which could have been a snort of derision, a bark of laughter or perhaps merely a strangled cough.

Conway said, "Yes and no, sir. Or, in a sense, the answer should be yes to both questions." He glanced at O'Mara to include the psychologist and went on, "It has to roll to stay alive—there is an ingenious method of shifting its center of gravity while keeping itself upright by partially inflating the section of its body which is on top at any given moment. The continual rolling causes its blood to circulate—it uses a form of gravity feed system instead of a muscular pump. You see, this creature has no heart, none at all. When it stops rolling its circulation stops and it dies within a few minutes.

"The trouble is," he ended grimly, "we may have almost stopped its circulation once too often."

"I disagree, friend Conway," said Prilicla, who never disagreed with anyone as a rule. The empath's body and pipestem legs were quivering, but slowly in the manner of a Cinrusskin who was being exposed to emotion of a comfortable type. It went on, "The patient is regaining consciousness quickly. It is fully conscious now. There is a suggestion of dull, unlocalized pain which is almost certainly caused by hunger, but this is already beginning to fade. It is feeling slightly anxious, very excited and intensely curious."

"Curious?" said Conway.

"Curiosity is the predominating emotion, Doctor."

"Our early astronauts," said O'Mara, "were very special people, too . . ."

It was more than an hour later by the time they were finished, medically speaking, with the Meatball astronaut and were climbing out of their suits. A Corps linguist was sharing the ferris wheel with the alien with the intention of adding, with the minimum of delay, a new e-t language to the memory banks of the hospital's translation computer, and Colonel Skempton had left to compose a rather tricky message to the Captain of *Descartes*.

"The news isn't all good," Conway said, grinning with relief despite himself. "For one thing, our 'patient' wasn't suffering from anything other than malnutrition, partial asphyxiation and general mishandling as a result of being rescued—or rather kidnaped—by *Descartes*. As well, it shows no special aptitude in the use of the thought-controlled tools and seems completely unfamiliar with the things. This can only mean that there is another intelligent race on Meatball. But when our friend can talk properly I don't think there will be much difficulty getting it to help us find the real owners—it doesn't hold any grudges for the number of times we nearly killed it, Prilicla says, and . . . and I don't know how we managed to come out of this so well after all the stupid mistakes we made."

"And if you are trying to extract a compliment from me for another brilliant piece of deductive reasoning, or your lucky guess," said O'Mara sourly, "you are wasting your time and mine . . ."

Mannon said, "Let's all have lunch."

Turning to go, O'Mara said, "You know I don't eat in public—it gives the impression that I am an ordinary human being like everyone else. Besides, I'll be too busy working out a set of tests for yet another so-called intelligent species . . ."

BLOOD BROTHER

T his is not a purely medical assignment, Doctor," said O'Mara when Conway was summoned to the Chief Psychologist's office three days later, "although that is the most important, naturally. Should your problems develop political complications—"

"I shall be guided by the vast experience of the cultural-contact specialists of the Monitor Corps," said Conway.

"Your tone, Doctor Conway," said O'Mara dryly, "is an implied criticism of the splendid body of men and creatures to which I have the honor to belong . . ."

The third person in the room continued to make gurgling sounds as it rotated ponderously like some large, organic prayer wheel, but otherwise said nothing.

". . . But we're wasting time," O'Mara went on. "You have two days before your ship leaves for Meatball—time enough, I should think, to tidy up any personal or professional loose ends. You had better study the details of this project as much as possible, while you still have comfortable surroundings in which to work."

He continued, "I have decided, reluctantly, to exclude Doctor Prilicla from this assignment—Meatball is no place for a being who is so hypersensitive to emotional radiation that it practically curls up and dies if anyone thinks a harsh thought at it. Instead you will have Surreshun here, who has volunteered to act as your guide and adviser—although why it is doing so when it was quite literally kidnaped and nearly killed by us is a mystery to me . . ."

"It is because I am so brave and generous and forgiving," said Surreshun in its flat, Translated voice. Still rotating, it added, "I am also farsighted and altruistic and concerned only with the ultimate good of both our species."

"Yes," said O'Mara in a carefully neutral voice. "But our purpose it not completely altruistic. We plan to investigate and assess the medical requirements on your home planet with a view to rendering assistance in this area. Since we are also generous, altruistic and . . . and highly ethical this assistance will be given freely in any case, but if you should offer to make available to us a number of those instruments, quasiliving implements, tools or what ever you choose to call them which originate on your planet—"

"But Surreshun has already told us that its race does not use them . . ." began Conway.

"And I believe it," said Major O'Mara. "But we know that they come from its home planet and it is your problem—one of your problems, Doctor—to find the people who do use them. And now, if there are no other questions . . ."

A few minutes later they were in the corridor. Conway looked at his watch and said, "Lunch. I don't know about you, but I always think better with my mouth full. The water breathers' section is just two levels above us—"

"It is kind of you to offer but I realize how inconvenient it is for your species to eat in my environment," replied Surreshun. "My life-support equipment contains an interesting selection of food and, although I am completely unselfish and thoughtful where the comfort of my friends is concerned, I shall be returning home in two days and the opportunities of experiencing multienvironment conditions and contacts are therefore limited. I should prefer to use the dining facilities of your warm-blooded oxygen breathers."

Conway's sigh of relief was untranslatable. He merely said, "After you."

As they entered the dining hall Conway tried to decide whether to eat standing up like a Tralthan or risk giving himself a multiple hernia on a Melfan torture rack. All the Earth-human tables were taken.

Conway insinuated himself into a Melfan chair while Surreshun, whose food supply was suspended in the water it breathed, parked its mobile life-support system as close as possible to the table. He was about to order when there was an interruption. Thornnastor, the Diagnostician-in-Charge of Pathology, lumbered up, directed an eye at each of them while the other two surveyed the room at large and made a noise like a modulated foghorn.

The sounds were retransmitted in the usual toneless voice saying, "I saw you come in, Doctor and Friend Surreshun, and wondered if we might discuss your assignment for a few minutes—before you begin your meal . . ."

Like all its fellow Tralthans Thornnastor was a vegetarian. Conway had the choice of eating salad—a food which he considered fit only for rabbits—or waiting, as his superior had suggested, on a steak.

At the tables around them people finished their lunches and walked, undulated and, in one case, flew out to be replaced by a similar assortment of extraterrestrials, and still Thornnastor continued to discuss methods of processing the data and specimens they would be sending him and the efficient organization of this planet-sized medical examination. As the being responsible for analyzing this mass of incoming data it had very definite ideas on how the job should be handled.

But finally the pathologist lumbered off, Conway ordered his steak and for a few minutes he performed major surgery with knife and fork in silence. Then he became aware that Surreshun's Translator was making a low, erratic growling sound which was probably the equivalent of the untranslatable noise an Earth-human would make clearing his throat. He asked, "You have a question?"

"Yes," said Surreshun. It made another untranslatable sound then went on, "Brave and resourceful and emotionally stable as I am . . ."

"Modest, too," said Conway dryly.

". . . I cannot help but feel slightly concerned over tomorrow's visit to the being O'Mara's office. Specifically, will it hurt and are there any mental aftereffects?"

"Not a bit and none at all," said Conway reassuringly. He went onto explain the procedure used for taking a brain recording or Educator Tape, adding that the whole affair was entirely voluntary and should the idea cause Surreshun mental or physical distress it could change its mind at any time without loss of respect. It was doing the hospital a great service by allowing O'Mara to prepare this tape, a tape which would enable them to gain a full and valuable understanding of Surreshun's world and society.

Surreshun was still making the equivalent of "Aw, shucks" noises when they finished their meal. Shortly afterward it left for a roll around the water-filled AUGL ward and Conway headed for his own section.

Before morning he would have to make a start on tidying up loose ends, familiarizing himself with Meatball conditions and drawing up some fairly detailed plans for procedure prior to arrival—if for no other reason than to give the corpsman who would be assisting him the idea that Sector General doctors knew what they were doing.

Currently in his charge were a ward of silver furred caterpillar Kelgians and the hospital's Tralthan maternity section. He was also responsible for a small ward of Hudlars, with their hide like flexible armor plate, whose artificial gravity system was set at five Gs and whose atmosphere was a dense, high-pressure fog—*and* the oddball TLTU classification entity hailing from he knew not where who breathed superheated steam. It took more than a few hours to tidy up such a collection of loose ends.

The courses of treatment or convalescence were well advanced, but he felt obliged to have a word with them all and say good-bye because they would be discharged and back on their home planets long before he returned from Meatball.

Conway had a hurried and unbalanced meal off an instrument trolley, and then decided to call Murchison. Reaction to his lengthy bout of medical dedication was setting in, he thought cynically, and he was beginning to think only of his own selfish pleasure . . .

But in Pathology they told him that Murchison was on duty in the methane section, encased in a small half-track vehicle—heavily insulated, jammed with heaters inside, hung with refrigerators outside—which was the only way of entering the Cold Section without both freezing herself to death within seconds and blasting the life out of every patient in the ward with her body heat.

He was able to get through to her on a relay from the ward's duty room but, remembering the ears both human and otherwise which were probably listening in, he spoke briefly and professionally about his coming assignment and the possibility that she might be able to join him on Meatball in her capacity as a pathologist, and suggested that they discuss the details on the recreation level when she came off duty. He discovered that that would not be for six hours. While she spoke he could hear in the background the ineffably sweet and delicate tinkling—like the chiming of colliding snowflakes, he thought—of a ward full of intelligent crystals talking to each other.

Six hours later they were in the recreation level, where trick lighting and some really inspired landscaping gave an illusion of spaciousness, lying on a small, tropical beach enclosed on two sides by cliffs and open to a sea which seemed to stretch for miles. Only the alien vegetation growing from the clifftops kept it from looking like a tropical bay anywhere on Earth, but then space was at a premium in Sector General and the people who worked together were expected to play together as well.

Conway was feeling very tired and he realized suddenly that he would have been due to start tomorrow morning's rounds in two hours' time if he still had had rounds to make. But tomorrow—today, that was— would be even busier and, if he knew his O'Mara, Conway would not be completely himself . . .

When he awakened, Murchison was leaning over him with an expression which was a mixture of amusement, irritation and concern. Punching him not too gently in the stomach she said, "You went to sleep on me, in the middle of a sentence, over an hour ago! I don't like that—it makes me feel insecure, unwanted, unattractive to men." She went on punishing his diaphragm. "I expected to hear some inside information, at least. Some idea of the problems or dangers of your new job and how long you will be gone. At very least I expected a warm and tender farewell . . ."

"If you want to fight," said Conway laughing, "let's wrestle . . ."

But she slipped free and took off for the water. With Conway close behind she dived into the area of turbulence surrounding a Tralthan who was being taught how to swim. He thought he had lost her until a slim, tanned arm came around his neck from behind and he swallowed half of the artificial ocean.

While they were catching their breath again on the hot, artificial sand, Conway told her about the new assignment and about the tape taken from Surreshun which he was expected to take shortly. *Descartes* was not due to leave for another thirty-six hours, but for most of that time Conway would have delusions of being an animated doughnut which probably considered all Earth-human females as shapeless and unlovely bags of dough, or perhaps something much worse.

They left the recreation level a few minutes later, talking about the best way of wangling her release from Thornnastor, to whose elephantine species the word romance was just an unTranslatable noise.

There was no real necessity for them to leave the recreation level, of course. It was just that the Earth-human DBDGs were the only race in the Galactic Federation with a nudity taboo, and one of the very few member species with an aversion to making love in public.

Surreshun had already gone when Conway arrived in Major O'Mara's office. "You know it all already, Doctor," said the psychologist as he and Lieutenant Craythorne, his assistant, hooked him up to the Educator. "But I am nevertheless required to warn you that the first few minutes following memory transfer are the worst—it is then that the human mind feels sure that it is being taken over by the alien *alter ego*. This is a purely subjective phenomenon caused by the sudden influx of alien memories and experience. You must try to maintain flexibility of mind and adapt to these alien, sometimes *very* alien, impressions as quickly as possible. How you do this is up to you. Since this is a completely new tape I shall monitor your reactions in case of trouble. How do you feel?"

"Fine," said Conway, and yawned.

"Don't show off," said O'Mara, and threw the switch.

Conway came to a few seconds later in a small, square, alien room whose planes and outlines, like its furnishings, were too straight and sharp-edged. Two grotesque entities—a small part of his mind insisted they were his friends—towered over him, studying him with flat, wet eyes set in two faces made of shapeless pink dough. The room, its occupants and himself were motionless and . . .

He was dying!

Conway was aware suddenly that he had pushed O'Mara onto the floor and that he was sitting on the edge of the treatment couch, fists clenched, arms crossed tightly over his chest, swaying rapidly back and forth. But the movement did not help at all—the room was still too horrifying, dizzyingly *steady*! He was sick with vertigo, his vision was fading, he was choking, losing all sense of touch . . .

"Take it easy, lad," said O'Mara gently. "Don't fight it. Adapt."

Conway tried to swear at him but the sound which came out was like the bleat of a terrified small animal. He rocked forward and back, faster and faster, waggling his head from side to side. The room jerked and rolled about but it was still too steady. The steadiness was terrifying and lethal. *How*, Conway asked himself in utter desperation, *does one adapt to dying?*

"Pull up his sleeve, Lieutenant," said O'Mara urgently, "and hold him steady."

Conway lost control then. The alien entity who apparently had control would not allow anyone to immobilize its body—that was unthinkable! He jumped to his feet and staggered into O'Mara's desk. Still trying to find a movement which would pacify the alien inside his mind Conway crawled on hands and knees through the organized clutter on top of the desk, rolling and shaking his head.

But the alien in his mind was dizzy from standing still and the Earth-human portion was dizzy from too much movement. Conway was no psychologist but he knew that if he did not think of something quickly he would end up as a patient—of O'Mara's—instead of a doctor, because his alien was firmly convinced that it was dying, right now. Even by proxy, dying was going to be a severe traumatic experience.

He had had an idea when he climbed onto the desk, but it was hard to recall it when most of his mind was in the grip of panic reaction. Someone tried to pull him off and he kicked until they let go, but the effort made him lose his balance and he tumbled head first onto O'Mara's swivel chair. He felt himself rolling toward the floor and instinctively shot out his leg to check the fall. The chair swiveled more than 180 degrees, so he kicked out again, and again. The chair continued to rotate, erratically at first, but then more smoothly as he got the hang of it.

His body was jackknifed on its side around the back of the chair, the left thigh and knee resting flat on the seat while the right foot kicked steadily against the floor. It was not too difficult to imagine that the filing cabinets, bookshelves, office door and the figures of O'Mara and Craythorne were all lying on their sides and that he, Conway, was rotating in the vertical plane. His panic began to subside a little.

"If you stop me," said Conway, meaning every word, "I'll kick you in the face . . ."

Craythorne's expression was ludicrous as his face wobbled into sight. O'Mara's was hidden by the open door of the drug cabinet.

Defensively Conway went on, "This is not simply revulsion to a suddenly introduced alien viewpoint—believe me, Surreshun as a person is more human than most of the taped entities I've had recently. But I can't take this one! I'm not the psychologist around here, but I don't think any sane person can adapt to a continually recurring death agony.

"On Meatball," he continued grimly, "there is no such thing as pretending to be dead, sleeping or unconsciousness. You are either moving and alive or still and dead. Even the young of Surreshun's race rotate during gestation until—"

"You've made your point, Doctor," said O'Mara, approaching once again. His right hand, palm upward, held three tablets. "I won't give you a shot because stopping you to do so will cause distress, obviously. Instead I'll give you three of these sleep-bombs. The effects will be sudden and you will be out for at least forty-eight hours. I shall erase the tape while you're unconscious. There will be a few residual memories and impressions when you awaken, but no panic.

"Now open your mouth, Doctor. Your eyes will close by themselves..."

Conway awoke in a tiny cabin whose austere color scheme told him that he was aboard a Federation cruiser and whose wall plaque narrowed it down to Cultural Contact and Survey vessel *Descartes*. An officer wearing Major's insignia was sitting in the single, fold-down chair, overcrowding the cabin while studying one of the thick Meatball files. He looked up.

"Edwards, ship's medical officer," he said pleasantly. "Nice to have you with us, Doctor. Are you awake?"

Conway yawned furiously and said, "Half."

"In that case," said Edwards, moving into the corridor so that Conway could have room to dress, "the Captain wants to see us."

Descartes was a large ship and its control room was spacious enough to contain Surreshun's life-support system without too much inconvenience to the officers manning it. Captain Williamson had invited the roller to spend most of its time there—a compliment which could be appreciated by any astronaut regardless of species—and for a being who did not know the meaning of sleep it had the advantage of always being manned. Surreshun could talk to them, after a fashion.

The vessel's computer was tiny compared with the monster which handled Translation at Sector General, and even then only a fraction of its capacity could be spared for translation purposes since it still had to serve the ship. As a result the Captain's attempts at communicating complex psychopolitical ideas to Surreshun were not meeting with much success.

The officer standing behind the Captain turned and he recognized Harrison. Conway nodded and said, "How's the leg, Lieutenant?"

"Fine, thank you," said Harrison. He added seriously, "It troubles me a little when it rains, but that isn't often in a spaceship..."

"If you must make conversation, Harrison," said the Captain with controlled irritation, "please make intelligent conversation." To Conway he said briskly, "Doctor, its governmental system is completely beyond me—if anything it appears to be a form of paramilitary anarchy. But we must contact its superiors or, failing this, its mate or close relatives. Trouble is, Surreshun doesn't even understand the concept of parental affection and its sex relationships seem to be unusually complex . . ."

"That they are," said Conway with feeling.

"Obviously you know more than we do on this subject," said the Captain, looking relieved. "I had hoped for this. As well as sharing minds for a few minutes it was also your patient, I'm told?"

Conway nodded. "It was not really a patient, sir, since it wasn't sick, but it cooperated during the many physiological and psychological tests. It is still anxious to return home and almost as anxious for us to make friendly contact with its people. What is the problem, sir?"

Basically the Captain's problem was that he had a suspicious mind and he was giving the Meatball natives credit for having similar minds. So far as they were concerned Surreshun, the first being of their race to go into space, had been swallowed up by *Descartes'* cargo lock and taken away.

"They expected to lose me," Surreshun put in at that point, "but they did not expect to have me stolen."

Their subsequent reaction on *Descartes'* return was predictable—every form of nastiness of which they were capable had been hurled at the ship. The nuclear missiles were easily evaded or knocked out, but Williamson had withdrawn because their warheads had been of a particularly dirty type and surface life would have been seriously affected by fallout if the attack had been allowed to continue. Now he was returning again, this time with Meatball's first astronaut, and he must prove to the planetary authorities and/or Surreshun's friends that nothing unpleasant had happened to it.

The easiest way of doing this would be to go into orbit beyond the range of their missiles and let Surreshun itself spend as much time as necessary convincing its people that it had not been tortured or had its mind taken over by some form of monstrous alien life like the Captain. Its vehicle's communications equipment had been duplicated so there was no technical problem. Nevertheless, Williamson felt that the proper procedure would be for him to communicate with the Meatball authorities and apologize for the mistake before Surreshun spoke.

"The original purpose of this exercise was to make friendly contact with these people," Williamson concluded, "even before you people at the hospital got so excited about these thought-controlled tools and decided that you wanted more of them."

"My reason for being here is not altogether commercial," said Conway, in the tone of one whose conscience is not altogether clear. He went on, "So far as the present problem is concerned, I can help you. The difficulty stems from your not understanding their complete lack of parental and filial affection or any other emotional ties other than the brief but very intense bond which exists prior to and during the mating process. You see, they really do hate their fathers and everyone else who . . ."

"Help us, he said," muttered Edwards.

". . . Everyone else who is directly related to them," Conway went on. "As well, some of Surreshun's more unusual memories have remained in my mind. This sometimes occurs after exposure to an unusually alien personality, and these people are unusual . . ."

The structure of Meatball's society until the fairly recent past had been a complete reversal of what most intelligent species considered normal. Outwardly it was an anarchy in which the most respected people were the rugged individualist, the far travelers, the beings who lived dangerously and continually sought for new experiences. Cooperation and self-imposed discipline was necessary for mutual protection, of course, since the species had many natural enemies, but this was completely foreign to their natures and only the cowards and weaklings who put safety and comfort above all else were able to overcome the shame of close physical cooperation.

In the early days this stratum of society was considered to be the lowest of the low, but it had been one of them who had devised a method of allowing a person to rotate and live without having to travel along the sea bed. This, the ability to live while remaining stationary, was analogous to the discovery of fire or the wheel on Earth and had been the beginning of technological development on Meatball.

As the desire for comfort, safety and cooperation grew the number of rugged individualists dwindled—they tended to be killed off rather frequently, in any case. Real power came to lie in the stubby tentacles of the beings who worried about the future or who were so curious about the world around them that they were willing to do shameful things and give up practically all of their physical freedom to satisfy it. They made a token admission of guilt and lack of authority, but they were, in fact, the real rulers. The individualists who were nominally the rulers had become figureheads with one rather important exception.

The reason for this topsy-turvy arrangement was a deep, sex-based revulsion toward all blood relations. Since the rollers of Meatball had evolved in a fairly small and confined area and had been forced to move continually within this area, physical contact for mating purposes—a wholly instinctive affair in presapient times—was much more likely to occur between relatives than complete strangers, they had evolved an effective safeguard against inbreeding.

Surreshun's species reproduced hermaphroditically. Each parent after mating grew their twin offspring, one on each side of their bodies like continuous blisters encircling the side walls of a tire. Injury, disease or the mental confusion immediately following birth could cause the parent to lose balance, roll onto its side, stop and die. But this type of fatality occurred less frequently now that there were machines to maintain the parent's rotation until it was out of danger. But the points where the children eventually detached themselves form their parents remained very sensitive areas to everyone concerned and their positions were governed by hereditary factors. The result was that any close blood relation trying to make mating contact caused itself and the other being considerable pain. The rollers really did hate their fathers and every other relative. They had no choice.

". . . And the very brief period of courtship," Conway added in conclusion, "explains the apparent boastfulness we have observed in Surreshun. During a chance convergence on the sea bottom there is never much time to impress an intended mate with the strength and beauty of one's personality, so that modesty is definitely a nonsurvival characteristic."

The Captain gave Surreshun a long, thoughtful look, then turned back to Conway. "I take it, Doctor, that our friend, because of the long training and discipline necessary to its becoming Meatball's first astronaut, belongs to the lowest social stratum even though unofficially it may be quite well thought of?"

Conway shook his head. "You're forgetting, sir, the importance—again this is tied in with the avoidance of inbreeding—which these people place on the far travelers who bring back new blood and knowledge. In this respect Surreshun is unique. As the planet's first astronaut it is top dog no matter which way you view it—it is the most respected being on its world and its influence is, well, considerable."

The Captain did not speak, but his features were stretching themselves into the unusual, for them, configuration of a smile.

"Speaking as one who had been inside looking out," said Conway, "you can be sure that it doesn't hold a grudge over being kidnaped—it feels obligated to us, in fact—and that it will cooperate during contact procedure. Just remember, sir, to stress our *differences* to these people. They are the strangest species we have encountered—which is literally true. Be especially careful not to talk about us all being brothers under the epidermis, or that we belong to the great, galaxy-wide family of intelligent life. 'Family' and 'brother' are dirty words!"

Shortly afterward Williamson called a meeting of the cultural contact and communications specialists to discuss Conway's new information. Despite the poor translation facilities available on *Descartes*, by the time the watch-keeping officers in the control room had been relieved for the second time they had completed plans for making contact with the natives of Meatball.

But the senior cultural-contact specialist was still not satisfied—he wanted to study the culture in depth. Normal civilizations, he insisted, were based upon the extension of family ties to tribe, village and country until eventually the world was untied. He could not see how a civilization could rise without such cooperation at family and tribal level, but he thought that a closer study of personal relationships, might clarify things. Perhaps Doctor Conway would like to take the Surreshun tape again?

Conway was tired, irritable and hungry. His reply was forestalled by Major Edwards who said, "No! Definitely not! O'Mara has given me strict instructions about this. With respect, Doctor, he forbids it even if you are stupid enough to volunteer. This is one species whose tapes are unusable. Dammit, I'm hungry and I don't want more sandwiches!"

"Me, too," said Conway.

"Why are doctors always *hungry*?" asked the CC officer.

"Gentlemen," said the Captain tiredly.

"Speaking personally," Conway said, "it is because my entire adult life had been devoted to the unselfish service of others and my wide powers of healing and surgical skill instantly available at any time of the day or night. The tenets of my great and altruistic profession demand no less. These sacrifices—the long hours, inadequate sleep and irregular meals—I suffer willingly and without complaint. If I should think of food more often than seems normal for lesser beings it is because some medical emergency may arise to make the next meal uncertain and eating now will enable me to bring a greater degree of skill—even laymen like your-

selves must appreciate the effect of malnutrition on mind and muscle—
to the aid of my patient."

He added dryly, "There is no need to stare, gentlemen. I am merely
preparing my mind for contact with Surreshun's people by pretending
that modesty does not exist."

For the remainder of the voyage Conway divided his time between
Communications and Control talking to the Captain, Edwards and Surreshun. But by the time *Descartes* materialized inside the Meatball solar
system he had gained very little useful information on the practice of
medicine on the planet and even less about its medical practitioners.

Contact with his opposite numbers on Meatball was essential for the
success of the assignment.

But curative surgery and medicine were very recent developments
which had become possible only when the species learned how to rotate
while remaining in one position. There were vague references to another
species, however, who acted as physicians of sorts. From Surreshun's de-
scription they seemed to be part physician, part parasite and part predator. Carrying one of them was a very risky business which very often
caused imbalance, stoppage and death in the patient's continually rotating
body. The doctor, Surreshun insisted, was more to be feared than the
disease.

With the limited translation facilities it was unable to explain how
the beings communicated with their patients. Surreshun had never met
one personally nor was it on rolling-together terms with anyone who had.
The nearest it could express it was that they made direct contact with the
patient's soul.

"Oh Lord," said Edwards, "what next?"

"Are you praying or just relieving your feelings?" asked Conway.

The Major grinned, then went on seriously, "If our friend uses the
word 'soul' it is because your hospital translator carries the word with an
equivalent Meatball meaning. You'll just have to signal the hospital to
find out what that overgrown electronic brain thinks a soul is."

"O'Mara," said Conway, "will begin wondering about my mental
health again . . ."

By the time the answer arrived Captain Williamson had successfully
made his apologies to the Meatball non-authorities and Surreshun had
painted such a glowing picture of the utter strangeness of the Earth-
humans that their welcome was assured. *Descartes* had been requested to

remain in orbit, however, until a suitable landing area had been marked out and cleared.

"According to this," said Edwards as he passed the signal flimsy to Conway, "the computer's definition of 'soul' is simply 'the life of principle.' O'Mara says the programmers did not want to confuse it with religious and philosophical factors by including material or immortal souls. So far as the translation computer is concerned if a thing is alive then it has a soul. Apparently Meatball physicians make direct contact with their patients' life-principle."

"Faith healing, do you think?"

"I don't know, Doctor," said Edwards. "It seems to me that your Chief Psychologist isn't being much help on this one. And if you think *I'm* going to help by giving you Surreshun's tape again, save your breath."

Conway was surprised at the normal appearance of Meatball as seen from orbit. It was not until the ship was within ten miles of the surface that the slow wrinklings and twitchings of the vast carpets of animal tissue which crawled over the land surface became obvious, and the unnatural stillness of the thick, soupy sea. Only along the shorelines was there activity. Here the sea was stirred into a yellow-green forth by water-dwelling predators large and small tearing furiously at the living coastline while the "land" fought just as viciously back.

Descartes came down about two miles off a peaceful stretch of coast in the center of an area marked with brightly colored floats, completely hidden in the cloud of steam produced by its tail flare. As the stern slipped below the surface, thrust was reduced and it came to rest gently on the sandy sea bottom. The great mass of boiled water produced by the flare drifted slowly away on the tide and the people began to roll up.

Literally, thought Conway.

Like great soggy doughnuts they rolled out of the green liquid fog and up to the base of the ship, then around and around it. When outcroppings of rock or a spiky sea growth got in the way they wobbled ponderously around it, sometimes laying themselves almost flat for an instant if forced to reverse direction, but always maintaining their constant rate of rotation and the maximum possible distance from each other.

Conway waited for a decent interval to allow Surreshun to descend the ramp and be properly welcomed by its non-friends. He was wearing a lightweight suit identical to the type used in the water breather's section of the hospital, both for comfort and to show as much as possible of his oddly shaped body to the natives. He stepped off the side of the ramp

434 · JAMES WHITE

and fell slowly toward the sea bottom, listening to the translated voices of Surreshun, the VIPs and the louder members of the circling crowd.

When he touched bottom he thought he was being attacked at first. Every being in the vicinity of the ship tried to score the nearest possible miss on him and each one said something as it passed. The suit mike picked up the sound as a burbling grunt but the translator, because it was a simple message within the capabilities of the ship's computer, relayed it as "Welcome stranger."

There could be no doubt about their sincerity—on this cockeyed world the warmth of a welcome was directly proportional to the degree of strangeness. And they did not mind answering questions one little bit. From here on in, Conway was sure his job would be easy.

Almost the first thing he discovered was that they had no real need of his professional services.

It was a society whose members never stopped moving through and around "towns" which were simply facilities for manufacture, learning or research rather than large groupings of living quarters—on Meatball there were no living quarters. After a period of work on a mechanically rotated frame the doughnut slipped out of its retaining harness and rolled away to seek food, exercise, excitement or strange company somewhere across the sea bed.

There was no sleep, no physical contact other than for reproduction, no tall buildings, no burial places.

When one of the rollers stopped due to age, accident or a run-in with one of the predators or a poison-spined plant it was ignored. The generation of internal gases which took place shortly after death caused the body to float to the surface where the birds and fish disposed of it.

Conway spoke to several beings who were too old to roll and who were being kept alive by artificial feeding while they were rotated in their individual ferris wheels. He was never quite sure whether they were kept alive because of their value to the community or simply the subject of experimentation. He knew that he was seeing geriatrics being practiced, but other than a similar form of assistance with difficult births this was the only form of medicine he encountered.

Meanwhile the survey teams were mapping the planet and bringing in specimens by the boatload. Most of this material was sent to Sector General for processing and very soon detailed analysis suggestions for treatment began coming from Thornnastor. According to the Diagnostician-Pathologist Meatball had a medical problem of the utmost urgency. Conway and Edwards, who had had a preliminary look at the data and a number of low-level flights over the planetary surface, could not have agreed more.

"We can begin a preliminary diagnosis of the planet's troubles," said Conway angrily, "which are caused by the rollers being too damned free with the use of nuclear weapons! But we still badly need a local appreciation of the medical situation and that we are not getting. The big question is—"

"Is there a doctor in the house?" said Edwards, grinning. "And if so, where?"

"Exactly," said Conway. He did not laugh.

Outside the direct vision port the slow, turgid waves reflected the moonlight through a curtain of surface mist. The moon, which was approaching Roche's Limit and disintegration, would pose the inhabitants of Meatball yet another major problem—but not for another million years or so. At the moment it was a great jagged crescent illuminating the sea, the two hundred feet of *Descartes* which projected above the surface and the strangely peaceful shoreline.

Peaceful because it was dead and the predators refused to eat carrion.

"If I built a rotating framework for myself would O'Mara . . . ?" began Conway.

Edwards shook his head. "Surreshun's tape is more dangerous than you think—you were very lucky not to have lost all of your marbles, permanently. Besides, O'Mara has already thought of that idea and discarded it. Rotating yourself while under the influence of the tape, either in a swivel chair or in a gadget built by our machine shop, will fool your mind for only a few minutes, he says. But I'll ask him again, if you like?"

"I'll take your word for it," said Conway. Thoughtfully, he went on, "The question I keep asking myself is where on this planet is a doctor most likely to be found. Suppose the answer is where the greatest number of casualties occur, that is, along the coastlines—"

"Not necessarily," Edwards objected. "One doesn't normally find a doctor in a slaughterhouse. And don't forget that there is another intelligent race on this planet, the makers of those thought-controlled tools. Isn't it possible that your doctors belong to this race and your answer lies outside the roller culture entirely?"

"True," said Conway. "But here we have the willing cooperation of the natives and we should make all possible use of it. I shall ask permission, I think, to follow one of our far-traveling doughnuts next time it sets off on a trip. It may be like having a third party along on a honeymoon and I may be told politely where to go with my request, but it is obvious that there are no doctors in the towns or settled areas and it is only the travelers who have a chance of meeting one. Meanwhile," he ended, "let's try to find that other intelligent species."

Two days later Conway made contact with a nonrelative of Surreshun who worked in the nearby power station, a nuclear reactor in which he felt almost at home because it had four solid walls and a roof. The roller was planning a trip along an unsettled stretch of coast at the end of its current work period which, Conway estimated, would last two or three days. The being's name was Camsaug and it did not mind Conway coming along provided he did not stay too close if certain circumstances arose. It described the circumstances in detail and without apparent shame.

Camsaug had heard about the "protectors," but only at second or third hand. They did not cut people and sew them up again as Conway's doctors did—it did not know what they did exactly, only that they often killed the people they were supposed to protect. They were stupid, slow-moving beings who for some odd reason stayed close to the most active and dangerous stretches of shore.

"Not a slaughterhouse, Major, a battlefield," said Conway smugly. "You expect to find doctors on a battlefield . . ."

But they could not wait for Camsaug to start its vacation—Thornnastor's reports, the samples brought in by the scoutships and their own unaided eyes left no doubt about the urgency of the situation.

Meatball was a very sick planet. Surreshun's people had been much too free in the use of their newly discovered atomic energy. Their reason for this was that they were an expanding culture which could not afford to be hampered by the constant threat of the massive land beasts. By detonating a series of nuclear devices a few miles inland, taking good care that the wind would not blow the fallout onto their own living area, of course, they had killed large areas of the land beast. They were now able to establish bases on the dead land to further their scientific investigation in many fields.

They did not care that they spread blight and cancer over vast areas far inland—the great carpets were their natural enemy. Hundreds of their people were stopped and eaten by the land beasts every year and now they were simply getting their own back.

"Are these carpets alive and intelligent?" asked Conway angrily as their scoutship made a low-level run over an area which seemed to be afflicted with advanced gangrene. "Or are there small, intelligent organisms living in or under it? No matter which, Surreshun's people will have to stop chucking their filthy bombs about!"

"I agree," said Edwards. "But we'll have to tell them tactfully. We *are* their guests, you know."

"You shouldn't have to tell a man *tactfully* to stop killing himself!"

"You must have had unusually intelligent patients, Doctor," said Edwards dryly. He went on, "If the carpets are intelligent and not just stomachs with the attachments for keeping them filled they should have eyes, ears and some kind of nervous system capable of reacting to outside stimuli—"

"When *Descartes* landed first there was quite a reaction," said Harrison from the pilot's position. "The beastie tried to swallow us! We'll be passing close to the original landing site in a few minutes. Do you want to look at it?"

"Yes, please," said Conway. Thoughtfully, he added, "Opening a mouth could be an instinctive reaction from a hungry and unintelligent beast. But intelligence of some kind was present because those thought-controlled tools came aboard."

They cleared the diseased area and began to chase their shadow across large patches of vivid green vegetation. Unlike the types which recycled air and wastes these were tiny plants which served no apparent purpose. The specimens which Conway had examined in *Descartes'* lab had had very long, thin roots and four wide leaves which rolled up tight to display their yellow undersides when they were shaded from the light. Their scoutship trailed a line of rolled-up leaves in the wake of its shadow as if the surface was a bright green oscilloscope screen and the ship's shadow a high-persistency spot.

Somewhere in the back of Conway's mind an idea began to take shape, but it dissolved again as they reached the original landing site and began to circle.

It was just a shallow crater with a lumpy bottom, Conway thought, and not at all like a mouth. Harrison asked if they wanted to land, in a tone which left no doubt that he expected the answer to be "No."

"Yes," said Conway.

They landed in the center of the crater. The doctors put on heavy-duty suits as protection against the plants which, both on land and under sea, defended themselves by lashing out with poison-thorn branches or

shooting lethal quills at anything that came too close. The ground gave
no indication of opening up and swallowing them so they went outside,
leaving Harrison ready to take off in a hurry should it decide to change
its mind.

Nothing happened while they explored the crater and immediate surroundings, so they set up the portable drilling rig to take back some local
samples of skin and underlying tissue. All scoutships carried these rigs
and specimens had been taken from hundreds of areas all over the planet.
But here the specimen was far from typical—they had to drill through
nearly fifty feet of dry, fibrous skin before they came to the pink, spongy,
underlying tissue. They transferred the rig to a position outside the crater
and tried again. Here the skin was only twenty feet thick, the planetary
average.

"This bothers me," said Conway suddenly. "There was no oral cavity,
no evidence of operating musculature, no sign of any kind of opening.
It *can't* be a mouth!"

"It wasn't an eye it opened," said Harrison on the suit frequency. "I
was there . . . here, I mean."

"It looks just like scar tissue," said Conway. "But it's too deep to have
been formed only as a result of burning by *Descartes'* tail flare. And why
did it just happen to have a mouth here anyway, just where the ship
decided to land? The chances against that happening are millions to one.
And why haven't other mouths been discovered inland? We've surveyed
every square mile of the land mass, but the only surface mouth to appear
was a few minutes after *Descartes* landed. Why?"

"It saw us coming and . . ." began Harrison.

"What with?" said Edwards.

". . . Or *felt* us land, then, and decided to form a mouth . . ."

"A mouth," said Conway, "with muscles to open and close it, with
teeth, predigestive juices and an alimentary canal joining it to a stomach
which, unless it decided to form that as well, could be many miles away—
all within a few minutes of the ship landing? From what we know of
carpet metabolism I can't see all that happening so quickly, can you?"

Edwards and Harrison were silent.

"From our study of the carpet inhabiting that small island to the
north," said Conway, "we have a fair idea of how they function."

Since the day after their arrival the island had been kept under constant observation. Its inhabitant had an incredibly slow, almost vegetable,
metabolism. The carpet's upper surface appeared not to move, but it did

in fact alter its contours so as to provide a supply of rainwater wherever needed for the plant life which recycled its air and wastes or served as an additional food supply. The only real activity occurred around the fringes of the carpet, where the great being had its mouths. But here again it was not the carpet itself which moved quickly but the hordes of predators who tried to eat it while it slowly and ponderously ate them in with the thick, food-rich sea water. The other big carpets unlucky enough not to have a fringe adjoining the sea ate vegetation and each other.

The carpets did not possess hands or tentacles or manipulatory appendages of any kind—just mouths and eyes capable of tracking an arriving spaceship.

"Eyes?" said Edwards. "Why didn't they see our scoutship?"

"There have been dozens of scoutships and copters flitting about recently," said Conway, "and the beast may be confused. But what I'd like you to do now, Lieutenant, is take your ship up to, say, one thousand feet and do a series of figure-eight turns. Do them as tightly and quickly as possible, cover the same area of ground each time and make the crossover point directly above our heads. Got it?"

"Yes, but . . ."

"This will let the beastie know that we aren't just any scoutship but a very special one," Conway explained, then added, "be ready to pick us up in a hurry if something goes wrong."

A few minutes later Harrison took off, leaving the two doctors standing beside their drilling rig. Edwards said, "I see what you mean, Doctor. You want to attract attention to us. 'X' marks the spot and an 'X' with closed ends is a figure-eight. Persistency of vision will do the rest."

The scoutship was criss-crossing above them in the tightest turns Conway had ever seen. Even with the ship's gravity compensators working at full capacity Harrison must have been taking at least four Gs. On the ground the ship's shadow whipped past and around them, trailing a long, bright yellow line of rolled-up leaves. The ground shook to the thunder of the tiny vessel's jet and then, very slightly, it began shaking by itself.

"Harrison!"

The scoutship broke off the maneuver and roared into a landing behind them. By then the ground was already beginning to sag.

Suddenly they appeared.

Two large, flat metal disks embedded vertically in the ground, one about twenty feet in front of them and the other the same distance behind. As they watched each disk contracted suddenly into a shapeless blob of metal which crawled a few feet to the side and then suddenly became a large, razor-edged disk again, cutting a deep incision in the ground. The disks had each cut more than a quarter circle around them and the ground was sagging rapidly inside the incisions before Conway realized what was happening.

"Think cubes at them!" he yelled. "Think something *blunt*! Harrison!"

"Lock's open. Come running."

But they could not run without taking their eyes and minds off the disks, and if they did that they could not run fast enough to clear the circular incision which was being made around them. Instead they sidled toward the scoutship, willing every inch of the way that the disks become cubes or spheres or horseshoes—anything but the great, circular scalpels which something had made them become.

At Sector General Conway had watched his colleague Mannon perform incredible feats of surgery, using one of these thought-controlled tools, an all-purpose surgical instrument which became anything he wanted it to be instantly. Now two of the things were crawling and twisting like metallic nightmares as they tried to shape them one way and something else—which was their owner and as such had more expertise—tried to shape them another. It was a very one-sided struggle but they did, just barely, manage to hamper their opponent's thinking enough to allow them to get clear before the circular plug of "skin" containing the drilling rig and other odds and ends of equipment dropped from sight.

"They're welcome to it," said Major Edwards as the lock slammed shut and Harrison lifted off. "After all, we've been taking specimens for weeks and it may give them something to think about before we broaden contact with shadow diagrams." He grew suddenly excited as he went on, "With high-acceleration radio-controlled missiles we can build up quite complex figures!"

Conway said, "I was thinking more in terms of a tight beam of light projected onto the surface at night. The leaves should react by opening and the beam could be moved very quickly in a rectangular sweep pattern like old-fashioned TV. It might even be possible to project moving pictures."

"That's *it*," said Edwards enthusiastically. "But how a dirty great beast the size of a county, who doesn't have arms, legs or anything else, will be able to answer our signals is another matter. Probably it will think of something."

Conway shook his head. "It is possible that despite their slow movements the carpets are capable of quick thinking, that they are in fact the tool users we are looking for and that their enormous bodies undergo voluntary surgery whenever they want to draw in and examine a specimen which is not within reach of a mouth. But I prefer the theory of a smaller, intelligent life-form inside or under the big one, an intelligent parasite perhaps which helps maintain the host in good health by the use of the tools and other abilities, and which makes use of the host being's 'eyes' as well as everything else. You can take your pick."

There was silence while the scoutship leveled off on a course which would take it back to the mother ship, then Harrison said, "We haven't made *direct* contact, then—we've just put squiggles on a vegetable radar screen? But it is still a big step forward."

"As I see it," said Conway, "if tools were being used to bring us to them, they must be a fair distance from the surface—perhaps they can't exist on the surface. And don't forget they would use the carpet exactly as we use vegetable and mineral resources. How would they analyze life samples? Would they be able to see them at all down there? They use plants for eyes but I can't imagine a vegetable microscope. Perhaps they would use the big beastie's digestive juices in certain stages of the analysis . . ."

Harrison was beginning to look a little green around the gills. He said, "Let's send down a robot sensor first, to see what they do, eh?"

Conway began, "This is all theory . . ."

He broke off as the ship's radio hummed, cleared its throat and said briskly, "Scoutship Nine. Mother here. I have an urgent signal for Doctor Conway. The being Camsaug has gone on vacation wearing the tracer the Doctor gave it. It is heading for the active stretch of shore in area H-Twelve. Harrison, have you anything to report?"

"Yes, indeed," replied the Lieutenant, glancing at Conway. "But first I think the Doctor wants to speak to you."

Conway spoke briefly and a few minutes later the scoutship leaped ahead under emergency thrust, ripping through the sky too fast for even the leaves to react to its shadow and trailing an unending shock wave which would have deafened anything on the surface with ears to hear. But the great carpet slipping past them might well number deafness among its many other infirmities which now, Conway thought angrily, included a number of well-developed and extensive skin cancers and God alone knew what else.

He wondered if a great, slow-moving creature like this could feel pain, and if so, how much? Was the condition he could see confined to hundreds of acres of "skin" or did it go much deeper? What would happen to the beings living in or under it if too many of the carpets died, decomposed? Even the rollers with their offshore culture would be affected—the ecology of the whole planet would be wrecked! Somebody was going to have to talk to the rollers, politely but very, very firmly, if it wasn't already too late.

All at once the horse-trading aspect of his assignment, the swapping of tools for medical assistance, was no longer important. Conway was beginning to think like a doctor again, a doctor with a desperately ill patient.

At *Descartes* the copter he had requested was waiting. Conway changed into a lightweight suit with a propulsion motor strapped onto his back and extra air tanks on his chest. Camsaug had too great a lead for him to follow on foot, so Conway would fly out to the being's present position by helicopter. Harrison was at the controls.

"You again," said Edwards.

The Lieutenant smiled. "This is where the action is. Hold tight."

After the mad dash to the mother ship the helicopter trip seemed incredibly slow. Conway felt that he would fall flat on his face if it did not speed up and Edwards assured him that the feeling was mutual and that they would have made better time swimming. They watched Camsaug's trace grow larger in the search screen while Harrison cursed the birds and flying lizards diving for fish and suiciding on his rotor blades.

They flew low over the settled stretch of coast where the shallows were protected from the large predators of the sea by a string of offshore islands and reefs. To this natural protection the rollers had added a landward barrier of dead land-beast by detonating a series of low-power nuclear devices inside the vast creature's body. The area was now so settled that doughnuts could roll with very little danger far inside the beast's cavernous mouths and prestomachs and out again.

But Camsaug was ignoring the safe area. It was rolling steadily toward the gap in the reef leading to the active stretch of coast where predators large, medium and small ate and eroded the living shore.

"Put me down on the other side of the gap," said Conway. "I'll wait until Camsaug comes through, then follow it."

Harrison brought the copter down to a gentle landing on the spot indicated and Conway lowered himself onto a float. With his visor open and his head and shoulders projecting through the floor hatch he could see both the search screen and the half-mile distant shore. Something which looked like a flatfish grown to the dimensions of a whale hurled itself out of the water and flopped back again with a sound like an explosion. The wave reached them a few seconds later and tossed the copter about like a cork.

"Frankly, Doctor," said Edwards, "I don't understand why you're doing this. Is it scientific curiosity regarding roller mating habits? A yen to look into the gaping gullet of a land beast? We have remote-controlled instruments which will let you do both without danger once we get a chance to set them up . . ."

Conway said, "I'm not a peeping Tom, scientific or otherwise, and your gadgetry might not tell me what I want to know. You see, I don't know what exactly I'm looking for, but I'm pretty sure that this is where I can contact them—"

"The tool users? But we can contact them visually, through the plants."

"That may be more difficult than we expect," Conway said. "I hate to attack my own lovely theory, but let's say that because of their vegetable vision they have difficulty in grasping concepts like astronomy and space travel or, as beings who live in or under their enormous host, of visualizing it from an outside viewpoint . . ."

This was just another theory, Conway went onto explain, but the way he saw it the tool users had gained a large measure of control over their environment. On a normal world environmental control included such items as reforestation, protection against soil erosion, efficient utilization of natural resources and so on. Perhaps on this world these things were not the concern of geologists and farmers but of people who, because their environment was a living organism, were specialists in keeping it healthy.

He was fairly sure that these beings would be found in peripheral areas where the giant organism was under constant attack and in need of their assistance. He was also sure that they would do the work themselves rather than use their tools because these thought-controlled devices had the disadvantage of obeying and shaping themselves to the nearest thought source—this had been proved many times at the Hospital as well as earlier today. Probably the tools were valuable, too much so to risk them being swallowed and/or rendered useless by the savage and disorganized thinking of predators.

Conway did not know what these people called themselves—the rollers called them Protectors or Healers or an almost certain method of committing suicide because they killed more often than they cured. But then the most famous Tralthan surgeon in the Federation would probably kill an Earth-human patient if it had no medical knowledge of the species and no physiology tape available. The tool users worked under a similar handicap when they tried to treat rollers.

"But the important thing is they do try," Conway went on. "All their efforts go toward keeping one big patient alive instead of many. They are the medical profession on Meatball and they are the people we must contact first!"

There was silence then except for the gargantuan splashing and smacking sounds coming from the shoreline. Suddenly Harrison spoke.

"Camsaug is directly below, Doctor."

Conway nodded, closed his visor and fell awkwardly into the water. The weight of his suit's propulsor and extra air tanks made him sink quickly and in a few minutes he spotted Camsaug rolling along the sea bottom. Conway followed, matching the roller's speed and keeping just barely in sight. He had no intention of invading anyone's privacy. He was a doctor rather than an anthropologist and he was interested in seeing what Camsaug did only if it ran into trouble of a medical nature.

The copter had taken to the air again, keeping pace with him and maintaining constant radio contact.

Camsaug was angling gradually toward the shore, wobbling past clumps of sea vines and porcupine carpets which grew more thickly as the bottom shelved, sometimes circling for several minutes while one of the big predators drifted across its path. The vines and prickly carpets had poisonous thorns and quills and they lashed out or shot spines at anything which came too close. Conway's problem now was how to drift past them at a safe altitude but remain low enough so as not to be scooped up by a giant flatfish.

The water was becoming so crowded with life and animal and vegetable activity that he could no longer see the surface disturbance caused by the helicopter. Like a dark-red precipice the edge of the land beast loomed closer, almost obscured by its mass of underwater attackers, parasites and, possibly, defenders—the situation was too chaotic for Conway to tell which was which. He began to encounter new forms of life—a glistening black and seemingly endless mass which undulated across his path and tried to wrap itself around his legs and a great, iridescent jellyfish so transparent that only its internal organs were visible.

One of the creatures had spread itself over about twenty square yards of seabed while another drifted just above it. They did not carry spines or stings so far as he could see, but everything else seemed to avoid them and so did Conway.

Suddenly Camsaug was in trouble.

Conway had not seen it happen, only that the roller had been wobbling more than usual and when he jetted closer he saw a group of poisoned quills sticking out of its side. By the time he reached it Camsaug was rolling in a tight circle, almost flat against the ground, like a coin in slow motion that has almost stopped spinning. Conway knew what to do, having dealt with a similar emergency when Surreshun was being transferred into the Hospital. He quickly lifted the roller upright and began pushing it along the bottom like an oversize, flabby hoop.

Camsaug was making noises which did not translate, but he felt its body grow less flabby as he rolled it—it was beginning to help itself. Suddenly it wobbled away from him, rolling between two clumps of sea vines. Conway rose to a safe height meaning to head it off, but a flatfish with jaws gaping rushed at him and he dived instinctively to avoid it.

The giant tail flicked past, missing him but tearing the propulsion unit from his back. Simultaneously a vine lashed out at his legs, tearing the suit fabric in a dozen places. He felt cold water forcing its way up his legs and under the skin something which felt like liquid fire pushing along his veins. He had a glimpse of Camsaug rolling like a stupid fool onto the edge of a jellyfish and another of the creatures was drifting down on him like an iridescent cloud. Like Camsaug, the noises he was making were not translatable.

"Doctor!" The voice was so harsh with urgency that he could not recognize it. "What's *happening*?"

Conway did not know and could not speak anyway. As a precaution against damage in space or in a noxious atmosphere his suit lining was built in annular sections which sealed off the ruptured area by expanding tightly against the skin. The idea had been to contain the pressure drop or gas contamination in the area of damage, but in this instance the expanded rings were acting as a tourniquet which slowed the progress of the poison into his system. Despite this Conway could not move his arms, legs or even his jaw. His mouth was locked open and he was able—just barely able—to breathe.

The jellyfish was directly above him. It edges curled down over his body and tightened, wrapping him in a nearly invisible cocoon.

"Doctor! I'm coming down!" It sounded like Edwards.

He felt something stab several times at his legs and discovered that the jellyfish had spines or stings after all and was using them where the fabric of his suit had been torn away by the vines. Compared with the burning sensation in his legs the pain was relatively slight, but it worried him because the jabs seemed very close to the popliteal arteries and veins. With a tremendous effort he moved his head to see what was happening, but by then he already knew. His transparent cocoon was turning bright red.

"Doctor! Where are you? I can see Camsaug rolling along. Looks like it's wrapped up in a pink plastic bag. There's a big, red ball of something just above it—"

"That's me . . ." began Conway weakly.

The scarlet curtain around him brightened momentarily. Something big and dark flashed past and Conway felt himself spinning end over end. The redness around him was becoming less opaque.

"Flatfish," said Edwards. "I chased it with my laser. Doctor?"

Conway could see the Major now. Edwards wore a heavy-duty suit which protected him from vines and quills but made accurate shooting difficult—his weapon seemed to be pointing directly at Conway. Instinctively he put up his hands and found that his arms moved easily. He was able to turn his head, bend his back and his legs were less painful. When he looked at them the area of his knees was bright red but the body around it seemed more rather than less transparent.

Which was ridiculous!

He looked at Edwards again and then at the awkward, dangerously slow rolling of the wrapped-up Camsaug. A great light dawned.

"Don't shoot, Major," said Conway weakly but distinctly. "Ask the Lieutenant to drop the rescue net. Winch both of us up to the copter and to *Descartes*, fast. Unless our friend here can't survive in air, of course. In that case haul us both to *Descartes* submerged—my air will last. But be very careful not to hurt it."

They both wanted to know what the blazes he was talking about. He did his best to explain, adding, "So you see, not only is it my opposite number, the Meatball equivalent of a doctor, but I owe it my life as well. There is a close, personal bond between us—you might almost say that we were blood brothers."

MEATBALL

Conway had been worrying about the Meatball problem during the whole of the trip back to the hospital, but only in the past two hours had the process become a constructive one. That had been the period during which he had finally admitted to himself that he could not solve the problem and had begun thinking of the names and professional capabilities of some of the beings, human and otherwise, who might help him find the solution. He was worrying so hard and constructively that he did not know that their ship had materialized the regulation twenty miles from the hospital until the flat, translated voice of Reception rattled from the control room's speaker.

"Identify yourself, please. Patient, visitor, or staff, and species."

The Corps lieutenant who was piloting looked back at Conway and Edwards, the mother ship's medical officer and raised an eyebrow.

Edwards cleared his throat nervously and said, "This is scoutship D1-835, tender and communications ship to the Monitor Corps survey and cultural contact vessel *Descartes*. We have four visitors and one staff member onboard. Three are human and two are native Drambons of different—"

"Give physiological classifications, please, or make full-vision contact. All intelligent races refer to themselves as human and consider others to be non-human, so what you call yourself is irrelevant so far as preparing or directing you to suitable accommodation is concerned."

Edwards muted the speaker and said helplessly to Conway, "I know what *we* are, but how the blazes do I describe Surreshun and the other character to this medical bureaucrat?"

Thumbing the transit switch, Conway said, "This ship contains three

Earth-humans of physiological classification DBDG. They are Major Edwards and Lieutenant Harrison of the Monitor Corps and myself, Senior Physician Conway. We are carrying two Drambon natives. Drambo is the native name for the planet—you may still have it listed as Meatball, which was our name for it before we knew it had intelligent life. One of the natives is a CLHG, water-breathing with a warm-blooded oxygen-based metabolism. The other is tentatively classified as SRJH and seems comfortable in either air or water.

"There is no urgency about the transfer," Conway went on. "At the same time the CLHG occupies a physically irksome life-support mechanism and would doubtless feel more comfortable in one of our water-filled levels where it can roll normally. Can you take us at lock Twenty-three or Twenty-four?"

"Lock Twenty-three, Doctor. Do the visitors require special transport or protective devices for the transfer?"

"Negative."

"Very well. Please inform Dietetics regarding food and liquid requirements and the periodicity of their meals. Your arrival has been notified and Colonel Skempton would like to see Major Edwards and Lieutenant Harrison as soon as possible. Major O'Mara would like to see Doctor Conway sooner than that."

"Thank you."

Conway's words were received by the being who was manning the reception board, whose translator pack relayed them to the computer which occupied three whole levels at the nerve-center of the hospital, which in turn returned them stripped of all emotional overtones to the scaly, furry, or feathery receptionist in the form of hoots, cheeps, growls, or whatever other odd noises the being used as its spoken language.

To Edwards, Conway said, "Unless you are attached to a multienvironment hospital you normally meet e-ts one species at a time and refer to them by their planet of origin. But here, where rapid and accurate knowledge of incoming patients is vital, because all too often they are in no condition to furnish this information themselves, we have evolved the four-letter classification system. Very briefly, it works like this.

"The first letter denotes the level of physical evolution," he continued. "The second indicates the type and distribution of limbs and sense organs and the other two the combination of metabolism and gravity-pressure requirements, which in turn gives an indication of the physical mass and form of tegument possessed by a being. Usually we have to remind some of our e-t students at this point that the initial letter of their classification should not be allowed to give them feelings of inferiority, and that the level of physical evolution has no relation to the level of intelligence."

Species with the prefix A, B and C, he went onto explain, were water breathers. On most worlds life had begun in the seas and these beings had developed high intelligence without having to leave it. D through F were warm-blooded oxygen breathers, into which group fell most of the intelligent races in the galaxy, and the G to K types were also oxygen-breathing but insectile. The Ls and Ms were light-gravity, winged beings.

Chlorine-breathing life-forms were contained in the O and P groups, and after that came the more exotic, the more highly evolved physically and the downright weird types. Radiation eaters, frigid-blooded or crystalline beings and entities capable of modifying their physical structure at will. Those possessing extrasensory powers sufficiently well-developed to make walking or manipulatory appendages unnecessary were given the prefix V regardless of size or shape.

"There are anomalies in the system," Conway went on, "but those can be blamed on a lack of imagination by its originators—the AACP life-form, for instance, which has a vegetable metabolism. Normally the prefix A denotes a water breather, there being nothing lower in the system than the piscatorial life-forms, but the AACPs are intelligent vegetables and plants came before fish—"

"Sorry, Doctor," said the pilot. "We'll be docking in five minutes and you did say that you wanted to prepare the visitors for transfer."

Conway nodded and Edwards said, "I'll lend a hand, Doctor."

The scoutship entered the enormous cubic cavern which was Lock Twenty-three while they were donning the lightweight suits used for environments where the liquid or gas was lethal but at reasonably normal pressures. They felt the grapples draw them into the adjustable cradle and staggered slightly as the artificial gravity grids were switched on. The Lock's outer seal clanged shut and there was the sound of waterfalls pouring down metal cliffs.

Conway had just finished securing his helmet when its receiver said, "*Harrison here, Doctor. The reception team leader says that it will take some time to completely fill the lock with water as well as making it necessary to carry out the full anticontamination procedure at the other five internal entrances. It is a big lock, pressure of water on the other seals will be severe if—*"

"Filling won't be necessary," said Conway. "The Drambon CLCH will be all right so long as the water reaches the top edge of the freight hatch."

"The man says bless you."

They let themselves into the scoutship's hold, carefully avoiding the self-powered life support machinery which kept the first Drambon rotating like an organic prayer wheel as they removed the retaining straps from the freight lashing points.

"We've arrived, Surreshun," said Conway. "In a few minutes you'll be able to say good-bye to that contraption for a few days. How is our friend?"

It was a purely rhetorical question because the second Drambon did not and perhaps could not speak. But if it could not converse it could at least react. Like a great, translucent jellyfish—it would have been completely invisible in water had it not been for its iridescent skin and a few misty internal organs—the Drambon undulated toward them. It curled around Conway like a thick, translucent cocoon for a moment, then transferred its attentions to Edwards.

"Ready when you are, Doctors."

"This is a much better entrance than your first one," said Conway as Edwards helped him maneuver Surreshun's life-support equipment out of the hold. "At least this time we know what we are doing."

"There is no need to apologize, friend Conway," said Surreshun in its flat, translated voice. "To a being of my high intelligence and ethical values, sympathy for the mental shortcomings of lesser beings and, of course, forgiveness for any wrongs they may have done me are but small facets of my generous personality."

Conway had not been aware that he was apologizing, but to a being to whom the concept of modesty was completely alien it was possible that his words had sounded that way. Diplomatically he said nothing.

Lock Twenty-three's reception team arrived to help them move Surreshun's wheel to the entrance to the water-filled AUGL wards. The team leader, whose black suit had red and yellow striped arms and legs making him look like an updated court jester, swam up to Conway and touched helmets.

"Sorry about this, Doctor," his voice sounded, clearly if somewhat distorted by the transmitting media, "but an emergency has come up suddenly and I don't want to tie up the suit frequency. I'd like all you people to move into the ward as quickly as possible. Surreshun has been through our hands before so we don't have to worry about it, just take charge of the other character wherever it is and . . . What the blazes!"

The other character had wrapped itself around his head and shoulders, pinioning his arms and nuzzling at him like a dog with a dozen invisible heads.

"Maybe it likes you," said Conway. "If you ignore it for a minute it will go away."

"Things usually do find me irresistible," said the team leader dryly. "I wish the same could be said for females of my own species . . ."

Conway swam around and over it, grabbed two large handfuls of the flexible, transparent tegument covering its back and kicked sideways against the water until the being's front end was pointing toward the ward entrance. Great, slow ripples moved along its body and it began undulating toward the corridor leading to the AUGL ward like an iridescent flying carpet. Less gracefully Surreshun's ferris wheel followed close behind.

"An emergency, you said?"

"Yes, Doctor," said the team leader on the suit frequency. "But nothing will happen for another ten minutes, so I can use the suit radio if we keep it brief. My information is that a Kelgian DBLF on the Hudlar operating theater staff was injured by a muscular spasm and involuntary movement of the patient's forward tentacles during the course of the op. The injuries are complicated by compression effects plus the fact that the constituents of that high-pressure muck which Hudlars breathe are highly toxic to the Kelgian metabolism. But it is the bleeding which is the real cause of the emergency. You know Kelgians."

"Yes, indeed," said Conway.

Even a small punctured or incised wound was a very serious matter for a Kelgian. They were giant, furry caterpillars and only their brain, which was housed in the blunt, conical head section, was protected by anything resembling a bony structure. The body consisted of a series of wide, circular bands of muscle which gave it mobility and served to protect, very inadequately, the vital organs within.

The trouble was that to give those tremendous bands of muscle an adequate blood supply the Kelgian pulse rate and pressure were, by Earth standards, abnormally high.

"They haven't been able to control the bleeding very well," the team leader went on, "so they are moving it from the Hudlar section two levels above us to the Kelgian theater just below, and taking it through the

MAJOR OPERATION · 453

water-filled levels to save time . . . Excuse me, Doctor, here they come . . ."

Several things happened at once just then. With an untranslatable gurgle of pleasure Surreshun released itself from the wheel and went rolling ponderously along the floor, zig-zagging slowly among the patients and nursing staff who ranged from squat, crab-like Melfans to the forty-foot long tentacled crocodile who were natives of the ocean-covered world of Chalderescol. The other Drambon had twitched itself free of Conway's grip and was drifting away, while high up on the opposite wall a seal had opened and the injured Kelgian was being moved in, attended by too many people for Conway's assistance to be either necessary or desirable.

There were five Earth-humans wearing lightweight suits like his own, two Kelgians, and an Illensan whose transparent envelope showed the cloudy yellow of chlorine inside. One of the Earth-human helmets contained a head which he recognized, that of his friend Mannon who specialized in Hudlar surgery. They swarmed around the Kelgian casualty like a shoal of ungainly fish, pushing and tugging it toward the other side of the ward, the size of the shoal increasing as the reception-team leader and his men swam closer to assess the situation. The Drambon jellyfish also moved closer.

At first Conway thought the being was merely curious, but then he saw that the carpet of iridescence was undulating toward the injured being with intent.

"Stop it!" Conway shouted.

They all heard him because he saw them jerk as his voice rattled deafeningly from their suit phones. But they did not know and there was no time to tell them who, what, or even how to stop it.

Cursing the inertia of the water Conway swam furiously toward the injured Kelgian, trying to head the Drambon off. But the big, blood-soaked area of fur on the Kelgian's side was drawing the other like a magnet and, like a magnet, its attraction increased with the inverse square of the distance. Conway did not have time to shout a warning before the Drambon struck softly and clung.

There was a soft explosion of bubbles as the Drambon's probes ruptured the Kelgian's pressure litter and slid into the already damaged suit it had been wearing in the Hudlar theater and through the thick, silvery fur beneath. Within seconds its transparent body was turning a deepening shade of red as it sucked the blood from the injured Kelgian.

"Quickly," Conway yelled, "get them both to the air-filled section!"

He could have saved his breath because everyone was talking and overloading the suit radio. The direct sound pickup was no help, either—all he could hear was the deep, water-borne growl of the ward's emergency siren and too many voices jabbering at once, until one very loud, translated Chalder voice roared out above the others.

"Animal! Animal!"

His strenuous swimming had overloaded the drying elements in his suit, but those words caused the sweat bathing his body to turn from hot to cold.

Not all the inhabitants of Sector General were vegetarians by any means, and their dietary requirements necessitated vast quantities of meat from extraterrestrial as well as terrestrial sources to be shipped in. But the meat invariably arrived frozen or otherwise preserved, and for a very good reason. This was to avoid cases of mistaken identity on the part of the larger, meat-eating life-forms who very often came into contact with smaller e-ts who frequently bore a physical resemblance to the former's favorite food.

The rule in Sector General was that if a being was alive, no matter what size or shape it might take, then it was intelligent.

Exceptions to this rule were very rare and included pets—nonviolent, of course—belonging to the staff or important visitors. When a nonintelligent being entered the hospital by accident, protective measures had to be taken very quickly if the smaller intelligent life-forms were not to suffer.

Neither the medical staff engaged in transfering the casualty nor the reception team were armed, but in a few minutes' time the alarm siren would bring corpsmen who would be and meanwhile one of the Chalder patients—all multitentacled, armored, thirty feet of it—was moving in to remove the clinging Drambon with one or at most two bites of its enormous jaws.

"Edwards! Mannon! Help me keep it off!" Conway shouted, but there were still too many other people shouting for them to hear him. He grabbed two fistfuls of the Drambon's tegument and looked around wildly. The team leader had reached the scene at the same time and he had pushed one leg between the injured Kelgian and the clinging SRJH and with his hands was trying to pry them apart. Conway twisted around, drew both knees up to his chin and with both feet booted the team leader clear. He could apologize later. The Chalder was moving dangerously close.

Edwards arrived then, saw what Conway was doing and joined him.

Together they kicked out at the gigantic snout of the Chalder, trying to drive it away. They could not hurt the brute, but were trusting the e-t not to attack two intelligent beings in order to kill an apparent animal who was attacking a third intelligent being. The situation was sufficiently confused, however, for a mistake to be made. It was quite possible that Edwards and Conway could have their legs amputated from the waist down.

Suddenly Conway's foot was grabbed by a pair of large, strong hands and his friend Mannon swarmed along his body until their helmets were touching.

"Conway, what the blazes are you . . . ?"

"There's no time to explain," he replied. "Just get them both to the air-filled section quickly. Don't let anyone hurt the SRJH, it isn't doing any harm."

Mannon looked at the being who was covering the Kelgian like an enormous, blood-red blister. No longer transparent, the blood of the injured nurse could actually be seen entering and being diffused throughout the Drambon's great, slug-like body which now seemed filled to bursting point.

"You could have fooled me," said Mannon, and pulled away. With one hand he gripped one of the Chalder's enormous teeth, swung around until he was staring it in an eye nearly the size of a football and with his other hand made jabbing, sideways motions. Looking confused the Chalder drifted away, and a few seconds later they were in the lock leading to the air-filled section.

The water drained out and the seal opened to show two green-clad Corpsmen standing in the lock antechamber, weapons at the ready. One of them cradled an enormous gun with multiple magazines capable of instantly anesthetizing any one of a dozen or more life-forms who came within the category of warm-blooded oxygen breathers, while the other held a tiny and much less ferocious-looking weapon which could blast the life from a bull elephant or any e-t equivalent.

"Hold it!" said Conway, slipping and skidding across the still-wet floor to stand in front of the Drambon. "This is a VIP visitor. Give us a few minutes. Everything will be all right, believe me."

They did not lower their weapons, neither did they look as though they believed him.

"You'd better explain," said the team leader quietly, but with the anger showing in his face.

"Yes," said Conway. "I, ah, hope you weren't hurt when I kicked you back there."

"Only my dignity, but I still—"

"O'Mara here," roared a voice from the communicator on the wall opposite. "I want vision contact. What's happening down there?"

Edwards was closest. He trained and focused the vision pickup as directed and said, "The situation is rather complicated, Major—"

"Naturally, if Conway has anything to do with it," said O'Mara caustically. "What is he doing there, praying for deliverance?"

Conway was on his knees beside the injured Kelgian, checking on its condition. From what he could see the Drambon had attacked itself so tightly that very little water had entered the pressure litter or the damaged protective suit—it was breathing normally with no indications of water in its lungs. The Drambon's color had lightened again. No longer deep red, it had returned to its normal translucent iridescent coloring tinged only faintly with pink. As Conway watched, it detached itself from the Kelgian and rolled like a great, water-filled balloon to come to rest against the wall.

Edwards was saying ". . . A full report on this life-form three days ago. I realize three days is not a long time for the results to be disseminated throughout an establishment of this size, but none of this would have happened if the Drambon had not been exposed to a seriously injured being who—"

"With respect, Major," said O'Mara in a voice oozing with everything else but, "a hospital is a place where anyone at any time can expect to see serious illness or injury. Stop making excuses and tell me what *happened*!"

"The Drambon over there," put in the team leader, "attacked the injured Kelgian."

"And?" said O'Mara.

"Cured it instantly," said Edwards smugly.

It was not often that O'Mara was lost for words. Conway moved to one side to allow the Kelgian, who was no longer a casualty, to climb to its multitudinous feet. He said, "The Drambon SRJH is the closest thing to a doctor that we have found on that planet. It is a leech-like form of life which practices its profession by withdrawing the blood of its patients and purifying it of any infection or toxic substances before returning it to the patient's body, and it repairs simple physical damage as well. Its reaction in the presence of severe illness or injury is instinctive. When the injured Kelgian appeared suddenly it wanted to help. The casualty was suffering from poisoning due to toxic material from the Hudlar theater environment infecting the wound. So far as the Drambon was concerned it was a very simple case.

"Not all the blood withdrawn is returned, however," Conway went on, "and we have not been able to establish whether it is physiologically impossible for the being to return all of it or whether it retains a few ounces as payment for services rendered."

The Kelgian gave a low-pitched hoot like the sound of a modulated foghorn. The noise translated as "It's very welcome, I'm sure."

The DBLF moved away then followed by the two armed corpsmen. With a baffled look at the Drambon the team leader waved his men back to their stations and the silence began to drag.

Finally O'Mara said, "When you've taken care of your visitors and if there are no physiological reasons against it, I suggest we meet to discuss this. My office in three hours."

His tone was ominously mild. It might be a good idea if Conway roped in some moral as well as medical support for the meeting with the Chief Psychologist.

Conway asked his empath friend Prilicla to attend the meeting as well as the Monitor officers Colonel Skempton and Major Edwards, Doctor Mannon, the two Drambons, Thornnastor, the Diagnostician-in-Charge of Pathology, and two medics from Hudlar and Melf who were currently taking courses at the hospital. It took several minutes for them all to enter O'Mara's enormous outer office—a room normally occupied only by the Major's aide and more than a score of pieces of furniture suited to the e-ts with whom O'Mara had professional contact. On this occasion it was the Chief Psychologist who occupied his assistant's desk and waited with visibly controlled impatience foreveryone to sit, lie, or otherwise insinuate themselves into the furniture.

When they had done so O'Mara said quietly, "Since the period of high drama accompanying your arrival, I have caught up with the latest Meatball reports, and to know all is to forgive all—except, of course, your presence here, Conway. You were not due back for another three—"

"Drambo, sir," said Conway. "We use the native word sound for it now."

"We prefer that," Surreshun's translated voice joined in. "Meatball is not an accurate name for a world covered with a relatively thin layer of animal life, or for what we consider to be the most beautiful planet in the galaxy—even though we have not as yet had an opportunity to visit any of the others. Besides, your translator tells me that Meatball as a name lacks accuracy, reverence and respect. The continued use of your name for our glorious planet will not anger me—I have too great an understanding of the often shallow thinking engaged in by your species, too much sympathy for these mental shortcomings to feel anger or even irritation—"

"You're too kind," said O'Mara.

"That as well," agreed Surreshun.

"The reason I returned," Conway said hastily, "was simply to get help. I wasn't making any progress with the Drambo problem and it was worrying me."

"Worry," said O'Mara, "is a particularly useless activity—unless, of course, you do it out loud and in company. Ah, now I see why you brought half the hospital along."

Conway nodded and went on, "Drambo is badly in need of medical assistance, but the problem is unlike any other that we have already met on Earth-human or e-t planets and colonies. On those occasions it was simply a matter of investigating and isolating the diseases, bringing in or suggesting where the specifics could be distributed most effectively and then allowing the people affected to administer their own medicine through local doctors and facilities. Drambo is not like that. Instead of trying to diagnose and treat a large number of individuals, the patients are relatively few but very, very large indeed.

"The reason for this is that within the past few years Surreshun's race has learned how to liberate atomic energy," Conway went on, then added, "Explosively, of course, and with vast quantities of radiational dirt. They are very . . ." he hesitated, trying to find a diplomatic word for careless, or criminally stupid or suicidal, and failing, ". . . proud of their new-found ability to kill large areas of the strata creatures and render the shallows around these living coastlines safe for their expanding population.

"But living in or under and perhaps controlling these strata creatures is yet another intelligent race whose land is quite literally in danger of dying all around them," Conway continued. "These people made the tool which came aboard *Descartes*, and judging by that gadget they are highly advanced indeed. But we still know nothing at all about them.

"When it became clear that Surreshun's people were not the tool makers," Conway went on, "we asked ourselves where they would be most likely to be found, and the answer was in those areas where their living country was under attack. It was in this situation that I expected to find their medical people as well, and I did in fact find our transparent friend here. It saved my life, in its rather disconcerting fashion, and I'm convinced that it is the Drambon equivalent of a doctor. Unfortunately it does not seem to be able to communicate in any fashion that I can understand and, bearing in mind the fact that anyone can directly observe its innards without the necessity for X rays, there doesn't seem to be a localized gathering of nerve ganglia or indeed anything at all resembling a brain.

"We badly need the help of its people," Conway added seriously, "which is the reason for bringing it here so that a specialist in e-t communications can succeed, perhaps, where the ship's contact experts and myself failed."

He looked pointedly at O'Mara, who was looking thoughtfully at the leech-like Drambon. It, in turn, had put one of its eyes into a pseudopod and had extended it toward the ceiling so that it could look at the fragile, insect-like figure of the empath Prilicla. Prilicla had enough eyes to look everywhere at once.

"Isn't it odd," said Colonel Skempton suddenly, "that one of your Drambons is heartless and the other appears to be brainless?"

"Brainless doctors I am used to," said O'Mara dryly. "I communicate with them, on the whole successfully, every day. But this isn't your only problem?"

Conway shook his head. "I've already said that we have to treat a small number of very large patients. Even with the assistance of all the Drambon medical people I would still need help in charting—and I do mean charting by photoreconnaissance—the extent of the trouble as accurately as possible and probing subsurface areas. X rays on this scale are impossible. A full-scale drilling operation to withdraw deep tissue samples would be of little use either, since the drill would be a short and impossibly fine needle. So we will need to investigate the diseased or damaged areas in person, using armored ground cars and, where possible, our hands and feet inside heavy-duty spacesuits. Entrance to the affected areas will be through natural body openings, and the exercise will go much faster if we have the help of people with medical training who do not need the protection of armored vehicles and suits. I'm thinking of species like the Chalders and Hudlars and Melfans who are armored already.

"From Pathology," he went on, looking toward Thornnastor, "I would like suggestions for providing a cure by surgery rather than medication. Present indications are that the trouble will be largely the result of radiation poisoning, and while I realize that we can cure even advanced cases these days, the treatment may well be impossible to apply to patients this size, not to mention the fact that the regenerative medication required for only one of them could represent the total output of that drug from a dozen planets for many years. Hence the necessity for a surgical solution."

Skempton cleared his throat and said, "I begin to see the scope of your problem, Doctor. My part will be in organizing transport and supplies for your medical people. I'd also suggest a full battalion of engineers to set up and maintain the special equipment . . ."

"To begin with," said Conway.

"Naturally," said the Colonel a trifle coldly, "we shall continue to assist you in whatever—"

"You misunderstood me, sir," said Conway. "I can't be sure just how much help we will need at the present time, but I had been thinking in terms of a full sector subfleet armed with long-range lasers, surface-penetrating torpedoes, tactical atomic weapons—clean, of course—and whatever other forms of frightfulness you can suggest that are both concentrated and capable of being directed accurately.

"You see, Colonel," Conway concluded, "surgery on this scale will mean that the operation will be military rather than surgical." To O'Mara he added, "Those are a few of the reasons for my unscheduled return. The others are less urgent and . . ."

"Can damn well wait until this lot are sorted out," said O'Mara firmly.

The meeting broke up shortly after that because neither Surreshun nor Conway could give any information on Drambo which was not already available in the Corps reports. O'Mara retreated into his inner office with the Drambon doctor, Thornnastor and Skempton returned to their quarters and Edwards, Mannon, Prilicla, and Conway, having first seen to the comfort of Surreshun in the AUGL tank, headed for the cafeteria reserved for warm-blooded oxygen breathers to refuel. The Hudlar and Melfan doctors went along to find out more about Drambo and to watch the others eat. As very recent additions to the hospital staff in the first flush of enthusiasm, they were spending every available minute observing and talking to e-ts.

Conway knew the feeling. It was still very much with him, but now-adays he was practical enough to use as well as admire the enthusiasm of the new boys . . .

"The Chalders are tough and mobile enough to hold their own against the native predators," Conway said as they distributed themselves around a table designed for Tralthan FGLIs—the Earth-human DBDG tables were all taken, by Kelgians—and dialed their orders. "You Melfans are very fast movers on the sea bed and your legs, being mostly osseus material, are proof against the poisonous plants and spines growing on the ocean floor. Hudlars, however, while slow-moving do not have to worry about anything less than an armor-piercing shell hurting them and the water all over the planet is so thick with vegetable and animal life anxious to attach itself to any smooth surface that you could throw away your food-spraying gear and live completely off the sea."

"It sounds like heaven," said the Hudlar, its flat, translated tone mak-ing it impossible to tell whether or not it was being sarcastic. "But you will need large numbers of doctors in all three species—far too many to be supplied by the hospital even if everyone on the staff was allowed to volunteer."

"We'll need hundreds of you," Conway replied, "and Drambo isn't heaven even for Hudlars. At the same time I thought there might be doctors—young, still restless, newly qualified people—anxious for e-t ex-perience . . ."

"I'm not Prilicla," said Mannon, laughing, "but even I can sense that you are preaching to the converted. Do you *like* lukewarm steak, Con-way?"

For several minutes they concentrated on eating so that the gentle breeze produced by Prilicla's wings—it preferred to hover during meals, claiming that flying aided its digestion—would not ruin everything but the ice cream.

"At the meeting," said Edwards suddenly, "you mentioned other, less urgent problems. I expect the recruiting of thick-skinned beasties like Garoth here was one of them. I'm afraid to ask about the others . . ."

Conway said, "We will need on-the-spot advice during this large-scale medical examination, which means doctors, nurses and medical techni-cians experienced in the processing and analysis of specimens covering the widest possible range of life-forms. I am going to have to talk Thorn-nastor into releasing some of his pathology staff . . ."

Prilicla side-slipped suddenly and almost put one of its pencil-thin legs into Mannon's dessert. It was trembling slightly as it flew, a sure sign that someone at the table was radiating strong and complicated emotions.

"I'm still not Prilicla," said Mannon, "but from the behavior of our empathic friend I would guess that you are seeking, and trying to justify, a much closer liaison with the pathology department and especially a pathologist called Murchison. Right, Doctor?"

"My emotions are supposed to be privileged," said Conway.

"I did not say a word," said Prilicla, who was still finding difficulty in maintaining a stable hover.

Edwards said, "Who's Murchison?"

"Oh, a female of the Earth-human DBDG classification," said Garoth through his translator. "A very efficient nurse with theater experience covering more than thirty different life-forms, who recently qualified as a pathologist senior grade. Personally I have found her pleasant and po-lite, so much so that I am able to ignore the, to me, physically repellent slabs of adipose overlaying much of her musculature."

"And you're going to bring her to Drambo with you, Conway?" The Monitor Corps and its officers had very old-fashioned ideas about mixed crews, even on long survey missions.

"Only," said Mannon gravely, "if he's given half a chance."

"You should marry the girl, Conway."

"He did."

"Oh."

"This is a very strange establishment in some ways, Major," said Mannon, smiling, "full of odd and peculiar practices. Take sex, for in-stance. To a large number of the entities here it is either a continuing, involuntary process as public, and giving the about degree of stimulation, as breathing, or it is physiological earthquake which rocks them for per-haps three days in the year. People like these find it hard to understand the, to them, bewildering complications and ritualistic behavior con-nected with pairing off and mating in our species—although admittedly there are a few whose sex lives make ours look about as simple as cross-pollination.

"But the point I'm trying to make," Mannon went on, "is that the vast majority of our e-ts just do not understand why the female of our species should lose her identity, surrender that most precious of all possessions, her name. To many of them this smacks of slavery, or at least second-class citizenship, and to the others sheer stupidity. They don't see why an Earth-human female doctor, nurse or technician should change her identity and take the name belonging to another entity for purely emotional reasons and neither, if it comes to that, does the Records computer. So they retain their professional names, like actresses and similar professional females, and are very careful to use them at all times to avoid confusions of identity with e-ts who—"

"He gets the point," said Conway dryly. "But sometime I'd like you to explain the difference between an amateur as opposed to a professional female."

"They behave differently in private, of course," Mannon went on, ignoring him. "Some of them are sufficiently depraved to call each other by their first names."

"We need a pathology team," said Conway, ignoring Mannon. "But even more we need local medical help. Surreshun's people, for physiological reasons, can give us only moral support, which means that everything depends on gaining the cooperation of our leech-like friends. This is where you come in, Prilicla. You were monitoring its emotional radiation during the meeting. Any ideas?"

"I'm afraid not, friend Conway," said the empath. "During the whole of the meeting the Drambon doctor was conscious and aware, but it did not react to anything that was said or done or engage in any concentrated thinking. It emoted only feelings of well-being, repletion and self-satisfaction."

"It certainly did a good job on that Kelgian," said Edwards, "and to a leech the pint or so of blood it syphoned off . . ."

Prilicla waited politely for the interruption to cease, then went on, "There was a very brief heightening of interest detectable when members of the meeting first entered the room—the emotion was not one of curiosity, however, but more like the increase of awareness necessary for a cursory identification."

"Was there any indication that the trip here had affected it?" asked Conway. "Impaired its physical or mental faculties, anything like that?"

"It was thinking only contented thoughts," replied Prilicla, "so I would say not."

They discussed the Drambon doctor until they were about to leave the dining hall, when Conway said, "O'Mara will be glad of your help, Prilicla, while he is putting our blood-sucking friend through his psychological hoops, so I would be grateful if you could monitor its emotional radiation while contact is being established. The Major may want to wait until communication is complete and a special translator pack has been programmed for the Drambon before contacting me. But I would like to have any useful information as you get it . . ."

Three days later as he was about to board *Descartes* with Edwards and the first batch of recruits—a very carefully chosen few who would, he hoped, by their enthusiasm attract and instruct many more—the PA began quietly insisting that Doctor Conway contact Major O'Mara at once, its insistence reinforced by the repeated double chime which preceded most urgent signals. He waved the others ahead and went to the lock's communicator.

"Glad I caught you," said the Chief Psychologist before Conway could do anything more than identify himself. "Listen, don't talk. Prilicla and I are getting nowhere with your Drambon medic. It emotes but we can't get it excited about anything so that we cannot even establish its likes and dislikes.

"We *know* that it sees and feels," O'Mara went on, "but we aren't sure if it can hear or talk or, if it can, how it does these things. Prilicla thinks it may have a low form of empathy, but until we can put a few ripples into its even disposition there is no way of proving that. I am not admitting that I'm beaten, Conway, but you have handed us a problem which may have a very simple solution—"

"Did you try it with the thought-controlled tool?"

"That was the first, second and twenty-eighth thing we tried," said O'Mara sourly. "Prilicla detected a very slight heightening of interest consistent, it says, with the identification of a familiar object. But the Drambon made no attempt to control the gadget. I was saying that you handed us a problem. Maybe the simplest answer would be for you to hand us another just like it."

The Chief Psychologist disliked having to give unnecessary explanations almost as much as people who were slow on the uptake, so Conway thought for a moment before saying, "So you would like me to bring back another Drambon medic so that you could observe and eavesdrop on their conversation when they meet, and reproduce the method on the translator . . ."

"Yes, Doctor, and fast," said O'Mara, "before your Chief Psychologist needs a psychiatrist. Off."

It was not possible for Conway to immediately seek out, kidnap or otherwise acquire another leech-like SRJH on his return to Drambo. He had a group of e-ts of widely varying dietary, gravity and atmosphere requirements to attend to and, while all three life-forms could exist without too much difficulty in the Drambon ocean, their quarters on *Descartes* had to have some of the comforts of home.

They also had to be given some appreciation of the scope of the medical problem they were being asked to help solve, and this entailed many copter flights over the strata creatures. He showed them the great tracks of living "land" covered with the tiny, long-rooted plants which might or might not serve as the strata beasts' eyes—the leaves rolled back tightly to reveal their bright undersides when the helicopter's shadow passed over them, and opened out again a few seconds after it had passed. It was as if their shadow was a high-persistency yellow spot on a bright-green radar screen. And he showed them the coastlines, which were much more dramatic.

Here the sea predators, large and small, tore at each other and at the periphery of the great land beasts, stirring the thick, turgid ocean into yellow foam streaked and stained with red. It was in an area like this, where Conway had judged the strata beast's need for protection had been greatest, that he had found the leech-like SRJHs and where, as soon as he could possibly manage it, he must look for another.

But this time he would have lots of willing and specialized help.

Every day there was a message from O'Mara, different only in the mounting impatience evident between the lines. Prilicla and the Chief Psychologist were having no success with the Drambon doctor and had come to the conclusion that it used one of the exotic visiotactile languages which were virtually impossible to reproduce without a detailed sight-touch vocabulary.

The first expedition to the coast was in the nature of a rehearsal—at least, it started out that way. Camsaug and Surreshun took the lead, wobbling and wheeling along the uneven sea bed like a pair of great organic doughnuts. They were flanked by two crab-like Melfans who were easily capable of scuttling along twice as fast as the Drambons could roll, while a thirty-foot scaled and tentacled Chalder swam ponderously above them ready to discourage local predators with its teeth, claws and great bony club of a tail—although in Conway's opinion one look from any one of its four extensible eyes would be enough to discourage anything with the slightest will to live.

Conway, Edwards, and Garoth traveled in one of the Corps's surface cruisers, a vehicle capable not only of moving over any conceivable topography but of going over, through or under the sea as well as being able to hover for a limited period in the air. They kept just far enough in the rear to keep everyone else in sight.

They were headed toward a dead section of coast, a deep strip of the strata beast which Surreshun's people had killed to give themselves more protected rolling space. They had accomplished this by lobbing a series of very dirty atomic bombs ten miles inland and then waiting while the living coastline stopped killing and eating and drinking, and the coastline predators lost interest in the dead meat and left.

Fallout did not concern the rollers because the prevailing wind blew inland. But Conway had deliberately selected a spot which was only a few miles from a stretch of coast which was still very much alive, so that with any luck their first examination might turn out to be something more than an autopsy.

With the departure of the predators the sea's plant life had moved in. On Drambo the division between plant and animal life was rarely sharp and all animals were omnivorous. They had to travel along the coast for nearly a mile before finding a mouth that was not either closed too tightly or too badly overgrown to allow entry, but the time was not wasted because Camsaug and Surreshun were able to point out large numbers of dangerous plants that even the heavily armored e-ts should avoid whenever possible.

The practice of extraterrestrial medicine was greatly simplified by the fact that the illnesses and infections of one species were not transmittable to another. But this did not mean that poisons or other toxic material secreted by e-t animals and plants could not kill, and on the Drambon sea bed the vegetation was particularly vicious. Several varieties were covered with poisoned spines and one acted as if it had delusions of being a vegetable octopus.

The first usable mouth looked like an enormous cavern. When they followed the rollers inside the vehicle's spotlights showed pallid vegetation waving and wriggling slowly to the limit of vision. Surreshun and Camsaug were rolling out unsteady figure-eights on the densely overgrown floor and apologizing for the fact that they could not take the party any farther without risking being stopped.

"We understand," said Conway, "and thank you."

As they moved deeper into the enormous mouth the vegetation became sparse and more pallid, revealing large areas of the creature's tissue. It looked coarse and fibrous and much more like vegetable rather than animal material, even allowing for the fact that it had died several years earlier. The roof began suddenly to press down on them and the forward lights showed the first serious barrier, a tangle of long, tusk-like teeth so thick that they looked like the edge of a petrified forest.

One of the Melfans was the first to report. It said, "I cannot be absolutely sure until Pathology checks my specimens, Doctor Conway, but the indications are that the creature's teeth are vegetable rather than animal osseous material. They grow thickly on both the upper and lower surfaces of the mouth and to the limit of our visibility. The roots grow transversely so that the teeth are free to bend forward and backward under steady pressure. In the normal position they are angled sharply toward the outer orifice and act as a killing barrier to large predators rather than as a means of grinding them into small pieces.

"From the position and condition of several large cadavers in the area," the Melfan went on, "I would say that the creature's ingestion system is very simple. Sea water containing food animals of all sizes is drawn into a stomach or prestomach. Small animals slip through the teeth while large ones impale themselves, whereupon the inward current and the struggles of the animal concerned cause the teeth to bend inward and release it. I assume that the small animals are no problem but that the big ones could do serious damage to the stomach before the digestive system neutralizes them, so they have to be dead before they reach the stomach."

Conway directed the spotlight toward the area containing the Melfan and saw it wave one of its mandibles. He said, "That sounds reasonable, Doctor. It wouldn't surprise me if the digestive processes are very slow indeed—in fact, I'm beginning to wonder if the creature is more vegetable than animal. An organism of normal flesh, blood, bone and muscle of this size would be too heavy to move at all. But it moves, and does everything else, very slowly . . ." He broke off and narrowed the beam for maximum penetration, then went on, "You had better get aboard so we can burn a way through those teeth."

"No need, Doctor," said the Melfan. "The teeth have decayed and are quite soft and brittle. You can simply drive through them and we will follow."

Edwards allowed the cruiser to sink to the floor, then moved it forward at a comfortable scuttling pace for Melfans. Hundreds of the long, discolored plant teeth snapped and toppled slowly through the cloudy water before they were suddenly in the clear.

"If the teeth are a specialized form of plant life," said Conway thoughtfully, "they occupied a very sharply defined area, which suggests that someone is responsible for planting them."

Grunting assent, Edwards checked to see that everyone had come through the tunnel they had just made, then he said, "The channel is widening and deepening again, and I can see another presumably specialized form of plant life. Big, isn't it? There's another. They're all over the place."

"This is far enough," said Conway. "We don't want to lose sight of the way out."

Edwards shook his head. "I can see openings on both sides just like this one. If the place is a stomach, and it looks big enough, there are several inlets."

Angry suddenly, Conway said, "We know that there are hundreds of these mouths in this dead section alone and the number of stomachs is anybody's guess—great, flat, hollow caverns miles across if that radar isn't telling fluorescent lies. We aren't even *nibbling* at the problem!"

Edwards made a sympathetic noise and pointed ahead. "They look like stalactites that have gone soft in the middle. I wouldn't mind taking a closer look."

Even the Hudlar went out to have a closer look at the great, sharply curved pillars which supported the roof. Using their portable analyzers they were able to establish that the pillars were a part of the strata beast's musculature and not, as they had earlier thought, another form of plant life—although the surface of all the muscular supports in the area were covered with something resembling outsize seaweed. The blisters were nearly three feet across and looked about ready to burst. A Melfan taking a specimen of the underlying muscle accidentally touched one and it did burst, triggering off about twenty others in the vicinity. They released a thick, milky liquid which spread rapidly and dissolved in the surrounding water.

The Melfan made untranslatable noises and scuttled backward.

"What's wrong?" said Conway sharply. "Is it poisonous?"

"No, Doctor. There is a strong acid content but it is not immediately harmful. If you were a water breather you would say that it stinks. But look at the effect on the muscle."

The great pillar of muscle rooted firmly to both floor and roof was quivering, its sharp curve beginning to straighten out.

"Yes," said Conway briskly, "this supports our theory about the creature's method of ingestion. But now I think we should return to *Descartes*—this area may not be as dead as we thought."

Specialized teeth plants served as a filter and killing barrier to food drawn into the creature's stomach. Other symbiotic plants growing on the muscle pillars released a secretion which caused them to stiffen, expand the stomach, and draw in large quantities of food-bearing water. Presumably the secretion also served to dissolve the food, digest it for assimilation through the stomach wall or by other specialized plants— they had taken enough specimens for Thornnastor to be able to work out the digestive mechanism in detail. When the power of the digestive secretion had been diluted by the food entering the stomach their effect on the muscles diminished, allowing the pillars to partially collapse again and expel undigested material.

Blisters were beginning to rupture off the other pillars now. By itself that did not mean that the beast was alive, only that a dead muscle could still respond to the proper stimulus. But the cavern roof was being pushed up and water was flowing in again.

"I agree, Doctor," said Edwards, "let's get out of here. But could we leave by a different mouth—we might learn something from a stretch of new scenery."

"Yes," said Conway, with the uncomfortable feeling that he should have said no. If dead muscles could twitch, what other forms of involuntary activity were possible to the gigantic carcass? He added, "You drive, but keep the cargo hatch and personnel lock open—I'll stay outside with the e-ts . . ."

A few minutes later Conway was hanging onto a handy projection as the vehicle followed the e-ts into a different mouth opening. He hoped it was a mouth and not a connection with something deeper inside the beast, because Edwards reported that it was curving toward a live area of coast. But before the lowering temperature of his feet could affect his speech centers enough for him to order them back the way they had come, there was an interruption.

"Major Edwards, stop the cruiser, please," said one of the Melfans. "Doctor Conway, down here. I think I have found a dead . . . colleague."

It was a Drambon SRJH, no longer transparent but milky and shriveled with a long, incised wound traversing its body, drifting and bumping along the floor.

"Thornnastor will be pleased with you, friend," said Conway enthusiastically. "And so will O'Mara and Prilicla. Let's get it aboard with the other specimens. Oh, I'm not a water breather, but . . ."

"It doesn't," the Melfan replied to the unspoken question. "I'd say that it was too recently dead to be offensive."

The Chalder came sweeping back, its tentacles gripped the dead SRJH and transferred it to the refrigerated specimen compartment, then it returned to its position. A few seconds later one flat, toneless, translated word rasped in their receivers.

"Company."

Edwards directed all his lights ahead to show a fighting, squirming menagerie practically filling the throat ahead. Conway identified two kinds of large sea predators who had obviously been able to batter a way through the brittle teeth, several smaller ones, about ten SRJHs and a few large-headed, tentacled fish that he had never seen before. It was impossible to tell at first which were fighting which or even if it mattered to the beings concerned.

Edwards dropped the vehicle to the floor. "Back inside! Quickly!"

Half-running, half-swimming toward the vehicle, Conway envied the underwater mobility of the Melfans so much that it hurt. He overtook the Hudlar who had the jaws of a big predator locked on its carapace. Just above him one of the new life-forms had an SRJH wrapped around it, the Drambon doctor already turning red as it treated its patient in the only way it knew how. There was a deep, reverberating clang as another predator charged the cruiser, smashing two of their four lights.

"Into the cargo hold!" Edwards shouted hoarsely. "We've no time to fiddle about with personnel locks!"

"Get off me, you fool," said the Hudlar with the predator on its back. "I'm inedible."

"Conway, behind you!"

Two big predators were coming at him along the bottom while the Chalder was shooting in from the flank. Suddenly there was a Drambon doctor undulating rapidly between the leading predator and Conway. It barely touched the beast but the predator went into a muscular spasm so violent that parts of its skeleton popped white through the skin.

So you can kill as well as cure, thought Conway gratefully as he tried to avoid the second predator. The Chalder arrived then and with a swipe of its armored tail cleared the Hudlar's back while simultaneously its enormous maw opened and crashed shut on the second predator's neck.

"Thank you, Doctor," said Conway. "Your amputation technique is crude but effective."

"All too often," replied the Chalder, "we must sacrifice neatness for speed . . ."

"Stop chattering and get *in!*" yelled Edwards.

"Wait! We need another local medic for O'Mara," began Conway, gripping the edge of the hatch. There was a Drambon doctor drifting a few yards away, bright red and obliviously wrapped around its patient. Conway pointed and to the Chalder said, "Nudge it inside, Doctor. But be gentle, it can kill, too."

When the hatch clanged shut a few minutes later the cargo hold contained two Melfans, a Hudlar, the Chalder, the Drambon SRJH with its patient and Conway. It was pitch dark. The vehicle shuddered every few seconds as predators crashed against its hull, and conditions were so cramped that if the Chalder moved at all everyone but the armor-plated Hudlar would have been mashed flat. Several years seemed to go past before Edward's voice sounded in Conway's helmet.

"We're leaking in a couple of places, Doctor—but not badly and it shouldn't worry water breathers in any case. The automatic cameras have some good stuff on internal life-forms being helped by local medics. O'Mara will be very pleased. Oh, I can see teeth ahead. We'll soon be out of this . . ."

Conway was to remember that conversation several weeks later at the hospital when the living and dead specimens and film had been examined, dissected, and viewed so often that the leech-like Drambons undulated through his every dream.

O'Mara was *not* pleased. He was, in fact, extremely displeased—with himself, which made things much worse for the people around him.

"We have examined the Drambon medics singly and together, friend Conway," said Prilicla in a vain attempt to render the emotional atmosphere in the room a little more pleasant. "There is no evidence that they communicate verbally, visually, tactually, telepathically, by smell or any other system known to us. The quality of their emotional radiation leads me to suspect that they do not communicate at all in the accepted sense. They are simply aware of other beings and objects around them and, by using their eyes and a mechanism similar to the empathic faculty which my race possesses, are able to identify friend and foe—they attacked the Drambon predators without hesitation, remember, but ignored the much more visually frightening Chalder doctor who was feeling friendship for them.

"So far as we have been able to discover," Prilicla went on, "its emphatic faculty is highly developed and not allied to intelligence. The same applies to the second Drambon native you brought back, except that it is . . ."

"*Much* smarter," O'Mara finished sourly. "Almost as smart as a badly retarded dog. I don't mind admitting that for a while I thought our failure to communicate may have been due to a lack of professional competence in myself. But now it is clear that you were simply wasting our time giving sophisticated tests to Drambon animals."

"But that SRJH saved me."

"A very highly specialized but nonintelligent animal," said O'Mara firmly. "It protects and heals friends and kills enemies, but it does not *think* about it. As for the new specimen you brought in, when we exposed it to the thought-controlled tool it emoted awareness and caution—a feeling similar to our emotional radiation if we were standing close to a bare power line—but according to Prilicla it did not think at or even about the gadget.

"So I'm sorry, Conway," he ended, "we are still looking for the species responsible for making those tools, and for intelligent local medical assistance with your own problem."

Conway was silent for a long time, staring at the two SRJHs on O'Mara's floor. It seemed all wrong that a creature responsible for saving his life should have done so without thought or feeling. The SRJH was simply a specialist like the other specialized animals and plants inhabiting the interior of the great strata beasts, doing the work it had evolved to do. Chemical reactions were so slow inside the strata creatures—the material was too diluted for them to be otherwise since its blood might be little more than slightly impure water—that specialized plant and animal symbiotes could produce the secretions necessary for muscle activity, endocrine balance, supplying nourishment to and removing waste material from large areas of tissue. Other specialized symbiotes handled the respiration cycle and gave vision of a kind on the surface.

"Friend Conway has an idea," said Prilicla.

"Yes," said Conway, "but I would like to check it by getting the dead SRJH up here. Thornnastor hasn't done anything drastic to it yet, and if something should happen to it we can easily get another. I would like to face the two living SRJHs with a dead colleague.

"Prilicla says that they do not emote strongly about anything," Conway added. "They reproduce by fission so there can be no sexual feeling between them. But the sight of one of their own dead should cause some kind of reaction."

O'Mara stared hard at Conway as he said, "I can tell by the way Prilicla is trembling and by the smug look on your face that you think you have the answer. But *what* is likely to happen? Are these two going to heal and resuscitate it? Oh, never mind, I'll wait and let you have your moment of medical drama . . ."

When the dead SRJH arrived Conway quickly slid it from the litter onto the office floor and waved O'Mara and Prilicla back. The two living SRJHs were already moving purposefully toward the cadaver. They touched it, flowed around and over it and for about ten minutes were very busy. When they had finished there was nothing left.

"No detectable change in emotional radiation, no evidence of grief," said Prilicla. It was trembling but its own feelings of surprise were probably responsible for that.

"*You* don't look surprised, Conway," said O'Mara accusingly.

Conway grinned and said, "No, sir. I'm still disappointed at not making contact with a Drambon doctor, but these beasties are a very good second best. They kill the strata beast's enemies, heal and protect its friends and tidy up the debris. Doesn't that suggest something to you? They aren't doctors, of course, just glorified leucocytes. But there must be millions of them, and they're all on our side . . ."

"Glad you're satisfied, Doctor," said the Chief Psychologist, looking pointedly at his watch.

"But I'm not satisfied," said Conway. "I still need a senior pathologist trained in and with the ability to use the hospital's facilities—one *particular* pathologist. I need to maintain a close liaison with—"

"The closest possible liaison," said O'Mara, grinning suddenly. "I quite understand, Doctor, and I shall urge it with Thornnastor just as soon as you've closed the door . . ."

MAJOR OPERATION

On the whole weird and wonderful planet there were only thirty-seven patients requiring treatment, and they varied widely both in size and in their degree of physical distress. Naturally it was the patient who was in the greatest distress who was being treated first, even though it was also the largest—so large that at their scoutship's suborbital velocity of six thousand plus miles per hour it took just over nine minutes to travel from one side of the patient to the other.

"It's a large problem," said Conway seriously, "and even altitude doesn't make it look smaller. Neither does the shortage of skilled help."

Pathologist Murchison, who was sharing the tiny observation blister with him, sounded cool and a little on the defensive as she replied, "I have been studying all the Drambon material long before and since my arrival two months ago, but I agree that seeing it like this for the first time really does bring the problem home to one. As for the shortage of help, you must realize, Doctor, that you can't strip the hospital of its staff and facilities for just one patient even if it is the size of a subcontinent—there are thousands of smaller and more easily curable patients with equal demands on us.

"And if you are still suggesting that I, personally, took my time in getting here," she ended hotly, "I came just as soon as my chief decided that you really did need me, as a pathologist."

"I've been telling Thornnastor for six months that I needed a top pathologist here," said Conway gently. Murchison looked beautiful when she was angry, but even better when she was not. "I thought everybody in the hospital knew why I wanted you, which is one reason why we are sharing this cramped observation blister, looking at a view we have both seen many times on tape and arguing when we could be enjoying some unprofessional behavior—"

"Pilot here," said a tinny voice in the blister's 'speaker. "We are losing height and circling back now and will land about five miles east of the terminator. The reaction of the eye plants to sunrise is worth seeing."

"Thank you," said Conway. To Murchison he added, "I had not planned on looking out the window."

"I had," she said, punching him with one softly clenched fist on the jaw. "You I can see anytime."

She pointed suddenly and said, "Someone is drawing yellow triangles on your patient."

Conway laughed. "I forgot, you haven't been involved with our communications problems so far. Most of the surface vegetation is light-sensitive and, some of us thought, might act as the creature's eyes. We produce geometrical and other figures by directing a narrow, intense beam of light from orbit into a dark or twilight area and moving it about quickly. The effect is something like that of drawing with a high-persistency spot on a vision screen. So far, there has been no detectable reaction.

"Probably," he went on, "the creature can't react even if it wanted to, because eyes are sensory receptors and not transmitters. After all, we can't send messages with our eyes."

"Speak for yourself," she said.

"Seriously," Conway said, "I'm beginning to wonder if the strata creature itself is highly intelligent . . ."

They landed shortly afterward and stepped carefully onto the springy ground, crushing several of the vegetable eyes with every few yards of progress. The fact that the patient had countless millions of other eyes did not make them feel any better about the damage inflicted by their feet.

When they were about fifty yards from the ship, she said suddenly, "If these plants are eyes—and it is a natural assumption, since they are sensitive to light—why should it have so many in an area where danger threatens so seldom? Peripheral vision to coordinate the activity of its feeding mouths would be much more useful."

Conway nodded. They knelt carefully among the plants, their long shadows filled with the yellow of tightly closed leaves. He indicated their tracks from the entry lock of the ship, which were also bright yellow, and moved his arms about so as to partly obscure some of the plants from the light. Leaves partially in shade or suffering even minor damage reacted exactly as those completely cut off from the light. They rolled up tight to display their yellow undersides.

"The roots are thin and go on forever," he said, excavating gently with his fingers to show a whitish root which narrowed to the diameter of thin string before disappearing from sight. "Even with mining equipment or during exploratories with diggers we haven't been able to find the other end of one. Have you learned anything new from the internals?"

He covered the exposed root with soil, but kept the palms of both hands pressed lightly against the ground.

Watching him, she said, "Not very much. Light and darkness, as well as causing the leaves to open out or roll up tight, causes electrochemical changes in the sap, which is so heavily loaded with mineral salts that it makes a very good conductor. Electrical pulses produced by these changes could travel very quickly from the plant to the other end of the root. Er, what are you doing, dear, taking its pulse?"

Conway shook his head without speaking, and she went on. "The eye plants are evenly distributed over the patient's top surface, including those areas containing dense growths of the air-renewal and waste-elimination types, so that a shadow or light stimulus received anywhere on its surface is transmitted quickly—almost instantaneously, in fact—to the central nervous system via this mineral-rich sap. But the thing which bothers me is what possible reason could the creature have for evolving an eyeball several hundred miles across?"

"Close your eyes," said Conway, smiling. "I'm going to touch you. As accurately as you can, try to tell me where."

"You've been too long in the company of men and e-ts, Doctor," she began, then broke off, looking thoughtful.

Conway began by touching her lightly on the face, then he rested three fingers on top of her shoulder and went on from there.

"Left cheek about an inch from the left side of my mouth," she said. "Now you've rested your hand on my shoulder. You seem to be rubbing an X onto my left bicep. Now you have a thumb and two, maybe three, fingers at the back of my neck just on the hairline . . . Are you enjoying this? I am."

Conway laughed. "I might if it wasn't for the thought of Lieutenant Harrison watching us and steaming up the pilot's canopy with his hot little breath. But seriously, you see what I'm getting at, that the eye plants have nothing to do with the creature's vision but are analogous to pressure- , pain- or temperature-sensitive nerve endings?"

She opened her eyes and nodded. "It's a good theory, but you don't look happy about it."

"I'm not," said Conway sourly, "and I'd like you to shoot as many holes in it as possible. You see, the complete success of this operation depends on us being able to communicate with the beings who produced the thought-controlled tools. Up until now I had assumed that these beings would be comparable in size to ourselves even if their physiological classification would be completely alien, and that they would possess the usual sensory equipment of sight, hearing, taste, touch and be capable of being reached through any or all of these channels. But now the evidence is piling up in favor of a single intelligent life-form, the strata creature itself, which is naturally deaf, dumb and blind so far as we can see. The problem of communicating even the simplest concepts to it is—"

He broke off, all his attention concentrated on the palm of one hand which was still pressed against the ground, then said urgently, "Run for the ship."

They were much less careful about stepping on plants on the way back, and as the hatch slammed shut behind them Harrison's voice rattled at them from the lock communicator.

"Are we expecting company?"

"Yes, but not for a few minutes," said Conway breathlessly. "How much time do you need to get away, and can we observe the tools' arrival through something bigger than this airlock port?"

"For an emergency liftoff, two minutes," said the pilot, "and if you come up to Control you can use the scanners, which check for external damage.

"But what were you *doing,* Doctor?" Harrison resumed as they entered his control position. "I mean, in *my* experience the front of the bicep is not considered to be a zone of erotic stimulation."

When Conway did not answer he looked appealingly at Murchison.

"He was conducting an experiment," she said quietly, "designed to prove that I cannot see with the nerve endings of my upper arm. When we were interrupted he was proving that I did not have eyes in the back of my neck, either."

"Ask a silly question . . ." began Harrison.

"Here they come," said Conway.

They were three semicircular disks of metal which seemed to flicker into and out of existence on the area of ground covered by the long morning shadow of the scoutship. Harrison stepped up the magnification of his scanners, which showed that the objects did not so much appear and disappear as shrink rhythmically into tiny metal blobs a few inches across, then expand again into flat, circular blades which knifed through the surface. There they lay flat for a few seconds among the shadowed eye plants, then suddenly the discs became shallow inverted bowls. The change was so abrupt that they bounced several yards into the air to land about twenty feet away. The process was repeated every few seconds, with one disc bouncing rapidly toward the distant tip of their shadow, the second zig-zagging to chart its width and the third heading directly for the ship.

"I've never seen them act like that before," said the lieutenant.

"We've made a long, thin itch," said Conway, "and they've come to scratch it. Can we stay put for a few minutes?"

Harrison nodded, but said, "Just remember that we'll still be staying put for two minutes after you change your mind."

The third disk was still coming at them in five-yard leaps along the center of their shadow. He had never before seen them display such mobility and coordination, even though he knew that they were capable of taking any shape their operators' thought at them, and that the complexity of the shape and the speed of the change were controlled solely by the speed and clarity of thought of the user's mind.

"Lieutenant Harrison has a point, Doctor," said Murchison suddenly. "The early reports say that the tools were used to undercut grounded ships so that they would fall inside the strata creature, presumably for closer examination at its leisure. On those occasions they tried to undercut the object's shadow, using the shaded eye plants as a guide to size and position. But now, to use your own analogy, they seem to have learned how to tell the itch from the object causing it."

A loud clang reverberated along the hull, signaling the arrival of the first tool. Immediately the other two turned and headed after the first, and one after the other they bounced high into the air, higher even than the control position, to arch over and crash against the hull. The damage scanners showed them strike, cling for a few seconds while they spread over hull projections like thin, metallic pancakes, then fall away. An instant later they were clanging and clinging against a different section of hull. But a few seconds later they stopped clinging because, just before making contact, they grew needle points which scored bright, deep scratches in the plating.

"They must be blind," said Conway excitedly. "The tools must be an extension of the creature's sense of touch, used to augment the information supplied by the plants. They are feeling us for size and shape and consistency."

"Before they discover that we have a soft center," said Harrison firmly, "I suggest that we make a tactical withdrawal, or even get the hell out."

Conway nodded. While Harrison played silent tunes on his control panels he explained that the tools were controllable by human minds up to a distance of about twenty feet and that beyond this distance the tool users had control. He told her to think blunt shapes at them as soon as they came into range, any shape so long as it did not have points or cutting edges . . .

"No, wait," he said as a better idea struck him. "Think wide and flat at them, with an aerofoil section and some kind of vertical projection for stabilization and guidance. Hold the shape while it is falling and glide it as far away from the ship as possible. With luck it will need three or four jumps to get back."

Their first attempt was not a success, although the shape which finally stuck the ship was too blunt and convoluted to do serious damage. But they concentrated hard on the next one, holding it to a triangle shape only a fraction of an inch thick and with a wide central fin. Murchison held the overall shape while Conway thought-warped the trailing edges and stabilizer so that it performed a balanced vertical bank just outside the direct-vision panel and headed away from the ship in a long, flat glide.

The glide continued long after it passed beyond their range of influence, banking and wobbling a little, then cutting a short swathe through the eye plants before touching down.

"Doctor, I could kiss you . . ." she began.

"I know you like playing with girls and model airplanes, Doctor," Harrison broke in dryly, "but we lift in twenty seconds. Straps."

"It held that shape right to the end," Conway said, beginning to worry for some reason. "Could it have been learning from us, experimenting perhaps?"

He stopped. The tool melted, flowed into the inverted bowl shape and bounced high into the air. As it began to fall back it changed into glider configuration, picking up speed as it fell, then leveled out a few feet above the surface and came sweeping toward them. The leading edges of its wings were like razors. Its two companions were also aloft in glider form, slicing the air toward them from the other side of the ship.

"*Straps.*"

They hit their acceleration couches just as the three fast-gliding tools struck the hull, by accident or design, cutting off two of the external-vision pickups. The one which was still operating showed a three-foot gash torn in the thin plating with a glider embedded in the tear, changing shape, stretching and widening it. Probably it was a good thing that they could not see what the other two were doing.

Through the gash in the plating Conway could see brightly colored plumbing and cable runs which were also being pushed apart by the tool. Then that screen went dead as well just as takeoff boost rammed him deep into the couch.

"Doctor, check the stern for stowaways," said Harrison harshly as the initial acceleration began to taper off. "If you find any, think safe shapes at them—something which won't scramble anymore of my wiring. Quickly."

Conway had not realized the full extent of the damage, only that there were more red lights than usual winking from the control board. The pilot's fingers were moving over his panels with such an intensity of gentleness that the harshness in his voice made it sound as if it was coming from a completely different person.

"The aft pickup," said Conway reassuringly, "shows all three tools gliding in pursuit of our shadow."

For a time there was silence broken only by the tuneless whistling of air through torn plating and unretracted scanner supports. The surface wobbled past below them and the ship's motion made Conway feel that it was at sea rather than in the air. Their problem was to maintain height at a very low flying speed, because to increase speed would cause damaged sections of the hull to peel off or heat up due to atmospheric friction, or increase the drag to such an extent that the ship would not fly at all. For a vessel which was classed as a supersonic glider for operations in atmosphere their present low speed was ridiculous. Harrison must be holding onto the sky with his fingernails.

Conway tried hard to forget the lieutenant's problems by worrying aloud about his own.

"I think this proves conclusively that the strata creatures are our intelligent tool users," he said. "The high degree of mobility and adaptability shown by the tools makes that very plain. They must be controlled by a diffuse and not very strong field of mental radiation conducted and transmitted by root networks and extending only a short distance above the surface. It is so weak that an average Earth-human or e-t mind can take local control.

"If the tool users *were* beings of comparable size and mental ability to ourselves," he went on, trying not to look at the landscape lurching past below them, "they would have to travel under and through the surface material as quickly as the tools were flying over it if they were to maintain control. To burrow at that speed would require them being encased in a self-propelled armor-piercing shell. But this does not explain why they have ignored our attempts at making wide-range contact through remote-control devices, other than by reducing the communication modules to their component pieces . . ."

"If the range of mental influence pervades its whole body," Murchison broke in, "would that mean that the creature's brain is also diffuse? Or, if it does have a localized brain, where is it?"

"I favor the idea of a centralized nervous system," Conway replied, "in a safe and naturally well-protected area—probably close to the creature's underside where there is a plentiful supply of minerals and possibly in a natural hollow in the subsurface rock. Eye plant and similar types of internal root networks which you've analyzed tend to become more complex and extensive the closer we go to the subsurface, which could mean that the pressure-sensitive network there is augmented by the electrovegetable system which causes muscular movement as well as the other types whose function and purpose are still unknown to us. Admittedly the nervous system is largely vegetable, but the mineral content of the root systems means that electrochemical reactions generated at any nerve ending will transmit impulses to the brain very quickly, so there is probably only one brain and it could be situated anywhere."

She shook her head. "In a being the size of a subcontinent, with no detectable skeleton or osseous structure to form a protective casing and whose body, relative to its area, resembles a thin carpet, I think more than one would be needed—one central brain, anyway, plus a number of neural substations. But the thing which really worries me is what do we do if the brain happens to be in or dangerously close to the operative field."

"One thing we can't do," Conway replied grimly, "is delay the op. Your reports make that very clear."

She had not been wasting time since coming to Drambo and, as a result of her analysis of thousands of specimens taken by test bores, diggers and exploring medics from all areas and levels of its far-flung body, she was able to give an accurate if not completely detailed picture of the creature's current physiological state.

They already knew that the metabolism of the strata creature was extremely slow and that its muscular reactions were closer to those of a vegetable than an animal. Voluntary and involuntary muscles controlling mobility, ingestion and digestion, circulation of its working fluid and the breaking down of waste products were all governed or initiated by the secretions of the specialized plants. But it was the plants comprising the patient's nervous system with their extensive root networks which had suffered worst in the roller fallout, because they had allowed the surface radioactivity to penetrate deep inside the strata creature. This had killed many plant species and had also caused the deaths of thousands of internal animal organisms whose purpose it was to control the growth of various forms of specialized vegetation.

There were two distinct types of internal organisms and they took their jobs very seriously. The large-headed farmer fish were responsible for cultivating and protecting benign growth and destroying all others— for such a large creature, the patient's metabolic balance was remarkably delicate. The second type, which were the being's equivalent of leucocytes, assisted the farmer fish in plant control and directly if one of the fish became injured or unwell. They were also cursed with the tidy habit of eating or otherwise absorbing dead members of their own or the fish species, so that a very small quantity of radioactive material introduced by the roots of surface plants could be responsible for killing a very large number of leucocytes, one after another.

And so the dead areas which had spread far beyond the regions directly affected by roller fallout were caused by the uncontrolled proliferation of malignant plant life. The process, like decomposition, was irreversible. The urgent surgical removal of the affected areas was the only solution.

But the report had been encouraging in some respects. Minor surgery had already been performed in a number of areas to check on the probable ecological effects of large masses of decomposing animovegetable material on the sea or adjacent living strata creature, and to devise methods of radioactive decontamination on a large scale. It had been found that the patient would heal, but slowly; that if the incision was widened to a trench one hundred feet across, then the uncontrolled growth in the excised section would not spread to infect the living area, although regular patrols of the incision to make absolutely sure of this were recommended. The decomposition problem was no problem at all—the explosive growth rate continued until the plant life concerned used up the available material and died. On land the residue would subside into a very rich loam and make an ideal site for a self-supporting base if medical observers were needed in the years to come. In the case of material sliding off shelving coastlines into the sea, it simply broke up and drifted to the seabed to form an edible carpet for the rollers.

Certain areas could not be treated surgically, of course, for the same reason that Shylock had to forego his pound of flesh. These were relatively small trouble spots far inland, whose condition was analogous to a severe skin cancer, but limited surgery and incredibly massive doses of medication were beginning to show results.

"But I still don't understand its hostility toward us," Murchison said nervously as the ship went into a three-dimensional skid and lost a lot of height. "After all, it can't possibly know enough about us to hate us like that."

The ship was passing over a dead area where the eye plants were discolored and lifeless and did not react to their shadow. Conway wondered if the vast creature could feel pain or if there was simply a loss of sensation when parts of it died. In every other life-form he had ever encountered, and he had met some really weird ones at Sector General, survival was pleasure and death brought pain—that was how evolution kept a race from just lying down and dying when the going got tough. So the strata creature almost certainly had felt pain, intense pain over hundreds of square miles, when the rollers had detonated their nuclear weapons. It had felt more than enough pain to drive it mad with hatred.

Conway cringed inwardly at the thought of such vast and unimaginable pain. Several things were becoming very clear to him.

"You're right," he said. "They don't know anything at all about us, but they hate our shadows. This one in particular hates them because the aircraft carrying the sea-rollers' atomic bombs produced a shadow not unlike ours just before large tracts of the patient's body were fried and irradiated."

"We land in four minutes," said Harrison suddenly. "On the coast, I'm afraid, because this bucket has too many holes in it to float. *Descartes* has us in sight and will send a copter."

The pilot's face made Conway fight the urge to laugh. It looked like that of a half made-up clown. Furious concentration had drawn Harrison's brows into a ridiculous scowl while his lower lip, which he had been chewing steadily since takeoff, was a wide, blood-red bow of good humor.

Conway said, "The tools can't operate in this area and, except for a little background radiation caused by fallout, there is no danger. You can land safely."

"Your trust in my professional ability," said the pilot, "is touching."

From their condition of unlevel flight they curved into a barely controlled, tail-first dive. The surface crept, then rushed up at them. Harrison checked the rush with full emergency thrust. There were metallic tearing noises and the rest of the lights on his board turned red.

"Harrison, pieces of you are dropping off . . ." began *Descartes'* radioman, then they touched down.

For days afterward the observers argued about it, trying to decide whether it had been a landing or a crash. The shock-absorber legs buckled, the stern section took some more of the shock as it tried to telescope amidships and the acceleration couches took the rest—even when the ship toppled, crashed onto its side and a broad, flickering wedge of daylight appeared in the plating a few feet away. The rescue copter was almost on top of them.

"Everybody out," said Harrison. "The pile shielding has been damaged."

Looking at the dead and discolored surface around them, Conway thought again of his patient. Angrily, he said, "A little more radiation hereabout won't make much difference."

"To your patient, no," said the lieutenant urgently. "But perhaps selfishly I was thinking of my future offspring. After you."

During the short trip to the mother ship Conway stared silently out of the port beside him and tried hard not to feel frightened and inadequate. His fear was due to reaction after what could easily have been a fatal crash plus the thought of an even more dangerous trip he would have to make in a few days' time, and any doctor with a patient who stretched beyond the limits of visibility in all directions could not help feeling small. He was a single microbe trying to cure the body containing it, and suddenly he longed for the normal doctor-patient relationships of his hospital—even though very few of his patients or colleagues could be considered normal.

He wondered if it might not be better to have sent a general to medical school than to give a doctor control of a whole sector subfleet.

Only six of the Monitor Corps heavies were grounded on Drambo, their landing legs planted firmly in the shallows a few miles off one of the dead sections of coastline. The others filled the morning and evening sky like regimented stars. His medical teams were grouped in and around the grounded ships, which rose out of the thick, soupy sea like gray beehives. The Earth-humans like himself lived on board while the e-ts, none of whom breathed air, were quite happy roughing it on the sea bed.

He had called what he hoped would be the final pre-op meeting in the cargo hold of *Descartes,* which was filled with Drambon sea water whose content of animal and plant, life had been filtered out so that the beam of the projector would have a sporting chance of fighting its way to the screen attached to the forward bulkheads.

Protocol demanded that the Drambons present opened the proceedings. Watching their spokesman, Surreshun, rolling like a great flacid doughnut around the clear space in the center of the deck, Conway wondered once again how such a ridiculously vulnerable species had been able to survive and evolve a highly complex, technology-based culture—though it was just possible that an intelligent dinosaur would have had similar thoughts about early man.

Surreshun was followed by Garoth, the Hudlar Senior Physician who was in charge of the patient's medical treatment. Garoth's chief concern was with the devising and implementation of artificial feeding in areas where incisions would cut the throat tunnels between the coastal mouths and the inland prestomachs. Again unlike Surreshun, it did not say very much but let the projector do all the talking.

The big screen was filled by a picture of an auxiliary mouth shaft situated about two miles inland of the planned incision line. Every few minutes a copter or small supply ship grounded beside the shaft discharged its load of freshly dead animal life from the coastal shallows and departed while corpsmen with loaders and earth-moving machinery pushed the food over the lip. Possibly the amount and quality of the food was less than that which was drawn in naturally, but when the throat was sealed during the major operation this would be the only way that large areas of the patient could be supplied with food.

Aseptic procedures were impossible in an operation on this scale so that pumping equipment drawing sea water from the coast was drawn through large-diameter plastic piping. It poured in a steady stream—except when tools cut the pipeline—into the food shaft, supplying the strata creature with needed working fluid and at the same time wetting the walls so that leucocytes could be slipped down from time to time to combat the effects of any dangerous plant life which might have been introduced during feeding.

They were seeing a drill, of course, performed at one of the feeding installations a few days earlier, but there were more than fifty auxiliary mouths in a similar state of readiness strung out along the proposed incision line.

Suddenly there was a silvery blur of motion on the ground beside the pump housing and a corpsman hopped a few yards on one foot before falling to the ground. His boot with his other foot still in it lay on its side where he had been standing and the tool, no longer silvery, was already cutting its way beneath the blood-splashed surface.

"Tool attacks are increasing in frequency and strength," said Garoth in Translated. "They are also displaying considerable initiative. Your idea of clearing an area around the feeding installations of all eye plants so that the tools would have to operate blind, and would have to bounce around feeling for targets, worked only for a short time, Doctor. They devised a new trick, that of sliding along a few inches below the surface, blind, of course, then suddenly extruding a point or a cutting blade and stabbing or swinging with it before retreating under the surface again. If we can't see them, mental control is impossible, and guarding every working corpsman with another carrying a metal detector has not worked very well so far—it has simply given the tool a better chance of hitting someone.

"And just recently," Garoth concluded, "there are indications of the tools linking up into five-, six- and in one case ten-unit combinations. The corpsman who reported this died a few seconds later before he was able to finish his report. The condition of his vehicle later supports this theory, however."

Conway nodded grimly and said, "Thank you, Doctor. But now I'm afraid that you'll have to withstand air attacks as well. On the way here we taught the patient how gliders work, and it learned fast . . ." He went onto describe the incident, adding the latest pathological findings and their deductions and theories on the nature of their patient. As a result the meeting quickly became a debate and was degenerating into a bitter argument before he had to pull rank and get his human and e-t doctors back to a state of clinical detachment.

The heads of the Melfan and Chalder teams made their report practically as a duet. Like Garoth they had both been concerned with the nonsurgical aspects of the patient's treatment. To a hypothetical observer ignorant of the true scope of their problem this medical treatment could have been mistaken for a very widespread mining operation, agriculture on an even larger scale and mass kidnapping. Both were strongly convinced, and Conway agreed with them, that the wrong way to treat a skin cancer was by amputation of the affected limb.

The amounts of radioactive material deposited by fallout in the central areas were relatively small, and their effects spread fairly slowly into the depths of the patient's body. But even this condition would be ultimately fatal if something was not done to check it. And, since the areas affected by light fallout were too numerous and occurred in too many inoperable locations, they had skinned off the poisoned surface with earth-moving machinery and pushed it into heaps for later decontamination. The remainder of the treatment involved helping the patient to help itself.

A picture appeared suddenly on the screen of a section of subsurface tunnel under one of the areas affected by fallout. There were dozens of life-forms in the tunnel, most of them farmer fish with stubby arms sprouting from the base of their enlarged heads while the others drifted or undulated toward the observer's position like great, transparent slugs.

For a living section of the strata creature it looked none too healthy. The farmer fish, whose function was the cultivation and control of internal plant life, moved slowly, bumping into each other and the leucocytes which, normally transparent, were displaying the milky coloration which occurred shortly before death. The radiation sensor readings left no doubt as to what they were dying from.

"These specimens were rescued shortly afterward," said the Chalder, "and transferred to sick bays in the larger ships and to Sector General. Both fish and leeches respond to the same decontamination and regeneration treatments given to our own people who have been exposed to a radiation overdose. They were then returned to carry on their good work."

"That being," the Melfan joined in, "absorbing the radiation from the nearest poisoned plant or fish and getting themselves sick again."

O'Mara had accused Conway of treating Sector General like some kind of e-t sausage machine, although the hospital was curing everything Drambon that they possibly could, and the Monitor Corps medics had merely looked long-suffering when they weren't looking extremely busy.

By themselves neither the hospital nor treatment facilities on the capital ships were enough to swing the balance. To really allow the patient to fight these local infections required massive transfusions of the leucocyte life-form from other, and healthier, strata creatures.

When he had first suggested the transfusion idea Conway had been worried in case the patient would reject what were, in effect, another creature's antibodies. But this had not happened, and the only problems encountered were those of transportation and supply as the first single, carefully selected kidnappings became continual wholesale abduction.

On the screen appeared a sequence showing one of the special commandos withdrawing leucocytes from a small and disgustingly healthy strata creature on the other side of the planet. The entry shaft had been in use for several weeks and the motion of the strata creature had caused it to bend in several places, but it was still usable. The corpsmen dropped from the copters and into the sloping tunnel, running and occasionally ducking to avoid the lifting gear which would later haul their catch to the surface. They wore lightweight suits and carried only nets. The leucocytes were their friends. It was very important for them to remember that.

The leucocytes possessed a highly developed empathic faculty, which allowed them to distinguish the parent body's friends from its foes simply by monitoring their emotional radiation. Provided the corpsmen kidnappers thought warm, friendly thoughts while they went about their business, they were perfectly safe. But it was hard and often frustrating work, netting and hauling and transferring the massive and inert slugs into the transport copters. Sweating and short-tempered as they frequently were, it was not easy to radiate feelings of friendship and helpfulness toward their charges. Circumstances arose in which a corpsman gave way to a flash of anger or irritation—at an item of his own equipment, perhaps— and for such lapses many of them died.

Rarely did they die singly. At the end of the sequence Conway watched the entire crew of a transport copter taken out within a few minutes, because it had been impossible for one man to think kindly thoughts toward a being who had just killed a crew mate—by injecting a poison which triggered off muscular spasms so violent that the man broke practically every bone in his body—even if his own life did depend on it. There was no protection and no cure. Heavy-duty spacesuits tough enough to resist the needle points of the leeches' probes would not have allowed enough mobility for the corpsmen to do their job, and the creatures killed just as quickly and thoroughly and unthinkingly as they cured.

"To summarize," said the Chalder as it blanked the screen, "the transfusion and artificial feeding operations are going well at present, but if casualties continue to mount at this rate the supply will fall dangerously short of the computed demand. I therefore recommend, most strongly, that surgery be commenced immediately."

"I agree," added the Melfan. "Assuming that we must proceed without either the consent or cooperation of the patient, we should start immediately."

"How immediate?" broke in Captain Williamson, speaking for the first time. "It takes time to deploy a whole sector subfleet over the operative field. My people will need final briefings and, well, I think the Fleet Commander is a little worried about this one. Up to now his operations have been purely military."

Conway was silent, trying to force himself to the decision he had been avoiding for several weeks. Once he gave the word to start, once he began cutting on this gargantuan scale, he was committed. There would be no chance to withdraw and try again later, there were no specialists that he could fall back on if the going got tough and, worst of all, there was no time for dithering, because already the patient's condition had been left untreated for far too long.

"Don't worry, Captain," said Conway, trying hard to radiate the confidence and reassurance which he did not feel. "So far as your people are concerned, this has become a military operation. I know that in the beginning you treated it as a disaster-relief exercise on an unusually large scale, but now it has become indistinguishable from war in your minds, because in war you have to expect casualties and you are certainly getting them. I'm very sorry about that, sir. I never expected such heavy losses and I'm personally very sorry that I taught those tools to glide this morning because that stunt will cost a lot more..."

"It couldn't be helped, Doctor," Williamson broke in, "and one of our people was bound to think of the same idea some time—they've thought of practically everything else. But what I want to know is—"

"How soon is immediately," said Conway for him. "Well, bearing in mind the fact that the operation will be measured in weeks rather than hours, and provided there are no logistical reasons for holding back, I suggest we start the job at first light on the day after tomorrow."

Williamson nodded, but hesitated before he spoke. "We can be in position at that time, Doctor, but something else has just come up which may cause you to change your mind about the timing."

He gestured toward the screen and went on, "I can show you charts and figures, if you like, but it is quicker to tell you the results first. The survey of healthy and less ill strata creatures which you asked our cultural contact people to carry out—your idea being that it might be easier to establish communications with a being who was not in constant pain than otherwise—is now complete. Altogether eighteen hundred and seventy-four sites covering every known strata creature were visited, a tool left unattended on the surface and kept under observation from a distance for periods of up to six hours. Even though the body material was practically identical with that of our patient, including the presence of a somewhat simplified form of eye plant, the results were completely negative. The strata creatures under test made no attempt to control or change the tools in any way, and the small changes which did occur were directly traceable to mental radiation from birds or nonintelligent surface animals. We fed this data to *Descartes'* computer and then to the tactical computer on *Vespasian*. The conclusions left no doubt at all, I'm afraid.

"There is only one intelligent strata creature on Drambo," Williamson ended grimly, "and it is our patient."

Conway did not reply at once and the meeting became more and more disorganized. To begin with there were a few useful ideas put up—at least, they sounded good until the Captain shot them down. But then instead of ideas he got senseless arguments and bad temper and suddenly Conway knew why.

They had all been both overworked and overtired when the meeting had started, and that had been five hours ago. The Melfan's bony underside was sagging to within a few inches of the deck. The Hudlar was probably hungry because the water inside the hold had been cleared of all edible material as had the floor, which would similarly displease the constantly rolling Drambon. Above them the enormous Chalder had been hanging in a cramped position for far too long, and the other Earthhumans must have been finding their pressure suits as irksome as Conway was finding his. It was obvious that there would be no more useful contributions from anyone at this meeting, including himself, and it was time to wind it up.

He signaled for silence, then said, "Thank you, everyone. The news that our patient is the planet's only intelligent strata creature makes it necessary for us to try even harder, if that is possible, to make the forthcoming operation a success. It is not a valid reason for delaying surgery.

"You will all have plenty to occupy you tomorrow," he ended. "I shall

spend the time making one last try at obtaining the consent and cooperation of our patient."

Modifications had been completed to a pair of the tracked boring
machines just three days earlier, making them as toolproof as possible
and extending their two-way vision equipment to allow Conway to view
and, if necessary, direct the operation from anywhere on or inside the
strata creature. It was the communications gear that he checked first.

"I have no intention of becoming a dead hero," Conway explained,
grinning. "If we are in any danger I shall be the first to scream for help."

Harrison shook his head. "The second."

"Ladies first," said Murchison firmly.

They drove inland to a healthy area thickly covered by eye plants and
stopped for a full hour, then moved on for an hour and stopped again.
They spent the morning and early afternoon moving and stopping with
no discernible reaction from the patient. Sometimes they drove around
in tight circles in an attempt to attract attention, still without success.
Not a single tool appeared. Their ground sensors gave no sign that anything was trying to undercut them. Altogether it was turning out to be
an intensely frustrating if physically restful day.

When darkness fell they switched on the digger's spotlights and
played them around and watched thousands of eye plants open and close
suddenly to this artificial sunshine, but still the strata creature refused the
bait.

"In the beginning the brute must have been curious about us," said
Conway, "and anxious to investigate any strange object or occurrence.
Now it is simply frightened and hostile, and there are much better targets
elsewhere."

The digger's vision screens showed several transfusion and feeding
sites under constant tool attack, and too many dark stains on the ground
which were not of oil.

"I still think," said Conway seriously, "that if we could get close to
its brain, or even into the area where the tools are produced, we would
stand a better chance of communicating directly. If direct communication
is impossible we might be able to artificially stimulate certain sections to
make it think that large objects had landed on the surface, forcing it to
draw off the tools attacking the transfusion installations. Or if we could
gain an understanding of its technology that might give us a lever . . ."

He broke off as Murchison shook her head. She produced a chart
comprising thirty or more transparent overlays which showed the pa-

tient's interior layout as accurately as six months' hard work with insufficient facilities could make it. Her features fell into their lecturing expression, the one which said that she wanted attention but not admiration.

She said, "We have already tried to find the patient's brain location by backtracking along the nerve paths—that is, the network of rootlets containing metallic salts which are capable of carrying electrochemical impulses. Using test bores taken at random on the top surface and by direct observation from diggers, we found that they link up, not to a central brain, but to a flat layer of similar rootlets lying just above the subsurface. They do not join directly onto this new network, but lie alongside, paralleling it close enough for impulses to be passed across by induction.

"Some of this network is probably responsible for the subsurface muscular contractions which gave the patient mobility before it took over this particular land mass and stopped climbing over and smothering its enemies, and it is natural to assume that the eye plants above and the muscles below has a direct connection since they would give the first warning of another strata creature attempting to slip over this one, and the subsequent muscular reaction would be almost involuntary.

"But there are many other root networks in that layer," she went on, "whose function we do not know. They are not color coded—they all look exactly the same except for minute variations in thickness. The type which apparently abstracts minerals from the subsurface rock can vary in thickness. So I would advise against artificial stimulation of any kind. You could very easily start a bunch of subsurface muscles to twitching, and the corpsmen up top would have localized earthquakes to contend with as well as everything else."

"All right," said Conway irked for no other reason than that her objections were valid. "But I still want to get close to its brain or to the tool-producing area, and if it won't pull us in we must go looking for it. But we're running out of time. Where, in your opinion, is the best place to look?"

She was thoughtful for a moment, then said, "Either the brain or the tool-producing area could be in a hollow or small valley in the subsurface where, presumably, the creature absorbs necessary minerals. There is a large, rocky hollow fifteen miles away, just here, which would give the necessary protection from below and from all sides while the mass of the overlaying body would save it from injury from above. But there are dozens of other sites just as good. Oh, yes, there would have to be a constant supply of nutriment and oxygen available, but as this is a quasi-vegetable process in the patient with water instead of blood as the working fluid, there should be no problem in supplying a deeply buried brain . . ."

She broke off, her face and jaw stiffening in a successfully stifled yawn. Before she could go on, Conway said, "It's quite a problem. Why don't you sleep on it?"

Suddenly she laughed. "I am. Hadn't you noticed?"

Conway smiled and said, "Seriously, I would like to call a copter to pick you up before we go under. I've no idea what to expect if we do find what we're looking for—we might find ourselves caught in an underground blast furnace or paralyzed by the brain's mental radiation. I realize that your curiosity is strong and entirely professional, but I would much prefer that you didn't come. After all, scientific curiosity kills more cats than any other kind."

"With respect, Doctor," said Murchison, showing very little of it, "you are talking rubbish. There have been no indications of unusually high temperatures on the subsurface, and we both know that while some e-ts communicate telepathically, they can only do so among their own species. The tools are an entirely different matter, an inert but thought-malleable fabrication which . . ." She broke off, took a deep breath and ended quietly, "There is another digger just like this one. I'm sure there would also be an officer and gentleman on *Descartes* willing to trail you in it."

Harrison sighed loudly and said, "Don't be antisocial, Doctor. If you can't beat 'em, let them join you."

"I'll drive for a while," said Conway, treating incipient mutiny in the only way he could in the circumstances, by ignoring it. "I'm hungry, and it's your turn to dish up."

"I'll help you, Lieutenant," said Murchison.

As Harrison turned over the driving position to Conway and headed for the galley, he muttered, "You know, Doctor, sometimes I enjoy drooling over a hot dish, especially yours."

It was shortly before midnight that they reached the area of the subsurface depression, nosed over and bored in. Murchison stared through the direct-vision port beside her, occasionally making notes about the tracery of fine roots which ran through the damp, cork-like material which was the flesh of the strata creature. There was no indication of a conventional blood supply, nothing to show that the creature had ever been alive in the animal rather than the vegetable sense.

Suddenly they broke through the roof of a stomach and drifted down between the great vegetable pillars which raised and lowered the roof, drawing food-bearing water from the sea and expelling, many days later, the waste material not already absorbed by specialist plants. The vegetable stalactites stretched away to the limits of the spotlight in all directions, each one covered with the other specialized growths whose secretions caused the pillars to stiffen when the stomach had been empty for too long and relax when it was full. Other caverns, smaller and spaced closer together than the stomachs, simply kept the water flowing in the system without performing any digestive function.

Just before they drifted to the floor Harrison angled the digger into diving position and spun the forward cutters to maximum speed. They struck the stomach floor softly and kept on going. Half an hour later they were thrown forward against their straps. The soft thudding of the cutter blades had risen to an ear-piercing shriek, which died into silence as Harrison switched them off.

"Either we've reached the subsurface," he said dryly, "or this beastie has a very hard heart."

They withdrew a short distance, then flattened their angle of descent so that they could continue tunneling with their tracks rolling over the rocky subsurface and the cutters chewing through material which now had the appearance of heavily compressed and thickly veined cork. When they had gone a few hundred yards Conway signaled the Lieutenant to stop.

"This doesn't look like the stuff that brains are made of," Conway said, "but I suppose we should take a closer look."

They were able to collect a few specimens and to look closely, but not for long. By the time they had sealed their suits and exited through the rear hatch, the tunnel they had made was already sagging dangerously and, where the wet, gritty floor met the tunnel sides, an oily black liquid oozed out and climbed steadily until it was over their ankles. Conway did not want to take too much of the stuff back with them into the digger. From the earlier samples taken by drill they knew that it stank to high heaven.

When they were back inside Murchison lifted one of the specimens. It looked a little like an Earthly onion which had been cut laterally in two. The flat underside was covered by a pad of stubby, worm-like growths and the single stalk divided and subdivided many times before joining the nerve network a short distance above them. She said, "I would say that the plant's secretions dissolve and absorb minerals and/or chemicals from the subsurface rock and soil and, with the water which filters down here, provides the lubrication which allows the creature to change position if the mineral supply runs out. But there are no signs of unusual or concentrated nerve networks here, nor are there any traces of the scars which tools leave when they cut their way through this material. I'm afraid we'll have to try again somewhere else."

Nearly an hour went by before they reached the second hollow and another three took them to the third. Conway had been a little doubtful from the beginning about the third site because it was too close to the periphery, in his opinion, to house a brain. But the possibility had still not been ruled out, on a creature this size, of multiple brains or at least a number of neural substations. She reminded him that the old-time brontosaurus had needed two, and it had been microscopic when compared with their patient.

The third site was also very close to the beginning of the first incision line.

"We could spend the rest of our lives searching hollows and still not find what we're looking for," said Conway angrily, "and we haven't that much time."

His repeater screens showed the sky lightening far above them, with Monitor heavy cruisers already in position, floodlights being switched off at transfusion and feeding installations and occasionally glimpses of Edwards, who had been transferred to the flagship *Vespasian* as medical liaison chief for the duration. It was his job to translate Conway's medical instructions into military maneuvers for the fleet's executive officers.

"Your test bores," said Conway suddenly. "I assume they were spaced out at regular intervals and went right down to the subsurface? Was there any indication that the black goo which the patient uses as a lubricant is more prevalent in certain areas than in others? I'm trying to find a section of the creature which is virtually incapable of movement, because—"

"Of course," said Murchison excitedly, "that is the big factor which makes our intelligent patient different from all the smaller and nonintelligent strata creatures. For better protection the brain, and probably the tool-production centers, would almost certainly have to be in a stationary section. Offhand, I can only remember about a dozen test bores in which lubricant was absent or present in very small quantities, but I can look up the map references for you in a few minutes."

"You know," said Conway with feeling, "I still don't want you here but I'm glad you've come."

"Thank you," she said, then added, "I think."

Five minutes later she had all the available information. "The subsurface forms a small plain ringed by low mountains in that area. Aerial sensors tell us that it is unusually rich in minerals, but then so is most of the center of this land mass. Our test bores were very widely spaced, so that we could easily have missed picking up brain material, but I'm pretty sure now that it is there."

Conway nodded, then said, "Harrison, that will be the next stop. But it's too far to go traveling on or under the surface. Take us topside and arrange for a transport copter to lift us to the spot. And on the way would you mind angling us toward Throat Tunnel Forty-three, as close to the incision line as you can manage, so that I can see how the patient reacts to the early stages of the operation. It is bound to have some natural defense against gross physical injury ..."

He broke off, his mood swinging suddenly from high excitement to deepest gloom. He said, "Dammit, I wish I had concentrated on the tools from the very beginning, instead of getting sidetracked with the rollers, and then thinking that those overgrown leucocytes were the intelligent tool users. I've wasted far too much time."

"We're not wasting time now," said Harrison, and pointed toward his repeater screens.

For better or for worse, major surgery had begun.

The main screen showed a line of heavy cruisers playing ponderous follow-the-leader along the first section of the incision, rattlers probing deep while their pressers held the edges of the wound apart to allow deeper penetration by the next ship in line. Like all of the Emperor class ships they were capable of delivering a wide variety of frightfulness in very accurately metered doses, from putting a few streets full of rioters to sleep to dispensing atomic annihilation on a continental scale. The Monitor Corps rarely allowed any situation to deteriorate to the point where the use of mass destruction weapons became the only solution, but they kept them as a big and potent stick—like most policemen, the Federation's law-enforcement arm knew that an undrawn baton had better and more long-lasting effects than one that was too busy cracking skulls. But their most effective and versatile close-range weapon—versatile because it served equally well either as a sword or a plowshare—was the rattler.

A development of the artificial gravity system which compensated for the killing accelerations used by Federation spaceships, and of the repulsion screen which gave protection against meteorites or which allowed a vessel with sufficient power reserves to hover above a planetary surface like an old-time dirigible airship, the rattler beam simply pushed and pulled, violently, with a force of up to one hundred Gs, several times a minute.

It was very rarely that the corps were forced to use their rattlers in anger—normally the fire-control officers had to be satisfied with using them to clear and cultivate rough ground for newly established colonies—and for the optimum effect the focus had to be really tight. But even a diffuse beam could be devastating, especially on a small target like a scoutship. Instead of tearing off large sections of hull plating and making metallic mincemeat of the underlying structure, it shook the whole ship until the men inside rattled.

On this operation, however, the focus was very tight and the range known to the last inch.

Visually it was not at all spectacular. Each cruiser had three rattler batteries which could be brought to bear, but they pushed and pulled so rapidly that the surface seemed hardly to be disturbed. Only the relatively gentle tractor beams positioned between the rattlers seemed to be doing anything—they pulled up the narrow wedge of material and shredded vegetation so that the next rattler in line could deepen the incision. It would not be until the incision had penetrated to the subsurface and extended for several miles that the other squadrons still hanging in orbit would come in to widen the cut into what they all hoped would be a trench wide enough to check the spread of vegetable infection from the excised and decomposing dead material.

As a background to the pictures Conway could hear the clipped voices of the ordnance officers reporting in. There seemed to be hundreds of them, all saying the same things in the fewest possible words. At irregular intervals a quiet, unhurried voice would break in, directing, approving, coordinating the overall effort—the voice of God, sometimes known as Fleet Commander Dermod, the ranking Monitor Corps officer of Galactic Sector Twelve and as such the tactical director of more than three thousand major fleet units, supply and communications vessels, support bases, ship production lines and the vast number of beings, Earth-human and otherwise, who manned them.

If the operation came unstuck, Conway certainly would not be able to complain about the quality of the help. He began to feel quietly pleased with the way thing were going.

The feeling lasted for all of ten minutes, during which time the incision line passed through the tunnel—Number Forty-three—which they had just entered. Conway could actually see the inward end of the seal, a thick, corrugated sausage of tough plastic inflated to fifty pounds per square inch which pressed against the tunnel walls. Special arrangements had been needed to guard against loss of working fluid because the strata creature's healing processes were woefully slow. Its blood was quite literally water and one important quality which water did not have was the ability to coagulate.

Two corpsmen and a Melfan medic were on guard beside the seal. They seemed to be agitated, but there were so many leucocytes moving about the tunnel that he could not see the reason for it. His screens showed the incision line crossing the throat tunnel. A few hundreds of gallons of water between the seal and the incision poured away—considering the size of the patient, it was scarcely a drop. The rattlers and tractors moved on, extending and deepening the cut while the great immaterial presser beams, the invisible stilts which supported the enormous weight of the cruisers, pushed the edges apart until the incision became a widening and deepening ravine. A small charge of chemical explosive brought down the roof of the emptied section of tunnel, reinforcing the plastic seal. Everything seemed to be working exactly as planned, until the immediate attention signal began flashing on his board and Major Edwards' face filled the screen.

"Conway," said the Major urgently. "The seal in Tunnel Forty-three is under attack by tools."

"But that's impossible," said Murchison, in the scandalized tones of one who has caught a friend cheating at cards. "The patient has never interfered with our internal operations. There are no eye plants down here to give away our positions, no light to speak of, and the seal isn't even metal. They never attack plastic material on the surface, just men and machines."

"And they attack men because we betray our presence by trying to take mental control of them," Conway said quickly. Then to Edwards, "Major, get those people away from the seal and into the supply shaft. Quickly. I can't talk to them directly. While they're doing that tell them to try not to think—"

He broke off as the seal ahead disappeared in a soft white explosion of bubbles which roared toward them along the tunnel roof. He could not see anything outside the digger and inside only Edwards' face and pictures of ships in line astern formation.

"Doctor, the seal's gone," shouted the Major, his eyes sliding to one side. "The debris behind the seal is being washed away. Harrison, *dig in!*"

But the Lieutenant could not dig in because the bubbles roaring past made it impossible to see. He threw the tracks into reverse, but the current sweeping them along was so strong that the digger was just barely in contact with the floor. He killed the floodlights because reflection from the froth outside the canopy was dazzling them. But there was still a patch of light ahead, growing steadily larger . . .

"Edwards, *cut the rattlers . . . !*"

A few seconds later they were swept out of the tunnel as part of a cataract which tumbled down an organic cliff into a ravine which seemed to have no bottom. The vehicle did not explode into its component parts nor themselves into strawberry jam, so they knew that Major Edwards had been able to kill the rattler batteries in time. When they crashed to a halt a subjective eternity later, two of the repeater screens died in spectacular implosions and the cataract which had cushioned their fall on the way down began battering at their side, pushing and rolling them along the floor of the incision.

"Anyone hurt?" said Conway.

Murchison eased her safety webbing and winced. "I'm black and blue and . . . and embossed all over."

"That," said Harrison in an obviously uninjured tone, "I would like to see."

Both relieved and irritated, Conway said, "First we should look at the patient."

The only operable viewscreen was transmitting a picture taken from one of the copters stationed above the incision. The heavy cruisers had drawn off a short distance to leave the operative field clear for rescue and observation copters, which buzzed and dipped above the wound like great metal flies. Thousands of gallons of water were pouring from the severed throat tunnel every minute, carrying the bodies of leucocytes, farmer fish, incompletely digested food and clumps of vital internal vegetation into and along the ravine. Conway signaled for Edwards.

"We're safe," he said before the other could speak, "but this is a mess. Unless we can stop this loss of fluid, the stomach system will collapse and we will have killed instead of cured our patient. Dammit, why doesn't it have some method of protecting itself against gross physical injury, a nonreturn valve arrangement or some such? I certainly did not expect this to happen . . ."

Conway checked himself, realizing that he was beginning to whine and make excuses instead of issuing instructions. Briskly, he said, "I need expert advice. Have you a specialist in short-range, low-power explosive weapons?"

"Right," said Edwards. A few seconds later a new voice said, "Ordnance control, *Vespasian*, Major Holroyd. Can I help you, Doctor?"

I sincerely hope so, thought Conway, while aloud he went onto outline his problem.

They were faced with the emergency situation of a patient bleeding to death on the table. Whether the being concerned was large or small, whether its body fluid was Earth-human blood, the superheated liquid metal used by the TLTUs of Threcald Five or the somewhat impure water which carried food and specialized internal organisms to the farflung extremities of this Drambon strata creature's body, the result would be the same—steadily reducing blood pressure, increasingly deep shock, spreading muscular paralysis and death.

Normal procedure in these circumstances would be to control the bleeding by tying off the damaged blood vessel and suturing the wound. But this particular vessel was a tunnel with walls no more strong or elastic than the surrounding body material, so they could not be tied or even clamped. As Conway saw it the only method remaining was to plug the ruptured vessel by bringing down the tunnel roof.

"Close-range TR-7s," said the ordnance officer quickly. "They are aerodynamically clean, so there will be no problem shooting into the flow, and provided there are no sharp bends near the mouth of the tunnel any desired penetration can be achieved by—"

"No," said Conway firmly. "I'm concerned about the compression effects of a large explosion in the tunnel itself. The shock wave would be transmitted deep into the interior, and a great many farmer fish and leucocytes would die, not to mention large quantities of the fragile internal vegetation. We must seal the tunnel as close to the incision as possible, Major, and confine the damage to that area."

"Armor-piercing B-22s, then," said Holroyd promptly. "In this material we could get penetrations of fifty yards without any trouble. I suggest a simultaneous launch of three missiles, spaced vertically above the tunnel mouth so that they will bring down enough loose material to block the tunnel even against the pressure of water trying to push it away as it subsides."

"Now," said Conway, "you're talking."

But *Vespasian*'s ordnance officer could do more than talk. Within a very few minutes the screen showed the cruiser hovering low over the incision. Conway did not see the missiles launched because he had suddenly remembered to check if their digger had been swept far enough to avoid being buried in the debris, which fortunately it had. His first indication that anything at all had happened was when the flow of water turned suddenly muddy, slowed to a trickle and stopped. A few minutes later great gobs of thick, viscous mud began to ooze over the lip of the tunnel and suddenly a wide area around the mouth began to sag, fall apart and slip like a mass of brown porridge into the ravine.

The tunnel mouth was now six times larger than it had been and the patient continued to bleed with undiminished force.

"Sorry, Doctor," said Holroyd. "Shall I repeat the dose and try for greater penetration?"

"No, wait."

Conway tried desperately to think. He knew that he was conducting a surgical operation, but he did not really believe it—both the problem and the patient were too big. If an Earth-human was in the same condition, even if no instruments or medication were available, he would know what to do—check the flow at a pressure point, apply a tourniquet . . . That was *it*.

"Holroyd, plant three more in the same position and depth as last time," he said quickly. "But before you launch them can you arrange your vessel's presser beams so that as many of them as possible will be focused just above the tunnel opening? Angle them against the face of the incision instead of having them acting vertically, if possible. The idea is to use the weight of your ship to compress and support the material brought down by the missiles."

"Can do, Doctor."

It took less than fifteen minutes for *Vespasian* to rearrange and refocus her invisible feet and launch the missiles, but almost at once the cataract ceased and this time it did not resume. The tunnel opening was gone and in its place there was a great, saucer-shaped depression in the wall of the incision where *Vespasian*'s starboard pressers were focused. Water still oozed through the compacted seal, but it would hold so long as the cruiser maintained position and leaned her not inconsiderable weight on it. As extra insurance another inflatable seal was already being moved into the supply tunnel.

Suddenly the picture was replaced by that of a lined, young-old face above green-clad shoulders on which there rested a quietly impressive weight of insignia. It was the Fleet Commander himself.

"Doctor Conway. My flagship has engaged in some odd exercises in her time, but never before have we been asked to hold a tourniquet."

"I'm sorry, sir—it seemed the only way of handling the situation. But right now, if you don't mind, I'd like you to have this digger lifted to map reference numbers . . ."

He broke off because Harrison was waving at him. The Lieutenant said softly, "Not *this* digger. Ask him to have the other one checked out and waiting when they get around to pulling us out."

Three hours later they were in the second modified and strengthened digger, suspended under a transport copter and approaching the area which, they hoped, contained the strata creature's brain and/or tool-producing facilities. The trip gave them a chance to do some constructive theorizing about their patient.

They were now convinced that it had evolved originally from a mobile vegetable form. It had always been large and omnivorous, and when these life-forms began to live off each other they grew in size and complexity and shrank in numbers. There did not seem to be any way that the strata creature could reproduce itself. It simply continued to live and grow until one of its own kind who was bigger than it was killed it. Their patient was the biggest, oldest, toughest and wisest of its kind. As the sole occupant of its land mass for many thousands of years, there had no longer been the necessity for it to move itself bodily and so it had taken root again.

But this had not been a process of devolution. With no chance of cannibalizing others of its own kind, it devised methods of controlling its growth and of rendering its metabolism more efficient by evolving tools to do the jobs like mining, investigating the subsurface, processing necessary minerals for its nerve network. The original farmer fish were probably a strain which were able to survive, like the legendary Jonah, in its stomach and later grow plant teeth for both the parent creature and the farmer fish to defend themselves against sea predators sucked in by the mouths. How the leucocytes got there was still not clear, but the rollers occasionally ran across a smaller, less highly evolved variety which were probably the leeches' wild cousins.

"But one point which we must keep in mind when we try to talk to it," Conway ended seriously, "is that the patient is not only blind, deaf and dumb, it has never had another of its own kind to talk to. Our problem isn't simply learning a peculiar and difficult e-t language, we have to communicate with something which does not even know the meaning of the word communicate."

"If you're trying to raise my morale," said Murchison dryly, "you aren't."

Conway had been staring ahead through the forward canopy, mostly to avoid having to look at the carnage depicted on his repeater screens where the tool attacks were taking an increasingly heavy toll at the feeding and transfusion sites. He said suddenly, "The suspected brain area is far too extensive to be searched quickly but, correct me if I'm wrong, isn't this also the locality where *Descartes* made her first touchdown? If that is so then the tools sent to investigate her had a relatively short distance to come, and if it is possible to trace the path of a tool by the scar tissue it leaves in the body material . . ."

"It is," said Murchison, looking excited. Harrison gave new instructions to the transport copter's pilot without having to be told and a few minutes later they were down, cutting blades spinning and nosing into their patient's spongy quasiflesh.

But instead of the large, cylindrical plug cut from the body material they found a flat, reversed conical section which tapered sharply to a narrow, almost hair-thin wound which angled almost at once toward the suspected brain area.

"The ship would have been drawn only a short distance below the surface, obviously," said Murchison. "Enough to let tools make contact with its total surface while supported by body material, instead of making a fleeting contact after bouncing themselves into the air. But do you notice how the tools, even though they must have been cutting through at top speed, still managed to avoid severing the root network which relays their mental instructions . . . ?"

"At the present angle of descent," Harrison cut in, "we are about twenty minutes from the subsurface. Sonar readings indicate the presence of caverns or deep pits."

Before Conway could reply to either of them, Edwards' face flicked onto the main screen. "Doctor, seals Thirty-eight through Forty-one have gone. We're already holding tourniquets at Eighteen, Twenty-six and Forty-three, but—"

"Same procedure," snapped Conway.

There was a dull clang followed by metallic scraping sounds running the length of the digger. The sounds were repeated with rapidly increasing frequency. Without looking up, Harrison said, "Tools, Doctor. Dozens of them. They can't build up much impetus coming at us through this spongy stuff and our extra armor should cope. But I'm worried about the antenna housing."

Before Conway could ask why, Murchison turned from the viewport. She said, "I've lost the original trail, Doctor—this area is practically solid with tool scar tissue. Traffic must be very heavy around here."

The secondary screens were showing logistic displays on the deployment of ships, earth-moving machinery, decontamination equipment and movements into and out of the feeding and transfusion areas, and the main screen showed *Vespasian* no longer in position above Tunnel Forty-three. It was losing height and wheeling around in a ponderous, lateral spin while its pilot was obviously fighting hard to keep it from flipping over onto its back.

One of its four presser installations, Conway saw during the next swing, had been smashed in as if by a gigantic hammer and he knew without being told that this was the one which had been holding closed the ruptured Forty-three. As the ship whirled closer to the ground he wanted to close his eyes, but then he saw that the spin was being checked and that the surface vegetation was being flattened by the three remaining pressers, fanned out at maximum power to support the ship's weight.

Vespasian landed hard but not catastrophically. Another cruiser moved into position above Forty-three while surface transport and copters raced toward the crash-landed ship to give assistance. They arrived at the same time as a large group of tools which were doing nothing at all to help.

Suddenly Dermod's head filled the screen.

"Doctor Conway," said the Fleet Commander in a coldly furious voice, "this is not the first time that I have had a ship converted to scrap around me, but I have never learned to enjoy the experience. The accident was caused by trying to balance virtually the whole of the ship's weight on one narrowly focused presser beam, with the result that its supporting structure buckled and damn near wrecked the ship."

His tone warmed a little, but only temporarily, as he went on, "If we are to hold tourniquets over every tunnel, and with tools attacking every seal it looks as if we will have to do just that, I shall either have to withdraw my ships for major structural modifications or use them for an hour or so at a time and check for incipient structural failure after each spell of duty. But this will tie up a much larger number of ships in unproductive activity, and the farther we extend the incision the more tunnels we will have to sit on and the slower the work will go. The operation is fast becoming a logistical impossibility, the casualty figures and material losses are making it indistinguishable from a full-scale battle, and if I thought that the only result would be the satisfaction of your medical curiosity, Doctor, and that of our cultural contact people, I would throw a permanent 'Hold' on it right now. I have the mind of a police-man, not a soldier—the Federation prefers it that way. I don't glory in this sort of thing . . ."

The digger lurched and for an instant Conway felt a sensation im-possible in these surroundings, that of free fall. Then there was a crash as the vehicle struck rocky ground. It landed on its side, rolled over twice and moved forward again, but skidding and slewing to one side. The sound of tools striking the hull was deafening.

Two vertical creases appeared on the Fleet Commander's forehead. He said, "Having trouble, Doctor?"

The constant banging of tools made it hard to think. Conway nodded and said, "I didn't expect the seals to be attacked, but now I realize that the patient is simply trying to defend itself where it thinks it is under the heaviest attack. I also realize now that its sense of touch is not restricted to its top surface. You see, it is blind, deaf and dumb but it seems to be able to feel in three dimensions. The eye plants and subsurface root net-works allow it to feel areas of local pressure, but vaguely, without detail. To feel the fine details it sends tools, which are extremely sensitive— sensitive enough to feel the airflow over their wings in the glider config-uration and reproduce the shape themselves at will. Our patient learns very quickly and that glider I thought at it has cost a lot of lives. I wish—"

"Doctor Conway," the Fleet Commander broke in harshly. "You are either trying to make excuses or giving me a very basic lecture with which I am already familiar. I have time to listen to neither. We are faced with a surgical and tactical emergency. I require guidance."

Conway shook his head violently. He had the feeling that he had just said or thought of something important but he did not know what it was. He had to stay with his present train of thought if he expected to drag it out into the light again.

He went on, "The patient sees, experiences everything, by touch. So far our only area of common contact are the tools. They are thought-controlled extensions of its sense of touch throughout and for a short distance above the patient's body. Our own mental radiation and control are more concentrated and of strictly limited range. The situation has been that of two fencers trying to communicate only through the tips of their foils—"

He stopped abruptly because he was talking to an empty screen. All three repeaters glowed with power, but there was neither sound nor vision.

Harrison shouted, "I was afraid of this, Doctor. We strengthened the hull armor but had to cover the antenna housing with a plastic radome to allow two-way communications. The tools have found our weak spot. Now we are deaf, dumb and blind, too—and missing one leg because our port caterpillar tread won't work."

The digger had come to rest on a flat shelf of rock in a large cavern which angled steeply into the subsurface. Above and behind them hung a great mass of the creature's body material from which there was suspended thousands of rootlets which joined and rejoined until they became thick, silvery cables writhing motionlessly across the cavern floor, walls and roof before disappearing into the depths. Each cable had at least one bud sprouting from it, like a leaf of wrinkled tinfoil. The more well-developed buds quivered and were trying to take the shapes of the tools which were attacking the digger.

"This is one of the places where it makes the tools," she said, using a spotlight as pointer, "or should I say grows them—I still can't decide whether this is an animal or vegetable life-form basically. The nervous system seems to be centered in this area, so it is almost certainly part of the brain as well. And it is sensitive—do you see how carefully the tools avoid those silver cables while they are attacking?"

"We'll do the same," said Conway, then to Harrison, "That is, if you can move the digger on one track to that overhanging wall with the cables running along it, without crushing those two on the floor?"

Damage in this sensitive area could have serious effects on their patient.

The Lieutenant nodded and began rocking the digger forward and backward along the shelf until they were tight against the indicated wall. Protected by the sensitive cables above, the cavern floor below and the rocky wall on their starboard side, the tool attack was confined to their unprotected port side. They could once again hear themselves think, but

Harrison pointed out firmly but apologetically that they could not climb the slope or dig their way out on one track, that they could not call for help and that they had air for only fourteen hours and then only if they sealed their suits to use their remaining tanked air.

"Let's do that now," said Conway briskly, "and move outside. Station yourselves at each end of the digger, under the cables and with your backs to the cavern wall. That way you will have to think off attacks from the front only—any tool trying to cut through the rock behind you will make too much noise to take you by surprise. I also want you far enough from my position amidships so that your mental radiation will not affect the tools which I will be trying to control . . ."

"I know that smug, self-satisfied look," said Murchison to the Lieutenant as she began sealing her helmet. "Our Doctor has had a sudden rush of brains to the head. I think he intends *talking* to the patient."

"What language?" asked Harrison dryly.

"I suppose," said Conway, smiling to show the confidence which he did not feel, "you could call it three-dimensional Braille."

Quickly he explained what he hoped to do and a few minutes later they were in position outside the digger. Conway sat with his back to the port track housing a few feet from a water-filled depression in the cavern floor. There was a hole of unknown depth in the center of the depression where a cable or similar ore-extracting plant had eaten its way into the rock. To one side of him a group of seven or eight tools had merged together to encircle and squeeze the vehicle's hull, and some of the armor was beginning to gape at the seams. Conway thought a break in the metal band and then he rolled it into the depression like a great lump of animated, silvery dough. Then he got down to work.

Conway made no attempt to protect himself against attacking tools. He intended concentrating so hard on one particular shape that anything which came within mental range would, he hoped, lose its dangerous edges or points.

Thought-shaping the creature's outward aspect was easy. Within a few minutes there was a large, silvery pancake—a small-scale replica of the patient—lying in the center of the pool. But thinking three dimensionally of the mouths and their connecting tunnels and stomachs was not so easy. Even harder was the stage when he began thinking the tiny stomachs into expanding and contracting, sucking the gritty, algae-filled water into his scale model and expelling it again.

It was a crude, oversimplified model. The best he could manage at one time was eight mouths and connecting stomachs, and he was very much afraid that it bore the same relation to the patient that a doll did to a living baby. But then he began to add the creeping motions he had observed in smaller, younger strata creatures, keeping the area around the central depression motionless, however, and hoping that with the pumping motions of the stomachs he was giving the impression of a living organism. The sweat poured off his forehead and into his eyes, but by then it did not matter that he could not see properly, because the sections he was shaping were out of sight anyway. Then he began to think certain areas solid, motionless, dead. He extended these dead, motionless and detail-less areas until gradually the whole model was a solid, lifeless lump.

Then he blinked the sweat out of his eyes and started all over again, and then again, and suddenly the others were standing beside him.

"They aren't attacking us anymore," said Harrison quietly, "and before they change their minds I am going to try fixing that damaged track. At least, there is no shortage of tools."

Murchison said, "Can I help—apart from keeping my mind blank to avoid warping your model?"

Without looking up Conway said, "Yes, please. I'm going to take it through the same sequence once again, but halt it at the point where the dead areas extend to at the present time. When I do that I would like you to think the positions of our incisions and extend and widen them while I seal the severed throat tunnels and think the feeding and transfusion shafts. You withdraw the excised material a short distance and think it solid—dead, that is—while I try to get across the idea that the remainder is alive and twitching and likely to stay that way."

She caught on very quickly but Conway had no way of knowing if their patient had, or could, catch on. Behind them Harrison was at work on the damaged tread while before them their model of the patient and the effects of their present surgery became more and more detailed— right down to the miniature corrugated seals and what happened to the creature when one of them was collapsed. But still there was no indication from the patient that it understood what they were trying to tell it.

Suddenly Conway stood up and began climbing the sloping floor. He said, "I'm sorry, I have to move out of range for a minute to catch my mental breath."

"Me, too," she said a few minutes later. "I'll join you . . . look!"

Conway had been staring at the darkness of the cavern roof to rest both his mind and his eyes. He looked down quickly, thinking they were under attack again, and saw Murchison pointing at their model, their *working* model.

Despite it being out of range of both their minds it had not slumped down or lost detail. Somebody was maintaining it exactly as they had been doing. All at once Conway forgot his physical and mental fatigue.

Excitedly he said, "This must be its way of saying that it understands us. But we've got to widen communications, tell it more about ourselves. Go collect a few more tools and think a model of this cavern complete with nerve cables—I'll shape the digger to scale with moving models of the three of us. They'll be crude, of course, but to begin with we only need to get across the idea of our small size and vulnerability to tool attacks. Then we'll move away for a short distance and shape a model of the digger in operation, then 'dozers, copters and scout-ship on the surface—nothing as big and complicated as *Descartes*, at least to begin with. We'll have to keep everything very simple."

In a very short time the shelf around the digger was carpeted with models which were being maintained by the patient as soon as they were completed, and more and more tools were rolling heavily but very gently toward them eager to be shaped. But their visors were becoming almost opaque with perspiration and their suit air was running out. Murchison insisted that she had time for just one more shaping, a large one using upward of twenty tools, when Harrison appeared from behind the digger.

"I have to go inside," said the Lieutenant. "Unlike some people I have been working hard and burning up my air . . ."

"Kick him for me. You're closer."

". . . But the digger will work at about quarter speed," Harrison continued. "And if it doesn't we may still be able to call for help. I used a tool to shape a new antenna—I knew the exact dimensions—so we may even get two-way vision—"

He stopped abruptly, staring at what Murchison was doing to her tools.

A little crossly she said, "As the pathologist of the party it is my job to tell the patient what we look, or rather feel, like. This model has a much simplified respiratory, digestive and circulatory system and, as you can see, articulation at all the main joints. Naturally, as I know a little more about myself than anyone else, this representative of mankind is in fact female. Equally important, I do not want to needlessly confuse the patient by adding clothes."

Harrison did not have enough oxygen left to reply. They followed him into the digger and, while Conway made contact with the surface, Murchison instinctively raised her hand in farewell to the cavern and the shapes of the tool models scattered across the shelf. She must have been thinking very hard about her good-bye because her last model raised its hand also and kept it there while the digger crawled slowly out of mental range.

Suddenly all three repeaters were alive and Dermod was staring at him, his face reflecting concern, relief and excitement in sequence and then altogether. He said, "Doctor, I thought we'd lost you—you blanked out four hours ago. But I can report progress. The incision is proceeding and all tool attacks ceased half an hour ago. There is no tool trouble reported from the tunnel seals, the decontamination teams, the transfusion shafts anywhere. Doctor, is this a temporary condition?"

Conway let his breath go in a long, loud sigh of relief. Their patient was a very bright lad despite its physically slow reaction times. He shook his head and said, "You will have no more trouble from the tools. In fact, you will find them of assistance in helping maintain equipment and for use in awkward sections of the incision once we make it understand our needs. You can also forget about digging that isolation trench—our patient retains enough mobility to withdraw itself from the newly excised material—which means that ships which would have been tied up in digging that trench will now be free to extend the incision more rapidly, so that our operation will be completed in a fraction of the time originally thought necessary.

"You see, sir," Conway ended, "we now have the active cooperation of our patient."

Major surgery was completed in just under four months and Conway was ordered back to Sector General. Postoperative treatment would take a great many years and would proceed in conjunction with the exploration of Drambo and the closer investigation of its life-forms and cultures. Before leaving, while he was still seriously troubled by the thought of the casualty figures, Conway had once questioned the value of what they had done. A rather supercilious cultural contact specialist had tried to make it very simple for him by saying that difference, whether it was cultural, physiological or technological, was immensely valuable. They would learn much from the strata creature and the rollers while they were teaching them. Conway, with some difficulty, accepted that. He could also accept the fact that, as a surgeon, his work on Drambo was done. It was much harder to accept the fact that the pathology team, particularly one member of it, still had a lot of work to do.

While O'Mara did not openly enjoy his anguish, neither did he display sympathy.

"Stop suffering so loudly in silence, Conway," said the Chief Psychologist on his return, "and sublimate yourself—preferably in quicklime. But failing that there is always work, and an odd case has just come in which you might like to look at. I'm being polite, of course. It *is* your case as of now. Observe."

The large visiscreen behind O'Mara's desk came to life and he went on. "This beastie was found in one of the hitherto unexplored regions, the victim of an accident which virtually cut its ship and itself in two. Airtight bulkheads sealed off the undamaged section and your patient was able to withdraw itself, or some of itself, before they closed. It was a large ship, filled with some kind of nutrient earth, and the victim is still alive—or should I say half alive. You see, we don't know which half of it we rescued. Well?"

Conway stared at the screen, already devising methods of immobilizing a section of the patient for examination and treatment, of synthesizing supplies of that nutrient soil which now must be virtually sucked dry, and for studying the wreck's controls to gain data on its sensory equipment. If the accident which had wrecked its ship had been due to an explosion in the power plant, which was likely, then this might well be the front half containing the brain.

His new patient was not quite the Midgard Serpent but it did not fall far short of it. Twisting and coiling it practically filled the enormous hangar deck which had been emptied to accommodate it.

"Well?" said O'Mara again.

Conway stood up. Before turning to go he grinned and said, "Small, isn't it?"